The Cursed King

A.M. Josephine

Contents

Welcome to Horcath	VI
Map	IX
Dedication	I
Prologue	2
1. KSEGA	3
2. SAKURA	16
3. SAKURA	27
4. KSEGA	37
5. SAKURA	44
6. KSEGA	53
7. SAKURA	62
8. KSEGA	72
9. SAKURA	83
10. KSEGA	96
11. SAKURA	107
12. KSEGA	114
13. ERABETH	124
14. GIAN	139
15. KSEGA	146
16. SAKURA	155
17. KSEGA	166

18. KSEGA 175

19. SAKURA 184

20. KSEGA 195

21. SAKURA 204

22. KSEGA 213

23. SAKURA 218

24. KSEGA 229

25. SAKURA 239

26. KSEGA 248

27. SAKURA 254

28. KSEGA 264

29. SAKURA 274

30. KSEGA 283

31. KSEGA 291

32. PEELER 303

33. SAKURA 311

34. KSEGA 318

35. SAKURA 325

36. SAKURA 334

37. KSEGA 344

38. SAKURA 352

39. SAKURA 359

40. KSEGA 365

41. ERABETH 376

42. SAKURA 391

43. SAKURA 401

44. Character Guide 405

45. Creature Guide 407

Acknowledgements   410

About the author   412

Welcome to Horcath

A guide to the kingdoms & their mage types (alphabetized), with pronunciation guide

BRIGHTLOCK

"bright • lock"

The second largest kingdom within the borders of Horcath.

Mainly supplies and exports ores and metals from the vast mines in the Shattered Mountains.

MAGE TYPE: Erru:

"air • oo"

The ability to manipulate and control the state of light. An erru-mage is rendered powerless when there is an utter absence of all light. Erru requires its mage to maintain clear and focused emotions.

CARLORE

"car • lore"

The third largest kingdom within the borders of Horcath.

Mainly supplies and exports timber, colorful clothing, and fruit tree saplings.

MAGE TYPE: Eirioth:

"air • ee • oth"

The ability to conjure fire, manipulate preexisting fire, and summon and control lightning. Some eirioth mages are capable of all three, but the majority are only capable of the first two. An eirioth-mage is rendered powerless if their body temperature drops too low. Eirioth requires its mage to have enough physical strength to keep it in check.

COLDMON

"cold • mon"

The largest kingdom within the borders of Horcath.

Mainly supplies ships and means of transport for cargo traveling between kingdoms.

MAGE TYPE: Aclure:

"ack • lure"

The ability to manipulate preexisting water, freeze preexisting water, and manipulate preexisting ice. The majority of aclure-mages are capable of all three. An aclure-mage is rendered powerless when there is no water nearby. Aclure requires its mage to maintain constant focus on the magic.

FREETALON
"free • talon"
The fourth largest kingdom within the borders of Horcath.
Mainly supplies and exports medicines and healing substances.
MAGE TYPE: Recle:
"reek • le"

The ability to create remedies that heal more than any remedy made without magic, to create poisons more potent than any poison made without magic, to heal external and internal wounds as well as poison someone with the touch of a hand. The majority of recle-mages are only capable of the first two, but there are a rare few capable of the third and fourth; almost no recle-mages are capable of the fifth. A recle-mage is rendered powerless when they are unable to access the ingredients necessary for their potions or when they have no way to physically touch another being. Recle requires its mage to have access to the tools necessary for their potions, at least a minor knowledge of healing, and strong focus.

OLD DUSKFALL
"old, dusk • fall"
The sixth largest kingdom within the borders of Horcath.
Since its downfall, the kingdom has remained largely secret, focused on resolving issues within itself. It occasionally supplies sandcat and Horcathian camel pelts to other kingdoms.
MAGE TYPE: Andune:
"an • dune"

The ability to manipulate preexisting sand and very fine grains, like salt or loose dirt, and the ability to host bone reading rituals, which have long been outlawed by the royals. Any mage found practicing bone reading is sentenced to life in prison or immediate execution. An andune-mage is rendered powerless when there is no sand nearby. Andune requires its mage to have a clear mental state and a strong connection to the earth.

OLD NIGHTFALL
"old, night • fall"

The smallest kingdom within the borders of Horcath.
Old Nightfall is supposedly the Glass City in the sky. Some don't believe it exists at all.
MAGE TYPE: Whorle:
"whirl"
The ability to manipulate certain aspects of the weather such as fog, wind, and clouds, and the ability to summon powerful storms. A whorle-mage is rendered powerless when in extremely dry or hot conditions. Whorle requires its mage to have a cool body temperature, a hydrated body, and a clear and calm mind.

WISESOL
"wise • sole"
The fifth largest kingdom within the borders of Horcath.
Mainly supplies and exports fish, fishing tools, stone, and slate-wolf pelts from the Slated Mountains.
MAGE TYPE: Bering:
"bear • ing"
The ability to manipulate the state of and grow preexisting plant life, the ability to calm and coax animals with their connection to life, the ability to see the 'life glows' of any living thing, and the ability to deeply connect to an animal through physical contact. All bering-mages are capable of these things but some more than others. A bering-mage is rendered powerless when there are no forms of non-human life around them. Bering requires its mage to have a clear and positive emotional and mental state.

The people born without magic are referred to as "underlings."

A guide to the characters and creatures within this story, as well as a pronunciation guide for them, can be found in the back of the book. Those guides will contain spoilers for The Cursed Mage & The Cursed King.

If you still pronounce Ksega's name "ka - say - guh," you didn't read the guides closely enough in The Cursed Mage, and we need to have a very serious talk.

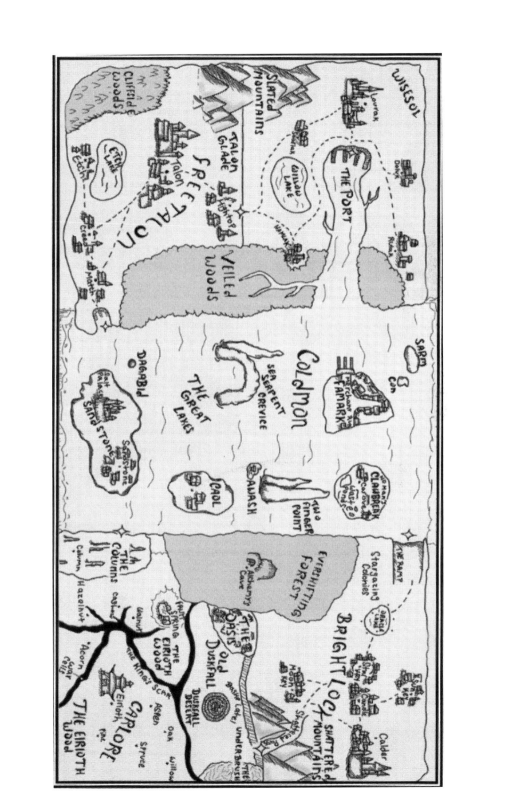

This book is dedicated to The Book Nook, and all the wonderful, creative minds that dwell there.
You guys are the best!

Prologue

*C*ontrolling the Curse cost him.

It wasn't just his emotional strength that was drained, it was all of it. It left him physically weak and ill. Sometimes he would have a fever, other times he would be as cold as ice. Some days it left him retching on his beautiful marble floors, others he would be starving so much he ate every morsel of food in his sight.

His friends weren't aware of his dark hobby. No one in the royal staff knew of his secrets, which he thought to be a partial good thing. The other part of him was furious at their ignorance. How could they not know the history of their people? How could they not know that it was their destiny to follow in the footsteps of their greatest ancestor, the one who had given them so much hope, so much prosperity in their land?

He would tell them. Not yet, but one day, he would, when the Curse was under control. Now, it was far too unpredictable. It ravaged the world around them, even to the point he could not stop it. He had tried, and he had failed, but he would not let that stand in his path. He would find a way. He would keep training, keep practicing until the Curse knelt at his side as the greatest weapon in all of Horcathian history.

Then, all would bow to him. He would no longer cower away from the world. He would make his stand and claim all the lands as his own. He would show the people the dream that the great king of old had possessed. He would share with all of them the glory of finally being one free people, and nothing was going to stand in his way, least of all the weapon itself.

He would tame it. He would find a way to control it, or he would die doing so. But he didn't believe he would die. He believed that it was too strongly connected to him. Despite its carnal nature, it did have magic within it, and it was a great magic. It knew who he was all too well, and it wouldn't risk killing him.

No, it needed him, and he needed it. They were one now.

And they were going to be unstoppable.

1
KSEGA

Magic had always been a confusing thing, even to people who believed they had mastered it. For someone like me, who had never spent more than a handful of days practicing with my bering, it was the greatest puzzle I'd ever faced.

To complicate the matter, my bering's strength had redoubled at least three times over the past week, and it was the most uncomfortable feeling I'd ever experienced. Even more uncomfortable than when Willa had accidentally spilled half a gallon of unfinished boiling perfume on me, leaving me drenched in sweet-smelling water, covered in slimy peach skins, and riddled with burns that didn't leave for two weeks.

Sitting in the makeshift camp on the shores of the Oasis, I was surrounded by sprawling life, life I never could have imagined would thrive in a place like the deserts of Old Duskfall. It pulsed and hummed around me, tugging at me and filling me with surety and safety. With a twitch of my fingers, I could bring the vines hanging overhead down to my side. Just by looking at them, I could make flowers expand into full bloom, or trees extend their branches to the skies. I could make moss creep over stones and roots curl into hands.

But these were all things I could have done before. Not with as much ease or precision, but I still possessed that power. What I really wanted to do was to master the art not of bending the living things, but the dead.

At first, the thought had made me uneasy. I was curious about it, but by no means wanted to touch a part of my magic that felt unnatural. I was content to leave it be with the things that made my power sing and soar, but after a Cursed runeboar had nearly killed me in Brightlock, I had used a part of my power I'd never been in touch with before. I had changed the form of dead wood. Not newly dead wood, which still had potential to be malleable, but wood that had been dead for years, that had seen lives come and go and felt hundreds if not thousands of feet pressed against its boards. Whatever life it had, whatever connection it would have had to me, was long gone, and yet, I had changed it so easily within seconds.

Since then, I hadn't been able to change anything dead, but not for lack of trying. I had reached out to the wood of the Duskan sand-sleds and the wood that was used to construct the homes and buildings in the City of Bones, but there was no connection there.

I had first learned of the art from Peeler, a peculiar bering-mage that made his living as a repairman for a pirate ship. I had once seen him take a pole of dead wood and create a thorn longer than my thumb by simply pulling it from the timber, pinched between two of his fingers.

I now sat on the sand beside the softly stirring waters of the Oasis, dragging patterns into the grains beside my bare feet as I tried to sense a piece of driftwood in front of me. I had been staring and poking and prodding at it for the past hour, but it had done nothing. I simply didn't understand it enough to master it.

"Any luck?" With a jump, I looked up to see Gian approaching me. I smiled broadly at him, hoping it looked encouraging and betrayed none of the pity I truly felt for him. He looked *terrible*.

"Not so far." I sighed, shaking my head and kicking the driftwood away and into the water. It bobbed beneath the surface, then floated gently away. "Sometimes I envy underlings. You don't have to worry about this stuff."

"Mages don't have to worry about it any more than we do," Gian pointed out, lowering himself to the sand beside me. He shut his eyes for a moment, face pinched, as if he were dizzy, then opened them and released a long breath. I tried to ignore the dark bags beneath them and the graying pallor of his cheeks.

"I guess so; but we feel a lot more obligated to worry about it. What's the point of having all this power if I never use it, anyway?" I tucked my legs beneath me and stared down into the water. Silvery fish flicked in and out of sight, reflecting the light of the sun on their shimmering scales. Brightly colored corals and writhing seaweed littered the distant bottom of the Oasis, dotted with slippery eels and swirling shells. If the thought of it didn't make my chest tighten in fear, I would've jumped in for a swim.

I didn't say it, but I was tempted to tell him about *my* power, especially. It had never been this strong before, but after I'd spent some time at sea, my connection to the land had seemed to enhance. I'd never heard of that happening with a bering-mage before. It made me wonder if I was somehow stronger than some of the other bering-mages. And if I did have stronger bering, wasn't it right that I try to find a way to master it?

"How're you feeling? Adjusting to all *this*?" I gestured at the Oasis around us, the towering trees and the vibrant flowers, eager to change the subject. Gian grunted but didn't reply for a moment, and I glanced at him. The weariness that had eaten away at him over the past two days was evident in everything: the way he stood, the way he moved, the way he spoke. He was exhausted, and we hadn't even gone anywhere or done anything.

"Little by little, yes, I am." He squinted his eyes at me, and I wriggled, not for the first time, under the intensity of his olive gaze. His eyes weren't the same steely, dark green as Sakura's. They were brighter and sharper and colder. Even with the shock and fatigue that enveloped his body, his eyes were as full of life and mystery and rebellion as they had been when I'd first met him.

"Tea helps," I said, looking out at the Oasis again. Its softly rippling surface glowed orange and gold in the light of the setting sun. "I always have a cup whenever I can. Soothes the nerves."

"I've never had tea." Gian admitted, rolling his shoulders. He groaned as they sagged and he lowered his head, shutting his eyes. "Does it help with a lack of energy?"

I shrugged. "Depends on what kind you have. If you really want some energy, you might want to try coffee. I've never liked it, but my friend Jessie is a big fan of it. You aren't likely to find much of it here, though. It's only produced in Brightlock and Carlore, and I don't think Duskans are a big fan of any brews other than ale." I rose to my feet and dusted sand off my pants. "We can always ask Beth if she's got any handy, if you want."

"No, it's alright." Gian rose unsteadily. I reached out to help him balance, but he held up a hand, shaking his head slightly as he squinted, trying to rise to his full height. "That woman intimidates me," he said, lowering his hand and blinking his eyes back open.

"That makes two of us." I smirked as I started back up the sandy little shore with him close on my heels.

Two days ago, after we had returned to the Oasis from our visit to Old Nightfall, Beth had called off the remainder of the small search party that had been combing the area for us. I wasn't sure how she'd sent them all away, but within a couple of hours, we had the entire Oasis all to ourselves. We had set up a campsite a little way off the shore of the great body of water that lazed its way through the Oasis's tropical luxury, tucked comfortably between a copse of palm trees. It consisted of three tents, a fire pit, and a large pile of our packs.

The rest of the day had mainly been catching Beth up on everything we had done and what we had learned. Gian was learning everything, too, but he was still a little foggy on the details, because he was very distracted by his new surroundings. After growing up in Old Nightfall all his life, he had never been to any of the other kingdoms, much less seen a tree or a bird other than an owl.

Speaking of owls, he had one with him. A purple one with thick black stripes across his wings and back. Gian had introduced him as Light Ray, and the two of them were inseparable. Light Ray seemed to have adapted just fine, but Gian was in need of some sort of root back to his home kingdom, and the owl provided that.

Light Ray and Taro, Beth's red-brown hawk, didn't get along very well, and because of that, Beth and Gian held unspoken grudges against each other. I thought it was ridiculous, but Sakura didn't agree. I wasn't sure if that had anything to do with the fact that her people typically had pet dragons or not, but I didn't bother to ask. Any mention of her life before she set off on this quest seemed to cause her pain, so I tried not to bring it up, despite the curiosity about her past that constantly plagued my thoughts.

A buzzing hum in the back of my mind told me Alchemy was waiting for us back in the camp, and when we pushed through the thick foliage, we saw he was the only one. He had discarded any form of clothing and was lying sprawled across a long rock, head resting on a clumped pile of moss. If I hadn't known he wasn't capable of it, I'd have suspected he was sleeping.

"Finally, someone is back!" he boomed when he noticed us, his ashy black skull tilting towards us. A spur of unease shook down my spine. I wasn't sure I'd ever get used to the pulsing green cracks that ran like broken veins across his bones, much less the constant eerie grin displayed across the bare front of his skull.

"Where are Beth and flame-fingers?" I asked, stretching my arms up above my head and sighing when my joints popped. I took a seat beside Alchemy, twirling my finger through the air to pull a few small buds into blossom. They would wither into dormancy in only a couple months, but they deserved to display their full beauty until them.

"I told you not to call me that, *Ka-sega*." A voice from the thick bushes around us made me jump back to my feet, whirling to see Sakura and Beth pushing their way through the broad leaves into our little campsite. Pushing strands of dark hair out of her face, Sakura glared at me.

"Stop calling me Ka-sega, and maybe I'll think about it." I retorted, lowering myself back onto the rock beside Alchemy and reaching for a satchel containing fresh fruit.

"Think too long, and we'll have to see if you can make your eyebrows grow back as easily as those flowers." Sakura snapped, and I winced away from her hand just in time to avoid an arc of golden fire that swirled from her fingertips.

Instinctively my hands reached up to brush along my brow, just to make sure she hadn't singed the hair away. I chuckled, hoping it didn't sound as nervous as I felt. I knew all too well that she would burn me if I irritated her too much. It would be a small burn, something I could recover from fast, but a burn nonetheless.

"If I hear one more bout of you two pretending not to adore each other, I'm going to start slitting throats," Beth snarled at us, her expression sour. I grinned sheepishly as heat crawled up my neck, but Sakura only rolled her eyes and disappeared into one of the tents.

"Are we heading out today?" I asked Beth, pulling an apple out of the satchel and scrubbing some of the sand off it with the end of my sleeve before crunching into it.

"Maybe." She squinted up at the sky. It was only a couple hours past dawn. "If we're lucky, it will be ready by the afternoon, but we don't want to get caught by sandcats. We can travel during the night. So long as none of the royal patrols stop us, it will be smooth sailing back to *Baske Latel.*"

I took another bite of the apple instead of replying. We all knew how dangerous it would be getting back into the City of Bones. For the past two days, we had been waiting. After falling through the magical well that transported us into Old Nightfall, the sandcats that had attacked us continued to wreak havoc upon the Oasis. Only two soldiers had survived, but one of them was severely injured. As for the man that had taken us to the Oasis in the first place, Kieran, and his Horcathian camel, Casper, they hadn't escaped the vicious beasts, and neither had the sand-sled we'd ridden on.

The entire thing had been reduced to splinters and broken boards. The sandcats had been driven wild by the scent of blood and their desperate craze to find more of it. When Beth and a small number of others had arrived, they had been faced with a gruesome battle against the creatures, barely escaping it without any deaths. They had managed to scare the cats away, but not before their own two sand-sleds were rendered useless, one of them cracked down the middle, and the other brought to nothing more than planks of wood sliding across sand. Their camels were alive and well, though, so once one of the sand-sleds was repaired, we were heading back to the City of Bones, the capital—and only surviving civilization—of Old Duskfall.

"You should all get some rest." Beth told me as she looked at the fire pit. Our fire from that morning had dwindled to nothing but sparking embers and swirling smoke, and Beth lifted and twisted her wrist, pulling an arc of sand up over the smoldering remains of the fire.

"We've been resting for days," I whined, swiping apple juice from my lips with the back of my sleeve. "I've got all the energy I need."

Beth raised an eyebrow at me but said nothing as she kicked the ashy remains of the fire and trooped into her tent. When she'd vanished, I looked up at the trees around us, wondering where Taro had gotten too. He was rarely with us, and when he was, he was perched on Beth's shoulder, watching all of us with narrowed, aggravated eyes. When he wasn't, there was no telling where he might be; there were plenty of places for him to hide comfortably away in the Oasis.

"Maybe you do," Alchemy said, sitting up and leaning towards me. He kept his gravelly voice low. "But Sky Boy doesn't." He flicked a finger towards Gian, who was sitting on a log across the little glade, head in his hands, massaging his brow. Light Ray was perched beside him, wide violet eyes looking all around. Ever since he'd left Old Nightfall, Gian had been growing steadily sicker with each passing hour.

"Maybe we can find a recle-mage to help him out when we're back in the City of Bones." I said through a mouthful of apple. I had my doubts about a recle-mage finding a home in Old Duskfall, after seeing its people and its culture, but I had to remind myself I had only seen the outermost ring of the City of Bones. The castle and the more sophisticated towns had yet to be explored, and I was sure the people there were more refined. It was a bit of a shame we wouldn't get to see any more of it for a while.

"I don't think we'll be there long enough to find one." Alchemy steepled the thin bones of his fingers together, absentmindedly tapping them together. "We need to get back to Brightlock as fast as we can. The Curse—"

"I know, I know, it's growing." I looked sidelong at him. "You and Sakura remind us constantly."

"Because it's important, Ksega." I paused at the tone of his voice. He was rarely very serious with me. "It isn't only growing. It's *changing*. The more powerful it becomes, the more it adapts to having that power. Whoever is in control of it is capable of commanding us for longer periods of time."

"You mean commanding the Cursed animals," I said. "You aren't one of them. You're able to resist it." And he was. Even though he spoke as if there was nothing human left in him, Alchemy was different from the other creatures the Curse claimed. He was fighting back, and not only was he fighting back, he was helping to bring about the destruction of the Curse once and for all.

Alchemy's only response to that was a sort of hoarse grunt. I would have pressured him to talk more about it—he rarely spoke of any parts of himself he'd rather keep in the dark, even when he pushed Sakura and I to embrace our own—but at that moment Gian rose to his feet.

"Are there any more of those apples?" he gestured to the satchel resting by my feet. I nodded and kicked it towards him. Hesitantly, he reached out to pick it up. I raised an eyebrow at him, and when he noticed, he grinned crookedly. "Sorry. I'm not used to being offered food so . . . *freely*." He squinted down at the apple he had pulled from the satchel. "No one has ever let me have fresh food, much less fresh fruit without some sort of payment, whether that's in the form of clothing or making an embarrassment of myself."

"That's alright." I smiled at him, hoping the expression was encouraging. "But you're away from all that now. We'll be your friends here. You're safe." I crunched into my apple, and after a baffled blink, Gian followed suit with his own.

"Safe might be the wrong word." Alchemy stood, towering nearly a foot over me. Gian's wary gaze locked on him. He was still afraid of Alchemy's true nature, even more so than Beth, who was the most superstitious out of all of us.

"Right." I rubbed the back of my neck, squinting into the distance. "Going on a deadly mission against the Curse. Maybe *secure* would be a better one. Is that Taro?" I pointed towards a small sliver of the Oasis's water, where a bird was swooping close to the surface before pulling up and away again.

"I think so. He might be trying to catch a fish," Alchemy commented.

"He'd better catch one for me, too," I muttered, looking at the last four bites of my apple. "I'm tired of only having old, dried meat."

"Well, you'll have to put up with it for a while longer," Sakura said as she crawled back out of her tent. Standing to dust the sand off the front of her pants, she added, "We don't have time to wait for him to finish his fishing."

"Beth said we aren't leaving until tonight, if the sand-sled is ready by then," I said, frowning at her. "That gives us the rest of the day to do whatever. Why not spend it fishing?" I wasn't by any means a fisherman, and any encounters I'd had with fishermen in the past had rarely been in a positive light, but I was always open to finding new talents. I only lacked a fishing rod.

"Because we're going to spend it planning." Sakura looped one of her feet through the straps of the discarded fruit satchel and kicked it up into her hand, reaching in to produce a slightly bruised pear. She stepped forward and took a seat on the log Gian had sat on moments ago, biting into the fruit. I raised an eyebrow at her.

"We are?"

"Yes. We are." She reached for another of the satchels we had stacked to the side, rummaging through it before pulling out a weathered piece of parchment. She unrolled it and set it down on the sand in the center of our rough circle, pinning the corners down with rocks. It was a map of Horcath.

Judging by the curling, torn edges, it was an old map of Horcath, but modern enough to show the correct borders of the kingdoms, after they had been severely altered by the wars of the Havoc Ages. The details in the tall peaks of the Shattered Mountains of Brightlock and the Slated Mountains across Freetalon and Wisesol were immaculate, with small slate-wolves etched into the paper, or even the small pebbles lining the Shattered Pass. The Evershifting Forest was like a sea of various types of trees and animals, displaying the broad possibilities of the forest's magic, and breaching the surface of the Great Lakes were the tall spines of jutting fins along the ridge of a sea wraith's back.

"What's this for?" I asked, stepping closer and sitting on the sand beside the map so I could get a better view.

"We need to have a solid plan for our journey. I'm tired of walking into things unprepared." Sakura clenched her hands into fists; I could see her thumb running over her knuckles as she glared down at the map. "When I was called in to talk to the king and queen of Old Nightfall, I was quite literally shaking in my boots. I'm not going to let that happen again, especially not in Brightlock. The Calderon family is too well-respected to let me march in there and claim they've created the Curse so boldly. We need to know what we're doing."

"First of all," I said, drawing her attention. "*You* aren't marching in there. *We* are marching in there. You're not alone in this, remember?" I gestured at Gian and Alchemy, who had huddled in around us. "You've got the three of us and Beth looking out for you."

"I hardly know Gian and Beth. No offense, but I don't think I'd trust either of them with my life." She replied, glancing up at Gian, who merely shrugged as he crossed the little camp to give Light Ray something to eat. I grinned at Sakura.

"So you're saying you trust me with your life?" I leaned forward, and she huffed and rocked back on her heels.

"Only if I'm left with no other choice, and you're willing to protect me as selfishly as you do that longbow." She nodded at the weapon that was lying safely unstrung and wrapped in leather beside my tent, lying beside my quiver of arrows. It was my most precious possession.

"Don't worry, I am." The second the words left my lips, I snapped my jaw shut. Sakura squinted at me, looking confused, and a snort-like sound escaped Alchemy behind me. I turned to glare at him over my shoulder and was grateful that Sakura had shifted her full attention to the map again.

"Beth can help us cross the Duskfall Desert, but we can't get through the Gates into Brightlock. With Beth and Gian added to the group, we can't scrounge up enough money to get us all through, and I haven't even tried to think of a way we could sneak Alchemy through." She frowned down at the map, as if it would give her an alternative path.

"Is there no way we can climb the cliffs we came down before?" I asked, recalling the descent into the desert. The craggy surface of the cliffs had given us plenty of stable hand and footholds. Even if it was risky, it was possible, and it cost nothing but our energy.

"You can climb, and I can climb, but . . ." Sakura looked up at me, then cast a meaningful glance at Gian, and then at Beth's tent. "I don't think we would be able to do it without sufficient climbing gear, and we don't have the time to obtain that. Even if we're spending another day in the City of Bones, it's only to get the final rations we'll need for the journey. We're so close to the end now. We can't get distracted. And besides, we don't have the money to get the supplies we'd need for that climb."

"So what's your master plan?" I quirked an eyebrow at her, scooting closer so I could see the map a little better.

"I have one in mind, but Beth won't like it." Sakura pursed her lips and squinted down at the map, reaching forward to tap the Oasis, depicted as a knot of palm trees, bushes, and broad-petaled flowers.

"Beth doesn't like much anyway," Gian commented as he returned to Sakura's other side, lowering himself down to the sand with us. Alchemy stepped forward from his rock seat and knelt on my other side.

"We could avoid going to the City of Bones altogether," Sakura began, letting her finger slide up north through the Oasis, cutting into the Evershifting Forest. "We already have an unguarded border right here beside us. It doesn't need a guard, because the Forest is so renowned for being full of deadly beasts. Normally, I wouldn't dare put us in such risk, but I think between the five of us, especially with Chem on our side, we don't have as much to worry about. We can go straight through the Forest and back towards the Stargazing Colonies where Ksega and I stayed before." Her finger trailed across the worn parchment, finally stopping over the little villages dotted around and on Oracle Lake, a series of intentional splotches that marked a portion of Brightlock.

"Don't we need supplies from the city?" Gian asked, voicing my own thoughts seconds before I could. I glanced up from the map at Sakura, expectantly awaiting her reply, but she didn't give one for a long moment, pressing her lips into a pale line and staring down at the map. When she spoke again, all she said was, "We don't need them."

"Explain why." I said, and she frowned at me, irritation forming a crease between her brows. "As much as you may want it, none of us can read your mind. You have to tell us your reasoning behind these kinds of decisions." She huffed but sat back to answer me.

"We have a good amount of rations, and it should only take us a couple of days to reach the little town where we were before. When we're close enough, we can send a few people in to gather any extra supplies we might need, then spend a day resting outside of any populated areas before we make our way towards the castle." She blew loose strands of dark hair out of her face. "It will give us more time to learn about what we need to do to get an audience with the king."

"You're right. Beth won't like that." I drummed my fingers against my knee. I wasn't saying Sakura's plan was a bad one. It was exactly the kind of unorthodox, unexpected sort of plan I'd pull out of my own back pocket. The problem was with executing it. On my own, it would be easy, but with this group? That was debatable.

"She doesn't have to like it to see the sense in it," Sakura pointed out, rolling the map back up. "It's quicker and better than going back to the City of Bones and trying to get through the Gates, *or* climbing up a cliff, and we all know it."

"Well, you can tell her all on your own," I stood and dusted sand from my pants. She scowled at me.

"Whatever happened to 'you're not alone in this'?" she huffed, standing. Gian and Alchemy both stood as well, and my lips split into a crooked smile.

"Being by your side when you're facing the man who might control the Curse? That's easy. Being by your side when you're changing plans on a short, angry Duskan? Not so easy." I shrugged and gestured towards Beth's tent. "Look, you're the only other girl, so naturally this responsibility falls on you. Don't worry, she'll understand. And in the meantime, I'm going to go see Mulligan."

She muttered something else under her breath, but I didn't hear as I turned away, already reaching for my longbow and quiver of arrows. I didn't think I'd need them, but it was a familiar reassurance to have the weight of them all the same.

"I'm coming with you," Gian said, falling in step beside me. I tensed, prepared to catch him if he lost his balance, but he only staggered for a pace or two before falling into the rhythm of walking.

I knew Gian didn't want me to be so ready to help him. I could tell he hated that all of us half expected him to collapse to the ground at any moment. I didn't blame him, after the way he'd been treated all his life. Being an underling on Horcath didn't make you much different from anyone else, even though the majority of people were a mage of some kind. Some mages had such weak magic or practiced so little that they were practically underlings themselves. Being born without magic only put you in a position that lacked advantage in certain situations, but while there may have been small acts of ill will towards underlings, violence or cruelty towards a person simply because they had no magic was unheard of, much less tolerated.

In Old Nightfall, the kingdom in the clouds, the Glass City that set itself apart from every other piece of Horcath, underlings were seen very, very differently. The tattoo on Gian's neck, a small black triangle beneath a rose, proved that.

For the majority of our time in Old Nightfall, I had been unconscious. According to Sakura and Alchemy, I had become terribly sick after reaching the well that allowed us into the kingdom. None of us knew why my body had reacted that way, but it was a mystery for another time. After everything had settled down when we'd returned to the Oasis, it had been explained that underlings in Old Nightfall, while they were called servants, were treated as slaves.

I still wasn't entirely sure I could wrap my head around that thought. Slavery was such a bizarre, old-age idea, I'd never considered it to be a problem in the modern world. I knew it happened, but it was on a small scale and highly illegal. Slave traders had thinned considerably over the past hundred years, as the Curse had taken hold, but it was still possible that some of them existed. It was a cruel way to live, and even crueler to be the one inflicting that life upon another.

Gian had always fought against those above him. As an underling, it had been the lot he'd been given in life to bend to those higher than him, yet it had been clear from the moment I'd met him that he spent every moment he could defying the powers he served.

Now, looking at him and seeing him reduced to the coughing, shaking, sleepless man he'd become, my heart twisted with pity. He took great pride in his independence, that much was clear, and I respected him for that. I was just afraid he didn't realize I possessed that respect, since he was so obviously weakened.

Being from Old Nightfall as he was, he'd never had contact with any sort of natural diseases or germs or sicknesses like I had, living in a mysterious kingdom so high into the clouds, and that meant, now that we had kidnapped him—which we most definitely had, even if I was the only one to call it that—his body, which had nearly no developed immune system, was faced with hundreds of new challenges.

"Why do you want to go see the camel?" Gian asked, drawing me out of my thoughts as we walked past the sandy banks of the Oasis's river. Overhead, Taro swooped and twirled through the light breeze, diving down at the water and skimming his talons through it before sweeping back up into the air. Light Ray watched him closely from his perch on Gian's shoulder.

"I've been wanting to try something with him the past couple days," I answered vaguely. Most people knew that bering-mages had connections to animals and that we could sometimes coax them to follow our will. This was all true, and it never required any physical contact, but there was a deeper aspect of it as well, one that did require you to come in contact with the animal you were connecting to. I'd only done it once, with Mulligan himself, and, if I was being honest, had been a little hesitant to repeat the experience. But I was ready. I wanted to learn more about my magic, now that it was getting stronger.

Gian gave me a strange look but said nothing as we continued towards the ruined gates of the Oasis. They had once been strong, sturdy gates made from thick wood, held together by strong twine and heavy support posts, but after the destruction left behind by the sandcats and the panicking Horcathian camels, they were little more than splinters and broken beams. A team of men had already begun to restore them, as well as the broken sand sleds, but it would be slow progress beneath the sweltering heat of the desert sun.

There were three Horcathian camels standing nearby, tethered to the thick trunks of palm trees that grew around the outskirts of the Oasis. One of them was Mulligan, Beth's camel, an antsy young creature with yellowing tusks jutting from his lips.

There were a few people, Duskans with their bronzed skin slicked with sweat and their hair flattened against their heads, but they didn't pay us any attention as we approached the camels. Mulligan and the other two camels twitched their ears at us as we came closer, but none of them made a move until I stepped up beside them.

"What are you going to do?" Gian asked, looking warily up at the beasts. He'd only seen them from a distance before, and I could see his fingers shaking as he looked at them, barely two feet from their trunk-like legs. It was startling how often I forget how little he had seen of the world.

"Honestly, I don't know. That's what I'm hoping to find out." I stepped up to Mulligan, looking into his big, dewy, black eyes. The last time I had connected to him—that's what I had begun to call it in my mind—I had been overwhelmed. His emotions had mixed with mine, his heartbeat had thundered in my ears, his pulse had raced through my veins. It had been exhilarating . . . and terrifying.

Gian watched hesitantly a few steps away as I came up beside Mulligan, slowly reaching my arm out to press my fingers into the coarse fur of his leg. I closed my eyes and let my bering flow through me, twisting and writhing like great vines through my body, searching and waiting for my command. I urged it to reach forward, and I flinched as a branch of bering burst from my chest. I gasped and opened my eyes, but the tether between myself and Mulligan was invisible, and only he and I could feel its pulsing life.

Emotions stronger than any I'd felt before thrummed inside of me. I could feel what he felt, sense what he sensed. I was off-balance and dizzy from the pounding of twin heartbeats in my ears and the rush of power in my veins, but some things seemed to be in extreme focus. The grains of sand beneath me, digging into my feet, despite my boots. The desert sun was suddenly more distant, not as intense and suffocating as it had been before. The gentle breeze tickled my ears and buzzed around my eyes. I could hear sounds I'd never heard, feel strength and energy like I'd never had before.

"Ksega?" The voice made me suck in a breath, but not like a gasp, more like a great tunnel sucking in a powerful gust of wind. It made me stumble back, coughing, and my entire world flipped upside down. My chest felt like it was being torn in two, and I wheezed as the breath left my body in a mighty rush. I felt myself falling but was only distantly aware of my body hitting the ground.

"Woah, careful! He's going to step on you. Are you alright?" The voice echoed around my head, ringing like bells in my ears. I groaned and pushed myself up onto my elbows, squinting as the earth swirled around me. A face formed before my eyes. Prominent cheekbones, but hollow cheeks; dark stubble against grayish skin; unkempt, shoulder-length black hair, and tired but sharp green eyes.

"Gian," I rasped, surprised at how dry my throat was. I coughed and pushed myself into a sitting position, looking up at Mulligan, who now towered so high over me it made my head spin and my stomach curl in agitation. I groaned, rubbing my hand against my temple to try and soothe the ache, and took deep breaths to try and loosen the tight stretching feeling still in my chest.

"Let's not do that again, shall we?" Gian stood and offered me his hand. I accepted it but gave myself an extra boost as I pulled myself up, aware of how weak he still was. He didn't seem to notice.

"Yes, let's not." I agreed, grimacing. He looked like he wanted to say more, but I held a hand up. "Another time. For now, let's go see if Sakura's delivered the unpleasant news to Beth." As we stepped away from the camels, my stomach growled, and I smiled sheepishly. "And if Taro's managed to catch me a fish."

2
SAKURA

Beth was sour with the suggested change of plans, complaining about all the work she'd gone through and the money she'd spent to get all of us back to the City of Bones safely, but even with all her swearing and dirty looks, she couldn't deny the practicality of my idea.

"We'll need to pack up and get out of here fast, then," she said once we'd agreed, her accented voice heavily laced with irritation. "They'll want me to give them more money for taking Mulligan home safely, but I'm not dropping another shin for their services. They care enough about the culture of our people to take him anyway, but if they can suck some more money out of us, they will." She led the way out of her tent and started to gather our packs and miscellaneous items together. Alchemy was leaning against a tree nearby, and I nodded with a small smile when I saw him. He returned the nod, although with his ever-grinning face, it was hard to tell if the smile had also been mutual.

I'd never tell him to his face—or skull, I suppose—how much he meant to me, but I was glad Alchemy was there. Since I'd met him, he'd filled a sort of void that had been left by my brother, but only halfway. He had been that confident, prodding arrow that acted as my guide as I continued on my journey. As much as I hated to admit it, Ksega had filled the rest of that void, replacing my brother's annoying sense of humor and stupidity with his own. Of course there was still room in my heart for Finnian. Nobody could replace him. But Finnian changed after the Curse had caused him to kill his eirioth dragon, Elixir, and the old Finnian that I had known was gone. The new Finnian would always be loved by me, but it was time I found a way to move on from his past and mine. Letting Alchemy and Ksega into my life seemed like the perfect way to do that.

I helped Beth break down the tents and pack everything into neat and manageable piles. There was no way we could bring all of it with us, but what was vital had been set aside. It wasn't easy leaving some of the tents behind, but they were too much dead weight, and even though there were more of us now, each of us could only carry so much. We would just have to share.

Just as we were finishing, I looked up to see Gian and Ksega returning. I wasn't sure exactly what they had gone to do, but I also found that I didn't really care, so I only nodded a greeting to them.

"Grab some packs, boys," Beth instructed, yanking on a strap to cinch a pack securely to a bedroll. "We're moving soon."

"We are?" Ksega raised his eyebrows, throwing me a questioning look. I nodded and pulled what I could over my shoulders, biting back a groan as the straps bit into my shoulders. It had been several days since I'd last carried them, but my muscles hadn't fully recovered from all the traveling I'd done over the past weeks.

"You're coming with us?" Gian's voice was chilly as he leveled his olive-green gaze at Beth. She met it with her own dark eyes, keener and sharper than his could ever be. His gaze dropped without further question. It had been heavily debated before whether she would come with us or not, but I always knew her curiosity would win out in the end. She wanted to see more of the world, no matter how much she denied it.

"We should hurry. We've wasted enough time on this wild raptor chase as it is," I said, hoping any arguments would be settled then and there. They both gave me an aggravated look, but I ignored it, satisfied that they would stop their squabbling.

I was ready to bring the Curse to an end. Ever since I met Alchemy, I had felt that we had a true chance of stopping it, and we had been hunting down its source every moment after. At first, we were just chasing our own hopes, the logic that wound itself outside the boundaries of magic, but the Curse *was* magic, and it was evil magic, which had brought our attention to the ancient andune of the Duskans. After a brief and unfriendly encounter with a witch, we had been led to Old Nightfall, a kingdom of supposed legend, where I had nearly given up my search, left with nothing but failure and embarrassment to take home with me, but Ksega had given us a new lead, which we were following now.

The Curse was created by someone, a powerful mage many, many years ago. The last war waged between kingdoms was almost two hundred years in the past, between Brightlock and Coldmon. Carlore, my home kingdom, had fought alongside Coldmon for much of the battle, but fell back when Brightlock's forces became too many. Coldmon had the natural barriers of the Great Lakes to assist their soldiers, but Carlore had no such protection, and they decided it was a losing battle. In the end, Brightlock was victorious, its power-hungry king expanding his lands across the Shattered Mountains and into the Evershifting Forest. Had he not died, he would have continued fighting for all of Horcath.

It made sense for someone like that to reach into the depths of forbidden magic to forge a weapon so powerful and savage that every victory was guaranteed. But the Curse was a wild thing. Alchemy had told us many times before that whatever source controlled the Curse only called upon it for hours at a time, bending all it possessed to one singular will.

When the Curse wasn't summoned by its source, it ravaged the world, creeping into all the kingdoms and spreading like a terrible plague through its creatures. It had been this way all my life, and for many years before then. It was growing stronger now, claiming powerful beasts like herds of runeboars and even the eirioth dragons that were so beloved to my people.

"Sakura?" The voice sucked me out of my thoughts, and I looked up to see Ksega frowning at me, a light of concern in his eyes. My scowl deepened at the expression. I was growing tired of how much he paid attention to me. Couldn't he tell he was being a distraction?

"What?" I snapped, glancing around to make sure everything was sufficiently packed up.

"Nothing. Sorry. You just looked a bit angry." Ksega leaned back, looking slightly hurt. I felt a prick of guilt but wouldn't apologize.

"Maybe I *am* angry. Did you ever think of that? Come on, let's go." I adjusted my boots and stepped into the jungle-like terrain of the Oasis, dodging branches and bushes and vibrant flowers, careful to move my feet deftly around the roots and twigs that broke through the sandy earth.

"Why?" Ksega asked as he followed. Beth, Gian, and Alchemy trailed after us. Light Ray and Taro swooped lazily overhead, too wary of each other to settle onto their respective perching shoulders.

"Why does it matter to you?" I grumbled at him, annoyed that none of the others bothered to come up and walk alongside me like he did.

"Because you're my friend, and you've been acting strange ever since we came back from Old Nightfall." Ksega replied, his voice hardening a little. I glowered at him, and he huffed and looked at the path ahead. "Not that you weren't abrasive and snarky and stubborn before, but . . . you seem different now. You weren't so devoted to this. You were purposeful, but not to the point you drove yourself over the edge. What's gotten into you?"

"Maybe I *should* have been this devoted," I bit back. "You act like this Curse doesn't affect you, but I know it does. Maybe there aren't as many Cursed animals back where you live, and maybe you haven't suffered from it as directly as I have, but there are people out there losing their lives and losing their loved ones, and you expect me to stop and let that happen?" I could feel my chest warming in anger but tried to keep my voice down. The last thing I needed was one of the older three to start lecturing me.

"I never said you should stop. Those things are terrible, and I want to help you bring an end to them, but it sounds like you're trying to justify all of this to yourself, because you know what you really want is—"

"Is what, Ksega?" I stopped walking, turning sharply to face him, ignoring the surprised halting of Alchemy, Gian, and Beth some distance behind us. Ksega slowed to a stop as well, watching me with wide and uncertain eyes. I glared at him, waiting, a sharp defense ready on my tongue, because I already knew what he thought it was I wanted. Everyone thought they knew, thought they understood how I felt, but how could they? Had they seen all but one of their family members brutally torn apart by Cursed animals? Had they seen the misery and terror in Finnian's eyes when he had driven his dagger into the heart of the animal he had loved and cherished since we were children? How could they *possibly* understand what this meant to me, how important it was that I was the one to finally make a difference, and fix this terribly broken world?

He held my gaze steadily, patiently, and for a moment I thought he would voice his thoughts; then something in his eyes changed. They weren't as soft and pitying as they had been before. Now, they were indifferent, their stunning, beautiful blue replaced with an icy wall.

"Nothing. Maybe I'm wrong. Maybe you aren't acting any different. But if you really want to help people, Sakura, I suggest you actually learn how to let them help you, too, because you won't make it anywhere on your own." Then he turned on his heel and continued walking, forcefully shoving low-hanging branches out of his way.

Grinding my jaw, I cast a warning look behind me, then followed him, my stinging eyes boring into his back as I tried not to let the truth of his words burn into my heart. But they did anyway.

Finnian had always taught me that each year of my life would bring new challenges; that each month would bring new heartaches; that each day would bring new struggles, and each hour would bring new losses. That was the mind of a warrior, he would tell me, to not only be prepared for those things, but to accept them. Being ready for the end of the world was different from being at peace with the end of the world.

I had never understood what he meant by that until recently, when every hour *did* bring new losses. When every little thing reminded me of home and the things I had left behind, and when every little thought shoved all my mistakes right back in my face. It was painful and it was hard, and I was tired of it all.

Finnian had also taught me how to be strong through those challenges and heartaches, and how to overcome those struggles and losses. He had taught me through waking me up long before the sun rose and taking me out to our training glade by the King's Scar to train with our swords or curls of eirioth. He had taught me through laughter-filled races on the backs of our dragons, winding through the twisting, knotted branches of the colorful Eirioth Wood. He had shown me the light in small victories and the peace in those safe moments with the ones I loved.

I desperately wished I could thank him for everything he had shown me. I had always yelled at him or hit him or scowled at him whenever he had done those things for me, because they were an inconvenience. Now, they were probably the only thing helping me retain my sanity.

It wasn't easy, obviously, but it was *easier* with Ksega and Alchemy by my side. I was still warming up to Gian and Beth—they were adjusting to us, too—but knew that in time we would all get along better than we did now. There was a lot of tension and confusion at the moment, and I still wasn't happy with Alchemy for dragging Gian along with us, but there wasn't much we could do about that situation now. The magical well that had served as a portal between the Oasis and Old Nightfall had closed and, according to Beth, moved on to a new location as a part of its protective enchantment. I wasn't going to put the effort into hunting down a magical well if all it would do was put Gian back into a world of slavery and rebellion, so he was left with us, even if that meant we would end up half-carrying his sickly body across Horcath.

I looked back at him now, walking alongside Alchemy, who was keeping his stride even with Gian and Beth's so he could stay between them. I wasn't sure what it was the two of them had against each other, but I suspected it had something to do with the fact that their birds didn't get along. The moment I had the thought, I glanced up to see Light Ray and Taro diving around each other, beating their wings at each other's heads and releasing disgruntled squawks as they tried to avoid the branches they flew past. Gian and Beth did nothing to stop them, instead throwing dirty scowls at each other.

I stumbled over a root, fumbling to catch myself, and kept my gaze trained forward after that. I didn't like being left alone with my thoughts, but it was better than falling face-first into the sand. Besides, we would be reaching the border between the Oasis and the Evershifting Forest—also the border between Old Duskfall and Brightlock—soon enough.

It was a few hours past noon when we reached it. I hadn't expected it to be so blatantly obvious that we had reached the tree line of the Evershifting Forest, but the change was so evident, it couldn't be missed. The sandy earth we had been traveling on, which was loose and patchy, came to a jagged stop against tightly packed dirt covered in happy green grass, sprinkled with gently waving tulips of lavender and pink. Rising tall and high above the spiky palm trees we had wandered past were elegantly pointed pines, littering the ground with warm green needles and pinecones. A wave of humidity passed over us when we stepped across the border, and I breathed in as a gentle breeze—cool and light, nothing like the harsh winds of the desert—blew through my hair. Already I could hear the excited chirping of birds and flitting of wings deeper into the forest, and a flower of joy and contentment bloomed inside me. The desert had been beautiful in its own way, but I was glad to finally be back in an environment I was suited to. The same could not be said for Gian and Beth.

When we stepped into the boundaries of the Evershifting Forest, Alchemy, Ksega and I all seemed to lower our shoulders in relief, but Beth grew more tense. I could tell from the way her eyes widened and her hand instantly gripped the handle of her cutlass that she had never left the Duskfall Desert before. I wasn't too worried about her, though, because if I'd learned anything about her, it was that she was a hardened warrior. She'd been through hardships before, and a change of surroundings wouldn't be what took her down. Gian, on the other hand, looked like he might fall over at any moment.

"We should stop for now," Ksega said from up ahead, slowing to a stop, and I could tell it had been because he'd looked back at Gian and seen his sweat-soaked shirt and dipping eyelids. He looked absolutely miserable, with his shaking hands and his ragged breathing, but none of us said anything, because we knew he'd hate it.

I stopped just a few feet behind Ksega and the rest of the group alongside me. I could have gone on walking, and I was sure Ksega and Beth could too, but we all knew Gian needed a rest, and we could all do with something to eat. I had skipped breakfast, after all.

"Who has the food?" I asked, shrugging my packs off my shoulders.

"I do, I think," Beth said, slinging her own pack off and crouching to rifle through it.

As I waited for her to find us something to eat, I looked sidelong at Gian. I had expected him to be finding a place to settle down and rest, especially with his labored breathing, but I was surprised to find him carefully holding a thin clump of his hair in front of his eyes, meticulously working out a small knot in the black strands. He caught me looking and scowled, turning away as he finished working out the knot and combed his fingers through the rest of his hair, making sure there weren't any others to be found.

"You care a lot more when you have long hair," Alchemy's whisper was like a husky rasp in my ear, and I raised an eyebrow at him, gesturing at my head, where my own long dark hair was fastened in a bun at the nape of my neck. I rarely did anything with it, other than putting it up to keep it from falling in my face or making my neck too hot. I hadn't even brushed it since I'd left home. Even when I'd been at home, I'd hardly ever brushed it, aside from when I washed it. Gamma always hated it, but I'd gotten good at keeping it in such a state that she couldn't tell if it had been brushed or not.

"You care a lot more when you're a *boy* and you have long hair," Alchemy corrected himself, shaking his head as I tugged my hair free of its bun, letting it fall loose and running my fingers through to try and separate the clumps. I blew some of the frazzled strands out of my face and grinned slyly at him.

"You had long hair?"

"Of course I had long hair. I'm a Talon." He sounded almost offended, but I knew he was only teasing. It was common knowledge that most Talons grew their hair out very long, typically fashioning it into thick braids or twisting crowns or intricate buns. Despite having known that he came from the kingdom of Freetalon, I had never imagined what Alchemy might have looked like before the Curse had turned him into what he was now.

"Hey, *Faja*," Beth tossed a strip of some sort of dried meat at me, and I clumsily caught it. I frowned at the name, still unsure of its meaning. "There's also some fruit, if you want that," she said, producing a number of other food items from her pack and passing them out to everyone but Alchemy.

"This will do. I'm going to go find a good place for us to camp." I looked up through the thick branches of the pine trees around us. The sky was slowly being enveloped in a veil of orange and gold as the sun sank farther to the west. "This place isn't very safe, and it's even less so after dark."

"I'll come with you," Beth said, setting her packs aside and whistling for Taro. He swooped down from one of the branches overhead to perch on her shoulder as she followed me into the dense forest.

"We won't want a big space," I said, craning my neck as I tried to keep a lookout for any potential dangers. It was one of those rare occasions when I wished Ksega was at my side, with his helpful ability to see living things around us that we normally couldn't spot.

"Couldn't we just sleep in the trees?" Beth asked, gesturing at the trees around us. She was looking at them a little wonderingly, and I had to remind myself she'd never been in a thick wood before. Eirioth trees were magical and unique, but they weren't the only kind of tree I'd been exposed to in Carlore. Growing up in the desert, Beth hadn't seen the variety of plants I had.

"The Evershifting Forest isn't very reliable," I told her, kicking a pinecone out of my path. "It can change everything about itself within minutes. Sleeping in the trees wouldn't be our safest option." I thought back to when I had first entered the Evershifting Forest. I had used a log as a bed one night, and in the morning, it was completely gone. The only thing I knew of that was unaffected by the forest's changes was Alchemy's cave, which he had informed me the forest left alone. It was strange to think a forest could know he lived there, but it was a powerful magic that the forest possessed, so I wasn't terribly surprised.

It didn't take us long to find a good place to camp. There was just enough space for four bedrolls and a small fire pit, and enough thick-trunked trees packed around our camp to give us good cover if it happened to rain. We marked it by jamming a stick upright in the dirt and began to make our way back to the boys. I was tempted to ask about Beth as we walked. I didn't know a lot about her, and that made me uneasy. She was a dangerous woman. She wasn't a very strong andune-mage, but because of that she had devoted her strength to mastering the art of the cutlass at her hip, using her skills to drive and protect one of the great Duskan sand-sleds.

But what else did I know about her? What about her family? I could ask the same questions about Gian and have no useful answers, but I intended to get some soon.

"How did you know Kieran?" I asked finally, pushing a drooping pine branch out of my path. Beside me, Beth tensed, her features twisting into an angry scowl, and Taro ruffled his feathers at her discomfort. I raised my eyebrows in mild surprise. Kieran had been the man that had taken us to the Oasis and sadly lost his life during the scuffle with the sandcats. It was Beth who had arranged for him to take us, and I had assumed they were friends, especially considering he had referred to her as Beth instead of Erabeth. I hadn't expected her to be so agitated at the mention of him.

"We've known each other since we were children," Beth spat, still glaring at the ground, fists clenched. She was silent for a long moment, and I dared to ask another question.

"Were you close?"

"Very." She snorted, shaking her head. "For a long time. It was just him and me, growing up without loving homes, without stable jobs, without useful magic." She pressed her lips together tightly, and I could see the muscles in her jaw flexing. "We made it work. We were happy." Her expression softened, her eyes turning to a warm brown that resembled the swirling coffees Gamma often made for people in Hazelwood Inn. "We were engaged. We were *in love*." Her eyes hardened, glimmering like the hot coals of a dying fire. "And then he left. For that *ista*'s daughter." Her lips peeled back in a mocking sneer as she roughly kicked the dirt beneath our feet, sending clumps of dust and pebbles skittering into the underbrush.

My eyebrows lifted in shock. I couldn't tell if I was more surprised that Beth, *Erabeth*, the fierce, thick-skinned warrior that never seemed to stop glaring, had actually been in *love* with someone and engaged to him or that he had turned away from her for . . .

"Mariem?" I asked hesitantly. Beth's scowl deepened, a look I had seen on her face the first time we had told her we needed to speak with a woman named Irina. Mariem was

Irina's daughter, and because of her illegal practices of bone reading, Irina was referred to as a witch—or *ista*, in Sandrun.

"*Yes*," Beth snarled, her hands curling into fists. On her shoulder, Taro fluffed his feathers and stared around us with narrowed eyes. "I only asked him to help you because . . . well, you needed the help. I thought the well may have been a myth. I thought maybe you would see that your quest was pointless and you would go home." She looked over at me, brows furrowed. "But I was wrong. You seem more determined than ever."

"Well, now that we have a pretty good idea of who's behind it, I'm eager to get to the end." I sighed, pursing my lips. We were so close. We just had to get an audience with a king, and then . . . I still wasn't sure what I was going to do once I reached that point, but I still had a week or two to figure it out.

"That makes sense. I'm glad you feel that way. Your enthusiasm is contagious." Her frown curled up into a sly smile on one side. "Your friends are more energetic than you are, but you have the true drive behind it all."

"I'm glad you're coming with us," I admitted, stepping away from her to avoid an unstable patch of earth before coming back to her side. "It will be nice to have another level-headed person on the team."

"Don't underestimate Bones and the archer." Beth remarked, and I raised an eyebrow at her. I knew Alchemy and Ksega were both capable fighters–they had proved that on more than one occasion—but making good decisions wasn't Ksega's strong suit, and Alchemy had been a hermit in the Evershifting Forest for so long, he wasn't much help when it came to current conversation.

We said nothing until we came closer to where we had left the boys. I could hear Alchemy's rasping laugh from somewhere up ahead, but he blended into the trees too well for me to spot him right away. Ksega was chuckling too, and I could see him leaning against a tree, holding a half-eaten apple. Gian was standing beside him, and I realized he was a few inches shorter than the Solian. He was still combing his hands through his silky dark hair, careful to keep the part perfectly in the center. None of them had noticed us yet, and I touched Beth on the arm to stop her. She glanced at me, a question in her eyes.

"I'm sorry," I said, and at her confused frown, I elaborated. "About . . . you know. Asking about Kieran. I just assumed he was a good friend, and now that he's . . . well." I bit my lip, internally wincing as I realized how insensitive I sounded, but Beth only smiled sadly and shook her head.

"It's okay, *Faja*. No need to apologize. He's a thing of the past now. For everyone." She ran her thumb lovingly over Taro's beak, and his eyes closed in pleasure as he turned his head to rub it against her jaw in appreciation.

"What does that mean? *Faja*?" I asked as we resumed our walk. Ksega caught sight of us and smiled, and I gave him a small wave of hello. He returned it, but only briefly, his head tilting to the side as his gaze flicked about the forest around us.

"In plain Sandrun, it means 'fire,' but when it's used as a title—or a name, in your case—it means 'of the sun.'" Beth's smile had turned warmer. "The sun blesses people with its warmth and light, but you are one of the few blessed with its own power." She nodded at my hands, which hung at my sides. Instinctively, I looked down at them, feeling my eirioth surge to the surface of my skin, warm and reassuring. "The honorary title *Faja* means that I have seen you use your power in a manner befitting one who shares the gift of the sun's fire." Before I had the chance to respond, she pushed forward to the others and knelt by the packs she had left, retrieving her own meal.

Light Ray and Taro both made uneasy noises at each other, and Gian and Beth gave each other cold glares as they maneuvered around the packs, careful not to come close to each other. I didn't blame Beth for being wary of Gian. Not only was his bird not a fan of her bird, but he was also a Nightfaller. Beth told us once that her people believed the magic of Nightfallers wasn't natural, and that the kingdom of Old Nightfall itself may have been a fable of old. It was anything but that, and its people weren't corrupted by evil, as she had believed, but it would take time for her to adjust to that knowledge.

"Find a good place for us to camp?" Alchemy questioned as I stepped up beside him, rolling my shoulders to try and relax my muscles.

"Yeah. It isn't far," I told them.

"Let's get there quickly then." Ksega tossed his apple core over his shoulder and rubbed his hands together, reaching down to pick his packs back up. I would have argued that I was still hungry, but there would be time to eat once we'd set up camp. Besides, Ksega was unnaturally antsy, and that set me on edge.

Gian looked to be steadier on his feet, but that was where the improvement ended. Beads of sweat dotted his brow and slid down his neck, soaking into his shirt and clinging to his skin. His eyes darted every which way, drinking in the details of the forest. I was a little worried he was experiencing too many new things and too many changes at once. His body's weak immune system was already taking a heavy toll on him now that he had left Old Nightfall, and I wasn't sure how much excitement he could take in his current state.

Once everyone was ready, Beth and I led them towards the place we had marked. As we walked, I noticed how skittish Ksega was acting. It made me nervous to see him so jumpy, so I let Beth take the lead, falling back so I was walking alongside him.

I was still irritated with him for what he had said earlier, but I tried not to let it seep into my voice when I asked, "What's going on with you? You're all shaky." He wouldn't meet my gaze, his eyes constantly moving over the trees and underbrush around us. It was similar to the way he had behaved when we were around the water, like the docks of Brightlock or Famark, but a little less terrified.

"It's my bering," he said, squinting. "The life glows here are different than they were before. Last time, I could sort of sense a distant life within the forest, but now it's strong. I can *feel* it. It's like everything has a heart and a pulse of its own." He grimaced, one hand reaching up to gingerly touch his earlobe. "It's deafening."

"Is there anything dangerous?" I asked, remembering the way he had sensed living things around us before, and when he had been able to sense multiple Cursed runeboars in the village around us. If there were any threatening beasts lurking in the shadows nearby, I'd like to know about it.

"Nothing yet. It's just a bit . . . eerie." He looked at the canopy of pine needles above us. "I'm sure the feeling will pass, or I'll just get used to it. Sort of like that buzz I'm used to with Alchemy." I often forgot how strongly Ksega's senses were tied to his bering. Eirioth relied heavily on physical strength, while many of the other mage types took root from emotional or mental paths.

"Okay . . . just let me know if anything changes." I started to go ahead, then hesitated, adding, "I think Beth has some tea leaves left. It might help, if you have a headache."

He nodded. "I'll try some." He pressed his lips together and shrugged his shoulders. "I just can't shake the feeling that the whole forest knows we're here."

3
SAKURA

*E*veryone's job—when it came to setting up camp, at least—went without saying. Each of us that had need of one set up our bedrolls in a sort of half-circle, leaving space in the center of the small clearing for a fire. Gian sorted and organized all of the packs while Erabeth rifled around to gather enough food for all of us to have some supper. Alchemy gathered stones that were large enough to arrange into a safety ring for our fire. Ksega used his bering to draw thick branches out of the trunks of trees and, with Alchemy's help, broke them apart to stack into a neat arrangement of firewood. I worked to dry them out with my eirioth so they would burn better. While I was doing that, Ksega pressed the tips of his fingers against the bark of one of the nearby trees, and when he slowly pulled his hand back, I watched, mesmerized, as thin twigs followed, each of them clinging feebly to the ends of his fingers. Then he repeated the process a few more times and snapped all of the twigs away, setting a bundle of kindling beside the stone ring.

"Back away," I instructed, placing some of the larger logs into the circle of stones and packing some of the kindling on top before standing and holding my hand steadily over the wood. My eirioth burned inside of me, like a constant well of flame lying in the pit of my belly, always eager for me to give it more leash. I did so now, letting the power flow up through my chest and down to the tips of my fingers. I took a bracing breath through my nose, carefully letting a tendril of yellow-orange flame curl out from the center of my palm. Eirioth was wild and demanding, especially of its wielder, who was drained of their physical strength the longer they maintained the fire. I coaxed the snake of fire down towards the kindling, entranced by its twisting motion, and a flower of pride bloomed in my chest as I remembered what Erabeth had said—*the gift of the sun's fire.*

"Very nice." Alchemy commented as the twirl of fire reached the wood at last, wrapping itself like glowing ribbons around the thin kindling until its heat ensnared them in its writhing grasp, erupting in a plume of bright red as it boasted its freedom. I lowered my hand, content that the flames would be satisfied with the wood they had been given to consume.

"Very *hot*," Gian corrected him, his lips curling into a frown as he stepped away from the flames, absent-mindedly swiping perspiration from his brow and combing his fingers once more through his hair.

"It might be best if you sweat it out," Ksega advised, giving the Nightfaller an apologetic look. "I'm not sure what exactly has made you sick, though."

"*Everything* has made him sick," Beth remarked, setting some small loaves of bread near the fire to heat up. "He's never left that *dasten* home of his. He's never experienced the heat of the desert sun, the prick of sand in his heels, the relief of wind in his hair." She curled her nose up at Gian. "He is like an infant. He must learn it all."

"What does *dasten* mean?" Gian snarled from where he had tucked himself into the shade of the pine trees, his voice enough to startle Light Ray, who was perched on a branch above him.

"It means 'dark' in my language." Beth spat. "That is what your kingdom was borne of. *Dasten limga*. Dark magic." She bent back to the bread, refusing to acknowledge him any longer. He sneered at her from the shadows.

"For once, I agree with you. That place is wretched." He crossed his arms, wearing a surly expression. "And I'm not an *infant*."

Beth snorted, but didn't respond.

I was prepared to argue the point that Old Nightfall wasn't wretched. Yes, it must have come from an ancient and powerful magic, possibly one that *was* dark and forbidden, like whatever had caused the Curse to come to life, but what it had become was anything *but* dark. It was bright and beautiful and happy. The buildings were made from sheer glass, the people were orderly and neat, owls were everywhere, and the roads were made of *clouds*. Everything I had seen was breathtaking and awe-inspiring. What I had learned there, specifically of its people, maybe a little less so, but nobody seemed to hate the Nightfallers as much as Gian did. I didn't blame him. The tattoo on his neck marked him as a slave, the property of the Nightfaller king, forced to serve those higher than him, and all because he had been born an underling, without any magic.

"I'm going to go patrol around," Alchemy said, shedding the clothing he acquired before we had left the Oasis, exposing the smith-tooth daggers strapped to the insides of his arms with what I assumed to be strips of homemade leather. It always made me uncomfortable to see him without anything on, and not even for the reasons most people might think. It was just *unnatural* to see someone so thin and spindly. There was no substance to him, and while it was still painfully obvious how thin he was when he wore the clothes, it was almost excruciatingly so when he took them off.

None of us argued as he wandered off into the growing shadows of dusk. We enjoyed a silent dinner, and patted the dust out of our bedrolls. Everyone began to remove their weapons. Ksega unstrung his longbow and set it to the side with his quiver of arrows, Beth set the sheath of her saber close to her sleeping place, I polished the iron of my flame-sword hilt and set it beside my pillow with my belt. Even Gian had something to remove: A small, thin dagger resembling an oversized sewing needle was produced from the inside of his shirt. We all tucked in for the night and lay there, looking up at the sky. There wasn't much of it visible, what with all the pine branches obscuring our view, but there was enough for me to pick out the dusting of silvery stars that peppered themselves across the blanket of purple-blue.

It wasn't long before Ksega was snoring on the other side of the dwindling fire, and eventually Beth's snoring joined it. Gian would cough every now and then, and I could hear Light Ray and Taro shuffling about in the trees around us, ruffling their feathers, clicking their beaks, and scooting around on their branches as they tried to drift into sleep.

I tried to join them, tried to let myself be lulled into the comforting embrace of unconsciousness, but it was a futile effort. The darkness closing in around me made me feel like I was being choked. I knew it was only my imagination making my chest tighten. I knew it was only the day's traveling making my shoulders ache and my toes go numb. I was being unreasonable, thinking something was out there, trying to find its way to me. Alchemy was patrolling around the camp. He didn't sleep, so he was always on alert. He would keep us safe. I could sleep.

So why wasn't I?

I closed my eyes, forcing myself to take a few deep breaths, trying to set my thoughts in order. I needed a way to clear my head, but not right now. Tomorrow, I would go and do some training with my flame-sword. We wouldn't start moving until later in the day. It would do everyone—especially Gian—some good to take a little break and just try to enjoy themselves.

A small voice in the back of my head whispered anxious thoughts at me, reminding me of my past fears of more and more people dying the more time we wasted. Yes, that was still a risk, but it was only half a day. Besides, I needed to sharpen my skills with the flame-sword; what good would I be in a fight if I no longer knew how to properly wield my weapon?

I woke up long before dawn arrived, sweat-slicked and shaking, fear and nerves coiling tightly in my belly. Beside me, the fire that had been lowered to an ember now roared, reaching its tendrils of flame so high into the air they brushed against the pine branches. Panic coursed through me as I saw it, hurriedly closing my fist to bring the eirioth down again, and it swooped down to the crumbling, ashen logs with a powerful hush.

Gasping, I forced myself to sit up, looking wildly around me. The dark forest lay to my right, rustling and shifting and whispering in the quiet. Beneath my shirt, which was plastered to my back with sweat, a chill slithered down my spine. Trying to calm my racing heart, I wriggled out of my bedroll and crawled to the pile of packs, searching for some water. When I found it, my shaking fingers fumbled to hold the water skin to my lips.

Nightmares weren't a common occurrence for me. Despite the haunting memories of my family that clouded the back of my mind, I had only dreamt of their awful deaths a handful of times. Sleep was often dreamless and peaceful for me, especially considering how little of it I managed to get.

The nightmares, when I did have them, always left me trembling. This time was no different. I remembered it vividly and despised myself for it. Who would want to hold onto such memories?

It was that terrible day twelve years ago, when I was walking home with Aurora. We saw the boards that once made up our home, now blood-stained, broken, and splintered. We went inside, and everything after that I would rather leave forgotten. But I couldn't. Even though I knew it was a memory, it didn't feel like one. It felt real and terrifying. The screams I heard, the leaping wolf, the blood staining the floorboards, all of it was terribly, cruelly real.

I forced myself to drink the water, shutting my eyes tight against the world around me. There could be Cursed beasts lurking just beyond the shadows, waiting for the right moment to slip in and tear me apart just as they had done to my parents and my sister, and if they did try, I would fight with every ounce of strength I had. Finnian and I had been robbed of our family, and now the Curse was trying to tear what was left of us apart. It had already taken Elixir from Finnian, and I wasn't about to let it take me, too.

Shuffling back to my bedroll, I shrugged into its warmth, ignoring the strands of hair that clung to my damp skin. I was tired, and even though fear still coursed through me, I could feel drowsiness seeping farther and farther into my body. As I turned over, facing the fire and the strange comrades I had come across, my heart twisted with emotion. I had to remember that I wasn't alone in this. While some of us may have different motives than others, we all had the same collective goal, and I knew that we were all willing to work together to destroy the Curse.

With that in mind, a calm settled over me, and as the eirioth fire before me slowly dwindled back down to its soft golden flickering, I finally let my eyes slide closed against the night.

I never would have thought of Alchemy as a cook, and even now that I'd gotten to know him a little better, it was hard to imagine him hard at work in a kitchen. But several times I had been proven wrong. The skeleton was full of surprises.

When I opened my eyes again, rubbing the weariness from them, the pine forest around us was gone completely. We were in a small glade of lush grass, dotted with gorgeous wildflowers and surrounded by a sprawling forest of silver birch trees, their leaves a vibrant green and their trunks shining brightly in the glare of the morning sun. The most pleasant change to our surroundings was the softly rippling lake that took up half the glade, its waters clear and pure.

"There she is," the gravelly voice drew my attention to where my eirioth fire still burned, roused back to a steady flame. Alchemy was crouched beside the stones, the slender bones of his fingers carefully handling slices of bread that appeared to be buttered and topped with small basil leaves.

"That smells good," I croaked, blinking the sleep from my eyes and pulling my legs out of my bedroll, sliding my feet into my boots before resting my arms on my knees and my chin on my arms. My eyelids started to droop.

Alchemy was looking at me, the bottom of his skull walled in by the folds of his cloak's hood. "You're up after Ksega. That's new." He chuckled hoarsely, the sound bouncing eerily around the glade.

"I didn't sleep well," I admitted, my eyes opening again to search the glade. It was empty except for us and Gian, who was feeding what appeared to be a field mouse to Light Ray. "Where are the other two?"

"Gone hunting. Ksega wanted something other than dried meat and fruit." Alchemy replied, carefully setting another slice of the delicious-smelling bread on the stones beside the fire to toast.

"Is that . . . tea?" I squinted at what appeared to be a teapot crudely carved from wood, set beside three equally rough wooden cups.

"Yes. I found some chamomile while I was keeping watch last night and used my daggers to make a pot and some cups. I figured Ksega might appreciate some. Do you want any?" Alchemy leaned over to peer into the pot, checking to see how much there was.

"No thanks. I don't like tea." I yawned and stretched, beginning to pack up my bedroll. "We'll stay here for most of the day. It'll give Ksega and Beth time to hunt." If he had any eyebrows to raise, I'm sure both of them would be rocketing skywards.

"We will?" he tilted his skull to the side, the glowing green cracks that ran through it like veins pulsing from the orange light of the fire. "I thought you were in a hurry."

"I am. We just need a rest." I wasn't about to tell him that what he said in the past had influenced my decision. I knew he was one of the people that thought revenge was what fueled my hunt for the Curse, and he thought I would stop at nothing to destroy it. I wanted it gone, yes, but I knew that I had my limits. Why was that such a big deal, anyway? I wanted justice, but maybe I wanted a little bit of revenge, too. Maybe that was what I needed to finally have closure concerning the deaths in my family.

"Alright then . . ." He watched me for another long moment before I cleared my throat and awkwardly nodded towards the toast on the stones before him.

"Your bread's burning," I grunted. He glanced down and muttered a curse as he pulled the bread away from a snaking twirl of fire.

"You did that on purpose." Avoiding the accusation, I leaned forward to see what else there was to eat. He had made several slices of the toast, but there were a few fruits left, and some pieces of the jerky Ksega was always complaining about. I opted for a fuzzy peach and a slice of the buttered bread. I wasn't entirely sure where Alchemy had acquired the butter, but it probably came from the packs Beth brought with her.

"I'm going to train a little bit after breakfast," I said, reaching for a skin of water. "I need to work on my flame-sword skills." I looked across the glade at Gian, who was now carefully cleaning the underside of his fingernails with that sliver of a dagger. "Do you know what anyone else plans to do?"

"I'm not sure how long Beth and Ksega will be gone, but Sky Boy over there doesn't seem to have any plans. I think he was considering taking a swim in the lake," Alchemy replied, nodding at the water beside us. The thought of jumping into it was tempting. I knew how to swim, but I hadn't had many opportunities to practice it growing up in the southwestern portion of Carlore. The Fruit Spring was where Finnian and I had first learned to tread water and swim easily beneath the surface. But I hadn't gone swimming in a long time, and I wasn't sure I wanted any of my companions to see me flailing aimlessly in the middle of the lake.

"Sounds good," I reached for my belt and clipped it into place, sliding my flame-sword's gleaming hilt into its appropriate pouch at my hip. If I was being honest, I was a little disappointed that neither Beth nor Ksega had tried to wake me to bring me along on their hunt. I needed a good reason to get up and start doing things in the mornings.

After I finished my measly breakfast, I stood, brushed the dust off my pants, and walked farther into the forest, pulling my flame-sword out as I did so. I could have practiced in the glade we camped in, but I wanted to find a setting with a bit more stone. The fewer things my eirioth could burn, the better.

It took me a little while to find a place that would work, but it was only about half a mile from our camp, and it would be a perfect place for me to train. Any training sessions I had been through in the past were with Finnian, and most of them had taken place in our training glade near the point of the King's Scar in the Eirioth Wood. Despite the Scar being a series of jagged slopes and outcroppings, there were few natural stone structures in Carlore itself.

The place I found was a neat little clearing with sparse grass and several moss-covered boulders. Only one or two of the spindly silver birch trees stood close enough to be at risk of being burned, but I was confident enough in my abilities to control my eirioth that it didn't cause too much concern.

I stood in the center of the clearing for a long moment, staring around me expectantly, and with a start I realized it was because I was waiting—waiting for Finnian to step out of the shadows of the trees, for Sycamore to give me an encouraging chirp from the tree line, or even for Derek to swoop down from above on Bear—but when none of those things happened, I released a sigh. I wasn't used to being on my own like this. It had been alright when I was first starting out, traveling towards the Evershifting Forest in the hopes of finding information about the Curse, but after Alchemy and Ksega had joined me, and now Beth and Gian, I found that, when company was an option, I much preferred it over quiet solitude.

Taking a steadying breath, I lifted my arm, my flame-sword's handle held tightly beneath my curled fingers and coaxed my eirioth forward. It spurred through my arm, erupting in a spitting tongue of orange and gold, curling and warping until finally it solidified into the beam of fire I had spent so many years learning to wield.

I went through a series of movements I had practiced when I was first learning, drills that served as helpful warm-up exercises for any training occasion. Once I was done with those, I moved on to more complex combinations, arcs and jabs and twirls, things that could also be practiced with a normal broadsword. A sweat broke out along my brow and on my arms as I danced around one of the boulders, whipping at it with the flame-sword, watching as the flames splayed out and twisted when they came in contact with the stone.

My muscles complained as I worked them, throbbing and aching and stretching as I twirled the fire through the air, but I wouldn't let them rest. Instead, I added another element to my training, letting the form of the eirioth change. It elongated into a writhing whip, snapping through the air as it hissed and bit at the stones. I practiced with it for almost two hours without stopping, ignoring the protests from my body as I jumped and feinted around the boulder.

"Mind if I join you?" The voice brought a groan to my lips, and I turned with an exhausted expression, sweat dripping off my chin, to see Ksega stepping into the clearing, longbow strung and in hand, quiver of arrows clipped to his belt at the hip.

Licking the salty perspiration from my lips, I flicked my wrist, letting the eirioth snake out before spinning in on itself as it spiraled back into the metal of the hilt, extinguishing itself coolly against my skin. I let out a rasping breath, pushing the flame-sword hilt into its place on my belt and stepping to the side to sit on one of the lower boulders, trying to still the trembling of my sore muscles.

"Do you have a target?" I quirked an eyebrow at him, reaching for my water skin and taking a swig. The water was warm, and I grimaced.

"The trees will do fine," Ksega answered, and my lowered eyebrow lifted to join its twin.

"They're hardly wider than my hand." I commented, and a sly grin pulled across his face as he lifted the longbow and pulled an arrow from the quiver at his side.

I hadn't seen him practice with his bow and arrow before, but I *had* seen him shoot. It had only been for brief moments, when we were fighting with the runeboars, but the long hours of training were easily visible in the way his hands slid into their familiar grip on the longbow and the few seconds it took for him to aim and fire. This time it was different—he didn't just glance and shoot. He took his time, knocking an arrow to the bowstring and pulling it back to full draw, his arms steady despite the pressure being put on his muscles. I watched closely as he narrowed his clear blue eyes, keeping them locked on one of the birch trees in front of him. They closed, only for a second, before they snapped open again and the arrow was sent hissing into the air. My eyes couldn't track it, but my ears could. It whisked past the place where I sat then buried itself with a heavy *thud* in the wood of one of the silver birch trees, almost exactly in the center. Before I had the chance to look all the way back at him, another thud followed. When my gaze returned to the tree, I saw that another arrow penetrated the bark just above the first one, and as I was watching, another joined it at the top. By the time he was done, Ksega had fired fifteen arrows and made clean vertical lines with them in three separate birch trees, all in the span of a couple minutes.

"Impressive," I admitted, nodding my approval as I rose from my boulder seat. I walked over to him, offering him the water skin. He accepted it and gratefully lifted it to his lips. Derek was a skilled archer, but even though he could hit a running Cursed badger with ease, I wasn't sure even he could pin a tree as thin as this, especially not from the distance Ksega had.

"Sure, when it's quiet and I can concentrate." He chuckled softly, handing the skin back to me and shaking his head as he pulled another arrow from his quiver, inspecting the sharpened tip with a slight frown. "I wish I could have such accuracy when there's more stress on me."

"You did fine with the runeboars," I reminded him. I couldn't recall any of the finer details, but I remembered him firing while running and still hitting his target. Many archers I knew wouldn't even attempt such a thing for fear of the arrow flying wildly askew.

"Yeah, I suppose." He shrugged and went to the trees he had shot, squinting at them. "You know, it never feels very good to shoot something I'm so connected to. It doesn't cause me any physical pain, but I definitely question whether or not I should do it at all . . . I mean, they are *living* things. The arrows don't really hurt them, only create a piercing in their substance. It's less of a wound and more of a shallow scratch, but it doesn't make me feel any better about doing it." He shrugged to himself. "Can't really be helped, though. Things live and prosper, but nothing can avoid a few scars here and there. At least I'm not killing them."

I said nothing, unable to find anything good to say. I couldn't relate to him, considering eirioth didn't allow its mages to have any special connection to it. Bering was much more mental and emotional than my own magic, which was part of why Ksega's personality and my own—and at times our morals—were vastly different.

I was about to ask how his hunt with Beth had gone when a branch snapped loudly in the shadows behind one of the taller boulders. I looked up sharply, half expecting to see a raptor or maybe a fox, something small. What I *wasn't* expecting was to find myself looking directly into the dripping fangs of a hungry smith.

With a yelp, I stumbled backwards, my hand instinctively reaching for the flame-sword hilt at my waist. The eirioth blade that spewed from the metal was strong at first, but it quickly died down, condensing to only half the size I would have preferred. I gasped, shocked at how much my strength began to wear down as soon as the flame was conjured.

"Back away from it," Ksega's voice came from behind me, high-pitched with shock. "I've got an arrow on him."

The smith's lips curled and dripped with blackish ooze, its red eyes sparkling with murder. My feet felt like lead, and my eirioth-flame was already sputtering as I struggled to concentrate on keeping it alive. I dragged myself backward, my heart thundering in my chest as I kept my eyes trained on the smith, still crouched in the shade.

"What are we going to do?" I asked softly, just loud enough for Ksega to hear me. I wasn't sure how far behind me he was, but I couldn't help but wish he were closer. "We can't fight it." Hundreds of stories had been told about the ferocity of smiths, the giant bear-like beasts that strongly resembled wolves, fearsome and vicious and deadly. The only person I had ever met capable of killing a smith was Alchemy, and I was sure that was only because he couldn't be killed himself.

"Don't worry." Ksega's voice was calm, which was more than could be said about my own voice. "If we can get close enough to the camp, the others can come help."

"Great plan," I rasped, a tremor working its way into the words. My flame-sword was as short as Finnian's favorite dagger now. "Let's let Beth and Gian get killed by the smith, too." I had hoped it would bring a little more light to the situation, but all it did was make my stomach knot in fear. The last time I faced a smith, I had barely escaped with my life, and all because the Evershifting Forest had given me a safe lead, and Alchemy had shown up to kill it seconds before it tore me in half. Something told me I might not get so lucky this time.

"Stop being so dramatic, nobody's going to *die*." His voice wasn't far now. I wanted to look back at him, to see how much farther I had to go, but I was too afraid to see what would happen if I took my eyes off the smith. It was low to the ground, its muscles bunched, but it was by no means small. It was almost as big as the first one I had been chased by, but scrawnier, with mousy fur. The fact that it looked sort of like an overgrown golden fox didn't make it any cuter.

"It's going to jump," I whispered, more to myself than Ksega. I could see the muscles twitching and flexing in its powerful legs. My eirioth-flame vanished in a wisp of smoke, and I gasped, shocked at how weary I'd suddenly become. One of my legs nearly gave out, and I stumbled back, my head swimming with the wave of exhaustion that swept over me. The smith tensed, its shoulders shifting eagerly, giving it the appearance of a cat waiting to attack.

"I've got you." A voice sounded in my ear, even though I was only distantly aware of it. Ksega's hand gripped my arm, steadying me against him. "Take a second to get your strength back." He adjusted the way he held his longbow, an arrow still knocked to the string. "Back farther into the woods. Get back to the camp. Alchemy can help. *Go*." With a gentle shove, he stepped away from me and drew his arrow back again. I blinked the bleariness from my eyes, stuffing my flame-sword back into its sheath and stumbling backwards until I was beyond a thin veil of birch trees. The farther I went, the more I could see of the smith, and my breath hitched when I saw its haunches, curling and blackened.

"Ksega," I called as quietly as I could manage. He kept his eyes on the smith, but angled his head towards me to let me know he had heard. "It's Cursed."

4
KSEGA

I uttered a swear under my breath the second the words left Sakura's lips. The Curse's corruption must have been very minimal in the smith, because none of it showed on the front half of the beast. Its eyes were red and lively, its fur silky and shining in the flashes of sunlight that dotted its pelt, and its defined muscles flexed and rippled beneath the golden coat. The Curse must have begun to spread through its back half, which I couldn't see.

"Just keep going," I called back to her, wishing I could look over my shoulder to make sure she was going but not wanting to give the smith an opening. "I'll be fine."

"I'll get Chem as fast as I can," she said, and then I heard her retreating footsteps, as soft as she could make them, as she ran into the woods. I pressed my lips together, my brows pinching with worry. I knew using her eirioth could drain her of strength, but I hadn't expected it to leave her so exhausted. The journey back to the camp wasn't terribly far, but in her condition, it could have been miles. I wished I could go with her, just to make sure she was okay, but there was no way I could turn my back on the smith.

It was growling, slobber dripping in blackened globs from its dark lips as it twitched and jerked anxiously. I would have put it up to the creature's nature before, but now that Sakura had pointed out that it was Cursed, I couldn't deny the obvious signs of its corruption. It might have given me an advantage. I'd never seen a smith before, but I'd heard vague stories of their ferocity. The Curse had different effects on different beasts, so there was no way to be sure, but if it had affected the smith's hind legs badly enough, I might be able to stay ahead of it long enough to do some damage with my bow and arrows.

It slunk forward, keeping close to the tree line, and I trained my bow on it, following it carefully and aiming for one of its glinting eyes. My heart was pounding in my ribcage, but my arms were steady as I tracked the smith's movements. I wasn't sure if it would go for me or try to chase Sakura, but I wasn't waiting to find out. I decided to take a risk, angling my bow to the boulders and releasing the arrow. It hissed through the air, sparking on the stone and careening off into the shadows. The smith's crazed eyes flew to the source of the screeching sound, a snarl tearing from its throat as it lunged for the boulders. I pivoted on my heels and sprinted after Sakura. Much to my dismay, she hadn't gotten very far, and when I caught up to her, I slowed my jog to match her pace. I didn't say anything to her, because I knew she understood the severity of the situation just as much as I did.

"Did you distract it?" she panted, glancing over her shoulder. I grimaced.

"Only for a moment. Keep going." I took off to the right, crashing through the woods, stepping on branches and dragging my longbow through bushes, anything I could do to cause noise. Sakura's muffled footsteps were inaudible seconds after I began running, which I took as a good sign.

Almost as soon as I started the ruckus, I heard the angry snorting of the smith, following me from scent and not sight. I saw it before it spotted me, its senses muddled by the Curse, whirling in circles as it tried to track me. When it did, my heart skipped a beat. I could see its back end now, patchy and blackened. One of its hind legs was gone entirely, with a crumbling black bone jutting from the stump. A twist of unease curled up my spine. I'd seen the Curse at work before, and not just in Alchemy and the runeboars we fought back in Brightlock. There had been a few young raptors, feisty and fighting as they hunted for living flesh. Sometimes it was little more than a limping carcass, so overcome by the Curse it could hardly move, but nothing I had seen could be compared to this. The smith was larger than the runeboars, and much larger than any raptor.

The beast let out a roar and charged for me. I already had another arrow knocked, and I let it fly, turning to run again before I saw where it hit. I knew it struck the beast because a high-pitched shriek tore through the air, a blood-curdling sound that such a creature shouldn't have been capable of emitting.

I thought the arrow had helped slow the animal down, but from the pounding sounds behind me, it had done little to deter it. Gasping, I pushed my legs harder. I'd never been much of a runner. I could climb and sprint away from assailants and angry shopkeepers when necessary, but long distance runs had never been my strong suit, and I knew I couldn't outrun the creature, so I turned to my bering. I wasn't sure what power had caused the jutting thorns back in the Stargazing Colonies, but I wished I did, because I needed it now.

I glanced over my shoulder and my breath hitched. The arrow was burrowed into one of its eyes, and thick blood poured in rivulets down its face. More terrifying than that was the fact that the smith was much closer than I'd thought. I swiped my free hand through the air, calling to the plant life around me. The spindly silver birch trees heard my call, curling sharply towards the ground and forming a pale tangle of trunks. Vines and roots erupted from the ground, clawing into the air to create a mesh of sharpened thorns. The smith crashed into them, snapping some of the thin trees clean in half, and I winced as I saw their life glows flicker and wither into a dull, grayish green. The smith had lost its momentum, but it was still fighting through the maze of wood, which I knew wouldn't last long against its strength. I muttered an apology to the trees under my breath, as well as a quick thanks, then turned and ran back towards the camp, ignoring the aches sprouting in my feet.

I half fell into the glade where Sakura was just stumbling and yelling to Alchemy. He was a good distance off, close to the lake and still crouched near the fire, with Gian and Light Ray at his side. I could tell from the way he stood and faced us, hands already angled towards the concealed daggers strapped to his arms, that he knew we were in trouble.

I was about to shout that there was a smith behind us—Sakura was so out of breath she could do little more than scream his name—but before I got the chance, a crash sounded behind me, and the smith thundered into the clearing, blood soaking into its fur from the wound the arrow had caused. As soon as he saw it, Alchemy ran towards us, passing Sakura and coming close to me, flicking one of the smith-tooth daggers free of its hiding place.

"What happened?" Beth was sprinting out of the woods to the side, rushing to the fire to meet us. Sakura practically fell to the ground in front of it, gasping for breath and grimacing as she hugged herself. I wanted to lean down and try to help her, but the smith wouldn't be distracted by Alchemy for long. He was another Cursed being; the smith wanted something living.

"A smith snuck up on us." I looked over my shoulder to see what Alchemy was doing. The smith hadn't slowed at all, but that didn't deter the skeleton. Leaping up at the last second, he met the beast head on. The clawing bones of his fingers snagged in the matted fur of the smith's neck, and he dragged himself onto its back, bringing the dagger deep into its chest. It roared and threw itself onto the ground, rolling violently in an attempt to crush Alchemy beneath it.

"Stay here and help her," Beth ordered, and I glanced back to see that she was addressing Gian. He stood rooted to the spot, petrified with fear, his eyes wide as he stared in horror at the smith. It was a reminder to me that he had never seen the Curse at work aside from in Alchemy, and he had never encountered a creature such as a smith.

I waited until Gian nodded numbly before I turned back to the tussle in the glade. The smith was back on its feet now, less interested in the limp black form beside it now that it had once again locked eyes on us. I could see Alchemy moving, but only barely, and with a twist of horror in my gut, I realized several of his bones were broken, and one of his legs was split clean in half. The magic that kept him alive would weave the pieces back together—I had seen it after the sandcat fight in the Duskfall Desert—but it would take more time than we had before the smith got to us.

"I'll keep it busy," I said to Beth as we ran towards the fight. I wasn't sure if I had a plan or not, but I knocked an arrow to the string and drew back. I lifted it up, trying to steady my aim. The rough course of my run, combined with the fact that the smith itself was moving, meant my shot wouldn't be as precise as I would like, but it would at least hit the monster. As I let the arrow fly, I was already pulling another free from my quiver, knocking it as I curved around to the smith's side. Beth went the opposite direction, saber in hand and muscles bunched. I didn't doubt that she had fought her fair share of sandcats throughout her life, but this smith was much larger than the agile cats she was used to. It may have been slower, but it was much, much stronger.

My first arrow struck the smith in the shoulder, but it didn't pierce all the way through the thick fur and fell to the ground within the animal's next couple strides. My second, sent soaring through the air seconds after the first, found better purchase, digging into the Cursed hide of the smith and drawing its attention to me. Its eyes blazed with fury as thick silvery-black blood began to gush free of the wound, and it swerved sharply, kicking up clods of dirt and grass as it changed its course to barrel straight for me.

A third arrow was ready on my bow, and I lifted it as Beth sprinted up to the smith's rear. Feeling my pulse thrum in my ears, I slowed my pace to ensure I made the shot. If I made a mistake, she could end up on the wrong side of those terrible fangs.

I released the arrow, tracking it while I reached for another from my hip as I stumbled forward. The smith was facing me, and it saw the arrow approaching. With spittle flying from its mouth, it snapped at the arrow, yelping in shock and pain as it tore through the soft flesh of its cheek. I winced as the arrow flipped through the air, falling to the grass just beyond Beth, having accomplished almost nothing.

With a grunt of effort, Beth swung her saber at the smith's hind leg. The blade sliced cleanly through the fur, sinking into the meat of the creature's thigh. Despite her small size, the Duskan possessed terrifying strength. The smith screeched as it stumbled as the cut ran deep into its leg. It tried to turn towards her, but it angled too sharply and fell heavily to the ground. Beth slid to a stop, backing hastily away as the smith struggled back to its feet. I was facing its back now, and I drew my arrow back to fire it into the Cursed hide. It lunged at Beth, and a loud screech sounded from overhead. My eyes flicked up to see Taro circling overhead, looping around and around. When the smith did the same, it stumbled, seemingly losing all control of its own limbs. Taro looped twice more, then released another cry before diving to intercept the smith before it reached his master. The next few seconds were little more than a blur. My arrow struck the smith in the rear, sinking in almost to the fletching just as Taro reached the smith's face, his sharp talons ripping savagely into the tender flesh of its muzzle, and Beth rolled to the ground, still clutching her bloodied saber.

I saw movement out of the corner of my eye as Sakura rose unsteadily to her feet, Gian close to her shoulder, muscles bunched and pitifully thin dagger in hand. Light Ray was nervously flitting about the campground, wide violet eyes watching everything.

"Don't," I panted, slowing to a halt, my grip tightening on my longbow, silently pleading Sakura to stay out of it. It had hardly been twenty minutes since she started resting her eirioth, and I could tell from how flushed she looked that she hadn't regained enough of her strength to try and battle the smith.

My attention was drawn back to the smith itself as another tortured roar ripped free of its throat, and it stumbled back to face me, a hissing sound rasping from between its teeth. Taro had almost entirely shredded its face, letting thick blood flow over its eye and into its mouth, blinding it, but its nose was twitching fiercely, trying to detect where I stood. When it finally had its head angled in my direction, another gargled snarl rumbled from its chest, and it charged forward, nearly losing its footing with every other step.

Seeking another projectile, my hand instinctively curled around the rim of my quiver, but my heart leapt into my throat as my fingers closed on empty air. I risked a glance down, and panic seized my chest as I saw that all my arrows were gone, most of them still buried in the birch trees. My only remaining weapon was my bering, but there was nothing for me to use, no roots just below the ground, no trees to draw into a safe cage, nothing but the soft grass beneath my feet.

The smith was almost upon me now, blood and foam and spit flying from its mouth, its whole body trembling and struggling against the Curse and the wounds that riddled its body. Its jaws snapped open and closed, teeth gnashing eagerly as it approached me. I was rooted to the spot, unable to drag my feet away, terror crawling through every inch of my body as I waited for the awful fangs to close on my flesh. The scent of blood and decay curled in my nose and pooled bitterly in my mouth, making me shudder. I closed my eyes and flinched away as its heavy footfalls pounded so close to me it sounded like thunder, waiting for the pain. But it never came.

A hiss and a crack rang out in the air around me, and my head snapped up, my eyes widening as I saw a snake of fire whip through the air and curl several times around the wounded leg of the smith. It cinched tight against it, the flames licking at the fur and setting it alight, creeping up its hide and along its back as the eirioth hungrily claimed more of the beast's body. The rope of flame drew taut and jerked backwards, causing the smith to lose its footing and fall back onto its haunches, widening the wound Beth had given it and letting more blood spill into the earth. A blur of black and green raced in close to the fallen monster, and with a final squelch of blood, Alchemy's bone dagger found its home deep in the heart of the smith, twisting and turning as it shredded the inside of the animal's chest when Alchemy buried it deep. The beast stumbled against the skeleton, snarling and groaning as it slowly sank to the ground, the green light coursing beneath its skin dimming into darkness.

Everything after that seemed to be in slow motion. Sakura's shoulders slumped, and in a shower of sparks, the whip of eirioth vanished. Gian's rigid posture sagged a little, and Beth dragged herself back to her feet, inspecting her blood-stained saber. Alchemy stood and staggered back from the body of the smith, his bone dagger still locked in place and the shadowy fibers of his bones still weaving themselves back together into glowing green cracks. I watched it all for a moment, numb, until the panic and action caught up with me and the fatigue set in. My knees felt like the fruity jams Willa loved to make, and I sagged to the ground, my breath escaping in a *whoof* of relief as I released my bow and lowered my head, shutting my eyes against the dizziness that washed over me.

I'd never experienced such an intense sense of urgency in any fight before, and it left me struggling to keep my breakfast down. At least I wasn't the only one it affected in such a way. Looking up, I could see Gian bent over by the shores of the lake, face pinched as he fought not to retch.

"Are you okay?" The voice came from to my left, and I turned to see that Alchemy had approached me, offering an arm to help me back up. I accepted it and pulled myself onto my feet, swaying softly back and forth. My pulse was still racing, booming in my ears, and I groaned as I rolled my shoulders free of their knots.

"Yeah, I'm okay. Is everyone else?" aside from Gian's puking and Sakura's visible exhaustion, I couldn't see that anyone was hurt.

"We're all fine," Alchemy reassured me. I gave him a brief once-over. He was still wrapped in his long cloak, but I could see where his skull had fractured and mended itself back together. New veins of green also scratched through the dark bones of his hands, and I knew a thick new band of the glowing magic was now on his leg, where it had been snapped in half. I wondered if it hurt him to have his bones broken like that, but I wasn't going to ask. If there was anything I'd learned about him, it was that he didn't like talking about himself, least of all matters pertaining to how he was Cursed.

"I'll need to retrieve my arrows from where I was training," I muttered, more to myself than him, as I cast a tired look in the direction of the small clearing, farther into the birch wood. I wouldn't bother to try and salvage the arrows I had fired at the smith; they were either covered in blood or broken, and I would rather fashion more on my own than try to restore them to the quality they were before.

"I'll fetch them." Alchemy gestured towards the camp. "I doubt it will be hard to find where you were, from the trail this monster left. Go and get something to eat." He looked over at the limp body of the smith and the growing puddle of blood beneath it. "When I get back, I'll figure out what to do with that thing."

I nodded, mumbling a "thank you" to him as I bent to retrieve my bow before marching towards the little camp. I settled myself onto the ground beside the fire pit, which now harbored smoking black logs and flickering embers. There were two hares and a quail lying beside the stone ring, the fruits of the hunt Beth and I had gone on that morning. The Duskan was already reaching for one of the hares to skin and prepare. Beside her, Gian was sitting closest to the lake, his grayish skin taking on a green hue as he stared disgustedly at the hare now being skinned with the short, glinting knife Beth had produced from one of her packs.

"I think we need to get moving as early tomorrow morning as possible," Sakura announced, leaning back on her bedroll and twirling the handle of her flame-sword around in her hand, seemingly to give herself a distraction. She looked ashen-faced and shaken, and I was sure I appeared in a similar state.

"Fine by me," Beth said, sliding her blade cleanly beneath the hare's pelt. Gian's face twisted, and he looked away. "I'm already sick of this place. How can you stand it?" She adopted a sour expression. "All these bugs, all this *wind*. It isn't natural."

"It is natural," I pointed out. "Just not the natural you're used to." I looked around at the silver birch trees lining the glade. "The Evershifting Forest isn't a natural that *anyone* is used to, I suppose."

"*That* definitely wasn't natural," Gian remarked, nodding at the body of the smith, already attracting flies. Alchemy would have to move it somewhere far enough away that any scavengers that found it wouldn't pose a threat to us.

"Nothing Cursed is natural," Sakura said, her brows furrowing. I frowned at her, recalling that she had spoken briefly of a Cursed eirioth dragon, and not just any dragon, but her brother's. I couldn't imagine what it must have been like for her to witness. The Curse being able to take a dragon was not a small piece of news. Dragons were not weak-minded creatures and shouldn't have been able to fall prey to the Curse. Then again, neither should a healthy smith.

"So what about Bones?" Beth asked, and I raised my eyebrows at her question, looking between her and Sakura. The Carlorian's features softened a little, and she shook her head.

"He's different. He's human." She sighed and set the handle of the flame-sword on the ground, lying back and closing her eyes. "What the Curse did to him outwardly is unnatural, but on the inside he's still a man. He has a conscience, a voice, a *life* inside of him that no animal claimed by the Curse can ever possess." She turned over, facing away from us. "Now hush. I'm trying to sleep."

5
SAKURA

My peaceful nap was short-lived. I was only able to sleep for half an hour before I was woken by Alchemy and encouraged to eat something to regain my energy. Beth was still preparing the hares with Alchemy's careful supervision, so I had to settle for fruit and dried jerky. I accepted some and chewed idly on it while I listened to the conversation around me.

Alchemy had removed the smith from the clearing, somehow managing to drag it farther into the woods all on his own. He had also retrieved any of Ksega's intact arrows he could find, but that only left the archer with eighteen that were still usable. He was currently sitting cross-legged beside the rejuvenated fire, carefully using one of Alchemy's elegant tooth daggers to shape new arrow shafts. Beside him, Beth was cleaning the gray pelts of the hares, meticulously removing every bit of dirt and grime from the fur. Taro was on her opposite side, his beak and talons cleaned of the blood and bits of smith flesh that had stained them earlier.

The only person not seated near the fire was Gian. He was on the shores of the lake, staring into the water, his elbows on his knees. Light Ray sat watchfully on his shoulder, eerily turning his head back and forth as he kept an eye out for any possible danger. The owl was adjusting to life outside of the Glass City much better than his master.

"I don't know what's up with him." Ksega had seen me looking at the Nightfaller, and now he was watching him too. "He's been quiet since the fight. I'm not sure what he's thinking about." He shrugged. "Whatever it is, at least it's distracting him from throwing up."

"When do you want to get moving tomorrow?" Alchemy poked me in the side, regaining my attention. I shrugged, wishing they had let me sleep longer.

"Right after breakfast, I suppose. We'll reach the Stargazing Colonies in a matter of days if we keep a good pace." I curled my hands into fists, running my thumb along my knuckles. "After that, we'll need to find a way to get an audience with the king."

"You plan to just march up there and accuse him of creating the Curse as a weapon to use on the other kingdoms?" Alchemy's skepticism was mirrored in the expressions of Ksega and Beth.

"No, of course not." I looked down into the embers of the fire. If I was being entirely honest, I hadn't thought that far ahead, but they didn't need to know that. I would find a way. At the moment, I was thinking I would try to find a clever way to question him, dancing around what I was really implying until he convicted himself. If I voiced that plan aloud, Alchemy and Beth would probably call it foolish, but I still had time to work out some finer details for now. Before any of them could interrogate me further on the matter, I stood and gave them a brief nod, keeping my eyes down and mumbling something about needing to get more firewood before stomping towards the tree line.

I wanted to be left alone with my thoughts for a while, but I knew the chances of that were low. After the smith attack, it was clear that none of my companions would let me wander too far away or go off on my own for too long. I didn't blame them; I would have done the same for any of them, as wild as that was. Before all of this, it wouldn't have crossed my mind to watch someone else's back so closely, aside from perhaps Finnian's or Gamma's.

I pushed my way through a small wall of bushes and farther into the woods, going just far enough that I was out of sight of anyone back at the little campground. I knew my departure would leave them with questions, but I was determined to have answers for them by the time I returned.

I wasn't certain that it was the Calderons—the royal family of Brightlock—that had created the Curse, although it made complete sense. Almost two hundred years ago there had been a great war between Brightlock and Coldmon, and my home kingdom, Carlore, had fought on the side of the Coldmonians until they saw the effort as a futile one. Brightlock had come out victorious, but not without major losses to their forces. For years, Brightlock slowly crept across Horcath, taking portions of the Shattered Mountains from Old Duskfall and pushing the borders of their kingdom farther into the Evershifting Forest. The growth of the kingdom had ceased after a while, and suspicions among the other rulers had been that they were preparing to mount a massive attack against one of the neighboring kingdoms, but before any attack could be launched, the Curse became a serious problem.

It would have made sense for the dots to have been connected by someone else long before anyone I knew had thought of it, except there had been one vital piece of information withheld from anyone before me: the Curse was *controlled*. Whether by some*thing* or some*one*, no one was sure, but from what Alchemy had told us about the calling force he had always fought against, I was willing to believe that someone had crafted the Curse as a weapon, and their plan had somehow gone horribly awry, leaving it to spread like a disease through all of the kingdoms. All that was left was to find who it was that had done it.

It was possible that King Kirk, the current ruler of Brightlock, wasn't the original master of the Curse, but it could have come from his bloodline or possibly one of the bloodlines in his court. An army general had every motive to reach into the depths of dark magic if it ensured the success of their endeavors, and even more firmly secure their position at a king's right hand.

The problem I was faced with now was finding a way to gain an audience with the king and his councilors. Confronting the king of Old Nightfall, whom we had originally suspected because of the rumors of ancient and dark magic surrounding not only the kingdom itself but also the people that dwelt there, had been a simple affair. As unexpected intruders, we had been brought before the king and queen to be questioned. Entering Brightlock through the Evershifting Forest meant we weren't passing through any of the Gates that barred passage between two kingdoms, and while our entry into it would most definitely be considered illegal, without anyone there to prove it, there was no way we could be arrested in a kingdom in which we were unwelcome.

I had never sought an audience with the king of Carlore, but in my modest education from Gamma I had learned enough to know it was a long and tedious process. Nobody could march in and demand to speak to such a powerful figure. One might be able to come before a duke within a day of the request, but there would be no such small wait to see a king. I had no doubt that the requirements for requesting to see the king of Brightlock would be just as precise, if not more so, than those of Carlore. There would be papers and officials and all sorts of complications that I had never dealt with before, nor did I want to deal with them, but I was afraid I would have no choice.

My moments of quiet silence were broken when a branch snapped off to my left. My head whipped around, my first thought that it was another smith or some other Cursed animal, and my second was that it was someone from the camp who had come to look for me. To my pleasant surprise, instead of being faced with a vicious beast or questions I still wasn't fully prepared to answer, there was a fox, its broad ears swiveled towards me, eyes wide and alert as it stared up at me. I could see its entire body, and it bore no signs of the Curse. It must have been young, because it was quite small, and far more curious than an adult would have been. I hardly dared to breathe as I watched it, stunned by the way the sun hit its orange coat in mottled patches of gold and copper. Its bushy tail flicked back and forth as its nose twitched, trying to smell me without coming any closer. I wished I could reach out and stroke the soft fur of its head, the vibrant orange color reminding me painfully of Elixir. At least it didn't have his aquamarine eyes to bring back my haunting memories of the dragon's death.

Before I was ready to have the little beauty vanish, I heard the sound of leaves and branches crunching beneath someone's boots behind me, and the little fox raced away into the bushes, disappearing from sight within seconds. I released the breath I had been holding and turned, wearing a nonplussed expression, to see Ksega coming closer.

"I didn't mean to scare it away," he admitted sheepishly, gesturing towards where the fox had run. "I didn't think it would be frightened of me."

"It isn't supposed to be, is it?" I raised an eyebrow at him. I hadn't known much about bering before leaving home, but now that I had spent some time with Ksega, I had a better understanding of it.

"Only if I'm actively trying to keep it calm." He shrugged. "I guess I wasn't focusing very well."

"It's fine. It should probably be developing a healthy fear of everything that comes crashing towards it anyway, right?" I crossed my arms. "What are you doing out here?"

"You said you were collecting firewood when there's still plenty of fuel for it back at the camp, *and* you can keep a fire going with no wood at all. Not the best lie you've come up with," he pointed out, and I rolled my eyes.

"It wasn't exactly made to fool you, you know. And I can't keep a flame going eternally. It takes up my own strength, remember?" I waved a hand in dismissal of the matter. "Forget it. Answer my question."

"We drew blades of grass to see who would come looking for you. I got the shortest."

"Curious for someone who can make blades of grass grow with the blink of his eye." I deadpanned. He grinned.

"Fair enough. Really, though, Chem is almost done cooking the hare, and we didn't want you to miss out on it. You know how good his cooking is. Unless, of course, you'd rather have all the dried fruit and jerky from the packs." He took a step back in the direction he'd come from, tilting his head in a question. With a sigh, I fell in step beside him, my stomach releasing a gurgle at the prospect of something Alchemy had cooked. I had been surprised to find that the skeleton was so adept at making masterpieces of food, but it wasn't a cause for complaint. If anything, it made me look forward to any meals that weren't a few bites of dried meat and fruit.

"Did you talk to Gian at all?" I asked, and Ksega shook his head.

"I plan to, but I didn't want to ask in front of Beth. She's already hurt his pride enough after calling him an infant." He opened his mouth to say something more, then closed it, hesitating.

"Go on, out with it," I pried.

"Were you watching the smith during the fight when Taro was flying over it?" he asked, and I paused for a moment, not expecting the change of subject.

"I guess so."

"Did you notice anything strange?" he pressed, his brows furrowing.

I frowned at him and asked, "What are you getting at?"

"Nothing. I mean, it might be *something*, but I'm not sure. I may have just imagined it. You know, from the adrenaline and all." He chewed his lip anxiously, watching the ground in front of us and letting his fingers brush along the fletching of the arrows that had returned to their home in his quiver.

"You weren't anywhere near stressed enough to start hallucinating," I said, earning another amused grin from him.

"True. Alright, I thought that when Taro kept looping around and around in the air the way he was, it made the smith's legs . . ." He blew air out through his cheeks, and mumbled, "This is gonna sound so stupid, but it *looked* like the smith's legs just *stopped working*. It tripped over itself and fell. Only after Taro started diving did it try to get up again." He said nothing for a long moment; or maybe he did say something, I just didn't hear it. His previous words had brought a memory swimming to the surface of my mind.

"What?" I asked, turning my head to face him and make sure I heard him right.

"Yeah, I told you it was gonna be stupid." He grimaced.

"No, I meant 'what' as in say it again. I think you might be onto something." I could feel my excitement bubbling inside of me as I realized what connection I was making. Ksega's eyebrows lifted in surprise and expectation as he watched me.

"Well, are you going to explain why?" he finally prompted.

"Oh, yes. I can do that. Just give me a moment to think." I focused once again on our path, rubbing my knuckles with my thumbs as I turned the thoughts over in my mind to make sure I had them in order. "The way he was going around and around, did it have any effect on you?" I asked, and he shrugged.

"It made me sort of dizzy, I guess, but other than that, no." His frown deepened.

"Maybe Cursed beasts are more sensitive to it," I muttered.

"More sensitive to *what*?" his voice had taken on an exasperated edge.

"I don't remember what it's called, but it's some big fancy word Chem taught me. The night we met you, actually," I slowed my pace as I thought, traveling back through my memory to when I had gone on that first little hunt to acquire some clothing for the skeleton. "I was out in the road on Clawbreak and there was a man wearing a strange shirt. Something about the pattern on it and the way he was swaying made me dizzy and sleepy, and before I knew it, he was right next to me with a knife. If Chem hadn't been there to snap me out of the trance, who knows what could have happened." I looked up at him again, sure now that I was right. "Something about the way Taro was circling in the air must have had a similar effect on the smith. We can ask Chem about it when we get back.

This might be something we can use against the Curse!" A grin split my face. "*Finally*, we might be making some progress!" Hardly unable to contain my excitement, I took off towards the clearing again with a confused Ksega right on my heels. For the first time in several days, I felt the comforting sensation of surety. At least we now had a chance to change *something* for the better.

*W*e didn't come to Alchemy about the matter right away. Beth had finished preparing the hare with some wild herbs she'd found, and it smelled delicious. We sat down to dig in, and I would have tried to discuss my latest revelation with Alchemy if another topic hadn't come up. We all sat there stuffing our faces with hare, except for Gian. He was quiet, poking at his meal and taking sparing bites, but then he spoke up, staring deep into the flames before him.

"I want to be trained." At first, I hadn't been sure he was the one who had spoken. It could have been Alchemy, and I had only tricked myself into thinking his voice was less hoarse than usual, but when we all looked up curiously, we saw that the skeleton was watching Gian.

"Trained?" Alchemy echoed, tilting his skull to the side. I stayed silent, watching with mounting curiosity as Gian slowly nodded his head.

"Yes, trained. I don't care how, I just need to feel less . . . *useless.*" Gian's lips curled into a scowl as he looked at the fire. "You saw what happened in that fight earlier. You were all doing your part, watching each other's backs and finding a way to bring that terrible beast down. And I stood here watching like a headless owl. I couldn't do anything. I don't know *how* to do anything." He lifted his glare to look into the dark pits of Alchemy's eye sockets. "One of you can teach me. I know each of you has your specialty, and I don't care which I learn, but please, one of you has to be willing to train me."

"So the Nightfaller finally humbles himself?" Beth said through a mouthful of hare. I cut her a warning look, but she didn't see it, her sharp gaze locked on Gian, who bared his teeth at her in a sneer.

"You could do with a little humbling yourself," he snarled.

"Admit it." She hissed, leaning closer, although it would do little considering they were on opposite sides of the fire. "Admit that you cannot do *anything* down here. Admit that while you may have been the greatest warrior or rebel or whatever saints-forbidden thing you thought you were in the sky, down here you are made no more than the mere infant I say you are."

He watched her closely from across the flames for a long moment, and I was afraid he might try to lunge at her, but even he wasn't that foolish. The knife she had used to skin the hares lay glinting by her side, and we all knew she wouldn't hesitate to use it on him if he tried to lay a finger on her.

"In Old Nightfall, I fought with everything I could," Gian finally said through gritted teeth. "But underlings are not allowed to wield weapons of any kind aside from these puny things." He pulled the thin knife from within his shirt. "I have not been given the opportunities to learn how to properly defend myself as you four have. I know I have a lot to learn." He lifted his chin stubbornly. "But I am still *not* an infant, nor am I equivalent to one."

"Your big words don't scare me." Beth said, unimpressed. "Why do you insist on using them?"

"In a place where formality is law, you develop the habit." He replaced the little knife in its home and turned his glare back to the rest of us, looking at each of us in turn. "Are none of you willing to teach me?"

We were all silent for a long moment. With the way Horcath was physically affecting him, any intense training might be a serious threat to his health, but it would also do him some good to start building up some strength. If he let the sickness eat away at his muscle, he would be even more hopeless than he was now.

"I don't have a real sword with me," I began, and everyone turned to look at me. "But Beth does, and if she's willing . . . I think a sword would be the most reasonable weapon for you to use, out of your options." I looked questioningly at Beth. I knew it was risky suggesting that we should force the two of them to put up with each other for several hours at a time, and even riskier suggesting that one or both of them be given a blade, but it made sense to me. If Gian wanted to help fight, who was I to tell him he couldn't?

"Yes," Beth said finally, her jaw flexing. "I agree with *Faja*."

"You do?" Gian's eyebrows raised in surprise, and I saw the look mirrored on Ksega's face. I wouldn't have been shocked if my own expression matched as well. Beth curled her nose at us.

"Yes, I do. If you really want to prove yourself worthy of working alongside us, you should know how to use a weapon." Her voice was like steel, cold and hard. I already knew she would be a relentless teacher, but Gian would be an equally stubborn pupil.

A silence followed her statement, broken only by Ksega dramatically ripping a bite of hare free from its bone with his teeth. I wasn't really sure what else to say. What more was there to be said? If Gian wanted to accept the offer, I would stay true to my word and help Beth train him. It would be strange, being the teacher for once. I had always learned from Finnian. Everything I knew had been drilled into my brain from the tips and tricks he and Walter and Derek had given me over the years, and from the midnight training sessions out in our little glade by the King's Scar. Was I ready to try and teach someone else?

"It's agreed, then." Gian said at last, nodding. "When will we begin?"

I looked to Beth for an answer. I still wasn't sure it was a good idea for Gian to try and take on something that required so much physical strength and energy, but he appeared to be certain about his decision, and if Beth wanted to get him started right away, that was her choice.

"When we set up camp tomorrow," Beth decided, tossing the bones of her bit of hare into the lake. "Try to conserve your energy when we're traveling." Then she stood and stretched her arms out. "I'm turning in. I'll see you fools in the morning." And with that, she shrugged into her bedroll and fell silent.S

The sun was dipping lower and lower into the sky, and I knew it would be wise for us to follow her lead and get some sleep, but I wanted to talk to Alchemy first. He was standing now, checking to make sure his cloak and smith-tooth daggers were in place before he began to walk away from the camp, assuming his usual position as the watch. As Gian grumbled something under his breath, tucking himself into his own bedroll and gently stroking the soft violet feathers on Light Ray's chest, I stepped around the campfire and followed the skeleton.

"Chem, may I have a word?" I asked, wrinkling my nose as we passed the place where the Cursed smith had died. The earth still bore a dark bruise made from the beast's blood.

"I suppose that depends on what the word is, Ironling." He responded, angling his skull up at the sky, which now had a few bright specks appearing across it.

"I don't actually remember the word," I said, glancing back over my shoulder. Ksega was watching us walk away, and I wasn't sure if he would get up to follow us. Turning back to Alchemy, I continued, "It was the one you taught me on Clawbreak, when that man in the strange shirt almost stabbed me. Do you remember?"

A hoarse sound that I assumed was a scoff escaped him. "When you've lived as long as I have, there isn't much you *don't* remember, as much as you might wish to forget it. Yes, I do remember. Hypnotism is what you're referring to. Why do you bring it up?" He looked away from the starlit sky to face me.

"Because I think it may have drastic effects on creatures that are Cursed. During the fight, Ksega said that Taro was flying in a loop over and over, and it made the smith fall."

My words came in a rushed jumble, so eager to get out that they almost escaped in the wrong order. The skeleton was silent for a long moment, and I was tempted to pry him for an answer, but I knew it would do nothing. He would give me a response when he wanted to, and not a moment before.

"It's an interesting theory. Do you know any way we can find more proof it will work?" he said finally. I was aware he already knew what I was thinking, and I wasn't sure how he would react to it, but we didn't have many other options if we wanted to test my theory.

"Well, we could try it with you . . ?" I wasn't sure if I should have phrased it as a question or not, but it was too late to go back now.

"We could," Alchemy agreed cryptically. "Do you think it would work?"

"There's only one way to find out, and there's no harm in trying. If it can work effectively as a weapon against the Curse, it could give us a major upper hand." I paused as a thought struck me. "Unless you think someone else has already tried it, and maybe it was just the right timing when the smith fell." Alchemy's long silence was almost unbearable.

"I doubt anyone has tried it against the Curse. Hypnotism is an old and lost art. I'm not surprised it's still alive on Clawbreak, because they keep all sorts of unthinkable things alive on that wretched island." He slowed to a stop, and I halted beside him, looking up into the dark pits of his eye sockets. "It's definitely worth a try. We'll test it out sometime tomorrow. I'll work on something we can use for it tonight. For now, you should head back and get some rest. We have a lot of traveling ahead of us." He lifted a slender arm, wrapped in the baggy clothing Beth had supplied him with, and hooked it around my shoulders, giving me a squeeze. "I'm proud of you for figuring this out, Ironling." I could hear the excitement in his gravelly voice. "I think the future holds good things for us."

6
KSEGA

*S*akura had made it a habit to wake me up by digging the tip of her boot into my ribs if I wasn't already up by the time everyone else was. I thought it was a cruel habit, but none of the others ever objected whenever she decided it was time to expand the bruise in my midriff.

Breakfast the following morning was small: some chunks of dried fruit and meat and whatever water was left in the water skins. Once we refilled them—the forest had decided not to change on us overnight again—we quickly packed up camp and began our march north. We were already in Brightlock, but how far we were from the edge of the Evershifting Forest was impossible to tell. According to Alchemy, it rarely altered the borders of the forest itself, so if I remembered my map of Horcath correctly, we were somewhere near the middle of it.

Conversation was minimal as we traveled. The first few hours went by quickly with only small grunts and groans of complaint from Gian, who was sweating profusely. He accepted water whenever it was offered to him but wouldn't let any of us support him as he walked. I wasn't sure what it was he wanted to prove—and whether he was trying to prove it to us or to himself—but I desperately wished he wouldn't push himself so hard. Light Ray even seemed on edge, flitting anxiously between the branches overhead as he tried to keep close to his master. It wasn't until after Gian had stumbled and fallen to his knees that Alchemy decided we should stop and rest for an hour.

"This will be a good time to try our experiment, Ironling," the skeleton said once we had located a good patch of shade to settle into for our break. I watched curiously as Alchemy pulled something from within his cloak. I was sitting too far away to be able to tell what it was, but it fit somewhat snugly into the palm of his leather glove.

"Ksega should come with us," Sakura said before Alchemy could lead her a little way off into the woods. She looked over at me, and I raised my eyebrows. "I told you you'd get an explanation," she told me, tilting her head to the side in a motion that clearly indicated I should follow her.

With a glance at Beth and Gian to make sure they would be fine on their own, I trailed after them into the silver birch trees, letting their life glows flow in and out of focus. It was almost blindingly bright to look at them directly, since all of the trees were so healthy and young, but it was a great reassurance to see them. Up in Old Nightfall, there had been no plant life for me to connect to. While it hadn't been as terribly disconcerting as being at sea, it was still a strange experience that left me feeling empty and twitchy. I was glad we were finally spending more time in a place where my bering was more comfortable.

"Hypnotism was what I was thinking about yesterday," Sakura told me as we followed Alchemy to a small patch of cleared grass.

"It puts people into a sort of trance," Alchemy explained as he turned to face us. "I've seen it coupled with magic in the past, and the results can be quite terrifying. People can be controlled to drastic degrees when under the spell of hypnotism."

"Is it a type of magic?" I asked, feeling my stomach squirm at the thought of not being in control of my own body.

"No. Anyone, mage or underling, is capable of learning and mastering hypnotism. It's much more dangerous when magic is at play, but to varying degrees depending on what type of mage is in control of it. No matter, though. If Ironling is right about this, and just simple hypnotism has more dire effects on Cursed animals than it does on humans, we won't need the aid of magic anyway." He began to pull his gloves off, and as I gave Sakura an uncertain glance, which she didn't see because she was watching Alchemy, he also shed his cloak and boots, leaving him in only the large shirt and pants that hung loosely on his frame.

"What did you make for us to use last night?" Sakura asked, and I saw that the small dark object was still in Alchemy's hand. Now, he held it up for us to see. It was a simple thing, constructed from vines, some pieces of sturdy tree bark, and a mostly rounded black stone. The stone was nestled snugly at the end of the vines, cradled in a basket of the natural twine with two pieces of the bark supporting it on either side.

"It's a pendulum," Alchemy said as he held it out to Sakura, who took it from the top of the vines and held it higher so she could inspect the stone. "It isn't the most effective type of hypnotism, as it takes longer to have any effects. Spirals are much easier to use, especially when you don't have a lot of time to get someone or something under your control. For now, though, this was the best I was able to do." He took a couple steps back and gestured at Sakura. "Hold it still at the top and let it swing slowly back and forth. If you ever want to try this on someone new, they will have to sync their breathing with the rhythm of the pendulum's swing as much as they can and focus on their breathing and their heartbeat and the swinging of the pendulum. They must be willing to be hypnotized in order for it to work, which is why this is the less effective method." He stood at his full height, clasped his hand bones in a confusing knot behind his back, and stood frighteningly still as he waited for Sakura to begin.

"Alright," she said, sounding a little unsure of herself, but not daring to argue with the skeleton. I kept silent as she held it high and as steady as she could. My pulse was beginning to pick up its pace, heart thumping in my ribcage as I waited with an uncomfortable mix of anticipation and dread. Whatever hypnotism was, it felt *wrong*. The thought of anyone trying to control a body that didn't belong to them chilled me to the bone.

"I'm ready whenever you are." Alchemy spoke calmly and confidently. How could he face the prospect of losing control of himself so easily? If I had been in his position, I would have been trembling in my boots. Had he been hypnotized before? Did he know how to escape its effects? He hadn't told us how to reverse the process. What if we locked him in a trance forever?

I was about to voice my concerns, but I didn't speak, because Sakura had set the pendulum swinging, and I didn't dare break her concentration. The black stone swung back and forth, back and forth. I tore my eyes away every few seconds, and even though there was no chance my rushed breathing could ever sync with its slow pace, I tried to keep track of it all the same. My eyes flicked back and forth between Sakura, the pendulum, and Alchemy. Because of his obvious lack of lungs and flesh, there was no way to tell if he had synced his breathing with the pendulum as he had told us was necessary, which made the process even more nerve-wracking. He hadn't told us how long it might be until we saw the results of the hypnotism.

The wait was growing unbearable. It couldn't have been more than a few minutes, but I was already getting antsy. Would we know when the hypnotism had taken hold on him? Would he be able to tell us? Would he mirror Sakura's actions, or ask for some sort of command from her? I wished he had told us more about the effects of the pendulum, and it irked me that he hadn't made us more prepared.

"How long do you think this will take?" I finally whispered when I noticed a small sweat break out on Sakura's brow. Her dark green eyes danced my way only for a moment before locking on Alchemy again, her wrist rotating ever so slightly every couple of seconds to keep the pendulum's rhythmic swing alive.

"I don't—" Sakura began to answer, but she didn't finish as her voice pitched up into a shriek. Through her scream, I heard a strange clattering sound that could only be one thing. My heart skipped a beat and my breath hitched in my throat as my gaze flew to Alchemy, where he now fell in a heap of bones and cloth to the dusty forest floor.

"He's dead!" I yelled before I could think, panic racing through me as I stared in horror at the pile of black bones, half hidden within the folds of his shirt and pants. I nearly choked on my own words. "You killed him!"

"I didn't kill him, he's *always* been dead!" Sakura snapped back, but I could hear her voice shaking as her wide eyes bored into the hollow sockets in Alchemy's skull. My gut twisted to see that his jaw was set at an awkward angle, pulled free of its sockets and jutting to the side.

"What did you do, then?!" I squeaked, worried that I was about to throw up my small breakfast. I couldn't bring myself any closer to the pile of bones, despite the part of me that wanted to step forward and try to piece them back together with some faint hope that it might restore him.

"I didn't do anything! Just what he told me to do!" Sakura's voice was higher than I'd ever heard it before, and there was more panic in her face than I'd ever seen in one person's expression. "What do we do? Is he gone? *What do we do?!*"

"I don't know!" I took a pace forward, gagged, and stepped back again, my shoulders shaking. What would we do if he was gone? Even though Sakura had a tendency to call the shots and usually knew where we were going, Alchemy was the most level-headed of anyone in the group. He was the one that had first believed I was worth adding to the team, in his own roundabout way. What would we do without him?

"Do something! You're the one that has all that life magic!" Sakura squeaked, and I stared at her, dumbfounded.

"What do you expect me to do?!" I chirped, already letting my bering cloud my vision with life glows. Hers was bright and flashing, pulsing with the racing beat of her heart, but Alchemy's was nothing. Of course it was nothing. He was *bones*. He didn't *have* a life glow because he wasn't alive.

"I don't know, *something*! Anything!" Sakura's panicked voice grew quiet, her shaking fingers curled tightly around the vines of the now still pendulum. We both fell silent, staring in disbelief and horror at Alchemy's bones. I didn't know what to do. I didn't know what we *could* do.

And then, without warning or explanation, the bones moved, snapping through the air, cracking against each other, shifting beneath the clothes and grating back into place until, to our amazement, Alchemy stood before us once more.

"Well, that wasn't so bad," he said simply in that low, grating voice of his, that ever-present grin once again facing us in its eerie familiarity.

After a short pause, Sakura and I did the only logical thing to do in such a situation: we screamed.

*H*ypnotism *did* have greater effects on Cursed beings, that much had been established. From what Alchemy had told us after we calmed down, he'd gone into a trance so intense it rendered him completely powerless until it had worn off. He was greatly amused by our panicked reactions, but neither of us could find the heart to join in his laughter, still stunned and shaking from his collapse.

When we returned to the others, we saw that Gian had fallen asleep leaning against one of the trees, his head tilted towards a ray of sun that shone through the canopy of leaves above us. Light Ray was, unsurprisingly, close at hand, having tucked himself snugly into the crook of the Nightfaller's arm. Beth sat nearby with Taro on her shoulder, carefully mending a hole that had somehow found a way to appear in her shirt's sleeve.

"What happened back there?" she asked, sounding like she could care less as she raised one of her thick black eyebrows.

"We were just playing around with hypnotism," Sakura answered quickly, giving Alchemy and me sharp looks that clearly indicated we weren't to share anything more. I was more than happy to comply, but I had my doubts about Alchemy keeping his silence.

"Hypnotism? Rings a bell, but it sounds like something *dasten*, so I probably want no part of it." Beth huffed, looking back down as she meticulously pulled the thread into a knot and sliced the excess away with her knife.

"Probably," Sakura agreed, picking up one of the packs to search for something to eat. I could see that she was still shaking from the shock back in the small clearing, but she was trying to hide it by avoiding eye contact and focusing on her breathing. Tricking people into believing there was nothing wrong didn't come as easily to her as it did to me, and while I knew that fact would irritate her, I saw it as a good thing. Lying and tricking and stealing were all things I was naturally good at, but it didn't mean they were traits I always took pride in.

"We should get moving again soon," Alchemy advised, looking up at the sky through the trees. "If we keep a good pace, we should be able to go into the Stargazine Colonies the day after tomorrow."

"Do you think we could get there any sooner?" Sakura's voice was fringed with despair and exhaustion as she looked up at him, her eyes almost pleading, as if the skeleton could magically move us closer to our destination.

"At this pace," he responded gently, gesturing vaguely at Gian. His brows twitched, but he didn't say anything as Alchemy went on. "I'm afraid it will. But it will give you more time to focus on beginning his training. It will require more breaks, yes, but I think it will benefit all of us more than it will hurt us." He was holding his gloves and cloak, which he had yet to put back on, and tucked them inside one of the packs. It was even more disconcerting to see him in only pants, a shirt, and a pair of boots than it was to see him shrouded in the folds of his cloak. The thin bones of his hands and neck looked out of place jutting out of the fabric the way they did, but there weren't many ways that could be helped, especially not while we were in a hurry.

I could tell his words made Sakura uneasy, because her thumb began to trail aimlessly over her knuckles. I doubted she was even aware she was doing it. I had often caught the action when she was nervous or anxious, or when she was deep in thought, trying to plan out our next steps as carefully as she could.

"We'll have a certain number of breaks we can take per day," I suggested. "For the rest of today, we'll get two more. One can be used for Gian's training. Tomorrow, we'll try for three and hopefully reach a good camping spot at the edge of the Evershifting Forest by nightfall."

"And what after that?" Sakura prompted, watching me expectantly.

I shrugged. "We'll be able to get some more supplies and stuff from the Colonies, and maybe find that recle-mage to help Gian." I held my hand up when I saw her open her mouth to say something. "I know, we're in a really big hurry to get to the king of Brightlock, but we can't exactly drag Chem along with us, and I doubt bringing Beth and Gian will make the task any easier. No offense," I added the last bit as Beth's dark glare snapped up to me. She rolled her eyes and refocused her attention on organizing her thread and her little needle into one of the leather pouches on her belt.

"So what are you proposing?" Sakura asked, her voice steely. Most signs of the ordeal with Alchemy's reaction to the hypnotism had faded now, replaced with her rigid need to have control of the situation. I kept my tone as calm and reasonable as I could without sounding patronizing.

"I'm saying maybe just you and I should go and try to gain an audience with the king." I could tell that she immediately didn't like the idea, and although she pretended to be irritated by the fact that she couldn't get her thread to roll back onto its tiny wooden spool correctly, I could tell Beth had begun to listen intently as well.

"That doesn't sound like a good idea," Sakura said through the grinding of her teeth.

I shrugged again. "Doesn't it? You and I are completely capable of finding a way in on our own, and it will be much easier to travel towards the capital without these three to worry about." I flicked a hand around us to indicate Alchemy, Gian, and Beth. Sakura glared at me, but didn't speak, so I went on. "It won't be for too long, and it's probably the best way to move forward with this. Gian can stay behind and continue practicing with a sword with Beth and resting up, and Chem will be there to keep an eye on things. Everyone will be safe, and we don't have to put any of them at risk. It will just be you and me, and by now I think both of us are willing to try it on our own." I crossed my arms now to show I was going to be stubborn about this. Sakura held my gaze for a long moment, and I returned the stare coolly. Finally, she sighed and lowered her eyes to the ground.

"We'll take the breaks, but I'm going to need to take some time to think about the rest of your plan." She reached down to grab her packs and nudge Gian with her boot, obviously done with the conversation. Resigned, I knelt to find my own snack and let the debate fall.

*T*ravel throughout the rest of the day, as well as the next, was surprisingly smooth. The second break we took was for lunch, and the third was used to begin Gian's training with a sword. I had my doubts about giving him a weapon, and they were doubled when Beth offered him her saber to see how he would wield it. The hilt of the saber had a protective guard made to protect the fingers and hand of the person holding the weapon, but because of that it could only be held comfortably and safely in the right hand. Gian was left-handed, and since he wasn't used to a blade that big—and was even less used to holding things in his right hand—Sakura decided to let him practice getting the hang of properly wielding it with the iron hilt of her flame-sword before he tried with a real weapon. Once he had it in his hand, Sakura told him that it wouldn't be the same as training with a real sword, so he had to try and remember that there would be a long, sharp blade attached to the end of the hilt.

At first, the training was a little boring as they guided him through the various ways to plant his feet for a secure defensive stance and how to hold the sword, but then it got interesting. They went on to some of the beginner moves and how he should hold himself as he moved through them. Since learning the way of a flame-sword, which was said to be similar to a broadsword, was very different from learning the way of a saber, neither Beth nor Sakura tried to teach him anything that would belong to one form of the art or another. Beth said that if he was going to learn to use a sword, they would have to get him one of his own, and only when he selected one would we know which style he should pursue.

I sat on the sidelines with Alchemy, Taro, and Light Ray, watching as the three of them hopped deftly around the glade, teaching and practicing feints and darts and jabs. I felt a little left out, itching to pull out my longbow and practice with it some, but also wanting to stay and watch Gian's training unfold before me. Parts of it were fascinating, like when Sakura took her flame-sword back and, with a flick of her wrist, brought the blade roaring to life before she performed a series of complex twists and stabs and arcs. Other parts of it were entertaining, like when Gian clumsily held the extinguished flame-sword hilt at such an angle that warranted a comment from Beth.

"You've just sliced your foot off at the ankle there," she snapped, rubbing at her temple in aggravation as Gian hurriedly corrected the angle of the invisible blade. Dragging her hand down her face, she looked at Sakura and said, "Maybe this isn't going to work."

But Sakura insisted it would pay off, so the training continued until our break had come to an end. Physically, Gian looked absolutely miserable, pouring sweat and shaking from head to toe, but there was something notably optimistic about his mood that hadn't been there before, a lively spark in his eyes that told me he thought it had been worth it.

The following day went by quickly, with another successful hour or two of sword training and some much-needed naps. The only eventful thing that happened was the Evershifting Forest deciding it was time for a change of scenery, morphing beneath our feet to replace the soft grass with hard-packed dirt and moss, twisting the silver birch trees around and around until they thickened into strong oaks. The day went by with such ease that I was actually surprised when we reached the tree line and stood beneath the shade to look out into the rolling plains of Brightlock.

"That was it? No raptor attacks? No Cursed ferrets leaping out of the trees?" I crossed my arms and nodded in satisfaction, speaking more to myself than anyone else. "Good. We've earned a day free of any unwanted surprises."

"We're not out of the woods yet," Alchemy reminded me. Looking up at the trees above us, he added, "Literally and figuratively, I suppose. We should probably find a place to camp a little farther in if we want to remain inconspicuous, especially if we're following Ksega's plan." We hadn't talked much more about what I'd suggested, but from what Sakura had been saying over the past day, I was fairly certain we were going through with it.

Everyone agreed, and as the sun began to sink further into the distant sky, we trooped back into the Evershifting Forest to find a good place to camp. It would have to be a place Alchemy, Beth, and Gian wouldn't mind staying for a while. We could always ask Jhapato to take Beth and Gian in as he had Sakura and me, but we already knew we wouldn't put him in the position of having to mediate between the two of them. It would be much easier to leave that job to Alchemy.

In the end, we found a suitable place and went through our now established routine of setting up the camp. By the time it was done, and we all had our bedrolls out and a fire roaring in the fire pit, it was dark. All of us but Alchemy were exhausted, especially Gian, so we settled for a small dinner before tucking ourselves in.

"Some of us should probably go into the Colonies tomorrow," I said as I lay in my bedroll, hands tucked beneath my head, staring up through the oak branches to the few glittering stars in the sky.

"That's a good idea." Sakura's voice was slurred with drowsiness. "We'll need some more supplies, and maybe we can find someone to help Gian." She yawned at the end, barely managing to add, "We'll worry about it in the morning," before she fell asleep. Not long after, the rest of us were asleep too, leaving Alchemy to stand stoically over us throughout the night.

7
SAKURA

*F*or the second time within the span of four days, I woke up later than Ksega. Usually I was dragging myself out of my bedroll long before either of the boys were, and Beth and I would enjoy a quiet breakfast while we waited for Gian to claw his way out of the depths of his sleep. Once the three of us were up, I performed my usual ritual of aggressively waking the loudly snoring Ksega. This morning, however, I found that I was alone in the campsite when I woke up, and the sun was already nearing its position in the center of the sky.

"Where in the world . . ?" I asked groggily, wondering if any of them were nearby, but there was no reply. I frowned, for a moment thinking I was dreaming, but then remembered what we had talked about the night before. They wouldn't have gone to the Stargazing Colonies without me, would they?

Scrambling out of my bedroll, I looked at the others'—Beth's was neat and tidy, Gian's slightly rumpled, and Ksega's was left in the messy heap it often was when he scrunched it up to crawl out of it. Holding a hand over the fire pit, I could sense no warmth. The fire had long since been put out, but they would have had to heat up their breakfast, and unless any of them could magically cool the ashes, breakfast had been several hours ago.

"Idiots," I grumbled, kicking one of the stones away from around the pit.

"Oh, you're awake!" The hoarse voice came from deeper into the forest of oak trees, and I looked up to see Alchemy making his way closer. He had once again shed the clothing I had acquired for him, leaving them folded neatly beside one of the bedrolls.

"Long after everyone else, I see," I spat, scowling at him. "Why didn't any of you wake me?"

"You were dead asleep, Ironling." There was a hint of amusement in the skeleton's voice. "We figured that if our conversations over breakfast weren't enough to wake you up, you needed the rest. But look on the bright side!" He came closer and spread his arms wide, and I got the feeling that if he wasn't constantly doing it anyway, he would be grinning. "You get to spend most of the day with me!"

"Where are the others?" I demanded, keeping my expression nonplussed as I crossed my arms at him.

"So much for wanting to spend some quality time with the first friend you made in this group," he huffed, dropping his arms. "They left for the Stargazing Colonies a couple hours ago. They said they might be back late and not to let you go looking for them unless they weren't back by the time you went to sleep again." He tightened the straps of the leather sheaths on the inside of his forearms, making sure the smith-tooth daggers were secure. I groaned, clenching my fists.

"And what exactly am I supposed to do all day?" I unfolded my arms to plant my hands on my hips, glowering at him. His shoulder blades slumped.

"You really don't think I'm worth spending some time with?" His voice seemed more scratchy than usual, almost as if he had a lump in his nonexistent throat. My expression softened as a worm of guilt squirmed into my gut.

"No, no, that's . . ." I grimaced. "That's not what I meant. I'm sorry. I just don't like when I'm not helping to . . . you know. Make progress with things." I smiled at him, hoping he could see that it was sincere. "I'm glad we can spend the rest of the day together. What should we do?" I wasn't sure he was entirely convinced, but at least he had lost his down-hearted tone.

"We could go hunting, but I'm not sure if the others plan to bring us more food." He looked up at the sky, judging how far the sun had gone in its daily journey. "Perhaps you should have some lunch first." Glancing back down at me, with my messy hair and eyelids still blinking away my sleep, he amended, "Or some breakfast, I guess. Here, there's still some fruit left." He went to the packs and produced a fuzzy peach for me. It was a little mushier than I would have liked it, but it was better than the last few strips of nasty jerky we had, so I accepted it.

As I was eating, he rambled on with a list of things we could do. Most of them were odd suggestions or things I would expect from someone who wasn't concerned with the current state of the world, things like picnics or spelunking or fishing. None of it sounded particularly appealing, but none of it sounded terrible, either. In the end, it turned out we would be doing none of those things, because just as I was licking the sticky peach juice from my fingers, a loud crash sounded from farther into the forest.

"We can go investigate whatever that was," Alchemy offered, and since everything else he had suggested sounded far too idle for my liking, I agreed to it. For all I knew, it could've been another Cursed smith, but at the moment it sounded better than fishing.

When we started off into the woods, following the sound of the crashing, we heard a roar, and I glanced up at Alchemy. There were no features for me to read, but what little body language I *could* read told me he was unconcerned, even as we heard another cry from ahead, this time more of a screech. I let my fingers rest lightly on the hilt of my flame-sword, just in case I needed it. I couldn't tell what manner of creature the sound was coming from, but judging by how much noise it was causing, it was big. It wasn't until we got closer that I realized it wasn't one but three creatures rolling through the forest, fighting each other. Moments after we came upon them, staying just out of sight, I recognized what they were: raptors.

Two of them were green, one much darker than the other, and the third one was a pale blue. The dark green and the blue raptor were violently clawing at the lighter green one, hissing and spitting and roaring as they tried to fight it. With a gasp, I realized that I knew the light green raptor.

"It's Wynchell!" I whispered to Alchemy, pointing, although I knew he was already looking. He arched his neck to try and get a closer look, but I knew I was right. His big, fanning tail and leaf-like wings beat at the two raptors, pushing them back far enough for Wynchell's head to be revealed. It was definitely him, and I was only more certain when I saw a piece of parchment fastened to his foreleg.

"What's he doing out here?" Alchemy muttered, already flicking his smith-tooth daggers free of their sheaths. I pointed at the raptor's leg, but it was hidden once more as the blue raptor pounced on him, sharp claws raking along his scales, trying to dig into flesh. Wynchell roared and threw him off but revealed the underside of his belly in the process, and the darker raptor darted in, slashing at him with its claws.

"He's got a message. Come on, we've got to help him." I pulled my flame-sword free of its sheath and stepped closer, glad that Alchemy followed without question.

As soon as we came into the small area where the raptors were fighting, which was littered with broken tree limbs and bloodied grass, the blue raptor let out a throaty hiss and threw itself at us. Alchemy and I dove in opposite directions, narrowly avoiding its attack. I whipped around and called to my eirioth, letting it roar free into my flame-sword as I raced in to swipe at the raptor's tail. The flames were hot enough to sear through the scales, cutting nearly all the way through the beast's tail. It screamed in pain, a high-pitched screech that made me wince. It used my moment of distraction to twirl around and lunge for me again. I side-stepped and spun on my heel to take a swipe at its webbed wings. Flame-swords didn't have as much substance as real swords, so when they came in contact with certain things like stone or thick bone, they only warped around it, but sometimes it was hot enough to push through it. Raptor wings were more bone than anything else, aside from the webbing that connected them, so my fiery blade only curled around the edge of the beast's wing, burning the scales. It let out another cry of rage and barreled at me once more. This time, I darted forward and to the right, tossing my sword into my left hand to drag it through the raptor's tender underbelly as I slid past. The smell of burnt flesh began to cloud the clearing as I staggered back, feeling my stomach turn as the beast's uncauterized innards spilled out onto the earth. It roared again, but unable to follow me anymore, it fell to the ground, whimpering.

Alchemy was wrestling with the dark green raptor. It was bigger than both the blue one and Wynchell and was attempting to crush Alchemy's bones, clawing and snapping and biting as it rolled across the clearing with him. He had lost one of his bone daggers in the tussle, but one was still firmly gripped in his hand, and I could see him trying to jab it into the raptor's heart through the struggle.

Instead of going to help him—I knew he would eventually tire the raptor out—I hurried closer to Wynchell. His golden eyes were wide and crazed, and he was losing blood from the gashes in his belly. One of his wings had a tear in it, and I could also see a cut along the top of his head. Hesitantly, I held a hand out towards him, hoping he would recognize me. He growled, and I retracted my hand, risking another step forward.

"It's okay, Wynchell." I kept my voice as reassuring as I could, ignoring the grunts of strain behind me as Alchemy fought the other raptor. "I'm a friend. I'm here to help." I reached my hand out again, and he hissed, digging his sharp talons into the packed earth beneath him. I pulled my hand back slowly, glancing over at Alchemy. He had pinned one of the raptor's wings into the ground with his dagger, and now he was retrieving the other. Ignoring the slashing claws that reached for him, chipping bits of his bones away onto the ground, he reached forward and drove the second dagger deep into the raptor's chest before slumping to the ground beside it, groaning.

"You alright?" he rasped once he'd found his voice.

"I'm fine. Wynchell's hurt and scared, but I think he'll be okay. What about you?" I gave him a worried glance. I'd never seen him show any sign of experiencing pain or exhaustion before. He waved a bone hand at me, and I noticed the bones of one finger were missing, lying with the other bits of him that were scattered around.

"Just give me a minute. I'll be as good as new soon enough," he replied before falling silent. I waited anxiously to make sure I could hear him breathing before I remembered that was pointless. Without lungs, I wasn't sure Alchemy breathed at all.

"Easy, Wynchell," I said softly as I returned my attention to the raptor. He was looking about frantically, eyes panicked as he stared at the bodies of the two raptors that had been attacking him. "We're going to help you. Just calm down. There you go . . . nice and easy." I pushed my hand closer to him, and through the fear in his eyes I saw a flicker of hesitation. A moment later, my fingers pressed against the warm scales of his nose, and he huffed an exhausted sigh, his whole body losing its tension as he sagged in relief.

"Poor guy," Alchemy commented, and I looked up to see that he had dragged himself into a sitting position, little flecks of him glowing brightly as whatever bizarre magic that possessed him worked to repair the damage done to his bones.

"All of the injuries he has are probably ones he can recover from, but he won't be able to run or fly on his own for a little while." My gaze trailed down to the body of the blue raptor, its eyes still open and staring blankly at the sky. "These guys must have just started attacking him, so he can't have been away from Theomand for very long. Should we look at the message?" I gestured at Wynchell's leg, where the parchment bound to his leg had begun to slide loose.

Alchemy shuffled up to my side and pulled it free of its binding, offering it to me as he said, "I don't see why not. It may have been for us, anyway, and if it isn't, we might be able to find whoever it *is* for." He reached forward tentatively to let his bone hand press against Wynchell's shoulder. The raptor's muscles tensed beneath the touch but relaxed soon enough when he realized neither of us were a threat to him.

I unrolled the paper and scanned it briefly. I was mildly surprised to find that it was once again addressed to Ksega and me, and butterflies began to appear in my stomach as I continued to read. Excitement bubbled up in my voice when I held it out to Alchemy, "Look! They're coming to Brightlock!" I waited for him to finish skimming over it, then took it back to glance through it once more, just to be sure I had read it correctly.

Ksega and Sakura,

Unfortunately, another sea wraith attacked us, and it grieves me to say that Orvyn *has been lost. Fortunately, I have found the pirates you directed me to. They were surprisingly welcoming to myself and Wynchell, which was a surprise. In my past experiences, pirates have been nothing but trouble-making scum. It's nice to see some other thieves and backbiters with a sense of dignity about them.*

I'm writing to inform you that the pirates and myself, along with two people who claim to know the three of you, are soon departing from Wisesol to travel across the Great Lakes back into Brightlock. If the three of you still happen to be in the area, the pirates and the two other travelers have made it clear that they wish to see you.

If Wynchell is able to track you, and this letter finds you, know that we are expected to arrive in Brightlock within a week. If we do not receive a reply by then, we will not expect to find you. Below is a message from one of the two travelers who say they are your friends.

Captain Theomand

Ksega!

It's been too long since I've seen you. There's so much we need to catch up on, but this is an awfully small piece of paper, and I can only say so much. I hope Captain Theomand's raptor finds you quickly so that we can see each other soon. Derek and I have been hard at work researching whatever we can about fighting the Curse, and we think we've found some good ways to combat it! None of it is guaranteed, but we need to talk to you and Sakura about it as soon as possible!

Willa sends her love and best wishes.

Jessie

"This must have been sent a few days ago," Alchemy remarked as I rolled the letter back up. "If that's the case, they'll be arriving soon." He cocked his skull at me. "Will you and Ksega still be leaving on your own, or will you wait around to see them?"

I bit my lip uncertainly, trying to work through it in my mind. I ached to see Derek again, if only because he was a piece of home, and I craved any amount of home I could find. If he and the pirates would be here within a couple days it might have been worth it to stay, but it could be days before they arrived at the Gates, and we couldn't afford to wait that long, especially not for the sake of a short reunion. The sooner we were able to gain an audience with the king, the better. Besides, if we went quickly enough, it couldn't take too many days before we were back in the Evershifting Forest again.

"We'll talk about it with him tonight," I answered finally, even though I already knew my preferred course of action. Ksega's friend was coming, too, as well as the pirates he was already acquainted with. Despite how much I might want to push on, this decision heavily relied on his input, and it was one of the few I was willing to hear him out on.

"For now, let's try to get this guy back and help him out a little," Alchemy suggested, lightly running his hands along Wynchell's scales and pressing every now and then to see if the raptor had internal injuries anywhere.

It wasn't easy to get Wynchell out of the clearing. He wouldn't follow us on his own, but we both knew better than to try and put some sort of leash on him. In the end, we had to settle for gently poking and prodding him in the rear until he went in the direction we wanted him to. It was a slow herding process, but we managed to get him back to our little campsite within an hour. There, Alchemy offered him the rest of the chewy jerky that nobody liked, and as the raptor wolfed it down, I tried to wash the cuts in his wings and abdomen. I knew it must have stung, but aside from a few hisses and growls of protest, he focused more on his meal than on what I was doing, and I managed to clean the wounds up pretty well.

"He should be okay, as long as he doesn't roll in anything that could infect it," I said once I was finished, looking up to see that Alchemy was seated in front of the raptor, supervising as he chawed through the last of the jerky.

"Well, now we've got something to focus on for the rest of the day," Alchemy said with a light chuckle, softly patting the top of Wynchell's head. The raptor huffed, narrowing his eyes at the skeleton. "You know what"— he moved his hand farther back to scratch behind Wynchell's ears—"I think I'm pretty good with animals, once they get over their initial fear of me." He shrugged. "If only I could find one stupid enough to ignore how predatory I look."

"You want a pet?" I snorted, finding it difficult to imagine any animal allowing itself to be cared for by Alchemy. He laughed, the sound startling Wynchell.

"I'm not opposed to the idea. Anything to make me feel a little more human." His voice tapered off at the end, and my own smile faded. This wasn't the first time he had talked as if he wasn't still human. There had been a time when I didn't see him as one either, but I had come to learn that he still had a conscience and that, while it may not have been there physically, a heart, and that made him human enough for me.

"The way you look isn't what defines you as a human. Your actions and who you are on the inside is what defines that," I told him, taking one of the water skins nearby and using it to wash Wynchell's blood off my hands. Alchemy looked out to the east, towards the Stargazing Colonies, although we couldn't see them from where we were camped, just deep enough into the thick of the woods to stay hidden from passersby.

"I suppose that's true," he said at length, his voice sounding weary. He released a sigh that rattled through his ribcage. "And that's what makes me the least human out of us all."

"Being a hermit and not really *having* any big accomplishments to your name doesn't make you inhuman," I pointed out, unsure if I was referring to what he was thinking about, but thinking the point needed to be made, nonetheless. "There's nothing wrong with having been hidden away for so many years. What's important is who you are to the people who know you now. What does your past matter to us, so long as you're our friend at this moment?"

"I think that, if you knew about my past, it would matter quite a lot to you," Alchemy rumbled, his hand falling away from Wynchell's head. I frowned at him for a long moment, waiting for him to elaborate, but he never did. Instead, he said, "But maybe you're right. Maybe it's best to leave the past in the past, for all of us." He stood, the cheerfulness returning to his voice. "Now, shall we try to find something suitable for dinner when the others get back? I'm not sure if they're getting some food in the villages, but it doesn't hurt to be safe." With a shrug, I stood with him.

"Okay. Should we just leave Wynchell here?" I asked, giving a questioning look down at the raptor, who looked to be on the brink of sleep.

Alchemy shrugged again. "I think he'll be alright on his own for now. We shouldn't be gone too long, anyway." Alchemy started off into the woods, and with only a moment's hesitation I followed him.

He was right. We weren't gone for very long. Alchemy managed to catch two rabbits by throwing his daggers with expert aim, and I was lucky enough to have a snake cross my path, where it met a swift and crispy end. When we returned to the campsite with the fruits of our hunt, Wynchell was soundly asleep at the edge of the fire pit, and the sun had gone so low I could no longer see it over the trees. If the others weren't back soon, I would insist on going looking for them, whether Alchemy liked it or not.

We sat on the side of the fire pit opposite from Wynchell to give him his space, and I lit a fire with what wood we had collected as quietly as I could manage so as not to disturb the raptor. With the low fire burning, Alchemy carefully began to skin the rabbits and work the edible meat from the snake without damaging its ebony scales. I had never worked with freshly killed animals, only whatever raw meats had been sold to Gamma at the Hazelwood Inn, and it was fascinating to see Alchemy use his bone daggers so surely, even after so many years during which he wouldn't have cooked. Why would he, if he couldn't eat? The only reason I could see for him to skin the animals would be to use their skins and pelts for other various things.

When the rabbits and the snake were cooking over the fire, I sighed and looked up at the stars. There hadn't yet been a night when I'd been camping with only one other person. The first night I hadn't been alone after leaving home had been with Derek and Alchemy, when Derek and I had taken turns sleeping to make sure Alchemy wouldn't try to harm us in our sleep. It was strange to think how quickly I had come to befriend the skeleton. Now, I hardly even thought twice about the dangers of the night when I went to sleep. As long as Alchemy was there to keep watch, I was confident no harm would come to me.

"I'm glad you're here," I said, finding the need to voice my thoughts. "You're a good friend, Chem, and you've taken good care of us. I'm glad you decided to help me." I looked up at him. Even sitting, he seemed to loom over me like an ancient, withering tree. "Even though I had a friend in Derek back home, it wasn't the same kind of friendship I have with you. He and I weren't really friends by choice. It was more a friendship of necessity." I looked down into the flickering flames before us. "After I lost my family, I felt like nobody but my brother, Finnian, really understood what I had gone through. When Derek's family was killed, I knew I wasn't alone in the loss anymore. We didn't really get along the way

normal friends do. We were there as a confidant for the other whenever one was needed."
I lifted my gaze to face him again and saw that he was looking at me. "But with you, it
is a choice. I didn't ever have to accept that you were anything more than just a Cursed
man, and even though I didn't want to in the beginning, I eventually did. You're wise and
helpful, and always know what to say. Everyone needs to have a friend like you in their
lives, Chem." I hadn't yet shared so much with anyone in our small group, but I was glad I
was now. Perhaps in time I could come to trust in the others as much as I did in Alchemy.
I knew Ksega wanted my trust, and to a great degree, he had it; I just wasn't sure if I was
ready to share everything with him yet.

"You're wrong about one thing," Alchemy said, and I raised an eyebrow. "I don't know
exactly what to say all the time. I can't, because I don't know exactly what to say right now.
But I am truly flattered, Ironling. Words can't express how grateful I am to have been
accepted by you." He put a bone arm around me and hugged me to his side. I'd never
hugged the skeleton before, and it was a bit of an odd experience as I hugged him back. I
had never wrapped my arms around someone so awkwardly thin, but even though he had
no flesh, there was a certain warmth to the embrace that made me feel just a little bit more
at ease.

"The others should be getting back soon," I said, pulling away to peer into the darkening
woods. A shiver of uncertainty blanketed me as the shadows grew longer. I hated when it
got dark.

"They'll be here," Alchemy said, unworried. "They aren't in any danger out there."

"What about the runeboar attack that happened last time we were in the Stargazing
Colonies?" I challenged, raising an eyebrow at him. They weren't pleasant memories of
mine, the ones from that day. It had started off alright, but quickly gone downhill when
our breakfast was interrupted by several Cursed runeboars wreaking havoc upon the village
we were in. Ksega nearly got killed, and I would've been dead myself if it hadn't been for
Alchemy.

"They didn't just appear within the Colonies, though," Alchemy pointed out. "I saw
them charging in from the Evershifting Forest. How else do you think I knew to come
there to help you fight them?"

"What about Gian? Do you think people will ask about him or Light Ray?" I pressed.

"Stop worrying, Ironling. They're all capable of taking care of themselves, and you know
it. For once you need to stop thinking and analyzing and planning and just enjoy the
moment." He tilted his skull back to gaze up at the stars through the branches of the oak
trees. I did the same, trying to let go of the prickly feeling I got whenever I turned my back
on the shadows.

"Worrying has just been my first instinct for so long, I don't think I know how to stop; but I'll try." That wasn't entirely true, and it was obvious that he knew it; I was too afraid to try and stop worrying, because what if I succeeded? If I stopped worrying, then maybe I would miss things. Opportunities would be passed up, and bad decisions could be made. It was always easier to worry about things, and while it may not have been the best thing for me, it was something I had grown used to, and I wasn't comfortable enough in drastic change to try and adjust to something so different right now.

"Well, at least that's something," Alchemy muttered, and we fell into a peaceable silence. I heaved a contented sigh as I realized that, for once, with Alchemy at my side and my gaze lost in the stars above, my skin was no longer prickling with the fear of the darkness around me.

8
KSEGA

When I left the camp with Gian, Beth, and their birds, I already knew we would be paying a visit to Jhapato. To my knowledge, Beth didn't know Jhapato, but I wasn't afraid of them not getting along. From our visit to Irina, I knew the witch and her daughter were not fond of Jhapato, and considering the fact that Beth was not fond of Irina and her daughter, I suspected they might get along well.

When I stepped out of the Evershifting Forest, I gasped in surprise. Maintained by its living magic, the Evershifting Forest was a constant place of light and life, even when it changed the weather within its borders, but outside of the forest, the world was subjected to the natural rotation of the seasons. It was getting close to late autumn, and the whole world was muted and going to sleep. I could feel myself being pulled slowly into a state of drowsiness and shook my head to clear it as we walked on.

It was easy to remember which of the Colonies Sakura and I had stayed in before, because it was the one on the southernmost shore of Oracle Lake. That specific Colony was called Arvos, named after the founder of the first Stargazing Colony, and when I told Beth, she said she knew a lot about the Colonies.

"The people of Old Duskfall are a very superstitious people, although we tend to find that particular term offensive," she began as we reached the main, well-beaten road that wound towards the Colonies. "The people who founded the Stargazing Colonies are similarly superstitious, if not even more so. They had close ties to people in the City of Bones, and through a series of minor miscommunications, they somehow formed the belief that Oracle Lake served as exactly that, a mirror into the realm of the dead, delivering omens and prophecies from the saints." She pursed her lips and frowned in disapproval. "The founders were less of a colony and more of a cult, but over time their descendants, as well as those who came to reside in their newly formed 'Stargazing Colonies,' fell out of the habits of worship they had for the lake. It's still very sacred among their people, but it is no longer considered a portal to the wisdom of those past." As we came closer to one of the outermost Colonies, she scrutinized it through thick lashes. "Although it wouldn't surprise me if we came across the occasional extremist or two."

"What exactly are we going to be looking for here?" Gian asked when we stepped into Arvos, receiving several welcoming smiles and greetings from the villagers. He reached up to where Light Ray was perched on his shoulder, petting the owl's soft feathers as he watched the villagers with narrowed and slightly fearful eyes. I wasn't sure what he expected them to do, but Light Ray's company seemed to help calm his nerves a bit. Gian himself was looking better than he had in a couple of days. His skin was still grayish, and there were dark bags beneath his eyes, but he was in a good mood after having completed his sword training each day. Even through his profuse sweating, he made a great effort to keep himself in high spirits, and for the most part it had done wonders for his mental state, which in turn helped him stay more energetic despite his sickness.

"A number of things," I answered him, casually resting one of my palms on the quiver at my hip. I had brought my longbow along, although I didn't expect that I would need it, so it was strapped, unstrung, to my back. "To start, some real food. I have a hankering for a good apple pastry right about now. Beth, how much money do you have?"

"Around three hundred shins, I think," the Duskan replied, running her fingers over the two leather pouches of coins hanging from her belt. She narrowed her eyes at me. "Wouldn't *Faja* disapprove of you spending our money on something as frivolous as apple pastries?"

"Good thing she's not here then." I winked at her and led the way towards the central street of Arvos. The last time I had been here, I hadn't paid much attention to the market, as I had been more focused on acquiring a bed for the night, but now I let my gaze roam over the stalls to see what was for sale. There were lots of wares suited for life on a lake, like water tunics made from cheap water-resistant fabrics, rubber boots, sturdy fishing poles and other baubles and fishing trinkets, and tools made specially to make cleaning and gutting a fish a quick and easy task. There were also items that could be used elsewhere, like daggers and hunting knives—all of which had been left dull until someone purchased one and sharpened it themselves—and even some arrows and longbows. I was tempted to buy some more arrows, since I only had twenty-two in my quiver that could hold thirty, but I knew I could make more when we went back to the forest, so I resisted the urge.

"You might be able to find something good over there," Beth suggested, pointing to a stall that was littered with steaming fruit pies, glazed honey buns, chocolate-covered cream puffs, and so many other sugary delights that I began salivating at the sight of them. Desserts were a rare delicacy in Willa's home, not only because the professionally made ones were expensive, but because she had wanted to try and curb the incessant sweet tooth I developed when I was small. It had never worked, and I still loved sweet things with all my heart.

"I'll *definitely* be able to find something good over there," I said with a grin, already heading towards the stall. Gian started after me, but Beth grabbed his sleeve and made a *tsk*ing sound, as if he were a misbehaving animal.

"Not you, owl boy. We're going over there." She lifted her arm, unsettling Taro, and pointed to another stall across the road, one that had a number of dulled swords and sabers on display. Gian cast a longing look at the pastry stall, then released a resigned sigh and stepped back to Beth's side.

"Don't worry. I'll grab something for you, too," I said, accepting the coin pouch Beth offered me and leaving them to their sword shopping as I stepped into the surprisingly short line in front of the stall selling the desserts.

"Hello, sir," the man running the stall said when it was my turn. I stared hungrily at the array of delicious treats laid out in front of me, my nose twitching at their sugary aromas. "What'll it be for you?"

"Do you have anything with apples?" I asked, although by now I had decided I didn't want *just* an apple pastry. Those bite-sized cherry pies looked quite appetizing. So did the custard-filled dough rounds, and the gold-crusted berry tarts, and the mini chocolate cakes topped with thick icing and sugar crystals, and—

"We certainly do!" The man's voice cut through my thoughts, and I snapped my gaze up to him with a start. I was glad I hadn't started drooling all over the edge of the stall table, because the last thing I needed was another reason for Beth to pick on me. "Would you like some?"

"Absolutely!" I said enthusiastically. "And throw in a couple of those little puff pastries while you're at it. And maybe a berry tart or two." I bit my lip, telling myself not to get too greedy. It wasn't my money I was spending, after all. Still, I hadn't had anything to satisfy my sweet tooth since I had been in Old Nightfall, and I had certainly done enough helpful things since then to earn myself a treat.

"Alrighty." The man wore a bright smile as he gathered my requested desserts onto a small disposable plate and held it up to me. I gratefully accepted it as he said, "That will be three gold coins or fifteen silver coins."

"Uh, do you take shins?" I asked in a small voice, worried I was about to lose the wonderful little rolls of deliciousness that I was so close to putting in my stomach. I held up the pouch Beth had given me.

To my relief, the man nodded, keeping his smile. "I do! It will be eight shins." He held his hand out as I pulled the small copper pieces free and let them fall with a series of clinks into his palm. "Thanks for coming by!" he said, and I nodded a grateful farewell as I stepped away from the stall, already stuffing my face with one of the puff pastries.

Gian and Beth were waiting for me in the center of the road. Gian was holding a brand new leather sword scabbard with buckles and a belt, and I could see the handle of a sword jutting out from within it. It was a simple craft, nowhere near as flashy as the twirls and feathers molded into Sakura's flame-sword hilt or Beth's gleaming gold saber, but it would do for the purposes he needed it for.

As I came closer, I saw that he was eagerly eyeing the fruit tart I had bought. I winced inwardly, having forgotten I'd promised him one of the desserts. Hoping my hesitation was successfully masked, I held the plate out to him. He gratefully and eagerly took the fruit tart, but before he could take a bite, Beth reached out and plucked it out of his hand. He stared at her for a long moment, and she took a bite while meeting his gaze. I could have sworn I saw his eyes flash and fill with tears. I held the plate out to him again, hoping the other puff pastry would appease him. Grumbling, he took it while I grabbed the other tart.

"What now?" Gian asked through a mouthful of pasty. He was hungrily devouring the entire thing, and I had to remind myself that, because of his poor treatment in Old Nightfall, it was doubtful he had ever had something like the pastry, much less one that was freshly baked.

"Now, we get food that will last a little while. We'll need enough for mine and Sakura's to the capital, but you two should be fine staying in the Evershifting Forest. You'll be close enough to the Stargazing Colonies to come buy more if you need it, plus you'll be able to hunt more in the forest itself," I replied, looking around to see what other stalls were selling food. "You two can find that. I'm going to go say hi to a friend and see if I can't find a recle-mage." I began to walk in the direction I thought Jhapato's house was in when Gian's voice stopped me.

"Why do you need a recle-mage?" he asked, narrowing his steely green eyes.

"Actually, it's *you* who needs the recle-mage," I corrected. I put my hands up, palms-out, causing the crumbs left on the plate to tumble to the ground. "Look, I know you don't want help from us, but trust me, a recle-mage will help you feel a hundred times better than you do now. Besides, it'll help you stay stronger for training with that." I gestured at the hilt of his new sword. Gian's lips twisted into an unsatisfied frown, but he didn't argue.

"We'll meet back here in half an hour," Beth decided, gesturing for me to keep the pouch of shins when I offered it back to her. "Keep it in case you need it, but no more pastries. You may find a good use for it when you and *Faja* travel to the capital."

With another nod, we went our separate ways. I meandered through Arvos for a short while, finding a place to discard the little plate along the way before I stumbled upon the familiar house. It was more worn down and ragged than the buildings around it, although it was by no means falling into a state of disrepair. It was simply lived-in and well loved. I stepped up the faded steps onto the porch and knocked on the door. The last time I had come to Jhapato's house—while conscious, that is—he had been sitting in one of the rocking chairs on the porch. Today, though, I didn't see him, and I wondered if he was home. My question was answered a moment later when the door swung open, and I saw his tanned, leathery face looking curiously up at me. I grinned, and seconds later recognition flickered in his dark brown eyes. He smiled and opened the door farther, stepping out of the way and gesturing for me to come inside.

"Ksega! It's good to see you again, my friend." His gaze trailed curiously to the empty air behind me, and when he glanced back up at me, I saw the question in his eyes before it escaped his lips.

"She isn't with me today," I explained. "She stayed behind with a friend. We're only here in the Colonies for today, and then we need to get moving again, but I wanted to come say hi." My grin widened, as did Jhapato's.

"Well, as long as you're here, let's make the most of it. Come in, come in, I've just finished making some lunch. Elana is expected to come visit within the hour." He paused as he led me to his dining room, which was just as neat and modestly furnished as I remembered, and looked back at me. "You won't mind that, will you?"

"No, of course not," I replied, adding, "I was actually hoping she would be around. We've made a few new friends since we last talked with you, and one of them is pretty sick. It would be nice if Elana was able to give him something to make him feel a bit better. We have money." I produced the pouch of shins to show him, but he waved his hand as he ushered me into one of the seats around the table and disappeared into the kitchen.

"Don't bother with paying, she'll be more than happy to assist you for free," he called back to me.

"We'd all appreciate it," I said politely, memories flashing into my mind of Sakura getting onto me the last time we had been here. I had never practiced my manners very much, but now I was doing my best to show Jhapato that I respected him, and I secretly hoped Sakura would be proud of my efforts.

"So how did things go with Irina? I'm assuming you spoke with her?" He returned a moment later, making two trips with a pitcher of water and three large dishes, one being a bowl of what appeared to be green beans, and two plates, one which bore delicious-smelling chicken breasts and the other laden with cuts of ham, cheese, and bread. It appeared Jhapato had come into better fortunes since the last time I had been in his home.

"They went as well as could be expected, I suppose," I answered, trying to conceal my eagerness to eat as he set the dishes on the table before me. "You conveniently forgot to mention that you weren't on good terms with her," I added, remembering the way Irina the witch had reacted when we had mentioned Jhapato's name. The old Duskan shrugged.

"It wouldn't have done any good if I'd said anything about it. My history with her and her family is complicated and better left in the dark." He took one of the other seats around the table and gestured at the food. "Please, dig in. Elana will be here soon, but she wouldn't want us to wait up for her."

I dished some of the ham, cheese, and chicken onto my plate, muttering a thanks to him as he filled my glass with water from the pitcher. We didn't talk much, but it didn't matter, because within ten minutes, Elana stepped in the door. She was a Talon, so she was of exceptional height, and her long, blond braid almost reached her knees. She was a beautiful woman, but most people from Freetalon had a natural beauty to them, at least from what I had seen. She elegantly swooped into the dining room, taking quick note of the food on the table and my place before it. Her pink lips lifted into a pleasant smile as she recognized me.

"Ah, the young traveler returns. It's good to see you in excellent health. I trust your leg is no longer troubling you?" She took her seat at the table, politely lifting some food from the serving dishes onto her plate.

"Not anymore it isn't, thanks to your remedy," I confirmed.

"He has a friend who is in need of your talents, if you're able to assist them," Jhapato said through a mouthful of bread. Elana arched a delicately shaped eyebrow.

"Oh? I'd be more than happy to offer my services." She returned her emerald gaze to me. "Is it the girl who was with you before? The Carlorian?"

"No, not her. She's doing well," I said quickly. I wasn't sure why the attention from the Talon unsettled me, but something about her calm demeanor set me instinctively on edge. It was like her gaze made little invisible bugs crawl over my skin, never able to be slapped away.

"I'm happy to hear it. Who is in need of healing, then?" She reached for her glass, taking a sip of water so small I wondered if it even served her in any way. I didn't know much about Talons, but I did know they had rigid education systems. Was this some way of simply showing that she was putting Jhapato's hospitality to use? If it was, it was an odd way to go about it. In a place like the Stargazing Colonies, such formality wasn't common, much less required.

"My friend, Gian. He's—" I paused, unsure if I should go on. This would normally be where I let Sakura take the lead. While I knew I was more than capable of making my own plans, she was the one in charge of most of the ones I had followed over the past weeks, and I wasn't sure how much about Gian she would want me to disclose. I wouldn't have had any hesitation sharing it with Jhapato, but there was something inherently suspicious about Elana that made me hold my tongue.

"He's . . . sick?" the healer prompted, her eyes narrowing slightly, like she knew I was hiding something.

"Yes. He's quite sick. He has been for about a week now. Grayish skin, trouble sleeping, lots of sweating. He's thrown up a lot, too. He's . . ." I pinched my face, searching for the right words. I didn't want to give away where Gian was from. "He didn't grow up in a place where he had much of a chance to develop an immune system, so since he started traveling with us, it's gotten progressively worse." I lifted my eyes to hold her gaze, letting a nonchalant expression settle over my features. "Think you can give him something to help with that?" She watched me in silent scrutiny for a long moment, and I couldn't tell if she was thinking about what she could do to heal Gian, or if she was trying to decipher what I wasn't telling her. I kept my expression neutral, and eventually she nodded and looked back down at her plate.

"Yes, I can make something to help the fever recede, and even strengthen his immune system. I can have it done in a matter of minutes, if Jhapato has some specific ingredients I'll need." She looked over at the Duskan, one eyebrow quirked.

He shrugged and waved a hand at the doorway behind him. "You may use whatever you need," he said, and with that irritatingly demure smile, she stood, hardly having touched her food, and stepped into the kitchen to prepare her concoction. I would have been hesitant to give anything she gave me to Gian, except she had helped me once before, and I could think of no reason why she would wish harm upon any one of my friends, so I was forced to put my trust in her.

The rest of the meal was completed in silence, and as Jhapato was clearing away the dishes, Elana returned with a thin vial of some sort of purple-gray liquid. She swirled it around, examining it in the light, then nodded and handed it to me, her smile, for once, seeming more genuine than I had seen it yet.

"That should do," she said. "It will begin to take effect by the end of the day, and he should be feeling like himself again before the day's out tomorrow." Her eyebrows lifted daintily as she asked the question, "Will you be staying nearby so that you can come to me if there are any issues?"

"He will be, yes, and I'll direct him here if the need to see you again arises," I said as I stood, carefully holding the vial against my chest so I didn't accidentally drop it. "But this should do. Thank you again for your help, and Jhapato, it was nice to see you again." I smiled at him, and he returned it.

"Tell Sakura 'hello' for me. I'll always enjoy a visit from the two of you," he said, and for a brief moment, I was tempted to give him a hug, but Elana stood in my path, so I stepped towards the door instead.

"Goodbye." I waved farewell and stepped back out onto the road, carefully cradling Elana's remedy in my hand. For a moment, I stood there, looking up at the sky to see what time of day it was, then taking a deep breath, relishing the various scents that wove through the air, the scents of life and people and a town that was thriving despite the broken world it lived in.

Rolling my shoulders, I went down the steps and had just begun to walk towards the place I had agreed to meet Beth and Gian when a small sound stopped me. I paused, turning in a circle, trying to identify the source of the sound. At first, I didn't see anything at all, but then the sound came again, and my gaze dropped to the sandy earth in front of me. For a moment, I wasn't sure what I was looking at, and then the soft little noise came again, and I realized it was a kitten. He didn't exactly *look* like a kitten; he was so small I could've cupped him in the palm of my hand, and his black fur was so frizzy and spiky that it shot out in every direction. He had bright green eyes, but something about them seemed a little off. As I leaned down to peer at him closer, I realized that one of them was stuck looking to the right, leaving only his left eye functioning normally.

"Aww, you poor little guy," I said, crouching down and holding my free hand out to him. "Where did you come from?"

The kitten wobbled forward, so unsteady on his feet he veered too far to the left and missed my hand entirely. I moved it over so he could sniff it, then gently gave him a pat on the head. He released another pitiful mew, stumbling forward so that his head knocked softly into my boot.

"He's been here for a couple days now." Looking up at the voice, I realized Jhapato was standing in his doorway, watching me pet the little cat. "He doesn't have a family. I've fed him whenever I can, and I'm honestly surprised he's still alive. He needs someone good to take care of him." Before I got the chance to say anything to that, Elana's voice echoed out from somewhere deeper in the house, and Jhapato stepped back inside and closed the door.

"Well," I said, looking back down at the scruffy little kitten, "I'm not sure how to take care of a cat, but I'm sure we can figure it out." I carefully curled my fingers under the kitten's belly and lifted him up, cradling him against my chest like I had the vial of medicine.

It was easy to find the place I had agreed to regroup with Beth and Gian, but I didn't expect to be waiting there as long as I was. Eventually, I took a few steps to the side of the road to stand in the shade and out of the main path, trying to find a secure place for the vial of Elana's remedy while also calming the disheveled kitten. Almost twenty minutes later,

I heard Beth's familiar snarking nearby, and I looked up to see her and Gian approaching with a sack of food each.

"C'mon, little guy," I muttered to the kitten, holding him close as I stepped over to my companions, comfortingly cupping the shaggy furball in my hand. "Hello, you two," I said to gain Beth and Gian's attention. Instantly, Beth's eyes dropped first to the vial, then to the cat.

"What in the name of the saints is *that*?" She scowled at me. "I wish Sakura would have warned me to tell you not to pick up roadkill. Why are you carrying it around? Here, Taro will enjoy it for dinner." She reached her free hand forward, the hawk on her shoulder already having narrowed its eyes at the kitten.

"No!" I stepped back, holding the little cat closer. "He isn't *roadkill*. He's still alive, just a little . . . ragged. A bit worse for wear. But he's alive, and he's coming with us," I said, jutting my chin out at her to prove my point. Gian arched a dark eyebrow at me, and I huffed at him and Light Ray, adding, "And he isn't a snack for either of the birds."

"You're not bringing it with you and Sakura. You know she'll never allow it," Beth remarked. I sniffed at her, conceding the point.

"Then I'll leave it with Alchemy. He'll make sure you don't let your birds eat him. Now come on, we should be heading back." I looked up at the sky. It was getting dark. I could already see stars flickering to life across the blanket of deep pink and magenta, which was slowly being overtaken by the darker purples and blues of night.

Beth made a disapproving sound in her throat, but didn't argue as I led the way back towards the Evershifting Forest. As we walked, I gave Gian the remedy and explained to him how soon it should start working. After a moment's hesitation, and some careful scrutiny of the contents of the vial, he downed it in one gulp, pinched his face as if it was sour, and discarded the empty vial in a rubbish bin near one of the market stalls.

We walked in companionable silence as we returned to our campsite. By the time we reached the edge of the forest, it was dark out, and the little kitten in my arms had mostly settled down. His claws were still digging into the fabric of my shirt and the skin of my arm as he clung on for dear life, his breathing erratic and his one functioning eye snapping every which way as we walked.

We reached the little clearing where the camp was set up just as the sky got as dark as it would get for the night. At first, everything seemed normal. There was a healthy fire blazing in the fire pit, and Sakura and Alchemy were sitting beside it, the former gnawing on what appeared to be the remnants of more rabbit. It wasn't until Beth and Gian had set their packs down and Beth let out a startled cry that I realized there was someone else in the clearing. My heart skipped a beat in fear when I saw the curve of horns and the arc of wings, but as my bering instinctively cloaked my eyes and the life glows flared brightly in my vision, I realized that I recognized this raptor.

"Wynchell!" I cried, my lips splitting into a grin as the beast lifted his head to look at me, blinking his bright amber eyes. I didn't know if he recognized me, but he seemed far more docile than the last few times I'd seen him. It wasn't until I got closer that I saw he was wounded. I looked over at Sakura, a question already on my lips, but she held a hand up, and I could tell from the tense look on her face that my questions would have to wait until after hers.

"First of all, I can't believe you would all go to the Colonies without me." She looked between all three of us as Gian, Beth and I stood beside each other awkwardly, not willing to meet her gaze. "I would have at least wanted the chance to see Jhapato," she added, and her sharp look cut to me. I grimaced, feeling guilt bloom inside my chest. I had suggested that we wake Sakura up before we left, but Beth had insisted we let her sleep instead, and I, not wanting to cause an argument, had agreed to it.

"And second of all?" Beth urged her, clearly eager to hurry through Sakura's scolding so we could deal with the matter of Wynchell. Neither she nor Gian had ever met the raptor, and I could sense the unease rolling off of them in waves. Gian shuddered every now and then, and while I suspected it was fear at being so close to the raptor, I wouldn't have been surprised if it had something to do with what Elana had given him as well. She had said it would help strengthen his immune system, and who knew how strange that might feel?

"Second of all, we got another note from Theomand." Sakura lifted her hand to reveal a folded piece of parchment pinched between two of her fingers. Gian and Beth both had unreadable expressions. We had explained most of our journeying to them, but we hadn't gone very far into Theomand's portion of the story, and we hadn't mentioned Wynchell at all. The two of them were completely unmoved by the news, but giddy excitement swelled up inside of me. The last time we had heard from Theomand, he said he might go try to find the pirates of *The Coventry*. I wouldn't exactly call their entire crew my friends, but I was confident enough in admitting that some of them were rather fond of me.

"What does it say?" I asked eagerly, wanting to step forward and snatch the paper out of Sakura's hand to read it myself. She narrowed her eyes at the squirming wad of fur in my arms before she lifted her gaze to mine and answered.

"Theomand found the pirates, and apparently, they're all coming here to Brightlock. He also found Jessie and Derek with them, and they're coming too." Even before she had finished speaking, I knew I was grinning like an idiot. Jessie was my dearest friend in the entire world, the sibling I never had, the half–stand–in parent alongside my grandmother Willa, and while I knew it had hurt her more than it had me for us to be away from each other, I thought my heart might burst with joy at the idea of seeing her again soon.

A moment later, though, my grin began to fade away. I could already see by Sakura's expression that she was about to ask a pressing question.

"They might be here tomorrow, or they might be here in a few days. We have no way to be sure when the message was sent, because when Chem and I found Wynchell, he was being attacked by two other raptors. There's no telling how long he had been flying or trying to get away from them before they caught up with him, so we have two options. One, we can go ahead and leave, just you and me, like we'd planned. That's what I vote for. We could be out and back in a week, and still have time to see Derek and Jessie. Or option two, we can stay here and see them first, *then* go try to gain an audience with the king." She paused, taking a deep breath that made me wonder if she was going to regret the words she was about to say, then finished with, "The choice is entirely up to you."

I pursed my lips, already turning the ups and downs of each option over in my mind. My first instinct was to just go with option two and call it done. I wanted to see Jessie and learn what she had been up to, and there were so many things I wanted to share with her about what I'd been up to over the past month. Besides, I knew Sakura would want to see her friend Derek as well. But the other part of me knew I had to try and be rational. Leaving sooner rather than later was our best option for getting to the bottom of whether or not the Locker king was indeed in control of the Curse or not as fast as possible, and Sakura was right about it only taking a matter of days. As much as waiting longer to see Jessie again pained me, I knew which Sakura would rather do, and I knew which one I would rather go with when it came to the long run.

"We'll go with option one," I said, scratching my fingers through the matted fur between the kitten's ears. My heart squeezed with my words, guilt worming its way through me, but I stamped it down. I could wait a little longer to see her, and I was sure she could too. "We'll leave tomorrow for the capital."

9
SAKURA

*B*efore any of us crawled into our bedrolls, I insisted that Ksega and I write a note for Gian or Beth to take to the pirates when they arrived, confirming that it was okay for them to stay with our group until we returned. I also had to remind them both that the pirates didn't know about Alchemy, and Jessie had never seen him, so it was probably best for him to stay out of sight until we returned and figured out if and how we wanted to introduce him to the others.

After that, I shrugged into my bedroll, letting the fire die down a bit so that it wasn't so overwhelmingly bright and hot, and tried to fall asleep, which wasn't exactly easy when Ksega kept grunting and muttering to himself from somewhere off to my left. When it had gone on for almost ten minutes, I propped myself up on my elbows and hissed in his general direction,

"Will you *shut up*? Why are you being so loud?"

"It isn't my fault!" he replied in a hoarse whisper. "It's this silly little cat. I don't know what's wrong with him. He keeps trying to stumble over into the fire." I squinted towards his shadowy form and saw that the mysterious little scruff of fur I'd seen him holding was indeed waddling towards my eirioth flames until Ksega lifted it by its neck, set it beside him, and watched as it wobbled off again.

"Put the poor thing out of his misery," Beth snapped from the other side of the fire. "He clearly isn't going to last very long. He would do better in Taro's stomach than he would out here with us."

"Stop being so mean to him," Ksega huffed, lifting the kitten to his chest and squirming farther into his bedroll. He cinched it around his shoulders so the animal couldn't get free. "He's just a little special, that's all."

"Well, let him be special in *silence*," I grumbled, tightening my bedroll around me and turning so that I was facing away from the fire. It was unsettling to look into the dark, shadowy underbrush of the forest, but once I closed my eyes and focused on the safety and surety that came with knowing my power was close at hand, some of the fear ebbed away, replaced with a bone-deep tiredness that trembled through me. I wasn't sure when I'd become so exhausted, but I was grateful for the chance to rest.

After a few more minutes of near-silent struggling, the kitten seemed to settle down, and seconds later a loud rumbling noise escaped from beneath Ksega's bedroll. After that, with the little cat's purring serving as a sort of fake thunder sound, sleep was not only easy to find, but it came running to greet me.

Ksega and I woke before dawn. We packed our things together and settled for the absolute minimum luggage. We didn't want to be weighed down too much by our packs, so we left most of it to be watched over by our companions.

Alchemy was, as always, awake and nearby, and he was more than happy to help us prepare to leave. Almost as soon as he joined us, Ksega shoved the little kitten into his bone hands and demanded he take care of him and not let him be eaten by Light Ray and Taro. Alchemy made a great show of being hesitant about it, even though he had already expressed to me that he sort of wanted a pet. Eventually he gave in and held the tiny creature tightly against his rib cage, very carefully and very gently petting him so that he released that roaring purr again, his one working eye locking on the skeleton's skull as his little fuzzy tail twitched back and forth.

"He likes you," Ksega told Alchemy when we finally finished packing up. The skeleton didn't deny it, still patting the cat on the head. I gave him some directions for caring for Wynchell and making sure the note Ksega and I had written reached the pirates alright, and then we were off, marching through the break of dawn towards our meeting with the king of Brightlock.

We were quiet until we left the Evershifting Forest, now trekking through the golden waves of tall grass that spread like a heavy blanket across Brightlock. It wasn't a very mountainous kingdom, so the traveling would be fairly easy, which was another reason why I knew it would be better and faster for just Ksega and I to go, as much as I hated to admit that he had been right.

"Do you want to go through Arvos to see Jhapato first?" Ksega asked me once we were out in the open. I couldn't see anyone close by aside from a group of carts and caravans and horses being driven and ridden towards the Stargazing Colonies, coming from the direction of the Gates.

"No," I answered eventually. "Maybe on the way back, but for now all I want to do is focus on getting to see the king." And that was all we said for several hours.

It was odd being left alone with my thoughts for so long. Normally, I could hardly get a moment of silence when Ksega was around. We skirted around the Stargazing Colonies, staying as far out of sight as possible, and heading towards the bigger towns. I had seen maps of Brightlock before, and it was one of the largest kingdoms in Horcath. The capital city, Calder, was located near the eastern cliffs, to the north of the Shattered Mountains. It was surrounded by its capital town, Candle, and there were three other larger towns established between Candle, the Stargazing Colonies, Brightlock's northern border, and the Shattered Mountains: Sun Key, Moon Key, and Star Key, collectively referred to as the Keys. I hadn't learned very much about the Keys, and had never really thought I would need to, but now I wished I had studied them more. I knew that each of them had their own particular type of imported goods that they specialized in and that Brightlock traded in. That meant one would mainly supply metals, ores, and stones, most likely the one nearest to the Shattered Mountains. Another would mainly supply horses, bred and trained to form the finest cavalry—Lockers took great pride in their esteemed horses. And the final Key would mainly work in heavy weapons for battle, like battle-axes, claymores, and full-body shields.

The road that connected all the towns of Brightlock was thick, well-worn, and easy to follow. Once we were past the Stargazing Colonies, we shifted over onto the road, staying to the side as we marched on towards the Keys. I could see the first one, the one in the center, and beyond it the tall gray spires of the royal castle, but the other two Keys were harder to spot. One lay far to the north, only just visible, with smoke belching out of what I assumed to be the chimneys of forges. The other Key was farther to the south and closer to the Shattered Mountains, almost invisible against the ominous black peaks.

We only stopped twice, once to have a quick lunch and once to just catch our breath and give our tired muscles a rest. Even after having managed several hours of sleep over the past two nights, I was inexplicably exhausted. I wondered if it had anything to do with the anxious thoughts that swirled through my head at the prospect of standing before the Locker king. I still didn't know what I would say, and even though I knew we would find a way to gain an audience with him, I was beginning to wonder if it was a good idea at all. Of course, our theory that he or someone in his court was behind the Curse made complete sense, which was why I knew we had to do this, but I was hesitant. Standing and pleading your case in front of such a powerful person introduced a whole new level of fear.

By the time we reached the very edge of the center Key—a helpful sign told us it was Star Key—it was night. The sun had set nearly an hour ago, and Ksega and I were both eager to get some sleep. We had some money from Beth and used a few shins to purchase a warm dinner, but rooms at an inn were expensive, so we settled for finding an empty building which appeared to be undergoing some remodeling. When we got there, we threw our bedrolls down and stretched out on top of them. Ksega sighed, popping his knuckles while his eyes slid closed.

"Finally, a rest," he murmured. It had been a long and quiet journey, and we'd mostly kept silent to save our breath, but now that we had slowed to a stop the weariness was catching up.

I looked over at Ksega, tempted to try and strike up a conversation but not wanting to disturb him. He was breathing slowly, undoubtedly on the verge of sleep, and if anything I had learned how much he loved his sleep; it was almost as much as he loved bacon. Aside from that, I noticed that I didn't know a whole lot about him. He had never seemed too keen on talking about himself, although there was surely a lot to tell; not that I would pry him about it. Now that it was just the two of us, anytime we talked it felt almost *too* private. I was slowly coming to the realization that I had depended on Alchemy and Ksega to initiate conversation, and now that I was alone with Ksega I didn't know what to say.

"What're you thinking about?" Ksega asked, surprising me. His eyes were still closed, his hands folded on his stomach; I had thought he'd fallen asleep.

"How do you know I'm thinking about anything?" I avoided answering, turning my attention to the ceiling and trying to let my own exhaustion lull me towards sleep. Ksega snorted.

"When are you *not* thinking about something?" he retorted, and I conceded the point.

Sliding my eyes shut, I said, "I'm thinking we should go to bed. The sooner we get some sleep, the sooner we can be on the move again."

"Yeah," Ksega agreed through a yawn. "And the sooner we can have breakfast."

I woke up to the sound of heavy boots thumping down on wood. At first, I didn't remember where I was, and I squinted blearily at the dark wooden boards around me. Then, rising onto my knees to look out one of the empty window frames, I remembered that we had reached the Star Key the night before. We were in one of the upper rooms of a building being renovated, and it sounded like the people doing the renovating were here to work for the day.

"Ksega," I hissed, reaching over to shake him awake. He squinted up at me, mumbled something, and turned over. "Ksega, wake up! There are people here." I snatched my boots and belt and quickly tugged them on, checking to make sure everything was secure in its place before starting to pack up my bedroll. Ksega sat up and rubbed his eyes, grunting.

"What?" he finally croaked.

"Be quiet! We have to sneak out of here." I finished with my bedroll, scowled at him, and stepped closer. He opened his mouth to protest, but I ignored him, grabbing the bottom of his bedroll and yanking it away from him. He frowned at me but went about grabbing his boots and longbow while I rolled the bedroll up and fastened it in place.

"Where are we going to go?" he asked, rising to his feet so quietly I knew I wouldn't have heard him if I hadn't known he was there. Not for the first time, I was surprised—and a little jealous—of his ability to be so naturally stealthy.

"We have to keep moving towards the capital."

"It will take us all day to get through Star Key," he pointed out.

"All the more reason to get going now. Come on." I led the way towards the door, but he stopped me by lifting his hand. He narrowed his eyes at the boards of the wall, then shook his head, whispering as he led me back to the window.

"There are people out in that hallway. Go this way. We can climb down the wall." He poked his head out the window frame, looking up and down the little alley there. Once he saw that it was clear, he lifted himself over the sill and began to scale down, easily finding hand and footholds in the boards. Throwing a hesitant glance at the door behind me, I stepped up onto the sill after him. Just as I was turning to climb down, the door opened and a burly man with the largest black beard I'd ever seen stepped in. As soon as he saw me, his eyes widened, and he turned to yell back into the hallway. Before I could see what happened next, I scaled halfway down the wall then let myself drop to the dusty ground, following Ksega as he sprinted around a corner.

"Will they look for us?" I asked, hurrying after him as he rushed through the morning crowd of people trying to bustle their way to first in line at the various market stalls around us. I lost sight of him a handful of times but then spotted his mop of blond hair popping up in a new place, and I shoved through the sea of people after him.

"Almost certainly, but we can lose them," Ksega said confidently, swerving and ducking and twirling around the people as he raced through the crowd with me struggling to keep up, always checking behind me to see if the burly man was following.

We went on that way for several minutes, bobbing and weaving and occasionally stepping into an alleyway to find another central road. Unlike the Stargazing Colonies, which were little more than villages, the Keys were massive towns, possibly even able to be referred to as cities. We were still wandering through the outer edges of it, and I doubted we would reach the center before noon if we continued on this maze-like path.

As we jogged, I looked around me, drinking in the architecture and culture of Brightlock. The Stargazing Colonies were made up of a completely new and different culture than any other place I'd seen, but it was also in the poorest area of Brightlock, meaning that there wasn't much visible culture on display. Here in the Keys, though, there were people with steady, well-paying jobs, and as we pushed deeper into Star Key, it became evident.

The houses we passed were nothing like those in Carlore. These were tall and sleek and pale, with dark trim and extravagant moldings and windowsills and flower boxes, and neatly kept yards and brightly painted fences. The pathways were clean and, for the most part, cobbled. Everything was pristine and stylish, and it was all in bright shades of brown and gold and white, vastly different from the deep, rich, expressive colors you would find on the buildings in Carlore.

As we drove our way farther into the Key, the roads broadened, and it was no longer just crowds of people forcing their way down them, but horse-drawn carriages, unleashed dogs,buggies, and wagons, all jostling for a spot in the throng. Ksega guided me to the edge of the road, and we finally slowed our pace to a brisk walk. He checked over his shoulder every now and then but seemed to be satisfied that we were safe now.

We came to a central plaza with a stunning fountain in the center. It had three white stone tiers, and on top of it was a rearing bronze horse with a broken bridle on its face. Water flowed around its planted hooves and down into the lower levels, but I could sense another magic at work in the sculpture: eirioth. I squinted at it, wondering why I could feel the tug from the bronze horse, and a moment later I realized there was steam seeping out of the beast's nostrils. It was impressive work, and I glanced around the plaza to see if I could find the person maintaining it, but there were simply too many people to single someone out. I searched for fellow Carlorians, but that was of little use. Since the Curse had begun to affect all the kingdoms, disputes between them had settled into a mutual struggle to work together for the common goal of survival, and now it was even more often that you found people moving into new, safer kingdoms. That meant that this plaza was teeming with not only dark-skinned Carlorians, but also the bronze Duskans and the pale, tall Talons, and even though Solians and Coldmonians didn't have such obviously distinctive physical features, you could tell who was the seafaring type and who wasn't.

Aside from the fountain, the plaza bore many other equine decorations, not all of them the rearing horse crest of the royal family. There were bronze statues of galloping horse herds, murals on the walls depicting noble horses and their soldier riders, even small wrought iron horse busts on fence posts. There were stores for horse tack, and a smith that specialized in bits, stirrups, and horseshoes, as well as a cute little shop decorated with carrots and apples and sugar cube paintings that I assumed was a place you could go to purchase horse treats. There were also a number of clothing stores, but they appeared to be selling riding gear and things jockeys would wear rather than practical outfits. Ksega and I moved on past them and continued until we got hungry enough to sit down on a bench and eat some breakfast, which technically should've been called lunch, because the sun had gone past the midpoint of the sky. The bench we sat on was near the outdoor seating area of a cafe, and as I sat munching on a sandwich of lettuce and turkey, I noticed Ksega had angled his head to the side so he could listen in on a conversation held by two obviously wealthy women gossiping loudly at one of the cafe tables. I was tempted to smack him to get him to stop, but from the expression of excitement that spread over his face from whatever he was hearing, I resisted the urge and waited for him to share what he had learned. When he was finally finished listening, he stuffed the last bite of his sandwich in his mouth, chewed it up, swallowed it, then grinned at me.

"Did you hear that?"

"No." I lifted my own sandwich to take another bite, stopping just before I did to ask, "Why? Is it something interesting?"

"The traveling entertainers are in town! We can go see them!" he exclaimed, and I paused, staring at him to see if he was serious. He shrugged off my nonplussed scrutiny. "Look, I know you're in a hurry and all, but what can it hurt? Please? It's only one night."

Something about the way his fluffy blond hair glinted in the sunlight and his big blue eyes shone with such pure joy made me want to agree immediately, because how could I say no to him? But I had to be reasonable, so I stamped down the weird, fluttery feeling and said in the calmest voice I could muster, "Ksega, we can't spend our money to see a puppet show. We might need it, and who knows how long it will take us to get an audience with the king?" I knew that Alchemy would disapprove of the statement. He would want me to take a break for some fun and relaxing, even if it delayed me a little bit.

Thinking of Alchemy's disapproval made my thoughts turn to the way Finnian would encourage Ksega's suggestion, and my heart twisted with the thoughts of my brother. I missed him so much. I would've given almost anything in that moment to have him at my side, helping me navigate this journey I had stumbled into. Some of my homesickness must have shown on my face, because Ksega's grin wavered.

"I mean . . . if it's honestly that important to you, then I guess we can skip the entertainers." He seemed to be choking the words out, as if it pained him to say them. I felt another twist in my heart, but this one was of guilt. I hated when Ksega got all frowny. It just wasn't who he was.

"No, that's not why I—I mean—" I paused, trying to put my thoughts in order. One of his brows lifted in a question. I cleared my throat and continued, "I was thinking of someone from back home. Someone that would want me to go see the entertainers, just to help . . ." I frowned. "Well I'm not sure what it would help, but he would be convinced it would help *something*."

"So," Ksega said slowly, a note of eagerness creeping into his voice, "we *can* go see the traveling entertainers?"

I grimaced, wishing I hadn't backed myself into a corner. On the one hand, I wanted to keep moving. It would still take us a number of days to make our way through to the center of Calder in the first place, and I didn't want to waste any more time than we already had. How many more dragons back home had been corrupted by the Curse? How many would have to stay locked up in the War Cells longer because of my delaying? But on the other hand, Ksega had a point. What *could* one night of fun hurt? It would only put us a few hours behind. Besides, Ksega had such a hopeful expression on his face that this time I really couldn't bring myself to let him down again.

"Fine, we can go see them. But only one night." I reached for the pouch of shins Beth had given us to see how much money we had left.

"One night," Ksega promised, his smile widening again. Rolling my eyes, I set about finishing my sandwich and wondering what the traveling entertainers' show might entail.

*T*he very center of Star Key was devoid of any major buildings, instead being a giant cleared field with various pens for horses, a couple small stables, an announcer stand, giant rings of bleachers, and a huge racetrack looping around the field. I'd never seen anything like it before. Dragon races were common in Carlore, and there were even annual dragon races for the champions to compete in, but they always took place in the air, with complex tracks that twisted through the Eirioth Wood and wound through the tricky cracks of the King's Scar. I wasn't sure why it had never occurred to me that horse races *had* to be conducted on the ground.

By the time we arrived at the racetrack it was already growing dark, and the whole field was flooded with people coming to see the performers. The racetrack itself had been shut down and cordoned off with temporary fencing, and a massive golden tent had been erected in the grassy center of the track, glowing with dozens of lights that flicked about from the inside. There were a number of other, smaller golden tents dotted around the rest of the field, probably home to the performers and various props the entertainers would use during their show.

Ksega led the way through the crowd of people, trying to forge a path that would let us get closer to the entry gate. It was a small opening, just wide enough for two people to pass through abreast, and there were two burly guards standing there, the garments they wore bearing the rearing golden horse crest identifying them as Locker soldiers. There was also a wiry Carlorian man wearing a festive black–and–purple–striped suit, along with a matching hat adorned with an obnoxiously large purple feather. He was scrawling notes with a quill onto a piece of parchment and accepting payment as people went through to find their seats in the golden tent.

The line was long, but not unbearably so, and it moved quickly. I wasn't uncomfortable speaking with strangers, but this seemed more like the type of situation Ksega would be at ease in, so I decided to let him take the lead. He looked excited, and I couldn't blame him, because the emotion was mirrored in me, only it was accompanied by lots of buzzing nerves, and I found myself running my thumbs anxiously over my knuckles.

"Hello, hello! Welcome to the grandest show you'll ever watch!" It was our turn to pay and get our tickets. The Carlorian man had a booming, excited voice and a broad grin as we stepped up to his little table. "May I get some names?"

"Ksega and Sakura," Ksega answered, and the man bent over his parchment to scribble it down. I noticed Ksega's eyebrow twitch as he watched the man write his name as *Sega*, and I held back a snicker.

"Should've said *Ka*-sega," I whispered, and he glared at me. A moment later, the Carlorian man stood again, still smiling widely.

"Wonderful to meet you! How will you be paying for your tickets tonight?" His dark eyes flicked expectantly to the leather pouch in Ksega's hand.

"Shins," Ksega replied.

The man glanced down to check his notes before slipping two white tickets off the top of the stack beside his parchment. He held them out to us and said, "That will be thirty-four shins."

Ksega dumped some of the shins out onto the table and quickly counted out thirty-four, scooping the rest back into the pouch. It was now about half as full as it had been when Beth had sent us off with it, so I made a silent promise to myself to watch how we spent it from here on out, only using it when we absolutely had to.

The man ushered us on through the little opening in the fence, and we marched towards the giant tent. As we walked, we were jostled by the moving crowd. The big golden tent wasn't the only thing that had been set up in the field. Vendors selling wares and souvenirs of the show shouted and waggled their merchandise at anyone who would give them a passing glance. The scents of fried cakes and popping corn and roasting meats rolled through the air, and all the stalls were getting plenty of attention, forcing us to walk so closely together that our shoulders maintained constant contact and our hands kept bumping into each other. After it happened a few times, Ksega threaded his fingers through mine, and I didn't pull away.

We hadn't had dinner, so the stalls selling foods were enticing, but I ignored the temptation to buy something. I didn't want to get into the tent late, so we kept a steady pace moving towards it, only stopping or slowing when the crowd got too thick. Finally, we reached the great opening and, after showing our tickets to the three guards stationed there, we were allowed inside.

The tent seemed even bigger on the inside than it had on the outside. There was one massive support post standing in the very center of a huge circular arena, and tall, collapsible wooden bleachers set up around the ring. Erru-mages dressed in flashy golden silks strutted about on the edge of the arena, manipulating the light and bringing the flashing beacons up and down and around in intricate patterns, or maybe just in any whimsical way they fancied. Either way, it made the otherwise drab golden tent all the more lively. The bleachers were already packed with people, and all the good seats were taken, but after some searching, Ksega and I found a good spot on the corner of one of the benches, about halfway up the bleachers that allowed us a relatively good view of the proceedings.

As we sat, I awkwardly slid my hand out of his, using it to instinctively reach for my flame-sword hilt, only to brush against empty air. I had forgotten that we had left our weapons and packs behind, safely hidden in an empty barn we had decided would be our next camping site so that we didn't have to worry about them being confiscated upon our entry. Even though I knew they probably would have been taken away from us anyway, I was still a little irked that I didn't have my weapon beside me. At least they couldn't strip me of my eirioth.

It was only about ten minutes later that an echoing voice announced that the outdoor vendors would be closing, and some of the salespeople would begin marketing their wares by walking around the tent itself with trays of their goods to sell. Shortly after that, Ksega convinced me to let him buy a bag of popped corn and a sweet roll, and then the show began.

A tall, pale man strode out to the center of the arena wearing a neat forest-green coat and matching pants, his long blond hair set in neat plaits all the way down his back. He spread his arms wide, grinning and turning in a circle, basking in the roaring applause, whistles, and shouts of excitement from the crowd.

"Welcome, one and all, to the fifty-eighth show of the Golden Tree performers!" the man shouted, his voice booming over the cacophony of the crowd with the help of a Nightfaller woman who stood beside him, carefully adjusting the sound waves so that the ringmaster's voice could be clearly heard by everyone in the tent. At his words, the crowd screamed even louder. He held his hands up for silence, still grinning, and slowly but surely, the shouting of the throng died down enough for him and his dark-haired assistant to continue.

"This will be a show like none you've ever seen," the Nightfaller woman promised, and high-pitched whistles and whoops erupted around the tent. "Prepare to be amazed! And please, feel free to enjoy the various sugary delights we have on sale for your pleasure while you watch the show!" with that said, she and the Talon man retreated to the sidelines, and the show started.

It was nothing like I'd imagined. People ran out doing cartwheels and flips and splits mid-jump, instantly gaining the crowd's rapt attention. As they twirled and danced and flipped, the gold-dressed erru-mages turned their magic towards the peak of the tent, revealing hoops and strings and bars hanging from the top of the tent or attached to the main support post. On these were performers, dressed in vibrant greens and golds, balancing and twirling and swinging, completely ignorant of the dangerous fall below them. Some of the bars were swinging, two of which held women upside-down, their legs hooked over the bars as they swung. One woman held the hands of a man who was swinging himself back and forth, gaining more and more momentum, and when he reached the peak of his next swing, he let go. My breath caught as he flipped through the air . . . and caught the waiting hands of the other woman. The crowd cheered and clapped with delight, and Ksega and I joined in, grinning at the impressive feats.

A few more minutes passed with similar tricks, but then, they lit some of the floating hoops on fire and let the swinging performers tuck and flip through them before they were caught by their partners, safe and untouched by the flames. It was enough to make your breath catch in your throat with fear and anticipation, and my hair stood on end with each increasingly dangerous performance.

After that, they brought out more mages from all across Horcath. The erru-mages were already on full display, walking casually on the thin rails of the arena as they flashed their power throughout the tent. The eirioth-mages were next, running out into the arena and performing a series of complicated flips and twists like the others had done, only now they were surrounded by bright orange flames that matched their shimmering clothing. The crowd cheered them on as the next group entered the arena: andune-mages. They were dressed in a more auburn-colored gold, and they kicked up mini tornadoes of dirt and sand around them as they danced around the eirioth-mages.

Moments later they were all joined by bering-mages wearing vibrant greens and bringing vines crawling up the main post and flowers blooming across the arena. It was nothing compared to what I had seen Ksega do on the ramp from the Gates between Brightlock and Coldmon, but it was still impressive, and Ksega was loudly cheering for the people that shared his magic. Finally, two Nightfallers dressed in pale gold ran out and funneled more of their power into the andune-mages' tornadoes, making them swell taller and thicker, and they were joined by four aclure-mages, who controlled great swirls of water. They curved them into leaping dolphins and blooming flowers and froze them into giant snowflakes that made the crowd scream even louder in approval.

It was all incredible and engaging, and I couldn't take my eyes off the performers. The show had gone on for nearly an hour now, and nobody was getting tired of it. The mages continued to turn and flaunt their powers, and the people on the suspended poles and hoops went on with their dangerous tosses and twirls. I thought the show would end soon, because what else could they possibly have to show us? But I was proven wrong as the performers slowly made their ways down and out of the arena, and the Talon ringmaster and his Nightfaller companion returned to make another announcement, both smiling and enjoying the excited cheers and cries for more from the crowd.

"We're delighted that you've enjoyed our show thus far," the Talon said, "but now it's time for the true spectacle. Behold, ladies and gentleman, I present to you the beasts of the Golden Tree performers!" Once again, he and his companion retreated to the sidelines as six more performers, five dressed in dramatic green garb and one in flashing gold, stepped out into the arena, bowing and drinking in the applause they were delivered from the crowd.

Everyone seemed to have expectations for what was about to come, but I wasn't sure what the ringmaster meant. I cast Ksega a questioning look, but he only grinned and shrugged, turning his eyes back to the arena. I let mine follow, waiting excitedly to see if they would bring out some powerful horses or even a young smith or runeboar. The cheering of the crowd reached its deafening crescendo as the back entrance to the tent widened, and the sound of heavy footfalls boomed into the tent. Everyone was on their feet now, and a hush fell over the bleachers. Shadows darkened around the entire tent, the mystery enhanced by the erru-mages magic, but the entrance remained clear as everyone held their breath.

Then the eirioth dragons swooped into the tent.

10
KSEGA

*I*didn't believe what I was seeing at first. I had only seen one eirioth dragon up close before, and it was an elderly one that lived with its master in Rulak. At first, I wasn't even sure that that was what had flown into the tent, because they were covered in fine silks and drapery, wearing extravagant costumes, but once I saw the great feathered wings sprouting from their shoulders and the sharp talons at the ends of their legs, I recognized them as dragons. One was a deep crimson color, with scarlet freckles dotting its face and legs, and the other was one solid shade of blue. They were both decorated with folds of golden fabric, and as they made loops around the tent, the crowd erupted into whistles and shouts once again.

I found myself grinning and watching the majestic beasts along with everyone else, amazed at their natural grace and beauty. They tucked their wings and spun through the floating hoops, whirling up and over the bars attached to the support pole and flaring their wings as wide as they could go, earning more screams of excitement from the audience.

The dragons circled each other and flashed through some of the flaming hoops, spotlit the whole time by the erru-mages on the sidelines and watched closely by the six men down in the arena. It was then that I realized what they were holding in their hands: coiled black whips. My grin lessened as I narrowed my eyes at them. Just as I was watching the men, one of the dragons—the red one—dipped towards the arena ground looking tired of twirling through the air. A man in all green stepped forward and snapped his wrist out, flicking the whip into the air so fast I only heard the resounding crack as it smacked just beside the dragon's face. The animal screeched and bolted back into the air, and the whole crowd roared once more in approval, working the blue dragon up into a tizzy. It started to fly erratically around the tent, but more cracks from the men's whips quickly tamed it back to its trained routine. My smile had completely faded at their cruelty. My gaze flicked to the side to see Sakura's reaction, and my heart pinched with sympathy the moment I saw her expression. Her eyes sparked with anger, and I could see the hot tears pooling in her eyes, threatening to spill down over her cheeks. I reached out and grabbed her hand, giving it a gentle squeeze.

"They can't do this," she said, almost too quiet for me to hear over the crowd. "They can't treat them this way." Her voice cracked at the end, or maybe it was just another snap echoing from one of the whips. I couldn't imagine how painful it must have been for her to see an animal that her people loved so much, that her people respected and claimed to connect to in life-long bonds, subjected to such a terrible fate.

More snaps and screeches sounded from the arena. The crowd's cheering swelled again. The erru-mages flashed their lights, and the vendors wandered around, still selling their goods to those that would buy them. Now, the thought of eating anything, even the popped bag of corn lying on my seat, made me sick to my stomach.

"We'll go," I told Sakura, unable to listen to the tortured cries of the dragons any longer, and unable to see so much hatred and sorrow swimming in her eyes. "We'll leave. Come on." I let go of her hand and moved my arm around her, pulling her close to me as I led her away from the bleachers and towards the exit of the big golden tent. She did nothing but mutely hug herself and glare at the ground.

"Leaving so soon?"

One of the guards posted at the tent entrance snickered as we walked past. Sakura snapped her glare up to him, but I pulled her closer and led her on, muttering, "Ignore them. It's late, and we're tired. The best thing we can do right now is go and get some sleep." I waited for her usual practical response of agreement, but she didn't offer one, so we walked back to the little abandoned barn we had found in silence. Once there, I released her and began setting up our bedrolls. She sat on an old tipped-over crate and stared at the wall, and I let her be.

As I sorted through our packs, making sure we had everything and setting our weapons by our respective pillows, I kept stealing glances at her. At one point, I caught the glint of the moonlight reflecting on tears that had streaked down her cheeks, and I finally stood and walked over to sit beside her. For a long time, we sat there, quietly watching the old wooden walls of the barn, listening to the soft rustlings of unseen creatures in the dusty corners and the groaning of the building's ancient structure settling. Finally, she spoke.

"I've heard of animals being treated unfairly," she said, her voice soft and low, "but I never imagined anyone could be so cruel to them, least of all to an eirioth dragon." She shook her head, more tears sliding down her face. "They're such peaceful creatures. They didn't do anything to those performers to deserve that." She wrapped her arms around herself, biting her lower lip to keep it from trembling.

"I know they didn't. People can be nasty and evil for no reason sometimes, and other times they just want the money that they believe is worth more than the animal's life." I grimaced at the memories of all the criminals and thugs I'd come across in the Port back home in Wisesol. There were many of them who owned vicious dogs or foxes who were only so aggressive because of the terrible treatment they received in their homes.

"Those dragons could've *belonged* somewhere, Ksega," she said through a sob. "They could've belonged *to* someone. Maybe they did. Maybe they had riders who loved them." Her shoulders shook with another wave of tears. "Maybe they were bought or stolen from their homes and left to this terrible way of living. That could have been a dragon I knew. That could have been *my* dragon." Her voice hitched at the end, and a shuddering whimper escaped her as she lifted her knees to hug them to her chest.

I scooted closer and wrapped my arms around her, wishing I could provide more comfort, but what could I say? When I had been there for her in Jhapato's house, she had been missing home. I could relate to that. I had family and a friend to go home to, and of course I missed them, but I didn't have any pets or life-long animal companions to worry about like Sakura did. So I only held her tightly and hoped she knew that I was there if she needed me.

I grew drowsy after almost half an hour of sitting there, and Sakura's crying had slowed to a shaky hiccup. I sighed, trying to keep my eyes open. It was far later than the time I had wanted to turn in, but I wasn't going to wait any longer. I lifted my hand to tilt Sakura's chin up so I could look at her. Tears still gleamed in her eyes, but she seemed too tired to shed them.

"It's probably time to try and go to sleep," I said, my voice scratchy with tiredness. She only nodded silently and climbed to her feet, angrily wiping the streaks the tears had left away. She shuffled over to her bedroll, kicked off her boots, and curled up inside the covers. I waited until her shoulders were rising and falling in steady rhythm to stand up myself and make my way over to my own bedroll. I sank down to the covers slowly, lying and staring up at the rickety roof of the barn. I felt guilty for putting Sakura through the pain of seeing the eirioth dragons suffering at the tent. I tried to reason that I hadn't known that would happen, but I still couldn't shake the feeling, and I fell asleep wondering if I was the only one out of the two of us who blamed me.

*W*e both woke up late, which wasn't unusual for me, but it was definitely something Sakura wasn't used to. Throughout our short breakfast, I noticed she was developing bruises beneath her eyes, and her usual relatively tamed hair was starting to frizz and stick out. She was wearing it in a messy braid, and some of the strands had escaped to frame her face. Even despite being so miserable, she looked quite lovely.

Shortly after breakfast, we packed our things and began our march to leave Star Key. The racetrack was located roughly in the center of it, but the city was thicker to the east, where we were headed, so it would take us a little longer to forge our way through it. We weren't planning to stay in any inns; the current plan was to find another empty building to camp in or find a soul kind enough to take us in for the night like Jhapato had.

Sakura was quieter than usual, which was saying something, and I could tell that thoughts of the mistreated eirioth dragons were weighing heavily on her mind. Again, I wished I had some way of offering her comfort, but I didn't, so I only stuck close to her as we marched through the bleary dawn.

We gave the racetrack and the big golden tent a wide berth as we headed for the eastern side of the Key. From the rumors I had heard, the Golden Tree performers would be remaining at the racetrack for another two days to put on their shows. Once they had flaunted their magic and their poor, captured eirioth dragons to all who would see it, they would move on to some other part of Brightlock to do the exact same thing and bleed the towns dry of their money.

Star Key was a fascinating place, especially the eastern portion. It was where most of the breeding ranches and training areas for the horses were, so there were lots of barns and stables. The smell was rather unpleasant, but the sheer number of stunning horses and pristine buildings we passed made up for it. Everything, horse or building, was kept at a shimmering gloss and shown off in any way possible. The people were dressed informally compared to their surroundings, but they were covered in the dirt and grime that came with their jobs, so it made sense for them not to wear anything very expensive.

Most of our day was spent navigating the tight twists and turns, avoiding the big streets mainly used for horse transport and trying—and, for the most part, failing—not to get turned around. There were a number of small plazas boasting the rearing bronze horse fountain, but we somehow managed to wind up in the same one four separate times. At that point, we had been walking for hours, and the sun had passed the midpoint in the sky, so we decided to sit on one of the stone benches around the fountain and take a short break to eat some fruit while we planned what to do next.

"They probably won't have any inns near the outer parts of the Key," Sakura said. It was one of the few things she'd said all day, and just like the other short sentences she had uttered, it only had to do with us moving forward.

"Should we look for one nearby and just wait until tomorrow to keep moving?" I asked, taking a bite of a fuzzy peach. It was a bit overripe, and peach juice flooded over my lips and chin, dripping onto my shirtfront and into my lap.

Sakura raised an eyebrow at my mess before saying, "Maybe. I don't want to spend any more money than we have to, so maybe we should see if someone will take us in. I thought . . ." she paused, her gaze drifting towards one of the roads we had been on several times in our attempts to make our way east. I raised my eyebrows, waiting for her to go on. "I thought I saw a house that looked like it belonged to a welcoming host. We'll stop by and say hello after you're finished bathing in peach juice."

I grunted and took another bite of the fruit, ignoring the rush of juice that flowed over my palm and down my arm. I hadn't spotted any houses that looked very friendly as we walked. They all looked like they belonged to stuck-up rich people who would rather preen over our asking for help than actually welcome us in for a meal and a warm bed for the night.

I finished my peach and attempted to wipe the sticky juices off on my clothes, even though it didn't help very much at all, then we stood and made our way down the street Sakura had been looking at. I let her take the lead, since she seemed to know what she was looking for.

I was about to ask what it was that made her think the house may have been a safe place for shelter when she stopped in her tracks. It was so unexpected, I walked right into her back, nearly knocking her over. She scowled at me over her shoulder, and I offered an apologetic shrug. A man leading two fine-looking bay horses gave us an odd look as he passed, but we both ignored it. By now, we were used to being singled out as outsiders.

"This way," Sakura grumbled, stepping onto a small path that wound between two tall stables filled with curious horses. Some of them were huge, almost twice the size of Tooth and Dagger, Jessie's two caravaning horses. I awkwardly ducked around their heads as I trailed after Sakura.

"Where in the name of the Endless Sea are you going?" I asked her, convinced she was just wandering aimlessly now in hopes of finding someplace to stay the night. We had already been walking for a handful of hours, and my muscles were starting to tire again.

"Hang on . . . I know I saw—aha!" she stopped again, and this time I managed to scrape my boots into the dirt quick enough to avoid bumping into her again. She bent down and then twirled around to show me something she had picked up. I quirked an eyebrow at her, unimpressed.

"It's a feather," I commented, and she nodded, smiling. Even if I had no idea why she was excited by this, it was good to see her smile again.

"Yes, it's a feather."

"What's so important about a feather?"

She waggled it in front of my face, saying in a tone lighter than any I'd heard her use all day, "What kind of feather *is* it?"

I opened my mouth to answer, then closed it, squinting at the feather she held. It was long and brownish-yellow, nothing very impressive. It could've come from any old hawk, but then I realized it was bigger than a hawk feather and looked to be softer, less stiff than one you might find on a bird's wing.

"It's a dragon feather," Sakura answered herself before I could open my mouth again. I licked my lips and frowned at the feather. It had clearly been trampled underfoot a few times but couldn't have been lying on the ground for very long.

"What does that mean for us?" I asked, turning my frown to her.

"It means there's an eirioth dragon somewhere nearby, and if you've ever been with a Carlorian meeting another Carlorian outside of Carlore—which I highly doubt you have—then you know this means we have a guaranteed place to sleep for the night. Come on." She spun on her heel and stalked farther along the little path, twirling the dragon feather in her fingers. I had no clue what she was talking about but was left with no choice but to follow her, so I took a few long strides to catch up.

"Are you sure about this?" I asked, hating to voice that I doubted her but knowing my doubt needed voicing anyway. Sometimes Sakura was a little too headstrong in her ideas.

"Absolutely. Just trust me."

After only a few more twists and turns, Sakura stopped in front of a gloomy-looking house tucked away behind all the horse stables and the shops and fancy houses. It was still nice, of course, with neat trim and fresh paint, but it was very dark and very lonely looking. Sakura didn't seem to mind, her gaze roving over the little house. There was some sort of lean-to structure beside it, but it must have only opened to the small yard in the back, because I couldn't see anything in or around it.

"Does anyone even live here?" I asked, stepping up beside Sakura to squint through the window panes. They were clean and clear, but there were no lights on within the home, and I couldn't see anyone moving around inside. Maybe it was another house that had recently been cleaned up, now waiting for someone to come along and buy it. Maybe it would work as a place for us to sleep in anyway.

"Yes, someone does. Quit being creepy and get out of the way." Sakura roughly pulled me away from the window and stepped up to the door, rapping her knuckles loudly against it a few times. We stood and waited for several seconds, and all was silent inside the house. I gave Sakura a doubtful look, but she only shook her head and knocked again. Once more, there was no sound. I opened my mouth to tell her I had been right, but of course, at that exact moment, the door swung open.

"Hello?" The woman standing before us was very, very elderly, even older than Jhapato. She had skin darker than Sakura's, lined and weathered with age, and silver hair with streaks of black in it. She seemed far too thin to be living in such a rich city, shaking as she peered cautiously around the door.

"Excuse me, we don't mean to interrupt," Sakura said, her voice kind and softened now, and I resisted the urge to roll my eyes. She was always so kind and motherly to everyone but me. When would it finally be my turn to get some free compassion out of her?

"But?" the old woman probed, shrewdly narrowing her eyes at us.

"But we need a place to stay the night," Sakura finished, holding up the dirty feather. I made a face at the back of her head, but neither she nor the Carlorian woman noticed my mocking. I thought Sakura was supposed to be the one with manners and the experience of talking with strange people. Did she really expect that to work?

"In that case, come on inside." The woman stood a little taller, which hardly made any difference, considering she was shorter than both Sakura and I, and stepped backward to let us inside. I gaped at Sakura, not bothering to hide my confusion. She gave me a mysterious little smile and stepped into the home after the woman.

"Okay," I stepped closely after her, whispering to her as I glanced around the dark little entry room we were in. "How did you do that?"

"Tell me all your secrets, I'll tell you mine," she replied, also keeping her voice low. I scrunched my eyebrows together, unsure what she meant. I didn't keep any secrets. I was an open book. Well, aside from that little matter of me developing fluttery feelings for her, but that was a secret I most definitely wasn't sharing.

I set the matter aside for the time being, making a mental note to bring it up later when we had the chance to speak in private. For now, I turned my attention to my surroundings. The house was small, only one story, and had very few furnishings. There were three rooms: a kitchen that also served as a dining space, a cramped little living room, and a bedroom visible through the open doorway on the other side of the building. There was another closed door off to the left, presumably a closet or washroom of some sort.

"Are you hungry? I've just finished making dinner." The woman looked over her shoulder at us from where she had stepped into the dimly lit kitchen, gesturing at a somewhat small pot that was warming over a tiny fire.

"If you have enough to share, that would be wonderful," Sakura said, and at the mention of food my stomach growled loudly. I'd forgotten it had been several hours since we'd eaten lunch, and now the sun was dipping farther and farther into the horizon.

"I think we can make that work." The woman began to dish out some bowls of the stew, and I watched the thick, steaming broth hungrily, already eyeing the softened carrots and chunks of meat resting in the bowl.

"I'm Sakura, by the way." Her voice drew my thoughts away from the food temporarily, and I blinked as Sakura gave me a prompting nod.

With a start, I said, "I'm Ksega. Spelled with a K." I added the second part before I even thought about it and did my best to ignore Sakura's ensuing smirk. The Carlorian woman craned her neck to give me a sharp look, as if she wasn't sure whether to take me seriously or not.

"My name is Maki." Her eyes narrowed at me. "Spelled with an M." She approached the table, setting the bowls of stew down on the top and gesturing for us to join her. "May I ask what's brought you to the Star Key?"

I took my seat and hurriedly shoveled a bite of stew into my mouth, forcing Sakura to answer as I savored the overflowing flavors and spices that wound through the broth. Sakura gave me a sour look, politely taking her seat much slower than I had and making eye contact with Maki as she answered.

"We want to speak to the king. It's a very urgent matter." She lifted a spoonful of stew to her lips, ignoring the judging look Maki gave her. The woman's dark gaze cut to me, equally suspicious and judgmental, and I dropped my gaze to my soup, wanting to stay out of it.

"It must be for you to be traveling directly to the capital. Tell me, do you know how you're going to gain an audience with him?" Maki returned her attention to Sakura. "I know that you two are young, but surely you understand that a man of his position is constantly busy, and your request for a formal audience with him wouldn't even be glanced upon by his officials for a number of months." She calmly took a bite of her stew as I looked over at Sakura, my eyes widening. I had known that it might be a long process, but a number of *months*? We didn't have that kind of time to spare. Sakura drew in a breath and slowly delivered her response in the form of another question.

"We know that. That's the most direct route. But aren't there . . . *other* ways to gain an audience with him?" the way she said it made it sound like she knew what she was talking about, like she was hinting at something she knew to see if Maki knew it as well. If I hadn't known she had no clue what she was babbling about, I probably wouldn't have been able to see through the bluff. I couldn't tell if Maki believed it, but she slowly replied.

"Yes, there are. There always have been, but that doesn't mean they're easy, nor are they wise." Her gaze was sharp as it trailed over the two of us. "It takes a long time to gain an audience with His Majesty unless you are facing trial for some terrible crime or you've somehow managed to make your case dire enough for the guards or officials to bring you before him ahead of everyone else on his list." Her voice was stern, carrying a clear warning as she spoke.

I ignored it, asking, "What would someone have to do in order for that to happen?" it was easy to keep my voice openly curious and innocent, but something about Maki's knowing gaze made my stomach turn with unease, as if she could see clearly through my façade of nonchalance.

"Bring warnings of an attack, information on a well-known criminal, an inside view of an assassination plot, news of plague, forbidden magic, or a drought or famine, the list goes on, but it must be deemed important enough for his council to bring it to him immediately. Even *being* that well-known criminal or that assassin would land you in his presence easily enough, although I wouldn't want to be in the shoes of anyone facing the king's council after being caught by the guards." She took a calm spoonful of her stew, waiting for one of us to make a comment.

Sakura was the first of us to speak. "Right. Naturally. No one would." Sakura bent over her soup again, seemingly content to leave it at that. Instead, when she spoke again, she spoke of her home. "I'm from Hazelnut. Where are you from?" her dark green eyes were filled with something more than just curiosity, something close to longing as she watched Maki expectantly. I wondered if it was because she was eager for some faint connection back to her home, because as of yet, only the belongings she had with her provided that.

"I am from Willow. It is unlikely I have ever crossed paths with a member of your line." Maki's eyes grew even sharper, and I noticed Sakura stiffen in her seat. I cast a questioning look at her, but her gaze was locked on the other woman, something akin to terror creeping into the rough edges of her expression. I tried to decipher Maki's words, and why they might warrant such a reaction from Sakura, but they meant nothing to me. I knew there were many villages in Carlore, but the only location I knew of with 'Willow' in its name was the shimmering Willow Lake just outside the city of Soarlak in Wisesol.

"Yes, that . . . well." Sakura stopped, at a loss for words. I couldn't remember ever seeing her so flustered. She simply sat there, jaw clenched, hands anxiously clasped in her lap with, if I had to guess, her thumbs rubbing over her knuckles.

"Nevertheless," Maki spoke firmly, and there was still evident defense glittering in her eyes, but I detected a note of hesitant kindness behind her words. Sakura's fear trembled in her eyes, waiting. "I will provide the two of you shelter for the night. Not more than one breakfast will be served for you at my table, is that clear?"

"Yes," Sakura said immediately. "Perfectly. Thank you." I blinked at her, a little shocked by her curtness. She had always made such a point out of being polite, at least when it came to strangers.

"Good." Maki nodded once. "Finish your supper. Then, I suppose, you'll be wanting to meet him?" she raised a thin, dark eyebrow, and I found myself frowning at her. Sakura still wouldn't meet my gaze, instead allowing a sheepish smile to spread across her lips as she watched the other Carlorian.

"I would love to, if you're alright with that." *There* was the politeness. Maki only nodded once more, then dug into her stew.

*D*inner was over within the next twenty minutes. I had wolfed down my stew faster than the other two, and as punishment had been forced to sit in awkward silence as I waited for them to finish. Once they had, Maki gathered our dishes and put them away to wash later, then instructed us to set our bedrolls up in the living room. When that was done, she beckoned Sakura to her side beside the small door I had assumed led to a closet.

"It is getting late, so he will be tired." A wry smile stretched across the woman's lined face as I took a step closer, unsure if I was welcome in their little conversation. "He's belonged to me longer than either of you have been alive. Sleep is very precious to him, so try not to make too much noise." Her expression turned a touch sterner as her gaze slid to me. "Particularly you." I bit my tongue to keep my lips from twisting into a disapproving frown. Between the two of us, I was more stealthy than Sakura was. But, of course, Maki didn't know that. Still, it hurt a little that she assumed *I* was the loud one.

Sakura seemed to be buzzing with nerves and excitement. I, on the other hand, was completely lost. Who were we meeting? Why did we have to be quiet? What was beyond the little door, and why was I the only one who couldn't seem to figure it out? Moments later, as Maki eased the door open and carefully lit a small lantern hanging beside the frame, I had to resist the urge to slap my palm against my forehead at my own stupidity. There, lying curled in the corner of the lean-to on a bed of hay, was a magnificent brown-and-gold eirioth dragon.

"He's beautiful," Sakura whispered, and Maki gestured for her to go closer. She did, crouching beside the dragon's head and gingerly lifting her hands to run her fingers along his mottled feathers. I, too, came closer, making a point of being as quiet as possible. The dragon was clearly very old, with some of the color fading from the feathers around his eyes and beak and claws, but he seemed to be in good health. His green eyes were bright and alert as they took in the three of us, and he blinked slowly a few times once he realized we were safe to be around. He was bigger than the two dragons we'd seen in the Golden Tree performers' tent, and almost three times the size of most of the horses we had passed while traveling through the Key.

I stopped a short distance away from the dragon, realizing Sakura had tears pooling in her eyes as she cradled his head. My chest ached with sympathy for her. What must she be feeling in that moment, to be able to touch a beast like this, knowing all the while that she had left one of her own when she had embarked on this journey?

I risked a glance at Maki, but she was watching Sakura and the dragon, her expression having softened into something like compassion. She made no move to comfort Sakura, and neither did I. For a long time, all of us were silent but for Sakura's soft sniffles as she pressed her forehead to the dragon's. Then, finally, Maki spoke.

"His name is Zan. What did you name yours?" her voice was gentler than I'd heard it yet, and Sakura lifted her tear-streaked face to look at her.

"Sycamore," she replied, in a voice so quiet I almost didn't hear her. I felt a pinch in my chest as I realized she'd never told me the name of her dragon before. Why was she so willing to speak to this stranger she'd only just met, but not me? Granted, she didn't know me *that* well, but we were at least closer than Sakura and Maki. At least, I *thought* we were. Maybe she didn't feel the same. I swallowed back the lump that had appeared in my throat, blinking and looking out the small window of the lean-to into the darkness of the night, not wanting Sakura to catch my gaze.

"Sycamore," Maki repeated. "A beautiful name." A long silence stretched out, and pressure mounted in my chest. I wasn't sure what it was, but it burned and clawed inside me, and I cleared my throat, taking a step back towards the door.

"I'm pretty tired. I think I'd like to retire now." I kept my voice and expression neutral, not looking at Sakura, although I could see her watching me out of the corner of my eye. Maki looked me up and down once, then nodded and stepped to the side to let me in. Without another word, I went inside, welcoming the dark quiet of the living room. With a relieved sigh, I tore off my boots and other accessories, then shrugged into my bedroll and shut my eyes tight, hoping sleep would come soon and steal me away from the fiery pain blooming inside my chest.

11
SAKURA

Would you like to take a bath?" Maki's voice drew me out of my dreary stupor, and I looked up at her, not bothering to conceal the answer I knew was shining in my eyes. "I'll draw one for you," she said with a kind smile, retreating into the house with nothing more than whispered instructions to put out the lantern when I came inside.

I wasn't sure how long I sat out there, my head resting against the wall of the lean-to and Zan's resting heavily in my lap. I stroked the soft feathers of his head, scratching behind his big, fanning ears. Sycamore didn't have visible ears. The thought of her only made my heart feel even more like a squeezed lemon, shriveled and torn and hanging on to whatever scraps of juice and broken peel it could, trying to remain whole but knowing it couldn't. I tried not to think about home, about Sycamore and Finnian and Gamma and Walter, and even Derek, although I knew he wasn't any closer to home than I was, but the thoughts came anyway. I wondered what they would be up to. The inn would undoubtedly be getting lots of business, thanks to all the eirioth dragons being locked away in the War Cells, trapped in the yawning depths of the King's Scar. She would be very busy, probably working far too hard for her own good. She'd likely be putting Finnian and Walter to work in the kitchen, despite neither of them ever having shown any talent in the culinary arts. Maybe she'd even brought in Violet, Derek's sweet younger sister, to keep an eye on her just as much as to have another person helping around the inn. All in all, the inn would be faring well enough, and everyone would be busy. Maybe it would provide them all with a welcome distraction from darker thoughts, like wondering if any more eirioth dragons had been taken by the Curse or wondering where in the name of the stars and clouds *I* had managed to find myself. Maybe they weren't worrying about anything more than what type of soup would be served in the inn for supper.

I drifted in and out of my thoughts, sometimes sinking so deeply into them I hardly noticed my surroundings, other times emerging to the sensation of a chilly night-time gust of wind swishing between the boards of the lean-to.

I contemplated going inside. I was desperate for that hot bath, and I didn't want to wait and let it get cold, but I wasn't able to bring myself to wake Zan again. His eyes were closed peacefully, his breathing rhythmic. I pressed my fingers against his smooth feathers, still soft and sleek despite his age. I knew I should go inside. It was late, and I needed a good washing. Besides, if that alone wasn't reason enough, I also had to check on Ksega. Something had upset him, and I wanted to help him if I could. He had been there to comfort me more than once when I was feeling down, and I owed it to him to offer him that same service.

Sighing, I wriggled myself free from Zan's head. He huffed in protest, but didn't move much as his head nestled into the pile of straw on the floor. Muttering a soft good night to him, I put out the lantern and stepped back into the living room. My eyes had adjusted to the soft golden light of the lantern, so when I shut the door, I stood leaning against it for several minutes, blinking and waiting until the blurring shadows began to take on vague forms. Once they did, I saw that Ksega was already in his bedroll, no more than a long lump of darkness on the floor. I couldn't be sure if he was asleep, but he didn't move, so I let him be. I crouched by my pack and blindly fished out a change of clothes, one of the very few I had brought with me, and made my way towards the door to Maki's room, which had slivers of warm yellow light shining beneath it. Before I could even lift my hand to knock, it opened just a crack. Once she saw it was me, she opened it more and beckoned me inside before shutting it with a soft *click*.

The room was small and neat, with a cozy-looking bed, a wardrobe that rose from the floor to the ceiling, and a small side table. Off in the corner, there was a curving bar with a curtain hanging from it, and around the fabric of said curtain, I could see soft curls of steam rolling through the air.

"I just finished heating it." Maki gave me another secretive smile. "Being an eirioth-mage sure has its advantages." I looked at her, my eyebrows raising.

"You're a mage?" I wasn't sure why it hadn't occurred to me that she might be.

"Of course I am, silly." She waved a hand in dismissal. "It doesn't matter. Go ahead and take your bath. I'll help you brush your hair when you're done. It looks like a weasel found it and tried to make a nest." Before I could comment, she roughly shoved me behind the curtain with a towel and slid the fabric to the side to close any gaps. A few moments later, I heard the turning of pages from across the room.

As I slid out of my grubby clothes and eased into the blissfully hot water, I couldn't help but think about what Alchemy and the others were up to. Had Derek and Jessie and the pirates joined them yet? How was Gian's sword training progressing? Had Taro managed to eat the odd little kitten Ksega had brought back yet? I hated missing out on those things, but I knew it would be alright in the end. Soon, Ksega and I would have an audience with the king, and once we had pleaded our case . . . well, who knew what would happen then, but at this point, I didn't really care. I just wanted all of this to be over.

But how *would* we gain an audience with the king? From what Maki had told us, there was no legal way to do it without waiting almost, if not more than, a year. I turned the thoughts over in my mind as I washed the filth off my body. I'd never thought a bath could feel so good. Dunking my head briefly beneath the water and yanking my hands through my hair to try and free it of the grime it had collected, I tried desperately to come up with a solution. All I could think of was finding some way to magically pop up in the king's court without looking like assassins, but unless we came in from the sky, or had Theomand's sneaky mist trick by our sides, I wasn't sure how we could get into the castle so easily.

I sat up abruptly, causing a small wave that nearly sent the water swelling up and over the lip of the tub. That was it. I had it. We could get to the king if we—

"Everything alright in there?" Maki's voice called out, and I jumped, having forgotten I was even in the same room as her. Suddenly very aware of that fact, despite the curtain between us, I sank awkwardly back into the water so that only my head was above the surface. The temperature had cooled considerably now, signaling that I had been soaking in it for some time.

"I'm fine." I answered, sputtering bathwater off my lips. "Just finishing up." I dragged myself out of the water, shuddering at the sudden wave of cold, and began bunching my thick, dark hair in my fists and wringing it out as best I could before swinging the towel around my shoulders.

I dried myself and as much of my hair as I could before pulling on my clean clothes. It felt wonderful to wear something not covered in itchy dust. I pulled the curtain back and began to gather my dirty clothes into a bundle to carry back into the living room, but Maki stopped me.

"Don't worry about those. I'll wash them tonight and have them returned nice and clean to you tomorrow. Come here, let me do something with that hair." She was sitting on the end of her bed, a brush in hand, and she patted the spot beside her. Leaving the clothes, I went and sat beside her.

We didn't say anything as she carefully picked through the knots and tangles with her fingers first, working them out as gently as she could before going in with the brush. It was a very motherly gesture, and I couldn't help but swallow back a bout of tears at the thought. I barely remembered my mother. She had died when I was five years old, in the same Cursed attack that had taken my father and sister. I knew there had been moments like this between us, even if I couldn't remember them. But just because I didn't remember her brushing my hair or tucking me into bed at night didn't mean she was totally forgotten. I remembered having picnics and tea parties with her and my sister Aurora in the twisting branches of our pink eirioth tree. I remembered going with her to visit Gamma and helping to knead the dough for fresh rolls, playing in the flour and making a complete mess of the Hazelwood Inn kitchen that Gamma was so proud of. I remembered practicing eirioth with her in the safe space of our front yard, and learning to climb trees on my own, with her beneath, ready to catch me if I fell. Those memories always carried with them a sense of safety and happiness and warmth, a sense that I could rest and not worry, because I knew someone was there, taking care of me.

I hadn't felt that in a long time, aside from in those memories and right now, here on the foot of Maki's bed, with her tenderly brushing my hair out. How had I managed to get here, tangled up in all this mess and knotted there just as tightly as the strands of my own hair were in the brush?

"I don't know what's brought you to the conclusion that you need to go before the king," Maki said softly, trying not to pull too hard with the brush as she worked through my hair. "But I want you to be careful. You and the boy are very young, and you have your whole lives ahead of you. Even in a world torn by the Curse, there is life and hope and peace. Whatever it is you are looking for, you don't *have* to be looking for it. You can find happiness without it, if you'll only give it a chance."

I bit back the words that rested on my tongue. The ones that said she sounded just like everybody else, the ones that said I was doing it for revenge, the ones that said the hole in my heart wouldn't close just because the Curse was gone.

But maybe it would. Maybe, just maybe, it would be enough to satisfy me. Maybe that was what I needed. Maybe it was okay if I wanted a little bit of revenge, because who wouldn't? Didn't I deserve to avenge my family? Wasn't I allowed my fair share of grief, and for that grief, my own want to make things right?

"I know it's difficult for you, being so young," Maki continued, "To comprehend some of the things of this world can be . . . daunting. It shouldn't have to happen for people your age, but it does, and I can see that it has. You have been through a lot, and I am sorry to see that." The brush paused in its work, and Maki's voice adopted a sorrowful tone. "I can only hope you have set yourself on a path that you know has a worthy end."

I said nothing. There was nothing for me to say, and there was nothing more for Maki to say. She worked through the rest of my tangles in silence, and when she was finished, I wrung my hair out into the tub once more before bidding her goodnight and slipping back into the silent shadows of the living room.

It was late, and I was exhausted. I half crouched and half fell onto my bedroll, barely having the strength to kick my legs beneath the covers as my head flopped onto the pillow. Somewhere on the floor beside me, Ksega was snoring loudly, and for once I didn't have the energy to be irritated about it.

I woke up in utter darkness, which meant I hadn't been asleep for very long. As annoyed as that made me, I only had myself to blame, because I was coughing so violently my throat felt like it was on fire.

"Sakura—" I heard Ksega's voice repeating my name over and over, groggily at first, but then more concerned as I felt his hand on my shoulder. I waved a hand at him, letting him know I wasn't choking. The cold winter air always made my throat aggravatingly scratchy.

"I'm fine," I rasped eventually, clearing my throat and massaging my neck as I waited for that burning tickle in the back of my throat to go away.

"I'll get you some water," Ksega said through a yawn, rising to his feet and shuffling towards the kitchen. I only coughed again in response. When he returned, I didn't bother to question how he had retrieved the water so easily, only downed it gratefully and sank back into my bedroll with a groan. I had always hated having a raw throat.

"Sorry for waking you," I croaked, shutting my eyes and wriggling further into the bedroll. When he said nothing, I opened them again. Beside me, Ksega was still sitting, one side of his body illuminated by the moon's glow shining in thick beams of silver light through the window.

"It's okay," he said finally. I waited, sensing he had more to say. "I . . . you said something about secrets earlier. That I had some. What did that mean?" I blinked, a little taken aback by the question.

"Uh, I'm not sure. I mean, you have plenty of secrets. It's not like you've told me your life story." I licked my lips, wishing he'd brought more water, but taking the hint that he was in a crankier mood than usual, I decided against asking.

"No. And you haven't told me yours. But you seem just fine with telling it to people you just met today." His voice was chilly, and I frowned.

"What are you talking about?"

"Nothing. It's nothing. I'm probably just overthinking things." He scooted back towards his bedroll and slid his long legs beneath the covers, lying on his side so that he was facing away from me. I pushed myself up onto my elbows.

"No, tell me. If something's bothering—" my voice trailed off into a scratchy hiss. I cleared my throat and tried again. "If something's bothering you, I want you to tell me. You can trust me, Ksega."

"Yeah, only as much as you trust me," he snapped back.

I rolled my eyes, making sure he could hear it in my voice when I said, "Now you're just being dramatic. Come on, we're tired, and it's been a stressful couple of days. What's wrong?" I lowered myself back onto my pillow. "Is it because I've taken a liking to Maki?" I whispered, finding it easier and less painful than speaking. Ksega grunted. I sighed. "I know it isn't natural for me to warm up to someone so fast, but . . . she's very nice, you know, and she sort of reminds me of my mother." I grimaced. "I mean, not *really*, because I don't remember her much, but . . . you know what I mean, right? I can't help but enjoy being around her." To my surprise, Ksega rolled over to face me, his bright blue eyes taking on an ethereal hue in the moonlight that was breathtaking. I doubted I would ever stop marveling at his eyes.

"No, actually, I don't know what you mean. According to Willa, my mother died when I was born." He said the words so simply, so blatantly, that I almost thought he was joking. How could anyone be so emotionless about such a topic?

"I'm sorry, I . . . I didn't know." I said softly. "That's one of your secrets, I suppose."

"The strange thing," Ksega went on, turning to lie on his back so that he was looking up at the dark ceiling. "Is that I *feel* like I remember her. Not a lot, obviously, but . . . there are glimpses, like flashes of memory. Blond hair, fair skin. I even remember hearing a laugh. But I'm probably just imagining it." He shut his eyes. "I can't possibly remember her if she died giving birth to me." I watched him for a long moment, trying to read what I could of his expression, but it remained aggravatingly blank.

"Maybe you should ask Willa about it," I suggested at last, and his eyes fluttered open, darting towards me.

"Maybe," was all he said. Then he inhaled sharply and turned to face me again. "Okay, it's your turn to share a secret. Explain how you got Maki to let us stay here." I drew in a long breath, bracing myself for the rasping pain in my throat as I answered him.

"There's a custom that's taught to all young Carlorian children. I never really thought it would apply to me, but-"—I shrugged—"here we are. Basically, if a Carlorian is leaving the kingdom, they can leave a feather belonging to their dragon with any friend of theirs, and if they present that feather to the Carlorian that left, then that Carlorian is obligated to provide them with food and shelter for as long as they need it. The neat part is that the feather can be passed down as an heirloom through bloodlines, so the descendants of the friends of the departed Carlorian, assuming said Carlorian is still alive, will be given the same treatment their ancestors would be." I paused, watching him closely to see if he was still following. I saw no signs of confusion in his expression, so I continued, a little bashfully, "I wasn't entirely sure if picking the feather up off the road would work, but I knew it was a dragon feather, and I figured . . . well, why would she question it? And she didn't. Up until that little bit where she said she was from Willow." Once more, I shrugged. "We got lucky that she's so kind, I guess."

Ksega was silent for a long moment, as if processing all of this, then he asked, "Would any other Carlorian have butchered us or something?"

"No," I chuckled. "But they would have kicked us out. Just because we're from the same kingdom doesn't mean we're all allies." I closed my eyes, feeling another wave of tiredness batter into me. "Okay, it's time to go to sleep now. I have a plan to get to the king, but it'll have to wait until tomorrow." I curled up beneath the covers of my bedroll. "Good night, Ksega."

"Technically, I think it's morning," he replied, then, after grinning at my responding glare, he added, "Good night, flame-fingers."

12
KSEGA

Maki was in the kitchen when I woke up, cooking something that smelled delicious. Beside me, Sakura was still asleep. The cup I had used to fetch water in during the night was gone, presumably taken by Maki when she came out that morning.

"Rise and shine," Maki said from behind me, and I looked over to see her setting dishes out on the table. She didn't meet my gaze as she turned to go back into the kitchen, working something that smelled like bacon at the stove.

"What time is it?" I asked, looking towards the window, trying to gauge where the sun was, although all I could see was the backs and roofs of more buildings of Star Key.

"Early." She watched me closely as I stood, raking my hands through my hair and trying to pull out any of the curly knots I found. "I'll be leaving to go to work shortly after breakfast. Will you two be gone by then?"

"I don't know," I answered honestly, glancing back at Sakura. "She told me she had a plan last night but fell asleep before she could share it. We can ask her when she wakes up." Maki's only response was a grunt.

I went and sat at the table, not bothering to pack up my bedroll until I was told to do so by Sakura. I had wanted to learn more about her plan as soon as I'd learned she had one, but two things had barred my lips from asking. The first was that she had clearly been very tired, and I didn't want to keep her from getting her rest. The second was all the thoughts that had been sent swirling through my head after our midnight conversation. I wasn't entirely sure I understood the concept of the feather and promise of safety and shelter between Carlorians, but I could always ask her to explain it to me further when she was less drowsy, and when there weren't so many pressing matters to deal with. Aside from that, she had set my thoughts awhirl with whatever small memories I could recall of my parents. There weren't many. As I'd told her the night before, Willa had told me my mother died in childbirth, so there was no way I could remember her. And yet . . . it made me feel crazy whenever I thought about it, but I could've sworn I remembered *something* about her. Golden hair and pale skin, and maybe even the dimples of a smile. I remembered a musical, lilting laugh, and a soft, gentle voice. There were never any specific words formed, but I knew that the mysterious voice didn't belong to anyone I knew. The only logical owner I could think of was my mother, but I knew that couldn't be possible.

Then there was my father. Willa rarely spoke of either of my parents, and she'd never told me their names—I'd never even cared to ask—but out of the two of them, she spoke the least of my father. I knew that he was her son, and talking about him must have been difficult. The details of his death were still in the dark to me, but I knew it had been some sort of sickness caused by an accidental injury. Beyond that, and the fact that he had died within a year of my birth in some foreign kingdom, I knew nothing of him. I knew the memories of him were real, even though they seemed even fewer than those of my mother. I remembered a deep voice and a big frame.

And that was everything. All I could recall of my parents wrapped into a miniscule kernel of knowledge and tucked away somewhere in the back of my mind. I didn't even know if anyone else in Rulak knew them and remembered them, or who my other grandparents were. I knew Willa had been married to a man named Lance, but he had died before I was even conceived, and I didn't ask about him. Any talk of deceased family members seemed to cause her pain, and considering the fact that I couldn't remember any of them, I saw no reason to bring them up. Now, I was beginning to wonder what all there was to learn about my family.

Sakura didn't have her family around, aside from her brother, but she still knew what happened to them. She still knew who they were before they died, and she still found the strength to talk about them, even if it was only for brief moments. What was I so afraid of learning about my own family's past? Why couldn't I bring myself to ask Willa about them? Yes, I didn't want to hurt her any further, but I had a right to know about my own parents, didn't I?

"What's troubling you?" Maki's voice drew me out of my thoughts, and I blinked, realizing she had set a plate of eggs and bacon in front of me. I looked up at her, a little shocked she had bothered to read my pensive expression. Her face was as sharp and judgmental as it had been the day before, but I could see a light of curiosity shimmering in her eyes as she took a seat at the table and dug into her own breakfast.

"Nothing. I'm worried about my family," I admitted, hoping she wouldn't ask me to expand on the half-truth. I could see the suspicion in her eyes, so I added, "I left rather suddenly, with very little warning. They should be fine, but—" I cut myself off abruptly, licking my lips as my thoughts turned to Willa, running her little perfume business all alone for the weeks I had been gone. It made my heart pinch to think of how much she would be thinking about me. "But I still worry," I finished lamely.

"Suddenly and with little warning," Maki echoed, her voice monotone. I nodded, looking down at my eggs, finding I had little appetite. "Whatever it is you're wanting to see the king for must be mighty important. Tell me, how far from home have you traveled?"

"We came from Coldmon." Again, it was only a half-lie. "And yes, it is very important that we see him."

Maki looked dubious, and I expect she would have pressed me further if a groan from the living room hadn't drawn our attention to Sakura, who was forcing herself up into a sitting position. She dragged a hand through hair, blinking groggily at her surroundings until her eyes landed on us.

"Good morning," I said, as cheerily as I could muster. I was still a little irked with her, or at least I was trying to be, but the more I thought about it, the less I could remember *why*.

"Something smells amazing," she said, ignoring me and watching Maki expectantly. Her voice was scratchy, but not as much as it had been during the night. She rose to her feet and stepped up to the table, slumping into one of the seats as the older woman presented her with a plate of food.

"When are you planning to leave today?" Maki asked, not acknowledging Sakura's compliment. Sakura glanced over at me, and I raised an eyebrow at her, hoping my expression captured the *you haven't told me either* look I wanted it to.

"Not long after breakfast, I'd imagine." Sakura said, picking up the glass of water Maki had set before her. "We'll pack up our things and be on our way as soon as we're finished eating." She tipped the glass back and drank it all, clearing her throat as she set it back down.

"Good." Maki nodded curtly, scraping at her eggs with her fork and casting her gaze down at her plate. "I'll be leaving soon as well for work. Where will you be going?" Her eyes cut up again, expectant, like she was waiting for Sakura to slip up in a lie.

"To see the king," Sakura said simply, and I could tell she would be offering no further explanation. Maki must have picked up the same hint, because she said nothing more on the topic.

We finished our meal in companionable silence, then Maki went to check on Zan before she left for the day. By the time she was heading out the door, Sakura and I were finishing packing our things. The moment the door clicked shut behind Maki, Sakura dropped her packs and walked over to the door leading to Zan's little stable. I narrowed my gaze at her.

"Where are you going?" I asked, setting my bedroll on the floor and standing. I strode over to where she was easing the door open, holding a finger to her lips to signal for me to be quiet. She slipped as silently as she could into the stable, then I followed, slipping as silently as *I* could after her. It made me cringe every time her boots crunched against straw or clicked on wood, reminding me again and again of how much skill she lacked when it came to stealth.

"Hello, Zan," Sakura said calmly, and I blinked up at the dragon. He was standing now, towering over us and arching his neck to track our movements without having to move himself. A prickle of unease rolled down my back as he watched us, getting the distinct feeling that he knew we weren't supposed to be here.

"Sakura," I said in warning, but she ignored me. There was a second space in the lean-to, hardly even qualifying as a room. It was separated by a thin wall that was very unstable in appearance. On the other side of it, there was a big stable door that presumably led out into Maki's small backyard. There were also a number of wooden pegs and shelves installed in the wall, and on them were pieces of tack, although they were like no pieces of tack I had ever seen. The saddle was enormous, and the bridle oddly shaped. It took me a moment to realize that they were meant to go on an eirioth dragon, not a horse.

"This is what I was looking for," Sakura said, her fingers delicately tracing the thread work on the saddle. She inspected each piece of the set closely, fiddling with clips and belts and buckles, all the while setting me more and more on edge. What if Maki forgot something and had to come back? What if she was planning to come back for Zan anyway? What if we got caught?

"Why?" I whispered, unsure why I felt the need to keep my voice low. She glanced over her shoulder at me, irritation in her gaze until she saw how uncomfortable I was, and then the irritation was replaced with amusement.

"Aren't you supposed to be the sneaky thief? The stowaway? I didn't expect you to get so rattled." She coughed once, cleared her throat, and turned back to the tack, lifting the bridle off its hook to test its weight. I scowled at her, although she didn't turn to see it.

"I'm fine with stealing stuff, just not from people I *know*. Or sort of know, I guess. Wasn't it just last night you were saying Maki reminded you of your mother? Why are you stealing from her now?" I looked worriedly over my shoulder, spying Zan watching with slitted eyes. He released a breathy huff, taking a heavy step forward as he sensed my growing discomfort. I leaned away from him, warily eyeing his sharp gray beak.

"Relax," Sakura placed the bridle back on its peg and turned to me, rolling her eyes. "I'm not actually *stealing* it. We're going to borrow it later. Hopefully. Come on, we need to get moving."

"What?" I couldn't conceal the confusion in my voice, but instead of giving an explanation, Sakura pushed past me and went back into Maki's house. I hurried after her, and when I shut the door behind me, she already had her things together and slung over her shoulder. I didn't get the chance to ask her any more questions until we were both back out on the bustling street, squinting through the morning sunlight and trying to orient ourselves.

"Okay," she said over the ruckus of the morning. It was still early, with sunlight just beginning to stream down onto the cobbled roads, but there were plenty of people up and about, opening their stores and beating their rugs and hanging their laundry and leading their muscled steeds up and down the street. It almost seemed even more alive than it had been at noon the day before.

"Okay," I repeated, side-stepping off the pathway as a wagon rattled loudly down the cobbles, loaded with barrels and sacks and two howling dogs. The people of the Star Key were unfazed by the cacophony that rang up and down the streets so early in the morning.

"Go ahead, ask your questions." Sakura led the way down the street, her gaze dancing over the various shops and houses we passed, searching for any she may have recognized as she attempted to navigate through the maze of crisscrossing alleys and backroads and main streets.

"Why are we going west?" I bit my tongue to keep from letting all my questions flow like a tumbling waterfall from my lips. If she was willing to take them one at a time, I could be patient enough to go through them slowly.

"Surely you don't expect us to waltz up to the castle and go right inside to see the king," Sakura said, squeezing between a small throng of people. I refrained from telling her that my initial idea of our meeting the Locker king had indeed looked something like that. Instead, I said,

"That doesn't tell me why we're going backwards."

For a moment, I was afraid she was creating an entirely new plan, one that didn't involve us going to see the king at all, but seconds later that fear was squashed as she replied, "We can't sneak into the castle without looking exceptionally suspicious, and even if we could, it would be a lot harder to explain why we were there after magically turning up inside the walls." Sakura looked back to make sure I was close behind her so she wouldn't have to speak any louder than necessary. "It will be far easier if we're confronted as soon as we're inside."

"That doesn't make any sense," I said, frowning at her as I turned the idea over in my head. She was finding ways to connect all the dots, but I wasn't sure I could even see all of them.

"It will, once we get what we need. Ah, look, we've found the plaza." It was, in fact, only one of the many plazas that were dotted throughout the town, but it was one I recognized. The fountain in the center had stone benches pressed up against it, and my gaze fell on the one Sakura and I had sat on after getting ourselves turned around for the umpteenth time.

"What do you mean 'what we need'?" The more she talked, the more confused I became. Jessie and Willa had always said I was exceptionally clever, and it was true that I was unusually adept at finding ways out of tricky situations and rather talented at solving puzzles and codes. At one point, I'd even begun to learn how to read lips. But whatever Sakura was thinking had me stumped. I knew everything she did. We had to get into the castle in a way that was—preferably—legal, but the only way to do that and succeed in gaining an audience with the king would mean waiting months. What other option was there but to sneak in?

"I don't think we'll be able to get in on ground level. The place will undoubtedly be crawling with guards, and trying to scale any walls without getting caught is too risky, so we'll just have to go in over them," Sakura said, leading the way through the plaza.

"Doesn't that require scaling them?" I asked, growing exasperated with her little game. Why wouldn't she just tell me?

"Not if we fly," she said matter-of-factly, and as soon as the words left her lips, I stopped dead in my tracks. It took her a few paces before she realized I wasn't following, when she stopped and looked back at me, planting her hands on her hips as she waited, but I ignored her, finally putting everything together.

"You can't be serious," I said finally, concluding that, despite how much I didn't want it to, it made sense. Sakura walked back up to me so she wouldn't have to speak loudly.

"Why not? It's a smart plan. Genius, even, if you ask me." She shrugged, as if we were discussing something as trivial as the latest catch of fish being brought into Port to be sold. I clenched my jaw, still struggling to grasp the details of her plan.

"How do you plan to get it?" I asked thinly.

"You're a thief, aren't you?" she prompted, her eyebrow lifting again. My eyes widened, and I did nothing to try and temper the panic in my voice when I said,

"I've never stolen a *dragon*." I threw my gaze around the plaza, thankful nobody was paying much attention to us. I reached out and grabbed her arm, tugging her to my side and guiding her towards one of the shady corners of the ring, just to be sure.

"Look, we've got to try." She was already beginning to plead her case before we'd reached the shadows, tugging her arm free of my grip. "If we can fly over the walls, we'll have a better chance of getting brought before the king than we would with anything else."

"You mean we'll be arrested and brought forward in trial," I deadpanned. She pressed her lips into a thin line, but didn't argue my point. I sighed, shaking my head. "It's too dangerous, Sakura. This is reckless. We can find another way." Before I'd even finished, I could tell she wouldn't agree.

"No, Ksega, we can't. We can't wait any longer. We can't give the Curse any more time to grow, and we can't—" She broke out in a fit of coughs, grimacing as she cleared her throat. I reached out to steady her, but she shook her head, so I dropped my hand. When the fit was over, she spoke in a rasp. "I'm fine. I always get like this when it gets cold." Her face pinched with determination. "Ksega, we can't leave those dragons with those performers. You saw how they were being treated. You know what those dragons mean to my people, to *me*. You can't possibly expect me to turn my back on them when not only do I have the chance to help them, but in doing so, I might be able to help myself, too." Her expression was pleading.

"I know," I said quietly, although I wasn't entirely sure that I did. With a groan, I combed a hand through my hair, trying to keep it from falling into my eyes as I let my hand fall back to my side. I looked at her, unsure what to say. She held my gaze steadily, as stubborn as ever.

"Please, Ksega." She spoke in little more than a raspy whisper.

"Okay." I shut my eyes, hardly believing I was agreeing to this. "Okay, we'll do it. Come on, we need to get back to that racetrack by nightfall." Before I could talk myself out of it, I was moving, leading the way through the plaza and back onto the confusing streets. I'd never stolen anything living before, and I was hesitant to do so now. Anything I'd stolen in the past had been something small and relatively harmless to the victim, like some food or maybe a shirt or pair of pants. On one occasion, I'd snatched a man's golden timepiece, and on another a pouch of silver coins from some nobleman's wife, but they had left me feeling rather guilty, so I'd decided to never steal valuables only for the sake of stealing valuables again.

I tried not to think too much on it, focusing instead on navigating my way through the maze of the Key. From what I knew, the performers never stayed in one place for very long, so they would be moving on soon, if they hadn't left already. I doubted they had, because it would take some time to pack away all those tents and poles and hoops, not to mention the animals and their props, but they would probably be preparing to leave soon, so we had to act quickly.

My confidence in Sakura's plan was slim, but I wasn't going to voice my worries. It wasn't exactly like I had any better ideas, anyway. If flying over the walls on a dragon was our best chance to see the king quickly, I was willing to take the risk.

*D*usk was upon us by the time we found ourselves jogging through the field towards the racetrack, where the great golden tent stood in the center, no different than it had been before. We weren't going to go in the big tent this time, though. Instead, we had our sights set on one of the smaller gold tents behind the central one, where props and performers and animals would be when they weren't on display during the show. We knew this because of the animal handlers coming in and out of the tent. We didn't want to pay our way in again, but we also didn't want to appear too suspicious lurking around until the show started, so we made our way around the borders of the tent, being as inconspicuous as possible as we tried to find another way in. There were several Locker soldiers stationed at regular intervals around the perimeter of the racetrack, keeping their eyes peeled for any signs of trouble. A temporary fence had been set up around the track, with only one entrance at the front. Aside from the Lockers, it seemed that the performers had their own security force: A team of men and women, about twelve total, were patrolling the stalls and pathways and around the tents, marching throughout the racetrack and checking randomly for tickets. As long as we avoided them and got in around the Locker guards, we would be fine.

Sakura had plenty of talents, but being stealthy—and remaining inconspicuous while being stealthy—was not among them. I was constantly reminding her to stop furrowing her brow or to quit rubbing her knuckles anxiously. They weren't automatic tells of guilt, but they certainly came off as suspicious, and I knew that the soldiers and hired security would be taking note of them.

"Just try to relax," I told her. "Act natural." I wasn't sure what acting natural meant to her, but based on how she forcefully lowered her shoulders and plastered a blank expression onto her face, I knew that she would need some help understanding. "You're trying too hard," I pointed out.

She scowled at me, squaring her shoulders again, and snapped, "I'm not used to being without my weapons, and you aren't exactly giving me great directions here."

"I'm trying." I massaged my brow with my fingers, trying to think. I hadn't been taught by anything but experience, and my natural skills had been something I had honed and trained over the years. Finding a way to put those same skills into words for someone else was surprisingly difficult.

"Tell me what you want me to do." She slowed to a stop, and I halted beside her. We had been milling about through the streams of people making their way towards the entrance, but always detaching ourselves from the crowd before we reached it to make another lap.

"Stop looking so . . . afraid. Angry. Calculating. That's what they're looking for." I pursed my lips thinly, looking her up and down and trying to find out what it was that exuded suspicion about her. "Okay," I said at last. "Hold my hand. We'll go under the guise of being a young couple coming in to see the show. You'll drag me towards stalls and games, and point excitedly at all the cute, fluffy plushies they're selling, and you'll ask me to buy you a sweet treat, and you'll bounce on the balls of your feet and shake my arm when you see something exciting." I couldn't help but grin as I spoke, already finding the pictures of her performing such actions so far beyond ludicrous that I had to bite my tongue to keep from laughing. From her expression, I could tell she did not share in my amusement.

"I'm not going to act like a child," she said firmly.

I shrugged, accepting it. "Fair enough. But you have to sell it all the same. Try not to do it all *intentionally*. Forcing the actions will only make them appear more unnatural." I held a hand out to her, and after a brief hesitation and another glower sent my way, she took it, and we started walking again.

It didn't take us very long to find a portion of the temporary fence that was relatively unguarded. It was facing a part of Star Key that wasn't pouring out eager members of the show's audience, and wasn't close enough to the main attractions that the hired security was paying much attention to it, giving Sakura and I the perfect opportunity to easily hop over the fence and calmly stroll right into the throng of people. Avoiding the random ticket checks wasn't going to be impossible, but with how uneasy Sakura was, I had to work extra hard to keep us under the radar. To her credit, she did sell her act quite well. She held my hand and noted various wares and knick-knacks that caught her eye, and did on one occasion stop me by one of the vendors to ask if she could have a sweet roll. I bought it for her on the condition that she at least shared some of it with me. Aside from that, it was really only a matter of waiting until the show started and all the other guests made their way into the central golden tent.

We did a good job of keeping ourselves away from any ticket checks, and the only thing that really got me worried was when Sakura had one of her coughing fits. She quickly smothered them in the crook of her elbow, trying to keep as quiet as possible. Even over the roaring din of the crowd and the vendors and the announcers inside the tent, soldiers still tracked each and every sound they detected, even if it was with their eyes alone. Any signs of suspicious activity would have them on the move.

Finally, the ten-minute warning called from inside the tent and forced ourselves to the edge of the eager jumble of people. We still headed for the entrance of the tent, but as soon as we were confident no one was paying much attention, least of all the guards stationed beside the entrance, checking tickets and ushering people in, we darted to the side and wound our way back towards the furthest vending stalls, which had already been shut down for the night. Avoiding the merchants was easy, and most of the Locker guards had taken up more leisurely positions, sitting on crates or leaning against the fence, confident their work was over for the time being. As for the performers' own security, they still patrolled the area, and without the crowd to shield us, we would have to be completely invisible. There was a lot of ground to cover around the racetrack, and there were only so many of them. The problem was that they had no set rotation, meandering around whichever way they pleased, poking through some of the wares, rifling through crates, organizing the leftover sheets of pastry that hadn't been purchased, not paying much attention to their surroundings but still alert enough that they posed a threat to our plans.

"Alright," I whispered to Sakura as we crouched behind a stack of crates. I looked over at her. "Here goes nothing. Ready?"

She nodded, swallowing as she peered wide-eyed around the corner of the crate.

"I'm not sure I am," I muttered. "But if we stick around to wait, I never will be. Let's go."

13
ERABETH

*G*ian and I had gone to the cliffs above the ramp over the Gates every day to watch for a pirate ship pulling into the quay. The great ramp that led up from the docks was broad and, most mornings, left the other side half invisible through the dawn mist. Every trek through roughly a mile of the Evershifting Forest, only to be left disappointed, made me increasingly irked. Granted, it had only been two days, but as I woke up on the third morning, I wasn't feeling particularly enthused.

"Why don't you go check today?" I grumbled to Bones as I poked at the embers of the previous night's fire, wishing they could retain a little more warmth. Winter was coming. That in and of itself meant very little to us Duskans, considering we lived in a desert and, for the most part, winter didn't drastically affect us. It got a little chillier, and maybe a few snowflakes would fall, but it rarely changed much. Out here, though, without the hot sands and the heat of the sun on my skin, it was *freezing*. How did anyone live like this? Did they just bundle up in thick fur coats and huddle by fires? Where was the room for freedom, for adventure?

"You know I can't," the skeleton replied from where he was sprawled languidly beside the fire pit, clad only in his long cloak. I glared into the abyss-like depths of his empty eye sockets, hating that he was right. Not only was there too great a risk of him being seen, but there was also the matter of the injured raptor lounging on the far side of the camp, eyeing the other animals with shining eyes. He hadn't moved very much, which I was grateful for, and Bones had been his primary caretaker since he had been brought into the camp.

"At the very least, don't make me take Sky Boy with me again," I grumbled, glancing over at where Gian was still curled in his bedroll. Bones had taken to referring to him as Sky Boy, and at some point, the nickname had stuck, just like 'Bones' had. I knew Sakura and Ksega called the skeleton Chem, which was short for something, although I didn't remember what, but 'Chem' didn't seem to fit him very well in my eyes.

"It will be better if you both go. Besides, he's the one holding onto the letter from Ironling and Ksega," Bones pointed out, and I groaned. To convince the pirates that we really were with Sakura and Ksega, we were carrying both their letter and one from

Theomand to prove . . . something. I couldn't remember the exact details. In my opinion, it was a faulty plan. We easily could have stumbled across the letter from Theomand on our own and had now hatched a plan to exploit the pirates of whatever riches they may have had, legally obtained or otherwise. Still, everyone else seemed confident in the plan, and I didn't have much ground to argue, so I went along with it.

I muttered to myself about how idiotic Gian was and listed at least seven different reasons in my head on why it would be better for me to go alone, but I wouldn't voice them. While aggravating others had never bothered me, the thought of getting on the bad side of Bones was not a pleasant one. Whatever had claimed him, it was *dasten* magic, and I wanted no part of it.

Dawn's light was just beginning to filter through the trees, splaying out in whirling patterns on the yellowing grass. Despite its magical abilities, the Evershifting Forest had decided to merge its current state with that of the world, enveloping its landscape in the soft gold and brown hues of late autumn. Elegant maple trees flowered out around us, their red and orange leaves littering the forest floor and their sweet scent crawling through the air on the chilling autumnal breezes. I wrinkled my nose at the cloying smell every time I detected it, longing for the tang of sweat and metal and wood dust that wrapped itself around the City of Bones like a prickly blanket.

Our campsite had changed twice over the course of the past two days. In the evening of the day Sakura and Ksega had left, I had been thrown to the ground as a knobbly hill rolled up from the ground where our fire pit had been. The trees had shrunk into thorny berry bushes, and the air had swelled with summer heat. Then, when we had awoken the following morning, it was gone, replaced with the maple forest and a crisp creek that tinkled merrily in little waterfalls down a slope beside my bedroll. It was this creek's water that I used now to wash my face and smooth my hair back as I carefully pulled it into a tight bun at the nape of my neck.

"Breakfast for the birds!" Bones declared from behind me, and I looked back to see him lifting two fat lizards in his skeletal hand, letting them dangle over the eagerly waiting beaks of Taro and Light Ray. He dropped them, and the birds set upon their prey viciously. "And," the skeleton continued, "a little something for the small one." He produced a small vole from the depths of his cloak and turned around to offer it to the spiky ball of black fur behind him. The little cat pawed at it curiously, missing the first few times before finally clawing it. I watched with a nonplussed expression as Bones carefully helped the kitten through his meal.

"That thing is pitiful," I snarled at him, scowling at the little creature. "He can't even eat on his own! Put him out of his misery. Taro could use the protein." I rose from my crouched position at the side of the creek to go stand beside the skeleton and his bizarre companion.

"Are you sure he's not poisonous?" Gian groaned from his bedroll, blinking bleary-eyed in our direction. "Judging by the looks of him, there's a good chance he's diseased."

"Good point," I conceded. "We'll feed him to the raptor instead."

"Stop it, both of you. You're so heartless," Bones huffed, rising to his feet after giving the cat a quick pat on the head.

"I'm sorry, *we're* the heartless ones?" I echoed, raising an eyebrow as I gave a pointed look to his blackened rib cage. He huffed again but said nothing more as he stepped back to sit on one of the large rocks that had ended up around our campsite.

"What's for breakfast?" Gian asked as he finally sat up, combing his hands through his hair and shaking the waves loose. He made his way over to the creek to wash it, just like he had the morning before, as Bones reached for one of the packs and I took a seat on the side of the fire pit opposite him.

"Well, you have options. A bruised apple, some sort of jerky, or the last bit of rabbit," Bones said, still rummaging through the packs to see if there was anything else.

"Or the cat," I offered, and even though he didn't have eyes to roll, I knew that was exactly what he'd be doing if he did. "Speaking of the cat . . ." I mused, following the stumbling fuzzball with my gaze. "Bones."

"Rabbit sounds fine." Gian pulled his hands through his wet hair, now engrossed in carefully wringing the water out and retaining the thick waviness of his locks.

"I'll set it by the embers to heat up," Bones said, setting about the work.

"Bones," I said again, a little louder this time, a small smile pulling at my lips.

"Yes, yes, what is it?" he angled his skull towards me.

"Your cat is trying to waterboard itself."

"Hook—no!" the skeleton jumped to his feet faster than I would have thought possible, kicking up dust and pebbles as he skidded towards the creek. Indeed, the little critter was there, half-stumbling half-rolling down the stony bank towards the water. Gian ducked out of his way, avoiding the Cursed man as he splashed into the water, dunking his hands beneath the surface before reappearing with the sopping kitten clutched between his fingers, looking no less fazed than it always was.

"Hook?" I asked, not bothering to conceal the amusement that oozed into my voice as he stepped out of the creek, lifting his arms to assess how sodden his cloak was.

"That's what I named him," Bones explained, lifting the kitten up. The cat's one working eye was darting all over the place, as if taking in his surroundings for the first time. "I was inspired by the idea of meeting the pirates. Ksega's told me one of them has a hook for a hand, and I thought it fit him perfectly."

I only grunted in response, then turned to look at Gian, who was frowning in distaste at the drops of water falling from his hair onto his shirtfront. He glanced up at me, and before I could even open my mouth to speak, he rolled his olive eyes and held up a hand.

"Yes, yes, let's get going. Let me grab my sword." He mumbled something else beneath his breath, but I didn't catch it as he went to retrieve his weapon. I narrowed my eyes as I tracked him but said nothing. In fact, I was secretly a little proud of him. Before he'd begun training with the blade, he hadn't been half as assertive as he was now, and while it sometimes bordered on aggravatingly stubborn, the attribute suited him. Even though mild sickness still plagued him, he was learning to work around it, and the medicine from the Talon in the Stargazing Colonies had done wonders for his health. Now, it was little more than a strong fever and occasional bouts of coughing that really affected him.

As Gian fastened his scabbard to his belt, I double-checked the contents of my own, making sure my saber was in easy reach and that all my pouches were sufficiently full of my spare supplies. I was a little surprised that nobody had asked about them as of yet, but then again, I had to remind myself that the people I was traveling with were nowhere near as suspicious as those in *Baske Latel*. Not that there was anything bad in the pouches, of course. It was mainly small things that I had regular use of, like the whetstone or needle and thread. The only thing one might be suspicious of was the small palm-sized shiv

"Ready to go?" I asked, looking him up and down as he came to stand by my side. He was bedraggled and messy, and his clothes were smeared with dirt. The only pristine thing about him was his hair, which he had diligently washed and combed and cared for daily. He'd even trimmed it with my skinning knife on one occasion, careful to keep it just above his shoulders.

"Yep," he said none too enthusiastically, but I'd grown accustomed to it. There were few things Gian got excited about, and so far, the only routine thing he enjoyed was sword training.

The walk to the cliffs and back usually took us an hour and a half, depending on how tricky it was to get through the Evershifting Forest, but at least it was a pretty walk. I had never done much traveling, especially not outside of Old Duskfall, and whatever short trips I had gone on had only been through the Shattered Mountains of Brightlock. Maple trees—and all the other trees the Forest had displayed, now that I thought about it—were a novelty to me. I wasn't used to the humidity or the bugs or the rain or the wind, and I definitely wasn't used to the abundant wildlife and lush greenery, but I couldn't bring myself to dislike it. I'd never been one to want change, nor to go along with it when it came, but this was one I was willing to welcome. I'd known accompanying Sakura and Ksega would bring changes to my life, possibly even ones I wasn't quite ready to make, but if I was being honest, I was a little surprised at how pleasant some of those changes were turning out to be. Most of all, I was surprised about the changes involving Gian.

The Nightfaller got on my nerves to no end. He was whiny, mostly uncooperative, and cared more about his precious hair than he did anything else. Any words that left his lips were either a complaint or an insult, and while the words that fell from my own were rarely much better, I found myself wishing to cut his tongue out on more than one occasion. After Sakura and Ksega had left, he hadn't gotten much better. If things weren't about him, he didn't care what was happening. It was only when it was time to practice with his sword that his mood and behavior changed for the better.

Most days, we spent several hours sparring in whatever glade or clearing we could find. There wasn't much to do, and while the option was there, we never wanted to go down to the Stargazing Colonies, each for different reasons. Bones, obviously, couldn't risk being seen, and Gian was hesitant to socialize any more than was strictly necessary. I personally didn't want to associate myself with anyone from the Colonies. The superstitions about those people ran deep in the City of Bones, and they were just as deeply ingrained in my mind.

Gian's sword training, however, was improving greatly. I'd never been a teacher before, and that was one of the greatest changes of them all. Not only having to turn all I had learned into comprehensible words, but also being seen as a mentor was a curious challenge to me. Gian had no prior experience with weapons whatsoever, meaning he was wholly relying on me to teach him properly. This was an even greater challenge when you factored in the variables of him using a broadsword and being left-handed.

He carried the weapon with him just about everywhere he went, which I found to be respectable. When I had first begun training with my saber, the last thing I wanted to do was bring it with me. I kept forgetting it was there and knocking my wrist on it or whacking it on various table legs and walls and people that I passed, leaving me and those around me annoyed. But through time and discipline, I had grown used to it, and now it was as much a part of my body as my arms and legs. Gian didn't appear to have the same issue, though, as if carrying the blade with him everywhere had automatically become second nature.

We left for the cliffs with our birds, leaving Bones to deal with his waterlogged rodent. Conversation was a rare thing on the walk. Gian didn't like to share much about his life, and I was no different. From what Sakura had told me, Gian had been enslaved to the rulers of Old Nightfall, and the tattoo on his neck proved it. Aside from that, I didn't know much about the man, but I wasn't sure there was much to know. His life, while unfortunate, seemed uneventful up until the point Sakura, Ksega, and Bones had met him. The same could not be said for me.

I had a steady career driving sand-sleds with Mulligan, bringing in just enough money to keep up with the rent for my ramshackle home and to feed myself and Taro. I tried to avoid the darker sides of *Baske Latel* when I could, not caring to get caught up in any illegal affairs. I had been snagged in the web of gambling debts once, and it had been enough to encourage me to steer clear of any similar situations in the future. That had been during a rough time of my life, right after my brother and father had left and my mother declared that she didn't know me. I had fallen into a pit of self-hate, doing anything I could to distract myself, and gambling had quickly become an obsession of mine. But owing money to one of the most ruthless drunkards in town had given me the jolt of sense I needed to set myself straight again. That had been when I'd met Kieran.

At first, he had been a nuisance, always hanging around and nagging me, asking about Taro, and being an all-around pain. But once we started to get to know each other, we became friends, and then we became more. It was us against the backstabbers of the Bones, against the pompous nobles and the sneaky orphans, against the *world*. We lifted each other up in everything we did, and for a while, it didn't matter that I didn't have a family or that one of us had the occasional thug following us down a dark alley, trying to bludgeon our heads in. For a while, everything was perfect.

And then that wretch Mariem had come in, stolen his heart, and ruined it all. I blamed it on her mother, of course, that blasted *ista*. She must have learned that her daughter was hopelessly in love with the man who had promised to marry me and cast one of her *dasten* spells to turn his heart away from me and towards her own evil offspring.

Not that any of it mattered, of course. Kieran was dead now, although he had died to me a long time ago, and all of that was in the past. I would still hate Mariem and Irina until the moment my last breath escaped me, and then for all of eternity, but now that he was really, truly gone, I didn't harbor the same hatred for Kieran. If it had been a spell cast upon him that made him stop loving me—and I still chose to believe that was what had happened—then it was not his fault, and I could not continue to hate him if he had done no wrong.

Thoughts of Kieran were rare for me now, and I was grateful for that fact. He was as much a part of my past as my parents and brother, and I was glad to leave them there. Here, in this moment, walking beneath a canopy of auburn and gold leaves and breathing in the crisp air of autumn, I could let the memories of them flutter away on the biting gusts of wind, never to be remembered again.

"When do you suppose our two troublemakers will get back?" Gian's voice drew me out of my thoughts, and I looked over at him. He was still fussing with his hair, trying to work out the last of the tangles and make sure it was drying thoroughly.

"Who knows?" I replied, wishing he wouldn't try to make idle conversation. He did it from time to time during the breaks between our sword lessons, and it always made me inwardly cringe. He was *terrible* at making small talk. Even being the more private person I was, I still knew how to carry a decent conversation. Gian, on the other hand, was a complete mess.

"When do you suppose the pirates will get here?" he asked, and I rolled my eyes.

"They might be here today, for all I know. Have you got the letters?" my gaze dropped to his chest, where I knew he kept the letters tucked into the inner pocket of his leather vest.

"Yes," he said, absent-mindedly lifting his hand to pat the place where they sat over his heart, just to be sure they were still there. I had wanted to keep track of them at first, not trusting him not to lose them, but he had insisted that he could be responsible, and after a few minutes of arguing, Bones had pitched in to tell me I should try to have a little more faith in others. After seeing Gian's smug smirk, I had cursed both of them and retreated to my tent, not-so-graciously admitting defeat.

We didn't speak again until we were close to the cliffs. Exiting the Evershifting Forest was always the slowest part of the trip. The edge of it was a safe distance from the main road, and it was completely invisible from most of the ramp, but there were two tall watchtowers tucked into the corners of the harbor, almost unnoticeable from the sea, and difficult to spot unless you knew they were there. Gian had pointed them out the first day we had come to check for the pirates, and since then we had been extra cautious whenever leaving the Forest. It wasn't like we were doing anything wrong exactly, but two people waltzing out of the most dangerous wood on Horcath was bound to warrant a little bit of suspicion, especially since one of them was a Duskan. Illegally crossing the kingdom borders was greatly frowned upon across all the lands, and aside from certain portions of the Veiled Woods, the only places it was really possible were hidden within the boundaries of the Evershifting Forest. Most people wouldn't be stupid enough to enter the Forest, much less wander so far into it that they ended up in a different kingdom, but if you looked at our odd little troupe, we weren't exactly 'most people.'

I wasn't sure if the watchtowers actually monitored the activity on the cliffs, but it didn't hurt to be cautious. We crept forward slowly, waiting for any signs of alarm from below, and when we didn't hear any for several minutes, we finally relaxed a little, and hurried up to the edge of the cliffs.

The docks weren't very large. There were slips for up to five ships, and just enough room for everyone to stand around without being shoved off into the churning waves. There was only one person managing the payment stand, slowly filing everyone through one group at a time. Every now and then, a signal would be given to the soldiers stationed near the great black iron gates, and they would swing open just enough for a crowd of people and wagons and animals to fit through, spilling out onto the ramp.

Each day, there were usually a handful of ships in the quay. Some cargo ships, maybe a fishing boat, nothing very extravagant. From Ksega's description of *The Coventry*, it wouldn't be hard to spot. A great big pirate ship with three masts—with the crow's nest at the top of the center one—and a slate-wolf figurehead at the front. We hadn't seen anything remotely close to that yet, and I was beginning to wonder if the pirates would show up at all.

As we crept up to the craggy edge, lowering ourselves close to the ground and easing our way forward, our birds hopping irritably about our backs. My eyes were already scanning the docks, seeking out the locations of the fifteen Locker soldiers on duty and the status of the man in charge of waving people through. While I did that, drinking in as many details as I could from the docks themselves, Gian's eyes were turned towards the water, rolling over it in search of the pirate ship. Almost as soon as we peered over the edge, and when I was only at twelve on my soldier count, he gasped beside me.

"There it is. That's it, right? That's got to be it. There's no way it isn't," Gian said, squinting. Morning mist was swirling softly over the water, clawing at the ships and curling over their rails, but even through it, there was no mistaking the great vessel.

"Shush. Yes, that's it." Until a matter of days ago, I had never seen an actual boat in person, and when I'd first come to the cliffs with Gian, I had been overwhelmed with the size of them. Gian, too, seemed perplexed at the appearance of them, having never been this close to one either. *The Coventry* was something entirely new. It was at least twice the size of the boats around it, possibly three times so, and it almost seemed to glow in the dawn's light. People bustled about on its deck, and some blond-haired fellow was lounging up in the crow's nest beside what looked to be a massive crossbow, mounted so that it could swivel in all directions.

"Who are we supposed to talk to?" Gian whispered, and I licked my lips, unsure how to reply. That was the one thing Ksega hadn't had a good answer to. He wanted us to slip in and confront one of them after they exited the ramp, drawing them away from the crowd to present the letters as proof that we knew him, but *who* to confront had been unclear. He had told us that a man named Howard was the captain, but he didn't care for Ksega's company very much, so it would be best to go after one of the three mates: a ginger-haired man, his wife, or his brother. If we couldn't find any of them, we were to talk to the ship's navigator, the one with the long blond hair and the hook for a hand.

"We'll figure it out," I replied, scooting back from the edge. "Come on, we'll wait near the end of the ramp." There was no real need to go there this early, but I was fidgety and needed a reason to move. I always got like this before something exciting happened.

We jogged lightly towards the end of the ramp, looking for a place where the sun's warmth would bathe us as we waited for the pirates to be let through the iron gates. We would be waiting for a little while, but I didn't mind. Gian would no doubt complain about the sun affecting his fair skin, but I didn't have such worries, my skin already bronzed by years of hard work in the open desert. And besides, the sunlight was a welcome shield against the chilly gusts of wind that battered their way over the plains.

I embraced the golden glow of the sun, finding myself a somewhat comfortable knoll on the ground and lying back with my arms behind my head, shutting my eyes against the light. Taro had found a place to settle beside me, letting the sun shine on the feathers of his back. Beside me, I could hear Gian grunting and struggling to get comfortable with his sword still clipped to his belt as well as Light Ray's screechy protests to his jerky movements. Finally, he seemed to find a position that he found acceptable, and he sighed as he lay back on the grass beside me.

"Don't fall asleep," I reminded him, already feeling the sun's warmth soaking into me and making me drowsy. Out in the Duskfall Desert, the heat was so unbearable you couldn't bring yourself to sleep unless you were in the shade. Here, though, the sun's heat was greatly lessened, and coupled with the rolling winds of autumn, it created a perfect blanket to sleep beneath.

"You might have to slap me," Gian muttered, sounding closer to the brink of sleep than I was.

"I'll take great pleasure in that," I informed him, and when he didn't reply, I wondered if he'd already been lost to the depths of sleep. I feared I wasn't far behind him. I swayed in and out of consciousness, sweeping through a dip between the waking world and that of dreams. Because of this, there was no way to tell how long I lay there, eyes closed, lost in the strange magic of the sun's beams.

I was awoken suddenly by the sound of beating footsteps nearby.

"Gian," I hissed, shifting my elbows beneath me and rubbing the sleep from my eyes before I'd even identified the direction the noise was coming from. I blinked furiously, silently scolding myself for having fallen asleep, and elbowed the Nightfaller roughly in the ribs. He jumped into a sitting position with a yelp, one of his arms swinging out instinctively to ram into my chest. I was knocked back onto the grass, and the breath left me in an *oof*. Taro let out a squawk of protest, his feathers puffing out defensively, and if Light Ray hadn't clicked his own beak in warning, the hawk probably would have latched onto Gian's face and gouged out his glinting steely eyes.

"Huh? What? I—oh." He squinted down at me, rubbed his palms against his eyes, and groaned. "Seriously, you could stand to be a little gentler when you wake someone up."

His lips curled into a frown as he gently combed his hands through his hair, working out the small tangles and blades of grass.

"And you could stand to learn how to control your instincts a little better," I snarled back, forcing myself up again and rubbing the place where he'd struck me, wondering if it would leave a bruise. Instead of apologizing, which would have been the decent thing to do—although knowing the kind of person he was, I didn't really expect it of him—he scoffed and rolled his eyes, encouraging Light Ray up onto his shoulder and rising to his feet. I followed, bringing Taro with me, and dusting grass and dirt off the back of my shirt and pants before scowling up at him. I had never really minded being shorter than Bones and Ksega and Sakura, but the fact that Gian was able to literally look down on me made my blood boil.

"What's going on?" he asked, his gaze roving over the ramp, although from where we stood, we couldn't see down it all the way. Despite that, there was no real need for me to answer his question; the dust and rhythmic sound of footsteps coming from the ramp was evidence enough.

"Come on," I said, walking closer to the side of the road. Gian hesitated before following me, looking back towards the Evershifting Forest. Hiding away in its cover before coming out would make us seem a little less suspicious, but it was too far back from the road, so our best option was to stand here and wait until we saw the pirates. I wasn't sure how easy it would be to spot them, but I soon found out, and learned I shouldn't have had any doubts.

A few people gave us skeptical looks as they passed, but for the most part we went unnoticed. Those sharing the road were from all walks of life. There were dark-skinned Carlorians, colorfully-dressed Coldmonians, elegantly preened Talons, even a few bronze-skinned Duskans. There were carts and wagons and horses and leashed dogs and giggling children and crates of chickens. The smell of sweat and the sea clung to the crowd like the tendrils of mist that had clawed at the boats, twirling around them and making me wrinkle my nose as they passed. I had never smelled the saltiness of the sea until I visited the cliffs, and it had been an overwhelming sensation that burned my nostrils. From his expression of displeasure, Gian hadn't liked it either, and I could see him hiding a similar repulsion now, shrewdly scrutinizing everyone that walked past us.

When about half of the crowd had passed us, I saw them. They were a large group, and I guessed their number to be about thirty in total. They weren't dressed much different from everyone else, clad in baggy and grubby clothes, stained from work and sweat and torn or patched in various places. Many of them had weapons, but even more noticeable than that was their lack of body parts. The navigator was one of the first I saw, using his glinting silver hook to pick something out of his teeth as his remaining hand fussed with his ponytail of golden hair. Then, I noticed the others: a man with an eyepatch, a shirtless boy with sun-bleached bones protruding from his back, a legless man, a monster of a man missing an arm, a nasty-looking fellow with a metal hand and curls of pale white smoke winding around him; the list went on. There were only a handful of them that seemed to be whole, and the only ones of note were a grim-faced man with close-cropped blond hair and an imposing presence that made me guess he was Captain Howard, a spritely man with a flop of bright red hair, a sharp-eyed Carlorian woman, another red-haired boy—this one with tight curls and curious blue-green eyes—and two other people that hovered near the back, keeping close to each other and flowing in and out of my view so that the only details I could see were glimpses of pale skin. Aside from that, there was also a leashed brown eirioth dragon, casting suspicious eyes across the people that swelled around it as if they were pesky insects.

"That's our group," I murmured to Gian, and he nodded beside me, his eyes on the crew as well. As if sensing our gazes upon them, several of the pirates glanced up at us. One of them was the metal-handed man, and he smacked the navigator on the arm to get his attention, speaking in a lowered voice to him before gesturing in our direction. I plastered a look of open indifference onto my features and tried to ignore the knot of tension that formed in my gut when the pirates altered their course and made to join us on the side of the road.

"Are you Ksega's friends?" I asked, my gaze roaming over the group as they came up to us. The two I had caught glimpses of before stood in front of us now, and I looked them up and down. The first, the girl, was several inches taller than me, and pale-skinned. She wore a loose-fitting long-sleeved shirt to protect herself from the sun, but there was a smattering of red-brown freckles across her nose and pinkened cheeks. She had a very beautiful face, with a petite nose and sparkling blue eyes, framed by the two long fire-red braids that hung over her shoulders.

The other, the boy, was just shorter than Gian, and even paler than both the Nightfaller and the red-haired girl. His eyes were dark beneath his mop of shaggy black hair, glittering with suspicion and taking us in just as warily as we were him. He was dressed in baggy trousers and a tight-fitting, sleeveless black shirt that revealed bulging biceps, one of which had a tattoo of an eirioth dragon flying around a bolt of lightning. He also had a longbow and a quiver of arrows slung across his shoulder, not very unlike the kind Ksega had.

"We are," the girl confirmed. She must have been Jessie, Ksega's friend from Wisesol.

"Who are you?" the black-haired boy, whom I assumed was Derek, crossed his arms and glared at us. Beside him, the eirioth dragon was mirroring his look, huffing hot breaths out of his nostrils and lashing his feathered tail.

"We're also his friends," I replied, unsure if it was actually the truth or not. It had been a long time since I had considered someone a friend, but I doubted Ksega was the same way. Perhaps he already counted Gian and I as friends.

"Where is he?" Jessie asked, her blue gaze flying over the plains behind us, searching for him. I could see that the pirates, too, were scanning the area in search of any other companions. The one with the metal hand, especially, seemed suspicious.

"He isn't with us at the moment," Gian answered, watching the pirates warily. "He and Sakura went off to see the king. It's a bit of a long story, but the important things are detailed here." He produced the letter from his vest, passing it over when Derek held out his hand. The boy skimmed through it, eyes narrowed, then glanced up at us.

"Well?" the navigator asked, leaning to read over Derek's shoulder. "What's it say?"

"They've gone to see the king about the Curse," Derek said dryly. Jessie peered over his arm to look at the letter, worrying her lip as her eyes roved over the paper.

"That's Ksega's handwriting, for sure," she said.

"How do we know it isn't a fake? They could've copied it," the man with the metal hand said. From Ksega's stories, I assumed this was Theomand, the thief they had encountered. He still had those curls of wispy fog twirling through his fingers, and I was beginning to suspect it was the result of magic.

"Could anyone copy it so perfectly?" Jessie asked skeptically.

Theomand shrugged. "I've seen it done before."

"We thought you might say that," I said curtly, gesturing for Gian to give them the other letter. He rummaged through his vest and handed it over. As he did so, Jessie pulled another letter from within the pocket of her checked blue dress. She and Derek held the letters up on either side of the first one Gian had given them and compared the three.

"This is definitely the letter you sent to them, Theo," Derek said, tapping the second letter Gian had passed over with his thumb.

"And the handwriting from my letter from Ksega is an exact match," Jessie added, tilting the letters to the side so the metal-handed man could see it. The navigator was still teetering between the three of them, sticking his head in over their shoulders to try and get a good look at the papers. Captain Howard was standing to the side, arms crossed, watching us closely. As for the other pirates, they were regarding us with a mix of curiosity, suspicion, and irritation.

After a moment of considering the pieces of parchment, Theomand grunted and stepped closer to the teenagers to speak with them in a lowered tone. Derek's eyebrows scrunched together as he spoke, and his head lifted so that he could run his gaze along the plains and the edge of the Evershifting Forest. When he failed to find what he was looking for, he stepped closer to me, brushing past his dragon and unsettling Taro as he leaned down to whisper, "Where is the skeleton?" from his secrecy, I knew that the pirates didn't know about Bones yet, but just as Ksega and Sakura had informed us, Derek, Jessie, and Theomand did.

"In the forest," I answered, rubbing a finger across Taro's chest to calm his nerves. "He's watching our little camp. There's enough room there for all of us. We expect Sakura and Ksega to return in the next few days." My eyes shifted to rest on Captain Howard, whose attention was on me as I lifted my voice for all of them to hear. "They wanted us to invite you to come and wait with us. They have information they wish to share with you."

"So do we," Jessie said, stepping up beside Derek so that she was closer to Gian and I. "We've been looking into the Curse, hunting through the western kingdoms to see what we can find, and it seems like there are more and more Cursed animals appearing in the Slated Mountains. Even the big creatures, like adult slate-wolves and mountain goats and birds of prey." My hand tensed against Taro's feathers as she went on. "There have even been Cursed runeboars coming from the Veiled Woods. Now, I know other big creatures have been taken across Horcath, but with the Curse growing, it's important that we find where it's coming from."

"Which is what we were researching," Derek continued for her. "We found some interesting clues about the history of—"

"That's enough." I held up a hand. "You can save it for when our two little explorers get back. They'll want to hear it all from you. Until then, we need to know if you plan to stay with us at our camp while we wait for them." I looked expectantly between the captain and the other pirates, trying to ignore Gian's fidgeting beside me.

"Give us a moment to discuss it," the navigator said brightly, flashing us a smile as he stepped back to join his crew. The pirates crowded around him, the captain, and the three mates. The only people that didn't join them were Derek, Jessie, and Theomand and his odd tendrils of fog.

"Whatever they decide doesn't matter for us," Derek said simply. He shared a questioning look with Jessie, and she gave him an almost imperceptible nod, so he went on. "We'll stay with you. The whole reason we did all of this was to help Sakura with her mission to find the source of the Curse."

"Do you think the king of Brightlock has anything to do with it?" Jessie asked, and I pursed my lips. There was a lot of catching up to do with these two.

"Have you not found anything to point the search in that direction?" Gian asked before I could answer her. I gave him an annoyed glare, but only Light Ray caught it, watching me with his pale purple eyes.

"Not really. Most of what we looked into focused on Wisesol and Freetalon," Jessie replied. I frowned. From what I knew, there wasn't anything to tie the Curse to either of those two kingdoms, aside from the old and dead theory that it was some sort of disease that could be cured by Talon magic.

"What have you found?" Derek asked.

"Not a lot of solid information," I said before Gian could answer. "But we have some interesting leads. Sakura and Ksega started by looking into Old Duskfall and our secretive ways, and from there, they were led to Old Nightfall."

"The royals there were suspect because they might stand to gain a lot by eliminating all of the lower kingdoms with the Curse," Gian pitched in. I raised an eyebrow at him.

"'Lower kingdoms'?" I echoed. He shrugged.

"That's what we called all the kingdoms down here," he said simply, earning him another once-over from all three of the people standing before us.

"The point is," I went on, "the Nightfallers know even less about the Curse than anyone down here does, but we did gain the theory of the Curse having something to do with the kings and the old wars."

"The wars? As in the Havoc Ages?" Derek frowned before continuing. "But those were over two hundred years ago. The Curse has been around for almost a hundred years, and there haven't been any notable wars since."

"Think about the last war," I said, letting my gaze hover over the ramp as I heard the groan of the iron gates, signaling the end of the stampeding crowd. "Between Coldmon and Brightlock."

"Yes, I know of it. Carlore played a part in the war before they retreated," Derek said. Jessie seemed to be trying to follow the conversation, as was Gian, who had never received any formal education about the history of Horcath, but neither of them seemed to understand it quite the way we did. Theomand, on the other hand, was following easily.

"The Locker kings have always wanted power. They stole land from the Duskans and the Carlorians, and before the Curse halted them, there were negotiations between Brightlock and Coldmon about building a Locker city on the water between the docks here and in Clawbreak." I had never been a big fan of politics, but in the City of Bones rumors flew just as thick and noisy as the flies, and I had always been a vessel waiting to be filled with knowledge, sitting in the shadows so that no one knew I was listening.

"You think the royals of Brightlock had something to do with the creation of the Curse?" Jessie asked, her voice heavy with doubt. When she put it that way, it did sound a little ridiculous, but there was substance to our theory, and it only needed to be revealed.

"The Curse works like a weapon." I leaned closer to them to make sure the pirates couldn't overhear. "Bones has told us that the Curse controls them, at least for small periods of time. They can be guided towards one specific target, but it's almost as if whatever has them in its grip can't keep its hold on them for long. That's how the Curse spread far and wide, instead of functioning like the weapon it was supposed to be." I rose onto the tips of my toes, ignoring Taro's feathers ruffling in annoyance, and looked at the passing crowd of people. They were starting to give us odd looks.

"Who's Bones?" Jessie was frowning. I opened my mouth to answer, then stopped, still unable to recall his real name.

"Alchemy. The skeleton," Gian answered for me, and I glanced at him, equally thankful and annoyed that he knew it.

"So let me get this straight." Derek had been staring thoughtfully into the distance while I spoke, and now his gaze refocused on me. "You think that the power-hungry royals of Brightlock created the Curse to use as a weapon against the other kingdoms, and the current king is still in control of it today." I nodded, and he licked his lips. "It's a thin theory, and it doesn't exactly line up with what we've found."

"Well, that's fascinating, but I think we should get going before we dive into that." I waved a hand towards the crowd of people. "If we stand around huddling and whispering any longer, they're going to think we're up to something and call up some of the guards. Let's go ahead and get to the camp, then we can talk more."

14
GIAN

*I*t didn't take long to get an answer from the pirates, and then we were on the move, a group of thirty-something people marching towards the Evershifting Forest burdened with sacks of food and supplies and several fake limbs.

I had heard of pirates before, but never seen them with my own eyes, nor had I imagined that the reality of their peg legs and eye patches and metal hooks could be such crude devices. Most of them didn't seem to mind the bits of wood and iron attached to their bodies, surgically or otherwise; in fact, they acted as if they had lived with the fraudulent body parts their entire lives. It was hard to think of all the possible ways they could have suffered injuries severe enough to cause the loss of a hand or even an ear, but several came to mind unbidden before I could stop them.

I kept close to Beth as we walked, one hand resting on my sword hilt, the other loosely in my pocket. I was running through my sword training in my mind, trying to remember everything she'd taught me about what it was like to enter a real fight. The only issue was that she had primarily taught me how to fight and defend in a sword duel, not against the wide array of maces and claymores and crossbows and daggers that sat looped and strapped and wound on the pirates' chests and backs.

I wasn't sure what to make of the three outliers. Ksega had told us several things about each of them, not just to help us identify them, but also to use when speaking with them. To start, there was Jessie, his best friend since he was a little boy. He had described her very accurately: long red braids, blue eyes, pale skin and freckles. He hadn't mentioned that she was tall and lithe, with a posture that suggested she had been given an education from a young age. He had told us that she was not a fan of the sea, though she enjoyed watching dolphins, and that she was almost certain to engage in conversation if you brought up bunnies, horses, or wildflowers.

He didn't know as much about Derek, but now that I had met him, I wasn't very surprised about that. Dark hair, dark eyes, dark mood, that had been how Ksega had described him, and he had been exactly right. Derek said very little, staying close to Jessie's side and occasionally whispering something to her. Sakura hadn't seemed to know a whole lot about him either, despite having known him for many years. She'd told us that he used a longbow, had a younger sister, and was very protective of his eirioth dragon. Speaking of his eirioth dragon, the brown beast was much friendlier than his master. He was covered in rich brown feathers, with keen eyes and broad wings. He hopped playfully at Derek a couple of times, and once we had been walking for a short distance, Taro and Light Ray had both taken flight to come closer and investigate the dragon. It made me nervous for my owl to be so close to the beast's powerful talons and razor-sharp beak, but the dragon only seemed interested in skipping around in the grass and playing with the birds. It made me wonder how long he had been cooped up on a ship with the pirates.

"His name is Bear." Jessie had seen me watching and sidled closer to me. Beside her, Derek was also watching his pet, his watchful eyes following the movements of both the dragon and the birds.

"The owl is Light Ray," I said. I looked at Beth, wondering if she would introduce her own feathered companion, but she was in conversation with the blond-haired navigator, whom Ksega had told us was named Wendell. His silver hook glinted in the sunlight as he gestured through the air. Beth didn't seem to be very interested in whatever he was talking about, but she remained politely silent.

"And the hawk?" Derek asked, and I started, having forgotten I was speaking to someone at all.

"Taro. That's Taro." I looked up to see that we were very near the edge of the Evershifting Forest now, its golden and orange leaves splaying out on the tree limbs and lying scattered across the woodland floor. As we stepped past the tree line, we were instantly wrapped in the muffled blanket of autumn winds.

Many of the others shivered with the breeze, but I welcomed it. It did nothing to help with my sicknesses, of course, making my nose drip and my cough worsen, but it was familiar. Growing up in a kingdom so high above the earth, my people were really only affected by two seasons: summer, when the days were long and warmth rolled over the clouds as a welcome friend, and winter, when night fell early and the bitter fingers of cold made the clouds like stiff stone, tracing frosty patterns along the elegant glass buildings of our city. Spring and autumn were simply the lesser versions of the two seasons, never reaching high enough to touch Old Nightfall.

We hadn't really made a plan for getting Alchemy hidden away before the pirates arrived at the campsite, but we were making enough noise that he would have plenty of time to realize who was with us and what he had to do. I worried about it until our bedrolls came into view, and the stone ring full of chilled ashes had no thin black and green frame sitting behind it. There was no sign that the skeleton had been there at all. Hook was gone, along with the bundles of extra-large clothes, boots, and gloves that had been set aside for

Alchemy to wear when he went out. Oddly enough, there was also no sign of the green raptor. When we stepped into the campsite, I shared a look with Beth, and the only people who seemed to notice were Derek, Jessie, and Theomand.

"Where is he?" Theomand demanded, his voice low and husky.

"Not here," Beth answered, keeping her own voice lowered. "The pirates don't know about him, do they?" when he, Jessie, and Derek all shook their heads, she went on. "That's what I thought. He's staying outside of the camp. We can go find him while the pirates are settling in."

That seemed to satisfy Jessie and Derek, but there was still an anxious urgency behind Theomand's eyes, and before I could ask him about it, he hissed, "Where is my raptor?" the question hung between us for a long moment, and Beth and I shared a tense stare. Alchemy could have taken him, or he could have left him behind, and the raptor wandered off on his own once he was alone.

"I'm not entirely sure," Beth replied slowly. "But I'm assuming he's with Bone—or, uh, Chem. Alchemy." She frowned, as if the other names for the skeleton left a bad taste in her mouth. I didn't blame her. Not only did the skeleton himself seem other-worldly and eerie, but to be named after the art of alchemy, something long believed to be dark and forbidden—and possibly tied to evil magic—made him all the more terrifying.

"Then let's go find them," Theomand said, already starting for the forest. Beth held a hand out to stop him.

"Wait a moment. I'm going to talk to the pirates, then we'll go. Find a place to set your things down." She didn't even wait to see if they had anything else to say, marching towards Captain Howard with Taro once again on her shoulder.

Derek immediately went about unpacking things from Bear's saddle, and Jessie went to help him. Theomand didn't move for a long moment, watching us with narrowed us. I couldn't place why, but he seemed familiar. His dark hair was shaved so close to his head it almost wasn't there, and there were jagged scars on his neck and his one non-metal hand. He was a bulky man, with big shoulders and thick arms. But despite his beady dark eyes and his twisted frown, there was no denying the natural symmetry to his features, the way he seemed like a person that had tried to hide the truth of who he was, but had never succeeded in destroying the persistent beauty of his own bloodline. Plus, there was the little matter of the whorle he had been controlling out on the plains, anxiously working a thread of mist between his fingers. There was no denying that he was a Nightfaller, but that only made me more confused.

The customs of Old Nightfall were direct and clear, and one of the greatest had to do with hair. For complicated reasons concerning our kingdom's history—reasons that I thought were beyond stupid—the king was the only man that was permitted to have exceedingly long hair; all other men in the kingdom were to have hair that was above their shoulders, but below their ears. To let one's hair grow past the shoulders would be to insult His Majesty beyond imagining, and to cut one's hair so close to one's head would be to openly defy the royal family and claim no connection to the Glass City. Theomand's hair being shaved so close was an act of treason. He was lower than the low, to be treated even more poorly than the underlings. It only served to raise more questions. Had he left Old Nightfall? Been banished? Run out of the kingdom? What had happened to his arm that had left him with a mechanical version?

"What're you staring at?" the man growled, fisting his metal hand. I jumped, surprised to find that I had leaned closer to inspect him.

"Nothing. Sorry." I turned awkwardly away, instantly wishing I had gone the other direction as I saw his eyes latch onto the left side of my neck. There, tattooed just below my jaw, was the mark that identified me not only as a Nightfaller, but as a slave.

"You're an underling," he said bluntly. I grimaced, leveling my gaze at him.

"Yes. What of it?" I prepared myself for the usual onslaught of insults and reminders of my lowly status. Hot anger boiled in my chest, and my hands curled into fists as I braced for his words, arguments already perched on the tip of my tongue.

"My sister was an underling," Theomand said. I drew a breath to defend myself before I realized what he had said. My jaw snapped shut. He must have misread the surprise on my face. "I know, I'm not supposed to know that." He dragged his metal hand over his head, then pulled it away to examine it, not meeting my gaze. "My mother told me. She said I must never tell anyone else, and I must never go looking for her."

"But you did," I guessed. It wasn't difficult to see where he was going with this, but my only question was *why* had he bothered? When there was a birth in Old Nightfall, the baby was kept in a number of private chambers with his or her mother until they became old enough for the overseers of that particular child to determine whether or not he or she was a mage. If the child was an underling, they were taken away from their family to be raised as a slave, eventually tattooed with the same mark I bore on my neck. If the child was a mage, they would be taken to the rest of their family to grow up in the same lush, pompous lifestyle as all the other magical Nightfallers.

"Of course I did," Theomand said gruffly, squinting at me as though he was appalled by the notion that he hadn't. "She was my sister. My own flesh and blood. You think that just because I was lucky and she wasn't means I didn't love her?" he challenged. I watched him for a long moment, trying to understand.

"You're not *supposed* to love underlings," I said through gritted teeth. "We're here to serve and grovel and be walked on by the filthy feet of everyone else, because if you can snap your fingers and make a plant or a tongue of fire bow before you, then surely you can make people do it too." A long silence stretched between us. Theomand seemed to be searching my face for something, but I wasn't sure what he hoped to find.

"She was the kindest person I've ever known," he said quietly. I hesitated, unsure why he wasn't immediately arguing with me. "She endured the worst treatment imaginable, and still she had a heart purer than gold. She was judged because of what she couldn't do, and yet she was capable of more compassion than any mage I've ever met."

"Then she was foolish," I snapped. His eyes flashed angrily, but I pressed on. "The mages of Old Nightfall deserve no kindness. They deserve to be beaten and bruised the way we have, to be spat on and marked as another's property. They should wash glass floors until their bones ache and be forced to starve in silence while everyone else feasts right in front of them." The longer I spoke, the hotter my skin became. How could he speak as if he understood his sister's suffering the way I did?

"You misunderstand me, boy," Theomand said, his voice low. "I agree with everything you say, but she believed that there was good in every heart. She was too trusting, too forgiving, and in the end it's what got her killed." His metal hand clenched. My gut twisted. His eyes seemed to bore through mine as he said, "I was forced to watch her be beaten until she died, all because she called me 'brother' in front of a palace official. She was punished for merely knowing who her family was. That's why I left Old Nightfall, and why I will loathe it until the day I die. You hate it too, for what it's done to you, but that only begs one question." He reached out and grabbed a strand of my hair. I glowered at him. "Why haven't you forsaken its customs as I have?"

"I *have* forsaken its customs," I snarled, slapping his hand away from me and taking a step back. "But I also have the sense not to make myself look like an egg," I deadpanned. Theomand's nostrils flared, and he looked like he might shout at me, but we could now hear voices approaching. As Beth, Jessie, and Derek came closer, I added, "Besides, my hair is too perfect to cut."

"Are you two trying to see who has the best 'I'm-about-to-murder-you' face? Because you're both awful at it," Erabeth commented as she stopped beside us, looking unimpressed. Both Theomand and I stayed silent, and we all fell in step behind Derek as he led us into the woods to find Alchemy. We didn't say much as we got ready to go, and soon enough, we found ourselves wandering through the autumnal forest, waiting for the skeleton to appear.

"We aren't going to find him," Beth said, leading the way. "He'll come to us, once he knows it's clear."

And sure enough, once we had been walking for a little less than ten minutes, the skeleton emerged from the trees beside us, now fully dressed with the big long cloak hanging over his shoulders to complete the look. It was unsettling to an unnamable degree to look at his body and see nothing but a thin man, then look up a little further and see that ever-grinning black skull, riddled with shining green cracks and punctuated with gaping black holes where eyes should be.

"Hello, friends." His grating voice seemed to come from everywhere at once, and Jessie gasped beside me. A quick glance at our little group told me that Derek and Theomand had their hands on their weapons, and Jessie had backed behind Derek, watching Alchemy with wide eyes.

"There's no need for that," Beth said, having noticed the same things I had.

"Quite so." Alchemy added, tilting his skull to the side. "I have no intentions of hurting you. Look, I even got all dressed up just for this. It would be a shame to wear such nice clothes if I was going to get them covered in blood." He slipped his gloved hands into his pockets, speaking as casually as if we were discussing the weather. A small squeak escaped from Jessie, and Derek's muscles flexed, but Theomand seemed to have completely forgotten about Alchemy, because someone else was coming out of the bushes beside him.

"Wynny!" he cried, stepping forward to wrap his arms around the raptor. The beast made a grumbling noise deep in his chest, somewhere between a growl and a purr as he accepted his master's embrace.

"Yes, you're welcome for saving him," Alchemy commented, nodding in satisfaction. "He was a bit of a mess when Ironling and I found him, but he's all patched up and better now. He got in a scuffle with some other raptors."

"I appreciate it," Theomand grunted, not sounding like he appreciated it much at all.

"Bones, watch out." Beth's voice caught all our attention, and she pointed to the leaf-littered floor beneath our feet. "You'll step on your rodent."

"Oh, Hook, there you are!" the skeleton bent to pick up the little cat, cradling him in his gloves and petting his head lovingly. The cat's functioning eye blinked and twirled and watched all of us, fogged over with confusion even as a shaky purr like a rainfall of pebbles shook his tiny chest.

A little "aww" sound came from Jessie, and Alchemy's skull lifted to face her. He held his arms out, offering the kitten to her, and after only a moment's hesitation, she stepped forward and reached up to scratch the thick fur between Hook's ears.

"Where are Sakura and Ksega?" Derek asked, unmoved. His hand still gripped his longbow, ready to fire if Alchemy caused any trouble even though, from what I had heard, he had known the skeleton the longest, aside from Sakura herself.

"Gone to see the king," Alchemy answered. "We expect them to be back within a few more days."

"They put in a request to see him?" Derek questioned.

"No." Alchemy said smoothly. "But they're clever people. I'm sure they'll figure something out."

15
KSEGA

The dragons were kept in the largest prop tent, which happened to be located in a ring of other, smaller prop tents. The entire place was crawling with performers, waiting for their cue to go and display their acts for the audience. The reason we knew the dragons were kept there was because we saw the animal handlers coming in and out of it, as well as heard the sounds of beasts beyond the golden tarp. Sakura had whispered in a voice growing huskier and huskier that she recognized the cries of at least one eirioth dragon coming from within the tent, so we had spent the past ten minutes creeping closer.

"Two guards at the front entrance," I reported, peering around the side of another prop tent. I took a quick peek inside, since it had been empty and unguarded, and it was full of spare hoops and poles and thick cables for the acrobats and their performances.

"Can't we just crawl under the tent fabric?" Sakura rasped, squinting at the base of the tent. She was rubbing her knuckles so roughly it was a wonder they weren't raw. I followed her gaze and saw that the tent had no floor and was only secured to the ground in a few places by wooden stakes to keep it from blowing away in the wind. There was probably enough loose fabric for a body to wriggle beneath.

"Maybe. That depends on if there's anyone on the other side." I pressed my lips together. The area with the prop tents was cordoned off from the rest of the racetrack, with portions of it concealed in shadow. Slipping through the dark patches was an easy task, but once we were in, things got trickier. Here, the watch was a little bit heavier, and there were guards stationed in front of specific entrances. The big golden animal tent was a protected tent, and from the sounds coming from inside, I couldn't tell if it was to keep strangers out or to keep the beasts in.

"What other options do we have?" she hissed. "We're running out of time." It was true. The mage performers were already queueing up to go inside the giant tent, and the dragons would be escorted out after them.

"Fine. Hurry." I jumped out of the shadows, making for the side of the animal tent. The guards were just around the bend, but they were facing away from us. There were performers milling about, but we avoided the beams of moonlight and snuck around to the back. Just beyond the fabric, I could hear the rustling of large animals, the thumps of massive feet, and the clattering rattle of heavy chains.

"How many do they have in there?" I mumbled, and Sakura shrugged. She reached for the bottom of the tent, hesitantly lifting it, and I dropped onto my stomach to look beneath, trying to ignore the thundering of my pulse in my ears.

"Is it clear?" Sakura whispered anxiously, watching a couple of glittery aclure-mages saunter past the tent we had just been hiding behind.

"It's clear. Come on," I grunted as I crawled forward, dragging myself beneath the tent before holding it up for Sakura to follow me. As soon as we were both inside, I let it drop and turned to look at my surroundings. There wasn't much to see, considering we were huddled behind walls of hay bales and neatly stacked barrels.

"Are we alone?" Sakura asked. I held up a hand for her to be quiet and rose onto the tips of my toes, holding onto the hay bales to steady myself as I peered above them.

"Not quite," I said, my eyes widening. A couple grunts and a small struggle later and she was beside me, peering over the hay to look into the tent. She gasped when she took it all in.

The tent had four enormous cages in it, all made from sturdy bars of iron and complete with thick shackles and heavy bolts. The support pole of the tent rose like a barren tree in the center, surrounded by baskets and barrels of straw and animal food and a huge wagon overflowing with colorful fabrics. I recognized them as the hideous costumes the dragons had been forced to wear during the performance.

"The poor things . . ." Sakura croaked, and I looked sidelong at her. Her eyes were glistening with unshed tears as she stared in horror at the cages.

The first cage was empty, its door open, and the second housed two fully-grown slate-wolves, their rat-like tails lashing angrily at the iron floor and their silky silver fur matted with grime and sweat. The last two cages held the eirioth dragons, and unlike the slate-wolves, both of them were held in place by the shackles. Without the costumes on, the mistreatment they had gone through was evident. The crimson dragon was the worst out of the two, with thinning feathers and bloodshot eyes. Patches of dark brown showed the dried blood around the dragon's feet, where the shackles had sliced into its flesh, and part of one of its wings seemed bent at an awkward angle, as if it had been broken and reset improperly. The blue dragon was in better condition, but not by much. They were both pitifully thin, lying on the cold iron floors of their cages, their wings drooped and their eyes dim as they watched the snarling slate-wolves from across the tent.

"Those chains are thick," I pointed out. "We can't get them out without the keys."

"The handler has them." She spat. "He'll be coming in here to get them soon."

"He'll have help," I reminded her. "There's no way he's going to get both of these dragons out to the tent on his own. He'll have those men with the whips, no doubt." My memory turned back to the night of the performance, when the dragon handler had swaggered out into the arena, drinking in the attention and smiling smugly as he flashed a smile as bright as his golden suit, surrounded by his five lackeys.

"We can take them," Sakura said, and I raised an eyebrow at her. "If worst comes to worst, we'll at least go out fighting."

"Look at you, being the optimist," I deadpanned, and she huffed. "There are too many people. We can't fight a whole troupe of traveling performers."

"Well, what do you suggest?" she snapped. I scowled at her, then looked around the tent, racking my mind for ideas. The tent was empty except for the cages, the animals, the food, the dragon costumes, and the dust and weeds that served as a hard-packed floor.

"Hang on a second. I think I've got something." I squinted, letting my vision swim in and out of focus until I could see nothing but the glows of life around me. Sakura and I were bright and as alive as could be, but the dragons and the slate-wolves were a low pulse of light, the crimson dragon not much more than a vague wisp of green. But the weeds popping up from the dirt were also there, trying with all their might to persevere through the lack of sun and water.

"Hurry," Sakura whispered, breaking my concentration so that the life glows faded into the background and my vision returned to normal. "Can you hear the announcer? It's almost time for the dragons to come in."

"I'm trying. Keep watch for me, will you?" I stepped away from the hay bales and crept around them, snaking closer to the cage of the blue eirioth dragon. As I came closer, my boot knocked gently against the side of the cage, and the dragon lifted its head, its chains jingling. As soon as it saw me, it tilted its head to the side, its entire body tensing, eyes wide and fearful. And he wasn't the only one that sensed me.

"Ksega—" Sakura's rasping voice came a moment too late. When I stepped into the light of the lanterns, reaching for the lock of the cage to inspect it, I realized that the tent had gone quiet. The snuffling and pacing of the slate-wolves had stopped. I whipped my head around to look at them just in time to see their noses twitching and ears swiveling until finally they turned to face me, white eyes like blank pearls. Then they started to howl.

"Feed them!" I shouted back to Sakura, gesturing wildly at the barrels of food near the tent pole. My voice barely carried over the howling of the wolves. They barked and snarled, throwing themselves against the bars as they tried to reach me.

I turned back to the blue dragon, who had now risen to his feet and was puffing his feathers out in agitation. Out of the corner of my eye, I saw Sakura racing for the tent pole, rummaging through the first barrel she reached. She gagged as she lifted some sort of weasel from the depths of the barrel, rushing over to the slate-wolf cage and tossing it through the bars. They ripped eagerly into the rodent's body, making all sorts of disgusting noises as they fought over it. Between the two of them, I knew it wouldn't last very long.

"Keep it going!" I yelled, holding a hand out to the nearest weed. Instantly, it sprang upward and curled up the iron bars of the cage, growing thicker and thicker until it was the width of my thumb. Inside the cage, the dragon shifted uncomfortably, snapping his beak agitatedly as he watched the growing weed. Across the tent, Sakura was running back and forth, carrying dead weasels to the slate-wolves to keep them satisfied. With how much noise they made, I wasn't surprised when the two guards stationed at the entrance came running in, each carrying a club.

"Hey!" one of them yelled, spotting me immediately and charging. The other followed his lead, and I was forced to release my bering. The weed stopped, curling around the iron bars and halfway up to the lock.

"Woah, easy there." I put my hands up, palms out, and smiled warmly at them. "What's the trouble, gentlemen?"

"Don't try to talk your way out of this," the first guard said, reaching out to grab my shoulder once he was close enough. I tried to take a step back, but gasped when his grip tightened, his fingers digging painfully into my skin.

"Ouch, alright! Loosen up, would you?" I grimaced, trying to wrench myself free, but it only served to cause me more pain. The other guard stepped up in front of the blue dragon's cage, inspecting the weed.

"What's this?" he grunted. I licked my lips, not answering as my fingers began to go numb. The man sneered at me, leaning forward so that he was in my face and I could smell the stench of sweat and alcohol radiating off of him. "What is it?" he repeated. I stayed silent.

"A suitable distraction, apparently." Sakura's voice rasped from behind them, and a moment later something heavy and shiny was slammed into the side of the guard's head. His eyes rolled back, and he collapsed to the ground at my feet.

"Wha—" the first guard let me go and wheeled to face her, lifting his club, but I jumped at him first, one knee lifting to dig into his groin. He yelped and stumbled back, doubling over with a groan, and Sakura stepped forward to bring her weapon down on the back of his head, leaving him sprawled on the ground beside his companion.

"Good work," I said, wincing as circulation returned to my hand. She glanced down at it in question, but I waved it away. "I'm alright. Keep those wolves distracted."

"Ksega—"

"Trust me, I've got this. Go." I reached out and grabbed her arm to push her towards the slate-wolves when I realized what she was holding. I gave her an exasperated look. "You brought your *flame-sword*?"

"What, you're telling me you left *all* your weapons in that barrel?" she yanked her arm back and pulled her waistband out, sliding the iron sword handle in against her leg. I gawked at her, disbelieving.

"*Yes*! Yes, of course I did! If someone stopped us and searched—" I cut myself off with a growl of annoyance. "You know what, it doesn't matter. We need to keep it down if we're going to get away with this. Just go over there and keep them quiet." She did as I asked, and I returned to the front of the blue dragon's cage, stepping around the fallen forms of the guards. There was no telling how long they might remain unconscious.

The blue dragon tossed his head agitatedly as I reached for the bars again, but I ignored him, centering my attention on the weed once more. I took a couple deep breaths, calming myself and trying to focus on things and memories that would give me more pleasant emotions, ones that would make controlling my bering easier. Since my power had grown so much, I didn't always have to hone in this way, but it was a force of habit to do it anyway, especially when I was under too much pressure to think everything through.

I coaxed the weed up further, letting it thicken as it did. Finally, it reached the lock and snaked inside. I couldn't see it clearly through the metal, but just like with any life form, I could sense where it was and when it hit any barriers. It didn't take long to unlock the mechanism and slide the bolt to the side. I swung the door open, untangling the weed from it as I did so and bringing it inside with me. At this point, the dragon had stopped trying to back further away from me, either accepting his fate or realizing that I wasn't here to harm him.

"There you go," I mumbled, holding up a hand to keep him settled. "Nice and calm, see? I'm not going to hurt you. Just hold still for a minute and . . . there we go." I set a hand on the first band of the shackles, pushing the weed inside and pouring my magic into it. The shackle locks were slightly more complex than the one on the bolt, but it still only took me a matter of seconds to unlock it. As soon as the band clattered to the floor, the dragon stood upright and held still, letting me move on to the next band.

It was tedious work. The whole time, the dragon's tail and wings were rustling and moving, and he made soft cooing noises from deep in his throat. Additionally, the crimson dragon was grumbling and shaking and banging against the bars of its cage, jealous of the attention I was giving to the blue eirioth dragon.

"Faster!" Sakura called from across the tent, as loudly as she could without being heard by people beyond the fabric. "I'm running out of weasels out here, and those two are going to wake up soon."

"I'm trying," I called back through gritted teeth, trying to keep my focus on the locks. Band number four fell to the bottom of the cage, and the dragon stamped his freed feet, shaking the smushed feathers loose. I stepped back and out of the cage, dragging the weed with me. It was now almost twice as long as I was and stretched easily to the other dragon's cage. I slid it into the lock and got to work.

"Ksega, what is he doing?" looking over my shoulder, I saw Sakura gesturing at the blue dragon, who was stepping out of his cage and shaking himself, fluffing his feathers and twitching his great, fanning tail across the dust.

"I don't know, you tell me. Just . . . get a rope on him, or something. I'm trying to get the other one." I bit my lip, sliding the bolt to the side and stepping inside. Sweat trickled down my neck and back, beading on my forehead and falling into my eyes as I blinked. I could hear approaching voices from outside the tent, and my fingers fumbled as I tried to get the plant into the first shackle band.

"The handler—" Sakura was following a long strand of rope on the ground, trying to find where it came from. In the end, she stopped near the tent pole, lifting the coil that was knotted around it. Instead of trying to untie it, she pulled the sword from her waistband and flicked a dagger-length flame to life, slicing through the rope before extinguishing all the fire and replacing the sword handle. I didn't watch any more after that, only listened as she chased the blue dragon down. Luckily, he had only stuck his head into the open weasel barrel and was easy to catch.

Two shackles were left on the crimson dragon, but I knew we were out of time. Across the tent, the slate-wolves began howling again, and finally, the golden-suited dragon handler strode into the tent. His eyes flew from the fallen guards to me to the wolves and then to Sakura, who was looping the rope around the blue dragon's neck as he sniffed around the barrels.

"They're stealing the dragons!" he screamed, and his five companions, dressed in green and armed with thick black whips, ran into the tent, unfurling their whips as they raced towards us.

"Get the dragon out the back!" I yelled to Sakura, jumping away from the crimson dragon's cage as the men with the whips came closer. I dove to the ground just in time to avoid the snap of a whip, its tip cracking the air where I had stood a moment before.

"What about the other?!" Sakura shouted, and I scowled at her as I pushed myself back up, but she wasn't looking, once again pulling her flame-sword free as she led the blue dragon towards the only unblocked portion of the tent's walls.

"Sakura, just get out!" I didn't look to see what she would do next. I sprinted across the tent, throwing a hand out and calling to the other plant life scattered across the dusty tent floor. Two little vines shot out of the ground, spurring towards the front of the slate-wolf cage and latching onto the lock over the bolt. Within seconds, they had crawled into the keyhole and clicked it open. I wasn't able to focus on my bering and slow my momentum at the same time, and I crashed into the front of the cage, knocking my cheekbone and hip forcefully into the iron. I threw the bolt to the side, swung the door open and scrambled away as fast as I could. The slate-wolves sprinted free, ignorant of their jutting ribs and sagging skin.

"No!" the handler screamed, pulling his own whip free. The other five men yelped and jumped away from the charging wolves, who thankfully seemed more focused on getting revenge than chasing a new scent.

The crack of whips, snarling of slate-wolves, and screeching of the still-imprisoned dragon roared around us, and a moment later was joined by another sound: the crackling of fire. As soon as I detected the sound, I smelled the smoke. Throwing myself back across the tent to reach the crimson dragon, I risked a glance in the direction Sakura had gone, and my breath caught as I saw that a hole had not been torn in the golden tarp, but burned open, leaving the flames to hungrily eat up the remainder of the tent. The smoking tear in the fabric was growing ever faster, and I stumbled as I avoided a pillar of smoke that billowed towards the sky.

Skidding to a halt in front of the crimson dragon's cage, I did my best to ignore the scream of pain from the man behind me as I picked up where I had left off. The fire, the wolves, and the crack of the whips had worked the dragon up into a frenzy, and he was now swiping his free feet around the cage and releasing strangled cries as it tried to tug free, so close to freedom.

"Don't let them escape!" the handler screeched, just as the third shackle band fell with a *clang* to the floor of the cage. "*No!*"

"Come on, come on—" I snarled, jamming the vine into the final keyhole. I cursed as I worked my bering through the plant, but my focus was broken and I was shaking from sweat and stress. The whips cracked behind me, and the sharp, tangy smell of blood mingled with that of the smoke as the slate-wolves set upon the handler and his assistants.

"Come here, you little miscreant—" a hand closed around the back of my shirt just as the lock clicked open on the shackle band. I cried out as I was jerked backward, falling heavily into the iron bars and knocking my head into the metal. I groaned as bright spots swam in my vision. The whole tent seemed to spin, and before I knew it, I had fallen onto the floor of the cage.

"Ksega!" Sakura's voice came from somewhere in the distance, but I couldn't lift my head. Everything felt light and heavy, hot and cold. I was worried the handler might start kicking me, but it turned out he had a more pressing matter at hand; the crimson eirioth dragon, now freed from his bonds, kicked viciously at the handler, and the stench of blood erupted through the cage, splatters of it flying across the bars and my back.

Shouts of alarm and panic were spreading throughout the racetrack now. I could hear people screaming and crying out, the slate-wolves savagely ripping at the men with the whips, the handler wheezing on the cage floor beside me. It all made my head flip, and I drew in a shuddering breath, trying to regain my senses.

"Ksega, I'm here. Come on, you've got to get up." Sometime, somehow, Sakura had pushed her way through the chaos to get to me. She grunted as she wrapped her arms around me, helping to pull me up into a sitting position.

"Where—" The crimson dragon barreled out of his cage and trampled one of the slate-wolves, snapping its spine with a sickening *crunch* as he thundered towards the gaping, smoking hole. One of the uninjured assistants snapped his whip at the dragon's retreating hide, and a puff of crimson feathers flipped into the air, but he didn't stop, charging forward into the night.

"He's safe. Let's go, quickly." Sakura helped me to my feet, coughing a little once she was upright, but whether it was due to the smoke or her scratchy throat, it was impossible to tell.

"He's safe. Let's go, quickly." Sakura helped me to my feet, coughing a little once she was upright, but whether it was due to the smoke or her scratchy throat, it was impossible to tell.

I didn't argue as she led the way towards the exit. More security and Locker soldiers were flooding in, but they were quickly faced with the problem of dealing with a highly agitated slate-wolf, blood dripping from its fangs and clumping in its fur. Sakura and I were able to stick to the edge, avoiding them and the flames and most of the smoke as we tried to slink away.

As we passed the smattering of crimson feathers, Sakura bent to pick one up, tucking it inside her waistband and then adjusting the way she was supporting me so we could keep moving. I was slowing her down, but we moved with enough urgency to make it out, me being half-dragged after her as she ducked beneath the flickering flames and led me out into the night.

"Over here." Sakura's voice was shaking as she led me behind another tent, where the blue dragon was standing in the shadows, tethered to a tent stake. I didn't have the energy to berate her for leaving him out in the open, so I only leaned against his side as she took the rope and began to lead him away from the tents.

"We need to move fast," I groaned, struggling to keep pace with them.

"We'll go to that barn." She altered her course to head for the barn we had slept in the night we had first seen the performers. I didn't say anything, saving my breath for the walk. Sakura stumbled nearly as much as I did, but I didn't speak to her.

The blue dragon was quiet and wary, avoiding as much contact with either of us as he could and flinching whenever we heard a loud noise. I reached for him, hoping I could calm him some more with my bering, but he jerked violently away. There wasn't time to wait until he would let me touch him, and I wasn't about to force it, so with a curse I let him be and kept moving. As far as I could tell, we hadn't been followed, although it wouldn't be long before parties were sent out to search for him; but we had time to prepare for that, and that was exactly what we needed, so we only walked silently into the darkness, leaving behind the burning golden tent and the tragedies of the night.

16
SAKURA

I couldn't stop thinking of the mistreatment of the two eirioth dragons, how one of them had an offset wing and both were sickly and pitiful. The crimson one had vanished into the night, and all I had left of him was a single feather, but I wished it could have come with us just like the blue one. At least then, I knew it would be taken care of. Now, it may have only run out into another poacher's trap. All the way to that dusty old barn I was on the verge of tears, a lump in my throat, my entire body aching with pain and fury. I knew Ksega was hurt worse than I was, so I didn't mention that I had been struck in the back with one of the whips.

When we reached the barn, I half-heartedly tied the dragon to one of the support beams and looked up at the patchy roof, blinking away my tears. Behind me, Ksega flopped to the floor, and when I turned to look at him, he was lying with his eyes closed on a pile of dirty straw.

"I'm going to find him some food." My voice was thick and scratchy. I tried to clear my throat, but it was of little use. "I'll be back soon enough." His only reply was a grunt, so I double-checked that the dragon would be satisfied before hurrying off back into the night.

I knew I wouldn't be back soon, but I doubted Ksega would stay awake long enough to realize that, and even if he did, he wasn't stupid enough to leave the dragon alone to come looking for me. At least, I hoped he wasn't stupid enough to do that.

I needed some time to myself, and going to retrieve our things seemed like a good way to achieve that. I would have to take a longer route to skirt around the racetrack, and I would have to be extra careful not to be spotted by any search parties that had already been sent out to look for the dragon. I wasn't very concerned about that. I had my flame-sword and plenty of anger to fuel my eirioth if I needed it.

Those monsters had abused two dragons that were sacred to me and my people. They were merciless demons, donning a guise of entertainment to make their foolish customers laugh and cheer for them instead of catching a glimpse through the facade to the ugly truth of their acts. How could people be so blind to what was really happening, especially to those poor animals? The slate-wolves hadn't been used in the performance Ksega and I had seen, but I had no doubts they were paraded around just as cruelly as the eirioth dragons were.

My path took me through dark alleys and narrow backstreets, behind stables and sleeping homes and neat little backyard gardens. I tried to ignore the prickling feeling that made the hairs on my neck stand up, the voice hovering in the back of my mind that whispered falsities to me, telling me there were beasts and monsters lurking in every shadow. I tried not to think of how these people were happily living their lives, something I could have—and *should have*—been doing. I tried to find a way to channel my anger, to let it flow out of me or at least hide it away behind some stony mask like Derek did.

Derek. I would see him again soon. Had he already joined the others at the camp? Was Bear still with him? What had he and Jessie learned about the Curse? Did it even matter now? Too many thoughts and questions battered around in my head, giving me a headache. There were so many things to worry about, but for the time being, the most important of them was focusing on getting everything back to the barn and gaining the dragon's trust. After that, we had to get some tack for him, and then, finally, we would fly over the walls around Calder and go before the king to present our case. I still wasn't entirely sure how I would go about accusing the king of Brightlock of being the man behind controlling the Curse. I still wasn't entirely sure how it had been created, if it was by one of his ancestors or if he had simply found it and a way to control it. Then there was the even more pressing issue of getting rid of it permanently. Did he know how to do that? Was it even possible?

I pondered the endless questions until I found the barrel where we had hidden our things, tucked snugly behind the lean-to of an unsuspecting donkey. With all of them still unanswered, I grabbed everything and found an uncomfortable but tolerable way to carry it all as I began the walk back to the barn. This time, I thought about the blue eirioth dragon. His trust of humans would be broken, that was certain, and I had no clue how I could win it back as fast as I needed to, but I had to at least try. Maybe once he had been given food and water and a comfortable place to sleep—with no shackles or whips—he would warm up to us a little more. There was also the matter of giving him a name.

Naming a dragon was not a task to be taken lightly. Every Carlorian I knew took lots of time and contemplation when giving their best friend a name. Some, like Finnian and I, had only thought about it for a matter of hours before the names came to us, but others, like Gamma, would spend several days letting their thoughts marinate and turning possible names over in their minds until they found the perfect one. It would be no different with the blue dragon. I considered many aspects of the dragon's life, what it may have been like before being confined to the life of imprisonment he had faced with the performers, what it may have been like if Ksega and I hadn't rescued him, what it must have been like to live with the fear of not seeing a tomorrow of freedom. That was when it came to me; as I staggered along beneath my burden, ignoring the stinging pain in my back from where the whip had hit me, I decided that I would pick a name that meant tomorrow; that meant hope, future. Freedom.

"Asuka," I mumbled under my breath, and the moment I did, I knew it was right. The blue dragon's name, from that moment until the end of his life, would be Asuka.

By the time I got back to the barn, dawn was close. The sun was tinged pink on the horizon, and the stars and moon had begun to fade. I barely managed to get the barn door open and stumble inside without dropping to my knees and falling asleep.

"Sakura?" Ksega mumbled from where he was curled up, still lying on the straw. He blinked groggily at me through the darkness.

"It's me. Go back to sleep." I dumped everything in a big pile by the door, slunk further into the barn to check on Asuka, who was lying down but still watching everything with wide eyes, and then flopped down on my own pile of straw. Ksega asked something else, but his words were slurred by sleep, and I was too tired to care what it was.

When I finally pried my eyes open again, sunlight streamed in dusty beams through the holes and gaps in the wood, casting warm streaks across my body. It almost made up for the knot of pain in my back and the bruises blooming across my shoulders and legs.

"Good morning." The voice came from startlingly close, and I arced my neck back to see that Ksega was sitting criss-cross beside my head, twirling a small knife in one hand and raking the other through his unruly hair.

"Hi." My throat burned with each word, and I winced, lifting a hand to rub my neck. "Where'd you get that?" I nodded at the knife.

"Went out and swiped it this morning. I've been meaning to do something about this hair for ages." He let his hair fall forward, dropping nearly over his eyes. I raised an eyebrow at him, but he only grinned.

"You're going to butcher it," I told him, pushing myself up into a sitting position and shifting around to face him. I looked up at the sunlight through the boards again. "Time?" I croaked.

"A little past midday. I already fed the dragon. Are you hungry?" he made to get up, but I shook my head and stopped him.

"No, I'm okay for now. How about you? Are you alright? You hit your head pretty hard." I squinted at him, trying to gauge whether or not he was in any pain. "That looks pretty tender," I added, lifting my hand to press my fingers against his cheek, where a dark bruise had formed. He froze, his face flushing crimson, and I hurriedly dropped my hand, realizing what I'd been doing. He cleared his throat, and I glanced down as I felt my own face go hot.

"I'll live. It's just a few bruises and a headache. You're sure you aren't hungry? You haven't had anything since that sweet roll last night." He leaned forward, frowning at me, and I wondered if I had bags under my eyes. I waved him away.

"I'll eat soon, but first, let me deal with your hair. I don't trust you with a blade."

"Hey, I've dealt with way more than you think I have." He smirked but held the knife out to me anyway. It was a simple hunting knife, probably not very expensive. I doubted whoever he had stolen it from even missed it.

"Have you cut your own hair with one, though?" I countered as I scooted around behind him, starting with the back of his head. I hadn't noticed until now just how long it had gotten, falling to the nape of his neck and framing his face. I combed my fingers through it a few times to make sure there were no tangles, then carefully began to trim it with the knife, which was dangerously sharp.

"Not too short," Ksega said instead of answering my question, his shoulders tensing. I rolled my eyes.

"Trust me, I know what I'm doing. I've cut my brother's hair before," I said, trying to clear the scratchiness from my throat. Granted, it had been a long time ago, and it had been messy, but with Gamma's help it had been cleaned up and made presentable.

He fell quiet as I carefully slid the blade through his hair, cutting it back until it returned to the shaggy mop it had been when we'd first met, curling around his ears and sweeping across his forehead but not over his eyes. It didn't take me very long, working my way around his head until I reached the final cut on his bangs. I chewed my lip as I slowly pulled the blade past the strands, keenly aware of him watching me. The thought made my heart beat a little faster, and I had to focus extra hard to make sure the blade in my hand didn't shake.

"There," I breathed, handing the knife back to him. I leaned back and released a low breath, avoiding his gaze and hoping my face wasn't as red as it felt. He ran a hand through his hair, grinning again.

"Thanks. That feels a lot better." He tucked the knife into a small leather sheath on his belt, one that I knew he hadn't had before. "Now, eat something." He stood and went over to the packs to find something for me to eat. While he did that, I looked over at where Asuka was still tethered in the shadows. He was lying down again, but his head was lifted, and he looked eager and alert, which was a good sign.

"Only a little bit, then we have to get moving. We need to see if we can borrow Maki's dragon tack," I told him when he returned, offering me a slice of slightly stale bread and a bruised apple. As I accepted them and crunched into the apple, he gave me a sly grin.

"I figured that out while you were still asleep. Oh, yeah, I took the dragon out for a little walk around the barn this morning to let him stretch his legs. He doesn't seem to have a whole lot of muscle on him, but he's in high spirits, and he even let me pet him." His grin only broadened as he finished, pride seeping into his voice.

"We'll need to keep him well fed and rested if he's going to manage to fly us both over the walls," I said through a mouthful of apple. Ksega hesitated, looking over at Asuka, who had cocked his head as if he knew we were talking about him.

"Will he be able to hold both of us?" he asked, the concern worming through his words. I pursed my lips and looked at the dragon again, taking in his size and stature, and guessing at his age.

"He should be able to, if we wait until we're a little closer to the walls before we take off," I replied finally, recalling the time Alchemy, Derek, and I had flown on Bear from the Evershifting Forest all the way to Clawbreak. Bear was a bit bigger and older than Asuka, but the flight wasn't as long, and there were only two of us to carry.

"Alright. If you're sure." Ksega still sounded doubtful, but I knew he wouldn't press the matter. Besides, it wasn't like we could turn back now. As long as we had Asuka with us, we may as well try and use him to our advantage.

Most of the day was gone, but if I went quickly, I would be able to reach Maki's house in time to catch her before she went to sleep. I wasn't sure if I would be able to convince her to let me borrow Zan's tack, but I had to try. I wondered if I would have to share all the details of our journey with her in order for her to let me take it.

"What are you thinking about?" Ksega's voice dragged me out of my thoughts, and I blinked up at him. He quirked an eyebrow. "I know that face. That's your scheming face."

"I'm not scheming anything," I said through a mouthful of bread. "I'm just thinking through the next steps of our plan. I'm going to go back to Maki's house to ask about dragon tack. I need you to stay here with Asuka." Before I'd even finished talking, I could see the argument forming on his lips. "One of us has to stay, Ksega," I said before he could speak. "He needs to warm up to us."

He echoed the dragon's name instead of giving me a straightforward reply. "Asuka?" my lips twitched in irritation, but I didn't challenge him for now.

"That's what I named him." I started to gather my things together, already preparing a list in my mind for what Ksega would need to do to take care of Asuka while I was gone. He took note of the action and pressed his lips into a thin line. I looked at him, not bothering to try and stop him from pleading his case.

"I'd feel better if we went together, you know." He looked over at where Asuka was preening through his feathers. "I know someone has to watch him, but there will also be people on the lookout for us. Someone was bound to have given the local authorities our description by now. It would be safer if we went together."

"For us, maybe," I conceded. "But not for him." I waved a hand at the dragon. "People will be hunting for him, and there might even be a reward offered for his return. There will be people combing every inch of the Key, and if they find him in here, he'll be no better off than he was before we stole him." A silence passed between us, and I shuffled awkwardly on my feet. "You should count yourself lucky. I'm cutting you a break. You don't have to actually spend time with me today." I lifted one of the smaller packs over my shoulder, content that it would provide me with enough food and water for the day. When I looked back up at Ksega, he was frowning.

"You put yourself down too much. I like spending time with you." He tilted his head to the side, crossing his arms as he studied me. "What makes you think others don't?" I tried not to let him see how flustered his words made me. Nobody ever said they *liked* to spend time with me, except maybe Gamma or Finnian, but they were family, so they were obligated to say things like that.

"I'm not the most sociable person," I answered finally, keeping my voice cool. "People don't often have to deal with me outside of business matters, so . . ." I shrugged as nonchalantly as I could. "They only see me as the local grump. The person so wrapped up in her own misery that it's less of a bother to just leave her alone." As soon as the words left my lips, I could see the wheels turning in his mind, the hesitation in his eyes as he debated whether to press me for more information or not. I knew I had said a lot more than I'd intended to, and now I wasn't sure where to go with the conversation. But he didn't pry any further.

"Alright," he said with a nod. "I'll stay with him. Just try to be back as soon as you can, okay? And stay out of trouble." He dropped his arms from their crossed position and bent to root through the packs, producing a piece of jerky to throw over to Asuka. The dragon blinked at it suspiciously, slowly arcing his neck to inspect it closely before finally snapping it into his beak.

"I should say the same to you," I said over my shoulder as I headed for the barn doors.

"Right. I'll see you later," he responded. My only reply was a grunt as I shoved the door open and stepped out into the evening sunlight.

*T*he journey back to Maki's was more difficult than I'd expected it to be. Word had spread quickly about the events at the Golden Tree performers' tent from the night before, and people were already keeping their eyes open for the two troublemakers that had stolen a dragon and caused the untimely deaths of six people. As soon as I caught wind of the deaths—the animal handler, a few assistants, and another performer that had been unlucky enough to cross paths with a ravenous slate-wolf—guilt squirmed in my gut. The animal handler had deserved it, I knew, and his assistants did as well for everything they had done to the dragons and the wolves, but the performer was only an innocent bystander that had tried to help and been killed for it. It reminded me of Keiran. He had simply been taking us to the Oasis and then lost his life for it. Just like his, all the deaths from yesterday hadn't directly been my fault, but I couldn't shake the feeling that I still bore the brunt of the blame.

Sticking to the shadows and staying out of sight was not my strong suit. Ksega was the one that was all sneaky and light on his feet. I was a fighter, someone who was always prepared for battle, and in battle it was more important to focus on attacking than staying hidden. While I wasn't technically in battle as I walked through the sunny streets of the Star Key, wrapping my arms around me to protect myself from the biting winds that swept through the town, I felt like I was. There were potential opponents all around me, and I couldn't afford to let down my guard.

My back bothered me as I walked. I had managed to avoid the brunt of the animal handler and his assistants' attacks, but one of the whips had just barely caught me between my shoulder blades. I had no way to get a good look at it and assess the damage, and there was no chance of me asking Ksega to check it for me, so I had pushed through a painful night of sleep and forced myself to wait. My awkward pace, coupled with my violent coughing fits, left me feeling more exposed and obvious than I would've liked.

I reached Maki's house, and when I knocked on the door, I was relieved that she answered almost immediately. Her dark eyes narrowed and looked me up and down, then hovered in the air behind me, as if she was waiting for Ksega to appear.

"He isn't with me today. I'm only here for a short visit," I said quickly, which only caused her eyes to narrow further.

"Have you put in a request to see the king?" she questioned, and I wet my lips nervously. Did I trust her enough to share the full truth of our plan with her? How else could I convince her that we needed the dragon tack? I was beginning to wonder if I'd thought this through thoroughly enough.

"Not exactly," I said with a frown. Maybe I had misunderstood our last encounter. Maybe she didn't actually have the soft spot for me that I had thought she did. Maybe this whole trip was a waste of my time.

"Come in and explain." Maki stepped aside and let me in. I thanked her and went to take a seat around her table. She disappeared into the kitchen for a few short minutes before appearing with a small loaf of bread and two cups of tea. She offered some to me, but I wasn't sure I could work up an appetite through my jumbled nerves.

"After we left, we went to get some supplies for our plan to see the king," I began slowly, carefully turning each word over in my mind before I let it escape my lips. "And we need something else to go with it in order to make our plan work, which is why I'm here." I pressed my mouth into a thin line, at a loss for how I should continue. Maki raised one eyebrow at me, unimpressed. "It's something you have." I added, as if that clarified anything. I shifted my position in the seat, realizing she was just letting me dig my own grave. She must have noticed that I had come to such a conclusion, because she sighed and said,

"You're leaving out some very vital details, young lady." Her expression became sterner. "Did you and that boy have something to do with the murders of those performers?" I sat up straighter.

"They weren't *murdered*, they were killed by the slate-wolves," I said defensively. Her eyebrow arched even higher, and I bit my tongue as I realized I had just revealed myself. She sniffed and broke off a piece of bread, stuffing it into her mouth and chewing thoughtfully for a long moment.

Finally, when she swallowed, she spoke again, keeping her voice level and impossible to read. "They never revealed how they were killed, you know. Just blamed it all on the two miscreants who burned down their tent, killed one of their prized dragons, and set the other free." She sipped idly at her tea. "I suspect now that you were one of those miscreants, and that you have the other dragon in your possession." She looked at me with sharp eyes. "The question is, what are you planning to do with him?"

I sighed, defeated. There was little point in trying to conceal the truth now, and lying would only dig me into a deeper pit. "He's going to be our way into the castle. He can fly us over the walls, and as long as we aren't immediately shot down, we'll probably be brought before the king." Once I said it out loud, and to an adult, it sounded a little far-fetched. Had all my plans sounded so ridiculous?

"Hm. Well, it's an interesting plan, and an ambitious one at that," Maki said slowly, tapping a nail against the side of her teacup. I blinked at her, a little surprised. She smirked at me. "Believe me, I'm well aware of the treatment those eirioth dragons went through. It's a shame you couldn't save them both." She drew in a long breath. "I believe that we both want to see the one that lived go on to enjoy life as much as he can. If I turn you in to the authorities, that cannot happen." She set her teacup down and folded her hands together on the table, looking deep into my eyes, as if she was searching for something. When she found what she was looking for, she went on, "I will give you what help you need as long as you promise me something." She leaned forward expectantly, and I nodded.

"What do you need?" I asked when she didn't continue. She waited another heartbeat before answering.

"You must promise that the dragon is given a safe and loving home—" she began.

I cut her off, "Of course I'll make sure—" I stopped abruptly when she held up a finger.

"---that is not with you." She leaned back in her chair, gazing coolly at me as I blinked in bafflement.

"What? Why?" I stammered. Her expression turned slightly pitying.

"You have your own dragon, child, and while I know that you would find it in your heart to love them both, that love can never be equal. Each eirioth dragon is deserving of that special bond it shares with its master. Once you bring him home, you must promise me that you will not keep him as your own." Her voice was grave, but I detected an underlying note of gentleness. I swallowed thickly. Even if I hadn't been around him much, I already felt a strong attachment to Asuka. How could I not? He lived in a world of despair and loss and confusion that was not very unlike my own. But Maki was right. The bond that formed between an eirioth dragon and its rider was an unbreakable one, and even the thought of trying to replace or share the bond I had with Sycamore made my stomach twist.

"Okay," I said heavily. "I promise."

"How can you make that promise?" Maki demanded. I looked into her eyes, unflinchingly holding her penetrating gaze.

"He will not belong to me. He will go to my brother." I wasn't sure if Finnian would actually want to have another dragon. Oftentimes, when a dragon died, its owner never replaced it, but some craved that loving bond enough to try and build it again with a new dragon.

"Does he have a dragon?" Maki asked doubtfully.

"He did, up until a short while ago." I said, my voice thinning. I looked away. "But he died recently. My brother will take Asuka in."

"You've named him already?" Maki huffed. I glared at her.

"Of course I named him. But . . . my brother can change it, if he wishes to." I cleared my throat and looked at her calmly again. "So? Will you help?"

She held my gaze for a moment longer, then nodded solemnly. "I know what you're here for. Come, you have a large task ahead of you."

Maki's tack was much more old-fashioned than I was used to. The trends and styles had almost certainly changed a handful of times since she had left Carlore, and it took me a couple of tries to figure out how to properly use her tack. The saddle models we used back at home were much sleeker and easier to manage than the bulky one Maki gave me, and the reins were designed to be far more comfortable than the tight straps Zan was used to. Still, I doubted Asuka would mind after having been forced to wear those hideous costumes during his performances.

Maki ran me through how to properly don the tack, then ushered me out and told me not to get caught. Before I left, she gave me some extra food and covered the dragon tack with old pieces of sackcloth to help me avoid suspicion. I was a little disappointed to have to leave her again so soon, but I knew Ksega would be getting antsy and it was getting late, so I hurried back towards the barn.

My back bothered me throughout the journey, and it was even more difficult working through the evening crowds without being noticed. On multiple occasions, I had been forced to duck out of sight or hurry into the shadows of an alleyway to avoid the sharp gazes of passing soldiers. I even caught the uniforms of some of the performers' hired security skulking around brandishing heavy weapons.

In the end, I made it back to the barn without issue, which Ksega would be pleased to hear about, but first I would have to get through the immediate complaints and questions as to why I was only just beginning to pull the heavy barn door aside almost an hour after the sun had gone down. It was for this reason that I was a little more than surprised when I opened the door to not only find Ksega already asleep, but to also find Asuka asleep beside him, head resting in his lap, eyes peacefully closed. One of Ksega's arms was draped lazily over the dragon's neck, his fingers still curled in a position that suggested loving scratches had been given shortly before they'd both dozed off.

I stepped into the barn as silently as I could, once again ignoring the buzzing of my senses that warned me of the cloying darkness surrounding me and setting the tack down and eating a small dinner before reaching for Ksega's rumpled bedroll. Trying my best not to disturb either of them, I settled the fabric over Ksega's legs and one of Asuka's feet. Even with the warmth of the straw and another body, winter was very close, and the nights were getting bitterly chilly. As soon as I was confident that they were both still soundly asleep, I wriggled into my own bedroll and sighed as I finally allowed myself to join them.

17
KSEGA

I woke before Sakura did. I wasn't very surprised at this fact, since I knew she must have returned to the barn late again the previous night. I didn't remember going to sleep with my bedroll over my lap, so she must have set it there. I was grateful for it, because at some point the night had grown bitterly cold, and I had startled Asuka by absent-mindedly curling into his chest. He had stamped away, swishing straw across the barn floor with his feathered tail to find a different place to sleep, leaving me to wrap myself in the bedroll.

It must have been early dawn, because pale slivers of white-gold light crept through the gaps in the old wood of the barn, illuminating specks of dust that danced around in the air. The air was still cool, but the streaks of sunlight gave enough warmth to leave me just drowsy enough to not want to get up.

I knew I should go do something productive, like start packing things together so we could finally leave this barn and head towards the king, but instead I just lay there staring at the boards of the ceiling, lost in my own thoughts. The quiet was eerie and unnatural. Something about silence had been bothering me recently, and now I finally figured out that it was the absence of a certain, constant sound that I had grown accustomed to. Alchemy's Cursed state meant that, while I couldn't see any life glow from him, I could still sense him with my bering through hearing. A dull, fly-like buzz droned in the back of my mind whenever he was within a certain radius of me, and I had learned to tune it out for the most part. Now that I was away from him, it was strangely empty without the lulling noise, and it meant I had more room to get swallowed up by my own thoughts. They were odd thoughts, pervasive ones that had never surfaced before. They brought up questions that I didn't know the answers to, but Willa might. They circled through my head, triggering memories and thoughts and curiosities that I hadn't touched in years.

I hadn't realized until now that I was jealous of the way Sakura spoke of her family. I didn't know the details of what had happened to them, but I knew that she at least had a few years with them before they were gone. She had known them, had loved them, had even been given the opportunity to make memories with them that would last forever. The same could not be said for me. I had never forced the topic on Willa, of course, because of the pain it caused her. Speaking of her son and his wife left her wallowing in memories she would rather leave behind her, and I wasn't going to bring her back into them. Even so, there was a hunger roaring within me, demanding that I go searching for answers. I deserved them, didn't I? I of all people deserved to know who my parents were and how they met their ends.

"What are you thinking about?" the whisper came from somewhere to my left, and when my gaze darted to the side, I saw Sakura watching me, still bundled beneath her bedroll. I sighed and closed my eyes.

"My parents," I replied. She mumbled, saying nothing. I licked my lips, unsure how to phrase the question that sat on the tip of my tongue. Throwing caution to the wind, I forced myself to ask. "What do you remember of yours? Were they . . ." I swallowed, opening my eyes again to stare up at the ceiling once more.

"Were they . . ?" Sakura repeated, prompting me to go on. I turned my head to look at her.

"Were they everything they needed to be? Loving? Nurturing?" I pressed my lips together, feeling my heart tug with emotions I hadn't let envelop me since I was a small boy. "Did they teach you how to read and write? How to use your eirioth?" my gaze darted over to where Asuka was sitting, head tilted to the side as he listened to our voices. "How to ride a dragon?"

Sakura was silent for a long moment, and when I looked at her again she was staring off into the distance, considering what I had asked. I didn't hold my breath, but I was close to it, trying to be as quiet as possible, as if the smallest sound might make her snap back behind her walls of distrust.

"Yes," she said finally, so low I wondered if I had imagined it. "They were very loving. They taught me a lot. I learned how to snap a spark to life from my father"—she lifted a hand and snapped her fingers, causing a bright flash of light to fly from them before vanishing into wisps of smoke—"and how to light a candle with my finger from my sister, Aurora." Her voice turned wistful. I knew she had a sister, but this was the first time I had heard her name. "My mother taught me how to climb the big eirioth trees, and I first learned how to ride on her dragon, Lavender." Sakura's eyes closed as she continued to talk. I watched her intently, trying to memorize the peaceful expression laid over her features, unable to recall a time she had looked so calm.

"And you always got along?" I asked quietly. She huffed a small laugh.

"No, of course we didn't. I once got so mad at my father for not letting me hold his flame-sword that I didn't talk to him for an entire day. The only reason I forgave him was because Aurora and Moma found me at our eirioth tree and convinced me that I would have my own flame-sword one day, and he was just worried that the day I held one for the first time would mean I was growing up too fast." Her eyes opened again, and I saw that they were dewy with unshed tears. I felt a lump in my throat and realized I was envious of the way she spoke of them, the feelings that she must have encountered at that moment. I couldn't share the same peace of mind—or the same grief—when I thought of my family.

"And you—" my voice broke, but I covered it with a cough. Clearing my throat, I went on. "You were all close?"

"Yes." Her voice was raspy, and I suspected it wasn't just due to her sore throat. "I've never been closer to anyone. Moma and Aurora and I used to have tea parties by our eirioth tree, and I used to watch Papa train Finnian with his flame-sword before I was old enough to use my own." Her words hitched, and she closed her eyes again, a single tear sliding down the side of her face. "I miss them," she whispered, biting her lip. I clenched my jaw, realizing my own eyes stung, but not because of grief. I was angry. How could I not feel anything when I thought of my mother and father? How was it that they meant so little to me in my life, when they should have been a major part of it?

A soft rumbling sound from behind me drew my attention, and I realized Asuka had come closer, snuffling curiously at my feet. I licked my lips and swallowed back my confusing feelings, dragging myself up into a sitting position and forcing myself to go and find some food for the dragon. Once he was satisfied and had allowed me to give him some affectionate pats on the head, I went back to the big straw pile and sat beside Sakura. Her tears were gone, but the morning light revealed where their streaks had dried on her face.

"I'm sorry if I upset you by asking," I said softly, tucking my legs up and crossing my arms. Sakura shimmied up so that she was sitting similarly beside me.

"It's alright. I've been wanting to talk to you about them, anyway," she said, and I glanced at her, but she was watching Asuka dig into his breakfast. "They were killed by the Curse, you know, my parents and Aurora. It's why I'm so determined to destroy it. Nobody else should suffer the way I have." I held my breath for a moment, grateful she was telling me this and uncertain about why she was. How long had she been wanting to talk about this? Had I done anything to give her the impression that I didn't *want* her to tell me this?

"And your brother?" I asked slowly. She pressed her lips together.

"His dragon was taken by the Curse, and the only option was to kill him. It broke Finnian to do it, and I left before he got better." She looked away from Asuka, maybe unable to look at a dragon as she recounted the tale. "I'm not going to let it happen to someone else I love. And we're *so close*. It's almost time to go home." She sighed, staring down at her feet for a long moment before she looked at me again. "What about you?"

"What *about* me? Willa is my only family." I knew she knew this already, but I couldn't help but wonder what she was really getting at.

"You said you were thinking about your parents, but you told me you'd never met them. Are you wondering what they were like?" she leaned closer, squinting at me as if trying to unravel the mystery of my expression. "Do you wonder if they were similar to mine?"

"I guess. My father must have been something like Willa, but I'm not much like Willa at all, so am I like my mother? Who were my mother's parents?" I furrowed my brows. "Willa's never spoken of them."

"You have lots of questions. Have you asked Willa more about them before?" Sakura asked, her brows furrowing. I shook my head.

"When I was younger, I used to, but I learned pretty fast that she gets really upset thinking about them. I know they were very important to her. I think they lived with her for a while, which is why I was taken in by her immediately when they both passed." I chewed my lip, staring hard at the floor to avoid meeting Sakura's gaze. "Do you think I should talk to her about it more?"

"Yes," Sakura answered. I nodded, unsure what else to say. Sakura took it as a chance to stand up and end the conversation, setting about getting things prepared for the day ahead.

The tack Sakura had borrowed from Maki was similar to horse tack, only on a much larger scale, and since I had helped Jessie with her horses in the past, we were able to work Asuka into the leather pieces with relative ease. I was mildly surprised that he didn't fight when we first lifted the saddle to go on his back. Maybe all those shows and rounds of being viciously whipped had made it a habit to stand still when things were being put on him. It was a sad thought, and one that I was determined to ignore as we finished fastening all the buckles and loops.

"It's a bit big on him, but it will work," Sakura said, standing back to observe the dragon. He looked uncomfortable but not afraid. Since I had been walking with him, feeding him, and giving him pats whenever he was looking particularly lonely, he had grown to trust us to some degree. Whether he trusted us enough to let us ride him or not was unknown, but we would be finding out soon enough.

By the time we had everything together and were leading the dragon out the back door of the barn it was almost midday. Sakura wanted us to make camp near Candle by nightfall and at the place where we would take off to fly over the walls the night after that, ensuring that we would have at least a couple full nights' sleep under our belts before we faced the king. I had asked if we would need to take turns keeping watch, but she argued in between bouts of coughing that we both needed rest more than we needed security.

Our biggest challenge as we headed towards Star Key was finding a way to get through without Asuka being noticed. It was the peak of day, and the Key was a blur of activity.

Merchants and workers and travelers and, much to our dismay, dozens of Locker soldiers and searching performers were crawling over the streets, packing the roads so tightly that even a short eirioth dragon would draw far too much attention. It would have been easier if we had waited until dark to move, but we would get too tired if we waited, and Sakura was clearly itching to keep moving. Our best option would be to force our way to the outside of the town and go around. Candle was the only town left between us and the capital city of Calder. Sakura wanted us to be on the outskirts of Calder when we took off, that way Asuka wouldn't have as far to fly with both of us.

There would be time to worry about the details later, because at the moment my job was to find a way to provide a suitable distraction so that Sakura could get Asuka through the streets. It was inevitable that someone would see him, but she had done a good job of cleaning herself up to the point that she looked somewhat professional, and she'd had concocted the lie that she was working with the performers. As long as one of the performers themselves didn't bump into her, I was confident that she could sell the authoritative act well enough to get through.

My job was a little more difficult. Coming up with a suitable distraction was a challenge in and of itself and enacting it without getting dragged down by the already on-their-toes guards added another level of complication. I could feel the pressure mounting on my shoulders, but somehow I was unbothered by the task. I already had an idea in the works, and if the fizzling excitement writhing just beneath my skin was any sign of how it would go, it was going to be easy.

The place we selected for her to cross through was the thinnest part of the Star Key we could find, where there were few streets and few people. Once Sakura and Asuka were situated and safely out of sight, I crept farther east, far enough away that any crowd I drew wouldn't be paying much attention to Sakura so far down the road. As I moved, I called up my bering. Even with the dulling of approaching winter, it wasn't hard to get its attention, since it had been impatiently simmering just beneath my skin for so long. I was still getting used to the amount of power I now held. I had never been able to control plant life to such a degree before leaving home, and now that I could, it was a mystery. Beyond that, there was also the mystery of how I had manipulated dead wood. One of the pirates of *The Coventry*, Peeler, was able to do it at will, but I hadn't been able to do it more than once, and that had been entirely by accident.

For the time being, though, those mysteries were to be set aside. I had to focus on distracting the people of Star Key. Thankfully, we managed to find a strip of the street that was mostly devoid of guards. There were one or two armed Locker soldiers patrolling up and down the street, but they weren't paying much attention to those around them, and I couldn't spot any of the traveling performers' hired security.

I scanned the buildings on either side of the road, absorbing the details before me and making a map of my planned path in my mind. My footsteps became lighter and quieter, my movements more intentional, each step bringing me only where I wanted to go. A quick count of heads told me there were roughly twenty people within a fifty-foot radius of me, and only two had taken notice of my presence: a woman and the child whose hand she held, both of them looking at me with wide, hesitant eyes. They weren't dressed in anything more than rags, and I guessed that they were waiting to see if I had anything to offer them. I did have something, although I doubted it would be anything they found particularly useful. Still, if it could add a touch of pleasantness to their day, I was more than happy to provide it.

I strode into the middle of the street, meandering a little way farther from the direction Sakura hid in and letting my gaze roam to see if I could find a good vantage point. It would have to be somewhere with a clear view of the entire street, but also a place well out of sight, where it would be difficult to spot me. It didn't take me long to find it, a small alcove between two buildings close beside each other. The gap between them couldn't even be described as an alley, it was so thin. It would be a tight squeeze, but there were bits of cloth and paper and other littered items that would provide a decent amount of cover, and if I worked quickly, I might be able to wriggle my way through to the other side before anyone noticed me crouching there.

I paused beside a storefront near my chosen hiding spot, pretending to inspect something I saw just beyond the glass panes. Instead of actually looking inside, I focused on the reflections, taking in each passing face to make sure nobody was looking before I ducked nonchalantly to the side and into the crevice between the buildings. It was mostly cast in shadow, due to the close proximity of the buildings, and I shuddered as a chilly wind rolled through it, lifting my hands and locking my gaze on a patch of plant life across the road. As I curled my finger, a weed grew tall and thin, spiraling in and knotting around itself over and over, growing a new inch with each passing second and twirling itself into the shape of a goat. A big goat.

The first startled cry came from a woman walking hand-in-hand with a man who was engrossed in a book he held with his free hand. He was so shocked by the sound that the book tumbled from his grip, but before it could fall to the dusty earth below, a hand of thin, frail wooden fingers caught it and held it up. Instead of accepting the fallen item, the man cried out in alarm and stumbled away from the plant being. I wasn't sure what it was, exactly, but it was vaguely humanoid, with thick antlers of bush branches jutting out of its head and an elegant cape of flower-spotted moss draping from its shoulders. Other people began to take notice of the plant creatures as well, and they were backing off to the sides of the road to watch the spectacle unfold while I created two more: a mighty horse and a pointy-eared dog. One of the small children on the sidelines giggled as the pup rolled playfully on the ground, exposing a soft belly of young grass and dandelions. Even with the chill of oncoming winter crawling through every inch of the world, I could bring vibrant life back into these plants for a while, and I couldn't help but smile as I saw one of the little girls step forward to pat the grassy dog on the head. With a twitch of my fingers, I set the dog's tail wagging wildly. A boy closer to my age stepped forward, frowning at the horse. I knocked my knuckle against empty air, and the horse tossed its head, stamping hoofs of rose petals and flicking a tail of wild grass as it assessed him.

Wondrous gazes and murmurs of awe rippled through the drawn crowd, and my lips split into a wide grin as I coaxed a small cat from the grass, then a long-necked crane, and even a broad-winged raptor. The gathered people looked around for the source of the magic, applauding and cheering their approval as they stepped forward to greet the creatures. It wasn't easy maintaining all of them at once, making sure they retained their life-like states, but with only seven, it was manageable—and it would hopefully be well worth the effort.

Using my magic like this felt good. Warm emotions bloomed inside my chest just like the flowers on the backs of the animals I controlled. Happy memories that I couldn't put locations or names to flooded my head, and for a few minutes everything was locked in that moment, just me bringing whatever joy I could to the people around me. Even the poor mother and her child had found a friend in the timid crane. It was a scene that I could watch for hours.

But time was not on my side, and I knew I would have to bring the show to a close soon. Sakura would be leading Asuka through the now mostly-abandoned street if she hadn't made it across already, and she would be expecting to meet me shortly afterwards.

I slowly spread the fingers on one hand, pressing my open palm down against the chilled earth beneath me and watching as my plant creatures slowed their movements, coming to standstills to the great disappointment of those around me. The girl that had been happily rubbing the dog's belly held a wavering smile on her face as she realized that they had once again become immobile plants. I left them in their creature-like positions, slowly backing myself out of the alley and ignoring the confused muttering that buzzed in the air.

Sakura was waiting for me on the outskirts of the Key, anxiously looking through the wide, empty plains of tall grasses. We could barely make out the sight of buildings and other structures further to the north, and some to the east and west, but none of them were close enough for anyone to see us without coming closer. We moved further out into the field and started to the east, where the elegant spires of the castle rose like the fingers of some great stone beast out of the earth. By the time we found ourselves on the outskirts of Candle, setting up a campsite a safe distance away behind one of the small, sloping hills, the sun was gone and the pale light of the moon was spilling across the ground, illuminating the silver waves of grass that rippled in the chilly late-autumn breeze. Winter was just around the corner, hardly even a week away, and Sakura had no choice but to light a small fire to keep us warm. Out in the open like this, neither of us liked the idea of it, but by the time dawn came, there would be no more than a soft curl of smoke, and hopefully we would be on the move early enough to avoid detection.

Sakura's coughing had gotten steadily worse, and by the time we had choked down a stale dinner, her voice was so raspy I urged her not to talk anymore. She huffed but obliged, letting me fill the silence with my own stories from back home. I had never been much of a storyteller before, since the only people who would care to listen to me were Jessie and Willa, and they often knew the details of all my adventures from other avenues before I even got a chance to see them and explain myself. Sakura, on the other hand, knew very little about my life before stowing away on a pirate heist, and I was free to justify my actions and embellish my heroics as much as I'd like. I told her about my first time stowing away on a ship and how terrified I had been of Willa finding out, only to successfully keep it a secret for nearly a year before admitting it to her when the guilt became too much. I told her stories about the things I'd stolen, and the reasons I no longer stole only for the sake of stealing. I told her about the old eirioth dragon that had lived in our town and about helping Willa tend to the fruit trees in our backyard. I told her about how Willa had taught me to make perfumes when I was very young, and I still hadn't mastered the art of letting the ingredients mingle and stew together perfectly.

"You're too impatient," she had always scolded me, clicking her tongue when she caught me straining the water too early. "You've got all the brains of a great perfume-maker, but none of the willpower."

I told her how I had earned the nickname 'Trouble' from Jessie, and how I had contemplated running away from home in search of a less monotonous life. I smirked as I admitted that it had been wise not to run away after all, because here I was, drawn into that less monotonous life whether I liked it or not. Sakura nodded along and listened closely, but there seemed to be very few of my stories she was actually interested in. She paid more attention to the ones that involved Jessie or Willa and less to the ones where I was all on my own, and I wondered if it was because all of her own stories of home involved her family and friends. I wished I could ask her about them, but with the state her voice was in, I wasn't going to push it at the moment. Instead, I stretched and sighed and suggested we turn in. She didn't argue, only scooted into her bedroll, shimmied closer to the warmth of the fire, and closed her eyes. It was some time before I saw her shoulders rising and falling in the steady rhythm of sleep, but I was used to that fact by now. It had taken me some time to work out why she hated sleeping out in the open, or even in tight rooms, but eventually I had concluded that she was afraid of the dark. I had never had such a fear, but I understood the way fears could worm into your mind and make things appear more vicious and terrible than they were, so I kept the fire alive a little longer, vowing that, at least for now, I would do everything in my power to keep the darkness at bay.

18
KSEGA

My streak of waking up before Sakura was broken the next morning. By the time I rubbed from my eyes and stretched the stiffness of sleep away, she had already prepared breakfast for both of us, fed and tended to the dragon, and had all of our things neatly set to the side so we could get moving as soon as possible.

"Eat," she croaked, and my lips twitched into a frown as I realized her voice was worse than the night before. Had a night of rest done nothing to soothe her throat? I made a mental note to try and use some of the little money we had to buy some honey for her whenever I got the chance.

I ate a quick breakfast, and then we were on the move again. The cold was coming in short bursts of wind now, chilling me through my clothes and making the tips of my fingers go numb. Sakura appeared to be unaffected by the changing weather, and I wondered if that had anything to do with her eirioth. Either way, I kept finding myself huddling close to Asuka as he was led along by Sakura, burying my hands in his feathers to try and warm them up a little.

The day was uneventful, although I constantly felt as though we were being watched. We spoke very little and only stopped when we needed to eat or take a short rest. By the time the sun was lowering into the west, we had almost drawn level with Candle off to our right. There were a few small man-made glades of trees and bushes on the outskirts of town, thick enough that we might be able to hide there for a night. It was extremely close to the buildings, but Sakura thought it would be worth the risk, so as the sun was dipping beneath the horizon, we forged a path through the dense foliage into a clearing just big enough for the three of us to settle in for the night.

There would be no fire this time, since we were so close to Candle. I had no doubts that the search for Asuka had reached this far, although it was more likely it would spread further to the west, assuming that anyone would try to make a quick escape after stealing a dragon. Still, the possibility of search parties being in Candle was too dangerous for us to risk a fire, so we tethered Asuka to a nearby tree and set our bedrolls as near to him as he would let us, then wriggled into them and curled up to stay warm. It didn't work very well in my case. Sakura seemed to fall asleep pretty easily, but I was soon shaking and chattering my teeth, vigorously rubbing my hands together to try and restore feeling to them. I used my bering to create a blanket of moss over me, but since I was unable to keep continuous focus on it while trying to sleep, it slowly turned gray and crumbled like dirt. It was a long time before I finally slipped into the depths of an uncomfortable sleep.

In the winter back home in Rulak, Willa kept a hearty fire roaring in the stove downstairs, and it kept the entire house sufficiently heated throughout the night. I had never gone a single winter night without that warmth, and I was sure that each time I woke up in a stiff, frozen state and began to drift off once more, I wouldn't open my eyes again. When I pried my eyes open, I was shivering badly, and my teeth were chattering together. I sat up stiffly, and Sakura glanced over from where she was on the other side of Asuka. As soon as she saw me, her face paled a little.

"I thought you looked bad before, but this . . ." It sounded like she said something else, but her raspy voice trailed off into a hushed whisper. She cleared her throat and crawled around towards me. Asuka eyed her closely for a long moment before returning his attention to something in front of him, presumably his breakfast.

"Hold still," Sakura commanded, pulling the covers of my bedroll away and setting her hands on my chest. At first, I wasn't sure she was doing anything, but after a moment, heat rushed back into my core, curling in my stomach and settling in my chest. I blinked, wincing at how painful it was, and she noticed. Her hands moved up slowly, hovering first over my neck, and then the sides of my face. As soon as enough warmth had returned to my features, I gasped a sigh.

"Thanks." I swallowed stiffly, my cheeks still hot even after she had moved her hands towards my arms. She only nodded silently, patiently warming my hands back up. My fingers still shook with the cold, and it hurt to curl them into fists after she had heated them. I was lucky I hadn't lost any of them. I had been sure to sleep in socks and boots, as uncomfortable as it was, but without being able to feel my feet there was no way of being sure my toes were in a similar condition.

Once the upper part of my body was back in working order, I scooted myself backwards out of the bedroll. Sakura reached forward and yanked my boots off, then my socks, and I cringed as I saw my gray feet. She seemed unperturbed and went about the work of warming them back up but waved a hand at my legs before she did so.

"Massage them. Get the blood flowing," was all she said, and obediently I began to rub feeling back into my legs. It was a shockingly slow and painful process, and I winced and groaned with unexpected jolts of pain as we worked, but finally, after what felt like hours, I could feel my entire body again, and I pulled my socks and boots back on before dragging myself unsteadily to my feet.

"I'm fine," I said quickly, when Sakura flinched at how much I was swaying. I smiled through a grimace as I straightened to my full height, hoping she couldn't see how affected I was by the searing needles of pain that stabbed into every inch of my limbs. I hurried to grab Asuka's tack and begin putting it back on him—we had removed it for the night so he could sleep comfortably—to distract us both, and she soon joined me, correcting me when I made the straps too tight or missed a buckle by pulling my hands away and finishing the job herself.

We were packed up and ready to go within the hour, and most of the stinging pain had receded from my body. This time, the packs were all bound to the back and sides of the saddle, and there would be no more trekking across the grassy flatlands of Brightlock. Today was the day we flew over the walls and went before the king. Hopefully.

Since Sakura was the one that knew how to fly the dragon, she would be riding up front. I watched closely as she gave Asuka a reassuring pat on the head before swinging herself easily up into the saddle. Asuka pranced anxiously but was quickly soothed again when I stepped forward to hold the reins. Sakura wriggled around until she was comfortable in the old saddle, then patted the seat behind her and nodded at me. Swallowing back my hesitant remarks about flying, I gripped the leather and pulled myself up, settling into the saddle behind her. It was an awkward place to sit, wider than a horse's saddle and rather cramped between the two of us and all the packs.

"Hold on," Sakura coughed, and I frowned.

"To what—" I was cut off by my own abrupt yelp as Asuka suddenly jerked forward, spread his wings, and launched us into the air. I instinctively hugged myself against Sakura, shutting my eyes as wind pummeled my face and roared all around me. I didn't dare to open them again until the whirling sensation in my stomach settled, and it felt like we were no longer going up, but flying in a relatively straight course. When I pried them open and looked up from where I had tucked my face against Sakura's back, my jaw went slack.

We were several miles above the ground, so high up in fact that tendrils of clouds reached down like searching fingers so close to us I could have reached out and touched them. The landscape rolled out below us like a magnificent tapestry, one full of bustling towns and swaying grass fields and idle livestock. The castle was ahead, still far off but getting closer, and its surrounding capital city sprawling out below it. The tall walls around the castle gleamed in the sunlight, both welcoming and foreboding at the same time. The wind was also bitterly cold, slicing into me with each gust like a dozen tiny knives, and I shivered as it rushed up through my sleeves and tugged at my hair.

"Will it be a long flight?" I yelled over the wind, squinting through it to try and gauge the distance to the castle walls. Sakura's shoulders lifted in a shrug, but she said nothing. I doubted she could say more than a handful of words at a time, with how awful her voice had sounded.

We stopped once to let Asuka rest, and for Sakura to check and make sure we weren't overworking him. He'd only met us a number of days ago, and while he seemed to trust us a fair amount, he still flinched each time one of us lifted an arm. It made my gut twist with anger whenever I thought of how cruelly he had been mistreated.

The sun had passed its midpoint in the sky when we finally passed over Calder. My head still spun each time I looked way down at the ground, and I wasn't sure how many people had seen us flying overhead, but there was no going back now, so I gritted my teeth and tried not to worry about falling or being shot down. The latter was likely to happen, but Sakura wasn't as concerned about it as I was, at least not until we were within firing range of the soldiers posted on the walls, and we saw them scrambling to reach for something. Seconds later, when crossbows were lifted into arms and propped against shoulders, Sakura finally seemed to realize what could be a fatal flaw in her plan.

"Land in the courtyard!" I shouted over the wind, tightening my hold around Sakura's waist as bolts were slid into place on the bows. Asuka squawked alongside my unease, and Sakura leaned low over his neck, urging him onward.

Sakura had put her hair in a tight braid that morning, but some strands had come loose and were whipped up wildly by the wind as we sliced through the air and swerved from side to side to avoid the loosed bolts. They hissed through the air beside us. These were no doubt trained soldiers, and I was a little surprised we were able to dodge them until I remembered that Sakura had been riding dragons since she was a small child, and in the land of twisting, curving eirioth trees, she was probably very good at evasive maneuvers. My thought was confirmed moments later as we suddenly began to flip, arcing upside-down to avoid another volley of bolts. Another set was sent whirring towards us, but Sakura had already pulled Asuka up and into a loop, letting the deadly bolts soar past.

"This wasn't your most well-thought-out idea," I yelled, looking down and squeezing my eyes shut. My bow was slung across my back, and my arrows were in easy reach at my hip, but we weren't here to hurt these people, and there was no safe way for me to shoot from the dragon's back. Besides, I had to keep one hand on the quiver to keep the arrows from shooting out as we spun.

We flew over the wall, but Asuka seemed to be off-balance, and we tumbled through the air, flipping downward and crashing through a copse of well-manicured trees. Branches whacked into Asuka's wings and raked across our shoulders, their tiny twigs whipping painfully across my cheek and neck. Sakura was moving, trying to regain control, but Asuka was trying to land, and their fighting caused us to do another roll before sliding down onto a path of cobbles and skidding across the stones. I grimaced as Asuka's claws scrabbled for purchase, but he lost his balance once more and fell, flinging Sakura and I into a painful and ungraceful dismount.

"Don't move!" A voice boomed around us, and I groaned as I lifted my head to look in the direction it came from. Armed guards were rushing into the courtyard, surrounding us.

"Not planning on it," I huffed in a quiet breath, staying in the position I had landed in: flopped on my back, my bow digging into me as I raised my hands palms-up to show I wasn't holding any weapons.

I forced my teeth to unclench, ignoring the pulse of pain in my jaw as I released a shaky sigh. I kept my hands up as the soldiers closed into a tight circle around us, crossbows raised and trained on our chests. Sakura was beside me, flinching as she slowly massaged her wrist. There was a thick line of blood on her face, where one of the branches had cut her. Asuka staggered back to his feet and shook his head, backing away from all the people with wide eyes. Sakura noticed the dragon's panic just when I did. I frantically gestured at him, then down at her throat. I looked around, singling out the man that must've been in charge—a short, stocky fellow with a drooping mustache of fiery red and pouchy eyes that sat in shadow.

"The dragon," I gasped, pointing at Asuka. "He won't calm down. Can I help him?" The man looked at us with narrowed eyes, then nodded once. I scrambled to my feet and stepped up to Asuka, my fingers seeking the little spot beneath his jaw where he loved to be scratched. He pulled away at first, but after a few seconds began to settle down. Finally his breathing slowed and his panicked foot-stomping ceased.

"State your names," the man with the mustache demanded, stepping forward, and I now saw that he held a heavy battle-axe at the ready. I gave Sakura a quick glance. She opened her mouth to speak, but only a weak, hoarse sound escaped. She rubbed her neck, giving me a worried look. Her voice was gone.

"I'm Ksega, and this—" I began, but the man cut me off.

"Each of you state your own names," he said sharply. I pursed my lips.

"She can't speak," I explained. "But her name is Sakura." The man wore a nonplussed expression, but when neither of us said anything more he set the battle-axe's head on the ground, resting the handle against his hip, and crossed his arms to glare at us.

"You two are hardly old enough to be out and wandering off on your own, much less out stealing dragons and invading castles." His eyes narrowed further, so much so that it looked like he had shut them. The other guards around us shuffled a little closer, waiting for a command. "From the looks of it, you aren't from around here, either. Who are you, and why are you at the castle?"

It was a long moment of silence before I realized I was the one who had to answer. I gave Sakura a panicked look, swallowing nervously. An easy lie had sprung to my lips, not believable in the slightest, but effective for keeping people distracted while I sought out an escape route. The problem was we were here to tell the truth, which was considerably more difficult, especially when truth was something that I often avoided.

"We must speak to the king," I said finally, looking the man in the eyes. "It's urgent." I added when his only response was lifting a bushy eyebrow.

"*Everyone* urgently needs to speak to the king. Why do you think we have such a complex system?" He shook his head, looking tired of this. With a wave of his hand, he called off the crossbowmen, and they all lowered their weapons.

"We don't have time to go through the system. We might know how to stop the Curse, and it's important that we speak to the king as soon as possible." I kept my voice as confident as I could without it bordering on authoritative. This man was already against us, but we needed him to take us to see King Kirk before he inevitably threw us into a prison cell.

"The Curse, hm?" the man grunted. "Do you know how many times I've heard that excuse? It isn't going to work. I'll let you off with no more than a warning, since you're just a couple of trouble-making kids, but you'd better not come back." His scowl, surprisingly, deepened. "You're lucky you didn't get shot down on your way in. If we hadn't realized you weren't a significant threat, you'd look like pincushions right now." He uncrossed his arms and hefted his axe back up into his hands, resting it over his shoulder. "Next time, we won't be so gracious."

"But—" I began, but he lifted a hand to cut me off.

"No excuses!" he barked, beckoning a handful of soldiers closer. "Escort them into the city." He ordered, and the soldiers shrugged their crossbows into place onto their backs before assuming positions on either side of us that were both protective and threatening at the same time.

"Wait!" Sakura cried, her voice so scratchy that it was difficult to recognize the word. Everyone turned to her in surprise, except for the red-haired man, who gave me a sharp glare. I ignored him, trying to make out what else Sakura was trying to say, but her voice had given up again, and it was impossible to tell what she wanted to share. In the end, she gave up with a grunt and pointed at Asuka, giving me a wide-eyed look.

"Oh, yeah, the . . . dragon?" I said slowly, still unsure what she meant. She rolled her eyes, angrily swiping the dripping blood off her face as she gestured at Asuka once more. "Ah . . . oh! Yes! The dragon!" I turned back to the man with the fiery mustache, who was watching with increasing irritation. "We stole him! Don't we have to be tried for that or something?" I could just picture Willa and Jessie's disappointment at such a statement, especially when it was said with so much excitement. Even Sakura looked mildly confused as she watched my grin broaden. As for the man with the axe, he opened his mouth, closed it, and opened it again. Finally, a defeated sigh escaped him.

"Yes, that is a crime that is usually brought to court . . ." He reached up and massaged his temple, a torn look deforming his face.

We waited impatiently, me tapping my fingers against my thigh and Sakura rubbing her thumbs over her knuckles until, at last, he looked at the soldiers on either side of us and waved them away. As they stepped back into the circle around us, I molded my features into an expression of placid gratitude, and Sakura did her best to mirror it.

"Come with me," the mustached man ordered, waving us closer to him. "The dragon will be taken to a stable for now." He eyed us closely as we came to stand beside him. "I won't go through the usual rigamarole that is required for an arrest but know that I won't hesitate to detain you in a very rough manner if you try anything." With that he turned on his heel and marched towards the castle with Sakura and me and a small entourage of soldiers in tow.

During the excitement of the crash and the events that followed it, I hadn't had a good chance to look at our surroundings, and I took the walk through the courtyard as an opportunity to soak in my environment. The plants were shriveled and brown with dormancy, and while I could still feel the life lingering deep down inside them, it would take some work to bring them back to their former vibrancy. Aside from the sleeping plants, there were winding cobbled pathways and elegant marble statues of rearing horses and small rabbits wearing cloaks of moss. The whole place was chilly and unwelcoming with the promise of winter in the air, but I couldn't help but imagine what it might look like in late spring, when the flowers were blooming and the bushes needed to be trimmed back every few days between rain showers. There would be birdsong and small rodents scurrying about, sticking to the shadows to avoid the wrath of hard-working gardeners. There would be servants hurrying through the winding pathways carrying baskets of linens for the nobles and brandishing prickly scrubs to polish the statues to a shine. The place would be crawling with life, and a part of me longed to see it, thriving and swelling with just a little help from my magic.

"I'm General Otis," the man leading us introduced himself as we ascended the stairs to the keep. I nodded but didn't have a good reply, and from Sakura's tensed jaw, I decided it would be safe to remain silent for now.

The heavy doors swung open to let us in. The room we entered was wide and relatively unfurnished, but there had been no lack of effort in its design. The ceilings were vaulted and heavily detailed with swirls and vines of plaster, and the marble floors were so clean they shone like a pool of speckled water. A set of double-doors sat in an elegant archway off to the left, and Otis led us through them into an even grander hallway, decorated with paintings of stunning landscapes and galloping herds of wild horses. The nobles of Brightlock certainly seemed to like their steeds.

"You," Otis barked as a servant made her way past us, carrying a silver tray of empty plates and goblets. She halted, looking wide-eyed at the general. "Find the herald and tell him to inform the king that a trial is in order. It is a matter of grand theft and takes priority over any other minor items on His Majesty's schedule today. Go." He waved the servant off, and she rushed away, presumably to find the herald, leaving us to stand awkwardly in the hall with Otis. He looked us both up and down, still clutching the handle of his battle-axe and chewing his lower lip thoughtfully.

"We're on His Majesty's top priority list, huh? Wow, I didn't realize criminals got such posh treatment," I said to break the silence, flashing the general my most charming grin. He arched a bushy eyebrow at me.

"Believe me, you two are a special case. Normally, I'd have you shivering your toes off in the prison cells until the court is open, but since you're young and rather inexperienced, and you don't seem to pose any imminent threat . . ." He sighed, rolling his eyes as if he couldn't believe he was ignoring protocol for the sake of two mischievous travelers.

Otis was quiet as we waited, watching us shrewdly as we shuffled around on our feet. I wasn't sure how long we would be waiting, but it didn't seem like we were going to be let out of the intricate hallway anytime soon, so I took the respite from excitement as an invitation to explore the room. Otis watched me closely as I began to pace along the wall, examining the paintings, but he made no move to stop me. The art wasn't half as interesting as it needed to be to keep my attention for long, but there was no better way to pass the time, so I looked them over thoroughly as I made my way down the hallway, and when I had gone over them all, I went back through the hall looking at the patterns in the floor and ceiling. At some point, Sakura fell in step beside me, nursing her wrist and occasionally swiping her fingers along her cheek to see if it was still bleeding. The injury was pretty nasty, but she didn't complain about it. Neither of us said anything, and there were no windows to let us tell how much time had passed. Otis stood stoically by the door we had come through, his eyes tracking each of our movements beneath his fluffy red eyebrows.

After what felt like hours, the doors at the opposite end of the hallway opened to reveal the young serving girl and a tall, wrinkled man with fraying white hair and a bulbous nose.

"Ah, Master Lars, there you are!" Otis's voice exploded through the hall, making me and Sakura jump from the sudden break in the silence. "Is His Majesty ready for us?" try as he might to conceal it, a note of impatience was evident in the general's voice.

"Yes." The man, Master Lars, had a deep and slow voice that resounded through the room like the low tolling of a bell. "But one thing first. Names." His dark eyes swooped down on us, just as shadowed and unfriendly as Taro's gaze when he wanted a portion of my food. Once again, I gave our names. Lars nodded once, cleared his throat, and spoke again. "Please, follow me." He turned at a painstakingly sluggish pace and began to walk on bowed legs down another hallway, not bothering to see if we were following. Otis ushered us forward until we were tailing Lars, struggling to match his leisurely stride without stepping on his polished shoes.

"Are we going to see the king now?" I asked, my eyes darting up and down and all around the new rooms we passed through. Everything was in the same style, making for a very confusing maze of corridors.

"Yes," Lars answered steadily. He tilted his head in my direction to arch a thinning eyebrow, but said nothing more, perplexed by the hint of excitement lacing my words.

We continued the walk in silence. I tried to memorize the path we took through the castle, but it was a vain effort, so I gave up and focused instead on what we would say to the king. Sakura hadn't gone into great detail when she explained everything to me, but I knew the rough details.

It wasn't until we came to the grandest set of doors we had seen yet, richly detailed with the rearing horse crest and plates of gold, that I remembered Sakura would be unable to help present our case to the king. My mouth went dry at the realization that I would have to do the speaking entirely on my own.

19
SAKURA

The throne room was long and wide, bigger than the throne room from the Glass Palace of Old Nightfall and even more intricately detailed. Thick pillars supported the tall ceilings, and stained glass windows sent distorted flashes of gold and silver dancing across the marble floors. A slightly raised dais sat at the end of the room, and upon it were two thrones, one tall and imposing, made from dark metal and gold velvet, and the other slightly smaller but no less striking. In the smaller of the two thrones sat a woman who looked to be somewhere in her fifties, with black hair streaked with gray and keen, dark eyes. In the larger of the thrones was a man who looked even older, perhaps in his sixties, with silvering hair and beady green eyes. Both of them were dressed in several flashy layers of black and gold, and both had twisting crowns of black metal resting on their heads. The queen looked unfriendly, but the king had a somewhat warm look to his features. Standing behind the king's throne, with one hand resting on its back, was a man who looked to be about twenty with a neatly combed swoop of ebony hair and sharp green eyes. He was dressed much simpler than his parents, but the silver band around his head clearly marked him as a member of the royal family.

"To be judged for the accusations cast against them, Ksega and Sakura have been brought before the thrones of His Majesty King Kirk, Her Majesty Queen Ola, and His Royal Highness Prince Blake," Lars drawled, circling my attention back to him and the situation at hand. "Their judgment will deem the accused innocent or guilty. Punishment and retribution may be decided from there." He placed a withered hand on one of my shoulders and one of Ksega's, gently guiding us forward until we stood closer to the dais. Then he continued in his low, droning voice, "The charges placed against them are theft of an international good, desecration of performer property, and accomplices to murder." As he listed off the charges, a cold chill rode down my spine. When they were put in those words and said before the king himself, it all sounded far more dangerous than I'd realized.

"And trespassing," Otis pitched in from behind us.

"And trespassing," Lars repeated with a nod and a haughty glare at Otis. He then turned his owl-like eyes towards me and Ksega and declared, "Present your case."

My gaze went from the stony expressions of the Calders to Lars' expectant face to Ksega. The latter was staring dumbly at the king in front of him, eyes wide and jaw clenched so tightly he must have been causing himself pain. I reached out and gave him a nudge with my elbow, reminding him that my voice had completely given out.

"Oh, uh . . . well," he began, "technically we aren't here to talk about stealing a dragon—"

Lars cut him off with an icy tone. "I'll remind you that using matters of trial as a way to get an audience with the king is illegal and would only add to your charges." The herald clasped his hands behind his back and faced the royals once more. All of them wore matching unreadable expressions but I could see Ksega's eyes working to dissect them, unraveling the small signs that inevitably got through their stony facade.

"But it could decide the future of Horcath!" Ksega argued, his voice bordering on desperate. Lars regarded him, his expression darkening with his increasing ire. "Please, hear us out. It's about the Curse, and—"

"*Enough.* You will present your case, or you will be judged without one." Lars cut him off sharply. Ksega pursed his lips, throwing me a helpless glance. I shrugged, racking my brain for any more ideas, but they wouldn't come.

"The Curse, you say?" The voice was low and rough with age, and it came from the lips of the silver-haired king. He was watching us with a curious light in his eyes. It made him look almost grandfatherly. Beside and behind him, his wife and son had similarly thoughtful expressions on their features.

"Yes, the Curse. We've been tracking its source, trying to find out where it originated," Ksega said quickly, eyes darting between the king and Lars, as if he was afraid the herald might revoke his permission to speak.

"And tell me, boy," the king said slowly, curling weathered fingers around the armrests of his throne as he studied us with a curious light in his eyes. "What have you found?"

"Well, uh—" Ksega licked his lips, giving me another look. I nodded at him, hoping it conveyed encouragement and not the growing sense of dread in my stomach. None of this had felt *real* until we were actually here, and now that it did, I couldn't help but wonder if our argument was very compelling. This was a *king*, after all, and we were a couple of kids with no importance to our names.

"Start from the beginning." The queen's voice wasn't as warm and weathered as the king's. It was cold as ice and clear as glass, ricocheting off the walls to land sharply in my ears, and her face was like stone. "You are clearly not from here. Tell us about your journey." It was almost as if she was trying her hardest to mimic her husband's gentler tone. Her eyes seemed to soften as she went on. "Perhaps if it is entertaining and fruitful, we will let you go without punishment." She paused, seemingly sensing that her statement wasn't helping to gain our trust. "You are young, after all," she added. Ksega wrinkled his nose at the words, and I bit my lip, hoping he wouldn't say something dumb. I slowly released my anxious breath when he licked his lips, sighed heavily, and began to tell the tale of our journey, beginning with how we had met in Clawbreak.

He went through most of it quickly, leaving out the fact that Alchemy, whom he kept referring to as "our friend Chem," was Cursed. He explained that we had gone to Old Duskfall, thinking maybe the Curse had been created by dark magic not unlike bone reading. It wasn't until he got closer to the part where we went to Old Nightfall that things started going wrong.

"So once we got a ride to take us there, we went into the kingdom of Old Night-fall"—Ksega plowed on, his casual air still mostly intact, but I winced, remembering the Glass King's words about not letting anyone know how to find his kingdom—"and . . . well, that basically did nothing for us. We sort of ended up kidnapping a guy from there, but he's okay with it, he just got really sick. I think he's doing a lot better now. Hopefully he hasn't tried to run away. Considering who we left him with, it's a good possibility, but I don't think he really has anywhere to g—" he grunted in surprise as I jabbed my elbow into his ribs. I hoped that one look at my pursed lips and fiery gaze would be enough to tell him it was time to move on, and with the perplexed and slightly doubtful looks creeping onto the royals' faces, I knew they thought so too. Before he could go on, the prince—what had Lars called him? Blake?—stepped out from behind the king's throne and addressed us.

"I'll bet I can guess why you're here." His voice was nothing like that of his parents'. Where his father's was warm and honeyed and his mother at least attempted to match it, his was just as sharp as the lines of his face. "It's a relatively straightforward line of thinking, and while it is logical in several ways, you've also missed a few key facts along the way."

"Ah . . . and those are?" Ksega's voice had risen with nervousness, bordering on a squeak. Blake lowered his dark brows.

"First, let me make sure. You think the Calder royal family is responsible for creating the Curse because it could function as a way to wipe out all the enemy kingdoms, correct?" He crossed his arms over his chest, rocking back on his heels as he stared down at us. He didn't need us to reply to know the answer. "You believe that the war two hundred years ago—between Brightlock and Coldmon—spurred my ancestors into creating a sort of weapon that would leave our family in control of Horcath for generations, but the weapon somehow managed to get out of our control, and it now plagues our entire world." He pressed his lips into a pale line, tilted his head to the side in thought, then nodded to himself and said, "Have I got that about right?"

"Exactly." Ksega sounded both relieved and worried that the prince had figured it out on his own. I shared his reaction. At the very least, I no longer had to panic about any incriminating details Ksega might share.

A tense silence filtered into the room. My thumbs scraped along my knuckles, and Ksega's boot was *tap tap tap*ping on the glossy marble floors impatiently. I absent-mindedly touched the cut on my cheek, wiping away drops of sticky blood. I wiped it away on my pant leg and looked into the dark eyes of each of the royals, then over at Lars and sidelong at Otis. The latter two wore slightly amused expressions, but those of the royals were entirely unreadable, at least to my eyes; one look at Ksega told me nothing good was coming.

Then, to my surprise, the king began to laugh.

"You are children indeed, if you think that," Queen Ola said through a light chuckle. Even the prince now wore a smirk on his lips. I shared a confused look with Ksega, whose cheeks were pinkening with embarrassment. He only shrugged at me. The king regained his composure and looked down at us with a smile, losing the appearance of the stolid king and taking on that of a wizened old man patiently explaining something to a confused toddler.

"You are young and rather inexperienced, the both of you, and it is understandable that you would make such assumptions, but you are thinking in terms of *what* and not *who*. *What* my great-grandfather was was a king, and a king does whatever he can to make sure his kingdom prospers, even if that means taking great risks and making sacrifices." King Kirk reached up and tugged at his thinning beard. "*Who* my great-grandfather was was a man who loved his people dearly and loved his family even more. He wasn't just a king, but a father and a husband, and that meant that the weight of taking risks and sacrifices was greater." He shook his head, sensing that we weren't quite following his words. "I can see this will not persuade you to understand. Come, I will show you something. Lars, drop their charges, and make sure the dragon is returned to its original owners." The king rose from his throne and stepped off the dais, motioning for us to follow him as he strode towards the great doors at the front.

Before he could reach it, though, and before the queen and prince could move to follow as well, I stepped forward, saying as loudly as I could, "*No!*" the word tore from my throat, raking and painful, and I winced, one hand instinctively clasping around my neck as if it could soothe the ache. A hand touched my back, and I looked up to see Ksega watching me worriedly, the king wearing a similarly concerned expression behind him. I gave Ksega a pleading look. He knew how much Asuka meant to me, and he knew that we could never let him go back to those performers, no matter what the king said. I would rather he die than return to a life of such torture.

"What that dragon was put through was unimaginable," Ksega said, addressing the king once more. Lars curled a lip at him, and even Otis stepped forward, prepared to silence Ksega if he kept arguing, but he ignored them and continued. "I know our word doesn't mean much, but the treatment he was given was cruel and evil. We stole him not just so we could use him to gain an audience with you, but to save him from the nightmare he lived in. Please, you can't send him back. Let him come with us. Sakura was raised around dragons, and she can give him the life he needs." Distress wove itself into Ksega's voice as he spoke, and I couldn't be sure if it was just his excellent acting skills at play or heartfelt anguish. Maybe I wasn't the only one who understood Asuka's misery.

"That doesn't change the fact that you *stole* him," Prince Blake pitched in, stepping off the dais and ambling over to stand directly in front of us. "Those performers are his rightful owners."

"I doubt they even bought him!" I yelled, although it came out as little more than a harsh whisper. Ksega's hand moved up to my shoulder and squeezed, and I knew he thought I should stop talking for the sake of my voice, but I didn't want to stop. I wanted to shout at these people until they understood how much that dragon meant to me and my people, and why it was so important that he stayed with us. I wanted to grab the prince by his pale ears and make him learn about the savage ways the performers really treated their prized animals. I wanted to drag him over to their flashy golden tents and let him see the starving slate-wolves and heavy iron chains. Even if they were all daydreams that could never come to pass, I would continue to dream of them until something was done about it.

"Nevertheless, Blake has a point," the king said, and I glared at him. How could he be so heartless as to let something like this occur in his own kingdom? "But . . . I will take it under advisement. Now follow me." He resumed his steady march towards the door, and after taking a shaking breath, I trailed after him, and Ksega after me.

King Kirk led us through the castle hastily. We wound through corridors decorated with tapestries bearing the royal crest, past chambers being cleaned by servants and halls adorned with shimmering stained glass windows. Otis and Lars tagged along, but the other members of the royal family had gone off in another direction. We didn't ask where we were going, and the king gave no sign that he was going to tell us.

After making our way through the maze of corridors and passages, the king stopped in front of a small, dark door. When he pushed it open, a well-lit staircase spiraling downward was revealed.

"The royal archives, Your Majesty?" Lars asked, his skepticism clear in his voice and the crease between his eyebrows. My gaze flicked over to Ksega, but he looked no less lost than I was.

"Yes. If these two young people honestly wish to know the truth—and after hearing the lengths they have gone to obtain it, I believe they do—then they must understand the history behind it," the king said curtly, beginning to descend the steps. After only a brief moment of hesitation, Ksega and I started after him once more, with a confused Otis and vexed Lars on our heels.

The staircase was long and must have gone deep beneath the castle, because there were no windows and the distant sounds of work slowly faded into the background. More than once I had the fleeting thought that he was only luring us down into the dungeons, but each time I dismissed the notion. All my fears were laid to rest when we reached the bottom of the stairs, entering a warmly lit room full of great bookshelves that ran from the floor to the ceiling and nearly from wall to wall. On the shelves were scrolls and leather-bound tomes and scattered papers, all of them thrown onto the shelves in haphazard disarray. I didn't get to look at many of the titles as we walked past them, still following the king as he led us into a small office off to the right, but there was no identifiable order to the pieces of literature.

"Damon," the king said as we entered the office. It wasn't exactly a small space, but it felt much more confined than it should have thanks to the stacks of books and papers lying in every corner, and the mess of boots and cloaks and hats tossed carelessly over cabinets and chair backs. The broad desk that sat in front of us was equally disastrous, with parchments and pens and empty ink wells strewn across its surface; off to one side sat a flickering oil lamp that barely managed to keep the room illuminated. In the tall wingback chair behind the desk sat a withering old man with wisps of white hair and hollow, sunken eyes set deep in his wrinkled face. His back was hunched from years of poor posture, and he had to tilt his head at an awkward angle to look up from his work and observe us.

"Your Majesty." The man, Damon, dipped his head respectfully, then nodded at the other two men in the room. "Sir Otis, Master Lars. How may I assist you?"

"I would like the records from King Therol's reign brought up for these two travelers to view." The king demanded. Nodding once more, Damon rose stiffly and slowly from his chair and shuffled around his desk. We all stepped out of the way, then filed into a line behind him as he shambled his way out of the office and between the rows of bookshelves. He paused a time or two to examine the spines or labels, then lurched on, his stooped figure blending in and out of the flickering shadows.

At last, he came to a shelf against one of the far walls and, after running his frail fingers over the spines, began to pull volumes out. He turned and began to shove them into Ksega's arms, and when his were full, he began to fill mine. Neither of us objected, although the books were far thicker and heavier than I'd first anticipated, and my arms began to strain beneath the growing weight. When he was finished, he simply bowed to King Kirk, nodded once more at the herald and the general, and shuffled away. We looked up at the king, and he gestured to a set of tables nearby, their surfaces slanted to make reading easier.

"Please, take a seat and start reading. The actions of the Locker kings have been recorded in great detail by the royal scribes for the last five hundred years. All but extremely private matters, such as what takes place between a king and his wife or within a king's personal letters, have been written down and preserved, not only to keep our history alive, but also to help prevent us from falling to any mistaken accusations." He lowered his thick, dark eyebrows as he looked down at us.

"You want us to read *all this*?" Ksega gaped, looking with wide eyes at the stack of books in his arms. King Kirk merely shrugged.

"I want you to read until you are satisfied that you are wrong. Therol's reign, from the day he was crowned king to the day he died, is recorded in those tomes. You will find that he fought valiantly in the war against Coldmon, and that when victory was his, he came home and made sure the kingdom was at peace once again. No plans to set out for world domination are ever mentioned." He rubbed his hands together and sighed. "Now if that's all, I will leave a couple of guards posted outside the archive door. Should you need anything, ask Damon. I will send someone to bring you your supper in a few hours, and later you will be taken to the guests' quarters to rest." Finishing with that, the king shrugged his broad shoulders and marched out of the archives. After sniffing indignantly at us, Lars followed, and finally Otis meandered along after them, leaving Ksega and I standing with our arms full of books and hours and hours of reading ahead of us.

I walked over to the tables and set my stack of books down beside it, kneeling so I could read the spines and find which one came first. Ksega set his stack beside mine, and I spotted the beginning of the set at the bottom of his pile. I worked it out, set it on the table, flipped it open, and began to read. I was hardly a few words in when Ksega groaned.

"Do we seriously have to read these?" he whined. I gave him a stern look. I wanted to find the truth, and if that meant reading through all these books, so be it. Besides, this is what we had come for, wasn't it? He sighed when he realized I wasn't going to give in, picked up the next volume, and sat beside me to start reading.

Supper was brought for us, and we ate it in silence, our eyes still glued to the pages before us. Hours and hours passed, filled with only the sound of flipping pages and the occasional cough or sniffle from one of us. The books weren't very interesting, and it took more willpower than I would have liked to focus on what was actually being said.

Finally, after what felt like forever, we had each made it through at least one of the volumes. Ksega was nearly finished with his second, but I was only about halfway through my second one. I slumped back in my chair with a heavy sigh, rubbing my eyes. It felt like they were starting to cross, and they were getting sore. It must have been late, and my body was ready to go to sleep, but my mind was too hungry for answers to let me give in.

"This isn't going to help us at all," Ksega muttered, placing an elbow on the table and leaning his head into it as he looked at me. I crossed my arms and raised an eyebrow, prompting him to elaborate. Now it was his turn to sigh. "Look, this is the account of the war. Most of this book has covered it. It wasn't Brightlock that began the war in the first place, but Coldmon. It looks like the Coldmonian king at that time, Calysto, wanted to take some more territory on land and decided that Brightlock was his target. Therol murdered his fair share of noblemen and royals, and he was about as power-hungry as they come, but he didn't initiate the war against Coldmon, and now that I think about it, that makes sense. What would a king who mainly sells and trades in ores and horses stand to gain from taking territory on the sea?" he clawed at his hair with his hand, chewing his lip as he worked all the pieces of the puzzle together in his head. "So the war raged and Calysto was killed, leaving the Coldmonians to back out. Ever since then, there's been unspoken tension between the two kingdoms, but none of the descendants acted on it. It even says in here that after Therol won the war he went back home and spent time teaching his sons the ways of a king, since he had come near death during the battle and realized that one of them might have to take his place soon." Ksega's other hand came up and tapped at the papers of the book he had been reading, and he sighed again. "According to the dates here, there's no way Therol created the Curse, and I somehow doubt any of his descendants would be responsible for it." He groaned and buried his face in both hands. "This was such a waste of time."

"Yeah," I agreed in a rough whisper, feeling tears burn behind my eyes. He was right. What were we thinking? We really were just foolish children grasping at any ideas that came to us. But there had to be *something* somewhere.

"I suppose we could look into the Coldmonian royal bloodline, but that sounds pointless as well." Ksega said through his hands. "As far as I know, they spend more time perfecting underwater suits of armor and weapons than they do paying attention to other kingdoms or even their own history." He leaned back in his chair and crossed his arms, his gaze rising to scan the shelves around us. "Although . . . as long as we're here, why don't we have a look around? Maybe we can find something useful in these archives anyway." He pushed his chair back and stood, walking past me and disappearing behind the shelves.

I cleared the scratchiness from my throat and called after him, "Are we allowed to do that?"

"I'm not sure, but His Shininess didn't say otherwise, so I assume so." I ground my teeth at his careless tone, but didn't object as he pulled things off the shelves. Instead of questioning him further, I too stood and made my way back towards Damon's office.

Ksega was right that we still might find something helpful in all these pieces of history, and I was willing to bet that the current royal scribe would be just the person to help me find it.

His office door was open when I reached it, and almost as soon as I stepped inside, the bony old man looked up at me, a question in his eyes. I tried to ignore how they bored into me like shiny black beads.

"Do you have any material on"—I paused to cough a couple times, clearing up my throat, but found that my voice wouldn't be cooperating. I glanced down at the pieces of paper on his desk, motioning toward them questioningly. He narrowed his eyes at me, slowly pushing a sheet of parchment across the desktop and setting a quill beside it for me. I quickly scrawled out my question: *do you have any material on the Curse?*

After reading the paper, Damon watched me closely for a long, unsettling moment. I gave him what I hoped was a polite and innocent-looking smile. He stood and made his slow way out of the office and in between the shelves. I took that as a yes and followed him.

"Here," he croaked, stopping in front of a bookshelf cast in shadow and gesturing at one of the upper shelves. "Just the top. Don't steal anything." He eyed me closely, then ambled away once more. As soon as he rounded the corner, I reached up and pulled everything off the top shelf. To my disappointment, there were only two thin books, but it was more than I had found thus far, so I went to one of the nearby tables, sat down, and started to read.

To my increasing chagrin, the first book was nothing more than the most recent speculation on the Curse, including theories on it being a disease, a poison, and even a jinx set upon the world by saints. The second book was utterly useless, a collection of letters sent between two researchers across two different kingdoms about how the Curse might be stopped, but they were all methods that had been tested. They worked well for killing those corrupted by the Curse, but I knew already that the Curse was a living magic of its own, and the beings corrupted were merely vessels for it. Once they died or decayed to the point that they were no longer functional, the Curse would simply move on and find a new host. With a sigh I returned the books to their shelves, losing hope of finding anything useful. As I slid the books into place, however, I spotted a scroll sitting on a lower shelf. Leaning closer, I read that it was titled '*The Cursed Mage.*' Another Cursed human aside from Alchemy? He would love to hear about this. It was dated to around three hundred years ago and was written by an author from Freetalon. I unrolled it eagerly and began to read.

From the personal journals of Aarold Olen,

A young man from Freetalon once made my acquaintance. He was a good fellow, honest and straightforward, with a hunger for knowledge and an exceptional talent for using recle. His name was Alec Galloway, and I would like to say we became friends quickly. For several months we spent time together, working side by side, testing our luck with the maidens, even going on a few exploratory journeys into the Slated Mountains. It wasn't until about a year after our meeting that Alec began to change. He wasn't satisfied with just recle. He wanted more.

I told him not to pursue other magic types, but he ignored my words of caution and dove into tunnels of research. He began to experiment with the other elements, even seeing how his own power affected them. I told him I wanted no part of it, so he said goodbye and went to find someone else who would be more supportive of his new obsession.

It was not long until all of Freetalon rejected him. Alec was shunned by all of us, for only those who have dark and evil hearts would dare to search for such forbidden powers. When this issue arose, he was given the choice to leave behind all his research and come back into the community, or to be exiled. As much as it saddened me and the woman who, despite all his wrongs, had come to call him her beloved, he chose the latter and disappeared into the mountains.

It has been several months since I've seen or heard from Alec. He used to send me letters by eagle containing updates on his experiments, but after I ignored them continually, he stopped. I somewhat miss having him around. He was a joyful man, someone that was easy to like and get along with, and he'd always had a knack for making others comfortable. It is a shame he has gone down such a dangerous path.

I fear what he will discover on his own in those mountains. He is a boisterous man, but he is not stupid, nor is he ignorant. Whatever future he has up there on his own, it is most certainly that of a cursed origin.

"That's it?" I whispered, frowning at the scroll. Something about the story unnerved me, but I couldn't place what it was. There was some aspect of it that felt *familiar*, but that couldn't have been possible. This clearly had nothing to do with the Curse; it was too old for the Curse to have existed, and these people would have known nothing of its coming. Unless . . .

The Curse *was* a forbidden power. It was evil magic, and perhaps only an evil and dark heart could have created it. But how was that possible? The Curse hadn't been around for three hundred years. Whoever this Alec Galloway man was, he couldn't have created it . . . could he?

Then things started to click. Words said carelessly, peculiar questions brushed aside, offhand statements that now held far more weight than they had when they were spoken. I knew why it was familiar to me, because in more ways than one I was reminded of someone when I read the scroll. Even the name was obvious, the similarities blindingly clear. Alec Galloway. Alec.

Alchemy.

20
KSEGA

*T*he royal archive of Brightlock contained far more information on bering than I would have expected. Scholars and researchers from Wisesol had obviously contributed greatly to the king's collection, and it didn't take me very long to find what I was looking for.

About an hour passed as I read through the materials I had selected, all of them centered on the oldest and most sacred teachings of bering-mages. As years passed, bits and pieces of information and magic inevitably slipped through the cracks of time and were lost to history, but thanks to King Kirk's diligence in expanding the royal archives, as well as the diligence of those kings before him, I was able to recover those bits and pieces.

I found teachings from all different ages and cultures, and it didn't take me long to locate a chapter focused solely on an art known as lamenting—the unique ability bering-mages possessed to alter the state of dead plants. I eagerly began to read, drinking in every morsel of knowledge I could on the subject. I had never been a particularly avid reader, but that hadn't stopped me from reading before. I had learned how to read partially from Willa and partially from my own exploring in Wisesol, where I'd been forced to pick talents up quickly. Until tonight, though, I had never read so much material in one sitting, and it was giving me a headache. Still, I pushed past the pain, more concerned about learning a new branch of my magic than giving my eyes a rest.

Lamenting was a talent that had been very common decades ago, but once bone reading was outlawed and the Curse became a problem people began to look at it as something akin to dark magic, and so it slowly fell out of practice. Very few people still remembered how to do it at will. It was strongly influenced by instinctive reactions, mainly self-defense, which explained why I had been able to use it only when I was in mortal danger. While normal bering required only the existence of emotions to function, lamenting relied on the body's physical reaction to them. The examples listed were things like an increased heart rate due to fear, anxiety, or attraction; another example went into great detail about how strong emotions of anger or mental pain could cause a person to black out or start shaking. It was even possible to use hunger as a fuel for the magic, if it affected your body and mind enough. Overall, it sounded extremely risky, nothing like what I'd thought it was. Peeler was the person I had first learned it from, when he had shown me how he could mold dead wood with the brush of a finger. I hadn't realized until now just how much physical and emotional exertion it must have taken him to use lamenting to fix the holes and injuries that *The Coventry* sustained.

I closed the books and put them back in their rightful places on the shelves, turning this new information over in my mind. I wanted to try it, because what bering-mage wouldn't? I was still learning to be familiar with the common-knowledge aspects of my magic, but I wanted to master *all of them*, and while it was an unorthodox one, lamenting was one of those aspects. The only issue was that I would need to trick myself to do it.

The sound of something clattering to the ground made me jump out of my thoughts. I leaned around the end of the bookshelf I was standing in front of and looked in the direction the sound had come from. Sakura was sitting at one of the reading tables, palms pressed against her eyes, a scroll crumpled on the floor near her feet. I couldn't be sure, but it looked like she was shaking. The dark line of crusted blood on her face mingled with fresh tears and dripped off her jaw.

"Sakura?" I asked hesitantly, walking over to her. I made to reach for the scroll on the floor, but before I could her head snapped up and she gasped, as if she hadn't heard me approach.

"Ksega, I can't—he—it was him. All along, it was him . . ." she stammered, shaking her head. I frowned.

"What was him? *Who* is him?" I asked, but before I could get an answer, we heard the sound of multiple footsteps approaching. I looked up to find a servant flanked by two guards. When she spotted us, she dipped into a polite curtsy.

"I'm here to take you to your sleeping chambers. His Majesty believes you've had ample time to review the documents he presented to you. Please, follow me." She turned and walked back towards the stairs. I looked at Sakura, unsure if we were going to listen, but she wouldn't meet my gaze as she stood, aggressively swiped her bloody tears off her face, and walked slowly after the servant. Sighing, I fell in step beside her, knowing I would be going to bed without answers.

*T*he king provided both of us with very comfortable sleeping quarters. We came to Sakura's first, and I told her a brief goodnight before she mutely shut the door, then followed the servant to my own chambers. It was a big room, with a four-poster bed, a washroom, a work desk and chair, and the biggest wardrobe I'd ever laid eyes on, somehow already filled with clothes that looked to be either my size exactly or very close to it.

Without much else to do I took a bath, wiped down my longbow, checked the condition of all my arrows, and finally flopped onto the bed. The curtains over the windows were closed, but enough silvery light spilled through the gaps to let me know it was still dark out, although how long that would last was unclear. I shut my eyes and tried to let sleep take over. It wasn't easy, because my thoughts were still clouded with worry. What had been on that scroll that upset Sakura so badly? Was it something about the Curse? And what about what *I* had read? Did I dare to try and use lamenting?

I tossed and turned in the sheets until I couldn't stand it anymore. I blew air out through my cheeks harshly, sliding out of bed and pulling on a robe before lightly blowing on one of the shrunken candles to coax it back into a bigger flame. Once enough light encircled the room, I began looking for something to experiment on. The bedposts were a solid option, but they were big, and that might mean it would be easy to lose control. A chair might work, but if I caused any irreparable damage to the piece of furniture, I doubted the king would be very graceful about it. In the end, I settled on a soap stand that I'd found in the washroom, something small enough that I could stay in charge of the magic and insignificant enough that few people would notice any alterations to its shape. The next step was actually performing the magic.

Out of the examples I'd read, the ones having to do with an accelerated heart rate had seemed like the least dangerous. The only problem I had with them was having to make my mind believe something was actually terrifying enough to warrant that reaction from my body. Unless I went with the alternative way to make my pulse race, which had to do with attraction. I felt stupid even considering it, but I knew it was a sure way to get the result I was looking for.

Pacing back and forth in front of the table I had set the soap stand on, I dragged a hand through my hair, worrying my lip as I stared down at it. I could no longer deny my own feelings to myself: I was falling for Sakura. I couldn't place the exact time I had started to notice the change, but it had been around the time we had arrived in Brightlock the first time, and ever since I hadn't been able to have a conversation with her or even be close to her without constantly losing track of my own thoughts. Then there were the moments like the one in the barn a few days ago, when she had cut my hair. It was a simple gesture of kindness, a friend doing a favor for a friend, and yet it had set my pulse thundering in my ears and sent heat crawling all over my face. And what about all those times we had held hands? Not all of them had really been in a *romantic* way, but normal friends didn't hold hands that often, did they? I had certainly never held Jessie's hand that much; just when I was small, and she wanted to make sure I didn't get lost in the bustling city of Lourak.

I realized that I had stopped pacing and was now bracing my hands on the table. Without doing it intentionally, I had managed to cause the exact reaction I had been anxious about creating. The only issue now was trying to focus on lamenting the soap stand without getting too distracted by my fluttery thoughts of Sakura.

I lifted the little object gently into my hands and took a steadying breath, smoothing my thumb over the surface and reaching as far as I could towards it with my bering. I didn't feel anything at first, and I was about to give up hope of it working when suddenly there was a light tug of connection. I gasped, surprised at its presence, and a sharp triangle of wood rammed out the side of the soap stand, jamming into my palm. I yelped and dropped the stand, hissing in pain as it landed on my bare foot. Grumbling a curse under my breath, I picked it back up and, with a shaky hand, tried again. I attempted to push the triangle back into the smooth curve of the soap stand, but instead, a second piece of wood rolled out from the opposite side, forming a gnarled knot on the corner.

"What in the name of the Endless Sea . . ?" I whispered, scowling at it. Two more attempts to fix the new knoll in the wood resulted in two *more* pieces of it curling out in the opposite direction. It was all working backwards. Peeler and the books in the archive had done a *fine* job of preparing me for that little detail. The soap stand wasn't even recognizable as a soap stand at this point, now appearing as more of an abstract star of wood, and while I was still fidgety, it was more from pent-up nerves than any true emotion, so when I next tried to mold the wood again nothing happened.

Sighing, I returned the deformed soap stand to the washroom, blew the candle out, slid out of the robe and crawled back into bed, no more satisfied than I'd been before. I shut my eyes and tried to let thoughts of sleep drown out the failures of the day.

I didn't wake up until someone pounded on the door to my chambers, shouting something about breakfast and a meeting with Otis and the cavalry captain. Groaning, I yelled at them to come in, and as I was propping myself up in the bed the door banged open and a young man stepped in, set a platter of delicious-smelling food on the table, and yanked the curtains open. I yelped as bright sunlight streamed into the room, stinging my eyes.

"Sorry, but I'm afraid you must rush through breakfast. General Otis and Captain Garris are awaiting your arrival at the stables. Your lady friend is already there, and they have requested your presence by the end of the hour, or they will start without you," he said briskly. I was about to ask what exactly they would be starting, but before I could, he left the room without another word.

Muttering to myself, I hopped out of bed, got dressed, and dug into my breakfast. It was delicious, just like the supper the night before had been, and I knew that if I wasn't careful, I would find myself addicted to the menu of royalty. As soon as I was finished, I hastily made my way out of the castle—it took some asking for directions and several wrong turns—and wandered about the grounds until I found the royal stables. The stables were grand, and while the majority of the stalls were home to many fine steeds, one of them housed a lilac purple eirioth dragon, and to my utter shock, another contained a giant gray smith. Just the sight of it sent a chill sliding down my spine, reminded of the Cursed smith that had chased Sakura and me in the Evershifting Forest. This one appeared docile, blinking lazily at me as I walked by and while that offered up a small sliver of comfort, it didn't do much to calm my buzzing nerves.

With the help of my bering, I was able to identify all the animals in the stable as ones in perfect health. Their life glows were vibrant, their eyes bright, their expressions attentive. There was only one beast in the very back stall whose life glow was slightly more diminished than the others, and by the fuzzy shape I could see through the obstacles between us, I knew who it was.

Rounding the final turn, I came face-to-face with Otis, who startled at my sudden appearance. He took a harsh step back, nearly knocking into a wiry man with uncomfortably broad shoulders and unnaturally low brows. The man was dressed in finery, although not the same way Otis was, with the army colors and the royal insignia emblazoned over his chest. Instead, he wore a more tight-fitting suit with polished bronze buttons and lots of flashy gold tassels and sashes. It was an outfit that was more for show than anything else. This man must have been the cavalry captain, a title just as much of a flaunt as the outfit. In a world where there were dragons and boats, and in a kingdom bordered only by cliffs and seas, what purpose did a cavalry captain actually serve?

"There you are," Otis huffed through his mustache. "I was just about to come looking for you. We're about to begin the negotiations regarding you keeping the dragon you stole." He crossed his thick arms over his chest and sniffed, his disdain for our request evident.

"He has quite clearly been through many years of poor treatment. Whoever has been in charge of his care has been exceedingly neglectful," the cavalry captain—Garris, if I remembered correctly—stated. Sakura, standing behind him with her arms crossed, raised a dubious eyebrow. I looked her up and down once, taking note of the line of red across her cheek and the way she stood with slumped shoulders. I wasn't the only one who had slept poorly.

"And that means?" Otis prompted. We all looked expectantly at the captain.

"That means that he cannot be taken back to wherever he was homed before," Garris stated plainly. Otis's features fell ever so slightly, although even he must have been able to tell from Asuka's ragged appearance that we had been telling the truth.

"So he comes with us, right?" I asked, my gaze darting over to Sakura to try and read her reaction. A little to my shock, I found she wasn't really listening, instead staring towards the ground, lost in her own thoughts.

"Are you capable of giving him the care he needs?" Garris's eyes narrowed at me. I huffed and crossed my arms, making sure to level my eyes with his own and add an arrogant jut to my chin. I debated allowing arrogance to flood into my voice as well, but the key to convincing people of your confidence was knowing how to not overdo it.

"Yes, we are. He's already in a much better condition than the one we found him in, and that's thanks to the few days he spent with us being well-fed and cared for," I said. Out of the corner of my eye, I saw Sakura lifting her head as she tuned back into the conversation.

"He will be safe with us," Sakura said, her voice still raw but no longer incomprehensible. Garris turned his doubtful face to her, but she didn't waver.

"Trust us," I urged. "Sakura has grown up with and raised eirioth dragons herself. She knows how to handle them." A long moment of silence passed between us before he finally nodded, satisfied with our answers.

"Very well. Otis, see that the dragon is returned to them. His Majesty also ordered that enough provisions be given to them to last their journey home. Good day." He stooped into a polite bow and turned to leave. Otis waited until he was gone before grumbling out a string of curses and gesturing at the stall where Asuka was.

"Go on, get your dragon ready to leave. I'll have the other necessary things set in order before your departure. Meet me in the courtyard in half an hour. Don't be late, or you're not getting the provisions." And then he was gone too, waddling his way out the stable doors after the captain. The first thing I did was turn to Sakura, but the first thing she did was push her way into Asuka's stall and wrap her arms around his neck, burying her face in his feathers.

"Are you alright?" I asked, following her into the stall. The tack Maki had given us was propped on the wall nearby, and I began to gather it together, patiently waiting for an answer I wasn't sure would come.

"Let's go. I want to get back as soon as possible. We have people waiting for us." She avoided the question, gently stroking Asuka's face as he shuffled his wings. He snuffled at her hands for a moment, then pressed his face closer to her. I didn't pry any further for the moment, although I knew I would be asking more questions soon enough, and I was fairly certain she knew it too.

On a brighter note, she was right. If everything had gone as planned, Jessie would be waiting with Derek and the pirates at the camp with Alchemy and the others. I couldn't wait to see her. As much as I was enjoying traveling with Sakura and Alchemy, and now Gian and Beth as well, a part of me was longing for a piece of home. Maybe it was all the conversations I'd been having with Sakura about family, or maybe it was just so much time apart that made my heart squeeze with excitement. Only a few more days and I'd be back with my dearest friend.

"Yeah," I agreed numbly, grunting as I lifted the saddle into my arms. Sakura fastened the bridle into place on Asuka's head while I strapped the saddle around his middle, leaving it loose for his comfort. I didn't have to talk to Sakura to know we wouldn't be riding the dragon for most of the trip. He would be carrying most of the packs and supplies for us. As much as I wanted to avoid more days full of walking, I knew it was the best option for Asuka, so I would accept it.

We met Otis in the courtyard, where he helped us load Asuka's saddle with sacks of provisions. I had been expecting to leave with only some new knowledge, but I wasn't about to turn down some of the castle chef's cooking if it was offered. Once we were ready to leave, Otis gave us a thick piece of parchment paper about the size of a bookmark. The royal seal was emblazoned on it, and the back had a scrawl of cursive writing across it.

"It declares both of you as the rightful owners of the eirioth dragon. All persons who own such a creature within the borders of Brightlock must possess one of these small deeds. That's how we catch poachers and smugglers." He sniffed at us, still maintaining his indignant demeanor. "That paper right there says that the performers are no longer the legal owners of this dragon. You lose that paper, you lose the dragon, understood? Good. Now get out of my sight before I decide to arrest you for something else." He skulked away, leaving us to make our way out of the courtyard and through the heavily reinforced gates on our own.

Neither of us said anything for a long time, focusing on putting one foot in front of the other and ignoring the strange looks given to us by anyone we passed. At least we weren't on the run from Locker guards anymore. We didn't speak until we arrived at an inn in

Candle and bought a room for the night. After Asuka had been given a small space in a lean-to in the back, we sat down to a meager dinner of game stew and stale bread and had our first conversation of the day.

"I found some pretty interesting things to read in the archives," I said. She grunted, stirring her stew with her spoon and staring into it.

"Me too." Was her only response.

"I read about bering. I've already told you about the life glows and stuff, and you know about how it can work with animals, but apparently there's also this thing called lamenting that allows bering-mages to manipulate dead plants." I slurped at my stew, waiting for a reaction from her. She kept stirring her food. I watched her for a long moment, taking in her features. Her left side was turned away from me, so I couldn't see how the cut on her cheek was doing, but she hadn't complained about it yet, and I wasn't going to pry about treating it. Instead, I continued. "I tried it last night. It's really weird. Everything about it is backwards; it's almost like learning how to use my bering all over again, just in reverse." I watched her closely, but again she didn't respond. I sighed heavily. "And then a sea wraith crawled through the window and ate my blankets, and I had to use one of the icicles growing from my hair to drive it out." Still nothing. I reached out and tapped her on the shoulder. Her eyes snapped up to mine, and she blinked.

"What? Yes. I'm listening," She mumbled.

"No you aren't." I frowned at her. "Something's going on. What did you find in the archives? What was on that scroll?" I couldn't think of anything that might affect her in such a way except information about the Curse. But if it was about the Curse, why wasn't she telling me about it?

"It was a journal entry," she said, staring down into her stew again. I hadn't seen her take a single bite. I waited patiently for her to continue. It took her a moment, but eventually, she found her words and went on. "It was written by a man from Freetalon. Chem is a Talon. You knew that, right?" she looked up at me, and I nodded. She licked her lips nervously, her hands tightening on her spoon and bowl. "Well . . . that journal entry was dated about three hundred years ago. You—" she paused, cleared her throat, and forced herself to meet my gaze. "You talk to Chem a lot. Has he ever mentioned his age to you?"

"Bit of an odd question," I said, trying to keep my tone light. I had no idea where she was going with this but turned my past conversations with Alchemy over in my mind to give her an answer. "No, I don't believe so," I said finally. Her eyes fell to her bowl again.

"I've asked him about it before, but he would never give me a straight answer, and when I first met him . . ." She worried her lower lip between her teeth, and I waited. "When we first met, he asked me how old he sounded, and he was surprised and . . . I guess the right word would be *happy* when I told me that it wasn't very old. I've never thought much of it until now, but after reading that scroll it all makes sense." She dropped her spoon and pressed her face into her hands, shaking her head. "I can't believe I never put it all together before. I can't believe I didn't *try*."

"Never put *what* together?" I asked, leaning closer. A shaky sigh escaped her lips, and she split her fingers apart so she could look at me between them.

"I . . . I'm not sure. Yet. I think I'm right, but the more I run through it in my mind, the more I wonder if I might be wrong." She dropped her hands, bunching them into fists in her lap.

"Why don't you tell me? Maybe I can help you figure it out," I offered, reaching forward. Slowly, I took one of her hands, uncurled it, and threaded our fingers together. She swallowed, looking down at our clasped hands, and was quiet for a long time. The activity of the inn buzzed around us, but I hardly heard the bouts of laughter and spritely music that flowed through the air.

"It hurts, Ksega." She closed her eyes, her jaw flexing. "What I think I've found . . . it hurts me, and it will hurt you too; but it's all based on an *if*." She drew in a long breath and looked up at me once more. "Give me a few days. Once we get back with the others, let me make sure I'm right, and then I'll tell you, even if I'm wrong." She squeezed my hand. "I trust you, Ksega. I'll tell you everything, but I don't want both of us to be upset over nothing. Does that make sense?"

"Yes," I lied softly. I doubted any of it would make sense until she told me, but I trusted that she was telling the truth, and that I would know it soon enough. Instead of pushing the conversation further, I used my free hand to push her stew bowl closer to her. She eyed it glumly.

"I'm not hungry," she muttered.

"You need to eat something. We both do, and then we need to get some sleep." I summoned the most encouraging smile I could. "Don't worry, we'll be back with our friends in a couple days," I reminded her. Oddly enough, that didn't seem to lift the mood in the slightest.

21
SAKURA

The days seemed to pass too quickly. Anxiety wormed through my gut with each step closer to the Evershifting Forest. I was excited to see Derek again, and I'd even found myself missing Beth and Gian a little too, but the joy I felt at getting to see them again soon was severely diminished by the fear of who I had to confront. I had missed Alchemy as well, because who wouldn't? He was funny and protective and caring and a *fantastic* cook. He was like a young father or a well-learned older brother. No matter what problem you had, you knew he could help solve it . . . but not this time. This time, he *was* the problem.

I wanted to tell Ksega about what I had found and what I thought it meant, but I couldn't bear the thought of being wrong and causing both of us so much distress over nothing. I had to be sure before I told him. The only downside was having to talk to Alchemy about it alone.

We stopped by Maki's house in the Star Key, where she insisted we keep the dragon tack because "she no longer had any need of it," and again at Jhapato's when we passed the Stargazing Colonies, where we were given a hearty dinner of soup and bread. Both times there had been quite a display of concern for our bedraggled state, but we refused to be doctored up. There wasn't time, and besides, the worst of our injuries was the slice in my cheek. It had scabbed over, and wasn't bothering me much, so it could be left alone.

The visits did little to lift my spirits, but I put an effort into raising my mood for Ksega's sake. I could tell he was worried about me, but I couldn't think of any way to put his mind at ease until I could give him all the answers.

It was dusk when we reached the edge of the Evershifting Forest. Ksega was practically buzzing with excitement, bubbling over with so much energy that it rubbed off on Asuka and set both of them prancing with anticipation. I was too busy trying not to throw up to get either of them to settle down.

The Forest had adopted the guise of thick pine trees and thistly bushes, cloaked in a low-rolling fog that glowed gold in the light of the setting sun. Our boots sent the fog whirling into the air in curious tendrils, brushing against our legs and leaving traces of dust on our clothes. I tried to keep my focus on navigating the surroundings and ignoring the prickly sensation that raised the hairs on the back of my neck. Was Alchemy waiting for us, keeping an eye on the tree line? Was he close by? I couldn't shake the feeling that he was watching us from afar, and that he knew I had discovered his secret.

If it's his secret at all. I had to keep reminding myself that there was a chance I was wrong. There was very little proof, aside from what existed in my memory of Alchemy's behavior and the entirely circumstantial connections from the journal entry. There was only one way I would know for sure what the truth was, and I was terrifyingly close to discovering it.

When we got closer to the campsite, my heart lifted for the first time in days. The sounds of people laughing and sharing stories curled through the air, painfully reminding me of life at the inn when the townspeople would eat dinner and enjoy entertainment and ale in the tavern downstairs. A warmth stirred in my gut as we came closer, stopping a short distance away to tether Asuka to a young pine sapling so he wouldn't be spooked by all the noise. I couldn't help the smile that split my lips when we pushed our way into the large clearing that was home to a sprawling campsite and filled with people.

The pirates were the first ones I noticed. It was hard to miss them, with their shiny metal body parts or their notable lack thereof. Theomand was also easy to spot, reclined against a tree with Wynchell curled protectively nearby. There were many tents set up around the clearing, and two separate bonfires were blazing on either side of the camp. I spotted Beth lounging beside one of them, gnawing aggressively on what looked to be a stale bread roll. Slightly to my surprise, Gian sat just beside her, eating another bread roll in a much more refined manner. For once, neither of them was giving the other a nasty glare; instead they were listening intently to a pale, ginger-haired man that I vaguely remembered from Clawbreak.

"*Trouble!*" a voice broke through the hubbub of conversation, shouting over everyone else's and drawing all eyes towards the shade of the pine trees, away from all the activity, where two people stood. Almost in unison, Ksega and I sprinted towards them.

"Jessie!" Ksega's legs were longer, and he beat me to them, throwing himself into the arms of the red-haired girl I recognized from Famark. She nearly fell over from his momentum but managed to keep her balance and return the embrace. Seconds later, I was crushed in a bear hug by Derek.

"You're okay!" he practically yelled into my ear. He shoved me roughly back to arms length and gave me a once-over. "You *are* okay, right?"

"Yeah," I wheezed, grimacing. Bruises would most definitely be forming from how tight that hug was. "Have you put on some muscle? By the stars and clouds, that kind of hurt." I rubbed my arm, looking him up and down. He was definitely bigger, and his shirt hugged him tightly enough for me to make out defined muscles. *Those* hadn't been there before.

"A bit, I guess," Derek admitted, rubbing the back of his neck as he took a step away from me, tossing a glance in Jessie's direction. "I've been practicing with lightning a bit more, and it requires a lot more physical strength, so I've been working out here and there."

"'Here and there', he says," Jessie hopped in, putting her hands on her hips as she stepped back from Ksega, who was still grinning from ear to ear. "Practically every day you'd be able to find him working on his muscles. You should've seen how often he'd flex at himself in the mirror." She smirked over at Derek, whose pale complexion was pinkening. "Yeah, I saw you."

"Hey, leave him alone, that's just a guy thing," Ksega said, flexing his own muscles and somehow widening his grin. Derek only scowled at him.

"Your hair is a bit longer, too," I observed. A lot about him had changed, actually, but I wasn't going to point every detail out. He seemed to be more outgoing than usual, although I couldn't explain why. It didn't matter anyway.

"I don't even know what to say," Ksega said through an awkward chuckle, echoing my own thoughts. "How've you guys been? What have you been up to? How long have you been with the pirates?" he turned and waved a hand at the crowd behind us, all now refocused on their meals or their conversations. Gian and Beth spotted us and gave us a wave but made no move to come and join us. I guessed they wanted to give us some time to catch up.

"There's so much to talk about. We've discovered quite a lot about the Curse, and—" Jessie began, but I cut her off.

"And it can wait until later. For now, I need to talk to Chem. Do you know where he is?" I ignored Ksega's confused look, watching only Derek.

His brows twitched in momentary confusion before he said, "The skeleton? Yeah, he's usually lurking somewhere over that way." He pointed into the woods, tilting his head to the side as he studied me. "Want me to go with you?"

"No," I said quickly. "I'll go alone. Besides, there's an eirioth dragon you need to take care of. I don't know where Bear is, but they might be good friends. Ksega can take you to where we left him. We'll explain everything later, but this has to come first." I gasped in a breath, surprised at how dizzy I suddenly felt. Had my hands always been shaking? I knew I must have been brimming with anxiety, and from the expressions of those around me, I could tell they knew it too, but I refused to let it get to me.

"Aaalright . . ." Derek was still frowning at me. I knew things had changed about me, too, but I had a sinking feeling that my inability to keep my emotions a secret was not one of them.

"Alright. I'll be back later, then." I started towards the woods, but a hand on my arm stopped me. I gave Ksega an irritable glance, hoping he would let this go.

An argument was perched on my tongue, but he surprised me by asking, "Do you want something for your throat first? I'm sure Jessie can whip something up quickly."

"I'm fine," I said, pulling my arm out of his grip. His smile had faded.

"You're sure? You've still been coughing these last few days . . ." He left the question hanging, but I wouldn't be won over.

"I'm sure. I'll be back later," I repeated, pivoting and marching into the darkening woods before another word could be said.

Winter was upon Horcath, and the Evershifting Forest had welcomed it heartily. As I hunted through the thickly packed pine trees, searching for any sign of Alchemy, it began to snow. Dustings of fine icy powder coated the pine boughs and settled on my shoulders after only a few minutes. I felt numb, but with my eirioth I knew it wasn't because of the cold. I wasn't sure how far I'd walked, and with the layers of snow now blanketing the earth, it was impossible to tell where I was, but I knew Alchemy would be making an appearance soon. I couldn't explain how I knew, but I did, so I kept walking until I found a large boulder tucked away beneath a pine tree, dusted as much snow off as I could, and sat down to wait. I pulled the crimson dragon feather from my belt and worried it between my fingers, trying to focus on its texture and how it felt in my hand instead of what I knew I had to do next. It was only a handful of minutes before he appeared.

"Ironling, you're back!" his voice, familiar in its unusual gruffness, was far too cheerful for the occasion. He materialized out of the shadows, draped in his long cloak and hurrying through the snow towards me with something bundled in his hands. He must have sensed that this would not be a pleasant visit because he slowed to a stop several feet from where I sat, veiled in the shadows of the snow-covered pine.

"Yes. I'm back," I said, surprising myself with how empty my own voice was. I had put a lot of thought into what I would say to him, but now that I was here and staring at those vein-like cracks glowing in the winter moonlight, I found that all the words had vanished from my tongue.

"And Ksega is too, right? Where is he?" he looked around, although it was obvious that Ksega wasn't here.

"Yes, he's back too. He had matters to tend to back at the camp." I dropped my gaze, rubbing numb thumbs over my knuckles. "Besides, I wanted to talk to you for a bit . . . Alec." It was the first time I'd said the name aloud, and immediately it felt all wrong. I wanted to take the word back and call him Chem instead and pretend I'd never read that stupid scroll. But how could I, when I was finally so close to getting some answers?

Alchemy's silence spoke for itself. He was deathly still, an ominously thin black figure painted on a canvas of white and gray. A small shadow squirmed in his gloved hands, and I finally made it out to be the little black kitten Ksega had brought back from the Stargazing Colonies. In all honesty, I was a little surprised it had survived this long.

"I learned all about you from your friend, Aarold," I continued, my voice steely. Alchemy took a few steps forward, seeming to grow taller and thinner and more imposing than ever before. I shrank back against my boulder but refused to drop my gaze, staring resolutely into the soulless pits of his eye sockets. When he spoke, his voice was so low and gravelly that it grated against my ears, seemingly coming from every direction at once.

"*Where did you hear those names?*"

"I found them." Finally, the iciness in my voice shattered, and my words quivered. I was leaning so far back into the rock that I could feel the melted snow soaking into the back of my shirt, although it wasn't the only reason my body was overcome with chills. My eyes now darted frantically between Alchemy's—no, Alec's—skull and his arms, which still cradled the kitten. Beneath that kitten and the sleeves of his shirt were leather sheaths strapped to his bones, and in those sheaths were twin daggers made from the canines of the biggest smith Alec had ever killed. I had witnessed firsthand how quickly he could end a life with those very blades.

"Where did you find them, Sakura?" his voice had settled just a little, but it still held the dangerous edge that set my thoughts skittering in terrified circles through my brain.

"The archives. They said . . . Chem, Alchemy, Alec, whoever you are"—I pushed myself further up on the boulder, inching towards the other side as he loomed balefully closer. The dragon feather slipped out of my hand—"you have to tell me if it's true." My voice broke again, my arms trembling from the cold and the fear that pulsed through me.

"Tell you *what?*" he demanded, the question made all the more hollow by the howling wintry winds that roared over the treetops. A broken mewling sound squeaked out from Alec's hands, but he didn't look down, his focus trained solely on me.

"Was it you?" my raw voice had broken down into little more than a whisper, hardly audible over the pounding of my heart and the whistling of the forest around us. I didn't need to say anything more, because he knew I had figured it out. A rattling sigh left him, and he leaned back again, turning his skull away to stare at the swirling snow.

"Yes," he answered. My breath escaped me in a choked sob. Emotions flooded me, clouding my vision, muddying my thoughts. My head spun, as if my body refused to comprehend what I had just been told.

Alchemy had *created* the Curse. It was the answer I had been hunting for, and yet I was left with more questions and more pain than I could have imagined. Pain and sadness and *rage*.

"How . . ." I shook my head, gaping up at him. My hands curled into fists, and I launched myself back up onto my feet. "*Why* would you help me?!" he jerked back, surprised by my anger. "What sort of sick, twisted animal are you?!" hot tears pushed against my eyes. "You killed them! Moma, Papa, Aurora, Elixir—all of them are dead because of you! You're a *murderer*!" the tears spilled over, running in frozen trails down my cheeks.

"Sakura, lower your voice. The pirates—" He stepped closer, reaching a gloved hand out for me but I stumbled away, avoiding him as if any contact would burn me.

"Stay away from me! You're mad!" I screeched, my throat burning with pain as I screamed it raw once more.

"I don't think *I'm* the mad one in this situation. Please, Ironling, let me explain—" he hugged the little kitten to his chest, and his voice shriveled into something almost meek, but I wouldn't fall for his lies anymore. I had been too forgiving and too ignorant before, and I would never let it happen again.

"*No*! There is no explaining this away!" I gasped in the frigid air, ignoring the piercing pain that sliced at my neck from the inside out. My vision swam with lightheadedness, and I stumbled even farther away from him, furiously shaking my head, refusing to believe it.

"Ironling," he said softly, and I roared with fury, swiping my hand out and sending an arc of flames rushing into him. He bowed away from them, but they caught his cloak and sizzled to life, eating through the fabric. He yelped and unclasped it, throwing it onto the snow. With a hiss the flames were doused, and a spiral of smoke rose into the frigid air.

"*Never* call me that again!" I fumed, my voice shaking. The tears were turning to ice on my face and neck, making my shivering worse, but the chill began to seep out of my body when I clenched my fists and let balls of eirioth spring to life around them. "I should've put it together right from the start," I blubbered. "As soon as you asked about the Talon king from generations ago, I should have known, but I didn't question it. I was so willing to believe that you wanted to help!" I yelled the last part, throwing one of the orbs of flame into the snow. It warped up into a wave of silvery orange before falling in an ashen mist.

"I *do* want to help." Alec tried to reason, taking hesitant steps away from me. "Just listen, Sakura, for one moment. I never wanted to hurt anyone, I swear, I thought I was helping people. I thought I was inventing a new type of magic that could solve problems."

His voice was turning desperate. The kitten squirmed uncomfortably in his arms. I glared at him, disgusted.

"You can't justify this! You're the reason for hundreds upon thousands of deaths, and you think you're *helping*?!" I hurled the other ball of fire at him, and he ducked away before it could catch on his clothes again. It barreled into a pine tree, licking hungrily at the wood, but finding only a damp wall that snuffed it out all too quickly.

"I'm not trying to justify this, Sakura, I never would." Alec argued. "It was wrong, and I see that now, and no words could ever express how sorry I am for the pain I have caused. I've lived with the knowledge of what I created for *three hundred miserable years.*" His voice cracked, but it was just another farce, another excuse to get me to trust him again. How could someone without a heart *ever* sympathize with those who had lost the people they loved?

"But you could stop it!" I screamed. "You made it, so put an end to it! Where's the source? Is it you? Why haven't you destroyed it if you hate it so much?!" I broke into a fit of sobs, my shoulders slumping with resignation. Why had he let this happen? Did he just want to see the world fall into shambles?

"I wish I could!" Alec cried, hugging himself tighter and causing the kitten to mewl in distress. "But it did something to me. The moment the Curse was created, it corrupted me, and all the years that it ate away at my flesh have been forgotten. I don't remember them. There's nothing but clouded, pain-filled memories of screaming people and lonely nights until finally I found a place I could hide. The Evershifting Forest was the only place that would accept me after that, and I've lived here ever since!" his skull fell, staring at the snow beneath his feet. "You and Ksega have been my only friends in hundreds of years." My breath plumed in uneven gusts before my face as I glowered at him, shaking from the cold and my own wrath.

"I didn't ask for you to grovel. I want an answer, Alchemy. *Where* is the source?" I practically shrieked over the wind. When he next spoke, it sounded like he was crying, but I knew that was impossible. I doubted he was even capable of feeling anything at this point.

"I don't know. I swear, I don't. I've always figured it must be somewhere in the Slated Mountains, where I worked to create it, but after years of searching, I gave up hope. If nobody had found it by then, why should I believe it could *ever* be found?" he turned to the side, angling his skull away from me. The moonlight illuminated his hand as he comfortingly rubbed the little kitten between the ears. Another sob tore from my throat, and a new wave of tears ran down my face.

"But why hasn't it existed all this time? If you've been Cursed for three hundred years, why hasn't it affected all of us for that long?" I asked, hugging myself to try and fight the whirling cold. My eirioth roared within me, desperate to be set free, but I knew better than to let it out. With my emotions in such turmoil as they were, nothing good could come of that.

"It was trapped. I locked it away, but somehow, it's been released." Alec's broad shoulder blades slumped in defeat. "I don't think it can be stopped again."

"So that's it? It was all for nothing?" I cried. Leaving Finnian and Gamma, running away from my kingdom when it needed me to stay and fight, going through all the pain and struggles of this journey—it had it all been in vain? Was Beth right from the start, that this was a suicide mission that would land us all nowhere?

"No, Ironling, it can't be. We've come this far, and—"

"There is no *we*," I shouted, cutting him off. The tears burned my skin, then they froze, and the ice burned it again. Everything would burn after tonight. "Leave," I rasped.

His skull snapped back to me. "What?"

"You heard me. *Leave.* Go back to your cave, you miserable pile of bones!" I was trembling as I said it, my heart feeling like it was being shredded to pieces by some beast's vicious claws. "I never want to see you again. You deserve to rot with what you've done, alone and in the dark until all of Horcath sinks into the Endless Sea!"

"Sakura?"

My head whipped around. Ksega was standing in the snow-filled clearing, his eyes wide and distraught and confusion etched into his face. He looked between me and Alec in bewilderment. "What's happening? Why are you screaming? We can hear you from the camp. I said I'd come look alone, but they might follow, and—" he stopped himself, stepping hesitantly closer to us but staying in the middle, unsure who he should go to. "What's going on?" he finished weakly.

"Don't worry about it, Ksega," Alec said shakily, an accepting tone lacing his words. "It appears I am no longer welcome here, so I'll be taking my leave. I'm bringing Hook with me, if that's alright." He clutched the kitten to his heartless chest. "I'd like the company."

"What? Don't say that, of course you're welcome—" Ksega began to object, but I spoke over him.

"No, Ksega, he isn't. He needs to leave. Now." My voice was so unsteady and I felt so dizzy that I was sure I'd fall over at any moment, but I wouldn't let myself until Alec was out of my sight.

"Very well." Alec stepped through the snow, going around Ksega and giving me a wide berth.

"No, wait, you're serious?" Ksega started towards him, then turned and gave me a pleading look. "Sakura—?" he squeaked. I merely looked away, unable to tolerate the pain and confusion in his eyes. He raised his voice. "No, Chem, wait. Please, stop!" the sound of the skeleton's boots crunching through the snow didn't cease. "No!" Ksega yelled. "Why are you doing this? We're friends! Sakura!" he turned to me, but I could no longer read his expression through my tears.

"I'm sorry. To both of you." Alec's hoarse voice echoed through the snowy clearing. By the time I turned to look at him, he was gone, leaving only a trail of footprints in the snow.

22
KSEGA

I'm sorry. To both of you." Alchemy's voice rumbled back through the clearing. The dull buzz in the back of my mind grew fainter and fainter as I watched Alchemy disappear into the forest, and all the while, a rift grew larger and larger in my chest.

"Sakura . . ." I hurried to her, my panic spiking as I saw her swaying back and forth. I reached out and steadied her, taking notice of the tears that ran in torrents down her face. The scar on her cheek was like a sliver of white against her skin, distorted by her tears. "What's going on?" I asked as softly as I could. She shook her head pitifully, only managing a choked sob as her head fell forward into my chest. I looked through the snow where Alchemy had vanished, desperate to chase after him and ask for an explanation, but Sakura wasn't stable enough on her own two feet for me to leave her. My chest tightened as I stared at Alchemy's bootprints, racking my brain for any reason this could have happened.

"Trouble?!" Jessie's voice pushed through Sakura's crying, and I looked over my shoulder to see her and Derek walking through the snow towards us, concern evident on both their faces. They were bundled in layers of clothing, and Jessie held two furry coats in her arms.

"We're okay. I think. Mostly," I told them, my voice tight with emotion as a lump formed in my throat. "Just cold," I added when Sakura shuddered as a bitter breeze rushed past us.

"Here, put these on. Quickly." Jessie wrapped one of the fur coats around my shoulders and laid the other over Sakura, who still had her face buried in my shirt.

"What's going on?" Derek asked, crossing his arms and narrowing his eyes as he took in the melted snow and burned cloak.

"That's what I'm trying to figure out," I answered. "Come on, let's get her back to the camp. She's hardly eaten in days, and she needs to rest." I shrugged the fur coat into a more comfortable position around myself, and Sakura backed up to do the same, attempting to keep her head down to conceal her tears.

"I'm fine. I don't need rest," she spat, although the moment I was no longer supporting her she began to sway again.

"Yeah, no one believes that," Derek deadpanned. She looked sharply up at him, her jaw set, but he only raised an eyebrow. "Don't make me carry you back. You know I will." She grumbled beneath her breath but stopped arguing. I put an arm around her so she wouldn't fall over, and we all began to walk back towards the camp. I considered picking up Alchemy's cloak as we passed it, but something told me we wouldn't be needing it.

"Where's the skeleton?" Jessie asked as we trudged through the snow. Sakura tensed under my arm, and I thought she wouldn't answer for a moment.

"He's gone," Sakura said after a moment. "For good." Derek tilted his head at her, and for a second, I thought he was going to pry about it, but he seemed to think better of it right before he opened his mouth. His gaze lifted to meet mine, but I had no more answers than he did, so we all remained silent the rest of the way.

*S*he's finally eating something." Jessie came out of Sakura's tent to join us by one of the fires. It was around midnight, perhaps a little after, and most of the pirates had already turned in. Theomand, Wendy, and Old Hank were keeping watch around the camp, and only a few people had stayed out around the bonfires. Gian, Beth, Derek, Jessie, and I were around one, and Chap, Molly, Thomas, and Peeler were hunched around the other. All the pirates and Theomand had their tents set up on the far side of the clearing, which meant the rest of us had been given whatever room was left. It was convenient for a private conversation between our little inner circle.

"Has she said anything else about her argument with Chem?" I asked, looking up from my plate of roasted salmon. Even if he wasn't as good a cook as Alchemy was, Knuckles, the chef and honorary "uncle" of *The Coventry*, was a talented master of the culinary arts, and anything he made was delicious. We were lucky he was there to cook for all of us. Unfortunately, I found myself with little appetite.

"Not yet. She says she wants to tell you about it first." Jessie sat between Derek and I, slowly pulling her braids loose. She looked tired, and I felt a brief pang of guilt as I realized I hadn't asked about how *she* was doing. There had been so much excitement that it had simply slipped my mind, but I should have remembered sooner how much of a hassle it could be dealing with the pirates for more than a day or two.

"Do you have any idea what may have started it?" Beth was stroking Taro's soft feathers as she listened, her dark gaze pinned on the flickering fire. Beside her, Gian was trying to fix his hair in the reflection of his sword.

"It's sort of a long story . . ." I dragged a hand over my face as I spoke, sighing into my palms as I turned the events of the last few days over in my mind.

"Don't worry, we have time. She'll be resting in there for a while," Jessie assured me. She gave us a sheepish smile. "I might have slipped a sleeping draught into her food. It's completely harmless, aside from making her sleepy for a couple hours and perhaps causing excess crankiness when she wakes up, but I figured she needed the rest before she tried to put all her emotions into words."

"Smart move," Derek muttered, groaning as he leaned back onto the frosted grass and looked up at the sky. "She's always been too stubborn to admit when she needs to take a break."

"Why is that?" I asked, absent-mindedly pulling an arrow from my quiver and turning it over in my hands to give myself something to do, and to distract me from the aching thoughts that threatened to overwhelm me.

"You first, archer. Explain why Sakura's been in such a bad mood." He peered at me over the fluff of his fur coat. Everyone else turned expectantly to me as well, and with another sigh I began the story.

I told them everything, from going to see the traveling performers to stealing Asuka to flying over the castle walls. Gian and Beth looked downhearted when I explained that the Locker family was not responsible for creating the Curse, but Derek and Jessie didn't seem so surprised. I was practically bursting with questions for them, but they refused to share anything until all of us could hear it, so I focused on mine and Sakura's tale. There wasn't much to tell after that, except the volumes of history on the Locker kings and the text I had found on bering-mages. I told them about Sakura and the scroll, and then about Sakura's strange behavior all the way back to the camp.

"And now she's sent Chem away, for whatever reason." I put the arrow away and raked a hand through my hair, staring into the fire. "I don't understand. She said that whatever she was unsure about might make me upset, and she must have been right, because we are both *definitely* upset." I let out a frustrated groan and looked over at Beth and Gian. "Has Chem done or told you anything strange while we've been gone? She must be mad at him for something big."

"Nothing aside from his usual jabbering," Gian said, combing his fingers carefully through his hair.

"And unnecessary affection for his little vermin," Beth added. She wrinkled her nose. "Did he take the poor thing with him?"

"Yes." I pulled my coat tighter around me to try and get warmer, but nothing seemed to dispel the cold. The fire was struggling to stay alive in the gusts of wind that swirled through the camp, and everyone was shivering despite being within its little circle of quivering light.

"Well, there's no sense in dwelling on it if we won't know until Sakura tells us. I guess I can explain a couple things about why she's here at all in the meantime." Derek sat up again, brushing flakes of snow from his coat.

"Are you sure it's your place to tell those things?" Jessie asked uncertainly, dragging her hands through her hair to make sure there were no tangles left now that she had taken out her braids.

"I'm not going into all the grim details, just the important things." Derek shrugged her question away. "The whole reason she went on this quest of hers was to find a way to destroy the Curse because of the threat it poses to the ones she loves. We risked our lives fighting her brother's dragon when the Curse claimed him, and she decided that was enough. She lost the rest of her family to the Curse when she was small, like I did, so I can understand her motives." He waved a hand at the fire before us, sending it roaring back to life. A wave of heat washed over us, so sudden I gasped and nearly toppled over backwards.

"I didn't know that about her," Gian commented once everyone had settled again.

"She doesn't like to bring it up, but if you ever want to know for sure if you have her trust, ask her to tell you the story." Derek steepled his fingers and gazed into the rejuvenated fire. I blinked at him, a little baffled.

"Just like that? If she trusts us, she'll tell us?" I questioned. I had asked her about her past enough times to be confident in the fact that it was not something she disclosed easily. I knew that the Curse had taken her parents and her sister, Aurora, but she hadn't told me how it had happened.

"Yes," Derek replied confidently.

"And that doesn't make you feel like you're crossing a line?" Jessie's brows pulled together as she studied Derek. He shrugged again.

"That's how trust works. Once you believe that someone will tell you the whole truth, you'll trust them enough to and ask." He rose to his feet and stamped snow off his boots. "If they trust you, they'll give you their answer. If they don't, they'll let you know they don't want you crossing that line yet. Now, I'm going to get some sleep. We'll all be getting some answers in the morning, and I have a feeling I'll want to be somewhat rested when we do. Good night." We were all quiet as he made his way to his tent and disappeared inside.

After a pause, Beth sighed and stood as well. "I guess that's our cue to get some sleep, too. I'll see you all in the morning." She dipped her head at us and slipped stealthily away to her own tent. Gian took his leave as well, which left Jessie and I sitting in uncomfortable silence beside the fire.

"A lot has changed, hasn't it?" Jessie asked finally. I nodded mutely. "We're doing something, though, and that makes all the change worth it. I was scared half to death about what was happening with you the whole time, but at least I had something to do to distract me from it."

"Yeah, I was worried too. But everything turned out okay in the end, I think. We didn't find the source of the Curse, but . . ." I trailed off with a sigh. I couldn't find a bright side to this that outweighed the failure.

"But we're back together," Jessie finished for me. "And we can go home, and you'll be with Willa, and everything will go back to normal." She leaned closer, watching me intently. After a long moment of scrutinizing, she sighed and shook her head. "Yeah, right. We all know nothing will be the same after everything that's happened."

"Nope." I agreed, hugging my knees to my chest. "It'll never be the same again."

23
SAKURA

*T*he moment I was fully awake, I knew Jessie had drugged me. It made sense that she would, and I'd even had my suspicions about it when she'd first handed me the bowl of stew, but I had been too hungry and tired to act on my instincts and ignore the food.

Grogginess muddled my thoughts and made my head heavy, but I forced myself upright to take in my surroundings. The tent I was in had been loaned to me by the pirates, as well as most of the things inside. My flame-sword sat beside my bedroll, along with my belt and a pile of warm clothing. I hurried to pull on the thick clothes, the fur-lined boots and the slate–wolf–pelt coat, stuffing a pair of fuzzy gloves into the coat pocket before crawling out of the tent. Icy wind slapped my face the moment I left the confines of the tent's thick fabric, and I shuddered as I wrapped my fur coat tighter around myself.

The camp was more alive than it had been the night before and teeming with people. The clearing the tents were set up in was by no means small, but with close to forty people occupying it, it quickly became crowded. Early morning light shone brightly into the clearing, reflecting off the glittering snow that bowed the pine tree branches and skirted every tent. The sound of fires crackling and people talking flooded my ears, unfamiliar after all the time I'd spent traveling with such a small group of people. The smell of salty bacon was drifting through the air as well, reminding my stomach that Jessie's sleeping tonic had not been enough to satisfy my hunger.

I approached the nearest bonfire, around which sat Ksega, Gian, Beth, Jessie, and Derek. Beth was the first one to see me coming, and she scooted to the side to make room for me in the circle between her and Jessie. The sound of my boots crunching in the snow drew everyone else's attention, but I ignored their burning gazes as I sat down and reached for the platters of steaming food that had been set out for breakfast.

"Did you sleep well?" Beth asked, pouring me a mug of what appeared to be steaming tea. It wasn't my favorite drink, but it kept my hands warm and would give me an excuse to keep my mouth closed if the need arose.

"Just fine, thanks to someone's recle," I answered, eyeing Jessie. If her pale cheeks hadn't already been flushed by the cold, I knew they would be pinkening now. "And the rest of you?" I asked, unable to tolerate their expectant silence.

A quiet murmuring of "fine" and "alright" shuffled across the circle before we all fell into uncomfortable silence again. I knew what they were all waiting for, so I swallowed the bile that was rising in my throat and told them.

"Chem's real name is Alec," I began, tapping an anxious finger against my mug. "He created the Curse about three hundred years ago, and it corrupted him. He lived in the Evershifting Forest until I found him, and now he's going back to his miserable little cave to rot for eternity." I ground my teeth together, knowing I was doing an infuriatingly bad job of explaining things, but how could I put it into words? What Alec had done was unforgivable, and I would hold it against him until the day I died.

The stunned silence around me lasted long enough for me to slurp at my tea and choke down a few bites of food. I didn't look up from my mug. The bacon was delicious and the biscuits impossibly fluffy, but I couldn't find it within myself to enjoy them properly.

"He . . . *created* it?" Beth echoed, her expression displaying more shock than I'd ever seen from her before. She quickly molded her features into a look of indifference, crossing her arms over her chest. "I should've guessed. I knew there was *dasten* magic at work in him the moment I set eyes on him," she spat.

"That sort of lines up with what Derek and I found," Jessie offered, wringing her hands in her lap. "I was going to tell you before, but . . . well, you know what happened. Anyway, we did a lot of research in Lourak, and we found some pretty interesting documents."

"They mostly talked about records of criminals who had been arrested for practicing illegal forms of magic or studying dark arts," Derek added through a mouthful of bacon. "There was talk of old cults that centered their focus on resurrecting the dead or mastering the power of life and death. Most of the people involved were reportedly Talons."

"The power of life and death?" Gian echoed, rubbing his hands together and holding them close to the fire to keep warm. "That's impossible. Who's stupid enough to believe that can be achieved?"

"Lots of people, actually. It's theoretically possible." Jessie pressed her lips into a thin white line. "We researched that as well, because we had the same thoughts you do."

She looked at Derek, and he sighed as he began to explain. "Mages get their power from the accumulation of exceptionally strong elemental energy. People can only absorb this energy when they're small, which is why you're dubbed an underling if you haven't shown signs of magical abilities by a certain age. This also affects which mage type is more common than others. For example, since they're on the sea and surrounded by water, most people born in Coldmon are aclure-mages, and most people who grew up in the grit of the desert are andune-mages." He waved a hand at Beth. "The point is, if you can gather enough elemental energy, it can be poured into a vessel. On general principle, this doesn't really work. Animals don't have the conscious ability to wield any more power than they're given at birth, plants can't sustain elemental energy other than bering, and by the time any human is old enough to formulate these ideas, they'll have left the window of absorbing elemental energy well in their past." He paused to reach for a slice of honey ham, and Jessie picked up the explanation for him.

"That's where the practice of dark magic comes into play. The most common form of dark magic—and the easiest to perform—is known as bone reading. It's the art of communicating with the dead and has been outlawed across Horcath. There are other forms, though, that are less well-known because they"—she paused to clear her throat—"well, because they typically end in death."

"But those aren't very important right now," Derek said through a mouthful of ham. "The point is there's a type of dark magic that allows the elemental energy to be *implanted* into a person." He made a twisted face. "It's a pretty nasty process, and from all the records we found, it doesn't look like it's ever succeeded."

"Mainly because they all died before it could be deemed successful or not." Jessie pitched in, picking at her own plate of food, although little more than scraps were left on it.

"Sounds pretty terrible," Gian turned his needle-thin dagger over in his hands. I hadn't even noticed him pull it out of the little pocket he kept it tucked in. "You think that's what Alchemy did?"

"More or less. Obviously, he must have done something different from all these cults and rebels, because it resulted in the Curse." Derek rubbed his chin thoughtfully, still chewing a piece of ham. Another silence fell over us. I looked across at Ksega, and my heart leapt into my throat when I saw how intently he was staring back at me. His eyes were like two pearls of water from the Great Lakes, filled to the brim with curiosity and confusion. He had been silent the whole time, and a muscle in his jaw twitched as he flexed it, clearly trying to find a way to put his thoughts into words.

I couldn't bear the silence, so I asked, "How's Asuka? The dragon?" I looked at Derek. He shrugged.

"Fine. Timid, but fine. Bear's practically adopted him. We got a little shelter set up for them that way." He jerked a thumb towards the snowy forest and took another bite of ham.

"I still have questions," Ksega said icily. I winced at his tone, but was unsurprised.

I looked at him again, curling my fingers even tighter around my mug as I met his gaze. Slowly, I nodded at him. "Okay," I said softly. "I expect I have answers. Let's go for a walk." I stood, pulling the gloves from my coat pocket and tugging them on. Ksega stood silently, still glaring at me. My gut turned at the thought of him being so angry with me.

"Hey, I have questions too!" Gian protested, but Beth smacked him on the arm.

"We'll get an explanation when the time's right. Give them some space, sky brat," she hissed at him, and he returned her scowl as I walked away with Ksega.

I knew all of them had questions, but I wasn't sure I could give any of them answers until someone else knew them too. Once Ksega could help me explain everything, it would be a lot easier for everyone to get on the same page.

Neither of us spoke until we had walked far enough away from the camp that nobody could see or hear us. Snow sparkled beautifully around us in the sunlight, casting rays of silver and gold into the misty air. It was almost as if the Evershifting Forest was trying to compensate for the cold with its breathtaking scenery, but there was nothing that could soothe the cold crust forming in my chest after the night before.

"You should have told me before you sent him away," Ksega finally said, staring down at his boots as we crunched through the snow. I swallowed the lump in my throat.

"I know. I wasn't thinking." I took a shaky breath, wrapping my arms around myself and blinking up at the pale sky to try and keep more tears at bay. "I just wanted to see if it was true, and then I was going to come get you and . . ." I sighed, my fingers curling into my coat as I tried to force myself to think through my words. "I got angry. He's responsible for the deaths of so many people. He's had three hundred years to find a way to go back and destroy what he'd created, but instead he sat back and waited for someone else to fix it for him, and when no one could, he gave up hope." My voice was still raw, but Jessie must have put something else in my food to soothe my throat, because it was easier to speak. Without the pain to make me hesitate, though, the words spilled out of my mouth freely. "He was a lazy, selfish man that spent all his time hiding. Nobody's been able to find the source, but if anyone could have, it would have been him. I understand why he didn't look for it immediately, because he managed to lock it away, but a hundred years ago something or someone set it free again, and he should have taken responsibility and done something about it." I stopped walking, glaring down at the snow as tears blurred my vision again. "He waited for someone else to find something. Countless explorers and researchers spent their lives trying to identify what it was, and it was all for naught. At the very least he could have gone and found someone who would listen to him. If he really cared and he really wanted to do something to fix it, he would have made more of an effort before now." A shuddering breath left me when I finished. I squeezed my eyes shut, waiting for Ksega to say something, but he took a long time collecting his thoughts.

"I'm sure he realizes that now. He does want to help us, Sakura. He wouldn't have been traveling with us otherwise." His voice was patient but thin.

"Don't defend him!" I snapped my head back up to glare at him.

"He's our *friend*, Sakura, that's what you do. You haven't even tried to see this from his perspective," Ksega argued.

"If I were in his shoes, I would own up to my mistakes, not let them sit and kill people for a hundred years!" I fisted my hands, once again feeling my eirioth surge to the surface of my skin. As if sensing my anger, Ksega reached out and grabbed my wrists. I tried to pull away, but his grip was iron.

"You're upset. I understand that, but you can't just go doing and saying rash things because of it. I'm mad at him, too. I agree that he needs to make amends, but that's exactly what he was trying to do! We've made it this far, thanks to his help, and now you're kicking him out because of his past. That's not fair." Ksega chewed his lip for a moment, studying me. I kept blinking away tears to try and read his expression better, but his face was like stone. "You're letting *your* past affect it, too." His eyebrows drew together. "The Curse killed your family, and you think that makes him personally responsible—"

"It *does*! He created it and he—"

"Does he know how to get rid of it permanently? Does he know where the source is?"

"No, but that's not the point! He could have looked for it! He's had plenty of time to search for a way to–to—" I let out a frustrated groan, trying furiously again to tug my hands free, but I was too tired to fight him. Ksega waited until I had exhausted myself and stopped, panting plumes of fog into the air before me.

"Sakura, how did the Curse kill your family?" he asked, and I gaped at him.

"That has nothing to do with—"

"Just tell me. Please." I stared at him for a long moment, opening and closing my mouth as I tried to find my words. A soft breeze rustled the branches around us, shaking loose a fine powder of snow that settled on our shoulders. His face was pleading, softer than it had been before. I squared my shoulders and glowered at him.

"I was going home," I said. "I was just walking home with my sister. Finnian was helping at a saddle shop, so he wasn't there. We got home and—" my voice broke. I had to pause and clear my throat to go on. "It was a mess. Half the house was in shambles, and there was blood and broken glass everywhere. Aurora ran inside, and then I followed and—" I shut my eyes as the memory swam across my vision. I swayed, clenching my jaw and reaching forward to grab Ksega before I could fall over. "And they were in Moma and Papa's room. Moma was already dead when I got there, and Papa was on the floor. There were two animals in there, a wolf and a badger." I bunched the fabric of his coat in my hands to try and still their shaking. "The wolf saw me and—" my tears were freezing to my face again, making my teeth chatter. "And it attacked. Aurora jumped in the way before it could get me." My voice fell away into sobs. Ksega let go of my wrists and put his arms around me instead. I leaned into his chest, curling my fists tighter into his coat. "There was so much blood," I whispered, my voice quivering. "And *screaming*."

"Shh, don't say anymore. I'm sorry I asked." Ksega bent his head down and hugged me tight.

"It's okay." I managed between choked sobs. "It's just . . . it's hard not to hate him when I know he caused it."

"Yeah," he whispered. He was quiet for a moment, then added, "I'm sorry. I didn't know you saw it."

"Not many people know." In fact, only a handful of people did. Gamma, Finnian, and Walter were some of the first to know when I had told them in a panic what had happened, but aside from them, there was only Derek and Lady Nala. And now Ksega.

"I guess I can see why hate his guts, then," Ksega said. There was a pause, then he added, "I mean, technically he doesn't *have* guts, but you get what I mean. It still doesn't excuse what you did, though." He gently pushed me back so he could look down at me. I blinked away the rest of my tears and returned his gaze, grateful to see that they had thawed from their icy emptiness into pools of concern.

"I'm okay," I assured him, although we both knew I wasn't really. I peered at him, desperate for a distraction, and noticed how pink his nose and cheeks were. "You're freezing." I said, pulling a glove off and lifting a hand to touch his face. His skin was like ice.

"Some of us don't have fire magic to keep us warm," he said through a chuckle. I hadn't realized until now that I had been subconsciously using my eirioth to keep my body temperature at a consistent level. I often forgot that not everyone was able to do that.

"We should head back and tell the others, then," I said. Ksega nodded, releasing me and shaking snow from his coat and hair and blowing on his hands to try and warm them. I handed him the glove I had taken off, and once he had put it on, I took his bare hand.

*E*veryone was filled in, questions were answered and breakfast remnants polished off within the next two hours, leaving us with the question of what to do next. It had sat in the back of my mind ever since I knew I had to confront Alec, and now that the time had come to make a decision, I wasn't sure which way to turn.

As much as I hated to admit it, Alec had been right, and so had Ksega. With Alec's help, we had made it this far. Before he left, Alec had said he assumed the source of the Curse would be somewhere in the Slated Mountains. People had scoured almost every inch of Horcath in search of it, but they didn't have everything we had.

When Derek asked what we would do next, I looked across the camp and collected my thoughts. The pirates were having a grand time, drinking ale and playing card games. One of the ginger-haired fellows was constantly making moon-eyes at his wife, and the other spent most of his time with the one-handed navigator. Most of them seemed to avoid us, but when they were with each other they had nothing to hide.

"We know more about the Curse than anyone else. I think we still have a shot at destroying it. The source is somewhere in the Slated Mountains, but it's well hidden, so we'll have to put all our heads together to find it." I nodded over towards the pirates. "If they're up to it, we can get the pirates to sail us to Freetalon, and then we can go into the mountains. Ksega's bering lets him hear Cursed things, so that might help us track it down." I looked over at Derek and Jessie. "Did you learn anything else about where it might be located?"

"No," Derek answered. "But it does make sense that it would be in the Slated Mountains. People have searched up there before, but certain parts of the range can't be explored due to how dangerous it is. Between avalanches, steep cliffs, slate-wolves and other predators, there's almost no chance of survival without a well-trained escort of soldiers."

"That doesn't mean there's some hidden place that hasn't been explored yet," Jessie pointed out. "We don't even know what the source of the Curse looks like or how it functions. Maybe it's never been found because it's invisible, or because it has some sort of host that nobody would suspect."

"Those are both very reasonable assumptions, which means they've probably been thought of before," Derek said as he crossed his arms. "With the skill sets in our group, though, we might just be able to find something that no one else has."

"The likelihood of that is extremely low," Jessie argued. "Our time might be better spent getting everyone home safely."

"There's hardly going to be a true home for anyone to go to if we don't do something now," I said, my voice a little harder than I'd intended for it to be. I shared a look with Derek as I said, "The Curse has been growing. It's taken dragons and smiths and runeboars now, and it isn't going to stop. If all the dragons become Cursed, Carlore will become a bloodbath. If the Curse starts corrupting sea wraiths, the Great Lakes will be too dangerous to sail on. Nothing would be able to work properly."

A grim silence fell over us, broken only by the crackling of the fire and the laughter from across the campground. I reached for the pot of tea that had been set beside the fire, pouring myself a mug only to have an excuse for avoiding eye contact with anyone else. After the quiet had stretched for too long, Ksega broke it by loudly clearing his throat.

"That makes our next course of action pretty clear, then. I'll talk to Wendy and Chap to see what the pirates can do for us. Sakura, you may want to go visit Peeler. He's been researching the Curse a bit and said something about looking for new ways to fight it. You might want to tell him about the—" He paused abruptly, his face pinching as he tried to recall the word.

"Hypnotism?" I guessed, and his face cleared.

"Yes, that. Alright, off I go then. We'll want to be leaving as soon as possible, I'm assuming, so I'll check in with the pirates and make sure any business they have here in Brightlock is concluded quickly." Ksega adjusted his layers of clothes and marched off to speak to the pirates. I waited a beat before turning to Derek. Before I'd even opened my mouth, he pointed towards a shaded spot near the edge of the clearing.

"Peeler's the one with the glasses. He has some metal teeth," he said. He rose to his feet and brushed snow off his pants. "I'm going to go check on the dragons. Care to join me, Jess?" he offered his hand to Jessie, who accepted his help, and shortly after, the two of them had disappeared into the woods.

Beth suggested she go and give Gian another lesson with his sword, and then the two of them were gone as well. Blowing air out through my cheeks, I set my untouched tea back on the stones around the fire and started towards Peeler. He was reclined against one of the pine trees, using an oddly curving dagger to whittle a stick into a spear. When he saw me approaching over the rim of his spectacles, he sat up straighter and nodded a hello.

"You must be Sakura. I've been told you might be paying me a visit." He smiled warmly as he spoke, revealing that he did indeed have teeth of gold and silver. I returned the greeting, my gaze darting over to where Ksega was speaking with some of the other pirates as I wondered when he would have had the time to tell Peeler to expect me.

"Yes, that's me. You're Peeler, correct?" I crossed my arms awkwardly, unsure what to do next. Luckily, Peeler didn't seem fazed by it. He nodded enthusiastically and pushed off the tree, gesturing towards one of the nearby tents.

"Yep. Come along, I'd like to show you what I've been working on." I fell in step beside him as he walked through the snow, continuing, "Ksega's told me that you've been familiar with the Curse for a while now. I didn't really dive deep into studying it until recently, but I've discovered a few interesting things. For example, any animal's weak points are a prime target for a hunter, but even more so if that animal is Cursed. While attacking said weak points might injure or hinder the animal, a Cursed animal would most likely die from such an injury." He pushed the tarp of the tent aside and held it up for me to follow him in. Inside was a short table littered with maps and notes, an oil lamp, and a rumpled bedroll and pillow, cast unceremoniously into a heap in the corner.

"Are these all the notes you've taken during your research?" I asked as I stopped in front of the table, considering the papers. The handwriting was a messy scrawl, and most of it was unintelligible to my eyes, but there were some things I did understand. Unfortunately, very little of it was useful.

"Indeed they are. I'm afraid it isn't much in the way of life-changing discoveries, though. I was hoping that you might be able to provide some helpful insight." For a pirate, he certainly had an eloquent way of speaking. I nodded slowly as I reviewed what I could of the papers, collecting my thoughts. I definitely had some helpful information to share with him, but speaking of it would remind me of the person who taught it to me. I had to compose myself before I turned to Peeler to share it with him.

"We've discovered that hypnotism is surprisingly effective on Cursed animals. They basically stop working completely when enthralled by it." I told him about how we had tested it out with a swinging pendant, leaving out the details of who our test subject was. I could see that he had questions, but few of them would be getting direct answers.

"Fascinating," was all he said, rubbing thoughtfully at his dark stubble.

"The only issue is we aren't sure how to turn it into a real weapon," I said, not really because it was helpful, but because I felt like something was needed to fill the silence. Peeler nodded slowly, tapping dirt-covered fingers against his chin.

"You tried using a pendulum during your experiment, correct?" he asked finally.

"Yes. I know there are other types, though." I wanted to ask him how he knew about hypnotism, since nobody I had met aside from Alec seemed to know what it was, but I couldn't tell him how I had learned of it either, so I resisted the urge to bring it up.

"Indeed. Spiral hypnotism is by far the most effective, and I expect it will be the same when used against the Curse." Peeler stepped past me and reached for a quill and a piece of paper, urgently scribbling something down. When he looked up at me again, his expression was pensive. "Turning it into a weapon is the issue, you say?" I nodded. He sucked on his cheek for a moment, eyes distant, then snapped his fingers and bent back over his papers. "I may just have a solution for that. Give me a moment." He leaned unnecessarily close to his parchment and began to sketch something. I tried to get a closer look, but his face obscured most of my view.

I stood by impatiently, tapping my foot on the ground and observing the rest of the tent. Aside from the messy table and the pile of bedroll in the corner, there wasn't much. A couple leather packs that appeared to carry extra clothes sat tucked into the corner opposite the mess of a bed, and a unique contraption rested beside them. It was made from wood and iron and was sort of L-shaped, with a small lever protruding from the short end. The whole thing was thick, but only the longer end was hollowed out. There were a number of bands and rods and odd bits and pieces across the whole thing, and I couldn't make sense of what it might be. Peeler caught me staring and made a dismissive gesture.

"Don't worry about that. It's a personal project I've been working on for a while." His expression soured. "Unfortunately, I haven't been making much progress." He shrugged and went back to his sketching. "Still, it is only a prototype. Plenty of room for improvement. There, how does this look?" he set his quill down and lifted the paper so I could see it.

"It's certainly . . . swirly," I offered, tilting my head to the side. The sketch depicted a black and white spiral as a pendant, resting in some sort of pouch connected to a cord. It looked like a bulky necklace. Peeler's bushy brows twitched at my comment.

"Well, yes, that is the whole idea." He set the paper back on the table. "The concept is a hypnotic necklace. With water, painted marbles, glass, and a few well-placed bands . . . yes, I think this is possible." He adjusted his glasses and started to write on the page again, drawing lines to the sketch and frantically writing down notes.

"A necklace?" I echoed, frowning at him. He nodded, but didn't look up from his work.

"Precisely. If we can make enough necklaces that are designed to draw an animal's attention and then hypnotize it, we would have an excellent chance of fighting them off. Statistically, I would say . . ." He paused, looking up at the roof of the tent as he calculated. "The chances of one person's survival against, say, a Cursed smith, would increase from about three percent to roughly fifteen percent." I gaped at him.

"Out of a hundred?" I squeaked. He blinked at me through his glasses.

"Yes, that is typically how percentages are measured," he said slowly. I swallowed.

"The survival rate is only three percent?" I asked, thinking back to the Cursed smith that had attacked us in the Evershifting Forest. Peeler nodded and bent back to his paper.

"Yep. The Curse is usually pretty consistent. Patterns show that it makes animals twenty percent more aggressive towards living things. Factoring in hunger, size, and general agitation, a Cursed smith is two percent more likely to kill you than a non-Cursed smith." He sighed and turned his head to look at me. "Now please, stop asking meddlesome questions and give me some space. I'm going to get to work on a prototype for these necklaces." He made a shooing motion with his hands, and I trooped out of the tent before he could ask again.

The winter wind enveloped me, making me shudder. I shuffled my feet awkwardly in the snow, unsure what to do. Even if Ksega got the pirates to agree to take us over the Great Lakes, we would be stuck in Brightlock packing up for another day or two at the very least, which gave me lots of free time. The only issue was I wasn't sure what to do with that time. I wanted to spend time catching up with Derek, but his practical self would probably spend most of it talking about the next steps of our plan and dodging personal questions. There was never any good way to get him to open up. Besides, he seemed to want to spend most of his time with Ksega's friend, Jessie, and I was content to give them their space. I could join in on Beth and Gian's sword lesson, but basic training drills didn't sound very appealing. That only left Ksega, but he was busy with the pirates, so I was left on my own. In the end, the only plausible option was to do some training somewhere on my own.

Making a stop at my tent to retrieve a band for my hair, I set off into the woods to find a nice remote place to practice with my eirioth. It was in times like these I missed the sword I used to carry on my back, because it didn't pose as much of a threat to the plant life around me, but it had been extra weight both physically and emotionally, and I didn't regret having Alchemy take it away. I tightened my jaw as my thoughts turned to him. Each time a memory of him surfaced or I found myself wanting to talk to him, he was Alchemy, as fun-loving and exuberant as ever, but then I was reminded of everything he had done, and he became Alec, a stranger I could never call my friend.

When I found a sufficient place to train, I shed my outermost layers of clothing and rolled my shoulders, reaching for my flame-sword. The cold stung my skin, seeping quickly into my extremities and making my fingers go numb, but I didn't worry about it. Using my eirioth would warm me up fast, so I bundled the clothes and set them on the driest place I could find, then I shook my arms loose, gripped my sword handle tightly, and let my power flow into the blade.

24
KSEGA

Captain Howard may have been the person in charge of *The Coventry* and its crew, but he was just about the least approachable person out of all of them. I avoided him and went to his second-in-command. The first mate of *The Coventry*, Chap, was one of my favorite pirates, despite his tendency to tell obscure lies about his many adventures aboard the ship. His wife, Molly, and his younger brother, Thomas, weren't as likable as he was, considering one of them was mildly terrifying and the other rather monotonous, but all were still preferable over the captain, so I was glad to see the three of them standing separate from the grim-faced blond man. Molly was the first to see me coming.

"There you are, little stowaway. It's been a minute since we last saw you." She put her hands on her hips and gave me a once-over as I stopped beside Chap. It was surprising how welcome the sound of her voice was—anyone's voice, really. Even though I had taken notice of the strange absence of Alchemy's Cursed buzzing in the back of my mind before, now it was even more prominent, as if a piece of my own thoughts was missing. It made me feel cold and exposed in a way I couldn't put into words, and I was unnaturally grateful for any other sound I could latch onto to forget about the emptiness sitting in the back of my head.

"You look well. Much better than you did on the sea," Molly went on as her lips split to reveal a pearl-toothed smile.

Chap slapped me on the back in welcome as I said, "Yeah, life on a boat definitely isn't for me." I nodded at Thomas, and he returned it, hiding beneath his broad-brimmed hat as he usually was.

"We didn't expect to be seeing you again so soon," Molly said, crossing her arms and giving me a questioning look. They must have sensed that I was here for more than just idle chit-chat, which made me feel slightly guilty. I at least should have thought about asking how they were before leaping into my request, but Molly seemed antsy to get to the point.

"It's a pleasant surprise," I agreed, fidgeting with the hem of my coat. "But we didn't reunite just for the sake of meeting again. We sort of need your help." Molly and Thomas nodded. Chap's grin grew wider.

"Help? Why, that's our specialty! What do you need? A burglary? A cover-up? A homemade cheesecake recipe? Knuckles has a great one." Chap jutted a thumb in the direction of the burly, tattooed chef, who was currently bent over a pot suspended above one of the fires, stirring whatever sat within it.

"Tempting, but no, it's none of those things. We actually need a ride." I looked between the three of them. Molly and Thomas looked to Chap. He crossed his arms, his face for once clouded by a more serious expression. Why Howard had made the most distracted out of the three of them his first mate, I still didn't have a clue, but at least he was able to be solemn when the situation required it.

"Overseas?" Chap guessed, and I nodded. He grunted as he rubbed his chin. A spray of ginger stubble had grown across his face since the last time I'd seen him, and it made him appear much wiser than he actually was.

"Depends how far overseas you're wanting to go," Molly pointed out, tapping slender fingers thoughtfully on her arm. "Howie won't go off his chartered course just because some acquaintances need transportation."

"But isn't that what you do? Transport things?" I was still confused about what class *The Coventry* fell into. From the very start, the crew had been in the business of "high-risk transportation," but further snooping revealed them to be pirates of a sort. Molly and Thomas especially had emphasized that they were *not* pirates, just a group of people that mainly consisted of former pirates and criminals that were trying to make an honest living transporting cargo from place to place. I knew this wasn't true, of course, because I had snuck onboard the ship and ended up in one of their little pirate heists. My pure, blind curiosity regarding what they had been up to was the reason I had been on Clawbreak and ran into Sakura for the first time.

"We transport what we *want* to transport," Molly clarified.

Thomas's lips peeled back into a wry smile as he added, "And usually, that means we've got goods onboard that need to be taken to a new location, often to avoid being tracked."

"Because they're stolen," I deadpanned, raising an eyebrow at him. His turquoise eyes sparkled beneath the hat.

"Exactly."

"Where do you need to go?" Molly asked, poking Thomas in the arm to remind him to behave.

"Freetalon," I answered, chewing on my lip. I knew it was a long trip, and it would be no small undertaking even for the pirates, but we didn't have the money on hand to go through all the rigmarole involved in traveling overseas. It was best to try and get in with the people who knew what they were doing and wouldn't charge us for the voyage.

Chap whistled, squinting his eyes as he thought about it. Molly and Thomas both frowned at him but said nothing. The first mate made a number of clicking and *tsk*ing sounds with his mouth, then finally nodded.

"That should be fine. The areas we absolutely have to avoid right now are any of Coldmon's popular landmarks and now Brightlock." His gaze flicked briefly to the tents behind him. I raised my eyebrows. They had only been here a few days, and they'd already stolen something?

"We'll bring it up with Howie for you," Molly assured me.

"Before that, though, why don't we sit back and catch up for a little bit?" Chap offered, gripping my shoulder. "We've gone through quite the adventure since the last time we saw you. We actually ran into *three sea wraiths* just off the shores of Two Finger Point and had a mighty battle with them! Wendy shot one through the heart with the bow, and Peeler and Ritch strangled one to death with the spare sails." He gestured animatedly with his hands as he spoke. "Old Hank and I got the last one with a pole through the eye, then we slit its throat with Howie's sword." Before he had even finished the story, Molly and Thomas were already shaking their heads and rolling their eyes. Once he was done, his wife gave me an amused look.

"We did run into *a* sea wraith, but it was already injured, and Wendy just finished it off with the bow. The other two 'sea wraiths' were a piece of driftwood and an overly curious tuna that Knuckles had us catch and kill for supper." Chap only smiled lovingly at her and didn't argue. It hadn't taken me long to figure out that most—if not all—of his stories were embellished, and he only told them because he thought that's what pirates do. Little did he know that most of the stories his other crewmates told were entirely true.

"Ah, I see. Well, as much as sticking around and talking appeals to me, I've got some other people to check in on. Besides, if you guys are taking us to Freetalon, we'll have plenty of time to chat then." I smiled at all of them and gave them a nod of farewell. "I'll see you later. Thanks!"

My next visit was to Gian and Beth. I hadn't talked to them much since I'd come back, and what I had said was of a particularly glum nature. I had seen them walking off with their blades drawn, so I wasn't surprised when I heard the sound of clashing steel shortly after I walked into the forest where they had gone. It didn't take me long to find where they were training. It was a small glade, fit for only two people practicing their swordsmanship skills. Beth and Gian were dancing around each other, catching the other's sword with the occasional glancing blow. Even in the chill of winter, both of them gleamed with sweat, and Gian's usually pristine hair had taken on a slight frizz. A large ring of damp, dead grass showed where their boots had shuffled the snow slowly away, giving them more purchase.

Beth was the first to notice me there, but our eyes only met for a brief moment before she was focused on Gian again. Both had shed their outer layers of clothing, but there was no bitter wind like there had been the night before, so they wouldn't get too cold too fast. Gian was completely locked on Beth, his sleeves rolled up to his elbows, brows knit together in concentration as he darted and feinted with his blade. The sound of their swords crashing into each other was sharp and fast, muted by the mounds of snow and the thickly packed pine trees. I paused to watch at the edge of the glade, absent-mindedly rubbing the fletching of one of my arrows between my fingertips as I observed. I'd tried to use a sword once, but that resulted in a deep gash in one of Willa's beloved fruit trees, and I quickly gave up on trying to master the weapon. Daggers and small knives, like the hunting knife strapped to my belt, were much easier for me to handle, but the longbow was still my preferred weapon. I had trained with it since I was small, entirely self-taught, but I wasn't sure I would be able to train another person. The arts of a saber and a sword were not the same, but, despite her initial misgivings, Beth had done her best to meld the techniques, and everything was turning out pretty good from what I could see. Gian was getting more and more comfortable using a sword. The only issue was the very prospect of anything gory seemed to make him feel ill.

The blades rang against each other again, but this time it wasn't just Beth's blade Gian had to defend against. She parried a blow from his sword, then swiped her free hand through the air, sending a rush of powdery snow cascading over him and temporarily blinding him. He flailed his sword in a panic, barely managing to deflect one of her strikes before the snow fell away and he could focus again. The move had surprised both of us. I often forget that Beth was an andune-mage, because the magic took enough of her attention that the rest of her was too vulnerable for her comfort.

A final clash of the blades rang out around the glade, then Beth lowered the tip of her weapon to the frozen ground with a nod of satisfaction. Gian followed suit. As I approached, Beth sheathed her saber and walked around Gian, adjusting the way he held the sword and poking him roughly between the ribs before allowing him to put his own weapon away.

"Hello there," I said as I came closer. Gian raised a dark eyebrow at me, combing his hands through his hair to work out the tangles and try to smooth it back down. Instead of replying, he let out a high whistle, and two shapes responded by shooting free of the pine branches, swirling through the frigid air before coming down to perch comfortably on their respective master's shoulder.

"Where's *Faja*?" Beth asked, her sharp eyes swooping across the space behind me.

"I'm not sure. She was going to see Peeler, but I don't think their meeting would have lasted this long. We can go looking for her later. I wanted to come and see how you two have been. Nothing interesting happened while we were gone, right?" I noticed Beth and Gian both beginning to rub their hands together to keep them warm, so I went to help them retrieve their other layers of clothing.

"Not really, other than Sky Boy over here actually becoming a decent swordsman," Beth answered, nodding at Gian. He was sweating quite a bit more than she was, but also shaking more, and I doubted it was only due to the cold.

"And Alchemy falling in love with that little kitten," Gian added, tugging his fur coat on. "I don't understand why he liked it so much."

"Probably to use as another rat to test his *dasten* arts on," Beth spat, her face twisting into a scowl. I didn't comment. My own reasoning had been that Alchemy connected with the cat because both of them were outcasts of a sort, so different from all the others that they never believed they could be accepted. Both had found a place to be accepted, and now they were gone.

"Do we know what we're doing next?" Gian asked, looking at me again. I pursed my lips, unsure if I had a straight answer.

"Sakura wants us to go to Freetalon to resume our search, as you know, and I think the pirates are going to be the ones to take us. If all goes well, we should be getting out of here soon." I shivered, cold despite my heavy clothes. It would be nice to get out of the constant, bitter air. Beth was about to say something in response to that, her face displaying her obvious displeasure at the prospect of having to squish in on a ship full of pirates, but I silenced her by lifting a hand. I had heard something. It was only a brief sound, quickly snatched away by the wind, but it was familiar and unmistakable. I'd grown used to it hovering in the back of my mind, but after being absent for hours now, I was easily able to pick out when it resurfaced. It was the distant buzz of the Curse.

"What is it?" Gian asked softly, throwing his gaze around the clearing. Now that I was paying attention, I could see that both Taro and Light Ray had ruffled feathers, and their eyes were locked on the shifting gray shadows beneath the pine trees. For a moment, I thought it might have been Alchemy, coming back when Sakura wasn't around to maybe explain the situation or plead for a way to come back, but then I noticed something unnatural about the buzz. At first I thought it was just slightly disjointed, then I realized that it wasn't just *one* buzz, but many. The sound made the hairs on the back of my neck stand up, and I instinctively unslung my bow and tested the tension of the string. In response to my action, Beth and Gian redrew their blades.

"Over there." Beth gestured with her saber towards a portion of the forest where the trees were packed so tightly together that almost all the snow beneath them was cast into shifting shadows. It wasn't just the shadows that were moving beneath them, though; as we watched, there were flashes of bright green and pitch black.

"What *are* those?" Gian squeaked, gripping his sword handle so tightly his knuckles were ghastly white. "They look like that thing that tried to kill us the first time we came into the Evershifting Forest, just smaller and . . . pointier."

"Pointier?" Beth echoed, shrugging her shoulders so that her coat hung loose around her small frame. "Are you telling me you've never heard of a wolf before?"

"Heard of? Yes. Seen pictures of? Occasionally. I thought they looked more like rats." Gian replied as the creatures slunk into the clearing. It was true that smiths did greatly resemble giant wolves, although in many ways they shared characteristics with bears as well, which gave them the bulkier, rounder shape that they typically had.

"You're thinking of slate-wolves," I said, flicking an arrow free of my quiver and knocking it to the string as the gray and white shapes poured out of the trees, shuffling through the snow to form a ring around us. "They're much uglier."

The time for conversation was over then, because the wolves now had us entirely surrounded, and they were closing in. Taro and Light Ray both took flight again, anxiously circling above us. I counted thirteen wolves, and all showed obvious signs of the Curse. Patches of silvery fur had fallen off, revealing blackened, cracked bones and oozing black insides. Globs of silver-green blood dripped and gurgled between exposed ribs and hollow chest cavities, staining the pristine snow beneath. Some of them were missing legs or tails, others ears and eyes. One of them didn't have a lower jaw. They were all thin and bony and snarling, shaking with the anticipation of a fight. It wasn't long before the fray began.

The first attack came from the wolf without a lower jaw, spittle and blood flying from its mouth as it leapt towards Gian's back. He raised his sword in a defensive position, but it was unneeded; one of my arrows had lodged itself deep in the wolf's chest mid-air, sending it toppling backwards into the snow. The other wolves had been driven into action the moment the first had lunged, and now we were all caught in a flurry of thick fur and gnashing teeth. The beasts howled and yelped in pain as sword and saber were driven through their flesh, and their once-beautiful coats became peppered with arrows and grime. Grunts and cries of exertion escaped the three of us as we fought. Beth gripped her saber in one hand, using it to swipe at an eyeless wolf on her left, while she used the other to ram her skinning dagger up to the hilt in the skull of a wolf on her right. Gian had three wolves jumping at him. One nearly caught him in the heel, but he dodged at the last moment and kicked out with his foot, hitting the wolf squarely between the eyes and sending it staggering backwards, right into my line of fire. It fell lifeless to the ground in seconds. The other two wolves around Gian quickly met similar fates when they tilted their heads back and exposed their throats to the arc of his blade. It all happened in a matter of seconds, and as soon as their companions lay twitching and oozing on the ground, the remaining seven wolves trotted out into a wider circle, now wary of coming too close to us.

"Anyone hurt?" Beth called over the growling of the wolves. Gian and I both responded with "no." "Good. Watch out!" two of the wolves had darted towards us, and Beth slid on the frozen ground to intercept them, lashing out with her saber. With a cry from above, Taro swooped down to tear at the tender flesh of the wolves' faces.

I ignored the pained howls from behind me, because three more wolves were skulking closer to me, and the last two had their eyes on Gian. When they dove, I almost didn't react fast enough. One of the wolves' claws snagged on my fur coat, ripping through it and tugging the garment free of my shoulders. I gasped as the cold slammed into me and stumbled sideways to avoid a second wolf's snapping jaws. I sprinted out of the glade, weaving instead between the trees with the three wolves on my heels, an arrow knocked to my bowstring. I skidded around another pine, sending a spray of snow into the air, and ran back into the clearing. With the path ahead of me momentarily clear of obstacles, I turned back and fired. A yelp, a puff of snow, and one of them lay dead on the ground. The other two swerved around their fallen comrade and continued to chase me. I could hear the ringing of claws and teeth on steel, but didn't dare look to see how Beth and Gian were faring until I was out of danger.

Snow was a beautiful thing. I had always been fond of wintertime, even if it wasn't my favorite out of all the seasons. At the very least, it was pleasant to look at sparkly frost glittering on a dormant garden or to see rays of sunshine brightening a ghostly landscape. The downside to snow was that it had a tendency to make you very, very cold and the ground very, very slippery. The bigger downside was that, in a thick forest full of snow, you couldn't really avoid that if you were running at full speed. It was thanks to this that in my mad sprint to escape the wolves, my boots inevitably lost traction on the ground beneath me and sent me spinning painfully into the trunk of a pine tree. The wolves caught up to me within seconds, and my only instinct was to grip my longbow against my chest, throw my arms up in feeble defense, and squeeze my eyes shut tight. Well, that wasn't exactly my *only* instinct, but it was the only one I was consciously aware of. The other one was one I wished would stop surprising me so much.

"By all the saints, Ksega, what did you do?!" Beth's voice was what shook me out of my paralysis. Dropping my arms, I felt my mouth run dry at the horrid sight before me. The trunk of the pine I leaned against had grown dozens of spindly fingers, most of them curving in to impale the drooping forms of the two wolves that had been caught mid-leap. Thick, silver-green blood ran in streams from the puncture wounds, trailing in rivulets along the grains of the wood and dripping down into the snow. From somewhere beyond the cage of wood, I could hear Gian gagging as he gripped a cut on his midriff.

"Sorry. That just . . . happens sometimes." I curled my nose at the foul smell that washed over me from the partially-decayed wolves. They'd already had enough holes in them to begin with, if you asked me.

"Well, get yourself out of there so we can go get *Faja*. I have a feeling she'll want to hear about this," Beth ordered. I agreed with her; a whole pack of wolves claimed by the Curse? That was unheard of. Three or four at most wouldn't have been much of a shock, but *thirteen*? That was far more than the Curse had been capable of claiming before.

Since the pine tree was still alive, I was able to guide the branches away from each other, creating a gap large enough for me to duck through. I wasn't used to my bering acting without me actively controlling it, but I wasn't going to complain about it saving my life again.

We left my torn coat, the dead wolves, and the bloodied glade quickly, hurrying back to our large camp to find Sakura. The only one of us who had sustained an injury was Gian, the one of us who was most vulnerable to the infections and diseases the Curse-corrupted beasts carried. We had to get him to Jessie as quickly as we could; by the time we reached the camp, he already had a terrible fever and could hardly stay on his own two feet.

Luckily, Derek and Jessie were by one of the bonfires when we returned, and they took Gian into one of the tents with her bag so she could get to work on helping him. Beth followed after them, so I hung back to not overcrowd the tent. Soon after, Sakura came back into the camp, sweaty and slightly disheveled, but with a light in her eyes that I hadn't seen for quite some time. It was dim, but it was there, and that was enough to make me grin as she walked up to me. She returned it a little less enthusiastically, but at least she was in a good enough mood to smile.

"You look like you've just rolled down a cliffside," she observed when she came closer, tilting her head to the side and raising an eyebrow at me. I ran a hand through my damp mop of hair and brushed snow off my shoulders with a chuckle.

"Oh, nothing as serious as that. I got into a fight with a giant lizard. You should have seen it. You would've been proud." I grinned, and a huff of amusement escaped her lips.

"Of you or the lizard?" she asked through a laugh, crossing her arms. It was good to hear her laugh again. "What really happened?"

"I only slipped on some ice and fell into a tree." I rolled my shoulders, already feeling the achy bruise forming between them. I could see the next question hovering on Sakura's lips, so I answered before she could ask it. "And that may or may not have been the result of me running from a bunch of Cursed wolves." Any trace of her laughter quickly vanished, replaced with the cold, calculated expression I was used to. I sighed as she leapt into the inevitable barrage of questions.

"Was anyone hurt? Was it nearby? How many were there?" she asked brusquely, her eyes flinty.

"Total? Thirteen. At the time I only had three on my tail, though." I rubbed the back of my neck, nodding at the tent the others had disappeared into. "Gian got a scratch in the ribs, but he should be fine. Jess is patching him up as we speak. Beth went in there to 'supervise,' whatever that means. Derek is in there too, if you want to talk to him." Before I had finished talking, she was already shaking her head.

"Thirteen is a lot more than it could have taken before. You don't think . . ." She bit her lip before she could resume the thought. My chest squeezed as I realized what she was suggesting.

"*No.* It wasn't him. He would never try to hurt us." My voice was a little harsher than I'd meant for it to be, and Sakura flinched.

"No, you're right. That was unfair." She scrunched her face into a sort of scowl, as if she were trying to berate herself mentally, but it didn't look like she was having much success. I knew it wasn't easy for her to finally know who was responsible for the Curse, but Alchemy was still our friend. She couldn't hate him forever, could she?

"How's your cheek?" I asked to change the subject. I lifted a hand to brush my finger along the pink line on her cheekbone. The cut had healed pretty well, but the scar would most likely remain for quite some time, if not the rest of her life.

"Fine. It only feels a little weird if I stretch the skin too much." She flexed her jaw, pulling her lips in and out of a smile to prove her point. I dropped my hand and forced a smile.

"It looks good. Scars suit you." She rolled her eyes, unable to muster the zeal to return the smile. Instead, she crossed her arms, still clearly weighed down by the thoughts of the Cursed wolves. I suspect an awkward silence would have stolen over us, but at that moment, Derek stepped out of the tent and saved us from such a fate. When he spotted us, he strolled over, shoving long black bangs out of his face as he did so.

"Ah, there you are," he mused, adjusting his fur coat as he stopped beside us. He nodded at me. "Sounds like your bow got a good run in, hm?" his dark eyes flicked to the weapon still on my back.

"Yeah, a couple shots, I guess." I rolled the shaft of one of the arrows at my hip between my fingers, eyes resting on the entrance to the tent. I was running out of the projectiles and would have to acquire some new ones soon. "How's Gian?"

"Fine. He'll live. Jess has got it under control and wants some privacy to work, but that Duskan is quite stubborn about staying." He raised an eyebrow at us. "Does she have a thing for him or something?"

"Or something," Sakura mumbled. She was rubbing her thumbs over her knuckles and had a sort of distant look in her eyes. I didn't like it.

"What are you scheming now?" I sighed. She smirked wryly at me.

"Whoever said I was scheming? I'm not a schemer." I would have argued against that point, but she went on before I could. "We need to get moving as soon as possible. Have the pirates agreed to take us to Freetalon?"

"Yes, we have." All three of us jumped, whirling around to see that Thomas had sauntered up behind us, a film of snow on his hat and shoulders. He smiled dryly. "We leave tomorrow."

25
SAKURA

*T*he camp was packed up and all traces of it removed before dawn. It was a real shame we were leaving since the forest had, at some point in the night, shifted back into a pleasant, springy guise of silver birch trees and bright wildflowers. There wasn't much time to marvel at its new beauty, though, because as soon as everyone was packed up, we were marching for the Gates.

The Coventry was a magnificent ship. It was huge yet elegant, intimidating but refined. The slate-wolf figurehead was the most imposing feature, its lips peeled back in a fierce snarl. A close second was the giant crossbow mounted in the crow's nest of the central mast. There were no other remarkable aspects to the vessel aside from its sheer size, but it didn't need any more to be recognizable. Pirates were a rare sight on their own, but pirates with an actual pirate ship? They were even more scarce. Piracy was an occupation best kept under the table, and from what I'd learned growing up around the Port, pirates themselves preferred less conspicuous vessels.

The process for going through the Gates changed depending on what kingdom you were coming from and what kingdom you were going into, and it usually took a while to get through. The only consistencies were that you had to pay something, and you had to have a peaceable reason for crossing kingdom borders. Luckily, we were leaving Brightlock, and the protocol required for that was very minimal. Because of how necessary the islands in Coldmon are to ships and their crews, the fee for entering the kingdom of the Great Lakes was considerably less than that for leaving it, so we were all able to get through and board *The Coventry* before the sun's light had finished spilling across the land.

As soon as we were onboard, the crew began to get the ship ready to set sail. Ksega and Gian were both gaunt-faced by the rails as they watched, hands anxiously gripping the grainy wood as the deck lulled and bobbed with the waves. Light Ray was perched nearby, watching with wide violet eyes. Jessie offered to give Beth and I a tour of the ship, and we accepted. She showed us where Bear, Asuka, and Wynchell were bedded for the trip, where we would be sleeping, where we would be eating, and all the other necessary introductions. There were three decks total, and I suspected it would take me a little while to familiarize myself with all the rooms and their purposes, but I had time for that. The trip to Freetalon would take—assuming we didn't run into any mishaps or take any emergency stops—almost a week. There was enough food and clean water on board to keep all of us and the animals alive until we arrived at our destination, but it wasn't sustenance I was worried about.

"Something's bothering you," Beth prodded once we got a moment of quiet. We had placed our things by our selected hammocks and were reclined in them, taking a rest from the morning's excitement. I sighed, letting my head drop back into the hammock and staring up at one of the swaying lanterns overhead.

"It's the Curse," I admitted, picking at a loose thread in my shirt with my fingers. In the edge of my vision I could see Beth nodding slowly. "That wolf pack that was corrupted is just another sign of its increasing power. It's only been a short time since we saw that Cursed smith, and before that Ksega and I encountered several Cursed runeboars." I groaned, shutting my eyes as if that could stop the thoughts swirling through my head.

"Mm, yes, whatever Bones did to the world has certainly left us in a tricky situation," Beth pondered aloud. I cracked an eye open to look at her, but her expression was unreadable, and she was looking away from me.

"Did you . . . like him? I mean, did you count him as a friend?" I asked slowly, leaning forward to try and gauge her reaction to the question. Her gaze flicked to mine, her expression remaining neutral.

"Bones?" she asked, and I nodded. She pressed her lips together, considering for a quiet moment before she answered. "Yes. He was strange and corrupted in more ways than one, but . . ." She tilted her head to the side, her eyes lowering to look down at the floor. "I believe he is good on the inside. His outward appearance is scary and big, but he has a soft heart. He's kind, even if he wasn't always like that." She looked up at me again. "Our pasts mold who we are, but molds don't have to define us. We all have things we would rather lose to time. You become a hypocrite when you say he is a monster, yet you have regrets in your own past." She rose to her feet and rolled her shoulders, walking away towards the upper deck before I could find the words to respond.

Her words echoed faintly in my head. Regrets? Yes, I had some, but they didn't result in *thousands* of deaths. I hadn't screwed up nearly as bad as Alec had.

Grumbling under my breath, I launched myself out of the hammock to go find something to occupy my mind other than depressing thoughts. It was a mistake, because at that moment *The Coventry* lurched away from the docks and set sail on the Great Lakes. My balance lost, I toppled to the floor, smacking my knees with a resounding *crack* on the boards. I rose to my feet again, hissing and cursing, and stormed towards the galley in search of something tasty enough to drown out my anger.

In the galley, I found a bowl of salted shrimp and stewed kale and beans, along with Derek, who had also come searching for a snack. We took our bowls of food from the intimidating, tattoo-ridden chef, and retreated to the darkest corner of the galley to eat. There weren't many other people down there, other than a few of the pirates, but we kept to the sidelines anyway.

"Have you heard any word from Finnian or Gamma?" I asked almost as soon as we'd sat down. Derek's brows lifted.

"Not even a proper hello for your oldest friend? That's a shame," He deadpanned. I pursed my lips, giving him a tired look, and he sighed. "No, I haven't heard anything. I was hoping they might try to contact one of us and maybe include something about Violet, but with no way to tell where we've gone, I doubt they've even attempted to send a message out."

"Yeah, probably not . . ." I sighed, gripping my fork tightly. I hadn't even thought about Derek's younger sister. How must it have felt for him to be away from her for so long? It couldn't have been easy. I knew Finnian would hate to leave me for even a week, much less several. I shouldn't have been surprised that he had heard nothing from home, but some childish part of me had been grasping a sliver of hope that maybe he had. Any word from Gamma or Finnian would do wonders to calm my nerves. I just wanted to know they were okay.

"It's been good to be away for a while, though. I mean, obviously it's hard being away from home, but . . . it's freeing." Derek shoved a shrimp in his mouth, chewing thoughtfully. I nodded in silent agreement, although I wasn't really paying attention to him. "It's good to meet new people, too," Derek went on once he'd swallowed. I raised my eyebrows at him.

"Really? *You* enjoy social interaction?" I was more than a little baffled. The Derek I knew hardly ever left home, and when he did, it definitely wasn't to go out and fraternize.

"Well, some, I guess. You could call it that." His usually ghostly pale complexion pinkened. "I didn't meet *that* many new people. I mean, there was Jess and Willa, and that was about it, really . . ." I smirked at him and his gaze dropped to his shrimp.

"Oh, so she's *Jess* to you, is she?" I teased. His scowl was automatic, but not genuine. I had a sneaking suspicion it was just to mask his embarrassment.

"That's what everyone calls her." He ate another shrimp to avoid saying more. I hummed thoughtfully, my smile widening.

"Yes, of course. Silly me. I should have known better than to think the surly Derek Plow had actually caught feelings for someone." I rolled my eyes dramatically, stuffing my face with food and ignoring his glower.

"And what about you, little miss independent?" he sniped. "You and Ksega seem pretty close. Are you sure I'm not the only one who's caught feelings?" now it was his turn to smile knowingly.

"Aha! So you admit you like her!" I said through a mouthful of shrimp.

"You're avoiding the question," he countered.

"Oh come on, you honestly think I like him?" I plastered an expression of indifference onto my face, ignoring the warm, fuzzy feeling in my chest. "Ksega's just a friend," I added firmly. Derek scoffed.

"Sounds to me like you're not entirely convinced of that fact," he remarked. I would have argued the point, except he held up a hand to stop me and went on. "At the very least, he's *definitely* interested in you. It's obvious to everyone. You should make up your mind about your feelings for him before you end up breaking the poor kid's heart by accident." He scooped the last of his food onto his fork and shoveled it into his mouth. This time, I scoffed.

"You're talking like you aren't only a couple years older than him," I told him, and he shrugged.

"Whatever. Trust me, he's going to need some sort of confirmation, otherwise he's gonna be confused about it for the rest of his life." He finished off his meal and looked over at my plate, which still had a few bites of food on it. With a sigh, I pushed it across to him, and he eagerly wolfed it down. When he was done, he stacked our dishes and said, "We should try to start planning out what our next steps will be once we're in Freetalon. Shall we go find the others?" he stood.

"Yeah," I answered distractedly, also rising to my feet and trying to hide how flustered I was. Derek returned the dishes to Knuckles, then we made our way towards the sleeping cabin. Beth was in there, lounging in her hammock, and she perked up when we walked in.

"At last, someone interesting! I was expecting a ship full of pirates to be a little more entertaining than this, but they're surprisingly dull." She swung her legs out of her hammock and rocked to her feet. She fell in step beside us as we headed for the upper deck.

"I'm guessing you haven't had any run-ins with Chap, then?" Derek looked sidelong at her. She shook her head. "Count yourself lucky. He's a yapper."

"We're looking for our group to make a plan for when we're in Freetalon," I explained to Beth. "Do you know where the others are?"

"Not sure where your ginger friend is, but Ksega and Sky Boy are up on the deck," Beth replied. A grin split her lips. "From what I gathered from that fellow with the glasses, neither of them is doing very well."

"Ah, yes. That would make sense," Derek smirked. "Jess said Ksega was prone to getting seasick."

"That tracks," I mumbled, remembering how uneasy Ksega was around the sea. I almost told them about the time he had passed out during a sea wraith attack but thought better of it. Beth didn't need any more things to use to antagonize people.

We arrived on the upper deck, and sure enough the two of them were hunched over the rail together. I couldn't see either of their faces, but I could see their hands gripping the rail so tightly their knuckles were white. Behind them, Jessie was tinkering with a number of glass vials and bundles of herbs. As we came closer, all three of them looked up at us. Both Ksega and Gian were gray in the face, but Gian was considerably worse. Sweat beaded both of their temples, but while Ksega's hair was merely damp, Gian's clung like a wet shock of fur to his scalp. Light Ray looked like he was about to try and eat it.

"Ouch," Beth commented dryly. "You both look awful." Gian shot her a glare before another lurch of the ship made both him and Ksega bend over the rail again in a series of groans and violent coughs.

"I'm working on it," Jessie said through gritted teeth. She was mixing the contents of her various vials, shaking them together until she had two small tubes of a blue-green liquid. "This is a lot easier when you only need enough doses for one person." The tip of her tongue was sticking out of her lips as she worked, adding a small shred of some sort of leaf to each tube before swirling it around with a sort of long stick. Behind her was a leather pack that unrolled to reveal pockets and pouches for all manner of tools and utensils. Without question or need for direction, Derek stepped beside her and began to help.

"How do *you* know anything about making remedies for seasickness?" I questioned.

"When you spend enough time with a recle-mage, you pick up a thing or two. Besides, it has the same base components as a remedy for your typical stomach bug," he replied without looking up.

"*I* spent plenty of time with a recle-mage, and *I* never picked anything up," Ksega pointed out just before another gag left him doubled over the rail once more.

"That's because you're as dense as a doorknob," Jessie said, not bothering to look up from her work to address him.

Several minutes of similar bickering ensued, punctuated with various sharp gags from Ksega and a reappearance of Gian's meager breakfast, before we finally got around to laying out our plan for Freetalon. The conversation lasted a long while, filled with much debating and requesting of snacks—all mention of food was quickly met with queasy protests from Ksega and Gian—and by the time it was finished, the sun was low in the sky and most of us were ready for a warm meal and a good night's rest. With that decided, we went our separate ways and left the pirates to sail us through the black waves beneath the stars.

*T*wo days passed, then a third, and then a fourth. On the evening of the fourth day, the sky was dark with heavy, rain-filled clouds. On the morning of the fifth day, the waves became riotous, and we were forced to slow our course. Over breakfast, Wendy informed us that we were expected to reach Freetalon's docks within the next three days, as long as the storm didn't get any worse. Luckily, the storm did not worsen for a while. Unluckily, lunchtime brought with it a much bigger, much scalier concern than thunder and lightning.

I was relaxing in the sleeping quarters, along with Derek, Jessie, and Beth, watching Taro chase a wooden bead around the floor, when Gian stumbled in looking like a rat that had just crawled out of a bowl of noodle soup. Before he could get a word out, Ksega and Thomas barreled in after him, followed by Chap, Molly, Captain Howard, and Peeler. All of them had an expression that was either grim or excited. Chap was the only one who bore the latter of the two. Ksega had neither, but there wasn't a good word to describe how he looked. Both he and Gian had been given several doses of Jessie's seasickness remedy, and while it had calmed their stomachs, neither of them looked very steady on their feet yet. I supposed it wasn't just their physical states that had been affected by the sea, but their mental states as well. I didn't understand why Ksega was so afraid of deep water, but I could tell it rattled him to the bone whenever he was brought to it, and that was enough for me to feel sympathetic.

Even so, all I felt at that moment was a spike of panic when I realized what a rush all of them were in. There was no time for an explanation, though, because almost as soon as they had come, they were gone. Captain Howard swooped into another room with the three mates on his heels, and Peeler had vanished into what I had thought to be a supply closet. All five reemerged and went back up the ladder. Ksega disappeared towards the galley, only to return moments later with a big cup of water which he proceeded to chug while Gian flopped, almost liquid-like, into his hammock. We stared at them for a long moment. Beth was the first to let her impatience get the best of her.

"Well? What's going on up there?" she demanded. Ksega was squinting at the wall, as if trying to keep his water down, and Gian lifted his head to give her a hollow look.

"Probably nothing but the storm. Wendy thought he saw something in the water, and they all freaked out. I think I heard Thomas mumbling something about a whale," he said boredly. His head drooped back into the depths of his hammock.

"Oh." Beth seemed to deflate a little. "From the way you all came racing down here like a herd of stampeding camels, I thought something fun was about to happen." She sighed and leaned back into her own hammock. "I guess I should've known I would be disappointed when I saw that the two of you were involved."

"Are we sure it isn't something a little more serious?" I asked, watching Ksega. I realized now that him staring at the wall was actually him concentrating on something. I didn't even think he was listening to us.

"I wouldn't worry about it too much. If the pirates aren't panicking, we shouldn't worry ourselves sick." Beth waved a hand, then cast an amused look at Gian. "Some of us are already there, anyway." He lifted his head to sneer at her before dropping it once more.

"There's something out there." Ksega's voice was cold and slightly detached, and there was a faraway look in his eyes. I hesitantly rose to my feet and stepped closer, leaning to peer at his face. He didn't look at me.

"Like, out in the water?" Gian sat up now too, his mossy eyes sparkling with new uncertainty. Beth rolled her eyes, but before she could argue, Ksega went on with a curt nod.

"Yes. I can't really see it or feel it, but . . . there's definitely something there. Something big." The blood drained from his already pale face. His breathing sped up. I reached out and gripped his shoulder, forcing him to look at me.

"Don't panic yet, alright? Maybe you're overthinking this. Maybe all the rocking has gone to your head. Try drinking some more water," I said, nodding at his empty water cup. It was true that *The Coventry* was swaying and dipping violently in the water, thanks to the storm. It had made all of us a little on edge, but there was no need to jump to conclusions yet.

"No." Ksega was shaking his head, his eyes wide. "It's out there. I think it's—" he was cut off by all of us yelling as we were suddenly thrown from the floor. We tumbled through the air, snagging on hammocks and swinging lanterns. Someone screamed in pain, and there was a sound of flapping wings. We struck the far wall, and I yelped as I landed awkwardly across Ksega, my shoulder digging into his ribs. He cried out, instinctively curling around me, which was fortunate because one of the lanterns snapped free of its chain and crashed loudly to the planks where his leg had been moments before.

"Sorry," I gasped, lifting my head. My hair had fallen over both our faces, and I hastily brushed it away. He grimaced, and I tried to shift my position, but the ship rocked again, and I fell back on top of him. Someone else's boot rammed into the side of my skull, and I groaned, shutting my eyes against the bright flecks that flew across my vision.

"Here. Wait, don't—" Ksega hissed as I tried to move again, and I realized one of the packs that had lain beneath my hammock was tangled around his leg. My boot was looped through the strap, and when I tried to move, it tightened around him.

"Hold still a minute," I muttered, bracing my arm against the wall so I could lift my head again. The whole cabin was tilted, leaving us all sprawled on the wall with our packs and any other loose items and fallen lanterns. The hammocks swung, but the ship was no longer heaving with the waves.

"What's happening?" Derek was the owner of the boot that had struck me, but he wasn't as upright as I was. "Is everyone okay?" he awkwardly crawled up to where Jessie and Beth were. One of them was making pained whimpering noises. There was a murmured answer, but I couldn't make out the words. Gian was flattened against the wall, eyes wild and possibly brimming with tears, his face stark white.

"Sakura—" Ksega shifted his arm so that he was half-lifting me off of him. "You're squishing me. Untangle the pack." I was surprised at how steady his voice was, because it was obvious he was scared out of his wits. We could hear yelling now, coming from above, and hurried footsteps, but there was no way to get to the ladder.

"I'm trying. Quit wriggling," I ordered. He was trying to shimmy up away from the pack, but with my boot keeping it taut, it wasn't working. I had to flip myself onto my side to reach it, which was awkward because then my head was tucked beneath Ksega's, and keeping my balance was incredibly difficult. He had to grab my back to keep me steady, but it didn't help much as I reached for the pack. My fingers closed around the strap, and I tried to tug it away from my boot, but it only served to pull on Ksega's leg. He yelped and instinctively kicked up, his knee slamming into my jaw.

"Just take the boot off!" Ksega rasped. *There* was the panic. Giving up on the strap, I took his advice and shoved the boot away. At that moment, *The Coventry* was harshly jerked to the side, as if it were a small dagger being twirled within someone's hand. We all shrieked again as everything slid towards the far wall.

Being in a line as we were, it would have resulted in all of us in a bruised pile in the corner if Derek hadn't kicked off the wall and grabbed one of the swinging hammocks, reaching out and snagging Jessie's hand before she could slide past. She screamed, grimacing as he hauled her up and into the hammock. I saw a dark stain on the front of her shirt, and it was growing.

Everything else happened too fast for me to make out the details. My back collided with the wall, knocking the wind out of me, and seconds later something heavy and warm crushed me. I gasped, my lungs squeezing, my vision blurring. When it cleared up, I found that the ship was now tilted in such a way that if you were to look at it from the outside, the slate-wolf figurehead would be pointing to the sky. I sucked in a full breath, my chest aching, and looking to the side. Gian had somehow managed to land away from Ksega and I, but he was curled into a fetal position near the hallway entrance. Beth had followed Derek's lead and was swinging lightly back and forth in a hammock. Ksega was on top of me, his hands curling around my arms so tightly it hurt. His whole body was shaking—or maybe that was mine, because I knew what was going to happen. The ship couldn't sail like this. We were going to sink, and then we were going to die.

26
KSEGA

I tried to keep from panicking at first, and for a moment I almost succeeded. It was sort of easy after the ship had tilted the first time, because there was a great big Carlorian distraction that landed right on my chest. The initial feeling was pain as her shoulder dug into my ribs, but the second feeling was an odd one that made my chest feel all tight and my face feel all warm. Thankfully, she couldn't see it because her hair had successfully fallen just about everywhere.

Everything after that was sort of fuzzy to me. I remember my leg hurting, her moving, and at some point me putting my arms around her. I accidentally kicked her in the face, then the pain was lessened and immediately we were falling. That was when the fear finally caught up to me.

I attempted to pay attention to what was happening, but it was futile. The moment the ship was somewhat steady again and we were all lying on another wall, cold rivulets of panic slipped through me, winding around my spine and sending a shudder through my whole body. I remembered when I had become aware of something beyond the walls of *The Coventry*, and I remembered what it must be. A sea wraith was flipping the pirate ship over, and then we would either drown or be eaten. The types of sea wraiths that liked to eat people were not pleasant at all. Some had venomous fangs, others rows and rows of sharp teeth that shredded you as you were swallowed. I really, *really* hoped I would drown.

I grabbed the nearest thing to me—Sakura—as tightly as I could and tried to block out all the sounds. At least she was here, and she was warm, and I didn't have to die alone. At least I wasn't the only one shaking with fear.

"Ksega, come on, *get up.*" The voice was literally right in my ear, temporarily dragging me up from the depths of my own morbid thoughts. I was frozen in place. Sakura spoke again, angrier this time. "You have to get off of me if we want to live. Hurry." Her hands were on my chest, trying to shove me up, and I finally came to my senses.

I shoved off the wood, rolling away from her onto my back and gasping as if I'd already been drowning. I looked up towards the ladder and instantly sunk back away from it, towards the darkness of the ocean below. A hand lightly touching my shoulder snapped me out of it. It was Sakura, pointing up, and now I could see. Derek, Jessie, and Beth were nearly to the ladder. They had climbed up through the hanging hammocks, and Derek was helping Jessie get to it. Water ran down the planks of wood at the top, dripping down at us first in a slow rhythm, then in a steady stream.

"The ship isn't going down," Beth yelled down to us. "The rain is just running inside. The whole thing is suspended somehow. I think we're stuck on a rock. Quit cuddling and get up here before you become fish food." She said nothing more, launching herself up onto the ladder after Jessie. Derek peered back down at us. Sakura gave him a nod, then stepped over me to approach a huddle of damp . . . bedsheets?

"Let's go. We're running out of time," she said as she nudged the pile with her still-booted foot. The pile moved. It was Gian. He looked like he was crying. "Both of you!" Sakura snapped, whirling back to me. There was enough urgency in her voice that I propelled myself up onto my feet, staggering on the slick boards. My head spun, my heart raced, and my arms were still shaking, but for the moment I was alive, and for the moment and the many moments afterward I intended to stay that way.

All three of us raced to get to the hammocks. I was the tallest, then Gian, with Sakura being the shortest. Gian easily jumped up and grabbed one and, despite being weaker than most of us, managed to pull himself up and into it. Out of sheer desperation, he rose shakily and climbed to the next. Sakura, standing nearly a foot shorter than me, couldn't reach the nearest hammock.

"Come here." I stepped beneath it. "I'll lift you up." I locked my hands together. She gave my trembling limbs an uncertain look, but I nodded at her and forced a grin that I hoped was believable. "I've got you. Don't worry. Besides, it's not like you have many other options." That convinced her. She placed one sopping sock into my hands and shoved off the boards with her booted foot. I grunted as I boosted her up, and her dark fingers closed around the ropes. She struggled for a moment, then started to climb. As soon as she got to the second hammock, it was my turn. I gripped the ropes and hauled myself up. Every inch of me was cold and quaking, but I forced myself up after her. Within minutes, all of us were out of the sleeping cabin and scrambling on soaked floorboards to reach the uppermost deck. It took a lot of shuffling and grumbling and slipping, but we all managed to pull ourselves and each other up into the rain to get a good look at the terrible situation.

The first thing I noticed was how bad the storm was. It was pouring rain, and thunder rumbled in the background, but for the moment there was no lightning. The next thing I saw was the sea wraith. It was huge, and a great portion of it coiled around the ship. Beth had been wrong about us being stuck on a rock. The wraith had lifted *The Coventry* entirely out of the water and was holding it vertically. I couldn't see its head yet, but I heard it screeching somewhere nearby. The worst part was that I now realized why I had been able to sense it before. I had mistaken it for the rain, but now there was no denying the presence of a crackling buzz in the back of my mind. Signs of the Curse riddled the scaled body of the sea wraith. Great chunks of scaly flesh had fallen off, exposing bone and gooey insides and slashes of bright green. Silvery blood pooled and congealed with the rainwater, oozing down the boards. The weight of the wraith's body was great, and part of the rail had splintered and snapped beneath it. Then there were the people.

Most of them had found perches where they were relatively stable. Chap had an arm around Molly and was hunkered down on the mast. Howard, Peeler, and Old Hank were squatting near the door to one of the cabins. The people in the worst condition were the two laying on the rigging and Wendy, who was dangling from the crow's nest, holding onto the rail as tightly as he could as his legs flailed in the air. As for us, we were all crouched uncomfortably against the wall of the opening we had come from, squinting through the rain.

"Is there anyone else below-deck?" Thomas had somehow appeared beside us, his hat gone, his hair a mess. There was a sword in his hand.

"I don't think so," Derek answered for us. He had an arm slung around Jessie's shoulders. On her other side, Beth was helping to support her. The wound in her stomach couldn't have been too bad, because she was still upright and very conscious, but there was a considerable amount of blood running down her front. The sight made me reel, knocking my shoulders into the wood behind me. Gian was there to keep me from falling over, although he didn't look far from doing it himself.

"Stay out of its line of sight, and you'll be fine," Thomas shouted over the din. He cast a worried look at Jessie's midriff, wincing. "Well, mostly fine. Leave it to us." He slid down the boards and was swallowed up by the rain.

I was content to leave fighting the wraith to the pirates, but I could see from the glint in their eyes that Sakura, Derek, and Beth were not. Even as Thomas was enveloped by mist, Beth was shoving Jessie into Derek's arms and wrestling the saber from her hip. Gian gave her an exasperated stare.

"You can't be serious," he groaned, and I was surprised when she heard him over the rain, whipping her head around to grin at him.

"The beast isn't going to kill itself!" she shouted over the cacophony, shoving off the boards and slipping after Thomas. Sakura looked down at her feet, her expression contemplative, then pulled her flame-sword handle free of its place in her belt and leapt after them, still only wearing one boot.

"All of you are idiots," Gian spat, most of his face hidden by the clumps of wet hair that clung to his pale skin. I would have argued that at least some of us retained a small amount of sanity, but my teeth were chattering too much for me to get a word out.

"We need to—" Derek began to yell at us, but the rest of his words were lost in the storm as the wraith lurched, rocking *The Coventry* back to its original axis.

We all tumbled onto the deck in varying degrees of pain. I struggled to my feet and gasped as my head spun. The sea wraith's body was contracting around the ship, and the sound of boards cracking and breaking splintered the roar of the storm.

"Here, keep her still while she works." Derek was already on his feet and guiding Jessie towards me. Before I could object, he sprinted away in the direction Sakura had gone. I could see her huddled close to Beth, Thomas, and Ritch, all of them clutching their weapons.

"What—" Gian began to protest, but it was too late for that. We each had an arm on one of Jessie's shoulders, but none of us was exactly steady on our feet. Jessie had her hands clasped against her abdomen, her face pinched in concentration and pain as she used her recle to mend the wound. She wasn't the most powerful recle-mage, so she wouldn't be able to do much with only physical contact, but she at least had the ability to save herself before she bled out or fell unconscious.

"Let's get her over there," I suggested, my voice thin as I tugged them both behind some strapped-down crates nearby. Gian gestured towards the doorway we had come from, but I was shaking my head before he could ask the question. "No, we're not going back in there. If the wraith flips us again, it'll flood faster than we can get out." My whole body seemed to squeeze and shrink as I spoke, my pulse thundering in my ears.

"What does it matter? We're obviously going to die out here anyway," Gian snarled, his free hand clenching into a fist so tight his hand began to shake. I wanted to argue with him, but I knew he was right. Even if we did manage to drive the sea wraith away, the damage done to *The Coventry* was already bad and getting worse. It wouldn't be able to sail, and the only land we were close to was Sea Serpent Crevice, a place renowned for being a popular nest for young sea wraiths and water raptors.

"Stop bickering. I'm trying to focus," Jessie snapped, which shut both of us up. I rose onto my toes to look over the stack of crates, trying to see what else was going on. My breath hitched when I saw a giant scaled head rearing back near the rails.

It was beautiful and hideous at the same time. Silver-gray scales lay plated in neat rows on a long, narrow face; the rainwater slid across them, shimmering in the faint beams of moonlight that pierced through the storm clouds. Milky blue eyes were set deeply beneath heavy, drooping antennae, flashing as the monster screeched and bared its venomous teeth. Part of the skull was revealed along the jaw, showing where the Curse had claimed it. Cracks of black and green split the blueish scales, creeping like roots across the wraith's face. It had two horns, but one had broken away, leaving only an ashy stump behind. The beast was in pain and extremely angry, and the various weapons being shot or plunged or stabbed into the coil of its body around *The Coventry* was doing nothing to lessen either of its problems. Not that it mattered, since the Curse would end the wraith's life anyway. The best thing we could do for it—and for ourselves—was to put it out of its misery.

The sea wraith let out another terrible wail as Davie drove a spear beneath its scales. It lunged, fangs snapping furiously as it reached for the deck. I flinched back beneath the crates, shutting my eyes. The whole ship pitched to the side before righting itself. Wood broke, someone screamed, and a loud *bang* echoed through the air. Rainwater clogged my nose and ears and made every surface slick. The ship was designed to be manned during bad weather, so the decks were rough enough that my boots could still find a decent purchase, but I knew it wouldn't last long with how much water there was. As long as the rails held out, the water would begin to pool around our ankles.

Another shout of alarm made me pry my eyes open and look over the crates once more. My heart leapt into my throat as I saw that the sea wraith had bitten an entire chunk out of *The Coventry*, leaving a gaping hole in the deck and rail. What was unmistakably human blood ran in thin rivers towards the opening, and my stomach turned at the sight. Gian had seen it too, and I could hear him making strained gurgling noises behind me.

So many things were happening that it was getting difficult to keep track of it all. Peeler had appeared near the mast and was fidgeting with something that glinted in the faint light. Wendy was trying to help the other two pirates down from the rigging. I could hear Bear, Asuka, and Wynchell roaring in the upper cargo hold. Chap, Molly, and Captain Howard were near the bow with Theomand, all of them gripping weapons and holding on tightly to whatever was nearby. Thomas and Ritch had disappeared, but Beth and Derek were still where I'd last seen them. My eyes scoured the scene for Sakura, but it was difficult to make out who was who in the rain. I could only hope the blood staining the boards wasn't hers.

"Jess," I said as I turned back to her, gripping her arms and looking into her eyes. It was hard to see through the torrential downpour, but I could tell she was still hurt and struggling to heal herself. "Are you going to be okay with just Gian?" I asked, my voice shaking. Gian whirled on me.

"What? You're leaving me too?!" his voice was little more than a squeak. I ignored him.

"I'll be fine. Where are you going?" Jessie tried to look over my shoulder, but I turned her around and pushed her against the crates instead, tucked into the corner where she didn't have many places to fall if the ship tilted again.

"Don't worry about it. Just stay here and stay safe." I stepped back, swallowed my hesitation, and gave Gian a pointed look. "Stay with her," I ordered.

"Like I would go anywhere." He scoffed, knuckles white as he clenched his fists. He didn't have his sword on him, and I could tell he felt naked without it. I, too, lacked my weapon and its comforting weight. I didn't know what I was planning to do with nothing but my bare hands and the hunting knife in my belt, but I had to do *something*.

I ran up the length of the ship to get a better vantage point and to get closer to Chap and the captain. They, at least, seemed to have an inkling of a plan. As I ran, I searched for Sakura, but I still couldn't see her. My stomach clenched as images of her being snatched up by the sea wraith or sent tumbling overboard flashed across my vision.

I was nearly to them when the wraith's head appeared again, this time over the rails at the head of the ship. The group I was approaching hastily retreated, scurrying away as the wraith struck again, ripping the slate-wolf figurehead from the ship and casting it away into the foaming waves. The sea wraith tightened its hold on *The Coventry* as its head snapped around in the air, searching for a new target. My heart dropped down into my stomach as it leveled its eerie eyes at me, releasing another ear-splitting screech before it dove. I was so frozen with fear that the most I could do was take a single step to the side, slip on the wet boards, and half-roll, half-slide down the deck, narrowly avoiding the beast's fangs as they bit viciously into the wood. They were as long as I was tall. I tumbled through rainwater and debris, rolling and flipping over myself until I slammed into the rails on the opposite side of the ship. Someone—or multiple someones—yelled my name, but the voices were lost in the ruckus. More than just the ship tilted in my vision, and black spots clouded around me. I flopped into the puddled water, shuddering and gasping until I had the strength to move again.

I groaned as I lifted my head, soaked and bruised and shivering from fear and the cold, and spotted Sakura near the mast, mere inches from the sea wraith's face. Her flame-sword was clutched in her hand, its red-orange blade flickering in light tongues of flame, their reflections dancing in the wraith's haunted eyes. She was pressed flat against the mast, her chest heaving, both boots and socks now gone. The wraith hissed as it opened its jaws, its yellowing, venom-filled teeth poised to sink into her chest.

"No," I sputtered, lifting myself onto my elbows and shifting my legs back beneath me. They were going numb. "No!" My chest contracted in horror as I saw Sakura's flame-sword flicker out of existence. She tilted her chin up defiantly, but lowered her arms to her sides. She was giving up. There was nowhere for her to go.

27
SAKURA

*T*he giant thorns of wood weren't there, and then they were. It was as simple as that, although with a little more screaming and a lot more blood and a pinch more lightning.

At first, I didn't really notice the change. My blood had run cold, my vision blurring. Everything seemed to fade into the background as I shrank into myself, coiling around that ball of eirioth in my stomach and shutting out the world as I waited for death. Somehow, I could still see the dreadful thing before me. It was shimmering like a mirror, stained and tarnished with time. The Curse held half of its face in a sickly caress. Long, sharp fangs rose in front of me, pointed at my heart, set in a mouth that hung agape. Then, before my end could come, the wraith collapsed. Its head smashed into the boards at my feet, lolling to the side as blood ran down its scales. Huge spears of wood jutted from its body in multiple places, each emerging from *The Coventry* itself and now sticky with the monster's blood. To my horror, the slitted eyes still flitted around before locking on me once more. The beast struggled to lift its head, teeth raking the air dangerously close to my body.

"Sakura, get down!" the voice barely registered, and I had only seconds to react before the air crackled around me. My knees were like jelly, and I let them give way so that I fell into the ankle-deep water on the deck just before a bolt of lightning lit up the sky.

Electricity buzzed around the ship, making the water tingle and my toes go numb. Another bolt snapped through the air, this time striking the wraith directly where it was tightened around the ship. Its head crumpled back to the boards, nearly crushing me, and I frantically pulled myself away, grabbing my flame-sword as my bare feet shoved me back along the deck.

"*Faja*, come here." Someone grabbed my arm, dragging me up from the water and planting me unsteadily on my feet. It was Beth, pulling me back towards where Jessie and Gian were hiding behind some crates. Jessie was leaning against the crates with bloodstains on her shirt, but she didn't appear to be in very much pain. Gian, on the other hand, was red eyed and green skinned.

"Where's Ksega?" Jessie asked, but I didn't have the strength to answer her. I flopped against the crates, grimacing as everything slipped back into sharp focus, throwing me off balance. My heart felt like it was going to jump out of my chest, and every limb was shaking. I looked around the deck as another spear of lightning crashed into the sea wraith. I spotted a figure slumped in the water against the rail, blond hair matted against his head. As I watched, he took a deep breath, and the giant thorns began to creep back into place in *The Coventry*'s frame.

Freed from the spears of wood and glowing with electricity, the corpse of the sea wraith slid silently into the churning waves, and the pirate ship was finally released.

I didn't remember much of what happened next, but I knew it was gloomy. The pirates took a roll call and discovered that three people had been killed and seven were unconscious, one of them being Ksega. He didn't appear badly hurt, just exhausted. The thorns he had created to save me must have taken most of his strength. I didn't recognize any of the names of those that had lost their lives. After a moment of silence was had for the lost, everyone debated what to do. Asuka, Wynchell, and Bear were brought out and comforted, but there was little comfort to be had with the knowledge that the water around us was slowly rising. *The Coventry* was sinking.

"Our options are few," Chap told us when he came to deliver the news. Beth, Gian, Jessie, Derek, and I were seated on the crates, shivering in the rain. The storm had calmed quite a bit with coaxing from Theomand's whorle, but it was still raining and cloudy.

"Is it even possible for us to survive?" Jessie asked. She was huddled under Derek's arm, trying to work with her recovered medicine bag to try and heal her wound some more. Everything was completely soaked, and I wasn't sure what was usable and what wasn't. She had offered to give me a tonic to calm my nerves after my close call with the sea wraith, but I'd declined. The last thing I needed was some magical medicine messing with my brain when I needed to be able to think clearly.

"Some of you, yes, if you take your dragons now." Chap crossed his arms and clenched his jaw, his gaze landing on Bear, who was sitting, sodden and grumpy, beside the crates.

Asuka was standing on his other side, making disgruntled noises at the water rising around his feet. At least he hadn't panicked and flown away yet.

"We're not going to leave you," Derek said firmly, and Jessie nodded in agreement. My teeth were chattering too much for me to say anything, but I was with them. I wasn't going to leave these people to drown at sea. Beth and Gian both seemed a little peeved at our loyalty to the pirates, but neither argued to leave. Light Ray and Taro, who had flown away during the chaos, had returned and were now perched beside their masters, shivering and dripping and looking rather emaciated with their feathers all matted down with water. They looked no happier than their owners did about the situation, but at least none of the four of them were complaining.

"The only way we could all make it out alive is if another huge ship magically appears out of the fog." Chap's voice was thin and serious, nothing like the voice I was used to from him. His typical jolliness was drained, replaced with a weighty dread that brought all of us into a sour mood.

"Howie! Chap! Come look!" a voice shouted from the rigging. We all looked up. It was Wendy, long hair a disaster, clothes drenched and ripped, pointing with his hook to the south. "I think it's a ship!" he yelled. "Magically appearing out of the fog!" We all jumped from the crates and sloshed through the water to the rail, squinting through the rain and mist.

"Well, I'll be." Chap's lips twitched into a smile.

"You really should've talked a magical savior ship into existence an hour ago," Beth snapped at him, but even through her snarkiness, I could hear the relief in her voice. It was on all our faces as the crew began to shout and holler, trying to gain the attention of what we could now see was most definitely a ship sailing over the waves. I shot a beacon of eirioth into the sky with what little strength I had left, sending orange light flaring in the mist around us. Slowly, the other ship began to turn towards us.

"It looks pretty big. What sort of ship would be out here in this kind of weather?" Jessie asked, worrying her lip between her teeth.

"That's not just any ship." Thomas was coming up behind us, limping slightly. He grimaced as he propped himself against the rail. "See the paint job? That flashy piece of gold on the side? That's the royal insignia." His face twisted into a scowl. "It's a member of the Coldmonian fleet."

"Part of an armada?" Derek guessed. Thomas shook his head.

"Worse. Look at it. It isn't built for warfare." He sighed. "No, this vessel is a part of the king's personal fleet. It isn't the big flashy one, so I doubt any member of the royal family is aboard, but whoever's captaining it at the moment is undoubtedly very important." He shared a look with his older brother, who was drumming thoughtful fingers against his chin.

"It doesn't matter who it is." Molly brushed past us, one of her hands bleeding from a cut on her palm. She placed her other slender hand on Chap's back and stared out towards the ship. "As long as we can get out of this alive."

The next hour was a blur of action. The other ship didn't bother with introductions. As soon as Captain Howard explained that we had been attacked by a Cursed sea wraith, the crewmates of the other ship, dressed in their bright gray uniforms, began to help us all get off *The Coventry* and aboard their own vessel. We brought whatever we could with us, but most of the items below deck weren't salvageable. The dead and unconscious were taken down below the main deck, but everyone else stayed up top for a while. As rain poured around us and thunder roared in the distance, we all watched grimly as *The Coventry* finally gave way to her wounds. The ship broke in two, sinking steadily beneath the foaming waves. There was a long, heavy silence as the mast dipped and bobbed before finally vanishing into the black waters. Captain Howard stared into the depths, Chap and Molly by his side, all of them with tears swelling in their eyes.

Nobody asked any questions until we were all out of the rain and anyone who was alive and conscious was gathered in the broad galley of the ship that we now knew was named *Waterlore*. It wasn't very different from the galley in *The Coventry* in terms of layout, although the design was considerably more elegant. The entire ship was made from a silvery-white wood—or perhaps it was just painted that way—with details and moldings of gold and silver. The entire thing was stylish and bright and far too nice to be taken out in such a storm for an ordinary late-night sail. However, our questions would have to wait until later, because as fascinating as this showy ship and its showy crew was, *we* were the ones with eirioth dragons and a raptor and several missing body parts, so it only seemed fair that we answer questions first.

Captain Howardand his mates were in charge of that, leaving the rest of us to chat with the rest of the crew. Most of the pirates didn't seem up for talking, their expressions grim and demeanors somewhat defeated, but some of them put forth a good effort. Wendy, despite the obvious pain he felt at the loss of *The Coventry*, was talking to someone with a forced smile on his face. Peeler was busy scribbling something down in a notebook someone had given to him, sketching what looked to be a replica of the drawing he had made for me back in the Evershifting Forest. I had completely forgotten about the hypnotic charms he was going to make. Had all his progress been lost?

"This was a rather dreary turn of events," Beth said. We were sitting around one of the tables in the galley, untouched plates of steaming pork and green beans slathered in garlic sauce set before us. None of us felt like eating.

"At least we're all alive," Gian pitched in, although there was little conviction behind his words. Yes, *we* were alive, but not everyone. The three pirates that had died weren't people I was familiar with, but to the other members of *The Coventry*'s crew, they had been family, and now they were dead.

"I know what you're thinking." An elbow in my ribs made me look over at Derek, who was seated beside me. His expression was stern and serious, but his tone was surprisingly soft. "It isn't your fault. They agreed to help us because they believe in our cause." As soon as he spoke the words, I knew he was right. I *was* blaming myself for what had happened to the pirate ship. I was the one who wanted them to take us to Freetalon.

"If they hadn't agreed to it, they wouldn't have been there. We could have taken another ship and another route, but because they were there, it was convenient to ask them for help." I grabbed my fork and stabbed at my slab of pork. "Maybe they all would have survived if we had taken another way."

"And maybe *other* people would have died if we had taken another way," Beth argued. She leaned forward and scowled at me. "You should stop thinking that your decisions affect the whole world. The pirates *chose* to help us. Any consequences of this journey are theirs to bear, not yours. Maybe their navigator should have picked a different route, or maybe we should have stopped for the storm. You didn't control their choices, so stop blaming yourself for what's happening to them." She tilted her head to the side, eyes narrowing as she contemplated something. "You know, it applies in the reverse as well. You should stop blaming others for the consequences of *your* choices, too."

"Can we try not to argue?" Jessie sighed, chasing a green bean around her plate with her fork. Everyone looked at her. She was pale and looking slightly withered. She had refused to let anyone treat her injury and, instead, had slowly been healing it herself, a plan that was clearly leaving her a bit weakened.

Derek slid an arm around her and said something to her quietly while Beth huffed and crossed her arms. She leaned against the wall and rubbed her thumb on Taro's beak. Gian stared glumly at his food. I tried not to throw my own plate at Beth. I knew she was talking about Alec. I had tried not to think about him, because each time I did, I felt like throwing up. He was a terrible person, and he had ruined so many peoples' lives; I hated everything he'd ever done and I hated *him*, but most of all, I missed him. I missed his cooking and his gentle nature and the way he was always looking out for us. I hated that I missed him, but I couldn't help it, especially not when I could tell everyone else missed him, too.

There's no changing what you've done, I reminded myself, grimacing inwardly. I had sent Alec away, and now he wasn't going to come back. He could if he wanted to, of course, and none of us could do anything to stop him, but I knew he wouldn't. He respected me too much for that, and even if his mind was all twisted and messed up, he would honor that respect by keeping his distance.

"I'm going to go check in with Peeler," I said through clenched teeth, pushing away from the table and standing without meeting any of their gazes. Derek asked me something, but I wasn't paying attention. At that moment, all I wanted was to find something interesting enough to distract me from my own thoughts, and maybe find an excuse to get away so I could go see Ksega. I was worried that he hadn't woken up yet.

"Ah, Sakura, there you are." Peeler saw me coming closer and beckoned me to his side. I slid onto the bench beside him, not meeting his gaze for fear of him reading the turbulence in my eyes. He gestured at the notebook in front of him. "I lost quite a bit of research, unfortunately, but I've been keeping my notes and prototypes of the hypnotic charm nearby." His fingers tapped the new sketch, which was slightly different from the one I had seen before. "My papers are now entirely useless, but I have a handful of the charms themselves on my person. I'm not going to bring them out now, though. I don't want them being confiscated." I finally looked at his face and saw that he was scanning the crowd with suspicion. "Anyway, I'm quite confident that most of them will work, if not all. The only issue is producing enough of them and educating enough people on how to use them for them to actually make a difference." He tugged on a tuft of his salt-and-pepper beard.

"Will it cost a lot to make more?" I asked, frowning as I tried to read the various notes on the pages of the notebook. It was a fruitless effort, because his handwriting was little more than a slanted scrawl; I would have been surprised if even *he* could read it.

"That depends on what quality you want them in. Each pendant requires a length of cord, some leather, glass, and painted marbles. A single pendant will require lots of time and labor, so you'll want multiple people producing them at the same time. All of that together can add up to a pretty hefty sum." Peeler began to write figures down on his notebook page, but once again I couldn't read it clearly enough to discern what it meant. I just nodded along and pretended to understand.

"Is it possible, though?" I asked, rubbing my knuckles with my thumbs. The fascination of conversing with Peeler was already beginning to wear off, and I needed a new distraction soon.

"On the scale we need? I'm not sure, but we can definitely get a few dozen made—at the very least, enough to keep all of *us* safe." He made a vague gesture at the buzzing galley around us, although I knew he was only referring to the people who had been aboard *The Coventry.*

"Well, we'll have to be thinking about it, then," I said in a tone that suggested the conversation was over. Peeler nodded once, then bent over his notebook once more and didn't say another word as I stood and slipped away.

I was given a few skeptical looks from the Coldmonian crewmates as I left the galley, but I ignored them. No one had told us we had to be confined to one room. Besides, the place I was going wasn't very far, so if any of them were curious enough to follow me, their suspicions would quickly be put to rest. The sleeping quarters on *Waterlore* were much more accommodating than the ones on *The Coventry*, although they lacked the roguish charm of the pirate ship's swaying hammocks. Instead, there were cots bolted to the floorboards and made up with neat silk sheets and fluffy pillows. It was a wonder the pillows weren't strewn all across the cabin, thanks to the turbulence of the storm. A small number of the cots were slightly different from the rest, having stark white silk sheets instead of light blue. These were the sickbeds, all five of which, along with two non-sick bed cots, were currently occupied by the injured and unconscious people from the sea wraith fight. Wrapped in white linens and laid silently by the wall were the three bodies. I tried not to look at them.

I walked past the empty cots and stopped at the foot of one of the sickbeds. Ksega was a deep sleeper, and even though we were in a place and situation that would usually have his whole body vibrating with anxiety, he looked very peaceful resting on the cot. There weren't any stools or seats in the room, but standing was nauseating with the swaying of the ship, so I stepped closer and sat on the edge of the cot. As far as anyone could tell, Ksega wasn't injured, only exhausted. Seasickness and worry had worn him out, and I knew that creating the giant thorns must have drained him immensely. The first time he had made thorns like that he had also passed out, although that time he had been hurt as well.

Thinking of the thorns made me wonder about his bering. I knew that he was still figuring out how to control it all, but I hadn't asked many questions. I was honestly curious to know more about his magic, although whether he would be willing to share or not was doubtful after how much I had been ignoring him.

"I could really use some of your optimistic advice right now, you know," I said quietly, scooting so that I could lean against the wall behind me. I shut my eyes and sighed, at last unable to keep evading my thoughts any longer.

So much had happened and *was* happening that it was hard to organize everything that was going on in my head. I wanted to move forward with our plan and keep everyone focused on our goal, but I kept getting dragged back into past events. I was guilt-ridden over sending Alec away, questioning my own motives and shredding my own heart in the process. I felt so *alone*.

"Please, wake up," I whispered, leaning forward to grab Ksega's hand. My eyes burned with unshed tears. "I know that's unfair of me to ask, but I really need you right now." I squeezed his hand. He stirred, his eyelids twitching. I bit my tongue so hard I tasted blood.

It would be better to let him rest. He wouldn't want to be awake during the storm any more than he already had been.

A crewmate loudly entered the room, boots thumping and shiny *adda* armor clinking, startling me. I gasped as I looked up, but he didn't even glance at me. He strode through the room, pausing only to kneel beside a cot and rifle through something beside it before rising to his feet once more and leaving. I watched the doorway, expecting him to return or someone else to enter, but a groan from beside me drew my attention back to the pillow. Ksega's eyes were open but unfocused as he stared at the ceiling. My grip on his hand instinctively loosened.

"I'm sorry. I didn't mean to wake you." I cringed inwardly at the lie. He blinked slowly, his gaze shifting over to meet mine. A tired smile pulled at his lips as he slid his hand back into mine.

"That's okay," he croaked. We stared at each other for a long moment until I blinked and looked away, loudly clearing my throat.

"We're on a Coldmonian ship called *Waterlore*. *The Coventry . . .*" I mouthed the words but couldn't muster the heart to say them. Ksega's throat bobbed as he swallowed, his eyes shutting again.

He was silent for a minute before he asked, "And the pirates?"

"Most of them are fine, and the ones that are hurt will recover." I drew a breath to deliver the most unsettling news but hesitated. His eyes opened and met mine again.

"But?" he prompted. The breath left me in a defeated sigh.

"But three of them died. I'm sorry, but I don't know their names," I answered in a low tone. I felt a pang of guilt, now convinced I should have tried harder to commit them to memory, names and faces that would now linger in memory and legend until they faded away completely.

"There are a lot of them," Ksega said in a thin voice. "They're easy to get mixed up." He sighed, sinking deeper into the pillow. "How's Jessie? And Gian?"

"Fine. Jessie is still working on healing herself from that cut she got, and Gian is looking no less sick than he was before the sea wraith attack." I rested my head against the wall of the ship, trying to let the rocking lull me, but all it did was add to the pain in my roiling stomach.

"And how are *you*?" the question wasn't exactly unexpected, but it caught me off guard, nonetheless. I didn't look at him, because I knew he could already tell something was wrong, and I didn't want to see the pity in his eyes.

"A little lost, if I'm being honest." I stared at the ceiling. The lanterns weren't hanging here like they were in *The Coventry*. Just like the cots, they were bolted securely into the wood. I gazed into the flickering light, telling myself the queasy tightness in my belly was just the lantern's flame calling to the eirioth inside me.

"Do you want to talk about it?" Ksega asked, his thumb running up and down my hand. I bit my lip. Yes, I did, but where to begin? There was simply too much to say and not enough time to say it. Sensing my muddled thoughts, he picked a topic to start with. "Is it Alchemy? You were pretty harsh with him, but anyone can understand why. Your actions were more than justified."

"Were they, though?" I looked down at him, feeling the tears resurface. "Beth says I'm a hypocrite because I have my own regrets, and I blame him for his mistakes and don't blame myself for mine." My throat tightened, but I forced the words out. "Even now, I keep trying to convince myself I'm doing all of this for the right reasons, but I'm beginning to suspect that revenge really is my only motive." The first tear ran down my cheek. "I want the Curse gone, but I keep saying that's because I want everyone else to be safe from the suffering I went through." I dropped my head, staring into my lap. "But that isn't true. I want it gone because it stole my family from me, and it keeps trying to take whatever I have left." I clenched my free fist, my vision blurring with my tears. "Maybe I'm no less of a monster than Alec is."

"Don't say that." Ksega shoved himself up so that he was sitting next to me, squeezing my hand. "Never say that. Neither of you are monsters. Maybe he wasn't a great man at one point, but he's changed. We all change. It's a part of life." I didn't have the strength to argue with him. He was the one with the magic closely connected to life, after all.

"What about those who never got the chance to change?" I looked him in the eyes again, even though my vision was still too blurred for me to read his expression. "What about my sister? She sacrificed herself for me, and I just *stood there* like a blade of grass while it happened. The only reason I survived was because she and my parents bought me time with their deaths, and for what? So I could waste my life worrying Gamma and Finnian by throwing myself into a quest that seems to have no end?" I curled my fingers, digging my fingernails into Ksega's hand. "They had so much more to live for than I do. My parents had each other and their love, and Aurora had a promising life and a stable job and a great reputation. I had everything in front of me, but nothing in that moment, and what's the point of everything without them by my side?" so many questions, and no good answers for any of them. I knew I couldn't keep living in the past like this, but how could I go into my future without them? At the very least I had their memories, however painful, to keep me company.

"It sounds to me like you're blaming yourself for their deaths," Ksega said slowly, and I blinked my tears away to see him better. "You were a *child*. It isn't your fault. Are you saying you wouldn't sacrifice yourself the way Aurora did for someone you loved?" his eyebrows twitched, and I swallowed. He was right. Why had I never thought of it that way before?

"Of course I would," I whispered. "But that doesn't make it hurt any less."

"I see that as a good thing. It means you still love them even though they're gone." His expression softened. "I know it seems insensitive, but I'm glad your sister saved you, otherwise I never would have met you." His lips curved up into a smile, but all I could do was stare at him blankly, running his words through my mind again and again, analyzing the meaning behind them.

Derek had been right. Ksega *did* like me. The thought made my head flip. How long had he liked me? Why hadn't I noticed before? Did I like him? The questions flooded through my mind faster than I could think to answer them. A light touch on my knee drew me back to the present, and I realized Ksega had leaned closer to peer at me.

"Are you okay? Sorry. That really *was* insensitive. I just thought . . . never mind." He grimaced, drawing back. He began to pull his hand out of mine, but I squeezed it before he could.

"No, it wasn't that. You're right. I've never thought of it that way before, that's all." I did my best to return his gentle smile. "I'm glad I met you, too. I'm even glad I met Alchemy." The smile disappeared. "I wish I hadn't been such a jerk to him. You're all right that he's changed, and all that stuff is in his past. He could have helped us more." I slumped against the wall again. I hadn't even realized I had sat up straight.

"I'm sure he's glad to have met you, too, even if he thinks you loathe him right now." Ksega adjusted the sheets on his lap, bending his legs so he sat crisscrossed. He looked up at me and grinned. "How about this: once everything is over, you and I will go back to the Evershifting Forest and find him and have him make us the biggest Chem-cooked feast ever." His eyes sparkled. "And we'll make sure he cooks *lots* of bacon." Despite my dreary mood, I laughed, and his grin broadened.

"Alright," I said through chuckles. "That sounds good. I'll have to hold you to it."

"Perfect," he agreed, then looked around the cabin. "Now I'm hungry. Have they got any food around here?"

"Are you sure you're up to walking around?" I asked, and he raised an eyebrow at me.

"Honestly, Sakura, I'm beginning to wonder if you know who I am." He nudged me until I stood, then slid out from beneath the sheets and rose to his feet beside me, still grinning. "If there's good food involved, I'm *always* up to walking around."

28
KSEGA

*T*he captain of *Waterlore* was one of the Coldmonian royal advisors, a wiry man named Traf Perle. His name sounded familiar, but I couldn't remember much about him, as was the case with most somewhat-famous nobles. Traf told us that he and his crew had been out hunting a Cursed sea wraith that had been harassing and destroying the fishing boats sent out from Coldmon's capital island of Sandstone. *Waterlore* didn't seem like the type of vessel to be taken out for such a dangerous task, but none of us were in a position to question it.

In spite of all our suspicious belongings and people, Traf altered the ship's course immediately and promised to bring us all safely to Sandstone, where we would be invited into the palace as His Majesty's honored guests. Many of the pirates seemed ill at ease with this arrangement, but even with all of Captain Howard's modest protests and pointed hints, Traf refused to let us get by with anything less than the best treatment he could provide.

For the most part, Sakura, Gian, Beth, Jessie, Derek and I were kept out of the loop, but Theomand and the three mates of *The Coventry* did what they could to keep us informed. None of us were being treated badly, although suspicion rolled off of *Waterlore*'s crewmates in waves. Wynchell, Asuka, and Bear were being kept in a cargo hold that was just too small for them, and none of them were happy about it, but with the storm still raging, it wasn't safe to bring them onto the deck to give them the room they needed. As for us, we stayed out of peoples' way. The crewmates all wore *adda* except for a handful of servants and the cooks, and most of them were equipped with a number of small daggers and throwing knives. At first, I questioned the absence of larger weapons before I remembered that the Coldmonian weapon of choice was an ice-whip. Even if it was no more than frozen water, the deadly reputation of the ice-whip was well-known across all of Horcath, and I had no desire to experience firsthand how it had been earned.

Sea Serpent Crevice wasn't far from Sandstone, and even with the weather conditions, we reached it in the early afternoon of our second day aboard *Waterlore*. It was safe to say that all of us were relieved to be back on land and able to separate ourselves from the

Coldmonians. At first, we were still squished fairly close together, because we were taken beneath the cliffs into the private ports of the Salt Palace, which were tucked neatly away in the caves. The caves themselves were accessed through a large gate of ice that was manned by several aclure-mages, which explained why the port was never infiltrated and why it hadn't been flooded by the storm.

The private port of the Salt Palace was like nothing I'd ever seen, and by now I had seen quite a lot. The whole place had been polished and smoothed, making the natural stone walls seem unnaturally man-made. The docks themselves were crafted from thick, frosted, and relatively unadorned ice, aside from thick strips of textured metal that had been inlaid in the frozen water to make walking upon it safer. The whole cave was hollowed out, and it was home to almost twenty vessels, all of them similar or identical to each other. While all of them had masts, few of them actually had sails. Manned by powerful aclure-mages, the ships didn't require wind or rowing power to sail.

Waterlore was one of many classy ships in the Ice King's personal fleet, and while it was very nice, it was hardly more than a piece of driftwood compared to the capital ship. It rose high above the other ships, slightly larger than *The Coventry* and much more stylish. It was made from the same pale wood as *Waterlore*, but its gold detailing was much more extravagant. While all the other royal ships bore a golden raptor figurehead, the capital ship's was that of a snarling sea wraith. It sent a shudder down my spine.

The port was crawling with people, most of them dressed in *adda* or regal finery. Even the people that were obviously servants wore brightly colored tunics that were well-crafted. The whole place was alive, and the sounds of voices and creaking wood and softly lapping waves echoed off the shining walls. The chatting and murmuring swelled as *Waterlore* pulled into the port and we all prepared to disembark. Derek was standing beside a stoic Bear, one hand resting on his chocolate feathers. Jessie stood on the dragon's other side, gently petting his wings to help settle his nerves. Wynchell was standing beside Theomand, his body so tense with anxiety that the gruff thief had felt the need to grip one of the raptor's horns in his metal hand. I was standing beside Sakura, who was holding one end of a lead. The other end was looped loosely around Asuka's neck, but Sakura held the rope close to the knot in case he spooked.

I didn't get to drink in all the details of the port, unfortunately, because as soon as we were off the ship we were shuffled through the crowd. Led by Traf, who was strolling confidently ahead in an obnoxiously bright silver tailcoat, we filed into one of the wide exits to the cavernous room and slowly slipped farther and farther away from the hubbub of voices and ships and crew people at work. The noise was quickly replaced with the steady pounding of dozens of feet and clicking of sharp claws on stone. The rhythm was occasionally punctuated with a cough or a small, muttered conversation, but for the most part the only noise anyone made was Traf's energetic whistling at the head of the group.

I stayed close to Sakura, helping to keep Asuka calm. With my bering, I was able to form a connection to him that was stronger than anything she was capable of, but it was only temporary, a mere second compared to the lifetime love formed from the bond of a dragon and its rider. Still, it felt like a lot more than a second to me. Each time he got antsy, I reached out and buried my fingers in his soft blue feathers, pressing my palm flat against his warmth and channeling my bering into him. There was a sort of invisible string tethering us together, tugging at both our hearts and filling each of us nearly to bursting with each other's emotions. If I concentrated, I was able to calm my own racing heart and let that peace flow into him, settling his nerves. The only issue was that concentrating on that meant I wasn't concentrating on walking, and I stumbled more than a few times before Sakura decided to hold onto my arm each time she saw me reaching for the dragon.

The walk wasn't very long. After passing several torches set at regular intervals in the wall, we reached a broad, gently curving staircase carved into the stone. Without missing a beat, Traf began to leap up the steps, chestnut hair bouncing, taking them two at a time and leaving all of us to hurry after him. He didn't even bother to look behind him and make sure we were all following, even though he hadn't instructed any crewmembers of *Waterlore* to accompany us, and not one of the soldiers in the port had decided to escort us. For whatever peculiar reason, the royal advisor seemed to have the utmost trust in us.

At the top of the staircase was another large chamber of the cave system, but this one wasn't just polished stone. Thick pillars of pale, shimmering stone supported the heavy rock above us, their bases and tops flowering out in zig-zagging spikes across the floor and ceilings. As we marched through the room, our footsteps echoing like the thunder outside, a chill stole over me. It wasn't until I passed one of the pillars that I realized it wasn't made from stone at all, but ice.

"The Ice King is certainly fond of reminding people exactly why he has that title," Sakura mused under her breath, just loud enough that I could hear it.

"I only hope the Salt Palace isn't made of ice. Can you imagine that? It would be like the Glass Palace but freezing cold and a lot slipperier," I said, rubbing my arms to dispel the cold from the frosty air.

"It isn't made of ice," Sakura said. I raised my eyebrows at her.

"Oh. That's good," I said bluntly.

"It's made out of salt," she went on, and I gaped at her.

"*What?* Really? That's even worse!" it took me a moment to register her unamused expression. "Ah, I see." I chuckled, feeling my face go red. "You were joking."

"Hey, you lot," Wendy was working his way through the throng to get to us, holding his hook high so he didn't accidentally scrape someone with it. He fell in step with us and grinned, speaking in a low voice. "Try not to draw a lot of attention to yourselves, alright? Out of us, you six are probably the least suspicious." He gestured at us, Gian, Beth, Jessie, and Derek. "Howie and Chap will handle most of the talking. Hopefully you'll just be given some rooms and left alone. Don't worry, though, none of us intend to stay here for very long." He winked at us. "As soon as we can figure out a plan to get you the rest of the way to Freetalon, we're out of this noble slush puddle and back to sailing the Great Lakes."

"On what ship?" Beth asked, and I winced. Derek and Jessie, too, seemed shocked by her bluntness, but Wendy wasn't fazed. Instead, he looked only slightly confused.

"You haven't heard? Traf has already ordered a ship to go back out to sea. They're sending a considerable force of soldiers in *adda* to go and retrieve as much of the wreckage as they can." His grin wavered slightly as he went on. "Not that everything can be recovered, of course, and she'll never quite be the same ship she was, but . . ." He gave a shrug, staring at the ground silently as we entered an upward sloping corridor on the opposite side of the room with the ice pillars. "Well, at least we'll have a ship," he said finally, forcing that beaming grin back onto his face. He was given several encouraging smiles from us, ranging from the obviously-fake-but-shown-out-of-polite-respect smile from Beth to the everything-is-actually-going-to-turn-out-okay smile from Jessie.

The winding cave tunnels ended shortly after that. We arrived in a spacious room with only one door set into the walls. The stonework here was most definitely man-made, and most of it was decorated with various shields and spears and banners displaying the royal leaping dolphin insignia. There were also several racks with weapons on them, and a handful of wooden mannequins, some of them clad in *adda*. Traf breezed past it all, still whistling, and pulled open the heavy wooden door to reveal a marble staircase. He turned back to us and made a dramatic gesture with his hand, smiling broadly with pearly teeth.

"Welcome, ladies and gentlemen, to the Salt Palace of Coldmon," he said proudly. Thomas crossed his arms and frowned.

"That's it?" he asked, running slender fingers through his fiery hair. They got caught in his curls, and he agitatedly yanked them free. "You're telling me that if someone wanted to raid the palace, all they'd have to do is break a wall of ice and shove past some guards?" my gaze darted over to Sakura, then pointedly at Theomand. When he had given us transportation from Famark to Brightlock, we had come across several barrels packed full of Coldmonian royal rupees on his ship. How he had obtained them and what he had done with them, we'd never discovered, but we had promised not to speak about it, and we knew it was wise to stay on the metal-handed man's good side. At least now we knew he wouldn't have had a tough time getting his hands on them.

"It isn't as easy as you make it sound," Traf told the third mate with a smug smile. "While it's true that before the Curse made declaring war a great risk to any kingdom, we had much greater defenses, what we have now is nothing short of exemplary in terms of keeping the Salt Palace protected. Our soldiers are, at this time, the most well-trained of any kingdom and the most well-armed. With alure on our side, entering any port, private or otherwise, leaves everyone else at a disadvantage." His blue eyes seemed to sparkle with fascination as he spoke.

Thomas's only reaction to Traf's short speech was an unimpressed grunt. Ignoring it, the advisor waved us all along after him as he began to ascend the steps, and we followed. It wasn't long before we found ourselves in the body of the Salt Palace.

"Impressive." Wendy commented with a low whistle. I mumbled an agreement under my breath and heard several others doing the same.

We were led through many corridors crafted from sand-colored stone and decorated with all sorts of elegant sconces and colorful tapestries. It was slightly cramped with so many of us, along with the two eirioth dragons and Wynchell, but we managed. The windows were tall and arched and allowed a beautiful view of dormant but sprawling gardens and cobbled pathways and a circular courtyard with a flowing fountain in the center. Even with the muddy aftermath of the rain, it was stunning. The ceilings were supported by frosty pillars of ice that appeared to be set in the walls themselves, and many other decorations we spied were frozen as well, including ice sculptures of sea wraiths with heads reared back and a majestic ship being tossed on the waves. Traf only chuckled at our awe and led us deeper into the palace.

We came to a door that Traf knocked on, and a petite serving girl answered, clad in a blue silk dress. She watched us with wide eyes, her gaze lingering on the fake limbs and eyepatches that punctuated our appearances. Traf cleared his throat to regain her attention, then ordered her to gather a handful of servants and have everyone but Captain Howard, Chap, Molly, Thomas, Wendy, and Theomand escorted to guest chambers. She dipped into a low curtsy and immediately turned to obey the command. Shortly afterward, I found myself in a room that had been introduced as a 'modest guest chamber,' although it was anything but that to thieving scum like me.

The room was brighter and airier than the one I had been given in Brightlock, made from the sand-colored stone and decorated similarly to the rest of the palace. The furniture was all made from pale wood, and the bed was draped in many folds of blue fabric, some of which bore intricate seashell patterns. Upon closer inspection, I saw that each shell had been carefully hand sewn into the fabric in silver thread. The rest of the room was full of other sea-themed details, like the shiny white strings of pearls hanging from the lantern sconces, and the red octopus mural painted above the gold-rimmed hearth. There were more of those tall, arched windows, accompanied by sea-blue curtains, and they afforded me a view of the neat palace gardens below. As I peered into the washroom, I spied a soap bar that was shaped like a clam shell and a circular porcelain bathtub with silver and gold seashells around its lip. The walls were painted to look like waves, and the sole window was stained a deep blue. I found that the theme both pleased and unnerved me.

One of the windows had been left partially open after the storm had passed to let in the fresh, salty air and a light breeze, rustling the ends of the curtains and the bedding. It felt a lot like being at home in the Port, passing the floating merchant stands and all the little fishing boats bobbing in the quay, but at the same time all the shades of blue and the seashell details and the paintings and carvings of sea creatures made me feel like I was standing at the bottom of the ocean. It made me shudder to think about it, so I tried not to, instead focusing on who was left standing in the room with me. It was the serving girl in the light blue dress. Her red-brown hair was pulled into a tight, braided bun on the top of her head, and she kept her blue eyes moving, as if she didn't like to make eye contact any more than necessary. When she realized she had my attention, she jumped slightly.

"I'm Talia." She curtsied to me. "If you should need anything, just ring that bell there." She pointed at a small bell hanging from the wall beside the door. I nodded and gave her a smile, but she only dropped her gaze. The action unsettled me, reminding me of the poor treatment of servants in Old Nightfall.

"Understood. The king isn't hoping to speak with me, is he? How long does he typically keep his guests in the Salt Palace?" I hoped the questions didn't pry too much. She flushed but answered.

"He will let you know if there is anything he needs from you. He doesn't often host guests, and he never has them long. His frequent bouts of sickness make it difficult to attend them." She stopped with a squeak, her cheeks turning bright red as she realized she may have said too much. I pretended that the words meant nothing to me.

"Thank you, Talia," I said in the friendliest voice I could muster. "I'll be sure to call on you if I think of something."

"Great." She gave me a tight-lipped smile that was obviously forced. "I'll come fetch you when it's time for dinner, and some others will come by with some clothes for your wardrobe and hot water for your bath before then." She curtsied again and left before I could thank her once more.

The rest of the daylight hours passed uneventfully. I soaked in a hot bath and changed into a sleek pair of black pants and a billowy light blue tunic. I had just finished combing my hair into a somewhat presentable manner when Talia knocked on my door and came in to inform me that it was time for dinner. I hadn't been expecting all of us to eat with the king, but it quickly became apparent that that was exactly what was going to happen. Talia led me into a long dining room with a pale wooden table running down the length of it. There was one other door, tucked into the far wall beneath a giant window, the glass stained into a picture of a leaping dolphin. At the head of the table sat the king's extravagant chair, currently unoccupied. As soon as I stepped across the threshold, a chill slithered over me, and I shivered. The pillars here were just like all the others in the palace: thick and frosty and made entirely of ice. I wished I'd picked a thicker shirt.

Almost everyone else was already here and seated. The table was long enough to fit everyone that had survived the sea wraith attack and then some, so most of the remaining members of *The Coventry*'s crew already sat at the table, along with Theomand, Beth, Gian, and Derek. I didn't see Jessie or Sakura. Near the head of the table sat Traf, two elegant women who appeared to be twins, and a short, stocky man wearing an exceptionally flashy set of *adda*. Aside from the stocky man, everyone was dressed similarly to me except Traf, who still sported his flashy silver suit, and Davie, who was, as usual, shirtless to accommodate the bones jutting out of his back. I walked into the room and took the seat one space over from Derek, leaving one between us for when Jessie arrived. When I glanced back at the elegant wooden doors, Talia was gone.

"Ah, welcome, boy. Welcome to the table of the Ice King!" Traf said enthusiastically, nodding to me and giving me a wide smile. "These are the esteemed Ladies Luella and Lola Tonn, my fellow advisors to the Ice King"—he gestured at the twins sitting on either side of him, then at the stocky man across the table—"and their brother, General Lennon."

I nodded a polite greeting to each of them. The general said nothing, watching me with dark, beady eyes and tugging thoughtfully at his chocolatey beard. The ladies shared a look with each other, then turned demure smiles to me.

"It is wonderful to have you at His Majesty's table," said one—I couldn't tell them apart—while the other folded her hands neatly together on the table before her. I considered thanking her, unsure if it would have been considered improper, but I was saved by the doors being opened once again.

We all looked up to watch as Jessie and Sakura entered the room, both of them dressed in long blue dresses with braided belts of brown leather around their hips. Sakura had her hair in a pretty plait down her shoulder, the dark strands accented with small, shimmering white pearls placed strategically throughout the braid. Jessie, on the other hand, had her long red hair down, although it still had shiny blue ribbons wound through it. She took the seat between Derek and I, clasping her hands together in her lap as Sakura sat on my left. They were given the same welcome I was from Traf and the other officials of the royal court. They both mumbled civil acknowledgements, then fell quiet again.

"Feeling better?" Sakura asked me softly as a handful of other guests entered the room. It was Chap and Molly, both of them also dressed in varying shades of blue. Traf and the Tonns repeated their little introductions once more.

"Yes, thank you. And you? Still shaken up over almost getting eaten, or did the excitement wear off quickly?" I gave her a playful smile, but her expression remained placid.

"I'll be fine," was all she said. Other small conversations were blooming to life around the table, but Sakura didn't seem interested in them. She was fidgeting with the fabric of her dress.

I didn't like her silence, so I said, "Your scar makes you look very battle-hardened." That didn't appear to be the reassuring thing to say. Her hand came up to her face, and even though I couldn't see it, I knew she was touching the pale line along her cheekbone.

"I don't *feel* battle-hardened," she admitted, letting her hand drop.

"You'll grow into it," I said with a grin.

The small door in the far wall opened, and as heavy boots thumped against marble, the murmured conversations all died away. The man who entered was immediately recognizable as a king. He wasn't as big as I'd expected him to be, but he was by no means a small man. The first thing I noticed was that he was tall. Taller than me, but not quite as tall as Alchemy. The next thing I took note of was his peculiar build. He was thin, but not in the sense that he wasn't fit. He had broad shoulders, but the rest of him seemed very narrow. His features were strong and prominent, making his face one that would not be easy to forget.

"Welcome, my guests," he said as he smiled, his voice booming around the room. He walked up behind his chair and placed beringed hands on its backrest. His eyes were dark but warm, and his hair was a sandy blond mop that sat surprisingly uncombed atop his head.

"It's good to see you again, Your Majesty," Captain Howard dipped his head politely. I'd never seen the captain so formally dressed, and that sight coupled with his use of proper manners was a little shocking.

"And you, Howard, I'm sure." The king smiled widely again, revealing pristine white teeth. His gaze swept the rest of the table, meeting each of ours in turn. "For the duration of your stay you are my honorable guests, and I won't have you twisting your tongues with such excessive titles. Please, call me Matthias." His tone was genuine, and there was no indication of surprise on any of the other nobles' faces, but the rest of us shared mildly baffled looks. The king took notice of it and laughed, a deep, slightly unsettling sound that echoed off the walls. "If it makes you uncomfortable, I have no qualms with the title itself, but you are under no obligation to treat yourselves as lowly in my court. As far as I am concerned, we are equals." He pulled his chair back and sat. He was dressed in clothes not dissimilar to the rest of us, aside from a heavy fur drape that rested over his shoulders, but there were obvious signs that he was royalty and we were not. For one, the many silver and gold rings and bracelets adorning his fingers and wrists. For another, the heavy sapphire amulet hanging from a silver chain around his neck, and for a third, the crown sitting on his head.

Despite feeling that it was a little impolite, I couldn't help but stare at the crown. I'd only seen two other crowns in my life, and they had sat on the heads of the king and queen of Brightlock. Those had been imposing, made from twisting rods of black metal and fashioned into pointed crowns. This one was more elegant, yet somehow more intimidating. It was crafted from bands of silver and beads of sapphire, curling into the shape of a clam shell with five sharp points jutting from its ridges. A thin film of frost sparkled across its surface, drawing my attention to the sharp icicles dangling from the silver. If there had been any question about it before, now there was no denying that he was the Ice King.

Dinner passed. There were several courses, and while most of it smelled and tasted delicious, the knowledge that I was eating squid tentacles and raw oysters didn't sit very well with me, so for the most part I stuck to eating the roast bird and stewed potatoes. The pirates, for their part, seemed to enjoy the meal; even Knuckles, the picky chef, put away several plates of food. The king, his advisors, and his general kept the conversations lively. The king spoke of his parents, the only blood family he'd ever known, and talked some about his childhood, recounting tales of his 'foolish acts of youth,' as he called them, even though he didn't appear to be very old. If I had to guess, I would've said he was in his late twenties or so, but something about that didn't make sense. I couldn't place why, and eventually gave up; all the thinking coupled with the boisterous conversation around the table was giving me a headache, so I reached for my drink and set the matter aside for the time being. When I lifted the cup to my lips, I frowned at the sour taste. Mulberry wine. I set it back on the table.

Dessert was my favorite part of the meal. Almost as soon as the servants came out carrying trays of bread pudding and sweet-smelling coconut curry and wildberry pies, I was salivating. They set the dishes on the table, and it took all my willpower not to grab the nearest plate of fluffy fruitcake and claim it as my own. Everyone waited for the king to serve himself a portion of spiced apple pie before they reached for any desserts themselves, and once they did, I gladly joined them. Sakura gave me a peculiar look as I stacked a number of honey rolls onto my plate, followed by a slice of chocolate cake and three bite-sized lemon tarts dusted with sugar crystals. Her own plate had only two small pastries, one of them shaped like a seashell and the other a fish. When she pulled apart the fluffy pastry, a gooey fruit filling oozed out.

"I'll have to get a couple of those, too," I remarked, stuffing one of the lemon tarts into my mouth. It was the perfect mix of sweet and sour. Sakura took a tentative bite of one of her fruit-filled pastries, then frowned at me, licking sugar from her lips before she took a long swig of her mulberry wine. I made a disgusted face; I didn't understand how she could enjoy the sour drink.

"You're going to eat yourself sick," she pointed out.

"That's the plan." I grinned. "Besides, I'm not the only one. Look at Wendy and Chap." I gestured across the table as I took a bite of my slice of cake. There, Wendy was guzzling down a small bowl of the coconut curry, and Chap was attempting to take a bite of a muffin while it was sandwiched between two pieces of cinnamon bread.

"Wendy has no one to tell him not to eat so much, and Molly is subjecting herself to a night of disturbance by letting Chap wolf down that much sugar. Someone should keep you boys in check," Sakura said, finishing off her first pastry.

"That's only because Chap is her husband, and they're sharing a bedroom. Last I checked, you and I aren't married." I had to bite my tongue to keep myself from adding "*yet*" to the end of that sentence. As soon as the thought crossed my mind, heat rushed up my neck. I shoved another lemon tart into my mouth before Sakura could notice. She didn't seem to have a response to that and turned her attention to her other pastry instead. Unable to stand the growing awkwardness, I turned to Jessie on my other side, hoping to find a distraction there. Instead, I found her sharing a cookie with chocolate chunks in it with Derek.

In situations like this, my preferred escape was to slip away silently and do my own thing. Archery was a welcome respite from dealing with people, but I had no longbow, and I doubted I would be allowed to use the palace gardens as a training ground. Besides, it would probably be rude to stand up and leave during a meal with the king. With a sigh I dragged a hand over my face, took a swig of the powerful mulberry wine, and rolled my shoulders. We were well into the dessert course now, so surely the meal would be ending soon anyway. All I had to do was sit there and be polite until we were allowed to leave.

29
SAKURA

*T*o my great dismay—and several other peoples' as well, from what I could see—the end of the meal was not the end of the evening. As the servants cleared away our dishes, the king called for entertainment and tea. I was exhausted and ready to turn in for the night, but it would have been disrespectful to leave now, so I decided to focus on figuring out when we would be allowed to leave. For the entertainment, servants came in and moved the table and all of the chairs to one side of the room, setting out blankets and cushions and pillows for us to sit on as jesters and jugglers and dancers performed. Steaming pots of tea were provided, as well as platters of fruit that were fresh despite the season.

Since we had all stood while the table and chairs were being moved, most of us ended up sitting with different people than we'd been beside during the meal. As the king sat down, his fur-lined coat swung to the side, casting an odd, dark shadow across his neck. I sat between Molly and Thomas, picking idly at a plate of grapes in front of me. Thomas and Chap, who sat on Molly's other side with an arm around her waist, seemed very relaxed. Thomas was lounging back on a mound of pillows, his broad-brimmed black hat resting low over his eyes as usual, and his arms propped behind his head. Molly was leaning into Chap's chest, twirling a strand of her black hair between two slender fingers. She was in a dress a few shades darker than mine, and her hair was down in its long, shiny waves, but it had pearls wound throughout like mine did. Beside Chap's unruly shock of red hair and already-rumpled shirt, she looked exceptionally beautiful and slightly out of place.

"Don't worry, you'll get what they have someday," Thomas said, and I glanced down at him. I was sitting upright, unable to let myself embrace the same lazy positions they did.

"Come again?" I asked, my brows drawing together. On the marble floor in front of us, a number of musicians began to play a lively tune. Thomas waved a hand towards his brother and sister-in-law.

"Trust me, I've seen it often enough. It's a girl thing. Deep down, you're all dying to get married." He pushed the brim of his hat up to watch me. His blue-green eyes unnerved me, reminding me of Elixir and sending a pinprick of pain blooming in my chest. I forced myself not to let it show, keeping my features as unreadable as possible.

"You can't be serious," I said through a half-hearted laugh. "I can assure you, marriage is the last thing on my mind." He arched an eyebrow.

"At the moment, maybe, but you can't say it's never crossed your mind," he pointed out. I rolled my eyes.

"It's crossed *everybody's* mind. What's your point? Are you saying *you* never think about it?" now it was my turn to quirk an eyebrow. He shrugged.

"From time to time, it'll cross my mind, but I don't worry about it too much. You don't meet many attractive girls being a pirate, you know." He smiled slyly. Before I could respond, he continued. "At the very least, I haven't met my special someone yet. I don't think the same can be said for you." He wiggled his eyebrows, looking pointedly across the room. I didn't have to turn my head to know he was looking at Ksega.

"Oh come on, not you too," I said, pursing my lips. "Everyone seems to think he and I are in love or something. Isn't it possible for us to just be friends?"

"With the way he looks at you? Absolutely not." Thomas grinned now. I blinked, a little taken aback.

"What does *that* mean? How does he look at me?" I asked, then reminded myself to lower my voice. Most people had gone silent now that the entertainers were entertaining, but I didn't much care about watching people dance or juggle. Their time would be better spent learning *useful* skills, like sword fighting.

"There's a specific way a man looks at a woman when he likes her. It took me a while to figure it out, but now that I know it, I see it everywhere." He flicked his fingers at his relatives once more. "For instance, it's the same way Chap looks at Molly." I glanced over at them, immediately feeling like I was intruding on their personal space when I realized their faces had suddenly come very, *very* close to each other. "Or how Ksega looks at you." Thomas grinned. I scowled. "Or how that Gian fellow looks at your Duskan friend." He went on, and I snorted. A few people gave me weird looks, but I cleared my throat and ignored them, turning back to the young pirate.

"I think you're mistaken on that one," I told him. "Gian and Beth don't get along at all."

Thomas's only response was another shrug as he pressed his lips into a thin line, reaching forward to pour himself a mug of tea. He sipped at it idly, and as he did my gaze skimmed the crowd, searching for my companions. I spotted them on a purple blanket together, sharing a plate of assorted berries. Gian was wearing loose-fitting black pants and a dark blue shirt. He had clearly put more effort into making sure his hair was shining and brushed to perfection than into his outfit choices. Erabeth, on the other hand, was more dressed up than I'd ever seen her. For one thing, she was wearing a dress of sea blue, with a fashionable sash draped over her shoulder. Her black hair was braided and pulled up into a tight bun, decorated with pearls and tiny seashells. For once, the red-brown hawk and the purple owl perched on their masters' shoulders appeared to be at peace with each other. Perhaps that was only because their masters themselves seemed to be getting along for an evening. They were the only two sitting on that blanket, sharing a plate of fruit and a pot of tea, and now that Thomas had pointed it out, I couldn't ignore the way Gian kept stealing glances at the woman beside him. My brow twitched with confusion when I saw it. How had I not noticed that before?

"Do you have any idea when we'll be able to get out of here?" I asked Thomas, hoping to push our previous conversation out of my mind.

"Out of this room? Not a clue. Out of the Salt Palace?" he glanced around, then leaned closer to me, keeping his voice low, although the nearest Coldmonian was Traf, and he was fully invested in the entertainment. "Hopefully soon. Wendy told me he's working on a plan to get a shipful of us out of here by tomorrow or the day after, if he can. Howie plans to stay behind with a few others to oversee the reconstruction of *The Coventry*." He rubbed his chin, staring absent-mindedly at one of the men playing a lute.

"Do you think we can do that?" I asked, and he threw me a questioning look. "Leave for Freetalon that quickly? Won't the king want to . . . I don't know, verify that we aren't a bunch of thieves?" as soon as the words left my mouth, I wished I could take them back. I bit my lip, but Thomas only chuckled.

"If he thought we were thieves, he would have found out who most of us are by now." His grin was wry and unworried. "Believe me, Howie does a thorough job making sure *The Coventry* has a wonderful reputation as a trustworthy transportation ship just about everywhere, and I don't mean to brag here, but the rest of us do a mighty fine job of keeping up the ruse." His eyes shone with mischief as he spoke. "Very few people are intuitive enough to see us for what we really are."

"Ksega isn't very intuitive, and I've heard he saw through your act pretty quickly," I said dryly. Thomas laughed again, but this time he wasn't the one to respond. At some point, Molly and Chap had begun to listen in on our conversation, and now the former drew my attention as she spoke.

"The only reason he and that Jessie girl figured it out is because we underestimated them." She smirked, dark eyes darting first towards where Ksega was sitting with Wendy and Peeler, then over to where Jessie sat with Derek. "It's rare we don't judge someone's character accurately from our first meeting, but it's not entirely unheard of. The people we believe to be foolish enough not to discover our *less legal* side jobs are the people we loosen up around. We have short, sweet dealings with them, and then we never see them again."

"And they never remember us as anything more than pleasant business people," Chap pitched in. Molly nodded in agreement. I looked between the two of them, then over at Thomas, still confused. The third mate read my expression and explained further.

"We didn't take Ksega and Jessie for the types to snoop into other peoples' business; that was our mistake. Out of the handful of people who have figured us out, I wasn't counting on Ksega being one of them." He pulled his hat off his head and spun it around in his hands thoughtfully. "He keeps surprising me, somehow. There are a lot more layers to him than one would originally think."

"Yeah," I agreed, slightly distracted. Ksega *did* have a lot of layers, but they weren't as difficult to dissect as Thomas might have thought.

The rest of the night's activities were few, but it felt like I was sitting there absent-mind-edly eating fruit and sipping flavorless tea for hours. The light had completely vanished beyond the window panes, and I was fairly certain Thomas had fallen asleep with his hat tipped over his eyes. Molly looked close to being in a similar state, her head tucked against Chap's chest and her lashes drooping. Across the room, Ksega had shuffled over to sit with Beth and Gian, and while the two boys seemed to be attempting to mimic the jugglers' talents with fruits, Beth was reclining on the pillows and watching them beneath slowly lowering eyelids. The only people still excitedly invested in the entertainment were the king, his advisors and general, Wendy, and the young boy with the bones sticking out of his back.

When we were finally dismissed, I was so tired I practically staggered all the way back to my chambers. They were beautiful, themed like the Great Lakes and filled with wondrous deep-sea treasures, like pearls and dehydrated coral. There was even a glass carving of a school of fish mounted on a marble pedestal near the door. I didn't spare any time to marvel, though, because as soon as I was alone in my chambers, I lit all the candles with a light tap of my finger, changed into a nightgown after pulling the pins and pearls out of my hair, and buried myself beneath the covers.

*T*hankfully, we weren't required to eat breakfast with the king the next morning, but that didn't mean I was allowed to sleep in. A servant banged on my door at the crack of dawn and barged in with a large tray of food platters. She set them loudly on my pale wood table, informed me that I was allowed free rein of the palace grounds, and left before I'd managed to sit up properly and push my tangled mess of hair from my face. I was tempted to sink back into the pillows and sleep some more, knowing that my nights in such a comfortable bed were numbered, but the smell of breakfast wafting through the air enticed me out from under the covers.

I was, to put it simply, a disaster. I had made the mistake of not thoroughly washing my hair during my bath the night before, having been eager to change and hurry to the dinner, even though I had still somehow managed to arrive late. Now, I impatiently dragged a brush through my hair until it was decently straight and pulled it into a quick ponytail. I splashed some water on my face from the basin in the washroom and tried to scrub the tiredness out of my features. It didn't really work, but at least the cold water woke me up some more. I scrutinized myself in the mirror, wondering when my face had gone from that of just a stubborn girl to one of a scarred warrior. My cheeks looked hollower than before, my brows lower. The pale line along my cheek made me look like a different person entirely. I hardly recognized myself. What would Finnian and Gamma think when I finally came home? Would Sycamore still see me as the same person?

I devoured some sweet biscuits, a few coins of sausage, and several balls of fried dough that were filled with what I assumed to be crab before I bothered to change into real clothes. Back home in Carlore, it was customary for people to wear thin robes of silk with long slits, easy to move in and lightweight enough to be comfortable in the hot seasons. Dresses of any kind were rare, and typically saved only for very special occasions. Here in Coldmon, however, it appeared that dresses were everyday-wear for women, so that was all I found waiting in my wardrobe. At least they appeared pleasant, and the one I chose—a pale, sea-green color—was just loose enough that it was comfortable to move in.

I didn't know where anyone's chambers were aside from Jessie's, since she was directly across the corridor from mine. I was tempted to knock on her door and ask if she wanted to explore the palace with me, but the idea of walking around talking to Ksega's closest friend felt awkward, so I slipped out of my chambers and hurried down the corridor to put the thoughts out of my mind.

Many servants bustled through the palace, coming in and out of doors that I didn't think were worth poking my head through. I did my best to avoid getting in anyone's way, although with how many people there were, it was inevitable that some toes were stepped on and elbows knocked together. The palace was beautiful, and I stopped on more than one occasion to marvel at the beauties decorating the hallways. There were vases filled with flowers made of ice, and flocks of seagulls sculpted out of brightly-colored clay. Tapestries depicting rolling waves and undersea wonders adorned the walls alongside elegant sconces with gently flickering flames. The views from the windows were better still. The storm had passed, and the sky was now clear and blue, dotted with fluffy, drifting clouds. From one side of the palace you could see the neatly manicured gardens, currently dormant for the winter, and from another you could look out over the craggy cliffs to where the roaring waters foamed and crashed against the island. Even with the cold weather, many of the windows had been left slightly open, allowing a chilled, salty breeze to rush through the hallways, tugging through my hair and reminding me of flying through the wind on Sycamore.

I was thinking of home as I walked, trailing my fingers along smooth stone walls and over frosty ice pillars. For once, the thoughts of home didn't make me feel like curling up and being miserable. Something about the airiness of the day had put me in a good mood, and I couldn't help but think of Finnian and Gamma and Walter in a similar state, enjoying pleasant weather and each other's company. I would have loved to be with them, but until I could go home, the eclectic companions I was traveling with would have to do.

I wandered my way through several floors of the palace, and it was safe to say that I was very lost. I would have asked one of the passing servants for directions, but each time one walked past I couldn't form the words fast enough. Everyone was in a rush to get where they were going, so I just kept walking until I found myself in a broad, long room. At first, I thought I'd wound my way back around to the dining room, or perhaps a throne room, but there was no dais or table to be seen. The entire room was empty of furnishings. There were no windows, only a large balcony with glass doors waiting at the far end of the room. The floors were glossy black, the ceilings pale and vaulted. Unlike the rest of the palace, the pillars supporting the roof here were made from stone instead of ice. In fact, there didn't appear to be any icy features in the room at all, making it a few degrees warmer than the rest of the palace.

It felt like somewhere I shouldn't be, and I was about to leave when I saw the walls. They were smooth and flat, painted in many different styles. I stepped farther into the room, my gaze roving over the images, trying to interpret what they meant. The paintings wrapped around the room, spiraling down the walls. Near the very top, there was a man being crowned with a crown of ice. Then there was a picture of a massive ship being built, made from pale wood. Beside the ship was a crowd of people celebrating on a beach. Farther down on the wall, there was a man standing in the center of a coiling sea wraith, and farther still, there was a woman being crowned. I drank in all the details I could, my head tilted to the side as I attempted to figure out why the paintings existed. I was so caught up in admiring the artwork that I didn't even realize there was another person in the room with me until he spoke.

"The history of the Dorsey line."

I jumped at the deep voice, whirling around and spotting, to my horror, none other than King Matthias standing behind me. I froze, knowing this must have been a very private room and that I should have left earlier. The thought of bowing crossed my mind, but then I remembered that women are expected to curtsy in front of a noble, and that caused memories to rush to the front of my mind of my many failed attempts to properly curtsy. In the end, I did nothing but stand rigidly in front of him, holding my breath. He smiled broadly, seemingly unaware of the pounding of my heart, although I could hear it so loudly in my ears, I was sure he must be.

"Don't worry, you're not in any trouble. Free rein of the palace, remember?" he quirked a sandy eyebrow, but I made no response. Surely 'free rein' of the palace didn't *actually* mean I could go anywhere I wanted. There must have been rooms that were personal to the king and his council members.

I was sucked out of my thoughts by movement, and I refocused my attention on the king as he walked towards the wall I had been observing. He was dressed much more casually than he had been the night before, wearing a midnight blue tunic and dark pants. He still wore much of his jewelry, but the frozen crown was no longer on his head.

"This room is very special to my people," Matthias went on, ignorant of my new discomfort. He clasped his hands together behind his back and appraised the murals. "Each painting depicts a memorable moment in the reign of each ruler from the Dorsey royal bloodline. When the Ice King—or in a handful of cases, the Ice Queen—dies, our record keepers add the most notable part of their reign on this wall. The first Ice King, for example, is most famous for his unconventional crowning ceremony." He lifted a finger to point at the painting I'd noticed first. "He and his royal council were trapped in a cave when they decided to declare Coldmon its own kingdom. They had no crown, so the soon-to-be king, Drax, crafted one out of ice." Matthias smiled fondly at the painting, as if recalling a pleasant memory. "That handful of people became the first and, for a long time, the only people to recognize Coldmon as its own kingdom." His pointing finger moved to the next image, the one of the ship. "Drax's son, Sul, was the next king, and it was he who successfully gained Coldmon the recognition it deserved by designing the strongest sea-faring vessel known to Horcath at that time. Once his invention gained recognition, so did he and the kingdom, and that is how we became who we are today—sea-people and tradesmen. Our customs have existed since almost the very foundation of this kingdom." He turned his pearly smile back to me, dropping his hand. "Fascinating, isn't it? All our greatest historic achievements, recorded right here in this room."

"What did that one achieve?" I asked, lifting my hand to point at one of the paintings I'd been eyeing. My heart hammered in my chest as the king's gaze followed my own, landing on a painting of a headless man. Over him stood another man wielding a battle-axe. The dead man and his fallen head were painted in pale blue, while the other man was just a silhouette of ominous black. As I watched Matthias's face, I saw his demeanor grow grim, and a chill of fear rode down my spine, afraid I'd brought up the one painting on this wall he would rather leave unnoticed. As he inclined his head, I caught a glimpse of his neck. I had thought there was an odd shadow cast across it before, but now I realized there was a band of darker skin around the Ice King's throat, almost like a peculiar tattoo. My gaze flicked back up to his eyes as he began to speak.

"Ah . . . that one isn't as much of an achievement, I'm afraid." He crossed his arms tightly over his chest, his expression pensive. "It was the most memorable thing the Ice King of that time did. He was a wonderful ruler, and one of the few who cared more about the people under his rule than himself." He sighed heavily. "Unfortunately, his many great acts were overlooked by our record keepers. I can't really blame them, considering that his final act was one of sacrifice." He waved a hand at the painting. "Calysto, one of the most fearless Ice Kings ever to live. He went to war against Brightlock, hoping to obtain property on the motherland for some of his people." He gave me a wan smile. "He died fighting for more freedom for his people. An honorable death, but one that affected our nation greatly." He clasped his hands behind him again. I stared up at the headless man, trying to picture him as a king. Why would they have such a gruesome death painted with the rest of their history?

"You make it sound like your people are trapped on the Great Lakes," I said, curling my hands tightly into fists as I forced the rest of my body to appear relaxed. I wasn't saying anything that would directly offend him, but some part of me felt like I was prying into a part of his family's history that I didn't need to know.

"Oh, it's nothing like that." Matthias laughed softly. "We just don't live like the rest of the kingdoms do. It's only to be expected that at a time or two in history we wanted to branch out into a new way of life, isn't it?"

"I suppose so," I murmured, unsure what else to say. He was silent for a long moment before he turned to me, shifting the conversation away from his family's legacy.

"I've been told that not everyone aboard that ship was a member of its crew. Howard informed me that a handful of you were seeking something in Freetalon?" his tone was light, but his words held another question. I shuffled on my feet, running my thumbs lightly over my knuckles as I considered my answer.

"Yes, we're looking for a way to stop the Curse," I said, observing him closely to try and gauge his reaction to my words. His smile didn't waver. The only change was a curious light that danced in his eyes.

"You truly believe that's possible?" he asked finally. I nodded, and his smile grew. "I'm glad to hear it. Not enough people are putting forth a good effort towards that cause anymore." His brows drew closer together. "If I may ask, what led you to believe you'll find something in Freetalon? I've expended many rupees and much of my time investigating the Curse, but nothing points to it being a disease."

"We don't actually know very much," I lied, hoping he wouldn't press me for more information. The last thing I needed was to slip up and accidentally reveal something we were trying to keep quiet. "We're hoping the people of Freetalon can help us try and identify what type of magic may have been used to affect creatures in such a way."

"Interesting," Matthias mused. "Yes, my studies have also led me to the conclusion that the Curse must be a work of magic. Tell me, have you been studying the Cursed up close?" his curiosity was making my skin crawl. How much could I actually reveal to him without him becoming suspicious about how much I'd uncovered? If he knew too much, he had all the power at his disposal to shut us down and hunt for the source of the Curse himself. He may have better chances of dealing with it, but he didn't know as much as we did, and I doubted he had many dealings with an informative Cursed skeleton.

"Only dead ones," I said, keeping my voice as steady as I could manage. It was in times like these I desperately wished for the skill Ksega possessed of lying smoothly and convincingly.

"I see . . . it doesn't sound like you know much more than I do, then." He smiled at me again and gave me a brief nod. "Well, I must be about my duties. I hope one day we will meet again, and perhaps have more optimistic news regarding the Curse. I wish you safe travels on your journey tomorrow."

"Tomorrow, Your Majesty?" I echoed, frowning. His brows lifted slightly.

"My mistake. I thought everyone had been informed. All of you except a few members of *The Coventry*'s crew are being taken by one of my ships to Freetalon tomorrow morning. You'll all be given clothes and weapons similar to the ones found in the wreckage, if not the exact same ones you had before. Some of them survived with minimal damage." With that, he gave me one more polite nod and strode out of the room, his heavy boots thumping on the shining floors.

30
KSEGA

*T*he ship taking us to Freetalon was called *Wakepearl* and was captained by a burly, rather nondescript man who introduced himself as Nark. *Wakepearl* was almost identical to *Waterlore*, the only differences being the people onboard and the fact that *Wakepearl* had a young sea wraith's head mounted above the entrance to the captain's cabin.

The trip was pleasantly short. Sandstone was the closest island to Freetalon's Gates, and within two days we were pulling into the docks of Match. Nark and his crew gave us some money—extra funds for our journey from the king, he called it—and sent us on our way before swiftly turning around and sailing back towards the Coldmonian capital after they were sure we'd muddled through the Gates.

Our first two days in Freetalon went quickly and rather uneventfully. Howard, Peeler, Davie, Old Hank, Paul, and Zan had been the only pirates to stay on Sandstone and oversee *The Coventry*'s recovery and recreation, along with Theomand and Wynchell; the rest of them had tagged along with us to Freetalon, and on the first night aboard *Wakepearl* we had discussed what to do about that. Thankfully, the pirates turned out to be more of a blessing than a burden. On the first day, we ate dinner and stayed the night at an inn in Match, and over our meal Molly had informed us that she could get all of us a place to stay in the capital city for free. We had our doubts about her being able to obtain a place for all of us without paying *anything*, but Chap assured us that his wife had her ways, then planted a firm kiss on her mouth. The next day, we traveled towards Talon, the capital. We trudged through snow and ice, our progress slowed by the cold. We reached Talon by nightfall, and while there was lots of activity, we spent little time marveling at our surroundings. It was dark and cold, and we were all ready to get some sleep, so we trailed after Molly as she led us through the city, finally stopping to knock on a door. The woman who answered was petite and pretty, with dark skin, like Molly's. That was where their similarities ended. Where Molly's hair was thick and wavy, this woman's was short and in tight coils. Her eyes were brighter than Molly's, and she appeared much younger.

"Molly! How wonderful to see you!" the woman cried. She threw her arms around the pirate's neck and gave her a tight hug, then turned to Chap and Thomas, who both wore wide smiles. "And my favorite boys! Welcome back!" she gave them both a hug, then turned to face the rest of us, her eyes widening. "My, my, don't tell me the family's grown this large."

"Not quite." Molly chuckled. "These are my friends. Do you think you'll be able to give us a place to stay for a little bit?" the woman's eyebrows lifted, and Molly hurriedly added, "It shouldn't be for very long, I promise."

"I suppose so." The woman stepped back and stood to the side so everyone could file in. The building she was in was hard to see clearly in the dark, but it was obviously several stories and very expensive. We all made our way into a large living space on the bottom floor. A fire was roaring in a stone hearth, and several of us made ourselves comfortable on the plush brown sofa and the two wide-backed chairs. Once everyone was inside and the dragons had been stabled in the back, the woman bustled past us into a kitchen, fussing over a kettle and retrieving trays of food. Sakura was the first one to speak.

"Molly, who is that woman?"

"My baby sister, of course," Molly answered smoothly. She was perched on the armrest of the sofa, beside Chap. "Her name is Fayola." Across the room, I saw Wendy's eyebrows rising. He gave Chap a confused look.

"I thought you said you didn't have any other family," Wendy said, sounding a little hurt. Chap opened his mouth, but Molly placed a hand on his shoulder and answered instead.

"She isn't my sister by blood, but she might as well be at this point," she explained. Thomas pitched in from where he sat on the floor in front of the fire, his hat in his lap.

"You know how we always convince Howie to let us spend at least a week of winter in Wisesol or Freetalon?" he asked Wendy. The navigator nodded.

"Of course, I do. You three always disappear for most of it and pop back up before we leave again." He scratched thoughtfully at his chin with his hook, his brows lowering. "Are you saying you always come here?"

"That's right." Fayola returned to the living room carrying a tray, which she set on the glass coffee table in the center of the room. "I first gave them a place to stay thanks to my connection with Molly's family." She offered mugs of tea and plates of sandwiches around, and when she handed me mine, I saw that she was wearing a necklace with a large red feather.

I gave Sakura a questioning look. She was standing beside me, and she leaned close to whisper, "I told you the whole feather thing was a custom of ours." She nodded at the necklace, then gave a polite smile to Fayola as she declined the offered refreshments.

We all sat or stood around, drinking tea and eating sandwiches until we were tired. The building Fayola owned was apparently some sort of inn, although it was like no inn I'd ever seen. We were given a number of rooms, and I ended up sharing one with Thomas and Gian. There were two beds, which were quickly claimed by Thomas and me; Gian didn't even bother to protest, falling over onto the small couch in the corner and groaning into one of the decorative pillows. Light Ray, who had been on his shoulder, flapped his wings irritably and hopped over onto the Nightfaller's back, hooting softly. Gian lifted his head to give me a thin-lipped look.

"Can we please stay in one place for more than two nights? I'm tired of moving around," he complained. I kicked my pack beneath my bed and ran a hand through my hair, glancing at the washroom and debating on if I had the energy to take a bath or not.

"That'll be up to flame-fingers," I said over my shoulder as I walked into the washroom, deciding a quick bath couldn't hurt. Gian huffed loudly from the room behind me.

"I thought she hated when you called her that," he grumbled. Before I could say anything, Thomas pitched in with a light laugh.

"Something tells me she'll let him get away with it." He was sitting on the end of his bed, pulling off his jacket and kicking his boots off his feet. Gian was standing now, and he wrinkled his nose at the pirate's hole-filled socks. Conversation died away as we went about our own business.

I pulled a long item wrapped in cloth away from the rest of my belongings. Nark had shown us all to a room aboard *Wakepearl* that harbored many weapons. Some of them were ones that had been recovered from *The Coventry*'s wreckage, while others were gifts from King Matthias in compensation for the loss of the originals. We had asked why the king was showing such generosity, but Nark's only response was that Traf had been out hunting a Cursed sea wraith and had failed to reach it before it attacked our ship. Traf had blamed himself for what we had lost and had insisted that he and the king help us to restore what had been swallowed by the sea. Because of this, I had been given a new longbow and quiver of arrows. They were similar to my old one, if not even better. I admired the craftsmanship of the weapon before carefully rolling it back in the fabric and setting it beneath my bed. I tossed a change of clothes into the washroom and then went to fill the tub. When I kicked the door shut and began to undress, I heard Gian and Thomas start talking again, but I didn't bother to try and figure out what they were saying. I was exhausted, and it took all my focus to make sure I didn't fall asleep in the tub.

When I came out of the washroom, I tossed my dirty clothes in a heap at the foot of my bed and collapsed onto the covers. Thomas was already beneath his and snoring softly, and Gian was sitting on the sofa, meticulously running a comb through his hair. I was too tired to wriggle my way beneath the blankets, so I let my head flop onto the pillows, and within moments I was asleep.

When I woke up, I was cozy from the warm air circulating through the building thanks to the fire downstairs. I got up and pulled my boots on and I found that Thomas had already left the room, his covers a rumpled mess and his belongings a disastrous pile at the foot of his bed. I stepped around them and shook Gian awake, trying not to let Light Ray bite me from where he was perched above his master's head. Once he was up, we went downstairs and sat down at a table in the kitchen with the other late risers and each ate a heaping plate of steaming hot pancakes, along with wolfing down several portions of crispy bacon.

Fayola's inn was called The Dragon House, and themes of Carlore wound throughout the interior. I had been too tired to notice the night before, but now I took in the feathers carved into the wood of the furniture and the colorful rugs and silk window drapes. Freetalon was a very refined kingdom, with a polished architecture and an easily identifiable style. The Dragon House stood out, and it made me wonder why Fayola had come here if she was obviously so ingrained in the customs of her people. I would have asked, but it was quickly made apparent that Sakura was anxious to get going.

When I stepped into the living room I was embraced by the heat from the fire and pierced by Sakura's thoughtful gaze. She stood beside the hearth, wearing a loose tunic that looked a size too big for her. Her iron flame-sword handle hung from its loop in her belt, and her dark fingers tapped it impatiently. Sitting on the sofa, Beth was twirling a knife in one hand, the other twisting through her black hair, which, for once, wasn't put up. Across from her, sitting in the chairs, were Derek and Jessie.

"Finally, you're both awake." Sakura crossed her arms and gave me and Gian a stern look. Gian scowled at her.

"You say that as if you gave us a specific time to be awake. If you'd wanted us to be up and about early, you should have told us," he said as he crossed his own arms.

"Of course, you'd have to tell us an even earlier time than that, since it takes Gian an hour to brush his hair," I added, smiling. He gave me a slightly baffled look, as if he'd expected me to help him argue his point. When I only met his bewildered expression with a grin, his scowl returned.

"It's not *just* brushing," he grumbled, reaching up to his shoulder to pet Light Ray's feathers. I glanced around, wondering where Taro was, but he didn't appear to be in the room with us. My attention was drawn back to Sakura when she began speaking again.

"Fayola told us that the city is preparing for the winter festivals, and by the end of today the whole place will be teeming with tourists and merchants. If we want to be well on our way towards the Slated Mountains by nightfall, we have to leave now." She gestured towards the floor behind her, and I realized now that several packs had been placed there, presumably belonging to her, Beth, Derek, and Jessie.

"Or we could stay here another night," Gian offered. Everyone gave him an unmoved stare. He sighed heavily and turned around to troop back up the stairs. "Fine. Leaving now it is." He had disappeared before any of us could put in another word.

We were all packed and ready within the next half hour, and then we were out the door and on the streets of Talon. We were leaving the pirates to do their own thing while we were gone, but Molly had promised that she and her family would stay with Fayola until we returned safely. We thanked her as we were walking out the door, and then were immediately swallowed up by the wonder of Freetalon's capital.

I had been to Freetalon before, but only for a day, and I had been much younger. If I had any memories of the capital city, I couldn't recall them now. It was like I was seeing it for the first time. The buildings were tall and elegant, made from bright white and gray stone. The windows were all pointed and shiny, glinting in the early sun's light. Snow sparkled on every surface. There were beautiful fountains that were frozen over and lamp posts made from swirling iron. People moved in waves through the street, gawking at merchandise through shop windows and pointing at the winter festival preparations. We were given a few odd looks, especially Asuka and Bear, but no one tried to stop us, too overwhelmed by the excitement weaving through the air. We had arrived just before the festivals began. Merchants were already preparing their temporary stalls on the side of the road, and great fir trees were being erected in town squares and between prominent storefronts. People wound garlands along windowsills and on the lamp-posts. Lanterns were set at regular intervals on the side of the street, and tinkling wind chimes in the shape of snowflakes were hung over door frames and overhead arches. The people themselves were dressed in heavy woolen garments. Talons were easy to spot in the crowd, tall and pale and with their long red or blond hair done in intricate braids and knots decorated with fake silver snowflakes. I tried to imagine Alchemy being among them as a normal person, preparing for the festivals and laughing jauntily as young children raced by with bundles of garland in their arms. It wasn't difficult to picture.

Talon wasn't very far from the Slated Mountains. We had been given enough rations to last all of us around a week and a half, but I knew Sakura would want us to be finished with the Curse well before we reached the end of our food supply. How likely that was, I couldn't be sure, but there was a sense of confidence about us as we marched through Talon Glade towards the looming peaks of the Slated Mountains. The majority of the mountain range actually lay in the borders of Wisesol, but since we knew Alchemy was from Freetalon originally, we reasoned that it would be wise to start with the southernmost peaks.

We camped one night in the Glade. After we had eaten dinner, Gian and Erabeth did some sword training, and Sakura and Derek kept a blazing fire going. We took turns keeping watch of the snowy landscape throughout the night, although it was safe to say that with the bitter cold air and the whistling winds, none of us got a lot of sleep. The next day, we reached the base of the Slated Mountains around the time the sun was passing the midpoint in the sky. Unlike the last cliff face I scaled, which had been the sandy drop from Brightlock into the Duskfall Desert, the mountains had natural trails carved into them from rain and time and possibly the wildlife that dwelt there. Along with that, there were plants. They were thin and sharp, some of them being no more than dead thorn bushes, but there were some living vines and a variety of berry bushes. With the help of my bering, I strengthened the vines and let them grow into long ropes. Secured in the stone, the ropes allowed us to make fast progress up the mountainside. There was little to no conversation as we traveled until we stopped to make camp and eat dinner.

"We haven't run into any animals yet," Jessie observed as she went through the food bag hanging from Bear's shoulder. Sakura and Derek were building a small fire pit in the center of our little campsite. We had selected a relatively flat space that could only fit two of our tents, so people would be sharing.

"I've sensed a few nearby, but they've all been small," I said, rubbing my gloved hands together in an attempt to warm them up some more. "At least we haven't seen any slate-wolves."

"It's only a matter of time until we do." Derek rocked back from his work with the fire pit and shoved a pale hand through his mop of hair. "Once we get further into the mountain range, I'm sure the place will be crawling with them."

"That is, if we even have to go that far." Gian pointed out. He and Beth were setting up the tents. She had already managed to get the girls' tent up and disappeared inside to set up their bedrolls. Gian, on the other hand, was experiencing a considerable amount of difficulty when it came to using the tent poles, and Asuka was sitting beside him, observing and clicking his beak as he watched the Nightfaller struggle.

"How are we going to cover every little bit of the mountains?" Jessie asked, turning to Sakura, who was now working with kindling in the center of the fire pit.

"We shouldn't have to. Wherever it is, it will have to be someplace accessible by your average human, and it will probably be spacious. Alec was experimenting and studying things up here, which means he'll have needed a lot of room." Sakura snapped a spark to life between her fingers, and it caught in the kindling, flaring into a plume of fire.

"Keep in mind, though, that was three hundred years ago," I told her, giving up on attempting to warm my hands and walking around the fire pit to help Gian with the tent. "The mountains will have changed a lot since then." I grabbed Gian's hand and pushed it away from where he was pulling on the tent tarp so tightly he was going to tear something. Asuka cooed curiously as I took over assembling the tent.

"Even so . . ." she mumbled, then trailed off, because she knew as well as the rest of us that there was no good argument for that.

"We're better equipped to find it than anyone else, though," I said more optimistically. Beth poked her head out of the tent she was in and raised an eyebrow at me. "I can hear the Curse at work," I elaborated, "so I should be able to sense it when we're in the right area. Plus, if we learned anything from finding the well that led to Old Nightfall, it's that I have a knack for sensing powerful magic." I finished setting up the tent and then went to help Gian retrieve the bedrolls that would go inside. He frowned at me as he handed one of them over.

"Didn't that nearly kill you or something?" he asked, and I only grinned in reply.

"Great," Sakura stood and dusted off her pants. "So if Ksega drops dead, we'll know we're close."

Conversation faded away as Jessie and Beth worked on making dinner. We had been given a number of fresh ingredients from Fayola and the pirates, and while they had frozen during our journey, they were easy to thaw with Sakura and Derek's eirioth. The meal they made was good, but paled in comparison to anything Alchemy would have cooked. It was one of the many things I missed about him.

We crawled into the tents and shuffled into our bedrolls a few hours after night had fallen. Derek was taking the first watch, sitting close to the fire with Bear lying on one side of him and Asuka on the other. As I hugged myself beneath my covers to keep warm, I looked across the shadowy tent to where Gian was packing a number of spare cloaks into a sort of nest for Light Ray to nestle into. He and Beth were so gentle with their pets, the same way Jessie was gentle with her horses or how soft Derek became around Bear. I wondered what it would be like to see Sakura interacting with her own eirioth dragon. I had never had a pet; the closest I had come to it had been Asuka. Buying a pet had rarely crossed my mind, but now I found myself wanting one. What could be better than a nonjudgmental companion that loved you for its whole life?

As I drifted off into sleep, I added it to my ever-growing list of things to ask Willa about when I finally went home.

31
KSEGA

When I woke up to the interior of the tent lit by the sun's early-morning glow, I had vague memories of Derek shaking me awake and mumbling something about taking over the watch before he flopped onto his bedroll and fell asleep. I had stayed up by the fire petting Asuka and Bear for a couple hours before I went to wake Gian for his turn. After that, I'd fallen asleep once more and hadn't woken up again until now. Something was bugging me, but I couldn't place what.

Gian and Derek were both still asleep, and Light Ray was watching me with tired eyes. I spent a minute or so making myself somewhat presentable and crawled past a drooling Derek to get out of the tent, following the scent of salty bacon. Sakura was the one cooking it, the tip of her tongue protruding from her lips as she carefully used her eirioth to make the strips nice and crispy. Her gaze flicked up to me briefly before refocusing on the bacon.

"Good morning," she said, shifting the way she sat so that she could face me a little better. She waved a hand towards the cliff. "Asuka and Bear were out frolicking in the snow over there. Could you go check on them and make sure they're still close by?"

"Sure," I croaked, my throat dry and raw from the cold air. I grabbed a waterskin from where it was sitting near the fire and drank a swig, then crept closer to the cliff's edge. The sleet and snow made the whole mountain slippery, so I had to be careful when approaching the cliffside. When I peered over the edge, I could see two eirioth dragons, one burly and brown and the other agile and deep blue. They were tussling in the snow, rolling down a gentle slope through mounds of frost. When they bounced back to their feet, both of them were coated in fine white powder.

"They seem fine," I said, returning to the fire and crouching beside Sakura. I reached out and snatched a strip of bacon, hissing as it burned my fingers and tossing it lightly between my hands. She raised an eyebrow at me, moving her arm so that I couldn't grab another piece.

"Everyone else needs to eat, too, you know," she said, and I shrugged, crunching through the bacon.

"We have other food." I pointed towards our pile of packs. We had left most of them near the fire so that their contents wouldn't freeze overnight. Inside were a number of meats and breads and herbs, and some miscellaneous items Jessie used for her recle.

Sakura's only response to that was a grunt as she portioned out the cooked bacon into equal shares. She pointed at one of the little piles and nodded at me. I greedily ate it all, then went to find some bread and water to wash it down with. When I looked up next, Beth and Jessie were shuffling out of their tent and eyeing the bacon. Sakura gave them their share and then yelled in the general direction of the tent I'd slept in. A few minutes later, Derek came out, disheveled and grim-faced, although I was quickly discovering that that was just how he looked.

"Go ahead and dig in, then we'll start packing up," Sakura told him, gesturing at the bacon. "Gian will still be a while."

As we were all finishing our breakfast and packing up, Derek whistled for Bear, and both of the eirioth dragons happily bounded back to our campsite, shaking snow from their feathers and stamping their feet on the frosty ground. Their breath froze in plumes in front of their faces as they huffed from their play-fighting.

"At least we'll be able to tell if the Curse is ever taking one of them," Beth said dryly. Derek and Sakura both gave her a harsh look, but she shrugged it off. "It's true. With how energetic they are, it would be hard not to tell when they started feeling less like themselves."

"Hopefully we won't have to worry about them being taken by the Curse at all. Or any other animal, for that matter." Sakura cinched a pack closed and lifted it to fasten to Bear's saddle, brushing wet snow off his hide as she did so. Asuka snuffled at her, pressing his beak against her hands. She gave him an affectionate scratch on the head before gesturing towards the tent Gian was still in. The other tent had been folded and packed already, as had everything else, including the bedrolls and packs that had been inside the tents. We were only waiting on him.

"I'll bet you ten gold coins he's sick again," I said, glancing at Jessie. She gave me a disapproving frown as Beth walked over to the tent and aggressively kicked at the tarp.

"Hey, Sky Boy! We're getting ready to move. Get out here," she snapped, her sharp Duskan accent lacing her words. There was a grunt from inside, then a muffled response that I couldn't understand. A minute later, Light Ray fluttered out of the tent, hopping on the snow until he got to the warm ground near the smoking pit where the fire had once been. Moments after that, Gian came out, combing his hands through his hair and wielding his small knife. I saw strands of black hair hanging from his shirt and raised my brows.

"Were you giving yourself a haircut?" I guessed, and he sniffed at me as he placed his toothpick dagger back in its place inside his shirt, beneath several other layers of clothing.

"You had a haircut not that long ago. Is it so unusual?" he sniped, turning back towards the tent to help Derek break it down. I didn't respond. I hadn't thought anyone else had noticed that my hair had been cut.

"On a snow-covered mountain, while we're hunting the source of the most *dasten* magic known to Horcath? Yes, Sky Boy, it's a little unusual." Beth crossed her arms, her lips pulling into a frown. Gian looked like he was about to argue, but then thought better of it. He retrieved his sword and fastened it in place at his belt, then nodded at Sakura.

"Okay, let's go," he said, and we began our hike for the day. We had discussed flying on the dragons before but had decided against it in the end. The air was too strong and too cold for anyone but Derek and Sakura to be flying in, not to mention they were the only two that actually knew *how* to fly a dragon, so we were all moving on foot.

It hadn't been ten minutes when I realized what had been bothering me before. I was near the front of our group, and when I stopped suddenly, Derek walked directly into my back. Bear stopped, then Asuka, then a chorus of grunts of surprise sounded from the back of our procession as everyone else stumbled into the dragons.

"Sorry," I said, turning to face Derek. He was frowning at me. We were on a steep cliff edge, and I inched further away from the lip of the drop. "I think I hear something."

"The Curse?" he asked, the annoyance on his face lessening. I pursed my lips in concentration, trying to pinpoint the sound I heard. There *was* the distant humming that I associated with the Curse, but it felt far away, just barely out of my reach. Closer, though, was the sound of something scrabbling on stone. Once I had identified the noise, I angled my head a few different ways, waiting until I could detect which direction it was coming from.

"Over there." I pointed in the direction we had been walking and slightly to the left. There was a rise of snow and a jagged outcropping that cast the ground below it in shadow. "There's something in there. I don't think it's Cursed, but there is *something* Cursed in the distance." I took off my gloves, unslung my bow and tugged an arrow free from the quiver at my hip, gently knocking it to the string. "I'll go check it out." Derek began to advise against it, but he was burdened with the packs that couldn't fit on Bear's saddle and everyone else was stuck behind the dragons. It was safest if I went on my own.

I jogged ahead, mindful of the slick rocks beneath my boots, and slunk towards the snowy mound. Over the past few months, my skills in both archery and sneaking around had been greatly refined, especially when compared to those of someone like Sakura. Snow, however, was not something I was adept at stealthily walking on, and I cringed as my boots crunched through it. There was no helping it, so I did my best to ignore the sound and focus on the scrabbling coming from ahead, my arms tense and ready to draw and fire the arrow should the need arise.

When I crested the little hill of snow, my heart started beating a little faster. The animal before me was easily recognizable by its shaggy, silvery pelt made up of fur so soft it was coveted around Horcath. If that alone hadn't been what told me that it was a slate-wolf, the naked rat-like tail would have, or the pearly white-blue eyes. It had its snout in a hole it had dug, its curling claws full of frozen mud and stone. It was sniffing very loudly in the hole, its tail lashing the ground. It appeared to be alone, which was a good sign. Slate-wolves were notorious for being very dangerous to hunt, because alone they posed a great threat, and when they were traveling in packs. . . well, you get the picture. Thankfully, this one was on its lonesome and very distracted as I lifted my bow, bringing it back to full draw. I'd never liked hunting just for sport, and I'd rarely done it back home in Rulak. When I had gone hunting, it had only been because Willa and I had needed something a little more substantial to get us through the winter. I tried to block out the slate-wolf's screech of surprise and pain when I let the arrow fly. I looked away when it struck, but there was no avoiding coming closer once it stopped wriggling.

"Slate-wolf!" I yelled back to where Derek was waiting. Beyond him, I could see Beth peering curiously around Asuka's rump. "I got it. You can come over here now." I turned back to the animal's body and dipped beneath the overhang, hoping to retrieve my arrow. When I came closer, I did my best not to look at the blind eyes, only watching my arrow as I wrestled it free of the wolf's silky fur. The hole it had been digging in appeared to be the entrance to some rodent's den.

"Ew." Derek had appeared behind me, and he wrinkled his nose. "That thing is hideous."

"Can we eat it?" Beth asked, leaning around him and creeping beneath the overhang with me. Now that they were past the narrow ledge, they were filing around the dragons to come get a closer look. I was happy to slip out of the overhang to wash my arrow in the snow and check it for damage.

"Do whatever you want with it," I said, making a face as some of the blood smeared across my hand. I looked up towards the gray sky, where flakes of snow were now falling, twirling through the air. I could still hear the Curse, but something about it was off. Cursed animals moved around. Alchemy had told us that the Curse moved with a purpose, and that even if it wasn't actively being controlled, corrupted animals would take it upon themselves to go hunt down living things. If I really did hear something Cursed, why didn't it sound like it had come any closer or gone any farther away?

"Hear something else?" Sakura had walked past the spectacle of the dead slate-wolf and was watching me closely. Behind her, I could see Beth meticulously beginning to skin the slate-wolf's carcass. Disgusted, I looked away and finished cleaning the arrow and my hand before I stood, wiping the cold snow from my skin and tugging my gloves back on.

"Nothing new. I'm just curious about whatever Cursed thing I heard. It doesn't seem to have moved." I tilted my head to the side, then added, "And I can't tell where it's coming from. Normally, I at least have a sense of what direction to look in."

"Do you think it's the source?" Sakura pried, a hopeful note weaving its way into her voice. I shrugged.

"If it is, it must still be a good way off, but at least I can hear it." I tucked the arrow into my quiver and checked to make sure my longbow was securely in place on my back.

"It's a good sign," Sakura said. The others finally moved on from the slate-wolf and came to join us. Beth was carrying a partially bloodied pelt. It could be cleaned and used as a blanket, or even sold for a lot of money if that was what she wanted to do, but for now it was a clump of messed-up fur. I curled my nose at it.

"Let's keep going, then," Derek said, scratching Bear's neck and tugging him away from where he was poking his head curiously at the overhang and the remains of the slate-wolf.

We all fell back into our steady rhythm, and before I knew it half the day had passed. We saw three other slate-wolves, but two of them had been farther down on the mountains and hadn't noticed us, and one of them was little more than a Cursed heap of bones. We had passed it quickly, ignoring the raspy wheezing noises escaping from its blackened lungs. At the end of our line, Beth pulled her saber out and ran it through the animal's heart.

I was so caught up in not slipping and falling down the mountainside that I didn't even realize the buzzing in my head had intensified until it hit me in a jarring wave. I staggered, shocked by the ferocity of the noise, and immediately felt a hand grip the collar of my shirt. One of my feet slid off the edge of the cliff, and I yelped as I was half pulled and half thrown back onto the small plane of stone we found ourselves on. I stumbled back, rocking back and forth on my feet until the world righted itself and I could stand upright again. When I could, I saw that everyone was watching me with terrified and mildly expectant expressions.

"Sorry about that," I said, forcing a grin. "I heard it. It's close." I furrowed my brow, concentrating on the noise. It was crackling in my head like lightning, making everything else fuzzy. How had I failed to notice it growing in volume until now?

"Could be that. Get down." Derek's voice drew my gaze to him, and I followed where he was pointing to see an animal so horribly disfigured, I couldn't name it. It was like a stumbling, lurching mass of black fur and muck, dripping and limping and dragging itself around the side of a boulder. I shuddered as I ducked just in time to let Derek's arrow soar through the air where I'd stood a moment before, sinking with a sickening *squelch* into the flesh between the creature's eyes.

"It wasn't that," I said as I stood again, still hearing the buzzing. "And I have a feeling we'll be seeing more of whatever that was." I grimaced, unslinging my bow again. Behind me, I could hear Gian and Beth drawing their blades, and I didn't have to look to know Derek still held his longbow and Sakura now held her flame-sword handle.

"I wish we had some of those hypnotic charms from Peeler," Sakura said, curling her lip at the oozing creature. "They might be helpful in situations like these, but he never let me test out any of the prototypes."

"We'll be okay," I told her, squinting through the snowy wind. "I'm sure we can all handle ourselves out here. Besides, once we're done, there won't be a need for him to finalize the prototypes." She grunted but said nothing in response.

We continued through the snow-filled mountain, and the farther we went the louder the sound was. I remembered when I'd found the well that served as a portal to Old Nightfall, how painful the noise had been. It had been enough to knock me out and leave me incapacitated for longer than I was happy about. I hoped that wouldn't happen again.

We kept our weapons at the ready, and it was a good thing we did, because once we rounded a bend and were faced with an ominous cave mouth, we were also faced with dozens of Cursed animals. They were little more than four-legged twigs, hobbling around on partially-eaten limbs and watching us with what remained of their eyes. They were so black they were like shadows peppered with silvery-green blood. Gian and Jessie gagged somewhere behind me. From within the cave roared the buzzing sound, but there was no need for me to tell that to the others. Deep in the darkness of the cave, there was a faint light. It pulsed and warped in the shadows, never staying the same for more than a second. My throat ran dry at the prospect of finding the source of it.

As soon as we were in the sights of the Cursed beasts, they were charging for us. We couldn't run from the onslaught, so we met it head on. Derek and I shot them down quickly, our arrows sinking easily through their skulls. Their bodies fell and broke beneath our attacks. When the ones that evaded our arrows reached us, Gian, Sakura, and Beth leapt forward to meet them. The sounds were horrendous. Along with the buzzing, there were grunts from us and all sorts of snarls and screeches and howls from the animals around us. Gian kicked one over the edge of the cliff. Beth sliced one's head clean off. Sakura's eirioth blade caught on a patch of surviving fur and sent what must have been some sort of Cursed goat rolling in the snow to extinguish itself.

Jessie didn't join in the fray. When I glanced behind us for a brief moment, she was disappearing around a bend, tugging Bear's reins and Asuka's lead. Taro and Light Ray were on Bear's saddle. All four of them were tipsy, and the dragons were stumbling, as if they were dizzy. Whatever power was coming from inside that cave, it was already affecting them. It may have been thanks to Jessie that they hadn't already succumbed to it.

The monsters came at us in wave after wave. Derek and I shot and shot until we were out of arrows, then he pulled a long dagger from his belt, and I tugged the hunting knife at my waist free. The range of our knives was poor, meaning we would have to get very close to the beasts to hurt them. Fortunately for us, the Curse had already done most of the work. The animals could hardly stand, much less move and attack, making them easy targets. The only issue was there were *so many* of them. They poured out from cracks and crevices, rolled down the mountain from the higher peaks, loped out of the shadows of the cave. Every time one died, ten seemed to rush in to take its place.

"How many can there be?" Beth yelled over the fray, letting out a scream of frustration as she chopped a Cursed slate-wolf's hind leg off then swung around to kick it in the line of Sakura's flame-sword. It howled in pain as the fire licked at its bones. Fire didn't do much to Cursed bones, but when it was hot enough it could break them into ashes. The Curse had already made these animals ragged and brittle, and it didn't take much to kill them.

"Not many more, surely," Derek shouted back. He had shed his outermost fur coat, and I could see the sweat lining his brow. "Even if all the creatures on this mountain have been called here and Cursed, there can't be many more." He was right. The mountains were an unforgiving terrain, and few animal species were capable of surviving there.

"We have to get into the cave," Sakura called, panting. She had put her hair into a braid that morning, but throughout the day strands had come loose, and they were now glued to her face with sweat. Beth was in a similar way, and Gian looked like his legs were about to give out. He had become a good fighter, but his body still wasn't used to this much exertion, and it hadn't entirely healed from whatever sicknesses had plagued him when we first brought him down to Horcath.

"Jess took the animals away," I said, ramming my knife's hilt into the side of a small fox's head and nudging its limp body over the edge of the cliffside. "We can't leave her on her own out here."

"I'll go back for her," Derek grunted as a heap of black fur and bones leapt at him and he ducked out of the way, bringing his arm up so that his dagger caught it in the chest. When he kicked the corpse away, his hand and weapon were sticky with black grime and silvery blood.

"Don't die," Sakura called to him as he turned and sprinted back the way we'd come. He replied, but none of us could hear him, and we didn't have time to ask him to repeat it. More Cursed animals were rushing towards us, and this time we didn't just wait for them to come to us. Huddling close together, we pushed through the throng, sending deformed creatures rolling and stumbling left and right. Teeth gnashed and jaws snapped all around us. I felt a tug on my cloak and instinctively kicked out, my boot heel connecting with something's jaw. It yowled and flipped backwards, tumbling down the rocky slope into a pile of snow.

We cleaved through the crowd of beasts, tripping over legs and tails and each other's feet as we raced for the cave entrance. It was big and looming, and a chill curled around my spine as we fell into its shade. The sun was lowering in the sky, casting us into darker shadows, and it made the Cursed animals harder to see. Thankfully, once we pitched into the cave and staggered towards the shifting light, the Cursed beasts hung back. They skidded to a stop in the dust, illuminated by the flashing light of Sakura's flame sword, snorting and snarling as they watched us with beady eyes.

"Come on, we have to keep moving," Beth said between rapid breaths, shuffling backwards through the snow and dirt. The cave yawned before us, and I saw now that there was a rough staircase carved into it, descending into the depths of the mountain. Broken pieces of pottery lay on the steps, filmed with frost.

We hurried down the steps, oblivious to the dangers before us and aware only of the slobbering monsters at our backs. It wasn't until we slowed to a trembling halt at the bottom of the staircase that we stopped to catch our breath. Sakura and Gian were shaking from exertion, and Beth was swaying slightly back and forth, her eyes closed and sweat dripping down her face.

"Here," I gasped. I could sense life-glows in the darkness around us, but aside from the ring of orange light cast from Sakura's flame-sword we couldn't see anything clearly. I reached out to a plant nearby and a bush burst to life, bright red berries popping out against the emerald leaves. I bent down and broke off a branch, holding it out to Sakura. She lit it with her flame-sword, then let the weapon flicker out of existence with a sigh of relief.

The Curse was roaring in my ears now, but I did my best to tune it out as I broke more branches off the bush and allowed each of us to hold one of the make-shift torches. Once we all had one, we finally took a look at our surroundings. They wouldn't last more than a handful of minutes, but Sakura could keep the room lit. The room was vast, and as far as I could tell it was the only chamber at the bottom of the staircase. It was mostly empty and filled with rubble. Chunks of the ceiling had fallen out and lay in heaps of broken stone on the ground. Measly plants grew in tiny sprigs here and there, but there was little sign of nature aside from that. There were, however, signs of human life. Not recent, of course, but they were there. Broken dishes, ash that didn't come from dirt or stone, an old, tattered piece of fabric that looked like it would crumble to dust if you so much as touched it.

"Well," Sakura said, her voice shaky as she lifted her torch to peer at one of the broken dishes, cracked and dirt-covered. "We've found where Alchemy worked." Her voice was distant, and if that alone hadn't told me she was very distracted by the situation, her use of 'Alchemy' would have. Ever since she'd discovered who he was, she kept referring to him as Alec, but every now and then she would call him Alchemy, as if the two parts of his history were two separate people.

The far wall was where the faint light was coming from, as well as the awful din that bounced around in my head. That was where most of the wreckage of the room was. Great boulders and mounds of fallen stone lay in piles against the wall. Through the cracks and crevices between them came the pulsing light. Something about the way the rocks seemed to have fallen was odd. Beth noticed it, too.

"It looks almost like someone blasted this rock down," she said, lifting her torch towards the ceiling, where a great wound had been gouged into the mountain.

"To cover a mistake, perhaps." Sakura said thinly, her lips pressed tightly together. She had told me that Alchemy sealed the Curse away when he'd first created it, but these rocks didn't look like they had been sitting here for three hundred years. Maybe only some of them had been sent down on top of the source, and the rest had slowly given way over time.

"Let's get to work, then." Gian put his sword away, making a face as the black blood and grime that coated his blade stained the sheath as well. The rest of us also put away our weapons and approached the fallen stone. I shuddered as the sound swelled. Sakura gave me a pressing look, but I waved her concern away.

"I'm okay. It's just loud. I'll be fine once we get rid of it." I grimaced against the noise and held my torch out to her. She took it with her free hand, and Beth took Gian's, then we went to work.

We rotated between the four of us. Two would work and two would hold the torches. We were all pouring sweat and wearing far fewer layers than we had been before by the time we reached the bottom of the stones and boulders we could move individually. There were three giant slabs of stone left to move, with gaps between them that could fit a small smith. Beyond those gaps, the silver-green light ebbed and flowed across the ground.

"Are we sure this is a good idea?" Gian asked as he sank to the ground, gasping for breath. Jessie had taken all of our food and water when she'd retreated with the dragons. "I mean, if this thing Cursed Alchemy, it can Curse us, too." Sakura's face was grim as she bent down to inspect the slabs of rock, peering into the gaps to see if there was another way in.

"If you want to leave and not risk your pretty little face and your glossy hair, be my guest, but I'm seeing this through to the end." She wedged herself between two of the slabs and grunted as she shoved against them with all her might. One of them shifted slightly, but then it stopped. She tried again, but it wouldn't give, and she slumped to the dusty ground, shutting her eyes and gulping in huge breaths of air as she half-heartedly peeled away the last coat she had on. She was down to just her pants and her tunic, both of them stained with Cursed blood and her own sweat.

"This place is pretty obvious," Beth mused, ignoring Sakura's statement. She, too, lowered herself to the ground. I didn't sit down. If I let myself rest, I knew I wouldn't get back up again. "It makes you wonder why nobody's found it before."

"Maybe they have," Gian groaned, half-reclined on the ground. He had himself propped up on his elbows, protecting his hair from the dust and dirt on the stone, although it was already a matted mess from the fight.

"Maybe they died," I finished the thought for him, letting my head hang and my eyes close. It was the most relief I could give myself without collapsing. The noise thundered in my ears, seemingly louder than ever before. I wondered if it would rupture one or both of my eardrums.

"If you guys aren't leaving," Sakura said softly. "Then can you help me move these rocks?"

We all pulled ourselves together enough to heave against the stone slabs. One of them fell with a deafening *thud* and an explosion of dust, and then another fell the opposite way. The third one cracked down the middle and folded over itself, and before we knew it, there it was, hovering in front of us: the Curse.

At first, I was a little underwhelmed. It was like a hovering oval of white-green light, haloed by rings of flashing silver. Magic rippled from it, making the light around us flex and bend unnaturally. I couldn't take my eyes off it. It was beautiful; it was light, it was *life*. I wanted to reach out and touch it, but a nagging thought in the back of my head stopped me.

It isn't life. It's death. I flinched away from it, then paused. More words echoed into my head, sweeter than honey and as soft as one of Asuka's feathers.

It is not death. It is life and love. It will give you all you desire. It will rejuvenate your strength, your health, your soul. You need never want for anything, if you only reach out to take it. All the power in the world will be at your fingertips.

My head spun. The buzzing was like a million flies in my ears. My heart pumped in my chest, making my pulse race. Every instinct within me told me to reach out and grab it, yet every instinct pulled me away. I was at war with myself. Or maybe I was at war with the lilting voice that kept luring me in, calling for me to reach out and take the . . .

My vision snapped back into focus. I squinted against the light, tearing my gaze away from the floating oval. It had no name. It wasn't anything but evil, and it had nearly drawn me right into it. Beside me, I now realized that everyone else was entranced the same way I had been. Beth wore a conflicted expression, and Sakura had tears running down her face.

Their eyes were locked on the source before them. Gian's arm had already begun to lift towards it.

I didn't know how to destroy the Curse, but I didn't have time to worry about figuring it out, so I yanked my hunting knife back out of my belt and drove it forward. The tip connected with the pulsating oval, and then everything flashed bright white. I was blown backwards, rolling over stone and crashing into the far wall. A rumbling, cavernous wind rushed through the room, whistling up the staircase and vanishing into the snowy mountain air. Our torches went out. The light was extinguished, and everything turned black.

I didn't know if I woke up or if I had been awake the whole time. Eyes opened or closed, it made no difference to what I could see. I heard things, though. Someone was grunting and moving, and moments after the sounds began, a small flame winked to life, creating a circle of flickering light at the base of the stairs.

I was lying on my back, my whole body tingling with pain. I groaned and winced as I forced myself to sit up. Sakura was sitting at the base of the stairs, her hair a disaster, blood trickling from her lip. Beside her, Gian was pushing himself up as well. I couldn't see Beth.

"Is that it?" Sakura said softly, staring towards the dark far side of the room. She held up her other hand and a snake of fire slithered from her palm, hissing across the floor until it lit up the place where the source had floated. It was empty.

"I can't hear it anymore," I said, flinching as my hands stung against the stone. Looking down at them, I saw that they were nicked and cut in several places.

"Is anyone hurt?" Sakura asked. Gian and I mumbled that we were fine. We all waited and listened. I saw Gian's pale face grow paler.

"Beth?" he said hesitantly. There was a quiet whimper from somewhere to his left. All three of us scrambled to our feet, gasping and cursing at our own pain but pushing through it as we raced for the corner of the room. Beth was curled there, bleeding from her leg. Her face was pinched in pain.

"Beth . . ." Sakura shook her head, sucking on her bleeding lip. I could already see a plan forming behind her eyes. "Okay, try to be as still as you can. We're going to help you up, and we're going to get you to Jessie. Here, grab my arm." She gripped the Duskan's hand, trembling at the strain it put on her muscles. All of us were shaking from exhaustion, but none of us complained as we helped to pull her to her feet. She yelled and cursed in Sandrun, hissing and grimacing and digging her fingernails into our skin as we pulled her up, but we managed it. Sakura's snake of flame was coiled in front of us now, and she stepped back to let Gian and I support Beth on either side.

"I don't know if we can make it up those stairs," Gian whined, his arm around Beth, her shoulder around his neck. Sakura gave us all a weak smile.

"We have to. Don't you see? That was it. That was the end. We're free. We can make it. One foot in front of the other. Let's go." She and the fire snake led the way up the stairs, with Gian and I struggling to lift Beth after us. We only stopped once to let our breath come back, but it didn't do much. Sakura's flame-snake was growing thinner and weaker by the minute, and we were all sagging and tripping as we made our way up the steps.

Finally, after what felt like hours of climbing and searing pain, we reached the top. What waited for us there made all our hearts sink. Dozens of shadowy, snarling forms, decayed but alive and prowling back and forth just beyond a line of frost. We all collapsed to the ground in a defeated heap, our energy spent. My head throbbed with a prickly hum.

The Curse had not been destroyed.

32
PEELER

THE DAY AFTER EVERYONE LEFT ON WAKEPEARL

*T*he Salt Palace was not a place a pirate could afford to get comfortable. It was full of treasures and high-quality items that in the right market would sell for thousands more than they were worth. I was constantly mindful of the wealth that surrounded me as I walked through the corridors, keenly aware that it would be all too easy to slip one of those precious items into my pocket without anyone taking notice of it. It was one big test of self-control.

At the very least, it was easy to keep myself away from temptation by worrying about the charms I was working on perfecting for Sakura. I only had three complete prototypes, each of them slightly different from the others, but I was confident all of them would work. The only issue was figuring out which design was the most practical when it came to using them. One of them focused more on the effectiveness of hypnotism. It allowed the spiral-painted marble to spin in the water behind a pane of strategically-angled glass more freely than the other prototypes did, but it required a bulkier pendant to rest in, which was awkward to move with. The second prototype focused on ease-of-use, with the cords that controlled the leather pouch and spun the marble within easy reach; the problem with *that* one was that, since it was made to be used comfortably, it was relatively small, and might not work as well as the third prototype, which was larger than the first two.

I was sitting in my chambers, tinkering with my other project while the charms sat on the desk before me, the glass panes glinting in the dying light of day. The concept of miniature cannons—or pistols, as they were sometimes called—had existed almost since the wonder of cannons themselves had entered the world. The mechanics behind them weren't hard to understand, but the amount of materials required to build one was beyond the reach of the common folk. As pirates, it wouldn't have been hard for *The Coventry* to obtain and install cannons, but Howie had decided it wasn't an avenue worth pursuing. While it would be useful to have such a weapon at our disposal, it wasn't worth the time and money it took to keep them usable and ready for action. We were fine as we were with the mages we had aboard the crew, our own weapons, and the crossbow mounted in the crow's nest. At least, we *had* been fine that way, back when we'd had a ship.

I tossed the contraption in my hands onto the table beside the charms. From what I'd heard about crafting pistols, it wasn't easy, and no prototype had ever shown promising results. It was never quite comfortable to hold in one hand, or it didn't shoot far enough, or it didn't shoot at all. My version was greatly modified, and I was on the eighth prototype. It was comfortable to hold in one hand, and while it shot plenty far, it didn't quite go fast enough. I was still perfecting the amount of blasting powder required to shoot it out of the chamber and at a speed that would be powerful enough to go through scales or armor. I had last fired it in the fight against the sea wraith, but it had only glanced off its shimmering body. There were still adjustments to be made before it was just right.

I removed my spectacles from my face and idly cleaned them on my shirt, staring thoughtfully at the devices before me. As I was sliding the glasses back on, the door to my chambers banged open. I jumped to my feet so quickly my chair was sent toppling backwards. One of my hands darted out to grab a cloth and drag it over the charms and the pistol before whoever had entered could see it.

Theomand strode into the room wearing warm layers of heavy blue fabric that covered almost his entire body and concealed all but the fingers of his metal appendage. His usually shaved head was now sprouting short black hair. "Hiding something?"

"Only if you were one of those stuck-up water people," I replied, pulling the cloth back. I had actually enlisted Theomand's help in the crafting of the latest pistol prototype. With the knowledge of the mechanics that allowed his metal hand to work, I knew he must have skills that would prove helpful to my endeavors.

"Right." Theomand laughed. He was a lot more at ease than he had been before, and I wondered what had changed. It wasn't long before I had my answer. "I've just come back from speaking with Howie. He's decided to welcome me in as a member of *The Coventry*'s crew. That is, if you'll all accept me." He grinned, dark eyes glittering. I returned the smile.

"'Course we will. A limbless outcast with a pet raptor and a fondness for stealing valuables?" I chuckled. "You'll fit right in."

"Good. But for the record, Wynny is not a *pet*." Theomand came close, his gaze glancing over the charms and the pistol, then rising to meet mine again. "Anyway, that isn't the only reason I came to see you. The remnants of *The Coventry* have been brought back, and we're to come and make sure everyone is ready for repairs to begin."

I nodded, righting my chair from where it lay on the floor. I didn't want to leave the hypnotic charms and my pistol out for anyone to find, so I slipped the charms into the leather pouch at my hip and tucked the pistol securely into my waistband, then followed Theomand out the door. We made our way through the palace, marveling as we went at the wealth that surrounded us, and finally found ourselves exiting onto the palace grounds. Theomand said that the place we had been instructed to go to was on one of the beaches, not far outside the walls of the Salt Palace. It had been the easiest place to bring the wreckage of the pirate ship, and it provided a large enough workspace for its repairs to be carried out. It took us less than an hour to walk there. On our way, we stopped by a stable harboring horses and eirioth dragons and even a number of muzzled slate-wolves. There, Theomand urged Wynchell out of a stall, and the raptor accompanied us the rest of the way to the sandy shore.

"Bit of a remote place," I commented as we stepped onto the beach. It was hidden by high black cliffs all around, with only one small pathway leading to it. When we arrived, my heart twisted at what I saw. It was a heap of bent wood and broken timber. Pieces of hammock and metal were wedged and knotted on the splinters. A giant crossbow, split in half, was pinched between two of the masts. It was a pile of broken wood to anyone else, but to me and my crewmates, it was our home.

Fresh stacks of timber and iron and stone lay at the ready on the driest portion of the beach, well away from the foaming waves that rolled up onto the shore. Beside the wreckage stood what members of the crew had stayed behind, along with one of the king's royal advisors, Traf. He beamed at us when we came closer, then gave Wynchell a wary look.

"Ah, finally, everyone's here! Welcome!" he said brightly. I nodded a greeting to him, my eyes already surveying the rest of the beach. I couldn't help but notice that it was devoid of the soldiers that had brought it here; there were also no workers here to begin the repairs of the ship. I distractedly glanced at all the wood around me, urgent memories floating to the back of my mind should I need to use them.

"She's not in as terrible shape as I thought," Howie admitted, crossing his arms as he looked at his ship. His blond hair had grown out a bit, since he had neglected to cut it. His sharp eyes softened when he looked at the broken pieces of the ship he had built his life and work around.

"Which means she'll be an easy fix!" Traf said cheerfully. We all gazed at him, unmoved. He cleared his throat awkwardly, then said, "So, shall I go fetch the workers and tell them to begin the reconstruction? They aren't far from here. It won't take me but a moment." His smile stretched even wider. The hairs on the back of my neck rose. I glanced up at the sky, now tinted in deep shades of pink and purple as the sun disappeared below the horizon. I was very aware of how far we were from any civilization and remembered seeing no encampment of workers as we had approached. Beside me, Wynchell's throat emitted a low warbling sound. Theomand tapped his head with one metal finger to silence him, but I could see his steely eyes already darting around the cliffs and narrowing at Traf.

"Yes," Captain Howard said coldly. He, too, was stiff and tense, just as all the rest of us were. His hand rested close to the sword at his hip. "Go to get them. They may begin immediately." Before the words had completely left his lips, Traf had already dipped into a bow and was trotting away, silver tailcoat flapping behind him. The moment he had vanished into the shadows of the pathway, Howard looked over his shoulder at us and said, "Be ready. They'll be coming any second now."

He was right. Seconds later, the attack began.

THEOMAND

I don't know what I'd been expecting, but Cursed animals wasn't it. The moment the black figures scrambled down, my dagger was in my hands and my heart in my throat. At first, I thought they were people, but then I realized they were too low to the ground or too hairy or not hairy enough. A stampede of them rushed onto the beach. All manner of creatures, they were, moving like waves on the sea. There was a horse, two foxes, an eagle, and at least four mangled cats, howling their pain and hunger at us. Baying hounds with exposed black ribs raced past the others, charging for us. We were fast, but we hadn't been expecting the Cursed, and we hadn't been expecting them in such numbers.

There were at least twenty of them, and there were only eight of us, including Wynny. We were prepared for an attack, but we were quickly overrun. The beasts rammed into us like a wall of death. My dagger dug through flesh and hammered into bone. Howie's sword slashed through the air, sending Cursed limbs tumbling to the earth. Peeler was by my side, he and Wynny working to wear down the Cursed horse with quick attacks. Sticky blood poured onto the sand, silvery-black from the Cursed beasts and shining crimson from the pirates. The sun's light was nearly gone now, giving the animals another advantage. My blood ran cold with fear as I saw more shadows appearing at the tops of the cliffs: a lynx, another eagle, two more hounds. How many were there? Why were they hunting us? Why was *this* the attack from Traf, and how had he managed to set it up?

The questions fell from my mind as a cry of pain rang out off to my left. I used my metal hand to punch one of the hounds in the face, crushing its jaw, and looked to the side. Old Hank was crumpled on the ground, a Cursed cat making awful noises somewhere close to his bleeding throat. Beyond him, I saw Davie stumble back into the salty sea with a scream as one of the foxes lunged, scrabbling at the ribs sticking out of his back and sinking its teeth into his shoulder, shaking its head violently to tear into the flesh. Howie leapt towards the boy with a cry of alarm, grasping the fox by the scruff and throwing it into the waves. It sank beneath the foam almost immediately. I stumbled towards them, but already I knew it was too late.

Howie gripped Davie as the boy's knees gave out. He was sobbing and screaming, his shoulder a mangled mess of blood and bone, already curling black and becoming infected. Howie said something, crushing the young boy against his chest in a futile attempt to comfort him. Davie's screams and sobs tired, and then he was limp in the captain's arms. With an enraged shout, Howie let the body fall and turned to the onslaught of Cursed animals. I stared in horror as the waves washed over Davie's body, temporarily cleansing it of blood. By the time I looked away, Paul and Zan had fallen as well. Peeler, Wynny, Howie and I stood against a dozen Cursed beasts and then some. I shuddered as I saw how many there were. Was there any way to escape?

"The sea!" Peeler yelled over the roaring of the monsters. He swiped at the Cursed horse again, his knife catching it in the throat. Sticky blood ran in thick rivers down its chest, but while the injury would have killed a normal animal, the Curse kept this one alive. It reared up and kicked at Peeler with its hooves, but he ducked away and Wynny leapt to his aid, drawing the creature's attention. Peeler fidgeted with something in his pocket, yanking out a wad of leather and pulling a string before holding it up towards the horse's face. The beast stilled, starting at it, then began to tremble. Theomand jumped forward, claws raking through the horse's loose flesh and snapping bones. The horse collapsed in a heap, its spine severed in so many places it could no longer stand properly. Peeler whirled away with his odd contraption before I could ask what he'd done.

"Go," Howie snarled through the air, gripping his bloodied sword tightly. "Get out of here while you can. Find the others." Peeler and I shared a look, then set our jaws and retreated into the waves. We both knew Howard would not survive.

The sea was freezing and full of salt that burned my nostrils and throat. Wynny, Peeler and I all struggled against its current, pulling and pushing us whichever way we went. We angled for the cliffs just off to the side of the beach, where a small outcropping could be seen. It was too cold to swim for too long, so we dragged ourselves back onto the sand and slumped into the shadows, ducking beneath the rocks to hide from the Cursed animals. We waited in silence, and after a moment I realized it really *was* silent. The sounds of the ravaging beasts had ceased. Peeler must have come to the same conclusion I did, because both of us lifted our heads to peer through the cracks in the rocks we hid behind, our bodies shivering and teeth clattering. He squinted, having lost his glasses in the fray. The Cursed animals were dead. All of them lay strewn about in heaps of black and glowing green. Howie stood stoically on the beach, staring ahead of him as two figures approached. My jaw went slack at who I saw.

Traf had returned, his silver tailcoat shimmering in the light of the moon and stars. Beside him, one hand gripping the advisor's shoulder for support, was King Matthias. I had encountered the man before, many weeks ago when I had been snooping around in his personal treasury. I had been uniquely disguised at the time, which accounted for why he hadn't recognized me at the banquet he'd hosted upon our arrival. At the time, I had stolen many barrel-fulls of royal rupees solely out of spite for his beheading my dearest friend. It was a deserved death, of course, because he had been a terrible man, but it still stung, and I wanted the Coldmonian king to feel loss, even if it was in something as frivolous to him as money.

Now, he seemed much different than he had before. His appearance didn't look much changed, though he was now slump-shouldered and breathing raggedly. There was something unspeakably unsettling about him now, as if he was on the verge of great power or great defeat. When he began to speak, his voice carried easily through the silent air, even over the gentle crashing of the waves.

"Captain Howard. A respectable tradesman, as I've heard." The king's voice was ever so slightly slurred, as if he were drunk.

"Your Majesty. A noble king, as I've always thought," Howie's voice responded, cold and clear.

"Oh? Have your thoughts on me suddenly changed?" the king mocked. Howie stayed silent. I saw even through the darkness that the king's brow furrowed. "Where are the others? There were seven of you, and a raptor."

"Your monsters killed them," Howie snapped, his sword quivering in the air with his barely restrained rage. "They've been dragged into the sea. One of them was only a *child*. Why have you done this?"

"Please, spare me the speech," Matthias clipped. "I know that you've only done what you believe to be right, and while I have no quarrel with that, your definition of right happens to conflict with mine." His voice turned thready for a moment, then strengthened as he grunted and rose to his full height. "I regret to do this to a man of such remarkable talents, but you've made it necessary. Fear not, your beloved ship will still be repaired and given just as it was to your remaining crewmembers. I fear, though, that the workers I've assigned may not be as talented in ship-making as one might like, and mistakes that could cause it to sink may be made." The king's shoulders lifted in a shrug. "Oh well. It will be yet another tragic accident at sea." Faster than I could blink, the king was directly in front of Howie, and before I could register exactly what was happening, the waves roared forward. Spears of ice froze in the air, the waves crackling against their frosted surface. The longest point jutted from the captain's chest. Howie didn't move; he didn't even make a sound. As the ice slid out of him, he sagged to his knees and closed his eyes. A gargled noise escaped his mouth, then he fell forward and was silent on the beach.

Peeler, Wynny and I were very, very still. My sodden clothes clung to me like sheets of ice, but I wouldn't let myself shiver. My throat was dry, despite the fact that it had just been full of seawater. Beside me, even though he couldn't see as far and clearly as I could without his glasses, Peeler's face was taut with internal pain.

"Dispose of the bodies," Matthias ordered, regaining my attention. I tried not to look at the bodies of the fallen, whom I had so recently begun to call my comrades. Matthias kicked one of the spikes of ice into his hand. "Make it all look like a Cursed attack."

"Yes, my lord." Traf bowed deeply as his king stabbed the point of ice deep into the wet sand, leaning against it for support. The advisor tittered nervously. "My lord, do you require assistance? Perhaps you should rest. It's been a while since you've commanded such a force."

Such a force. What did that mean? Surely Matthias couldn't have been the one who called the Cursed to come attack us. Then again, how else could he possibly be connected to it? Howie had certainly seemed to believe he was responsible right before he was run through.

"I'm fine," Matthias growled, heaving a sigh as he stood again. "I will return on my own and retire to my chambers for a few days, but I need you to attend to other matters."

"Anything, my lord." Traf waited for the king to regain his breath.

"I have told you that exploration into the Slated Mountains has ceased since my going there, but it has been a long time. I hid the source well, but it has been so many years that it may be revealed again." He groaned, stumbling as if struck by a wave of dizziness. Traf stepped forward to help him, but the king stopped him with a raised hand. "I'm fine. Just a little light-headed. Listen, Traf, the Curse does a good job of protecting itself, but with all those pirates and that stubborn Carlorian girl, I'm not sure it will be safe from them. Something already feels off. It's like I feel its fear of being discovered and destroyed." He ran an anxious hand through his blond hair. "It's in the northern borders of the Slated Mountains. We must reach them before they find it. I will rest and regain my strength so that I may use the Curse to rise against Wisesol, but you must stall in my absence." He pulled his ice spear free from the sand and tossed it into the waves. Traf's head cocked to the side.

"What will become of the people of Wisesol, my lord?" he asked. Matthias turned to him sharply.

"What does it matter what happens to them? If they stand in the path of my Curse, then it will deal with them." He shrugged his broad shoulders. "The calamity that will destroy their kingdom is of no consequence to me. If and when they fall, I will simply sweep in to pick up the pieces and play them as my own." He stepped towards his advisor. "It will require all of my strength, and you must tend to matters of the court for me. Do not let anyone else know of my plan. I will not have my people involved in the bloodshed that will come from this. Bar any passage of Coldmonians wanting to go to the western kingdoms.

Make up some excuse for it, just make sure it's done. By the end of it all, they will see me as their savior and the Curse as their greatest ally, because our people will be among others at last." He took a few unsteady steps, regaining his balance, then confidently walked off the beach with little more than a wobbly stagger. As he walked off, he said into the bitterly cold night air, "At long last, the wishes of my ancestors will be fulfilled."

33
SAKURA

When I woke up, I was sure I wasn't truly awake. I hadn't been a moment ago, so why would I be now? I had been standing rigidly in the corner of a small bedroom, its furnishings broken and tattered. My mother's body lay in a pool of blood on the floorboards. My father was standing in the corner, wielding a broken table leg as a sword as he slowly bled out from a wound in his leg. By the doorway, Aurora was crouched by a wardrobe, tears staining her skin, her beautiful hair a mess. And then there was me, only five years old, standing in the doorway and screaming. The Cursed wolf attacking Papa shifted its attention to me: young prey, an easy target.

Before, my memory always cut off when the wolf lunged and Aurora leapt in my way. This time, though, I wasn't that little girl in the doorway. This time, I was another being entirely, watching the scene unfold and unable to stop it. Unable to look away when the wolf's claws and fangs ripped into my sister. I saw myself turn and run away, still screaming at the top of my lungs.

Now, I was sitting up in a tent. I knew I hadn't been in a tent when I'd fallen unconscious, so either some monstrosity was about to rip a hole in the tarp and tear my chest out, or something drastic had happened to all those snarling Cursed beasts in the cave.

I spent a long minute sitting there, my thoughts racing fast and my heart racing faster. Tears stained my cheeks, and when I lifted my fingers to wipe them away, I knew I was awake. Somehow, that made things worse, because it meant I was back in a reality where the Curse existed. Even after we had destroyed what was most certainly the source, it was still here. How could that be?

"Do you think she's awake yet?" the voice sounded from beyond my tent tarp. I jumped at the familiar sound of it. It was Ksega, sounding antsy and impatient. I glanced around me, down at my grubby clothes and my darkened, bruised hands. Whatever cuts I had sustained from the blast and the fight before it had been healed, but that didn't mean I was without a hundred aches.

"You can go see but be quiet." Jessie's voice was patient and cautioning. I heard boots on stone and snow, then my tent flap lifted, and Ksega ducked inside.

The moment we locked eyes, his face melted with relief. He rushed inside and knelt beside me, his gaze searching as he watched my face. For a long moment, neither of us said anything. I took in his weary eyes, his dirt-stained clothing. His hands had a dozen tiny scars across them, and there was a tear in one of his earlobes.

"What happened?" I croaked finally, my voice raw. He had been looking me up and down, and I remembered the tears on my face. I hurriedly wiped them away, although I knew he'd already noticed.

"Derek and Jess came back. They killed the rest of the beasts. Well . . . sort of. I mean, they're all dead, but Jess cured one of them first." Ksega babbled on, then stopped, seeing something in my expression. He sighed. "I'm sorry. You've been unconscious all day, and there's a lot to take in. Here, give me a minute and I'll get you some food and water." He scooted back towards the tent flap, then pointed at a pack in the corner of the tent. "You can find a change of clothes in there, if you'd like. You'll feel a lot better once you're in a fresh outfit." He disappeared before I could point out that he himself hadn't changed yet.

I did my best to quickly remove my ruined clothes and change into new ones, although it did little to make me feel better. I was stiff and sore and slow, and I groaned with exhaustion as I sat back down on the bedroll I had been lying on. Ksega returned with a bowl of steaming stew and a waterskin. I greedily accepted them both and began to dig in. He sat beside me on the bedroll and started to explain everything.

"Whatever we found in that cave was definitely the source of the Curse, and when I destroyed it, it stopped being the living, active thing Chem always insists it is." The mention of Alchemy made my chest ache, but I didn't show it on my face as I slurped at my stew. "Now, it's just like a disease. When Derek and Jessie found us, Jess said that something about the life force had changed about them, and when she tried using recle to heal them, it *worked.*" His eyes sparkled as he spoke, smiling tiredly at me. I was still too foggy-headed to completely comprehend what he was saying. He must have realized this, because he cleared his throat and reiterated his words. "Before, if she had tried to heal one, it would have had no effect. Now, it can cleanse the animal of the Curse. Unfortunately, it doesn't reverse the damage done to the body. The slate-wolf she healed had been missing a lung, and as soon as it was free of the Curse it limped away and keeled over." He grimaced at the memory.

"But . . . it can be stopped, now?" I whispered, my voice still too hoarse for me to speak any louder. His smile brightened.

"Yes, it can. We did it, flame-fingers." He winked at me, and I rolled my eyes, not strong enough to get onto him for the nickname.

Instead, I asked, "How is Beth? And Gian? What about the dragons?" talking was making my head hurt, but I had to know they were okay before I could let myself rest more. Ksega most certainly sensed this, because his expression turned stern.

"They're all fine, and they're all going to be okay. We're heading back down the mountain if everyone is feeling up to it, but for now you need to lay down and sleep some more." He took my empty stew bowl and set the waterskin beside my pillow in case I wanted it again. I wanted to argue, but I knew he was right, so I only curled up and let myself sleep.

I slept through the rest of the day and all through the night, not waking again until Jessie coaxed me out of the depths of sleep and urged me to drink a tonic she had made to help my achiness go away. Once that was done, she left me to clean myself up as best I could and leave the tent on my own time. When I did, I emerged to see everyone else around a campfire. Beth's leg was bandaged up, but she seemed to be doing fine, heartily digging into a roasted bird leg. Sitting beside her and eating his own bird leg in a much more refined manner was Gian, Light Ray and Taro both bundled by his other side. Derek and Jessie were leaning against Bear, who was huddled beside Asuka. Ksega had been crouching near the campfire, and he rose to greet me with a smile as I came closer, eyeing the rest of the bird they had cooked. Before I allowed myself to eat or any of them to speak, however, I had to ask a question. It had been burning in my mind ever since I'd woken up, and perhaps even before that.

"If the source vanished completely, then the Curse should have vanished with it. Even if it's defeatable now, there's still something tethering it to this world. Is it possible there's some sort of secondary source?" I took my portion of bird, but didn't sit down, instead hovering close to Ksega's side. He gave me an odd look.

"I suppose it's possible. But why bother looking for that if we can focus on just removing the Curse from all the animals it's affecting? Won't it have the same result either way?" he asked. I shook my head.

"Maybe the secondary source can grow stronger and act the same way the first one did. It's too dangerous," I said.

"If there is a secondary source at all, that is." Beth pointed out. I nodded, conceding the point, but she hadn't sounded very convinced.

"Maybe it's not an *it*, but a *who*," Gian piped up. We all looked at him. He squirmed beneath our attention but went on. "Think about it. Alchemy was always saying that something tried to command and control him, right? But it could only do it for short periods of time. Maybe someone is linked to the source of the Curse and uses up their energy whenever they need the Curse to do something for them." A long silence followed that statement. I turned the idea over in my mind, and the more I thought about it, the more it made sense. A number of things would have to line up for it to work, but the list was far from unachievable.

"It would have to be someone with access to the Slated Mountains, and someone who has an active need for that kind of power," I said.

"And someone who's physically strong enough to keep using it, even when it drains them," Derek added.

"So someone who has a lot of money and possibly a lot of enemies who also, what, gets sick a lot?" Beth asked, her lip curling. "That's not much to go on."

"But it might be enough." Ksega straightened as a thought occurred to him. "Back in the Salt Palace, the serving girl Talia mentioned something about King Matthias's 'frequent bouts of sickness.' It must be him."

"Are you sure?" Jessie said sharply, her eyes narrowing. "You can't just go accusing kings of that sort of thing," she said. Ksega and I looked at each other, eyes wide and mouths shut tightly. Derek groaned.

"Right. You already did that with King Kirk. How could we forget?" he said dryly.

"That's beside the point. We didn't think to look at the Coldmonian royal bloodline before because it just seemed so pointless, but it makes sense now." I chewed a bite of bird thoughtfully. Once I swallowed, I went on. "In the Salt Palace, there was this room with a bunch of murals on it that showed the Dorsey bloodline's history. King Calysto's death was painted there." I saw recognition flicker in Ksega's eyes, and he picked up my sentence.

"That was the king that was killed in the war waged between Coldmon and Brightlock two hundred years ago. The Curse had already existed by then, but as we know from Chem, it was sealed away." Once he paused to think, it was Beth's turn to piece the clues together.

"Matthias must have discovered it and decided to play the role of an unsuspecting king. Why would anyone bother to look at him specifically, anyway? He's never done anything memorable."

"But his ancestors have," I said, taking the lead again. "He spoke of Calysto's desire to bring his people to the mainland and give them a life outside of islands and seas." As the conversation replayed in my mind, another memory surfaced. I cursed. "He knows where we are and what we're looking for. He *deliberately* played dumb with me, hoping I hadn't guessed anything important."

"But you have, and surely he knows that now." Derek began to rise. I nodded.

"Yes, and that means that the pirates who stayed with him are in danger." I saw Ksega's face grow paler.

"It also means *we* are in danger, and we need to get back to The Dragon House as soon as possible." Beth stood, too. "Leave the tents. Can the dragons fly us back?" everyone looked at Derek and I. Bear was strong. He had carried Derek, Alchemy, and I over the Great Lakes to Clawbreak before, and I had no doubts he could carry at least three of us now. I had to hope Asuka could manage the same feat.

We wasted no time. We threw our essentials onto the saddle. Derek hopped onto Bear's back, and Jessie climbed up after him. Gian rode with them as well, and that left Ksega, Beth and me to ride Asuka. While tack had been provided from King Matthias's generosity for Bear, none had been for Asuka, and that meant we were riding bareback. I climbed onto the blue dragon's back and gripped the lead, which I had hastily tied into a makeshift bridle. Ksega climbed up next, hugging me tightly as Asuka stamped his feet. Beth was up next, sucking in a sharp breath at the dragon's nervous movements.

"Everybody hold on tight," Derek ordered, and then we were off.

Flying bareback was a favorite experience of any Carlorian dragon-rider, but I couldn't say I particularly enjoyed it this time. Asuka wasn't comfortable with the weight of three people, and it made his flight rough and unsteady. Aside from that, while bareback was exhilarating and new for just one person, it was absolutely terrifying for three. I kept worrying that Beth would slide right off his back if he lifted on a wind current too quickly.

We were in Wisesole when we took off, but it didn't stay that way for long. Eirioth dragons were powerful creatures, and they flew fast. Even Asuka, who had only a short while ago been half-starved and horribly treated, matched Bear's pace as they soared through the frigid winter air. Snow battered past us in icy gusts, clinging to our hair and clothes and making everyone shiver. I kept my body bent lower over the dragon's neck, my hands buried in his feathers. We had been in such a rush that we didn't retrieve the tents or the things inside of them, my gloves included, but I didn't need them. I let my eirioth surge towards the surface of my skin, warming my hands and, through them, Asuka's neck. It took almost all my concentration to make sure I didn't burn him while flying.

The sun was low in the sky when we swooped over Talon. The winter festivals had begun and were now in full swing. Loud music rose to meet us, smoke curled into the air, lights danced and swayed, people twirled and laughed and ran up and down the snowy cobbles beneath us. If anyone was alarmed to see two eirioth dragons flying overhead, they didn't make a scene out of it.

Conveniently and true to its name, the Dragon House had a space for landing and stabling eirioth dragons out back. We landed heavily, leaping off the dragons and slipping through the ice and snow to bang on the back door of the inn. It was quickly answered by an alarmed-looking Fayola. We all started talking at once, stuttering and yelling over each other.

She held up a hand and shouted, "Enough! Get inside, all of you, you look like you're freezing to death." She stepped back and ushered us inside. We hurried through the door, trailing snow and dirt behind us. "You aren't the only ones with a story to tell. Two of the other pirates just got here. Go on, they're in the living room. I'll be in shortly with refreshments." She offered no other explanation as she waved us out of the little kitchen. We wearily staggered down the hallway into the living room, which was full of familiar faces. When they saw us, not one of their grim expressions brightened.

"Uh oh," Gian said, and we all followed his gaze to where two men sat on the sofa, one wearing a new pair of glasses and the other with a metal hand. Curled at their feet was the familiar leafy, green form of a raptor. If Theomand and Peeler were here, and they hadn't brought the other pirates that had stayed behind on Sandstone, something bad must have happened. Molly read the horror on our faces, because she rose from where she'd been sitting in one of the chairs and offered it to us. In the other chair, Thomas did the same thing.

"Great. More bad news, I'm sure," He deadpanned. I gratefully sank into one of the seats, and Beth eased into the other, grimacing as she bent her injured leg.

"We realized some things while we were on the mountain," Ksega began to explain. Peeler and Theomand looked up at him, and he winced. "If you guys are here . . . something happened, didn't it? With King Matthias?" They both nodded.

With a heavy sigh, Ksega sat on the floor, the only open space for him to rest his legs, and Gian did the same, then we listened. Theomand and Peeler took turns sharing the gruesome tale of how they had come to be at The Dragon House, barely escaping from Sandstone and only happening upon Chap when they reached Freetalon. The pirates showed little emotion, but I could see the pain and shock in their eyes as they heard of the deaths of their crewmates and their captain. At some point, Fayola had entered the room and was listening intently, one hand covering her mouth.

"That's awful," Gian said when they finally finished, looking like he was on the verge of retching. His hair was disheveled from our flight, and he was distractedly fussing with it.

"What're you going to do now?" Beth asked, as ignorant of others' suffering as ever. She sat with her arms crossed, one of them lifting occasionally to rub Taro's beak comfortingly. Everyone turned their head to Chap. He was standing near the hearth, arms crossed and jaw set. He looked more serious than I'd ever seen him. He was the first mate, and with Howard out of the picture, he would be the one to decide what to do with the ship and what was left of its crew.

"We can leave you to decide that for yourselves," Ksega said to break the silence, rising to his feet. He was shuffling uncomfortably, arms crossed and gaze downcast. He didn't look up as he went on. "We're all very grateful for the help you've provided for us. We need to go to Wisesol now, but as soon as we're finished there, we'll pay you however—"

"Oh, don't even start." Thomas cut him off loudly. We looked at him in surprise; all but the pirates, that is. They seemed to be of the same state of mind. The young man smiled thinly at us. "You can't get rid of us that easily."

"But the ship—" I began to protest. Chap held up a hand to stop me.

"Forget about it. It'll be sabotaged to sink, remember?" he shrugged, his voice thick when he added, "We'll just have to build a new one from scratch."

"So that means . . ." Beth prompted, her eyes narrowing.

Thomas dipped his head at her in a nod and, in case the rest of us were too dense to figure out what it meant—which was a distinct possibility, with the condition we were in—he said, "We're coming with you."

34
KSEGA

We were all itching to get to Wisesol as quickly as possible to prepare for the attack, but Jessie and me most of all. I could see the worry in her eyes and hear it in her voice whenever she spoke. My own chest was tight with fear for Willa.

Talon was a good distance from the border between Freetalon and Wisesol, and we didn't have the spare time to go on foot. We depleted almost all the money between us by borrowing horses and tack, but we didn't have time to worry about being low on coin now. Whether we were good at riding or not, we all mounted a horse, some of us riding double, and started towards Hightop, the town at the Gates between the two kingdoms. Asuka and Bear thundered on leads alongside us, free of riders after their exertion that morning.

We arrived in Hightop as dusk was falling. We were all antsy to keep moving, but Molly and Chap ordered us all to a stop, reminding us that both we and the horses needed a rest. We didn't have the money to get rooms in an inn anywhere, so we found a flat expanse of land just outside the town and set up a large camp. I hardly got any sleep, and when we were all woken up and ordered to pack our things the next morning, I could tell most of the others had struggled to sleep as well.

We spent all our money but two silver coins and five shins to get through the Gates, then we rode long and hard for the whole day. Night had fallen by the time we reached the town of Soarlak, beside Willow Lake. I hadn't been to Soarlak many times, although I had ventured through it before. It was an unimpressive town, being one of the smallest. Many travelers and traders passed through it when coming to or from Lourak, so it had lots of inns and taverns and markets, more than was necessary for its permanent population. We stopped for half the night, letting the horses rest while we foraged for dinner in our packs. After a few hours we wanted to get moving again, so we mounted and kept going, now at a slower pace for the sake of the horses, who were tiring quickly.

Lourak came into view a handful of hours before dawn. It was all tall silhouettes and shadowy outlines until the sun rose high enough to reveal its pale stone structures and all the neat little details dotting the city. We trotted in through a side street, leaving the horses somewhere they would be safe and eventually returned to their rightful owners before going the rest of the way on foot. The plan we had hashed out during our trip was rough, and the chances of it succeeding were slim, but the pirates were confident that it was doable. Chap said he had a considerable number of contacts within the city, and as soon as we arrived, he, Molly, and Thomas broke away from the rest of the group to seek them out. Wendy, too, said he knew people in high places, and took Theomand and Wynchell with him to seek them out. I wasn't entirely sure, but I thought he might have said "Toren," which was the name of Wisesol's army general. Derek and Jessie also said they knew some people from their time spent researching the Curse, and they left us to go find out what they could.

The rest of us were commanded to stay put in the central city and wait for one of the small groups to return with information. By the time we found a place to lie low, the sun was setting again, casting the sky in all shades of pink and orange and gold. It was unbearable, standing around and doing nothing. Lourak was an unsettling place to be without a purpose. It was quaint and pretty on the outside, but it was teeming with thugs and murderers. While I myself was a skilled thief, I had never been able to blend in with the rest of the Solian crowd. They were all big muscles and loud threats, whereas I was someone who preferred to stick to the shadows and go unnoticed.

Now, there was no going unnoticed. A throng of people missing many body parts and traveling with two full-grown eirioth dragons was not something that was easy to miss, and we received lots of greedy-eyed looks as we made our way through the central town square. There were small bridges hanging between buildings overhead, and flower boxes bursting with bright green life despite the season, courtesy of their bering-mage caretakers. Snow fluttered down in spirals and rested on our shoulders and the feathers of the dragons and Light Ray and Taro. I blinked them out of my eyelashes, keeping my gaze attentive to all the shifting shadows in the alleys and corners. Bear and Asuka were prime targets for smugglers and thieves, and I had no doubt that some of the pirates' fake limbs would fetch a high price when bargained for. Thankfully, nobody seemed quite confident enough to approach us, and we moved through the city swiftly.

I led the way, being the most familiar with Lourak. The Port would be the safest direction to go in, even though we had been told to remain in the city. The city had too many eyes and ears facing us, so I guided the group towards the road that wound through a small glade and a copse of trees and swerved down to the Port. We stopped on the side of that road, since it wasn't commonly used this late in the day.

"We should go ahead and set up a campsite," Beth told everyone once we'd stopped, letting our packs slump off our shoulders. We had borrowed some from the pirates, since we'd left most of ours on the mountains.

We went about setting up the campsite quickly, and once it was done the sun had sunk low on the horizon. A fire was started, and everyone gathered around it to warm themselves. Aside from Peeler, the pirates who were still here weren't ones I knew well, so conversation was slow and stilted. When we all talked, it was only about worrisome things, like the fact that Wisesol's entire army wouldn't be enough to combat the Curse on its own. It was a depressing topic, and none of us wanted to dwell on it for long.

The pirates chattered amongst themselves, their tones and expressions flinty. On our little side of the fire, Beth and Gian sat huddled close together, their birds in their laps. Gian's hand was surreptitiously inching closer and closer to Beth's every few minutes, and she was pretending not to notice as she nibbled on a piece of half-frozen jerky she'd found.

I was sitting beside Sakura, twirling my little hunting knife in my hands. The tip poked into my bare, numb fingers. I was thinking about Willa. It had been so long since I'd seen her. I had grown so used to the feeling of missing her that I wondered how surreal it would be to finally see her again. I was excited and scared at the same time. There were so many things I now wanted to ask her, questions I never would have considered voicing if it hadn't been for Sakura.

"Be careful." A hand settled over mine, gently pulling the knife away, and I looked down to see that I had slit my finger with the blade while I was distracted. It was only a prick on the end of my finger, and I licked the beading blood off it.

"Whoops," I said sheepishly as Sakura handed the knife back to me. I tucked it snugly back into its place at my hip. "Lost in thought, I guess," I admitted. She nodded slowly.

"Worried about Willa?" she guessed, and I dipped my head.

"Yeah. She should be pretty safe, though. Matthias is mainly targeting the Slated Mountains, where we're supposed to be right now, and Rulak is all the way in the northern corner of Wisesol." I folded my hands together, then separated and clenched them. I didn't tell her that I was certain Matthias would have the Curse run across all of Wisesol anyway. It was land he wanted, and if Wisesol was already going to be partially under his attack, why not spread his forces across the whole kingdom?

"Are you going to ask her about your parents?" Sakura asked. I looked up at the people around us, then gave her a tense look.

"Why don't we go on a walk?" I suggested. She blinked, confused, then nodded in agreement. As we rose to our feet, a few of the pirates gave us questioning looks, but none of them said anything as we trooped off through the snow.

I took her to the Port. At this time of night, and in this weather, it was entirely abandoned save for a handful of armored Solian soldiers watching the ships. They watched us as we passed, peering at us from within the halo of lantern light they stood in, but they didn't move to stop us. We walked down the worn wooden boards until we'd reached the end, standing over the dark, lapping water. When we turned around, Lourak was lit up before us. Lantern-light shone through window curtains, torches flickered from sconces on distant walls, small fires set in grates sent shadows and beams of light dancing in the corners of our vision. This had always been one of my favorite views, but I couldn't recall seeing it in the dark, when everything around me was so calm and still.

"It can't be easy to talk about your family when you don't even know who they are," Sakura said, crossing her arms and tucking her hands beneath them to keep them warm.

"It's not." I looked sidelong at her. Her eyes reflected the golden lights shimmering in the distance. "I'm sure it's not easy to talk about your family when you knew them so well, and now they're gone," I said.

"You know it isn't easy." She looked up at the sky. It was a cloudless night, and the wide expanse of stars twinkled above us. She sighed. "It's gotten easier, but it doesn't hurt any less, if that makes sense."

I nodded in mute understanding. We stood in silence for a long while, the chilly wind biting at us and snagging in our hair. Even with dangers the likes of which we didn't know preparing to attack us, in that moment, everything was peaceful. It struck me that I was actually *home*. Willa was just a few hours' ride by caravan to the north, and the market stalls and shops I had swiped harmless little trinkets from dozens of times were barely two miles from where I stood. Somehow, so many things in my life had managed to change since the last time I had stood on these docks, brazenly boarding a pirate ship with my closest friend.

"It's kind of hard to fathom, knowing how many people are at risk now," Sakura said quietly, drawing me out of my thoughts. I looked over at her. Her face was solemn, and I waited for her to go on. "At the start, it was just supposed to be me against the Curse. Other people weren't supposed to be in any more danger than they had been before." She pursed her lips. "I'm not saying that I'm not glad you and Chem and the others joined me, because I'm so grateful for all of you." She gave me a small, genuine smile, and my heart gave a little stutter. I hoped it didn't show on my face. "But now look where we are. How many pirates are dead now? Seven? Eight? And what about the people that died from the sandcat attack or from the slate-wolves when we freed Asuka?" she twisted the smile into a frown. If it hadn't been such a serious situation, I would have joked about her inability to keep track of numbers.

"You know it's not your fault that they're dead," I reminded her, recalling Beth's words aboard *Waterlore*. Sakura nodded.

"Yes, of course. At least, not for the first three." She dropped her arms, her hands balling into fists. "All of the clues were right there in front of us, and we didn't put it together until too late. Maybe we could have saved Howard and the others if we'd figured it out sooner."

"But we couldn't figure it out until after the source was gone," I pointed out. "Besides, even if we could, what good would it have done? With the source at his command, Matthias could just have the Curse keep growing and corrupting things, and we still wouldn't have been completely rid of the Curse. Now that the main source is out of the way and the Curse can be reversed, we stand a much better chance of facing him. It's only a shell of what it once was, tethered here only through Matthias."

She grunted to concede my point but said no more. Another silence washed over us, but now that she had said that, I couldn't help but wonder what would happen if things went badly. I licked my lips nervously, turning to face her. She raised an eyebrow in question, sensing that something about my demeanor had changed.

"Sakura, listen, I know that it's wildly unlikely anything bad will happen to you or Gian or Jess or any of the others, because you're all very skilled and capable on your own, but . . . well, maybe not Gian, but—" I hesitated, realizing this may have been a bad way to start. Her other eyebrow lifted to join its twin, and I cleared my throat and forged on. "That was slightly off topic. The point is, if any of us get hurt or killed—"

"You think one of us will be killed?" her brows twitched down again.

"No!" I winced, lowering my voice. "No, that's not what I meant. What I *meant* was that in the hypothetical situation where one of us dies, hypothetical me would feel that there were a lot of things I never got to say to hypothetical you or hypothetical Chem or hypothetical Willa, and you get the gist of it." I dragged a hand through my hair, feeling like my little speech was going downhill. Maybe this was a bad idea.

"I see . . ." Sakura said slowly, narrowing her eyes at me in a way that suggested she most definitely did not see. I cursed inwardly, wishing I could take it all back and start over.

"I just don't think I'd be able to live with myself if there were things that I wanted to say to you that I never got the chance to say because you were dead," I tried again, then clamped my mouth shut. Her eyes widened. I resisted the urge to bury my face in my hands, or the stronger urge to jump into the black water at our side and never come back up to the surface.

"I think I know what you mean," Sakura said, and I blinked at her, drawn out of my visions of what it would be like to literally die of shame.

"You do?" I squeaked.

"Yeah. There are things I wish I could say to Moma and Papa or Aurora that I'll never be able to tell them now." Her gaze fell to the boards at our feet. "I wish I could tell them how much I love them, and that any time I said something horrible to them, I didn't really mean it and I was only angry, but . . ." she paused, biting her lip as she searched for the words. "I think they knew that. I know I told them I loved them before their deaths, but afterwards I never felt like I'd said it enough; now I know that I didn't *need* to say it. Love isn't just expressed through words, and neither is hate. They knew I loved them very, very much because of my actions towards them, and they knew I never truly hated them for anything for the same reason." She tilted her head to the side, making a weird face and laughing. "Now I feel like *I'm* the one babbling."

"No," I said quietly. "No, that makes sense. A lot of sense, actually." I chuckled, my breaths fogging in the air in front of my face. She smiled again.

"Good. I'm glad. And it's for that very reason that I know you care, Ksega. I know you care a lot. You're a great friend to all of us." For a long moment, neither of us said anything. I couldn't think of anything to say. My heart was racing, my stomach was doing flips. My thoughts were scattered in every direction. I tried to think of what Alchemy might tell me to do in this situation. Tell her *she* was a great friend, maybe? No, that wasn't his style. Knowing him, he would probably tell me to kiss her. The moment the thought crossed my mind, everything seemed to freeze. We were both uncannily still. It would have been easy to just lean forward and kiss her. Unbelievably easy, really.

I craned my neck, leaning closer to her, my eyes sliding shut.

"That's it!" she gasped, and I flinched back, my eyes snapping open. Sakura was doing an excited hop on the balls of her feet. I was surprised by the action. Such excitement was not something she commonly expressed. At least she seemed distracted enough to avoid mentioning our closeness. "That's what we have to do. Even if the pirates can get Wisesol's army to prepare to fight the Curse, it won't go down very well. They're humans that haven't had much fighting experience in the past thirty something years, but if we can give them help from something with natural fighting instincts—not to mention something that can match the animalistic ferocity of the Curse—then we might stand a better chance." She was on a roll now, following a train of thought that I couldn't keep up with. My heart was thundering in my chest as I regarded her.

I tried to keep my voice level when I asked, "What exactly brought this on? Have you been thinking of battle strategies this whole time?" the question earned me an odd look from her, and she flushed, finally taking a good look at my face. It felt like my skin was on fire.

"Of course not. I hate using critical thinking when it's not needed," she said breezily, and I wasn't sure if it was a joke or not. I must have been rubbing off on her. The thought made me grin, albeit shakily. She returned it, continuing, "I wouldn't have thought of it if you hadn't said that thing about never getting to say stuff to people. It made me think of Finnian, and how I wish I'd said something more to him before I'd up and left to find the Curse's source." She was running her thumbs along her knuckles now, her excitement growing. "*That* led me to think about eirioth dragons, which reminded me that we have *hundreds* of them, and most of them and their riders are trained in combat. We could bring them here to help!" she was grinning nearly from ear to ear now, an expression that was so unexpected on her features that I didn't know what to make of it. I turned her words over in my mind, having to think them through multiple times before understanding her reasoning, but coming away with a distinct flaw.

"A lovely idea, Sakura, but there's a small problem. That's all the way on the other side of the Great Lakes." I watched her face for some sign of a disappointed realization, but her grin didn't waver.

"Doesn't matter. I've got a plan. I have to get back to the others now, because I need to talk to Peeler and Beth." She made to leave, then turned back to me, still smiling. Before I had a chance to say anything more, she leaned up and planted a kiss on my cheek. "I couldn't have done it without you." Then she pivoted on her heel and sprinted back down the dock.

35
SAKURA

When I arrived back at the little campsite, Derek and Jessie had returned and were standing by the dragons, feeding them. I cast my gaze around, searching for Erabeth or Peeler. Even though it was late and cold and I was exhausted, I felt invigorated and fuzzy inside, and for more reasons than one. I tried to ignore it all when I spotted Peeler near one of the tents, picking idly at a burr stuck in the tarp.

"Peeler!" I called out, and his head lifted, swerving to face me. His eyes were tired and weary, but he smiled as I came up to him.

"Ah, perfect, just the person I wanted to see," he said as he straightened. I cocked my head at his statement, wondering what that could mean. He reached into the depths of his coat, producing three necklaces. Upon closer inspection, I saw that the pendants on the necklaces were actually bags of leather with cords hanging from them.

"Are these the hypnotism necklaces?" I asked hopefully. I had forgotten all about them until I was formulating a plan in my mind on the docks. He nodded, grinning and revealing silver and gold teeth between his natural yellowing ones.

"Indeed, they are. I've only got these three finished, and they're in different styles, but I think this one's design is the one to go for." He tapped one of the pendants with a wrinkled finger. "I've got another handful of them in the works, but I only have the supplies for so many." He looked up at me through the lenses of his glasses. "There are undoubtedly people in the city who have the abilities and items required to produce more of them, but we'll need to find some way to hire them or get them on our side."

"We can figure it out. If Wendy really does have friends in high places, I'm sure it can be arranged." I lifted one of the pendants into my hand, tugging one of the cords. The pouch opened to reveal a painted black-and-white spiral. When I pulled the other cord, the painted marble spun dizzyingly.

"Good that they're easy to figure out. They should draw the attention of any Cursed beast you may be facing, and once their eyes are locked, you've pretty much won." Peeler smiled proudly at his invention, and I grinned up at them.

"They're perfect," I said. He nodded curtly, then raised a bushy eyebrow.

"I suspect you didn't just come to me about the charms, though. What's going on?" he tucked all but one of the charms back into his pocket while I collected my thoughts to answer.

"I have this idea. It might be kind of crazy, but I think it's doable. Human soldiers against an army of Cursed beasts is going to be dangerous, and our chances of victory will be increased if we have some beasts of our own on our side." I could see by the way he narrowed his eyes shrewdly that he was following closely, trying to see where I was going with this. "I want to fly back to Carlore. If Jessie can make some sort of potion to keep up Asuka's energy, I can fly him back within a day or two and then be back with the cavalry in the same amount of time."

"Do you think we've got that long?" he asked instead of pointing out any issues with my plan. I shrugged.

"Even if we don't, it will help boost our chances of victory."

"And what does this have to do with me?" Peeler questioned.

"I did come to ask about those charms. I wanted to know if they'll affect normal eirioth dragons like they would a Cursed beast. If these charms are on the people fighting the Curse, it might do more harm than good to bring the dragons to where they could see them," I explained. The pirate sucked on his lip thoughtfully for a moment, then nodded.

"I'll go experiment with Derek and Bear right now. You'd better go talk to that Jessie gal if you want to get moving soon." He didn't give me the opportunity to say more, because he lifted the charm he had left in his hand and walked over to where Derek was giving loving scratches to his eirioth dragon. When he got over there, he spoke with Jessie first and waved a hand vaguely in my direction.

"You wanted to speak with me?" she asked when she came closer. I saw her blue eyes flash in the direction of Ksega, who was now speaking with Gian.

"Yes. I was wondering if you might be able to make something that could rejuvenate Asuka's energy repeatedly enough to get me from here to Carlore in one flight," I told her, then paused to reconsider, adding, "Possibly two, if we stop for real food and water somewhere in Coldmon, but that's risky."

The recle-mage was silent for a long moment, one pale finger tapping thoughtfully on her lip as she mulled it over. When she came to a decision, she reached for her belt, which I now realized carried a number of small pouches for vials and beakers and sacks of herbs. She poked through her store of medicinal items, muttering to herself. Finally, she looked up and gave me a confident nod.

"I can do it. Give me a few minutes, and I'll have it ready." She hesitated, then asked, "Are you going tonight?"

"Yes," I agreed, before I even thought it through. The prospect of being able to see Finnian again soon was making my head spin, sending my thoughts whirling in so many directions that it was impossible to keep track of them.

"Okay. I'll meet you up beside Asuka once I'm finished," she said. I thanked her, then she gave me another smile and trotted towards one of the tents, already pulling things from her belt.

I went to Beth before I went to Asuka. She was standing near the much-diminished fire, Taro on her shoulder, watching as Ksega and Gian talked animatedly about something. When I came up to her side, I could tell that she immediately knew I was in a hurry.

"What's bitten your tail?" she asked, a light note of amusement in her voice.

"I'm going to Carlore tonight, and I need you to help keep things under control while I'm gone," I said, the words rushing out of my mouth so quickly they slurred together. She blinked in a way that clearly meant she hadn't understood a thing, so I slowed down and tried again. "I'm going to bring forces back from Carlore to help us fight the Curse, but I don't completely trust all the pirates to keep track of stuff while I'm gone, so I want you in charge. Do you think you can make everyone behave until I get back?"

"What happens if the Curse starts to attack before you return?" she crossed her arms.

"Then you do whatever you think is right at that moment," I replied coolly. She gave me a long, scrutinizing look, and I did my best not to squirm under her gaze. I always hated when she got all judgy.

"I can do it," she reassured me. I grinned. Maybe it was the freezing cold or all the near-death experiences getting to my head that had put me in such a loving mood, but *something* had definitely gotten into me because I threw my arms around her before I could talk myself out of it and gave her a tight hug.

"Be safe. Keep Gian in line," I said as I let her go. She laughed.

"I'll make sure he behaves himself, *Faja*. And as for you, be careful." She patted me on the shoulder, then went to join Gian and Ksega. I left them to their conversation and hurried up to Asuka. Derek and Peeler were still there, but their experimenting seemed to have come to a close.

"Ready to go?" Derek asked, raising an eyebrow. I nodded. He sighed, then went on, "Ready to argue about whether you can take my tack or not?"

"Ready to take your tack whether you tell me I can or not, actually," I chirped. He gave me a baffled look, and I didn't blame him. There was no good reason for my mood to have become so chipper so suddenly, but I wasn't going to complain about it, and I doubted anyone else was either.

"Fine, you can take it. Just be careful with it," he said with a sigh. I nodded, beginning to gather up the heavy pieces of leather and metal. Peeler helped me lift the saddle over Asuka's back.

"The hypnotic effects of the charms don't work very well on animals unaffected by the Curse. The dragons should all be safe," he told me, tightening the saddle straps and then stepping back. I thanked them both as he and Derek went back towards the campfire to warm themselves.

I finished tacking Asuka up, then I fastened some small packs to the saddle. They had food and water and room for an extra pair of clothes if I should need them. Asuka kept shuffling around as I worked, and by the time I was finished, he was blocking my view of the campsite, as well as the warmth from the fire.

"Getting ready to leave already?" the voice surprised me, and I looked up to see Ksega walking towards me through the snow. He wore a smile, but he looked worried.

"Yes. The sooner I can get there and back, the better," I answered.

"And you're sure you have to go alone?" he asked, the smile wavering just a little. I nodded. He sighed, surely knowing there was little point in arguing with me. "Okay. Just promise me you'll stay safe and won't do anything stupid." He took a step closer and looked down so that he was staring directly into my eyes.

"Out of the two of us, I'm more worried about *you* doing stupid things," I said with a light laugh. I let my smile grow small and leveled my voice out as best I could as I went on. "I promise to stay safe, and I promise I won't make too many stupid choices." He sighed again and rolled his eyes.

"I guess that's the best I'll get out of you, huh?" he didn't need me to nod to know the answer, but I did anyway. He shook his head, but didn't say anything else for a long moment. I reached out to pat Asuka's flank, eager for some sort of distraction.

I knew Jessie would be coming here soon to give me the potion for Asuka, and for some reason a part of me thought it would be far too awkward if she walked around to this side of the dragon and saw Ksega and I standing so close to each other. I told myself I should go ahead and start leading Asuka to her tent so I could pick up the potion and be on my way, but I didn't move. It was as if the snow had crept up my legs and frozen into ice, leaving me rooted to where I stood.

"Well," Ksega said so softly it was almost a whisper. His breath plumed in the air between us, "I guess this is goodbye for now." I nodded, giving him another small smile and hoping he wouldn't be so serious. I really could have used some of his bizarre humor to diffuse the tension between us at that moment, but it appeared that Ksega had ideas in mind other than humor. I was just about to break the terrible silence by saying I should get going when I realized I couldn't, because within a moment my lips had been sealed by his.

The kiss had been so unexpected that I hadn't fully registered it until it was over. I gaped at him, shocked, and he gave me a shy grin. I was too baffled to say anything as he took my hand and silently helped me up into Asuka's saddle. Once I was there, I could see Jessie coming closer, holding a palm-sized glass bottle.

"Stay safe. I'll see you when you get back." Ksega looked up at me and gave me a bright smile, but I was still too shaken to return it.

"But– you–" I stammered, searching for words I couldn't find. I gripped Asuka's reins tightly, staring helplessly down at Ksega. My stomach felt like it was tying itself into knots.

"It's okay. You don't have to say anything." He looked towards where Jessie was coming closer, then sheepishly back up at me. "I just wanted you to know that . . . well, I mean–" he paused, clearing his throat. My heart felt like it was running circles inside my chest as I waited. He went on, "I don't know what's going to happen, but I know that if I didn't find a way to let you know how I feel now, I might never tell you." He licked his lips nervously. My fingernails dug into the leather of the reins.

"Ksega, what are you saying?" I asked, my voice barely more than a whisper. He shrugged.

"I honestly don't know. I'm finding it hard to think straight." He chuckled lightly, reaching out to pet Asuka's shoulder. I reached forward and grabbed his hand. His gaze snapped up to meet mine. He swallowed, then said, "I just want you to know that you're very important to me, and after all this is over . . . I want to talk some more."

"Yeah," I said softly. "Me too."

"Here you go. Only give it to him when you notice him starting to tire." Jessie came around Asuka's backside, startling both of us. Ksega jumped back, and Jessie blinked, looking between the two of us. "Sorry, was I interrupting something?" she asked, eyebrows inching skyward as she took in our flustered expressions. I looked down at Asuka's neck, feeling heat crawling up into my face.

"Not at all," Ksega answered, clearing his throat. "Just saying goodbye." He gave me one more smile before walking away. I watched him go until Jessie cleared her throat. I looked down at her, biting my cheek when I saw her smirk.

"Thanks for the potion," I said, holding my hand out for it. She handed it to me, grinning.

"When you come back, we'll probably be in Rulak." She looked over at where Ksega had gone. "Are you sure you want to go alone?"

"Yeah. It's best that way." I tucked the bottle into a safe place and gave her a smile. "Goodbye, Jessie. Keep everyone safe for me."

"I'll do my best. You stay safe, too, alright?" she said, and I nodded. She stepped back to give me room to take off, and I urged Asuka forward and flew up into the night.

I may have overestimated my flying abilities when I decided to fly from Wisesol to Carlore in one go, but I wouldn't let myself stop. Icy wind whipped at my face and pulled at my braid, stinging my skin and making me go numb. I ignored it, centering all my attention on keeping Asuka focused on flying in a southeastern course. After his time in the traveling entertainers' possession, he was good at following commands quickly. That, at least, was something good that had come from his time with them. It was probably the *only* good thing that had come from it.

There wasn't any good way to pass the time. My mind tried to wander, tried to drag me into a whirlwind of complicated emotions regarding Ksega. I kept having to force myself to refocus on making sure Asuka wasn't tiring himself out too much, and on making sure I was heading in the right direction.

The weather was thick and freezing. Heavy clouds of mist rolled over the Great Lakes, making it difficult to see anything below me. I spent the time keeping myself warm and occasionally swooping lower in the sky to see if there was any good place to land. It must have been a few hours before dawn when I was flying past Sea Serpent Crevice. It loomed out of the fog on my right, and I hesitated for only a moment before steering Asuka towards the rocks. It was known to be a place fraught with dangerous sea wraiths and raptors, but I would take my chances with raptors over Coldmonian guards who would bring me to the man controlling the Curse.

Sea Serpent Crevice was made up of two natural stone structures, the first being a great arch of rock and the second a spike of stone that rose high into the air. Its name came not only from the beasts that were known to lurk near it, but also from its resemblance to a sea wraith that was diving back beneath the waves. I tried not to picture it as such a foreboding animal as we flew closer.

I guided Asuka through curious tendrils of mist and had him land on the top of the stone arch. It wasn't as thick as I'd imagined it to be, and when I dismounted, my boots slid on slick stone. I held onto the saddle tightly as I reached for the potion Jessie had given me. I pulled a thick strip of dried peach out of one of the packs and gnawed a divot into it. I poured the potion inside and carefully fed it to Asuka. I wasn't sure how much of his energy the potion restored, but it would have to be enough to get us to the smaller island to the east, Caol. From there, it wouldn't be far until I was finally home.

I flew through the rest of the night and into the dawn. Caol came into view shortly after midday, and I slowly let Asuka descend through the air to land on a patch of snowy earth on the northwestern corner of the island. I didn't know much about Caol, because it was a small and unimportant island, but I had always assumed it was just as plentiful and pleasant as the rest of Coldmon. It was jarring to see how wrong I was. The sky over the little island was thick with black smoke that belched out of the chimneys of a giant cluster of stone buildings. Huge fences made of iron and stone surrounded the compound, menacing and accompanied by unfriendly looking guards that patrolled the perimeter. I was far enough away that I wouldn't be spotted easily, but there was no large plant life to cover me if I was. A small town could be seen beyond the compound, its lights dim and its structures too small and frail-looking beside the imposing collection of buildings. Whatever was going on this island, I wanted no part of it.

"Here you go, sweet boy," I said softly, repeating the process I had before with the dried fruit and the potion. Asuka snatched it from my palm eagerly, blinking his big, dewy eyes at me as if asking for more. I relented, letting him have another handful of dried fruit and jerky strips. I took a swig of water out of my waterskin, choked down some food myself, then adjusted the tack and mounted once more. Almost every inch of me was sore, but I was *so close* to finally being home that I couldn't stop now. Besides, Caol didn't seem like the kind of place that would welcome visitors with open arms.

It was almost nightfall when the familiar, bizarre silhouettes of the Columns appeared up ahead. They were almost invisible, concealed above in the low-hanging clouds of dusk and hidden below by the broad cliff face. Long strands of pale yellow grass waved and bowed in the wind on the very edge of the cliffside, resilient against winter's cold embrace. The Gates weren't far from where I was, but I would be avoiding them. The Gates that allowed passage between Carlore and Coldmon were often avoided, not just because few people aside from traders and business-people actually had reason to go back and forth between those kingdoms, but also because the Gates themselves were tricky to get through on either side. If you were coming from Coldmon, you had to anchor a short way out from the cliffs and wait for a Carlorian officiant to row out to you. If you were coming from Carlore, you had to tread down an extremely dangerous path down the cliffside, and if you didn't have a boat waiting for you or willing to take you where you needed to go, you had to climb all the way back up.

Asuka rode the wind currents high up over the yellow-grass plains. We swooped past the ominous forms of the Columns, those strange pillars with rivulets in them that no one had been able to identify. Off to the south stood the small Carlorian town of Cashew. It wasn't far at all now. I could see the bright colors of the eirioth trees, just as vibrant as they always were, even in winter. Their thick, dark, twisting trunks rose up into the air, flowering out their branches like arms waiting to welcome me home. Perhaps Asuka recognized something in them as well, because he pumped his wings faster, eager to reach the Eirioth Wood.

We soared through the forest, chilly wind biting at our faces. I couldn't help but laugh gleefully as we whirled through the winding trunks, ducking and weaving between thick eirioth tree branches. We raced past Cashew, flying along the edge of the King's Scar and aiming for the southernmost town of Carlore. When it came into view, I didn't know whether to laugh or cry.

It was one of Carlore's smaller towns, but one of its most popular. The central town was a bustling place of life and color. The square was full of shops and workplaces, with a collection of big stone basins where people threw their scraps for the dragons to eat right in the center. It was painfully barren now, the basins empty and not a dragon in sight. I was reminded with a pinch in my chest that all of the dragons had been locked up in the War Cells to prevent any Cursed ones from causing damage.

A few people gave me odd looks as I flew overhead, but I ignored them. Some of them were people I knew or knew of, but if they had ever had anything to say about me, it wasn't good, so I made no time to stop and explain myself to them. I flew on past Duke Ferin's large temple and his larger, now empty dragon stables. My stomach churned with a mix of anxiety and excitement that made me feel slightly ill as I finally pulled back on Asuka's reins to slow him. He spread his wings out, catching the air beneath them and landing smoothly on the ground. In front of us, with lanterns blazing and loud voices echoing from within, was Hazelwood Inn.

Tears were freezing on my cheeks as I hastily dismounted from Asuka's saddle. I fumbled with the reins, looking towards where our dragon stable had stood before. They were gone now, having burned down during the fight with Elixir, and all remnants of it had been removed. Dark patches of earth still showed where it had once stood. I looked away from it as I led Asuka up towards the porch. Here, evidence of change after Elixir's death was apparent. Most of the boards and the rails had been replaced with newer wood, most likely the work of Walter. My chest ached when I thought of him and Gamma and Finnian, just beyond the door in front of me. I tried to catch glimpses of who was inside through the windows, but my tears blurred my vision. I wiped them from my eyes and tied Asuka's reins to the porch rail.

"I'll be back soon," I whispered to him, because I wasn't sure I could speak any louder. He stamped his foot on the ground and swished his tail through the air, content to stay put for now. Satisfied, I raced up the steps and gripped the front door handle with numb fingers, then I tugged it open and stepped inside.

36
SAKURA

*F*or a long moment, nothing seemed to change inside. It was like I had walked into any other tavern. There were all kinds of people inside, laughing and drinking and digging into hearty meals of stew and fresh bread rolls. A handful of men were playing instruments joyfully beside the roaring hearth and another was shouting alongside them, singing an old Carlorian folk song about baby eirioth dragons being born in the blooming flowers of springtime.

I shut the door behind me and stood just inside the threshold. A few people looked up at me curiously, but nobody I knew; everyone else was too caught up in the noise and excitement that thrummed through the room to notice that the door had been opened. At least the inn had been faring well while I was away. That let me release a shaky breath of relief, and another tear slid down my face as I let myself look through the room, trying to pick out any faces I recognized. Someone stood at a table near the corner, an older man with leathery features and spiky gray hair; Walter. He spotted me, and his eyebrows rose towards his receding hairline. I shoved through the crowd, knocking my legs on table and chair legs and bumping my shoulders into other people until I reached him.

"Lady Sakura!" Walter said with a smile as I threw my arms around him, hugging him tighter than I'd ever hugged anyone before. "Welcome home," he said, patting my back. "Welcome home."

"Walter," I said with a grin when I drew back. "I'm so happy to see you." The tears were running freely down my face now.

"And I you," he said with a light laugh, and it was with a start that I realized his own eyes glistened with tears. "The others will be delighted you're back. Come, come, are you hungry? Are you hurt?" he looked me up and down, but I waved his worries away as he guided me towards the kitchen. Over the serving counter, I spotted a glimpse of silvery hair and heard a short, familiar laugh echoing out from near the ovens.

"I'm fine," I said, although I doubted Walter heard me over the din. We went through the little gate between the eating area and the kitchen, and I took a deep breath, inhaling all the wonderful scents of home. Soft bread steaming on the counter, hot stew simmering on the stove, fresh greens lying on a chopping board, waiting to be added to a pot. It was all so instantly *right* that, for a moment, I forgot that I'd ever been gone at all.

"*Rura!*" the voice snapped my attention back to the present, and I realized it was Finnian who had shouted. There he was, sleeves rolled to his elbows and flour dusting his clothes as he helped Gamma around the kitchen. His dark hair was a shaggy mop that fell in waves just past his ears, having grown out since the last time I'd seen him.

"Finn!" I screamed, rushing forward. He met me halfway, crushing me in an embrace so tight I couldn't breathe. I wrapped my arms around him, sobbing into his shirtfront.

"You're home!" he shoved me back to look at me, as if he wasn't sure I was real. I laughed, nodding because I was unable to find the words to respond.

"Finn, what are you doing? Those rolls need to get in the oven and—oh!" around Finnian's arm, I saw Gamma appear, her silvery hair pulled up into a slightly messy bun on her head and her hands nervously worrying her apron as they always did when she got frazzled. As soon as she saw me, she dropped the folds of the apron and ran forward, doing her best to get her arms around both Finnian and me. For several minutes, we all stood like that, laughing and crying and hugging until the smell of something burning wafted through the air.

"Oh dear, now look what you've done." Gamma pulled away hurriedly, rushing towards the stove to stir the contents of one of the pots. "I'm burning my stew." She wiped tears from her eyes and gave Finnian what I assumed was the sternest look she could muster. "You need to go put those bread rolls in the oven." He nodded, giving me another tight squeeze before trotting off to obey.

"Is there anything you need me to do?" I asked, rubbing tears off my face with my sleeves. Gamma rolled her eyes at me.

"Like I'd ask you to do anything in your state. Get over by the fire, warm up, grab a bowl of stew. When did you last eat? Are you here alone?" she adjusted the pots on the stove, then came back to me to look at me more closely. Her eyes narrowed as she lifted a hand, one finger trailing along my cheek. I winced, having forgotten about the scar.

"I'm fine, Gamma, I promise. I came back alone, but there are people waiting for me. I need—" she cut me off before I could finish.

"Not now. Get some food, wait for the supper rush to get out of here, and then we can talk." She patted the side of my face and motioned towards where a stack of bowls waited to be filled with stew. I pursed my lips, wanting to argue, but I knew it would only be in vain.

I dished myself out a bowl of stew and stood in the kitchen as I ate it, talking with Walter about how things had been while I'd been away as we watched Finnian and Gamma manage the customers. Walter told me about how almost all of the dragons had been put in the War Cells. Some people had stubbornly refused to let their lifelong companions be put in such a place, and had hidden them away in places the authorities couldn't find them.

"They really aren't that bad, though," Walter said, gnawing on a bread roll. "They had a whole bunch of us go down there and clean them up nice and good before we put the dragons in, and they aren't locked up. They're all fed and watered plenty, and people are free to visit them whenever they'd like. So far, only one dragon after Elixir was corrupted by the Curse." His lips turned downward. "They killed him before it could spread too far. A shame, that it came to that. But now you're back, and with good news, I hope?" he raised thinning eyebrows at me expectantly. I slurped the broth from my bowl and nodded.

"Yes, lots of good news, but this isn't over yet, and I *really* need to talk to Duke Ferin." I shoved the stew bowl into his hands and went to tap Gamma on the shoulder. She looked up at me, and I resisted the temptation to hug her again. There would be plenty of time for hugging when this was finished.

"Sakura, you should go rest—"

"I have to take Finnian with me. It's urgent, and I'm sort of in a hurry. Will you be able to manage on your own for a little while?" as if sensing he was being spoken about, I saw Finnian's head lift from the corner of the kitchen. Gamma gave me a disheartened look.

"You're leaving again?" she asked in a small voice. I swallowed thickly and forced myself to nod.

"Not for so long this time, I swear," I said. Gamma was silent for a tense moment, then she nodded.

"I can manage. Walter and Violet will help." She held her arms out, and I leaned into them, returning the embrace. "Be careful," she said into my ear.

"I will." I drew back and looked over at Finnian, who was watching curiously. I motioned for him to come closer, and when he did, I could see the worry in his eyes.

"You're not leaving again, are you?" he asked.

"I am, but you're coming with me this time. Come on, we've got to hurry. We need to go see Duke Ferin." I grabbed his hand and dragged him out of the kitchen, saying a rushed farewell to Gamma and Walter.

"Why do we need to see the duke?" Finnian asked as I led him bodily through the crowd. I opened the door and stepped back outside into the dark, frigid air with him at my side. He made a strange noise when Asuka looked up at us.

"I'll explain on the way. Hop on." I gave Asuka a little more of Jessie's potion and untied his lead, hoping he'd be able to carry the two of us, and then swung into the saddle. Finnian blinked at me through the falling snow, baffled, then pulled himself up behind me.

"I hope you know what you're doing," he said. I didn't respond as I urged Asuka up into the air.

*D*uke Ferin was a cold, expressionless man. At least, that's how I remembered him. Before she and my parents had been killed, Aurora would take Finnian and I to visit the Duke of Hazelnut each week. This was because my father made decorations and trinkets for the duke to display in his temple, and Aurora was often the one to deliver them. Finnian and I tagged along, expected to learn the nature of the trade, and we usually had to tell Duke Ferin about what we had been learning in our educational studies that week. After that, Aurora would speak with the duke about business matters and we would be sent off to spend time with his wife, Lady Nala, who was always the best part of our visits to the temple. This time, however, we weren't here to spend time with Lady Nala.

Finnian was filled in on why I was back in Carlore by the time we landed in front of the duke's temple, although I could tell he had more questions waiting to be asked; he would have to be patient for a little while longer before he got all the answers he wanted.

Each town in Carlore had a temple, and that temple was a part of the estate belonging to that town's duke. Duke Ferin's temple was a deep, plum purple, accented with black and gold. The big double doors up front waited for us ominously. We left Asuka tied up out front beneath the boughs of an eirioth tree with some food, then padded up the path and knocked. As we waited, Finnian looked me up and down.

"I think you've grown taller," he commented. I snorted, knowing that wasn't true and that he was only trying to make conversation. I was glad that he was in a joking mood. The last time I had seen him, he had just killed his own eirioth dragon, and I had been afraid he'd never return to his normal self. I hadn't been back with him long, but I was fairly certain that he hadn't let Elixir's death affect him too greatly. As far as I could tell, he was only a little quieter than usual.

An attendant answered the door, dressed in purple silk. She looked between the two of us, then peered over our shoulders at where Asuka was snuffling in the snow. I recognized her, but only just. Her face was lined with age and her hair was shorter than I remembered it, but I knew she was familiar. I couldn't recall her name.

"May I help you?" she asked politely, looking between the two of us. I waited a beat before I remembered that I was the only one who knew exactly why we were here. I cleared my throat and answered.

"I need to speak to Duke Ferin immediately," I said. The woman blinked at me slowly, then stepped back and held the door open for us. We shuffled inside, where she urged us to shuck off our snow-covered coats.

"I will take you to the anteroom. He is in another meeting at present, but you will be allowed to speak with him after it is concluded." She took our coats and hung them up, then led us down familiar corridors to the big anteroom with green eirioth dragons painted on its walls. There, she left us with a promise that she would seek out some refreshments. We took our seats on the plush velvet furniture, our gazes raking over the paintings and small details about the room that I had memorized long ago during the then-agonizing waits for Duke Ferin to be available. There was a painting of a fruit orchard with a young girl in a white dress frolicking hand-in-hand with a boy in a red suit, and just below that painting was a bookshelf with a chip in one of its clawed feet. It had been so many years since I'd sat in this room, but as far as I could tell the only thing that had changed was the rug.

"How have you been?" I asked to break the silence, tugging on a loose thread in the cushion I sat on. Finnian was beside me on the sofa, his fingers steepled together and his boots tapping the floor impatiently. I hadn't expected things to be so awkward when I came back, but there were too many things to say for it to go smoothly.

"Good, actually. Worried sick about you, but good. I've been teaching Violet how to use a flame-sword, and Gamma's kept everyone busy with the inn." He looked over at me, a teasing smile pulling at his lips. "Derek would hate me for letting his sister anywhere near a flame-sword, but I'm calling it retaliation for him letting *my* sister run off into the Evershifting Forest on her own."

"Ah, right . . . that wasn't entirely his fault. I told him to stay behind and make sure you were okay," I frowned. "Of course, that didn't stop him from following me anyway." Finnian grinned, but I slapped my hand over his mouth before he could speak. "No, stop there, I know what you're going to say, and you're wrong. He followed me because he was worried I would get myself hurt, and for no other reason." I dropped my hand and glared at him. He chuckled and shook his head.

"Fine, if you insist. Still, there's no way you ran around Horcath with a boy for that long and don't feel *something* for him," he mocked. I tried not to think about Ksega, but it was impossible. Our last conversation replayed in my mind, making my stomach erupt in butterflies.

"I didn't run around Horcath with him for that long, actually," I told him, forcing my tone to remain even. "A certain number of events led to him going to Wisesol with some other girl, and I ended up traveling with a couple other people." I trailed off awkwardly at the end, unsure where to go from there. How did I explain to my brother that I had been traveling Horcath with a seven-foot-tall Cursed skeleton?

"*Oh*?" Finnian's eyes widened. "I didn't expect you to be out there making friends on your vengeful quest." His brows twitched as his expression shifted into a frown. "Where did Derek go, then? And who were you traveling with?" he pointed towards the door. "And where did that *dragon* come from?"

"It's a long story, Finn, and I don't have time to tell it now, but I promise I'll give you all the details when this is over." I gave him my most convincing smile, although he didn't look very impressed.

"At least tell me what's gotten into you," he said. "You're not the same person you were before, that much is obvious. You seem more . . . grown up." His smile turned a little sad. "I'm sorry I missed it."

"It's really my fault," I said, hating to see him upset. "I should have waited to ask if you wanted to come with me." I absent-mindedly reached up to touch the scar on my face. How odd was it for him to see me after I had changed so much? I wondered if he was as unsure about it as I was.

He opened his mouth to reply when the doors to Duke Ferin's study opened. A man I didn't recognize walked out, dressed in heavy blue garments. He nodded to us as he passed, and once he was out of the anteroom, Ferin appeared in the study doorway. He didn't look very different from how I remembered him. He was a stout man, with a long mustache and thin gray hair. His eyes were sharp and rather unkind, and he was always dressed in dramatic purple robes. Finnian and I stood to greet him, and his bushy eyebrows inched upward.

"The young Ironlans return. Shocking." He sighed heavily, then beckoned us forward into the study. It was a place we had been many times before and it, like the anteroom, had changed very little. A large wooden desk dominated the center of the room, tapestries hung from the walls, and there was a large bookshelf so full of tomes and scrolls that it constantly teetered on the edge of causing a disastrous mess of paper and leather. Behind the desk, a tall window looked out over an expanse of snow-covered gardens, one of the duke's greatest prides. A torch set in a sconce near the doorway burned brightly, but its ring of light didn't quite reach every corner of the room.

"It's been a while since we last saw you. You seem to be doing well," Finnian said. I winced, giving him a sharp look. He frowned. I had forgotten that I was now the one more experienced in speaking with people of noble blood.

"Yes . . ." Ferin said slowly, walking around his desk and settling into his high-backed chair. "I take it that you are not here to tell me what you learned about botany today," he said, watching us with narrowed eyes as he folded his hands together in his lap. Finnian opened his mouth, but before he could say anything I stepped forward and addressed the duke.

"No, your grace, we are not. I've actually come to ask you if you can give me your support in mobilizing a regiment of air-borne soldiers to Wisesol." I knew how silly the words sounded out loud. They always sounded silly, and yet, somehow, they often got me the result I wanted.

I expected the duke to laugh at my request outright, so I was mildly surprised when he only gave me a prompting look and asked, "And why, dear child, would I provide this support?"

"I know that there isn't much I can do to prove the truth of my story, but I have just come from Wisesol. I've spent most of this past year searching for the source of the Curse, and my friends and I finally found it and destroyed it. Unfortunately, the source wasn't the only thing keeping it alive. Someone else found it before we did, and instead of trying to destroy it, he harnessed its power. He knows we found the source, and he believes that we are still where we found it in Wisesol. He is going to attack the kingdom with the Curse, and he is going to show no mercy." I knew that, even though this was his second time hearing it, Finnian was watching me skeptically. It hurt that he would doubt my word, but at the same time I didn't blame him. It all sounded very far-fetched.

"Tell me," Duke Ferin said, so slowly that his agonizing pace could only be intentional. "Who is the man who controls the Curse?" the question hung in the air. I took a deep breath.

"Matthias Dorsey. The Ice King of Coldmon," I answered, then clenched my jaw. I was holding my breath, sure that he would rebuke me for speaking such a dangerous accusation.

Silence stretched through the study. Outside the window, snow fell in peaceful flurries. The torch on the wall flickered, its strength waning with the passing time. I felt that passage of time keenly, every inch of my itching to return to Wisesol as soon as possible. Had Matthias already attacked? Was the Curse already ravaging the kingdom?

"A bold statement, Ironlan girl." Duke Ferin leaned forward, planting bony elbows on his desk and staring at me with those cold, dark eyes. "You father was a just man. He believed in honor and honesty and always doing the right thing, no matter the cost." He tilted his head to the side. I tried not to let my shock show on my face. I hadn't expected him to bring up our father. "I would like to believe he instilled such values in his children. So yes, I will give you my support." He stood, barely giving me time to be relieved. He stepped around his desk again and approached me, leaning close as he spoke again. "Mark my words, children, I am choosing to *trust* you. If I discover that I've been lied to, know that the consequences will be more than severe."

"Yes, sir. Of course, your grace," I stammered, nodding vigorously. I felt light-headed, still reeling from the fact that he had agreed.

"Quickly, then, we must take action. This is an urgent matter." He opened the door to his study, startling the attendant on the other side, who had finally come back with a tray of steaming tea cups and plates of bread. We apologized to her, then bustled past.

The next hour flew by. Ferin ordered servants and sent word to other dukes, asking for others to join the cause if they were willing. He only had the residents of Hazelnut under his jurisdiction, the majority of which were not soldiers, but as word spread through the town, many people started to show up at the temple, ready and willing to help. Ferin did not expand on the reason for the sudden wave of urgency, but nobody questioned his authority. He sent us back to the inn to inform its current residents of the situation. By the time we regrouped at the temple, which was overflowing with people, Ferin told us that a group of people were going to the War Cells to retrieve the dragons, and we eagerly volunteered to go with them.

As dawn light filtered through the leaves of the eirioth trees, Finnian and I, riding on a haggard Asuka, landed in Acorn. A throng of people was already marching towards the thin path that ran down the side of the King's Scar, all the way to the heavily-guarded War Cells, a place that, before now, hadn't been inhabited since the Havoc Ages. We found a place in the crowd and moved slowly through it. Already, people had made it to the Cells and retrieved their mounts, and they flew up past us, arcing to the west and flying towards Cashew, where Ferin had ordered everyone to meet.

We reached the bottom of the craggy pathway at last, stepping past a number of Carlorian soldiers into the vast chambers of the War Cells. They were enormous rooms carved into the stone, with cages that could hold tens of prisoners at a time. Each cage was large enough for two eirioth dragons to rest comfortably, three if they were small. There were somewhere around twenty giant rooms full of these cages, made into a great labyrinth beneath the kingdom of Carlore. More than enough for all of the dragons that had been brought there.

Though I had never seen them previously, I knew that the War Cells had been drastically transformed. They were brightly lit by bonfires and torches, and all the cage doors were wide open, the shackles rusted and unused. All the dragons inside were untethered, flying or climbing or trotting around excitedly at all of the people pouring in. It was a shock of color and sound, a mess of tangled limbs and wings. I searched desperately for the familiar silver-white feathers of Sycamore.

"I'll take him off your hands," Finnian had to half-shout over the crowd to be heard. He was gesturing at Asuka, who was practically vibrating with excitement as he looked at all the dragons around him. I nodded, shoving his lead into Finnian's hand.

"Stay near the entrance. Once I find Sycamore, we'll get out of here," I told him. He nodded, then I disappeared into the chaos.

I shoved past people and dragons, tempted to shout her name, even though I knew it would accomplish nothing. My heart was hammering in my chest as I searched through the dragons, registering eyes and beaks and tails and talons and discarding them all because they weren't mine. I hunted through the flurry of feathers until I spotted something familiar: a fanning silver-white tail, sweeping across the cave floor. I bolted in its direction, tripping over my own feet with excitement.

"Sycamore!" I shrieked, as she barreled into me and knocked me to the ground. I wrapped my arms around her neck as she beat her wings happily, stirring up dust from the cave floor. Her feathers were just as warm and soft as they always were. I dragged myself up to my feet, burying my face in her shoulder. She huffed into my neck, hopping up and down and lashing the ground with her tail.

Instead of leading her back through the crowd, I pulled myself up onto her back and urged her forward. Even something as small as the way she walked was easy for me to recognize. I knew I was grinning from ear to ear as we came back up to Finnian. He returned the grin, although a little less enthusiastically, and I could tell he was thinking about Elixir.

"Let's go get her tack on, then we can meet the others at Cashew," he said, mounting Asuka. We pushed our way back out of the War Cells and took off into the air.

Ferin, despite his advanced age, insisted on leading everyone to Wisesol. He knew that the dragons couldn't make the flight in one trip, but they were all energized and fit, so they would make it pretty far. At the mark of three hours past midday, he planned to lead the flight all the way to Famark, where they would stop for the night to let the dragons rest. If the Coldmonian soldiers had an issue with it, there was nothing they could do in time to stop all of them, so he was unconcerned about any threat they may have presented.

When everyone was gathered in Cashew, he began to go through and sort them into smaller groups. There were close to two hundred dragons and their riders, and some of them had to stray out towards Hazelnut and Walnut to make room.

"This is exciting," Finnian told me. We were in Walnut, stopping by to check in on Derek's younger sister to make sure she would be alright. Walter was with us. We had gone back to the Inn and I had taken the opportunity to take a well-earned nap before we left. Walter had agreed to make sure Violet came back to Hazelwood Inn with him if she didn't have anyone else to stay with. The young girl didn't like being told what to do, but she was only twelve and couldn't be left unsupervised.

"It certainly is," I said, although my thoughts were distant. I was nervous, but not for the battle ahead. I looked over at Finnian, and he seemed to sense that something was off.

"You're changing the plan again, aren't you?" he guessed, and I nodded.

"Only slightly. I need you to go with everyone else when Ferin leads the way, but I have something else to do here before I can follow. I promise, I'll be there by the time you all reach Wisesol." I could see the argument forming on his lips, but he bit it back.

"Since when did you become so bossy?" he said instead, forcing his tone to be light. He cleared his throat, dropping his smile and nodding. "I can do that. How will you catch up with us, though?"

"This." I lifted a small vial that I had been holding onto. It wasn't the one Jessie had given me, although its contents were the same. I had split what remained of the potion into two smaller vials. I handed one to Finnian.

"What is it?" he asked.

"A recle-mage made it for me. Asuka has been flying a lot, but if you give this to him, it will keep his energy up enough to get you to Famark. I have some for Sycamore." I patted the pocket in my coat where the other vial was.

"Sounds good." He nodded, then reached out and crushed me in another hug. "By all the stars and clouds, I missed you, 'Rura."

"I missed you too," I squeaked, wrapping my arms around him. Something butted me in the back, and as Finnian released me, I turned to see that it was Sycamore. "Okay, some love for you, too," I said, chuckling as I scratched her head.

A few moments later, messengers arrived to inform us that Ferin was ready to take off. I said another goodbye to Finnian and Walter, and then everyone mounted their dragons and flew away. I wished I could go with them, desperate for another chance to ride alongside Finnian, but I had something more important to do before I could join them.

Rubbing the freezing cold from my fingers, I pulled myself up into Sycamore's saddle, urged her into the air, and steered her towards the Evershifting Forest.

37
KSEGA

Kissing Sakura had not been one of the things I thought much about before, but after she had flown away towards Carlore, there was little else I *could* think about. No matter who I talked to or how invested I tried to get in a card game with Wendy and Thomas, I couldn't stop replaying that brief moment in my mind. I wasn't used to drowning in repetitive thoughts this way, and I definitely wasn't used to the weird, fuzzy feeling I got in the pit of my stomach whenever I remembered that I had actually *kissed* her. I wished Alchemy was still here so that I could go tell him. I wished Sakura was still here so that I could go do it again.

Eventually, I realized that I hadn't eaten much and that it was important that I go do that. I went to find something to eat and instead found Jessie standing beside Derek, also looking for food. When she spotted me, Jessie gave me a bright smile.

"Hey there, trouble." She looked like she was about to say more, then hesitated. "Are you okay?" she asked.

"Why wouldn't I be?" I said with a smile, forcing myself to look as casual as I could. Derek gave me an odd look. I ignored it. Thoughts of the conversations I would have to have with Willa were making my stomach turn. I'd never been so scared to talk to her before.

"Never mind. I'm going to take you to Rulak tomorrow so you can see Willa," Jessie went on, turning back to the luggage she had been going through in search of food.

"Sounds good," I said, hoping she couldn't tell how nervous that made me. There were so many things I had to ask Willa about now, I wasn't sure how I would do it. Bringing up the past upset her, and I hated to see her upset, but didn't she hate to see me knowing nothing about my family? Surely, she must have been able to understand that I wanted to learn about my own history.

We ate as we talked about home. Jessie told me some more about what she and Derek had done during their research. Derek merely nodded along and watched her as if he could listen to her talk all day, no matter what she was saying. I wondered if that was what I looked like when Sakura was talking.

When our meal was done, we all turned in. I tried to think about practical things as I lay on my bedroll, like how Wendy had told us that the Solian army was taking the threat of the Curse seriously and actively preparing for a battle at that moment, but I couldn't keep my thoughts organized. I kept turning my worries over in my mind, dreading the conversation I would have to have with Willa and hoping Sakura was safe. At some point, the thoughts blended together until they made no sense, and I fell asleep.

The caravan ride to Rulak went by so fast I hardly remembered it. Jessie had retrieved her beloved horses—a speckled one named Tooth and a bay named Dagger—and had hooked them up to a caravan early in the morning. Instead of leaving Beth and Gian to deal with the pirates alone, we were all going to travel to Rulak. Derek, Jessie and I were the only ones taking the caravan, which was loaded up with all our packs and remaining gear. The others were burdened only with a few sacks of food and water to last them the walk from Lourak to Rulak.

When we rolled into the town, my heartbeat increased with excitement. We passed familiar houses and familiar faces, waving and saying hello as we went past. Jessie steered the caravan out to the west, where a small homestead waited, a dormant orchard in the backyard and a steady stream of smoke curling from the chimney. Before the caravan had even halted, I launched myself off the bench and raced through the snow up the steps. I threw the door open, not bothering to stomp the snow off my boots or shed my ice-crusted coat as I went inside. Willa was sitting in the tiny living room, a hand-knitted beanie on her round head and a book in her hands. She looked up with a start, eyes widening, before she recognized me.

"*Ksega!*" she cried, throwing herself out of the chair to come hug me. I squeezed her tight, partially picking her up off the floor. "Put me down, you troublemaker!" she swatted me on the back of the head, and I set her down, grinning. She was smiling, too, tears glistening in her eyes.

"You're welcome for bringing him back in one piece," Jessie said as she came up the steps behind me, leaving Derek to deal with the horses. Willa laughed and gave Jessie a hug as well.

"Oh, welcome home, my boy." Willa turned back to me and grabbed my hand, pulling me into the kitchen. "I wasn't expecting you, but there's some food if you need it. Have you had lunch yet?" she looked out the window, making sure her judgement of what time it was correct.

"Yes, I have, but I'll never say no to some more food." I peered into the pot on the stove. I couldn't identify what type of soup it was, but it smelled delicious.

"Help yourself to a bowl, then, and come sit down. Tell me everything." She waved Jessie into the living room, and when Derek came inside, she ushered him over as well. They sat together on the sofa while Willa went to make tea and I served myself a bowl of soup. When we were all seated, tea in hand, Willa watched me expectantly. I paused, looking over at Jessie. As if sensing what I wanted to ask, she said,

"I've told her what Derek and I were researching, and she knows *of* Alchemy." She sipped timidly at her tea, nodding for me to pick up the conversation. I took a deep breath, knowing that the tale was going to be a long one.

By the time I was finished with the story and all of Willa's questions had been answered, it was dusk. She made more food for all of us, and after supper it was time to turn in. The house was small, and we didn't have a spare bedroom, so Derek was to sleep on the sofa. Jessie went next door to her home, and Willa and I trooped upstairs to our rooms.

My room was much cleaner than the state I'd left it in. The bed against the far wall was neatly made, and there were no clothes scattered across the floor. My wardrobe and the compartment in the side for my longbow had been dusted and polished, and all the clothes inside had been washed. On the wall across from the wardrobe hung a small green blanket. I hadn't thought about the blanket in years, although it had sat folded on my wardrobe for as long as I could remember. It was a small quilt of green fabrics that Willa had made for me when I was born. With it, she had made a small beanie to match and knitted a pair of wooly green socks.

"I hope you don't mind that I tidied up." Willa was standing in the doorway, watching me. I turned to give her another hug.

"It's not what I'm used to, but I suppose I'll manage," I said. I looked down at her, struggling to find the words I wanted to speak. She must have seen something on my face because she motioned for me to go sit down on the bed.

"What's on your mind, Ksega?" she shut the door softly and came to sit beside me. I twiddled my thumbs, unable to meet her gaze.

"I've just been thinking about my parents," I said. Willa stilled beside me. I forged on. "I know you don't like to talk about them, but I don't even know their names. I know nothing about my own family, and I know that it's never bothered me before, but now . . . I'm desperate to know. I *have* to understand." I finally looked up at her. She was watching me with sad eyes, her lips pressed tightly together.

"I hate keeping things from you, Ksega," she said, reaching up to push her fingers through my hair, picking through the strands. I had never liked when she messed with my hair, but I didn't stop her. "This one is just . . . it's difficult. But I understand." She sighed heavily. "Your father's name was Rynne. You got your determination from him . . . and your height." She let her hand drop into her lap. "He was a mapmaker. He did lots of traveling for his work, so he wasn't home often. I've told you before that he died on a trip, right?" she didn't meet my gaze.

"Yeah, from some sort of accident," I said numbly. Why had she kept all of this from me before? Why did the name Rynne sound so foreign to me? Had I really never known his name?

"Yes, well . . . that was shortly after your birth. Your mother was Kira, a beautiful girl. You have her looks." Willa glanced up at me again, as if looking at my features for the first time. She sighed. "She stayed with me when Rynne traveled. She never complained about helping around the house, even when she was pregnant." There were tears in her eyes now, and my own were stinging.

"What were they like?" I asked. *That* was what I desperately wanted to know. I wanted to know how the room changed when one of them walked in, or how they acted when they were at home. I wanted to know how much like them I was.

"I'm sorry, Ksega, but I can't . . . not right now." She wiped the tears from her eyes, and I did my best to hide my disappointment.

"That's okay. I understand. But one day, right?" I whispered, reaching out to give her a hug.

"Of course, Ksega. Now get some sleep. You have some big events ahead of you." She kissed my forehead and ruffled my hair again before standing. "Good night, Ksega. I love you."

"Love you, too," I replied, flopping over onto my covers and closing my eyes. I fell asleep thinking of my mother, the woman I had never known, yet somehow remembered.

Willa woke me early, and I went downstairs for breakfast, eagerly following the scent of salty bacon. Derek was already sitting at our little meal table, his black hair disheveled and his clothes rumpled from sleep. He didn't look like he was fully awake yet.

We finished breakfast, then Willa announced that she had errands to run in town. Derek wanted to go check in on Jessie before leaving to meet the pirates. Offers were made for me to join either party, but I declined. I wanted to spend the day at home.

When everyone was out of the house, I spent my time tidying up. I cleaned the dishes from breakfast, then folded the spare blanket Derek had used and took it up to my room to tuck it into the wardrobe. When I came back into the hallway, I glanced at Willa's bedroom door. I had been inside before, when I was sick or when I had suffered from nightmares as a small kid, but for the most part I didn't invade her privacy, and I had certainly never considered snooping through her belongings; but then again, I had never had any good reason to before. Now, I knew there were things she wasn't telling me. She was keeping secrets about my past, and even though it may have hurt her to open up about those secrets, wasn't it more harmful to me that I didn't know the truth? Surely, she had mementos or keepsakes from Rynne's life that she kept close to her heart. Surely, they were somewhere in her room.

"This is ridiculous," I muttered, trying to talk myself out of it. She was my *grandmother*. She raised me and had never done anything to break my trust. She would tell me everything when she was ready.

But would she ever be ready? I hated to admit it, but she was getting on in years, and if she took the secrets of my parents to her grave, how would I ever know who they really were?

Just a quick look, I told myself. I would poke around until I found something informative, then I would leave. She wouldn't be home for hours yet. I had time.

Steeling myself, I crossed the hall and eased the door open. It was a small room, with a bed pressed against one wall and a wardrobe on another. A small nightstand stood beside the bed with an unlit lantern sitting atop it. There was a single window on the far wall, letting gray sunlight in through the thin, beige curtains hanging over the pane.

I took a steadying breath, ignoring the twinge of guilt that tugged at my heart, and started by checking all the obvious places. I looked in the drawers of the nightstand and in the wardrobe. I checked under the bed and on the windowsill. There was a small closet beside the wardrobe, but it was empty aside from some blankets folded on the floor and a heavy winter coat hanging on the rack. I sighed, feeling stupid for having thought this was a good idea. I scuffed my boot on the floor, contemplating my next move, and stilled. I tapped the floor again, listening closely. Frowning, I knelt and moved the blankets out of the way, feeling along the edges of the closet floor until I found what I was looking for: a latch. There was a hidden compartment beneath the boards, and from how rough the construction was, I was willing to bet that Willa had been the one to create it. Why would she bother to have it made unless she had something worth hiding?

I rocked back on my heels, hesitant to open it. Maybe there wasn't anything inside that would tell me more about my family's past, and I was just sticking my nose where it didn't belong. My curiosity had led me into bad situations before, and this could wind up being one of the worst, but I knew I would have regrets if I didn't take a look.

Keeping my breath as even as I could, I undid the latch and lifted the door. The lighting was poor, but I could tell there were things inside. I reached down and lifted them gently into my lap, rotating so that I was sitting with the sunlight illuminating the items. I stared at them for a long moment, trying to understand why they were here. The biggest one was a small quilt, folded neatly and covered in a thin layer of dust. There was a pair of tiny knitted socks, and a little beanie with a bow on the front. All of them, from the yarn in the socks to the patches of fabric in the quilt, were varying shades of pink. There was only one reason Willa would have made these: I had a sister.

When Willa, Derek, Jessie, and a handful of the pirates came back to the house, I was lying on my bed, staring at the ceiling. Beside me, the pink blanket lay folded with the beanie on top. I was holding the pair of tiny pink socks. I didn't know what time it was or how long I had been lying there, lost in my own thoughts. If Willa had made these for my sister, where was she? Was she older than me? Why did *Willa* have the items and not my sister? Why had I never been told she existed?

"Ksega!" someone shouted from downstairs. I didn't bother trying to identify whose voice it was. I wasn't going to go downstairs.

I listened to everyone bustling about below for a while, talking loudly. Pots clanged in the kitchen, and soon the smell of roast venison curled through the house. I stayed in my bed, looking at the little socks in my hands. Finally, I heard someone coming up the stairs. When my door opened, Willa stood in the hallway.

"There you are. Why are you sulking up here? I'm making—" she stopped abruptly as she saw what I was holding. I didn't look up at her. Her voice shrank. "Where did you find those?"

"Your closet." I pushed myself up into a sitting position.

"You went through my room?" she asked coldly. I swallowed the lump in my throat.

"I know it was wrong, but I felt like you were hiding something important from me. And you were. Who were these for?" I lifted the socks, looking up at her. Hot tears pressed against my eyes, threatening to spill down my face. She stared at the socks with something akin to horror in her expression.

"Ksega . . . I was going to tell you at some point, I swear, I just didn't know how." She stepped inside my room and closed the door, muffling the sounds of people below.

"So I have a *sister*?" I said, sliding my legs off the bed and rising to my feet. Willa bit her lip, then nodded. I sank back onto the covers, dragging my free hand through my hair. A *sister*. I had been wondering if it was true ever since I'd found the things in the hidden compartment, running other answers through my mind. Maybe Willa had made it before I was born, because she didn't know if I would be a boy or a girl. Maybe she had made it as a gift for someone else who wasn't even related to us.

"I've wanted to tell you for so long, but I could never find a way." Willa stepped closer, but I shook my head.

"You could never find a way? That's your excuse? How about 'Ksega, you have a sister'? That would have worked just fine!" I clenched my jaw, trying to remind myself to keep my voice down. I glared up at her through my tears.

"It didn't feel like the right way—"

"I had a right to know! You can't just keep these things from me. I never asked before because I knew it upset you, but you should have told me anyway, *especially* about this! Why would you never tell me I have a sister? Where is she? *Who* is she?" I jumped to my feet again, squashing the tiny socks in my fist.

"It isn't that simple, Ksega. Please, calm down." Willa held her hands out to me in a pleading gesture. I wanted to swipe them away and demand that she explain everything. I wanted to shout at her until my throat was sore and my voice was gone. I had spent all this time envying Sakura for having a close relationship with her brother, wanting to know what it was like to have a sibling, not knowing the entire time that I *did* have one.

"Tell me," I spat. "Tell me everything. Now." She spent a long moment staring at me, and I waited. At last, she sighed and nodded.

"Your mother did die in childbirth, just . . . not yours." Willa's gaze dropped to her lap, her hands clenched into fists. "She died when your sister came into the world, about a year after you did. We were in Lourak at the time." Her face pinched. "I never told you because I know you too well, Ksega. We stayed there for a few days to let your mother rest, but during the time your sister was . . ." she shut her eyes, as if that would make the unpleasant memory go away. "She was taken from us. The inn we were staying at was raided by a group of men dressed in yellow and black. They stole all the valuables in the inn, your sister, and a group of other people. Some of the stolen people were found dead over the next few months." Her voice trembled as she spoke. I gaped at her. How could she have kept all of this from me?

"Why?" I whispered finally, wiping the tears off my face with my knuckles.

"I knew you would want to look into the matter of her disappearance, but what point would there be? She was a newborn baby, Ksega. There's no way she would have survived that unless—" Willa stopped herself, shaking her head. "No, there's no chance of it," she finished. I forced myself to take deep breaths. There *was* a chance, as small as it may have been. We both knew it wasn't impossible. It was a childish hope, but it was hope, nonetheless.

"You never even tried to look for her?" I demanded.

Willa sighed. "I've always looked for her, Ksega, but it's not exactly an easy thing to do. Those bandits came out of nowhere and disappeared just as quickly. Nobody could track them." She looked at me through her own tears, her eyes wide. "I'm so sorry I never told you any of this before, Ksega. Please, forgive me."

"Get out," I snapped, tossing the little pink socks back onto my bed with the quilt and the beanie. Willa opened her mouth, but I glared at her until she closed it. I watched her coldly, keeping my voice as restrained as I was able. "I don't want to talk to you until I've made sense of my thoughts."

We stared across the room at each other for a long, tense moment. Then she dipped her head in acknowledgement, turned, and left the room. As soon as the door was closed, I slumped back onto my bed, tucked my face into my hands, and cried.

38
SAKURA

The Evershifting Forest was a body of magic in and of itself. Even though it shifted its shape and season and weather as it pleased, the only thing remained the same was a large structure of rock, hidden near the center of the forest and home to what was undoubtedly the most dangerous being within its borders. It wasn't difficult to locate. With Sycamore's help, I got a bird's-eye view of the forest, and in the dying light of day I made out the mound of stone. The last time I had seen it, it had been raining heavily and I had been running for my life from a smith. As we circled lower, I spotted the ledges I had leapt between in a despairing attempt to escape the monster that had been hunting me, and there, just above those ledges, was a cave entrance.

I left Sycamore perched on one of the stone outcroppings just below the entrance with a few things to eat. She seemed antsy, not wanting me to go into the cave alone, but I patted her reassuringly and climbed up the stone. The walk wasn't quite the same as I remembered. It was dark and chilling, that much was the same, but now I had a vague idea of where I was going. I thought I had taken a wrong turn after walking the long and winding path for a while, but each time I came to a new bend, I lit the space up with my eirioth to see only one option available to me. At last, I reached the end. This was the one space I remembered clearly. A small, somewhat circular room with a crack in the ceiling. The crack had been filled with some sort of glass, which now afforded me a view into the clear sky above; the Evershifting Forest had welcomed winter, but only its temperature, leaving the forest brown and wilted. On the other side of the small chamber there was a roughly oval-shaped door set into the stone. I walked up to it and, before I could talk myself out of it, knocked.

At first, all was silent and I wondered if anyone was here at all, then a small scratching sound came from the other side. The scratching intensified, and then there was a voice that I knew well, calling out from somewhere deeper within the cave.

"Hook? What are you doing?" the gravelly voice came closer, accompanied by the sound of bones clicking in stone. My heartbeat accelerated, memories of the night I had sent Alchemy away flooding the forefront of my mind. Would he hate me for the things I'd said? Would he even hear what I had to say? I hoped my terror didn't show clearly on my face as the footsteps sounded on the other side of the door. There was a mewing sound, then someone grabbed the door handle, and it swung open.

For a moment, it was as if history was repeating itself. I stood in a sliver of light, the only beam that shone down through the glass, and he stood in the shadows, just out of sight. Thin ribbons of green wound across his bones, glowing faintly. He towered over me, and I shrank back. Silence stretched between us. A small blob of blackness stumbled away near his feet, knocking against my leg. It was the little black kitten, wobbling around unsteadily and whipping the air with his scruffy tail.

"Ironling." Alchemy rasped, leaning forward. I swallowed nervously, realizing he must have known it was me before he'd even opened the door. I reached down to lift the little kitten into my arms as an excuse not to look at him. "What are you doing here?" he asked.

"We found the source," I said, scratching Hook between the ears. His whole body vibrated with his purring. Alchemy shifted the way he stood. Something rustled in the darkness behind him.

"Yes, I know . . . I sensed it. But it's still here, isn't it?" there was a curious note in his voice, something close to happiness. Why would he be happy about the Curse still being here?

"Yes. We figured out who's in control of it. As long as he's still around, I think the Curse will still exist. At least it's defeatable, though. Cursed animals can be cured by recle now." I finally looked up at him. My skin prickled at the sight of his empty eye sockets, his ever-present grin. Beyond his skull, I saw something shuffling around deeper in the cave.

"And you came all this way just to tell me that?" he asked, tilting his skull to the side. I dropped my gaze again, my stomach feeling like it was turning itself inside-out.

"No, not exactly. I came because . . . well, I figured that your assistance would probably be appreciated considering that we're about to have a war with the Curse's forces." I set Hook back on the floor, where he promptly flopped over, still purring happily. "I came to Carlore to get some help from the dragon riders, and since I knew you would be nearby . . ." I trailed off, unsure what my point was.

"I thought you never wanted to see me again," Alchemy said, his voice thin. I winced, but couldn't deny it.

"I thought so too, but after a while I realized that maybe I was a little too quick to judge." I crossed my arms and forced myself to look at him again. Whatever was behind him poked its head closer, and I could now see that it was the vague shape of an eirioth dragon. Pushing away my new questions, I spoke directly to him. "I'm not saying that I forgive you for keeping your past a secret, but I do understand why you felt the need to do it. I'm not without my own regrets, and neither is anyone else. It was unfair of me to send you back here. I'm sorry." I was a little surprised that I was able to keep my voice as steady as I did. Alchemy was quiet for a minute, then he leaned closer.

"*And?*" he prompted. I frowned at him.

"And what?"

"And you *missed* me," he rumbled, a smile clear in his voice. I rolled my eyes, but he kept talking. "I wasn't sure if you would, and I wouldn't blame you if you didn't, but you *did!* Does Ksega miss me? Is he here? How are things with everyone else? Is Sky Boy still sick?" now that he knew I wasn't here to yell at him some more, he was overflowing with questions. I held up a hand to stop him.

"Slow down, Chem. Yes, Ksega misses you lots, and Beth does too, if that means anything." I bit my tongue as I thought of what had happened with the pirates, what we encountered on the Shattered Mountains, when Ksega kissed me, *everything*. "A lot has happened since we split up, but I don't have time to explain it all right now. You're just going to have to trust me and let me explain what I can on the way, alright?" I looked down at Hook, who had pushed himself back upright and was sniffing a pebble very intently.

"You're taking me with you?" Alchemy sounded a little astonished. My pulse jumped with my anxiousness as I faced him again. In the shadows beyond, the dragon had come closer. It looked thin and frail, but I didn't dare try to change the topic now.

"Only if you want to," I said hurriedly. "You don't have to if you don't want to, I just thought . . . I mean, since you were helping before and all, but . . . you don't have to." I bit my tongue to force myself to stop talking, knowing I was only digging myself into a deeper hole. Alchemy only laughed, the sound unnatural but welcome to my ears.

"Of course I want to, Ironling." He bent down and scooped Hook into his hands, and the little kitten's purring redoubled as he smushed his face lovingly into the skeleton's fingers. "I'm glad you came back. We both know you didn't have to, but I'm very happy that you're giving me a second chance. I swear, I never intended for the Curse to become such a problem when I created it—"

"Save it. I know you regret it, and you know that I don't want to be reminded of it."

He nodded agreeably. "Right. Sorry. And I really am sorry, Sakura, for all the trouble I've caused you," he said earnestly. I nodded, accepting the apology, even though I had already forgiven him in my heart. "I feel like this moment needs a hug."

I sighed, but relented. "Yes, I think so, too." The embrace was awkward, thanks to the drastic height difference and the fact that there was a squirming kitten in his arms, not to mention how little of him there was to hug, but it served its purpose.

"We should probably get going then, correct?" Alchemy said when we broke apart, once again giving Hook all of his affection. The kitten's eyes were closed happily as he accepted belly scratches from the skeleton.

"Yes. Do you still have clothes, or are you planning to fly into battle naked?" I quirked an eyebrow at him, and he laughed again.

"I have them. Wait here. I'll be quick." He turned, then paused and looked down at Hook. "We can't leave him here on his own, and Hobble . . ." He was talking to himself as he looked back over his shoulder at where the dragon had inched even closer. I wished there was more light so I could see it properly.

"I can take a quick run back into town," I suggested, prying my gaze away from the dragon. "I know just the person to watch them."

Sycamore was antsy and eager when I raced out of the cave to leap onto her back, and she needed no further encouragement as I urged her up into the air. We soared back towards Cashew as quickly as we could, arriving just in time to spot Walter and Violet preparing to go back to Hazelwood to stay with Gamma. When Walter looked up and spotted me, a frown pulled at his lips.

"Lady Sakura? Why are you—"

"There's been a change of plans regarding Violet," I said, pulling Sycamore to a stop beside him. At Walter's side, the young girl crossed her arms and glared at me. She had the same black hair and pale skin that Derek had, but where his eyes were dark, hers were green.

"I'm not going somewhere to hide and wait for everyone to come home. I want to help!" she tilted her chin up at me stubbornly. Walter gave me a weary look, but I didn't acknowledge it. Instead, I patted Sycamore's saddle and nodded to Violet.

"Great. Get up here, then; I have a job for you." Both of them stared at me for a moment, then Violet's face split in a grin, and she eagerly hopped on her feet, hauling herself up into Sycamore's saddle behind me. Walter narrowed his eyes at me.

"You'd better know what you're doing, Lady Sakura," he cautioned.

I nodded. "I do. Don't worry, she won't come to harm. Violet, you have enough food and clothes for a couple of days, right?" I glanced back at her. She tugged one of the straps on the bag that was slung over her shoulder.

"Yes, right here. It's everything I packed for the inn," she answered, eyes wide and curious.

"Good. I'll explain more on the way, but for now just hold on tight. Walter, keep Gamma in line until we get back." I waved farewell to him. He nodded after giving me one more stern look, then I urged Sycamore forward and back up into the air.

By the time Violet and I swooped back down to Alchemy's cave mouth on Sycamore, it was dark out and the Evershifting Forest had molded itself into an array of golden maple trees that winked at us in the starlight. I had given her a basic explanation of what she would be doing and told her what to expect when we went into the cave. Unlike Derek and I, Violet was an underling, so she wouldn't be able to use eirioth to keep herself warm and keep the space lit. Thankfully, the Evershifting Forest was abundant with flammable materials, and I had given her the fire-starting kit from my saddle pack.

"So, I'll just be camping out in a cave?" Violet asked when we landed, leaving Sycamore behind as we marched into the shadows. I looked down at her.

"Does that worry you?" I asked.

She shook her head vehemently. "Of course not! I can do it just fine. No problem. Easy peasy." She nodded confidently, although I could tell she was trying to convince herself more than she was me. I had my doubts about leaving a young girl unattended in the middle of the Evershifting Forest, but she would be shut away inside a cave, and perhaps the Forest would keep her safe. It had respected Alchemy's home for this long, so surely, she would be alright.

"Remember," I told her as we came closer, passing through the room with the crack full of glass in the ceiling. "Alchemy is a skeleton, but he's not as scary as he looks, alright?" I stopped in front of the door. Beyond it, I could hear Alchemy and his animals moving around. Violet nodded, wide-eyed. I had explained to her that Alchemy was a Cursed man, but there was no way to describe the immediate horror one felt upon seeing him for the first time. I could only hope that she would still agree to look after Hook and the eirioth dragon after she had met him.

I opened the door and stepped inside. Alchemy had already lit a rusty lantern that appeared to be getting its first use in many years. The room was small and unadorned, with only a big wooden table and some tattered blankets and pillows in the corner. The bedding was littered with black tufts of fur and red feathers. When our eyes adjusted to the room's lighting, Violet and I both gasped.

Her gaze was trained on Alchemy, who stood near the table pressed against the wall. He was clothed now, but the cowl of his hood was around his shoulders, leaving his cracked, glowing skull bare. Mine was locked on the eirioth dragon. He was full-grown, but didn't look to be in the best condition. His crimson feathers, speckled with darker red, were tattered and frayed, and his golden eyes looked tired; he was the other dragon that had escaped from the performers' tent in Brightlock.

"This is Hobble," Alchemy said as he waved a hand at the dragon. "Named that because of his wing." He added, and I took in the dragon's bent wing. It didn't appear to be causing him any pain, but it couldn't have been comfortable. "I believe you know each other," Alchemy went on. He picked something off his desk and held it up in the lantern light. It was a crimson feather. "You dropped this, when . . ." he trailed off, twirling the feather between gloved bones.

"Yeah," I said. "I did drop it." An awkward silence stretched through the cave. I had forgotten the feather had been lost when I'd sent Alchemy away. When had he taken it?

"I found him in the Evershifting Forest after that," Alchemy continued. "I realized the feather must have belonged to him, and after some coaxing with food he seemed to trust me enough to come back home with me and Hook." He bent over and patted the scruffy kitten, who was flopped on his side by Alchemy's boot and purring loudly. I was surprised a cat with such a tiny chest was able to make such a sound.

"Right . . . anyway, this is Violet." I gestured at the girl beside me, who was hugging her pack close to her chest as she took in her surroundings. She started at the mention of her name. Alchemy waved at her.

"Hello there," he said, voice echoing eerily around the cave.

"Hi." Violet said in a small voice. I looked down at her.

"Are you sure you want to stay and help? We could have them brought back to Hazelwood Inn, if you'd rather have Walter and Gamma's help taking care of—" I began, but she cut me off.

"No! I can do it. I'll take care of them. Just show me when and how to feed them, and I can do it." She set her jaw stubbornly, taking a step closer to Alchemy and watching him expectantly. His skull angled ever so slightly towards me, and I nodded.

"Alright then," he said, and began to walk Violet through the process of caring for Hook and Hobble. "There's plenty of lantern fuel, and things to burn can be found just about anywhere if you go outside." He explained when he and I were finally standing by the entryway, preparing to leave. Violet stood beyond the doorway, holding Hook. He was squirming and making a futile attempt to scale up her shoulder.

"Will it be safe to go outside?" she asked timidly. I knew that Finnian had been teaching her how to use a sword, but she still didn't have one of her own, so she had nothing to defend herself with.

"The Forest will take care of you," Alchemy promised. "It's protected this cave since I first came here, and that was a long time ago. It should be perfectly safe. You can bring Hobble outside with you so he can stretch his legs, and he'll be able to sense any danger coming if that makes you feel better." He reached out to give the eirioth dragon a loving pat on the beak, then pointed at where Hook was now chewing on Violet's sleeve. "Just make sure that one stays inside, or if you do take him out, hold him the entire time unless he's doing his business. He's quite unreliable, and he likes shiny things."

"Got it." Violet nodded. She still looked a little queasy, but at least now that she understood her job and was certain that Alchemy didn't pose any threat to her, she was slightly more at ease.

"We should be going, then, if you're all set?" I looked up at Alchemy.

He nodded. "Yes, we can go now." I started to turn away, but he glanced back at Violet as he followed. "Make sure not to leave any of the full water bowls out where Hook can get to them, he might drown."

"I'll make sure he stays safe," Violet said, grabbing the door to close it behind us.

"And he likes to snuggle at night! He's very tiny, though, so don't crush him." Alchemy walked backwards at my side, making sure Violet understood. She bobbed her head in acknowledgement.

"I'll be careful," she said.

"And—"

I grabbed him by the arm and jerked him along after me. "Come on, Chem, we're short on time. They'll be okay," I said. He grumbled something but fell in step beside me as Violet shut the door. "Great," I said, picking up my pace to match Alchemy's longer strides. "Now that it's just us and we have a long ride ahead of us, you can finally give me some answers."

39
SAKURA

Sycamore was excited and ready to take off when we got to her. As soon as we took to the air, she was racing through the wind as fast as she could go. I paid close attention to how much she was wearing herself out, making sure I still had Jessie's concoction for when I needed to use it.

During the flight, I finally got answers out of Alchemy. It was hard to decide where to begin, but after I had filled him in on everything that had happened since we split up, he seemed to have found answers to questions of his own.

"I knew something had changed in the Curse roughly a hundred years ago," he told me. "That was when that feeling of being controlled or pushed in a certain direction started. I've always assumed that the Curse was just expanding and growing more powerful, perhaps having freed itself from its prison."

"But it was actually Matthias?" I asked over the wind.

"It must have been," Alchemy replied. "I know it's sort of confusing, but I'll explain it as best I can. When I created the Curse, I somehow managed to seal it away. How I did this, I have no idea. The moment the Curse began to corrupt me flows right into the moment I regained complete consciousness and awareness in the Evershifting Forest. While I was becoming whatever stars-forsaken thing I am now, my body and mind were in so much pain that I can't remember much of what I did at all. What I do know is that I *tried* to destroy it and ended up sealing it away instead." It would have been difficult to listen to him while also focusing on flying, but Sycamore and I knew each other so well that it required little more than our instincts to keep us racing smoothly through the air.

"How did it get out?" I asked.

"Since Ksega was able to destroy it so easily, we must conclude that whoever found the Curse and unleashed it almost a hundred years ago is the one that took part of its life force, weakening the source itself," Alchemy answered. "There is also the possibility that the Curse somehow escaped on its own and searched for a vessel to share its power with."

"Which would be Matthias," I said.

"Right."

"That's impossible, though, isn't it? He can't be older than thirty or so, and he surely isn't forty." I frowned as my encounters with the Ice King flashed through my mind. "How could he have kept his appearance so young? And if the Curse's power is within him, why doesn't he look more like you?"

"All perfectly reasonable questions to ask," Alchemy rumbled. "I'm afraid I don't have any answers. My best guess would be that the Curse is helping him keep up this facade. He must be at least a hundred years old, but with the Curse's help he continues to look young. There must be people inside his royal court that help keep up the charade."

The elaborate feast we had shared with the king and his council members had been an opportune time for me to examine them, but I had been too distracted with trivial thoughts to realize that. I wished I had paid more attention to them now.

"At least that explains just about everything else we've wondered about the Curse," Alchemy said optimistically. I nodded mutely, and we both fell silent. Somehow, having all of these answers didn't make me feel much better about the confrontations ahead.

*F*amark was to our north. Duke Ferin and all the others with him would most likely still be there, preparing for the later flight. I would regroup with them later. For now, I directed Sycamore towards Rulak. We were losing the cover of night to shield our arrival, so we skirted around the town and landed on the western fringes of it. There were a few small homesteads here, and two of them had a campsite full of pirates set up between them.

"Should I stay back here for a while?" Alchemy asked when we dismounted. He was concealed in his clothes again, but there was no hiding the fact that his skull was easily visible in the light of day, even beneath his cowl.

"No," I told him. "If you walk into the camp with me, nobody will attack us outright. You've been hiding from humanity for long enough. Besides, if you're going to be fighting alongside these people, it might be helpful for them to know what you look like."

Thomas was the first one to notice our approach. He was lounging on the snow, ignorant of the fact that his clothes were now soaked, and staring up into the gray sky. When we came closer, he lifted his head and raised his eyebrows at the shadows beneath Alchemy's hood.

"Wow," he deadpanned. "If I'd known the kind of company you like to keep in your spare time, I would have worried a lot more about getting on your bad side." He dragged himself to his feet, sweeping snow off his trousers and shaking it out of his fiery curls.

"This is Alchemy," I said, ignoring his jest and waving a hand at the skeleton beside me. Alchemy dipped his head in greeting. Thomas grunted, then motioned towards the rest of the camp.

"We've had people keeping a lookout for the Curse. They've shown up, but so far haven't attacked. It looks like they're waiting for more beasts to get here." He stomped his boots in the snow and fell in step beside us. "That Erabeth woman has taken charge, pretty much, even though there are some Solian army officials here to talk strategy with us." He gave me a mischievous grin. "Like us pirates ever cared about something as trivial as *strategy*."

"That sounds about right," Alchemy commented, and I nodded in silent agreement.

When we reached the campsite, we received several strange looks. We ignored them, plowing through until we found the place where Beth, Gian and Derek were gathered. They stood apart from Molly, Chap, and a man wearing important-looking livery. Beth was picking dirt out from under her fingernails with her hunting dagger. She glanced up from her work when we approached, her gaze instantly latching onto the skull beneath the cloak hood.

"Ah, *Faja*, you're back. And you brought Bones with you!" Beth looked between the two of us with surprise. I nodded mutely, scanning the crowd for other familiar faces. I spotted Jessie and Derek deep in conversation with Knuckles, but Ksega was nowhere to be seen.

As if sensing who I was looking for, Alchemy asked Beth, "Where's the other one? I've been told he's dying to see me again."

"He's still at his house, over there." Beth pointed towards one of the houses. "He's been in a bad mood as of late. I'm not sure why."

"Perhaps Ironling can help out with that." Alchemy prodded me in the shoulder, and I scowled at him. I hadn't even told him about what had happened when Ksega had said goodbye to me. I still wasn't sure how to make sense of it myself.

"He's sulking somewhere in the orchard, if you want to go find him. Breakfast's in an hour, and I expect both of you to be there," Beth said, pointing with her dagger towards the house again.

"Only if Chem helps with the cooking," I said. I was hesitant to leave them, but I wanted to go talk to Ksega as well, especially now that I knew he was in a bad mood. I wondered if he had spoken to Willa about his family yet.

I broke apart from the others and trooped through the snow towards the house Beth had indicated. Sycamore stomped along behind me. There was a dormant fruit orchard behind it, and as I came closer, I realized that there was a crate pushed up against one of the trees, and someone was sitting on it, resting against the trunk. When I reached the orchard, I recognized Ksega's fluffy blond hair. I slowed to a stop three trees away from where he sat. Sycamore nudged me with her head.

"Shh, alright, alright." I wrapped my arms around her neck as I thought. Maybe it would be best if I didn't think, because thinking only complicated these things. I bunched Sycamore's feathers in my fist and looked into her eyes, as if I could will her into telling me what to do. She blinked slowly back at me, then snorted. I winced, clapping a hand over her beak, but the noise had already been made. I waited a long moment, hoping it hadn't been too loud.

"Sakura?" Ksega's voice was thick. I looked over my shoulder. He was peering around the tree. As soon as he knew it was me, he jumped up and rushed through the snow towards me.

"Hey, what's—" the wind was knocked out of me as Ksega pulled me into a hug. I grunted, my arms instinctively wrapping around him. "What's going on?" I asked when I caught my breath. He was taller than me by nearly a foot, making the embrace slightly uncomfortable, very much so when he tucked his head against my neck.

He mumbled something incoherent, and I felt something cold on my neck. With a start, I realized he was crying. I wasn't sure what to do. I had cried in his arms before, but now the roles were reversed, and I was frozen. Luckily, Sycamore was there to shove her head angrily into my back, prompting me to stumble forward and push Ksega back towards the crate he had sat on. That gave me an idea.

"Why don't you sit down?" I suggested, poking him in the ribs to get him to focus. He nodded mutely, straightening and wiping at his eyes with the backs of his hands. Something in my stomach twisted at the sight of him so upset.

We shuffled through the snow, and he sat down on the crate. I scootched in beside him, and he rested his head back against the tree, releasing shaky breaths. Sycamore stamped her feet, walking in a few circles around us before settling down on the ground beside the crate.

"Did you talk to Willa?" I asked, sure now that that must have been the reason he was surly. He nodded. I waited patiently, recalling all the times he had done the same thing for me as I had struggled to find the words to properly express what I was feeling.

Time passed slowly. The sun moved across the sky, snow drifted along the ground, and the smell of breakfast cooking in the camp wafted through the air. Sycamore shuffled around every so often, sighing heavily but never getting up to go entertain herself. Ksega sniffled and shivered at my side, at one point reaching out to grab my hand and wind our fingers together. I let my eirioth surge to the surface of my skin, warming his frigid hands.

"I have a sister," he said finally. At first, I wasn't sure I had heard him correctly. I leaned away and turned to look at him, and he sat up straight to look at me. His eyes were red-rimmed, and his hair was a mess. I wondered if he had slept at all since discovering this news.

"You *what?*" I asked, hoping I had misheard. He sighed and leaned back against the tree trunk, closing his eyes.

"She might not . . . you know, be alive anymore, but I had her at one point." His throat bobbed as he swallowed. "Willa never told me because she knew I would want to look into what happened to her." He opened his eyes and new tears slid down his face. He shook his head numbly. "Why would she keep it from me for this long? I thought my parents were the only thing she hid from me, but this . . ."

"I'm sorry, Ksega," I muttered, unsure what else I could say. He nodded once, acknowledging my words, then suddenly sat up straight. He cleared his throat and wiped his eyes again, then looked at me.

"Enough of that, though. How are you? How did things go in Carlore? Where's Asuka?" seconds ticked by as I stared at him, puzzled. I shook my head, squeezing his hand.

"You can't just brush this aside, Ksega. What are you going to do?" I asked, searching his face to try and gauge what he was feeling. He blinked back more tears, chewing on his lip. When he spoke again, it was in a low, hoarse voice.

"Sakura, I appreciate your concern, but I really don't want to talk about it right now. It's all I've been thinking about for the past two days, and I have to find some sort of distraction." He brought his free hand up and pushed a loose strand of my hair back behind my ear. "I'm glad you're back."

"Me too," I said, and I meant it, even though I had been dying to go home for so long. For now, my brief visit back to Hazelwood Inn would be enough to get me through the battle I knew was fast approaching.

Ksega drew his hand away hastily, as if he'd only just realized what he'd been doing. He cleared his throat again, his gaze darting down to where Sycamore was lying, then out across the orchard. His leg began to bounce nervously. I was about to ask what was wrong when he faced me again, his expression serious.

"Sakura, about what happened before you left . . ." he cleared his throat, and I knew that the pink in his face wasn't only due to the cold. I waited, and he forged on. "I didn't mean for it to be"— he paused, searching for the right word—"*weird.*" He grimaced.

"It wasn't weird," I assured him, feeling my own face go hot.

"Good." Ksega rubbed the back of his neck. Another silence settled over us. I watched him closely, wishing I could read the subtle signs in peoples' faces like he could. He was able to mask what he was feeling so easily, and it unnerved me.

Sycamore lifted her head to look at us, sensing a change in our demeanors. She narrowed her eyes at Ksega, and I reached out to pat her head comfortingly.

"It's alright," I said. "He's a friend." I glanced sidelong at him. "More than a friend." The crimson on his cheeks deepened. I reached for his hand, pulling it towards Sycamore. She made a low noise in the back of her throat, and he flexed away from her. "It's okay," I coaxed both of them. "Be nice." I pushed his hand all the way against her beak. He relaxed a little, and after a beat so did she. "There. That wasn't so bad, right?" I said, dropping my hand. Ksega rubbed the dragon's beak with his thumb.

"Not terribly so. She's not as friendly as Asuka." He glanced at me. "Speaking of Asuka . . ."

"He's here. Well, he's on Famark right now. But he'll be here." I looked up at the sky. "We should probably head over for some food now. Chem is cooking." I rose from the crate, dusting snow from my pants. Ksega's head snapped up.

"Chem's here? At the camp?" he jumped to his feet.

"I brought him back with me," I said.

"Why didn't you lead with that? Come on, let's go!" he grabbed my hand and half-dragged me towards the camp. Sycamore scrambled to her feet to chase after us. There were still so many questions left for him to answer, but I knew they would have to wait.

We raced through the snow towards the camp but slowed to a stop before we reached it. Sycamore made a disgruntled noise as we looked to the south, towards the Veiled Woods. Black figures were streaming out of the forest and racing towards the capital. Dinner would have to wait.

The Curse was attacking.

40
KSEGA

An hour flew by. As soon as we spotted the Cursed animals rushing the capital, Sakura and I abandoned all thoughts of dinner and raced into the camp to inform everyone that Matthias's attack had begun. Sakura checked again to make sure I was okay, then mounted her dragon and disappeared into the air, going to find the other Carlorians and tell them what to expect.

I stood rooted in place, my thoughts racing, trying to figure out what I should do first. I spotted Peeler approaching me, carrying some sort of necklace in his hands. I recognized it as one of the projects he had been working on.

"Put this on. This string opens and closes the pouch, this one spins the marble. It's for hypnotizing the Curse." He pointed to the different strings hanging from the pendant, then shoved the necklace into my hand and hurried off to hand more out. I fumbled with the cord and pulled it over my head, spying Beth, Gian, and Alchemy standing not far off. I went to join them, feeling my grin widen as the skeleton turned to look at me.

"Ksega, my boy!" he spread his cloaked arms wide, and as I came closer, he hugged me to his side. "It's good to see you again." He patted my back as he released me, and I saw Erabeth rolling her eyes.

"It's good to see you, too," I said, biting my lip to keep from running my mouth with all the things that I wanted to tell him. Instead, I tried to focus on the more serious matters at hand. "What's our plan for fighting the Curse?"

"These charms will help us." Beth lifted her own hypnotic necklace. "But only a certain number were made. They've been given to us and the pirates, and what was left over was given to the Solian army. Bones, you'll want to avoid watching anyone on our side too closely," she advised Alchemy. He nodded in understanding.

"You should go get your longbow now," Gian told me, loosening his sword in its sheath. "We're about to start moving. The Solian army is waiting to take the attack head-on between Lourak and Soarlak, and we're going to take them from the rear." He tossed his head, moving his silky black hair out of his face. For once, there was no sign of him feeling sickly. If anything, he looked as spritely and alive as possible, eager for the action ahead. I hoped he wouldn't do anything rash enough to get himself killed.

"Be ready in ten minutes. We're all getting our weapons situated, and Gian and I are finding places to leave Light Ray and Taro where they'll be safe before we form ranks. We're moving out then."

I nodded, turning on my heel and beginning to sprint towards Willa's house. At the sound of footsteps behind me, I glanced back to see that Alchemy was jogging alongside me, easily matching my stride with his long legs.

"How have you been?" he asked. I gave him an irritated look, but he didn't seem to register the fact that where he could speak without running out of breath, I could not.

"Good and bad. Lots of stuff happened," I panted. I skidded through the snow around the back of the house. Willa was inside the living room, but I didn't want to talk to her right now. She had sought me out when she heard the Curse was nearby, and of course with the prospect of potential death looming over our heads, it had been a little easier to have a conversation; but not easy enough.

I climbed the pear tree that backed up to our house and wiggled my window open. Alchemy followed. When he stood in my room, he had to stoop to keep from hitting his skull on the ceiling.

"What sort of good and bad? Don't tell me Ironling turned you down." He looked down at the pink quilt folded on the foot of my bed, topped with the beanie and the pair of socks. I reached into the compartment in my wardrobe to retrieve my longbow and lifted my quiver of arrows to loop it to my belt.

"No, the bad stuff has nothing to do with Sakura. My grandmother was just keeping some secrets from me and . . ." I cleared my throat, not bothering to finish the sentence. Alchemy took the hint and avoided asking about the latter remark.

"So the *good* things are concerning Sakura then, right?" he loomed close to me, sending a flurry of snow cascading from his shoulders onto the floor. I tried to look at him seriously but couldn't. He must have read it in my expression because he laughed and pumped a fist into the air. "I knew it! She *was* keeping something from me! Go on then, tell me, what happened? You've got to give me details."

"Chem, this really isn't the time for such a conversation; we've got to get moving. Where is this coming from, anyway? I never realized you were a romantic." I pushed past him, clambering over my bed and back out the window. As I was scaling down the tree, more snow fell onto my head as he came clumsily after me.

"Well, we can always walk and talk. Did you tell her you liked her? Did you make a big dramatic heart of flowers that bloomed in the dead of winter?" his voice was far too giddy for the occasion, but his joy was infectious. I was so glad he was *here* and that we would all finish this together. I scoffed at his question, beginning to jog back towards the camp.

"Nothing as frivolous as that. I only kissed her." I took off through the snow before he could respond, the charm Peeler had given me thumping against my chest. He didn't miss a beat, plowing after me as his throaty chuckle tore through the breeze.

"No, get back here, you can't just *say that* and then run off!" he shouted. I didn't respond until we slowed down and stopped in the camp beside Derek and Jessie.

"It's work time, Chem. No time for chatting." I said between gasped breaths. Derek gave me an unamused frown as he adjusted the way his quiver of arrows sat on his back. Alchemy shook his head and crossed his arms.

"Fine, but the second it's over you're telling me *everything*," he said.

"Deal." I looked up as Beth came closer, fussing with her cloak until it sat on her in a way that allowed her easy access to her weapon. She looked us both up and down, then nodded in satisfaction.

"Let's go," she said. The pirates and the one remaining Solian army official were already on the move up ahead, keeping a steady pace while we followed a few meters behind in our own little group. Nobody had mounts except Derek, but he led Bear alongside us instead of riding him. I kept a constant lookout on the skies above, waiting to see Sakura and the other Carlorians. I hadn't had the chance to ask her more about how many she had brought back with her.

It wasn't long before we came up behind a legion of Cursed animals. While the target was in the Shattered Mountains, there were plenty of Cursed animals lurking in the north, and they would have to go past Rulak and Doluk and through Lourak to reach the mountains. As we traveled, we saw animals racing out of the small portion of the Veiled Woods that extended across the corner of the northern portion of Wisesol. There were wolves and badgers and raccoons and birds, and I spotted more than a few raptors among them. I looked for Wynchell in the crowd ahead of us, spotting him slinking alongside Theomand. It was good that we no longer had to worry about the Curse claiming him, Asuka, or any of the other animals while we fought.

The Cursed animals in front of us were heading a course towards Doluk, and we made to intercept them. Derek unslung his longbow and swung into Bear's saddle, taking to the air to get a better vantage point. There must have been almost forty beasts total, loping out across the snow, and some of them were turning to face us. They moved with more purpose than made sense, as if they were puppets being pulled on strings. When they realized they were being approached, then doubled around and raced for us instead, their gaits jerking and uneven thanks to missing limbs and dangling bones. Weapons were drawn as the wave of beasts reached us, and the fighting began.

SAKURA

The rush of eirioth dragons and their riders appeared above me in the clouds before I could even register that they were there. Wind from their beating wings battered past me as I pulled Sycamore higher into the air after them, searching among the rainbow of colors for a familiar one. There were several shades of blue, but no two were the same, and only one dragon was a solid shade of azure. Sycamore pumped her wings and brought us up alongside Asuka and Finnian. He looked a little surprised to see me appear beside him but got over his bewilderment and waved with a grin.

"There you are!" he yelled over the roar of the wind. I only nodded in response.

We were flying past Rulak and over the Port, heading for the great, moving black masses rushing towards Lourak. There were ranks of soldiers in bright silver armor waiting to meet them with spears and swords and crossbows, but the number of Cursed animals was more than any of us had anticipated. Stags tossed heads adorned with racks of broken antlers, raptors screeched and tripped over their ripped wings, birds lurched through the air as feathers drifted down from their bodies; it was sickening to watch, and that wasn't even all of it. My gut twisted as I realized that bigger beasts were moving alongside the others, ones far too big to be anything from the Veiled Woods. We flew closer, lowering through the wind towards the sounds of battle. As we came close, it became apparent that the giant forms were those of smiths and runeboars, all of them soaked in water. It was as we swooped down on the beasts, dragons roaring and weapons screaming as they were drawn from scabbards and sheaths, that I realized the figures I had seen swimming across the surface had been other Cursed animals, summoned from across the Great Lakes to join their fellow shadows of the Ice King.

We descended upon them in a flock of beating wings and slashing claws. The eirioth dragons had once been the mounts upon which Carlorian war soldiers would ride, and while few of the breed had experienced war in decades and most had never seen it in their entire lives, they leapt into the fight with agile ease. A wall of crimson and pearl and deep blue and bright yellow and a dozen other colors collided with a stream of jarring black and oozing green. Flame-swords blazed to life around me, blades being plunged down towards sticky flesh, arrows hissing through the air past my head, all within a matter of seconds. My own flame-sword was in my hand and roaring hungrily. I held it high to keep it from singing any of Sycamore's feathers, letting it elongate into a crackling whip to reach out and curl around the throat of a Cursed raptor. The creature thrashed and struggled, screeching in a way that shouldn't have been possible as the whip seared through fur and flesh and bone. Sycamore swiped out with her claws and severed the mangled neck, sending the raptor's head toppling into the snow. A Cursed deer jumped towards us as we landed amidst the fray, kicking out at us with cloven hooves. Sycamore snapped her beak at it irritably, shoving it backwards into the line of fire of one of the crossbowmen. A bolt sank deep into the deer's side, and it bayed in pain as it toppled over.

All around me, battle was raging. Dragons, soldiers, and Cursed animals tore at each other; steel blades screamed against bone, and teeth clashed against beaks and claws. Bodies were falling left and right, and cries of war swam through the air. It was like nothing I had ever seen before, and it made me feel sick to my stomach.

I pulled Sycamore back from the swarm of gnashing teeth and vying talons, retracting my flame-sword to its normal length once more. I saw Finnian and Asuka tussling with one of the sopping smiths. It was twice Asuka's size, and yet the young dragon appeared undaunted, flaring his wings as wide as they would go and rearing back to slash his claws over the beast's face. Half of the smith's skull was already exposed, revealing an empty eye socket and blackened teeth. Finnian had his flame-sword in hand, but he didn't bother to use it. Instead, he lifted his opposite hand and shot a steady stream of fire directly into the smith's chest. It raised up on its hind legs, snarling, and Asuka took the opportunity to pump his wings once, lifting himself just high enough into the air that when he dove down again and slammed his talons into the chest of the smith, the beast's spine bent in half with a nauseating *snap*. I winced, more than a little surprised at the dragon's ferocity. Perhaps all those years in meek service to the Locker performers had kindled a fire of quiet, unbridled wrath within him, and now he was finally presented with the opportunity to release it. I was glad I hadn't been on the receiving end.

There were dozens of us, but dozens more Cursed animals. They rushed from the Veiled Woods, pulled themselves out of the waves of the Port, flew in from the clouds, even stampeded in from Freetalon. Creatures of all kinds had been corrupted, undoubtedly more than ever before. Alchemy had said that Matthias may never have pushed the boundaries of his power over the Curse this far, and it made one question just how far that magic reached; as more and more beasts flooded the snowy landscape, I suspected that by the end of the day, we would have the answer.

KSEGA

I had thought that nearly forty Cursed animals was a lot, but when we finished them off and kept moving towards Lourak I realized how wrong I was. We went around the eastern side of Lourak, past the Port, and what we saw there left us slack-jawed and frozen in fear. We were just about past the copse of trees that blocked our view to the south when the waters of the Port erupted in frothy white waves. Boats were sent rolling over the docks, crates sliding off into the Port as the vessels flipped and crunched beneath the onslaught of water. Even though we were a safe distance to the west, freezing salt water sprayed down on us, and we all cried with alarm and gaped at the monster that had emerged from the depths. A sea wraith, its scales blackened and bones exposed through gaps in its flesh, was drawing itself up, baring cracked fangs as its head swung to face the distant Slated Mountains. It let out a furious bellow and dove forward, crushing boats and docks and floating merchant stores. Its scaled body slammed onto the earth as it slithered forward, plowing over trees and bushes and upturning boulders as it went, discs of ashy scutes falling in its wake. We surged after it, pushing through the small cluster of trees before us and slowing once we were beyond them to take in the situation. The din of the Curse thundered in my ears, giving me a pounding headache, but I was well-practiced in tuning it to the back of my mind. It didn't lessen the pain, but at least it didn't drive me mad.

The sea wraith was struggling across the ground, its body not made for traveling on land. It was still pulling itself out of the water, its thick body breaking through wood and stone and earth. It was smaller than the wraith that had attacked *The Coventry*, but no less daunting. It slid roughly across the ground, trying to join its fellow Cursed beasts. There were hundreds of them in all shapes and sizes and species, clashing with the soldiers of Wisesol and the airborne Carlorians. There were dozens of colorful dragons circling the air, diving and rolling and picking at the animals before them. Some of them gripped the smaller animals in their talons, flying them high up into the air before diving down and slamming them into the earth. Flame-swords blazed, crossbow bolts whizzed through the air, spears and shields flashed in the fading light of day. The fires from the Carlorians' weapons illuminated most of the battlefield, but soon night would be fully upon us, and we would be at a disadvantage. There was no way to end the fight quickly, so torches would be brought out soon enough.

Chap huddled us up and laid out a plan. The sea wraith's body blocked our view and our path farther south, and it posed a great threat to everyone, so it had to be the first to go. Derek was to take Bear and fly to the beast's head, drawing it away from the rest of the chaos with his arrows. He would take Jessie with him, and if the opportunity presented itself, she was to do her best to cure it of the Curse with her recle. The rest of us were split into two groups. Most of us were charged with the duty of trying to find alternate ways to kill the sea wraith, and the remainder of our group was tasked with joining the rest of the soldiers. Alchemy and I were put in the first group. Chap put Thomas in charge of us, and he led the others towards the fray.

Thomas had us split into smaller groups and take different portions of the wraith's body. Alchemy and I were a part of Thomas's team, along with Theomand and Wynchell. We approached one of the sections of the body where the flesh had fallen or been torn away, revealing blackened, mushy innards and cracked bones laced with glowing green. Wynchell growled loudly as we came closer, eyes wide and leaf-shaped tail lashing the ground anxiously. My own senses were on high alert, my bowstring taut and ready to fire the arrow I had knocked. We were near the front of the monster, and with a gut-lurching feeling I recognized what must have been a giant heart, still beating within the beast's body. It pulsed in a disgusting way, and Alchemy made an *eugh* sound beside me. I was glad that the sun had gone down, and it was too dark to make out any further gruesome details.

"The Curse will continue to keep it alive," the skeleton commented, fidgeting with the clasp of his cloak. "But giving it what would typically be a fatal injury will slow it down considerably, and if that red-haired girl manages to succeed with her recle, it will be dead in seconds." Thomas nodded, pushing the brim of his hat up to get a better look into the wraith's body. He wrinkled his nose as something squirmed inside of it, and I realized there were a number of fish and other sea-dwelling animals that had managed to slip inside the living carcass.

"Right then," Thomas looked up at me and slapped me encouragingly on the shoulder. "That bit's up to you, archer." He waved a hand dramatically towards the beating heart. I grimaced, glad I hadn't eaten dinner, because if I had, I had no doubts it would have been making a second appearance at that moment.

"Of course," I muttered, lifting my bow and taking aim. I shut my eyes at the last moment to avoid watching as the arrow flew through the air and sank into the sticky heart with an awful sound. A roar tore through the air as the sea wraith rolled angrily, trying to quell the pain in its core. We all scampered out of its way as its rough scales demolished the frozen earth beneath it, sending clots of mud and ice into the air as it jerked about in agony. All that was left now was waiting for Jessie to administer her magic to the beast. It didn't take long.

We were on our way to join the massive brawl between man, dragon, and Cursed monsters when the sea wraith's entire body convulsed violently. People yelled and dragons roared as the wraith slid along the snow, knocking into friend and foe alike and screeching all the while. I watched in a mix of horror and amazement as what remained of the wraith's scales slowly changed, the black and green bleeding out of them to be replaced with a hazy blue. The silver-green ooze surrounding the wounds across its body thinned into crimson blood, soaking into the snow and staining it an ugly reddish brown. The wraith's screams slowly withered into silence, and as its body stilled on the frozen ground, the other Cursed animals seemed to take pause, staring at their fallen comrade. Alchemy swayed slightly from side to side.

"Woah," he rasped. We all looked at him sharply. He shook his head, lifting a gloved hand to rub the face of his skull, as if something there was irritating him. "That was

. . . bizarre," he said when he let his hand fall. We watched him expectantly, and he explained, "I don't think that was Matthias's control over the Curse," he began, clenching and unclenching his fists as though he were trying to alleviate pent up anger. "I think that *was* the Curse. I don't think it's ever been attacked that way before." He pushed his hood back off his head, running his hands over the surface of his skull over and over. A prickle of unease ran beneath my skin when one of his boots started rapidly tapping the ground.

"Are you . . . okay?" I asked tentatively, and at my hesitation, I noticed that Theomand and Thomas both took involuntary steps away from the skeleton.

"Yes, I'll be fine. It's sort of like a bad headache." He lowered his arm and looked down at me. "Matthias knows that the Curse is wary of continuing this fight. He's going to redouble the effort, and that will put everyone in more danger. You and Ironling need to go to the source of this to stop it."

"Right." I nodded in agreement, still watching him uncertainly. "Where's that?"

"Matthias is in control, isn't he? So he's exactly where you would normally find him." Alchemy replied. I stared at him for a moment, my head still too fuzzy from the sound of the Curse roaring around me to comprehend everything he was saying. He groaned. "The Salt Palace, you dimwit."

"Oh, yes, of course. There." I peered around him, searching the flock of dragon wings to see if I could spot Sakura. I saw Asuka, but he was ridden by an unfamiliar man.

"She's over there." Alchemy must have noticed my searching, because he pointed towards the center of the fray, directly at a silver-white dragon that was locked in a fight with a Cursed smith. Standing in the midst of an ocean of black and vile green beside her dragon was Sakura, snapping her flame-sword out into a whip to pull the monsters around her to the ground, where they were promptly finished off by the other soldiers.

"Good luck," Theomand said, giving me a squeeze on the shoulder with his metal hand. Thomas nodded to me, and I returned it. Just as I was about to set off, Alchemy gripped my arm and leaned close.

"*Be careful.* He has some of us guarding him in the palace, and probably that advisor, too. Keep Ironling close, and both of you come back alive, understood?" his voice grated in my ears like gravel. I leveled my gaze at him.

"You're not one of them, Chem." I said firmly. His grip on my arm tightened, and I knew he didn't believe me. I gave him a quick hug and said, "I'll bring us both back safely." Then I ran into the center of the swarm of beasts.

SAKURA

*K*sega appeared by my side seemingly out of nowhere. I nearly hit him in the face with my flame-sword when he grabbed my arm, but he released me and ducked out of the way just in time. I gave him an exasperated look.

"What are you doing?!" I shouted. He pointed at Sycamore, who had finally gotten the best of the smith she was fighting and was now clawing viciously at its limp body.

"We have to go to the Salt Palace. That's where Matthias is," he replied. My eyebrows inched skyward.

"We have to kill him? Duck!" I swung my flaming blade in another arc, and he crouched below it so that the fire could slam into the chest of a cursed bird that had been diving for his back. The bird was batted away and sent under the feet of a nearby eirioth dragon, where it was crushed beneath its talons.

"Yep," Ksega answered, reaching for Sycamore's reins. She let out a low, rumbling sound from her chest, but didn't snap at him. I didn't have the time to argue as I climbed into the saddle, and he pulled himself up after me. We took off into the air, angling to the southeast, but we were blocked by another dragon. It was Bear, with Derek and Jessie on his back.

"Where are you going?" Derek demanded.

"To the Salt Palace. Once Matthias is dead, all this will stop," Ksega shouted back. I winced, leaning away from him so he wouldn't be yelling directly into my ear. Across the wind, Derek and Jessie both gave disapproving frowns, looking down at the battlefield below us. It was a complete mess, a tangle of human and animal bodies alike, living and dead, grappling for victory.

"You're not going alone," Jessie said.

"Fine, you can come too," I said with a nod. "Let's go." I dug my heels into Sycamore's sides, urging her forward, and she swooped through the air. Bear flipped around behind us and hurried after.

Wind beat against us as we flew, soaring over the dark waves that glistened in the moonlight. More Cursed animals still were swimming furiously for the shores of Wisesol, eager to join in the fight. How many more could there possibly be? Would our people stand no chance as more and more of Matthias's forces came? The worrisome questions made me push Sycamore harder; she responded by snorting and tossing her head, then redoubling her speed.

"Are you planning to just fly right in?" Ksega asked over the wind. I nodded, trying to map out the Salt Palace in my mind. There were balconies and porches all over, and plenty of very breakable windows, so getting in wouldn't be the problem.

I tried not to think of what we had to do as we swept through the air, flying so fast through the chilly air that my hands and face were beginning to go numb. I had almost asked Ksega why he hadn't brought Alchemy with him instead but discarded the question as soon as it entered my mind. Bringing Alchemy directly before the man who controlled the Curse probably wasn't my brightest idea. The thought of murdering the Ice King was a daunting one, and thinking of it made me dizzy. Would I actually be able to go through with such a drastic action? His releasing the Curse was the reason so many people had died in the last hundred years, so there was no doubt in my mind that assassination was no less than he deserved, but was my hand the one who had to commit it? A burning anger had simmered inside me ever since my parents and Aurora had died, and a silent vow that had grown ever since, a promise that one day I would find a way to destroy the Curse. Now I was here, and my motives were crossed and muddled. If I killed Matthias for the wrong reason—for revenge instead of justice—didn't that make me no less of a killer than he was?

Sycamore was flying faster than I had ever seen a dragon fly. It must have been the residual effects of Jessie's potion, because Bear wasn't able to keep up with her. I didn't let her slow down for them. If they continued to fly, Bear would be exhausted, but he would survive the flight, and I was sure I had more of the potion left if he needed it.

I had a pretty good idea of where we would find Matthias, but the issue was that I couldn't remember how to get there. I knew it was on one of the lower levels and that there was only one pane of glass to let in natural light, set in the door to a small balcony. But the balcony faced the east, and we were approaching from the northwest. If Traf was helping to keep a lookout for any potential dangers, we would be ousted before we even got in.

When the Salt Palace came into view, my heart jumped into my throat. I was certain that there were Coldmonian soldiers keeping a watch on the sea and the skies, but Matthias wouldn't have told them to look specifically for Carlorians. From how secretive he had sounded, based on what Peeler and Theomand had told us, he wasn't going to reveal his power over the Curse until *after* we were out of the way and Wisesol had been completely overrun, when he would announce himself as a "hero" to his people and expand his kingdom.

We looped around to the western side, which was mostly cast in darkness. Lanterns and torchlight flickered beyond window panes and closed curtains, and I saw several soldiers posted outside chambers and patrolling down corridors. I guided Sycamore through the air until we came to one of the larger balconies attached to a bedroom chamber, where she landed deftly on the stone. Ksega and I slid from the saddle, and he leaned close to the doors to see what he could through the glass panes.

"I think this is an empty guest chamber. Want me to bust the lock?" he glanced curiously at me, and I nodded. He crouched in front of the door, pulling one of his arrows free of his quiver and setting about the work of . . . if I was being entirely honest, I wasn't sure *what* he was doing, but he was being quiet and getting us inside, so I kept silent.

Bear was barely visible in the distant sky, little more than a dark smudge against the star-dusted blanket. We didn't have time to wait for them to arrive. I gave Sycamore an affectionate kiss on the beak and motioned for her to stay put, that way Derek and Jessie would be able to see where we had entered the Salt Palace. Hopefully they had the sense to have at least one of them stay with the dragons, because I knew that as sure as fire was hot, Ksega would follow me inside.

"Got it," Ksega whispered, his voice barely carrying to my ears over the whistling wind that brushed past us. I looked back to see him easing the door open and stepping into a dark room. I gave Sycamore another pat and then slipped in after him. It was hard to make out any details, since the moon was still in the eastern part of the sky and this room was on the west side of the palace, but enough silvery light shone in through the cracked balcony door and the windows for us to make out vague, shadowy shapes. The bed was empty and neatly made, and there was a table and a few chairs laid about the room. A wardrobe was propped against a wall beside an empty hearth, and across the room from it was the entrance to a small washroom. Aside from that and an uncomfortably lumpy rug, the space was empty.

"What are the chances we can just walk in and ask for directions to that big room with the murals?" I asked, tailing Ksega to the door. He gave me a peculiar look over his shoulder, trying to gauge if I was joking or not.

"Very low," he said finally, his voice tense. I nodded, knowing he was right, but it had still been worth it to hope. We waited another beat before he eased the door open, letting light spill in from the corridor beyond. Another wait, this time with even more tension weaving through the air, passed. I couldn't hear any approaching footsteps or nearby voices. No shadows appeared or moved across the hallway as Ksega pulled the door open a little farther. Nothing seemed disturbed. We shared another glance, nodded to one another, and stepped deeper into the Salt Palace.

41
ERABETH

*A*ll-out war was not something I had ever experienced myself, although a part of me had always secretly dreamt that the day would come when I would have the chance for exactly that. Fighting hundreds—if not thousands—of Cursed animals wasn't *exactly* what I'd had in mind, but I supposed it would do.

My saber was sticky with silver-green blood, and a rank smell curled through the air. It reeked of sweat, but I was used to such a scent from all my days spent in the Duskfall Desert. Gian, on the other hand, was not so accustomed to the smells. Already, he had pulled himself to the side several times to loudly retch before returning to the fighting. I didn't have the time to bother with sniping at him over it; besides, in a real battle like this, encouragement to your comrades was always valued over all teasing and nitpicking. That could be saved for the end, when everyone was safe and alive and the true danger was past, so until we reached that point, I watched Gian's back and made sure he wasn't overworking himself. A strong sweat had broken out on his brow not long after we joined the fight, and I could hear the exertion in his grunts and see the strain in his muscles whenever his blows met with those of a Cursed beast. He didn't slow down or stop unless he was throwing up, which I found both respectable and concerning. He had been like this from the very start, inexplicably desperate to prove that he was one of our equals, even though he was an underling and he knew practically nothing about how the world outside of Old Nightfall actually functioned. At first, I had admired the quality, especially when he persevered through his sicknesses and poured all of his strength and effort into learning the art of the blade, but at some point, I had realized it was less of an advantage and more of a barrier. He was too stubborn to admit when he wasn't strong enough for something, and it made me worry about him. Not that I would ever express such worry to him. The last thing he needed was to learn someone was pitying him in secret.

There was little time for worrying anyway, because birds swarmed us and foxes snapped at our ankles and runeboars flailed their tusks dangerously close all around, giving us plenty of things to keep ourselves occupied. My saber met tooth and bone and fur, slicing through flesh and snagging on thick coats. The heavy hypnotic charm beat against my chest as

I moved, and I used it whenever I was able. It was surprisingly effective, rendering the Cursed beasts helpless against our weapons. I tore mercilessly through anything that defied my blade, at some point shedding my heavy winter coat to move with more precision and ease. Gian had done the same some time ago, his hair plastered by sweat to his clammy skin. I watched him out of the corner of my eye as we fought side-by-side and sometimes back-to-back. One of the upsides of fighting alongside the person that you trained was that you automatically worked well together, and if anything, Gian and I were living proof of that. We moved fluidly, guarding each other's blind spots, blocking each other from slipping and falling on the snow, and taking each opponent as it came. Even in his weariness, Gian didn't slow down for a moment, staying sharp and alert. Around us, the pirates and the Solian warriors were fighting just as valiantly. I saw bent limbs and bloodied bodies lying beneath the stampede of feet, but it was impossible to tell if the corpses were anyone I knew with so many other living beings in the way.

The fight was gradually expanding, pushing out farther into the plains between Lourak and Soarlack as some of the Cursed horde pulled back to charge for the Slated Mountains. Another portion of the Solian army was waiting to greet them in the west, and as the Curse's forces spread out, so did ours. More openings appeared across the battlefield and then, before I knew it, both sides were spread thin across the snow. The little place we had been fighting in, a corner created by the body of the dead sea wraith and the make-shift "campsite" of the Solian army, was running dry of enemies, although a few still lingered, watching us with what remained of their hungry eyes.

"You stay here and help everyone clear them out," I ordered Gian. I had spotted Chap, Molly, and Wendy fighting one of the Cursed smiths, and it looked like they could use a hand. The smith was energetic, more so than most of its companions, and I could tell that Gian was nearly drained. I watched him closely, wondering if he could see through my words to my true intentions of leaving him out of larger harm's way, but he only nodded grimly and turned to face an oncoming Cursed timber wolf. I spun on my heel and sprinted through the snow to help the pirates.

Molly saw me approaching and made a gap in their defenses for me to slide in and join them. She was armed with a longsword, as was Chap, and Wendy wielded a vicious-looking messer. They were taking turns diverting the smith's attention; one of them would draw its focus, then the other two would attack, unless one of them had to turn away to defend against another approaching Cursed animal. When I joined the rotation, there were three of us on the offensive, giving us a much greater advantage. None of the three of them were injured, but they looked weary. The smith was still lively, bouncing around even though it only had three feet and half of its face appeared to have melted off.

No words were exchanged as we faced the beast. It lunged towards Molly, and she dodged out of the way while Chap stabbed with his sword. He only grazed it, and then we were back in a standoff. Next, it went for Wendy, and Molly and I both made clean cuts into its hide. It roared, whipping around to face us and dancing just out of reach of our weapons. It was a tiresome game that I had played several times throughout the night, and though I was growing irritated, I forced myself to stay calm and collected. One rash decision could lead to more deaths than just my own.

The smith feinted towards me this time, black slobber dripping from its mouth, then quickly swung its head to the side and snapped at Molly. She yelped from how close it came, but she had seen the attack coming and dipped out of the way just fast enough to avoid being bitten. Chap let out an angry roar and charged forward, ramming his sword nearly to the hilt in the smith's shoulder. It snarled, curling around itself to rip him away, but he released the weapon and stumbled backwards, rolling through the snow to avoid the beast's swiping claws. The sword jutted out of its flesh, blood sputtering from the wound. It swayed unsteadily on its feet but was no less invigorated as it leapt for Wendy. The navigator had been preoccupied fending off a horse that was mostly bones. Water had frozen on what remained of its pelt, sliding off in sheets as the animal moved around. Chap called out a warning at the last second, and without looking behind himself Wendy dropped to the ground, sliding along the snow to avoid the horse's stomping hooves. The smith's teeth closed around the horse's throat and, unaware that its attack was on its own Cursed brethren, the smith vehemently swung its head from side to side, separating bone and flesh and nerve and whatever else was there.

I grimaced as silvery blood splattered across the snow, staining it. There was a squelching sound, then a disgusted groan, and I looked down to see Wendy half-beneath the smith with his messer plunged deep into its chest. It growled furiously, dropping the horse, and raked its claws at the navigator. Before it made contact, its whole body stiffened. Clutched in Wendy's hand and spinning mesmerizingly was one of Peeler's hypnotic charms. Molly took the opportunity to step in and slide the monster's throat clean open. The smith's body sank slowly into the snow. The Curse probably wouldn't leave it for some time, but at that moment and for many moments afterward, it posed little to no threat to everyone else, so we allowed ourselves to relax.

It was a mistake.

I was no stranger to death, and I was no stranger to losing friends and loved ones, but each time I was faced with it, it was as if I was seeing it for the first time. Sometimes it seemed to happen in slow motion; other times it was as if it had happened in the blink of an eye. This time it was the former. We were all regaining our bearings, finding our footing in the snow, and then one of us was on the ground in a pool of glistening red. Molly was the first to scream, which only made sense since it was none other than her husband who had fallen.

"Chap—" Wendy choked out as both he and Molly collapsed onto the snow beside him. Retreating swiftly behind them, a Cursed bobcat hissed at me and scurried away, crimson blood staining its face. When I crouched beside the others, heart in my throat, I was shocked at how vicious the wound was. It had been a quick attack, and a silent one. The cat had gouged a hole in his side, digging its claws deep enough into the flesh that when it had pulled away it had taken most of Chap's midriff with it. I didn't dare look any closer for fear of what vile things I might see.

Molly was sobbing, her hands gripping his shoulders tightly. He was still conscious, but only just, his eyes unfocused and his head lolling to the side. I tried not to look at the growing puddle beneath him, tried not to let the fear prickling just beneath my skin show on my face. Unintelligible words were flowing from Molly's mouth, and Wendy looked so pale that it may as well have been his blood draining out into the snow.

"Don't leave," Molly was whimpering, over and over again. I hardly heard her over the din around us. I looked up, steadying my breaths and doing my best to ignore the sharp, tangy scent of blood that rose into my nostrils. Another Cursed animal was being drawn in by the scent, a doe with one leg dangling so loosely it couldn't have been working. I shakily rose to my feet, letting the roar of battle around me drown out Molly's cries and lifting my saber again as the deer came closer. Wendy and Molly paid me no attention as I dealt with the animal swiftly. When its body hit the ground and I looked back at them, Molly was bent over Chap's face, shaking silently, and Wendy was staring into the distance with an empty look in his eyes. Chap was no longer moving.

I swallowed the lump in my throat and forced myself to turn away. I hardly knew that man and his relatives, and yet, seeing his wife's sorrow pricked me in the chest. I made myself march away, back towards where I had left Gian, now concerned that something may have happened to *him*. The thought made me quicken my pace, and I jogged through the snow, stopping only once to swipe a Cursed vulture out of the air with my blade. I stumbled back to where I had left Gian before. He was nowhere to be found. My pulse began to race, hammering in my ears as I looked down to see—

By all the saints. I felt dizzy. There were bodies *everywhere*. Now that I knew one of us had died, it seemed hundreds of us had. Solians in bright silver and gold armor, now gashed and blood-stained, more of the pirates lying in broken heaps, all of them surrounded by the mutilated, twitching bodies of the Cursed. My gaze roved over each face, and I pushed down the twist in my gut as I met each lifeless stare until, at last, I spotted him. My heart dropped down into my stomach at the sight of his pale face half-concealed by his dark hair. He was lying on his back, his sword a few inches from his limp hand, blood trickling out from long claw marks that ran down his hip and thigh. My breath hitched at how still he was in the snow, how out of place he seemed with his pristine, glassy features. Someone so beautiful didn't deserve to be in a place so ugly.

I slowed down, walking at an agonizingly sluggish pace. I wanted to get closer, and I wanted to run away. I wanted to see his face, to see if his chest really was that still, to see what animal had done this to him. My heart felt like it was being squeezed from the inside out. He was *my* responsibility. I should have brought him with me to fight the smith. Maybe he would have seen the bobcat. Maybe he and Chap could both have survived.

I reached him. I knelt slowly into the snow, setting my saber down and reaching for him gingerly. My hands were shaking uncontrollably. Thoughts ran through my head faster than I had time to register them. Not another one. I can't lose another one. I *can't* lose him.

"Gian," I breathed softly, pushing his hair away from his face. His eyes were closed. My hand slid down, stopping on his chest. I waited, pushing my palm into him, my breath caught in my throat as the seconds ticked by. *Thump. Thump. Thump.* His heart was beating. He was alive. I didn't know whether to laugh or cry, so I did neither, instead slapping him hard in the face and shouting his name. He groaned, his body tensing, then his eyes opened slowly.

"Beth," he grunted. The word was heavily slurred. I glanced at his leg again. He had lost a lot of blood, and the wound was curling and black. I raked my hands through his hair again to get the last strands out of his face, and he curled his lip at me. "Don't . . . you'll mess it up . . ." he moaned. I glared at him, reaching for a nearby cloak—someone had cast it aside when they had gotten too hot fighting, I assumed—and tearing it into strips to tie around his leg.

"If you die on me, I'll be doing a lot worse to your hair than messing it up," I snapped, tying the first knot. He winced. I leaned closer to his face. "Like cut it all off." His eyes widened just a bit.

"S'pose that's a good reason to live, then," he whined, grunting again as I continued to bind his leg. When it was finished, I pulled off my other outer coat and tucked it around him. The bitter wind sliced into me, but it didn't matter.

"Stay here. I'll get a doctor." I rose to my feet.

"Not like I'm going anywhere," he spat back. At least he was awake enough to bicker with me.

"Smart-mouth," I grumbled. He grunted again and shut his eyes, so I added, "And don't die." Then I turned and sprinted as fast as I could for the nearest medical tent.

SAKURA

*K*sega and I crept through corridor after corridor, silently making our way towards the lower levels. I kept my eyes peeled for anything I remembered from my wandering through the palace before, and Ksega continuously scouted the path ahead with his bering, since I was, in his words, "too cumbersome to simply tag along right behind him." I had wanted to argue the fact, but it wasn't long after we had started moving that I realized my boots thumped on the stones and his did not, so I kept quiet.

We snuck around some guards and past some busy servants, hurrying down the stairs to the next floor. As soon as we were there, something felt off. I knew immediately that this was where we would find him. We walked slowly through the corridors, checking rooms and peeking around corners, but the entire place was empty. This whole level had been cordoned off for something. It wasn't long before we realized what that something was.

"I hear it. The Curse," Ksega said, frowning as he tried to focus on the sound. I waited patiently. He nodded to himself, then pointed down a hallway. "This way." He led me through a maze of turns, then stopped dead. I bumped into his back, then peered around his shoulder to see why he'd halted. A Cursed rabbit sat in the center of the hallway. It looked rather innocent, its fur still fluffy, although now black. A thin crack of green ran along its nose, and one of its eyes looked unusually swollen, but aside from that it could have been a normal black rabbit. Ksega unslung his bow and cautiously nocked an arrow. I had one hand hovering over the hilt of my flame-sword. The rabbit blinked at us slowly, making no move to attack us. Beyond it and around another bend, snuffling sounds echoed across the stone floors. I had an uneasy feeling riding up the back of my spine, and when I turned around, I found out why.

"Ksega, there's a problem behind us," I said as softly as I could. Sitting on the ground behind me was a dog, its head cocked to the side, ears pushed forward curiously at the sound of my voice. It had thick black fur that all seemed to be intact except on one leg, where a paw was missing, replaced with a stump of bone that oozed silvery blood. The empty eye sockets glowed green.

"And more in front," Ksega said, sounding much more relaxed than I was. I risked a brief glance away from the dog to see that some sort of black pig had rounded the corner in front of us, its nose twitching in our direction.

"Should we take them out? Do you think he'll notice?" I asked uncertainly, my gaze refocused on the dog. It may have been my imagination, but I thought it had moved closer.

"He's bound to notice us sooner or later." Ksega lifted his bow, and in reply, I pulled my flame-sword out of my belt. My eirioth had sensed my unease since we had entered the Salt Palace, and I had ignored how it pushed against the surface of my skin until now.

The second the fire hissed angrily out of my sword handle, the dog leapt at me. I reached up and yanked the cords of the charm around my neck, sending the swirled marble spinning rapidly. The dog stumbled, falling to the ground. I heard hooves on stone and a squealing sound but didn't look to see where it came from, swiping with my flame-sword at the dog. My eirioth hungrily encircled the animal's neck, tightening and twisting until I heard a *snap*. The magical flames snaked back into the blade of my sword, leaving the mangled dog on the ground. Looking behind me, I saw that Ksega had dealt with the pig and the rabbit.

It was always difficult to tell if you had actually *killed* an animal corrupted by the Curse, but most of the time a typically lethal injury would suffice, because it made the body lose all operation and, through that, made it useless to the Curse. From the way Alchemy had explained it, it seemed that because animals had such weak wills and feeble minds, the Curse worked through them quickly and rotted them to the point that they could no longer serve its purpose. Alchemy, on the other hand, was a Cursed human with a very strong will and a very strong mind, meaning that as long as he provided a consciousness for the Curse to feed on, the Curse would provide him with a functioning body; or at least, what remained of his body.

We now stood in a hallway with three dead Cursed animals, weapons drawn. We stood there for a long moment, listening and waiting. We hadn't made much noise, but it had sounded deafening in the moment. During the scuffle, we had managed to scoot down one of the corridors, and now I could just barely see the dark frame of a familiar door. I was just about to let myself breath again when a rhythmic clapping echoed through the hallway. Ksega and I both jumped, spinning around to look down one of the corridors. Traf was swaggering towards us, clad in his dreadfully shiny silver tailcoat, now with a sword gleaming at his hip. His vibrant eyes twinkled with something menacing as he strode closer, hands curving around the hilt of his weapon.

"Well, well, well, look what the tide brought in," he mused. Ksega tensed beside me and within the span of a few seconds he had a new arrow on his bow. Traf slowed to a stop, barely ten paces from us. A small smirk played at the corners of his lips. "You're unusually clever for young people, you know." He went on as if there wasn't an arrow now trained at his heart. I wondered if Ksega could bring himself to kill another human being.

"Maybe you're just uncommonly stupid for an old guy," Ksega spat back. I looked towards the frame of the door again. I was certain now that it led to the room with the murals, and I was certain that Matthias was inside. Traf noticed me looking and addressed me, ignoring Ksega's jibe.

"So you've figured it all out, have you? His Majesty's connection to the Curse? Is that why you're here?" he narrowed his eyes. "You never went to the mountains in the first place?"

"Oh, we went to the mountains," I told him, letting my flame-sword retreat into a curl of smoke for the time being. I was getting stronger with it, but as I grew so did my eirioth, and I was already beginning to sweat from the strain of keeping it alive.

"Did you?" Traf frowned, taking another step towards us. Ksega drew the arrow back farther in warning. The Coldmonian royal advisor held his hands up in a gesture of peace. "Easy there, boy, you don't know what you're threatening here." One of his hands settled on the hilt of his flashy sword once more. His gaze hardened as his smile reset into a thin line, ill-concealing his apprehension. "You don't understand what you're meddling with."

"We know *exactly* what we're meddling with, especially after our visit to the Slated Mountains," I snapped. Traf raised a bushy eyebrow. "Matthias is the one who didn't know what he was getting into when he unleashed the Curse. He's let this go on for far too long, and now it has to come to an end."

"No, you've got it all wrong." Traf's tone adopted a condescending air, as if he were scolding a couple of children. "He didn't know what he was getting into, but now that he has the power he does, think of what he can do for our kingdom! He has a weapon at his disposal that no other kingdom will ever have. He can take whatever he wants!" he took another step toward us. A muscle twitched in Ksega's jaw, but aside from that he didn't move.

"It isn't a *weapon*, it's literally a Curse! It's forbidden magic, and it's done more harm than good to *everyone* including his own people." I tightened the grip on my flame-sword. "There are people fighting and dying in Wisesol right now because of the selfish acts of your king."

At that, Traf *tsk*ed. "He wouldn't have launched that attack if he hadn't thought you posed a threat to the Curse's source," he said.

I pressed my lips into a thin line, knowing he was only trying to flip the table on us. Not only that, he was wasting our time. The door was down the corridor behind him, in sight yet out of reach. Ksega had seen it too, and he gave me an imperceptible nod. My stomach felt like it was tying itself into knots, but I kept my voice as even as possible when I spoke.

"He knows by now that we completely destroyed the source. The only thing left to do to remove the Curse from Horcath entirely is kill the Ice King." Traf made an unimpressed squeaking sound.

"I'm afraid I can't let you do that," he said, drawing his sword.

"I'm afraid you're going to have to," I said, and Ksega let his arrow fly. The aim had been adjusted at the last second, so the arrow only grazed his shoulder as it went past, whirring through the corridor until it sparked on the stone wall and fell to the ground. Traf yelped and jumped to the side, momentarily dropping his sword to grab the portion of his sleeve that was now marked with a growing spot of red. I took the opportunity to sprint down the corridor. He grabbed for his sword, but another arrow sparked across the ground in front of his hand, making him hastily draw back. Ksega lunged forward as well, his small hunting knife in hand. I sped past Traf and slipped around the corner, doing my best to ignore the sounds of metal clashing behind me and forced the heavy doors open. I slammed them shut behind me, slid the bolt into place, and held my breath.

At first glance, the room appeared to be empty. It was still dark out, and only one torch was lit in the corner of the room, its soft orange glow illuminating pitifully little. I waited a long moment, too afraid to release my breath. It took a second to see the other person in the room, huddling in the corner directly across from me, still in the shadows. He was hunched over, curled into a ball and breathing heavily. I scanned the rest of the room, but there was nothing else in sight aside from a longsword propped against one wall.

"Matthias?" I asked uncertainly. My voice echoed oddly off the walls, bouncing back into my ears louder than I had spoken.

The person lifted his head at the sound of my voice. He was mostly concealed by darkness, but it was undeniably the king of Coldmon. I shivered as his head tilted to the side. He pushed himself awkwardly along the floor, half-dragging himself closer to me. I moved towards the light, trying to put as much space between us as possible. He crawled after me.

"You . . . you're supposed to be dead." He chuckled, inching closer. I held my flame-sword up, although there was no elemental blade yet.

"Don't come any closer," I ordered, my voice hitching with horror as he came into the edge of the ring of light. I wanted to look away, but I couldn't. He was still big-shouldered and narrow-waisted, and his bright blue eyes were easily recognizable, but his skin was changing. Half of his face was jarringly black, laced with delicate cracks of shining green. Strands of his hair looked like ashy wisps of smoke, and one of his hands appeared to be crumbling like old stone. The strange band I had mistaken for a tattoo encircling his neck was pulsing a sickly green.

"Why? Do I scare you?" his lips split in a wide grin. The side of his face that wasn't marred by the Curse was glimmering with sweat, and his breaths were ragged. His non-Cursed hand was trembling against the floor. The Ice King was very, very sick.

"I think a lot of people are scared of you. I think you've even become a little scared of yourself," I said warily, wishing my voice didn't quiver the way it did. Matthias snorted, shakily pushing himself onto his feet. He groaned, swaying back and forth, and stumbled over towards the wall. My heart hammered in my chest as he picked up the longsword. He lifted it to point at me, then doubled over in a fit of coughing. He fell back against the wall until the bout was over, then pushed the sword into the floor and used it as a cane to walk back towards me. I began to circle the room, keeping distance between us.

"I have never been scared of *anything*, little girl. I am a *king*. I am the *greatest king*!" he shouted, his voice hoarse.

I curled my lip at him in disgust. "You have none of the qualities of a great king, much less the great*est*. Look at you. Look what you've become. Your body is giving in to the corruption of the powerful magic you made the mistake of messing with." I let my flame-sword surge back to life, and finally the room was lit up sufficiently. Matthias squinted, as if it was too bright for his eyes.

"I *own* this magic," he snarled. "It is at *my* command. It will not kill me."

"It's been slowly killing you for a hundred years, and you know it. It's eaten you from the inside until you're just a hollow shell of who you once were." I glanced at the doors. How was Ksega faring? Was Matthias bringing more Cursed animals to his aid? I had to make my move against him quickly.

"I am no shell," Matthias spat, pulling himself upright, although he still leaned against the sword for support.

"You *are*. You're a cup, a vessel for the Curse to fill with itself, and once it's full, it will take you over completely. It does not serve you. It's simply been biding its time, waiting for the moment when it can strike and seize power." I looked into his eyes, both of them still clear and blue, even the one that was surrounded by darkness. I felt a tiny pinch of sadness as I realized there was no point in talking to him. Even if I could convince him of the truth, what good would it do? The Curse already had him in its power, and I doubted any recle-mage would be able to extract it. The only option was to kill him, but did I have the strength to do that?

"It will not strike me down," Matthias snarled, his lips curling into a crooked smile. "In fact, it *saved* me." He tilted his head to the side, ominous shadows falling over his face. I watched him uncertainly, a worm of doubt wriggling into my stomach. I had felt the pull of the Curse when we had found its source, but surely Matthias didn't actually believe that it was something good, something healing.

"You're delusional," I said, continuing to circle the room and keep my distance.

He cackled maniacally. "You don't understand." He grinned, half his teeth flashing white, the others cracked and gray. "I'm not who you think I am." He tilted his head up, extending his neck so the glowing green band was fully visible. "You see this scar? It is a mark of my first and only defeat." He looked over at one of the muraled walls, lifting his sword to point at it. Without following his gaze, I knew which one he was looking at. A nauseous feeling began to swim around in my head.

"You're saying . . ." I glanced quickly at the wall, at the painting of the blue beheaded man.

"Yes . . . Matthias Dorsey never existed." The Ice King coughed, digging his sword tip back into the floor to support himself. "His supposed 'parents' didn't, either. It was all part of a bigger plan, you see, for me to finally fulfill my goal." He stepped closer to me. I stepped back.

"*You're* Calysto?" I guessed, my heart pumping rapidly in my ribcage. His grin sharpened wickedly.

"Yes, now you're catching on."

"That's impossible," I stammered, tightening my hold on my weapon. "The timelines don't line up, and the Curse couldn't have saved you. Calysto died two hundred years ago. The Curse was released well after that time." I kept circling the room, but his stilted course made me inch closer to the walls. Eventually, if I wasn't careful, I would end up cornered. Luckily, the Ice King—I didn't even know what to call him in my own head now—seemed more interested in making sure I had my facts right before he worried about killing me.

"It only looks that way to you because the Curse was dormant for a hundred years. It *needs* me, you see. It managed to break free of whatever prison it had been shut away in, and it searched for a body with a will strong enough to suit its needs." He winced as he spoke, his hand and face splitting with new glowing cracks. "It was drawn to the war, and even more specifically to me. It understood my drive, my understanding of true power, my vision for the future of Coldmon. It saved me, if only just, and as time passed and I regained my life and strength, my intricate lie began."

"You staged the disappearance of your own body?" I tried not to retch as my stomach turned. "You faked the lives of other members of the Coldmonian royal family?" across from me, he shrugged, as if it was a small matter.

"My son wasn't strong enough to be a proper ruler, but he was useful in his own way. He understood the sacrifices necessary for success, and he was willing to help me accomplish my dreams." He lifted the sword and flipped it in his hand, looking once again at the murals that followed the one depicting a decapitation. "All the 'rulers' after me were fake descendants of my line. It's a shame that the true Dorsey bloodline will not continue, but that is what is required in order for the kingdom to remain strong." He waved his sword at the murals. "I couldn't do it all on my own, of course. My son and a select few members of my court, like Traf and his father, were instrumental in setting it all up."

He was circling closer to me now, and I kept inching farther away. My head was reeling from all this new information. How had no one been able to identify the lie? How had Calysto managed to orchestrate it all?

"Now you see why the Curse chose me," he said through another cough. "Now you see why it won't take me. It can't survive without me, I can't survive without it. We serve each other as we need."

"It's *killing you*," I urged, but he roared and swung his sword, its tip scraping against the muraled wall. It left a white line through almost three entire paintings, ones that came before the faked ones. My chest tightened. He was beyond sense now. He believed in his head that he was serving his people, and yet here he was tarnishing their history in his blind rage. Here he was preaching a truth that had never existed anywhere but in his own mind.

"*Enough*!" Calysto screamed, grunting as he lifted his breaking hand to his temple. He shut his eyes tightly, as if he had a terrible headache. "Enough talking," he gasped, prying his eyes open again. "Now, we fight." He lifted the sword at me again. I clenched my jaw, but only lifted my own weapon in response. My gaze flicked briefly to the murals on the wall, many of which I now knew were nothing but a part of Calysto's elaborate lie. Would I be painted on this wall, marked forever as the murderer of an Ice King? Perhaps I would not succeed at all. Perhaps I would die today, and unless Ksega was able to complete the task, Calysto and the Curse would see their plan through to the end.

The king roared as he dove at me, sword swinging in a flashing arc over his head. I lifted my flame-sword to parry it.

Calysto was greatly weakened by the Curse, and yet he was incredibly strong. We danced around the room for several minutes, blocking and parrying and lunging. He was shaking and pouring sweat, his breaths little more than raspy gasps now. It was pitiful, and I was sure I could have ended the fight earlier if I hadn't been so hesitant to kill a man.

"If the Curse cares so much about you, why have no beasts come to your aid?" I gasped, hoping I could at least figure out if he was trying to bring more to attack us.

"*I* don't need any help to beat you." He sneered. "Traf, on the other hand, can't do much on his own, and I take it that since you raced in here the way you did, he's out there with one of your friends, isn't he? I'm sure he could use the help." His last words faded into a war cry as he lunged at me again, hacking the sword wildly about. I blocked one blow, deflected another and skipped backwards out of reach of a third. My heart was leaping in my chest now, beating so hard and fast I was sure it was trying to break free of its cage. Was Ksega fighting off more Cursed animals? There couldn't have been that many patrolling this floor of the palace, surely, and Calysto wouldn't have been able to bring any more in from outside the walls. I just had to hope Ksega could handle it on his own.

"Give up now," I said, trying to keep my voice as reasonable and calm as I could. "It will do so much good if you let this go. You want to help your people find happiness, but the truth is that they already have it! They are content with what they have and where they are. They don't need anything more from you." I cried out as he swung the sword again. His blade met mine, and the flames warped around the steel, holding it inches from my face. I slid to the side and disentangled the blades. Calysto staggered forward, falling onto his knees on the marble floors. There, he violently retched, and I tried not to gag.

"You're wrong!" he yelled, as if the louder his voice was, the truer his words became. "They always need more! Humans are greedy, girl, and they always, always, *always* want more." He dragged himself onto his feet again, small blackened bits of rubble falling from his breaking hand. He glared at me. "With the Curse at my side, I will give them everything they desire. They will want for nothing. I will be the most renowned person in all the lands."

"You'll be renowned," I said, grimacing as I ducked below another swipe of his sword. "But not for your valiant, kingly actions. No, you'll be the famous Cursed King. People will speak for generations about how you threw your life away trying to turn forbidden magic into a weapon." I twirled my flame-sword in my hand, knowing that my eirioth was draining my strength quickly. I looked at him pleadingly, hoping that somewhere in that corrupted mind of his he could see sense. "It doesn't have to be that way, you know," I continued. "If you give up now and willingly sacrifice yourself, this can all end. I swear to you that you will not be remembered as the king who wrought destruction on Wisesol. The people who know what you've done will promise by oath to never utter the truth. We can make it look like you're the hero of it all. You can have the legacy you so desperately want as a great and honest king. At least let your court have that, instead of all the shame that will come from your stubborn foolishness." I waited nervously as he swayed towards me, stopping when we were each just outside of reach from one another's weapon. His eyes were wide and contemplative. I thought I may have gotten through to him, but then his face twisted in fury.

"*No!*" he roared, stepping forward. I lifted my sword to block his, but he angled it down at the last second. I yelped in surprise, then again in pain. I had been a moment too slow, and his blade had caught me in the calf. My leg seized and I fell onto the ground, catching myself on my elbows. Pain exploded through my arms and, with my focus broken, my flame-sword extinguished, and we were plunged back into darkness. Calysto held his sword up, still yelling as he swung it down at me. I pushed myself across the marble floors, but there wasn't far to go. My head hit the glass-paned doors to the balcony. Would anyone be paying attention? Would anyone from the outside see their king murder me?

"Wait, don't—" I said, scrambling up into a sitting position as Calysto drew his sword back, preparing to run it through me. My pulse skipped, my vision swam. I was going to be killed. I waited for the pain, something far worse than the new throbbing in my leg or the tingling in my arms. I shut my eyes, bracing myself.

The next few moments passed startlingly fast. The door to the room banged open, slamming loudly against the wall. My eyes sprang open, but they weren't yet adjusted to the new dimness of the room, so I couldn't see who had entered. Calysto had paused to look up, but he hadn't even managed to turn his head to face the doorway. Sometime within those few seconds, an arrow tip had appeared in his chest, jutting out of him and dripping blood that ran silver and red. Droplets splattered onto my boots. He gawked at me for a moment, then began to fall, sword still poised over me. I screamed and rolled out of the way, sending new pain rushing up my leg. I jumped to my feet, ignoring the sting and stumbling back away from the body of the Ice King. The fletching of an arrow was visible poking out of his back. A cool rush of air swirled around him, then bloomed out in a flower of frost on the marble around his body. His skin became brittle and black all over, and the green cracks faded into blackness. Bit by bit, his already-crumbling hand began to disintegrate into dust.

"Sakura—" the voice came from near the doorway, and my head snapped around to see Ksega leaning against the frame, bow in hand. His eyes were wide. "Are you okay?" he gasped, wincing as his bow fell out of his hand.

"I'm fine. Are you—oh, by all the stars, Ksega, you *shot* him! You actually killed him, you—" I limped towards him, then inhaled sharply, taking in the dark stain on his shirt. "You're bleeding. Ksega, you're—"

"I know, I know," he groaned, sinking slowly onto the floor. I rushed over to him. My leg gave out when I was nearly to the doorway, and I grunted as I fell onto my knees, sliding across the marble to reach him. One of his hands was tucked against his side, thin streams of red slipping between his fingers.

"You'd better not die," I said, looking out the doorway. I couldn't see much, but I saw enough: black limbs, silver-green ooze, a mess of broken arrow shafts and one arm lying on the ground just around the bend, its silver tailcoat sleeve soaking up crimson blood.

"Jess . . . find her. Quick." He bit his cheek, his arm tightening around himself. "She's on this level."

"I'm not leaving you—" I began, but he cut me off.

"You have to, or I don't think I'm going to make it. *Find her.*" He took his free hand and gripped my arm, trying to pull me towards the doorway. I winced as pain spurred down my leg, but it was only a small cut, and I could push through it. I rose to my feet and ran out into the hallway, turning away from the tangy-smelling hallway and taking another corridor. I screamed Jessie's name as I ran, not caring if the other palace staff heard me or not.

"Sakura?" the reply finally came, and I hurried towards the voice. I staggered to a halt when one of the hallways was blocked. I swore under my breath as the Cursed fox turned around, ears alert as it faced me. I didn't have time to be bothered with a fight, but just as I was turning to take another route, the fox let out an unearthly screech. It wriggled and stumbled and hit its head against the wall. Its whole body shook violently and little flakes of black drifted into the air around it. It let out one more pitiful mewl and then flopped over, the green, pulsing light within it vanishing. It went still.

"Sakura!" Jessie's voice came again, this time much closer, and then she was there, rounding the bend beyond the dead fox. She stared at it, bewildered, then up at me with a question in her eyes. I shook my head.

"No time. Ksega, he's hurt—" I began to explain, then shook my head. "Follow me." I turned around and didn't even wait to see if she was on my tail, running as fast as my leg would let me back to the room with the murals.

42
SAKURA

*I*t took Jessie exactly twenty minutes to get Ksega doctored up enough to move, and then we were on the move. Jessie had taken a moment after she had finished with Ksega to tend to my leg, so my limp was lessened and Jessie and I were each able to help Ksega back up the stairs. I didn't remember the way back to the room we had started in, and Ksega was too delirious to be much help, but thankfully Jessie had been sensible enough to pay attention to where she'd gone. We made no attempts at stealth as we rushed back through the palace, eager to get out as quickly as possible, and fortunately for us nobody was paying us any attention at all.

Whatever had happened to that little fox was now happening all over the palace. Without Calysto's constant command reigning over them, the Cursed animals that hadn't been killed on that one floor of the palace had wandered off on their own. We ran into another two pigs, one of which had already fallen over and was ashen and black. The other was squealing in dismay as the green cracks along its body slowly faded into blackness. All throughout the hallways, similar animalistic screams of pain and panic cracked through the air, and Coldmonian soldiers and servants darted every which way. Nobody spared us a second glance, if they had even given us a first one at all.

My chest was tight with anxiety as we traveled. I didn't know what I'd been expecting when we finally destroyed the Curse, but it hadn't been this. I had been under the impression that it would just stop existing, and everything would go back to normal. I hadn't even thought of the possibility of it destroying anything already corrupted. Worst of all, I hadn't thought of what that would mean for Alchemy.

When we clumsily reentered the room we had snuck in through, Derek was pacing back and forth in the darkness. A single candle had been lit and set on the table, nearly completely melted by now. Sycamore and Bear were both lying down on the floor, claws folded neatly over each other and heads attentively turned towards the doorway, beyond which more chaos could be heard.

"Where have you been?! What's going on out there?" Derek demanded, rushing to help relieve us of Ksega's weight. He groaned as we helped him flop into one of the chairs. He had been whining more about the fact that we had left his longbow behind than the pain, so I hoped he wasn't suffering too much. Jessie had done rushed work, but she had stopped any internal bleeding and almost all of the external. As long as he didn't rip it open again, he would recover just fine, especially with the assistance of a talented recle-mage.

"The Ice King is gone, and the Curse is going, but it's under no one's control now. We have to get back to Wisesol," I said, hoping my tone conveyed how urgent this was. I was exhausted, my whole body aching and trembling with the strain of staying upright, but I needed to return to Lourak. It was true that the Curse had nobody guiding it now, and its actions would become even more scattered and unpredictable until the Curse faded out of all the animals. From the pattern I had picked up, it seemed to be rolling out in a slow wave from the place Calysto had died, which meant I would have to race it back to Wisesol, because while I had no intentions of coming face-to-face with any more Cursed animals, there was one particular Cursed human I had to get to before that wave did.

"You and Ksega aren't going anywhere," Jessie ordered. "He can't stand alone on his own two feet, and you barely can, so I don't want to hear it. They have the situation under control there, I'm sure." She put her bloodied hands on her hips and glared at the two of us. Her long red braids had become frazzled and partially undone in all the excitement, and the loose strands waved around in the light wind coming in from the still-cracked balcony door.

"But we have friends there we need to check on, and—" I began to argue, but Derek cut me off, crossing his arms over his chest.

"They'll be there tomorrow evening. For now, both of you need to rest and get more medical attention," he said firmly. Jessie nodded in agreement. I scowled at them both, about to keep arguing when Ksega picked up my point for me.

"We have to go . . . Chem. The Curse. He won't be around much longer." His eyes were open, but slightly unfocused. My heart beat a little faster at his statement, foolish hopes blooming in my chest that maybe, just *maybe* since he was the creator of the Curse, Alchemy would survive it. Maybe he would go back to his former self. Maybe he would stay a living skeleton forever. But maybe this really was the end for him, and if it was, I couldn't risk not having the chance to say goodbye.

"Trouble . . . you absolutely *cannot* fly. If that wound reopens, no one is going to be able to save you." Jessie set her jaw. I looked down at Ksega, contemplating joining Jessie's side and arguing that he should stay put. Sycamore could fly faster with just me, anyway, but that wasn't fair to him. He was Alchemy's friend too, and I knew he wanted to see him just as much as I did.

"We have to make a decision. We're running out of time. If I give Sycamore the rest of that energy potion, how will it affect her?" I asked Jessie. Her eyes widened, and I couldn't tell if she was more outraged at the thought of me giving my dragon a ridiculous dose of magic or that I wasn't arguing her side.

"She'll be extremely hyper and energetic for several hours," Jessie began to say slowly, then, realizing this was a time sensitive matter and that I wasn't going to take no for an answer, she sped up. "She'll be able to fly you faster than she ever has all the way to Wisesol, but it will take a lot of energy and focus from you as well." Her expression turned stern, but she went on grudgingly, "I highly advise against it, but if you do take Ksega with you, he has to ride in front of you and you have to drive."

"That's going to be problematic considering he's taller than me," I said, trying to make my voice light and joking, although I couldn't achieve it with the worry that was turning in my gut.

"Have him lay down on her neck, and *do not let him fall off.* If he dies on your flight back, you as good as killed him, got it?" she snapped. I nodded, then held a hand out to Ksega. He took it and I helped him to his feet, then we both limped over to Sycamore. She rose to her feet, cooing curiously at us.

"Go ahead and help him climb on," I instructed Derek as I retrieved my little vial of Jessie's potion. While the boys did that, I uncorked the vial and held it up to the dragon. "Sorry if this tastes bad, but it's going to help us. Just one more time." I carefully fed her the remaining contents of the vial. She stamped her feet anxiously, tossing her head back and forth for a moment. Her pupils grew larger than I'd ever seen them, and I gave Jessie a worried look. She waved it aside, her attention fixated on Ksega, who was swaying in the saddle.

"She's fine. Get going, quick. She'll be bone-tired when it wears off and won't fly for a few days, so get moving." She waved at us with her hands, and I climbed into the saddle behind Ksega. Holding the reins in such a way was very awkward, but with Ksega leaning over onto Sycamore's neck I could at least control the dragon properly.

"We'll follow when we can. Bear is still tired. We'll be able to keep ourselves hidden long enough to let him rest," Derek said, sounding none too pleased about the situation but not about to argue. His voice softened when he added, "I'm sorry that the skeleton isn't going to make it. I was starting to warm up to him."

A lump formed in my throat at his words, and I could only manage a nod of farewell to them as I tapped Sycamore in the ribs, causing her to leap forward onto the balcony and up into the air.

The flight was much faster than any flight I had flown before. Sycamore's wings moved at an almost impossible speed, her breaths quick and sharp, her movements calculated despite her chaotic speed. It went so fast I almost didn't have time to worry about Ksega falling or me losing focus on flying. It made me wonder why recle wasn't used more often in the world of war before I remembered that recle-mages didn't often enter that world. When they did, they were always soldiers of great importance to any army thanks to the benefits they brought.

We reached Wisesol by the time the sun reached the midpoint of the sky. Everything was a disaster; bodies of all kinds littered the ground, blood soaked into the earth, much of the snow had melted or been stomped away, and what remained was in muddy chunks of ice. The Solian army was still mostly intact, attempting to herd the scattering Cursed animals into one central area. Carlorians rode their dragons around, using them to help the effort. All of the beasts were still corrupted, which was a strange relief to me. My gaze devoured every inch of the plains, searching for someone I recognized. I could hear the Cursed beasts beginning to cry out in pain and surprise, meaning we hadn't been fast enough to beat the fading by very much.

We landed roughly in the camp the Solian army had set up, and we both practically fell from the saddle. A familiar voice came from behind us, followed by the sound of human footsteps and heavy dragon footsteps.

"'Rura, you're back!" someone crushed me in a hug from behind, but I wriggled free and turned to face Finnian. Asuka stood behind him, head cocked to the side as he watched Sycamore. She was fluffing her wings and swishing her tail and clawing at the ground with her talons, the potion still coursing through her body.

"Finn, hi. Are you okay?" I asked the question only because I wasn't sure what else to do. I hadn't seen Alchemy or Beth or Gian—where were they?

"I'm fine. Are you?" my brother's voice took on an edge of concern as he looked me up and down, taking in my bloodied pant leg, then the big stain on Ksega's shirtfront.

"We're fine. Or, we will be, once we get some rest, but first I need to see Chem. Do you know where he is?" I asked. Confusion flickered across his face, and I groaned, remembering that Finnian had never met Alchemy before. "The big skeleton? Surely you saw him out there fighting, right?" I prompted. Recognition registered on his face.

"Oh, *him*. Yeah, he's out there somewhere. I think he was near the edge of Lourak when I spotted him, over that way." He pointed. "But listen, 'Rura, you're both hurt. Wait a second and—"

"We can't wait a second. Ksega, can you walk that far?" I looked over at him. He gave me an unconvincing thumbs-up. I would argue for him to stay here, but I knew he would never listen, and we were running short on time.

"Rura, please—" Finnian tried again, but I stopped him by holding up a hand.

"Finn, I swear that I'll rest for an entire week after this, but I *have* to go see him. Come on." I grabbed Ksega's hand and tugged him after me, half-jogging through the snow in the direction my brother had pointed. Ksega's long legs matched my stride easily, although walking pained both of us.

We passed dead bodies of every kind. I searched for familiar faces and was shocked to find some. They were pirates whose names I couldn't remember, but the fact that they were there and dead was jarring all the same. Ksega clearly recognized them, but he kept his mouth firmly shut as we marched on.

"There he is," Ksega grunted. I snapped out of my thoughts, looking up at the little slope we were climbing. Alchemy was at the top, although it was hard to identify him at first. He was on his knees in the snow, skull bent and as unnaturally still as ever. In the background, Cursed animals shrieked and wailed in pain. I glanced towards where they were being herded, my heart skipping a beat as I saw that many of them had already fallen into black heaps on the ground.

"Chem," I called as we came closer. His head lifted slowly. The cracks across his skull seemed dimmer than usual. We slumped to the ground beside him, both of us grunting in pain.

"Ironling. Ksega." Alchemy's voice was even more hoarse than usual, grating in my ears. "You made it back . . . mostly in one piece, it seems." He laughed, although it was humorless.

"Chem . . . I didn't even think about you, about . . ." I scooted through the snow closer to him, ignoring the cold seeping through my clothes.

"It's okay. It's time." A rattly, wind-like noise sounded, and I realized that was his equivalent of a sigh. "I've been this way long enough. At least I get to go knowing you two saved Horcath." He leaned back and lifted his arms, gripping each of us on the shoulder. "I'm very proud of you two." His voice wavered, as if he was in pain. The green in the jagged cracks of his skull flared and then died down until they were so dim I almost couldn't see them.

"Chem—" Ksega's own voice was thick with emotion. My chest felt like it was being burned, like someone had covered my heart in tar and set it aflame.

"Is it awful of me to want you to stay?" I sobbed. After all these years, living with all his guilt and struggles, he must have been ready to let go, but I wasn't ready for him to go yet. I had only just forgiven him. He had been watching my back from day one of this quest, and now we were here, and it was *over*. He couldn't leave now, not when this was supposed to be such a happy moment.

"No," he said softly. He made a low, scratchy sound, almost like an animal's growl. "I think I need to lie down." We helped him lean onto his back in the snow, hood beneath his skull. He folded his gloved hands over his empty ribcage. "This is better." His voice was growing weaker. I bit my lip to keep from crying too loudly. I could hardly see him clearly through my tears now.

"Chem . . . I'm sorry," I said, trembling. He began to shake his head, but I pushed on. "I said so many things that were out of line and I want you to know that I wholly forgive you, okay?" I sniffed, wiping my face with my sleeve. "And thank you," I added. "For everything. You're one of the greatest friends I've ever had."

"We never could have done it without you," Ksega pitched in, his own voice quivering. He shook his head, sending loose flakes of snow drifting out of his fluffy hair. "This feels so wrong . . . I hate goodbyes."

"It's only a goodbye if I'm completely gone, and you know I never will be." Alchemy lifted one hand and poked Ksega in the chest. "As long as you remember me—and after all we've been through, by all the stars and clouds you had *better* remember me—I'll never truly be gone." He let his hand flop back over the other. He released another sigh, the lights in his skull growing fainter and fainter. "This is good," he said weakly. "A much better place to die than my first time." He huffed a small laugh. Neither Ksega nor I joined him. "Thank you both for being my friend." His voice was nearly inaudible now. We both leaned closer to hear him. "You let me redeem myself. I will forever be grateful. And promise me . . ." His words were stilted and slow, like he was struggling to force them out.

"Anything, Chem. What is it?" Ksega breathed.

"Promise me . . . you will take care . . . of Hook." The skeleton's words were little more than a rattling whisper.

"We promise," I said, and Ksega was nodding beside me. Alchemy seemed satisfied with that, because his skull gave the smallest of nods, and then he went eternally, peacefully still.

A week passed. I told no one of the truth behind the Curse, the elaborate schemes Calysto had woven with the traitorous people of his court and the evil magic that kept him alive. It was simpler to let everyone believe Matthias was the one responsible. The Curse was gone, the mess of the battle was cleaned up, and most of the dead had been properly buried. The Carlorians that had died were to be sailed back with a trustworthy Solian escort to Carlore, where their funerals and burials would be conducted traditionally by their families. The Solian king paid a visit to the army camp after the event was over to speak with the general, but promptly left when he found it to be uninteresting. As for me and my friends, we spent the entire week resting and mourning.

Derek stayed relatively busy with Finnian and the handful of other Carlorians who had decided to stay to help clear up the damages done by the Curse and to help rebuild anything that had been destroyed. Jessie kept up her work with other recle-mages, hosting multiple healing sessions every couple of hours for anyone who was still recovering. Gian was one of the more critically injured people that she tended to. He had suffered from a brutal smith attack and was being transported around on a chair with wheels until both his legs were healed enough to walk on; the contraption had been created by Peeler specially for the Nightfaller. Erabeth had hardly left Gian's side. Both Light Ray and Taro had claimed a shoulder, and all three of them could often be found lurking near the healer's tent or trailing after Gian as he pushed the wheels of his chair, refusing to accept that it would be simpler if he let someone push him around.

As for Ksega and I, we spent most of the time resting. Whenever we crossed paths, one of us was on the brink of sleep or idly nibbling on food. We exchanged a few words and some soft smiles, but neither of us had the heart to carry out any real conversations. Asuka spent lots of time with Ksega, tucking his head beneath the Solian's arm and pushing his head into his chest while Ksega scratched his scalp lovingly. The mood felt heavy and damp whenever I looked around and saw everyone but Alchemy enjoying themselves. There was a large piece of dark cloth folded in the corner of my tent, and inside that cloth were the neatly sorted black bones of a skeleton. I wasn't sure what Alchemy would have wanted me to do with his bones, but Ksega told me that Alchemy would have trusted me to pick a suitable place to bury them. I tried not to think about the weight of that responsibility, focusing instead on letting myself rest and thinking about what the future would hold for all of us now.

KSEGA

*T*he day we were set to leave Wisesol and sail to Carlore on a ship called *Sands of the Sun*, I woke up early and walked through the chilly winter mist to the big, now-full graveyard. It was between Rulak and Doluk, and there were over one hundred plots that had been given to the dead. They had been visited daily over the week, but only two people came at such a ludicrous hour of the morning to sit by one of the freshly dug graves.

I knew they knew I was coming, because I made no effort to conceal the crunching of my boots through the snow, but neither of them looked up at me as I approached. Molly, bundled up in a heavy woolen coat, sat with her knees tucked beneath her and her hands folded together, and Thomas, in his long, thick jacket and broad-brimmed hat, stood with his arms crossed. They were both staring at the gravestone Wendy and Peeler had carefully constructed. It was the rough shape of *The Coventry*, and on it was engraved:

Chap Blackwood
Brother
Husband
Forever a Pirate of The Coventry

"I'm sorry you lost him," I said as I came to stand beside them. I had seen them out here each morning and debated joining them, but it had always felt like I would be intruding. Now, we were preparing to leave, and I didn't know if or when I would get the chance to see either of them again.

No more words were spoken for several minutes. We stared solemnly at the gravestone. I hadn't realized until now that I had never been told their family's last name. I didn't know any of the pirates on a personal level, but out of them I had always considered Chap to be one of the ones I was closer with. Now that he was gone, I wasn't sure how to feel. What would the rest of the crew do without him? What would they do without Howie and all the others they had lost? I looked sidelong at Thomas. His eyes were red-rimmed and puffy. Below us, Molly was sniffling.

I took a slow inhale and asked, "What will all of you do now?"

"There aren't many of us left." Thomas shrugged. "We may all go our separate ways now." He looked over at me, his eyes dim. "I hope we meet again, though. You're a good man, Ksega, and I enjoyed getting into trouble with you." He smirked, although it lacked mirth.

"Likewise." I nodded and did my best to return the smile. Molly looked up from where she sat. Her face also bore signs of continued crying.

"Goodbye for now, Ksega," she said, still sniffling. I bowed my head at her.

"Goodbye for now, Molly, Thomas." I politely let them be, my farewells complete for the time being.

I met up with the others at the Port, one hand holding my pack and one wrapped around my midriff, applying pressure to the bandages there in an attempt to lessen the aching pain beneath. We all boarded the ship and found places to wait until we set sail. I sat next to Sakura on a crate, leaning back against the wall of the cabin. She looked curiously at me.

"Did you say goodbye to Willa?" she asked.

"Sort of," I replied vaguely. She stared at me until I relented with a sigh. "I left her a note."

"You can't stay mad at her forever," she told me.

I nodded, dragging a hand over my face. "I know, and I won't, I swear, I just . . . I need some more time to process everything, and I can't be around her while I do that." I dropped my hand and gave her a quick look. "It's okay if I stay with you for a little while, right?" she blinked, surprised by the question, but nodded.

"Yes, of course. There are plenty of rooms at the inn, and I'm sure Gamma won't mind letting you have one as long as you promise to help with the chores." She cringed as she added, "I'm afraid you'll have to be okay with lots of taunting from my brother, though. About . . . us." She gestured awkwardly at the air between us. I raised my eyebrows.

"You . . . told him about that?" I squeaked.

"No, no, of course not. I haven't told anybody. But he likes to make assumptions. Besides, I've been told it's rather"—she paused, cleared her throat—"obvious."

"Ah." I felt my face turning bright red. "Yes. I've been told the same."

"Anyway . . . what are you going to do now? You can stay with us for as long as you want, but what about Willa? You know you're going to come back to her at some point." Sakura eagerly switched the topic, and I was glad to join her.

"I know I will, but I need to cool off first. Maybe I'll try to find out what really happened to my sister." I knew it was ambitious, but there was a burning curiosity inside me now that I knew she had existed and still might. Didn't I owe it to her as her older brother to do everything I could to find her?

"Well, whatever you decide to do, if it ever involves going on another adventure," Sakura said, fidgeting with her fingers, "you can count me in."

"And me." Gian rolled up in his wheeled chair, olive eyes sparkling mischievously. Beth stood behind him, and both the birds were perched on his chairback. "Once I can walk, that is." He lifted one hand to smooth down his hair, even though it was, as always, groomed to perfection. There was a rumor that had begun floating around about him surviving the smith attack purely because someone threatened to ruin his hair. Whether it was true or not, it was definitely realistic.

"Are you going to stay in Carlore with us?" I asked, looking between the two of them. Derek and Jessie had already decided that they would return to Carlore with us, but not permanently. They planned to "come back to Wisesol eventually," whatever that meant. As for Beth and Gian, their plans were unclear.

"Yes, why not?" Beth said, shrugging. "We've somehow managed to grow attached to you idiots." Her lip curved into a sad frown, a look that was unusual on her face. "It's a shame about Bones, though. He would be happy to see us all going home together."

We all muttered a quiet chorus of agreement, then fell silent as *Sands of the Sun* set off on the waves.

43
SAKURA

I stood before the oval door in Alchemy's cave for the third time, but this time was nothing like the others had been. This time, I would be greeted with warm lantern light; somehow, it felt colder than it had ever been before. Still, there was a small kitten, a young girl, and an eirioth dragon inside that couldn't be abandoned, so I opened the door and stepped into the little hallway.

Inside, the atmosphere was cozy and welcoming. It was a small room, decorated only with a wooden desk and some blankets and tattered pillows for the animals to sleep on, but it had been made quite homely by Violet. A pot of peace lilies was flowering on the desk, beside a stack of papers and something that shimmered in the lantern light. Violet's bedroll had been set up near the opposite wall, accompanied by some books and a half-knitted shawl. Violet herself was sitting on the dragon's bedding, leaning into Hobble's wing as she sketched something on a pad of paper. Patting her ankle repeatedly with his paw, Hook was laying upside down by her foot.

"Hello there," I said wearily as I came inside, smiling as Violet's head snapped up. Her face brightened when she saw me. Beside her, Hobble blinked curiously at me, and Hook rolled onto his front so he could unsteadily wobble his way towards me.

"You're back!" Violet cried, setting her sketchpad down and leaping to her feet. Hobble slowly rose as well, shaking dust from his crooked wings.

"I'm back," I confirmed, bending down as Hook teetered over to my side, bumping his head into my boot repeatedly and purring loudly all the while. I scooped him gingerly into my arms and held him against my chest, rubbing him between the ears lovingly. Had he formed an attachment to Alchemy? Would he be able to recognize that the skeleton was never coming back? For the sake of his barely-maintained consciousness, I hoped not.

"Is Derek here?" Violet asked eagerly, patting Hobble's shoulder as he stepped up to her side. I nodded.

"He is. We'll go to meet up with him now. We're actually—" my voice broke, and I paused to clear my throat. "We're going to a burial. He's helping with it." I looked around the little cave, then back at her. "You can pack your things now, and whatever the animals will need as well. They're coming with us." I didn't need to explain why. I could see in her eyes and the way she looked at the empty hallway behind me that she had guessed why Alchemy was missing.

Violet quickly packed her things together, as well as the dishes she used to feed the animals and was soon by my side with a lead tied loosely around Hobble's neck. I double-checked to make sure we had everything and that Hook was securely in my arms before leading us towards the door. We were just about to leave when the shining thing on the desk caught my eye. I hesitated, not wanting to pry, but also knowing that Alchemy was no longer here to tell me his secrets, so if I wanted to know them, I had to find them myself. I told Violet to wait a moment while I went back in. In the end, it wasn't another secret. It was my sword. I gasped when I saw it, nearly dropping Hook from surprise. I had told Alchemy to take the sword into the Evershifting Forest and get rid of it. It had been a reminder of home and extra physical and emotional weight I didn't want to carry with me, and he had brought it *here* to his home to keep safe. There were a number of folded papers on the desk beside the sword, and I set Hook down momentarily to flip one open. My eyes stung as I began to read.

Ironling,

I know you may find it difficult to forgive me for my wrongs, but I swear to you I never meant harm

The first letter stopped there. I opened the next.

Sakura,

I'm so, so very sorry for all the secrets I kept from you. It was wrong, and I should have come clean from the very start, but I was afraid. I desperately wanted a friend, and when you said you were setting out to destroy the Curse, I was sure I finally had a chance to make things right again, and no one would have to know the truth. How foolish I was to believe that. You've taught me that the truth is always more important, no matter how hurtful it may be. I never wanted to upset you or ~~Sega~~ Ksega, and I'm deeply regretful that I have. I wish I could

Again, the letter ended before it was finished. There were nearly a dozen of them, all expressing sorrow and regret for lying to me. There was even one addressing Ksega instead of me, where he wanted Ksega to plead for my forgiveness on his behalf. I had never realized

I meant so much to the skeleton, but I supposed when one went without friends for three hundred years, he would take what he could get.

I neatly folded the letters and set them on a stack on the corner of the desk. I looked down at my sword, then picked Hook up and left with Violet. I had already let go of the sword, and I didn't want to bring it back with me. Besides, I didn't have time to worry about getting the sword back to Hazelwood Inn and finding a place to put it, because we had a burial to attend.

*A*lchemy's skeleton was buried at the foot of the great pink eirioth tree where I loved to spend time alone with my thoughts. Ksega, Finnain, and Derek had already dug the pit by the time we got there, and Gamma, Walter, Violet, Jessie, and Beth had Alchemy's bones prepared to be laid inside. It was a small affair, and it was quick. The bones were buried, the earth packed tightly on top, and the gravestone set in place. It was unique, a tall rectangle with the inscription:

Alec Galloway
"Alchemy"
Visionary, Protector, Friend
The Skeleton with the Greatest Heart of them All

The rectangle had a squared hole beneath the engraving, in which sat a unique wrought iron stand. When the time came, I handed the squirming, purring Hook to Ksega and stepped forward, pulling two smith-tooth daggers out of my pocket. I placed them carefully but securely in the stand and stepped back, my vision blurred by tears once more. Ksega put an arm around me, and on my other side Finnian took my hand. Behind us, Asuka huffed at Sycamore, and both dragons stamped their feet. Beth and Gian stood—and sat—solemnly near the trunk of the tree, staring distantly at the grave. We all stayed there for a long time, but at last everyone began to break away and head back towards the inn.

Ksega and I stayed the longest. Somehow, the longer I stayed, the less sad I felt. Life was going to be drastically different now for all of us, and yet, it seemed promising. Individually, we all reached an ending we were happy with, and even now that those endings were past, new stories would begin. As off-putting as it seemed to embark on those stories without Alchemy by my side, I knew he would be proud of me for doing it anyway. Besides, I still had Beth and Gian and Ksega, and all the people from home.

"Let's go get some food," I said to Ksega, gripping his free hand. He smiled down at me. In the crook of his arm, Hook latched his claws onto the fabric of his shirt and began to purr loudly.

"Best suggestion I've heard all day," Ksega said as we turned around to troop through the snow, leaving behind us the fresh gravestone and its two smith-tooth daggers, crossed one over the other.

THE END

44
Character Guide

A guide to the main characters within the story (alphabetized), with pronunciation guide

Please remember that these guides contain spoilers for the contents of The Cursed Mage & The Cursed King.

ALEC "ALCHEMY" GALLOWAY
"aleck, alchemy, gallow • way"

Description: *A Cursed seven-foot-tall black skeleton; brightly glowing green cracks run through many of his bones—these are the result of the bones being broken and damaged over time*

Age: *Approximately 340*

Mage Type: *Underling*

Home: *A cave deep within the Evershifting Forest; previously Talon, the capital of Freetalon*

Specialties: *Fighting, with or without his twin smith-tooth daggers*

ERABETH CAWSON
"air • uh • beth, caw • son"

Description: *A five-foot-tall Duskan woman with bronzed skin, long black hair, and dark brown eyes, often accompanied by her red-brown hawk, Taro*

Age: *Twenty-five years old*

Mage Type: *Andune-mage*

Home: *City of Bones, the capital of Old Duskfall*

Specialties: *Fighting with her curved saber and driving a sand-sled*

GIAN PAWN

"gee • an, pawn"

Description: *A six-foot-tall Nightfaller man with pale skin, thick black hair that comes to his shoulders, light stubble on his chin, and olive green eyes, often accompanied by his purple and black owl, Light Ray*

Age: *Twenty-seven years old*

Mage Type: *Underling*

Home: *Glass City of Old Nightfall*

Specialties: *Making smart remarks*

KSEGA COPPER

"say • guh, copper"

Description: *A six-foot, three-inch-tall Solian boy with light skin, shaggy blond hair, and bright blue eyes*

Age: *Seventeen years old*

Mage Type: *Bering-mage*

Home: *Rulak, a town in northern Wisesol*

Specialties: *Archery, sneaking around, and stealing things*

SAKURA IRONLAN

"sakura, iron • len"

Description: *A five-foot, four-inch-tall Carlorian girl with dark skin, long, dark brown hair, and dark green eyes*

Age: *Seventeen years old*

Mage Type: *Eirioth-mage*

Home: *Hazelnut, a town in Carlore*

Specialties: *Fighting with a sword or with her flame-sword*

45
Creature Guide

A guide to the creatures within the story (alphabetized), with pronunciation guide

EIRIOTH DRAGONS
"air • ee • oth, dragons"

Description: *Large dragons, typically ranging between eight- and ten-feet-tall at the shoulder; broad wings; covered in colorful feathers; sharp beaks, and long scaled feet with sharp claws*

Breeds/Variations: *All eirioth dragons are the same breed, but their feathers can be a mix of any and all colors; their beaks and claws can range from yellow-gold to black, or even mottled; their tails can be long and whip-like or broad and fanning*

Where They Can be Found: *Eirioth dragons no longer exist in the wild, but are bred and raised in Carlore, and often make life-long bonds with one human*

Temperament: *If raised properly, an eirioth dragon is undyingly loyal and loving; the tempers of eirioth dragons strongly resemble those of pet dogs*

HORCATHIAN CAMELS
"hor • kay • thian, camels"

Description: *Giant camels, typically ranging between nine- and twelve- feet tall at the shoulder; big chests and long, thick legs; thick, sand-colored fur to keep them safe from sandcats; flat backs, lacking any humps; broad, flat heads with tusks, horns, or both*

Breeds/Variations: *The only variations in Horcathian camels are height and whether they have tusks, horns, or both*

Where They Can be Found: *Horcathian camels are only able to survive in the Duskfall Desert*

Temperament: *Horcathian camels are very calm and gentle*

RAPTORS

"raptors"

Description: *Winged reptiles that are typically the size of large dogs or wolves; some are able to breathe fire, others able to breathe ice, and some have no special abilities*

Breeds/Variations: *There are many types of raptors that have adapted to various parts of Horcath, such as water raptors, which are various shades of blue with webbing in their wings and feet; there are forest raptors, which are various shades of green with branches for horns and moss growing on their scales; there are mountain raptors, which have pale scales and icy claws and horns; there are fire raptors, which are various shades of red and orange*

Where They Can be Found: *All across Horcath*

Temperament: *Very violent and aggressive, to be avoided at all costs*

RUNEBOARS

"rune • boars"

Description: *Giant wild boars with tens of tusks and horns curling from their heads and mouths*

Breeds/Variations: *The only variations are the unique numbers of tusks and horns*

Where They Can be Found: *In the Evershifting Forest and the Veiled Woods*

Temperament: *Very aggressive and unpredictable, to be avoided at all costs*

SANDCATS

"sand • cats"

Description: *Giant cats with coarse, sand-colored fur, tall ridges of fur along their spines, long, thin tails, and jagged black stripes on their sides*

Breeds/Variations: *Some sandcats have longer manes than others, and none has the same striping as another, but aside from that they are almost identical*

Where They Can be Found: *Sandcats are only able to survive in the Duskfall Desert*

Temperament: *Very wild and aggressive, to be avoided at all costs*

SEA WRAITHS

"sea, wraiths"

Description: *Giant sea serpents that lurk in the Great Lakes and it is speculated, though not confirmed, the Endless Sea; they can range from only five feet to almost fifteen feet in diameter, and can be up to nine- or ten- miles long; most sea wraiths have spines or fins on the ridge of their backs, and their tails thin into whips*

Breeds/Variations: *There are only four documented types of sea wraiths; they can be various shades of blue, silver, and green, with highlights of pink and purple on their spines or scales; the four types of sea wraiths are not named officially, but have been given nicknames by sailors; the first type is commonly referred to as the "drowning rain" wraith, which is able to store large amounts of water in its mouth and spew it out with enough force to break bones; the second is known as the "screaming lady" wraith, which lets out a terrible sound much like that of a screaming woman as it wraps itself around its victims, crushing them in its vice-like grip; the third is known as the "viper" wraith, which has long, venom-filled fangs that contain enough toxins to kill a full-grown Horcathian camel within minutes; the fourth and final type is called the "leech" wraith, which has thousands of razor-sharp teeth coating its throat to shred its victims to bits when swallowed*

Where They Can be Found: *The Great Lakes*

Temperament: *Extremely aggressive, to be avoided at all costs*

SLATE-WOLVES

"slate, wolves"

Description: *Large wolves covered in long, silky, silver fur that is highly coveted across all of Horcath; long, bare tails that resemble those of a rat; ugly, narrow faces with a strong nose and broad ears; all slate-wolves are completely blind, but have the benefit of heightened hearing and smell; long, thin legs that end in bare claws, somewhat resembling a bird's*

Breeds/Variations: *Aside from size, one slate-wolf cannot be told from the next*

Where They Can be Found: *The Slated Mountains*

Temperament: *Very wild and aggressive, to be avoided if not trained to encounter them*

SMITHS

"smiths"

Description: *Giant beasts that resemble wolves and bears; thick, matted fur that is difficult to penetrate; aside from great size and strength, smiths vary greatly, with some possessing more wolf-like traits, while others are more similar to bears*

Breeds/Variations: *No smith is the same as the next; they can be any number of shades in the black and brown color range, sizes can differ, and physical abilities can differ; some smiths that are more bear-like can stand on their hind legs and swipe with their front paws, while some that are more wolf-like are swift and agile*

Where They Can be Found: *The Evershifting Forest and occasionally, though it is exceedingly rare, the Veiled Woods*

Temperament: *Unpredictable and aggressive, to be avoided at all costs*

Acknowledgements

Writing a book is no easy task, and being able to say I've written several and published two is a huge accomplishment. I'm elated and the tiniest bit heartbroken that the Curse of Horcath duology is complete. Over the last couple of years, these characters and this story have become very important to me, and it's going to be so weird moving on. There will definitely be more books in the Horcathian realm in the future, but it won't be quite the same with a different main cast.

I'm very grateful for everyone who had a part in bringing The Cursed King to life, especially my mom, who made the cover, my dear friend Cass, who was one of my proof-readers, and J. Mills at Word Mill Editing, my fantastic line editor. All three of them helped me make this book the best it could be, and I'm so thankful for all of them.

Thank you to Aunt Laura for encouraging me to keep writing book two (I know you had an ulterior motive), and to Mima, Pipa, Gran, and Papa for supporting me so much throughout the publication and journey of both books.

Thank you to my friends at East Side Church of Christ, namely Natalie and Murray, for always showing an interest in my writing and making me feel like it's worth it to keep writing. I'm sorry for making you cry, but it had to be done.

Thank you to all of my friends from The Book Nook, all of whom are constantly helping me learn and grow as a writer. The motivational boosts I get from seeing you guys freak out over the smallest details or slightest dropped hints (I'm sorry for terrorizing you about Gian, but not really) are unmatched. Thank you Cass, for cheering me on from day and one and believing in me from the very start. Thank you Faith, for all your amazing writing advice and your encouragement. Thank you Scrip, for being a great role model (you underestimate how much I look up to you). Thank you Olli, Ro, Iskaï, Stormy, and everyone else; it's impossible to name everyone who encouraged me to finish the book.

And thank you to all my other awesome friends who bought my book and continue to show their love and support for me (I'm looking at you, TWLians).

And I have to thank all of you readers who have given this duology a chance. It's a great encouragement to me, and I'm glad I've been able to share this story with you.

Also, thanks to Monkey for 1. being so supportive and 2. naming a character in TCK in the best possible way. For anyone who didn't catch it, Traf's name is a completely different word when spelled backwards. You can thank Monkey for that one.

This last bit is for Opal:

THANKS FOR BEING A SUPER AWESOME FRIEND AND GETTING MY BOOKS, EVEN THOUGH YOU'RE DYSLEXIC! AND JUST LIKE THAT YOU'RE A CHEESEBURGER!

About the author

Abigail "Muddy" Josephine is a teenage author from Cleveland, TN. She spends much of her time immersed in books, and can often be found typing away at her own project or with her nose in a book. She loves reading, writing, and spending time with those she's close to. She can be reached by contacting the email: amjosephineauthor@gmail.com